THE
OTHER SIDE
OF EVE

THE OTHER SIDE OF EVE

Sometimes to tell one story ...
two must be told.

Written & Illustrated by
PAUL IKIN

Gaze Akarr

This edition published by Paul Ikin & Gaze Akarr,
Melbourne Australia.

First Edition: March 2015
Copyright © Paul Ikin 2015
Story, Illustration, Design & Formatting by Paul Ikin

www.theothersideofeve.com

ISBN: 978-0-9925346-3-9 (Hardback)
ISBN 978-0-9925346-1-5 (Paperback)
ISBN 978-0-9925346-0-8 (Mobi/kindle)
ISBN 978-0-9925346-2-2 (ePub/ebook)

Proofread by MJ Editing: http://www.mjediting.com
Content Edited by Zoë Watts: https://www.linkedin.com/in/zoewatts

1.2

forever Mum

Many thanks to my family and friends,
who are always there for me.
Melissa-Jane, for casting the first stone of
editing over this monster of a manuscript.
And to my love Zoë,
for without her crooked fascination with
life, cartoonish sense of humour, tremendous
support and fervour with content editing this
book, it would be completely unreadable.
(So she reckons)

Contents

PART ONE — The Little Fear

Chapter 1 - Asleep and Awake   1

Chapter 2 - The Nights Day   11

Chapter 3 - The White Creature   20

Chapter 4 - The Rock in the River   31

Chapter 5 - The Weatherman   34

Chapter 6 - The Rule   45

Chapter 7 - Milton Carmon   51

Chapter 8 - It is Not my Birthday   61

Chapter 9 - Calam and the Jewel   69

Chapter 10 - Lucky Number Thirteen   81

Chapter 11 - Nerves   90

Chapter 12 - Astina Francis   105

Chapter 13 - Krin   112

Chapter 14 - White Picket Fence   123

Chapter 15 - The King   133

Chapter 16 - Behind Closed Doors   142

Chapter 17 - Goodbye   153

Chapter 18 - The Orphans   158

Chapter 19 - Pet Store   172

Chapter 20 - Outside Inside Out   180

PART TWO — Together Apart

Chapter 21 - A Cloud of Sand   191

Chapter 22 - The Queens Gardens   193

Chapter 23 - Treasure   207

Chapter 24 - Transformation   213

Chapter 25 - The Tip Trip   223

Chapter 26 - Scissor Salt   232

Chapter 27 - Hidden   239

Chapter 28 - The Woven Woods   251

Chapter 29 - The Shadow Leech   259

Chapter 30 - The Last Day   271

Chapter 31 - The Golden Cicadas   283

Chapter 32 - Tjaman and Palice   295

Chapter 33 - Family   304

Chapter 34 - The Occupants   310

Chapter 35 - Food   319

Chapter 36 - Night Terrors   324

Chapter 37 - Not the End   328

Chapter 38 - Gretn Maramon   334

Chapter 39 - Weather or Not   340

Chapter 40 - Dark Swamp Kind   342

Chapter 41 - Odger and Mune   344

Chapter 42 - Beetles and Bridges   350

PART THREE — Lost & Found

Chapter 43 - Goodbye Again   358

Chapter 44 - The Tunnel   364

Chapter 45 - Libraries are too Noisy   377

Chapter 46 - Unlucky or Not   384

Chapter 47 - Snapdragon   389

Chapter 48 - The Return of the Great Gonzo   400

Chapter 49 - Into the dark light   410

Chapter 50 - Whirlpool and few Demons   414

Chapter 51 - Two Tailed Treat   419

Chapter 52 - Wompig   425

Chapter 53 - Woodsmen   433

Chapter 54 - Downwards Spiral   442

Chapter 55 - Trapped   449

Chapter 56 - Fate   459

Chapter 57 - The Boiler Room   463

Chapter 58 - The Centacean   468

Chapter 59 - My Self   474

Chapter 60 - Escape   478

Chapter 61 - Which Witch   486

Chapter 62 - Escape is nigh   493

PART FOUR — Face to Face

Chapter 63 - Kikaan Returns   500

Chapter 64 - Reunited   504

Chapter 65 - The Seed of Doubt   509

Chapter 66 - Reunion   514

Chapter 67 - The Nightmare of Truth   519

Chapter 68 - The Vision   523

Chapter 69 - Under Below   526

Chapter 70 - A Problem   531

Chapter 71 - Prepare for the Worst   533

Chapter 72 - Poskar's Pain   536

Chapter 73 - Two-Tailed Friend   539

Chapter 74 - Haunting Eels   546

Chapter 75 - Calam is Sentenced   550

Chapter 76 - Danté Disappears   554

Chapter 77 - The Sea of Tears   557

Chapter 78 - Home sweet Home   562

Chapter 79 - Abreaction   564

Chapter 80 - The Inner Child   568

Chapter 81 - Death and Revival   576

Chapter 82 - Girl of the Wind   586

Chapter 83 - Weatherman   589

Beyond the Yellow Tree

There is a place called Mare-Marie,
A place unlike any—as you shall see;
It's because of the schoolgirl, Evelin Boots,
From the vicious ocean, to the nectarous fruits.

She created the weather, the land and the sky,
—but never she'll see it, never she'll spy;
A parallel world, conjured up for her child,
To be free, to laugh and dance in the wild.

But as Evelin's fears take over her mind,
Marie-Marie suffers and all of its kind;
Its princess is cursed, full of fury and rage,
Remaining inside, her castle her cage.

The witch and her creatures are out of control,
Born from the sorrow in Evelin's soul;
Unless there is change in the young girl's mind,
Mare-Marie's doomed and all of its kind.

—The Weatherman

Let's begin shall we ...

— PART ONE —

The Little Fear

Evelin Boots slumped heavily upon her pointy white elbows, her sleepy head propped within her open palms as she gazed along desks of flowing pages. There was little to be seen this far out at sea and the chalky black horizon was forever looming.

"He's back!" she gasped.

Evelin's docile eyes ignited, unlatched to catch a rare glimpse of the spiked, red-tipped dorsal fins of the treacherous and dual-jawed creature known as, The Infamous Ruegeris Bimatherous.

Before she could scream, it caught her deep blue eyes, stole her breath and dove deep, whipping its oily feathered fins into the air and twisting them below.

In an instant, sound had all but vanished and what remained was a vacuum of panic in which Ruegeris had placed within her. The stillness hid all traces of the demon that stirred below.

Evelin froze, even though her mind raced, wanting her to kick like mad.

Through clenched teeth, she growled, "Where are you Ruegeris? Come on you … you horrid beast, show yourself!"

"Shhh!" came a hush from behind like a blast of air escaping from a slashed tyre.

Damn … spoke out loud.

Evelin refrained herself as she received the usual clueless stares and familiar daggers. The pupils in the class returned one by one to the test paper on their desks; her antics bored them, and they were none the wiser to know what imminent danger lurked beneath them. But Evelin knew it was too late, Ruegeris had found them, he smelt their anxieties, their worry, and she knew he would not go back to the depths below without a child in his stomach.

Nervously she pushed back her seat and stole a quick glance under the desk, but the cunning Ruegeris hid below in the ever-moving shadows. All she could see was the white stockings of her naive classmates, wading, luring and inciting the beast.

What is worse? she thought, *Observing the horrific creature in full sight or not at all?*

Definitely not at all, she concluded. The anticipation of his silent attack was too much to bear. *Where are you Ruegeris? Maybe he's gone away, back to his underwater cave.* Evelin smirked, knowing full well this was the last thing on his agenda.

Ever so slowly she peered back up. With sourness tightening in her stomach, she felt something terrible was about to happen, and as her eyes rose above the desk her fears came to fruition. In a flash, only two rows in front of her, Ruegeris' shimmering black eel-like body tore through the surface of the sea revealing his majestic emerald blue and ruby red-speckled throat. Like a car crash, Ruegeris appeared to be moving in slow motion as he unlatched his jaws before the class to reveal four rows of razor sharp teeth gnashing out like a bricked window frame. No one moved a muscle. Evelin met its glazed eyes with clenching fear as he stared deep into her soul and strangled it tight. With a slashing roar, Ruegeris arched his spine against the fabric of gravity and pierced the air around it. A layer of goose bumps instantly sprang up across her entire body. Ruegeris paused above the students like an exhibit in a museum. Portrayed in an all-encompassing and menacing exposition, a rippling current of neon specks glistened along his pitch-black skin, his gills flaring with each and every breath. Evelin's heartbeat timed his final descent, a countdown to demise. As the invisible wires snapped from his immense weight, he lunged with jaws gaping, plummeting with full force taking poor Febe and Rose Listner in one ferocious bite.

It was as if the twins had never come to class.

Evelin sat speechless and in the blink of an eye it was over. The beast had to eat, and she agreed with Ruegeris, if any of them were to be sacrificed, it would be without a doubt the soft and fleshy twins of whom would be most palatable.

No one batted an eyelid and to Evelin it was just another classroom sacrifice. Once again, she had been spared by the beast.

It will not be long, she thought, confident. *Next time it will be me.*

Evelin sighed as she did these days; time ticked over ever so slowly, and there was little more to be seen. Like a carnival ride, one way or another, her imagination had come to an inevitable halt. The watery horizon had vanished back into dreary walls, the sea around her and Ruegeris had vanished, and the habitual classroom in all its stale clarity surrounded her once again.

Reality, only one way to escape, she sighed.

It had been a long afternoon and an even longer week; it was as if there had been two Mondays and at least three and a half Wednesdays.

Did I even go home this week? she thought with a depressed moan and she gazed around the classroom as she had done so many times before.

Am I actually bored? Has it come to this? Is this what bored really feels like? I can't remember. It's definitely in the vicinity, but this is something else, it's in the same category I suspect, she thought curiously. She hated to be bored, let alone unable to decipher her emotions, which she was told were chemically unstable for any twelve-year-old.

Maybe this is a unique emotion no other has ever felt. Maybe I am the only person who can ... feel this way. Outside the spectrum of all known human emotion, like an undiscovered colour or shape. She paused for a moment, thinking of all the varied shapes that there ever was and will be and started to scribble abstract prisms on the inside of her textbook until the lines converged into a dark ink-like whirlpool.

I doubt it ...

Evelin's eyes returned to the clock above the blackboard, then down again, glazing over the back of her maths paper, trying to make sense of the surreal scribbles she had drawn earlier. Within the spiralling black ink, creepy faces appeared and disappeared; a witch with horns screaming into a cracked mirror, a raven with extra long legs taking flight, a pair of black horned beetles dancing with wiry wings out wide and several small creatures of unnameable sorts peering through the inky darkness.

Evelin woke from her daydream. It was of course Ursula who was seated beside her, forever coughing in Evelin's ear. The students were amused and began a coughing wave. Next was Sarah with a tight fur-ball of a cough, then Petra in the far corner, wheezing and splattering across her papers, and then she passed it to Ellen who was sitting in the front row. Ellen coughed until what seemed like a thick green oyster had come to the surface. Intrigued by the unpleasant chorus that appeared to jump across the room from one student to another, Evelin began to imagine a stylish cigar wielding man as he appeared and disappeared from within their desktops, each time exhaling a thick white puff of smoke straight into the girls' faces. She raised a sleepy smirk and leant down on her desk. With a lead pencil she began to shade in the initials of her name, now etched deep into the pine on her school desk top. The desks had been passed down from student to student, year after year, and now they were no different from the unsightly doors in the girls toilets; scratched up and tagged. She smiled at the words; *Milton was here!* Scored deep into the desk and wondered what he was up to today, *probably irritating the headmaster no doubt.*

Carefully Evelin placed the point of her pencil within one of the many small holes stabbed across the desk, and it seemed to balance as if it had come from outer space. With her hands out front, she waved them around as if she was holding the pencil up by magic alone, and for a split second, Evelin was content.

"Pst ... Eve, Milk! What the hell are you doing?" scowled Ursula Fradel, the unkempt, horse-faced girl sitting at the desk beside her. Underneath her enormous nose, her head melted into her neck as one and in an unusual way her eyes seemed closer to her ears, unlike most other people.

Evelin ignored Ursula as they were not friends. Like many of the girls, Ursula was a classroom associate with whom Evelin gave little acknowledgement other than what basic manners demanded.

Evelin fixed her gaze and returned to her pencil balancing act.

"Number sixteen, what is it?" demanded Ursula, nudging her head in close for a peek.

"Get stuffed Ursula, do your own test," said Evelin. *Is she only up to number sixteen? Half of it is multiple choice for god's sake.*

"Just guess!" whispered Evelin.

"Don't be such a snob Milk, you finished ages ago."

"Not my fault you're obtuse."

"What?" said Ursula, with a confused expression.

"It means stupid."

"You are! Just spit it out already," scoffed Ursula.

Evelin peered up towards the teacher, Mr Brackenback. He seemed preoccupied with a book and in a smooth motion she looked under her test sheet, then back to Ursula's frustrated face.

"Don't ask for anymore," said Evelin.

"Whatever, what is it?"

"Six thousand, four hundred and twenty-three," she quietly whispered. It was the first string of numbers that came to her head. If Evelin wasn't so drained, Ursula wouldn't have taken her seriously, but she was, and Evelin's flat facial expression seemed somewhat serious.

"See Milk, that wasn't too hard was it?" snorted Ursula curling her lips up. She scribbled in the answer before it leaked out of her head with the rest of her knowledge.

In an instant, a hundred coloured pencils, pens, ballpoints, protractor and eraser exploded on the chequered floor. "Aghh not again!" Evelin cursed as the students turned their shoulders towards her.

Evelin shrugged, but they didn't care, the girls were a pack of wolves and she had always been the black sheep.

Ursula pointed at the floor with a light cackle. She didn't need to point. Evelin closed her eyes for a few seconds and took a deep breath; she pictured her paralysed pencils with their fractured spines sprawled across the hard tiles.

"Thanks a lot, might as well leave them there," Evelin huffed.

"Boots! Try to encourage your pencils to stop leaping from your desk. The life of a pencil can't be all that bad," quipped Mr Brackenback.

"But ... ah yes, of course, Sir."

I wouldn't want to be a pencil, Evelin mused, imagining her head being sharpened and her feet being gnawed on.

Looking down at the colourful mess, it was exactly as she had pictured it. She needn't look at Gertrude Cohne and give her any satisfaction.

Gertrude smiled down at her as if her thin lizard-tail lips were glued together. Evelin wished they were stuck together on most occasions.

Down at this level Evelin noticed Gertrude's stocky and manly legs; the non-existent ankles and a sweaty pattern of patchy dark curly hair created a mesmerizing pattern. Gertrude was enormous and solid like her dad; he worked in the cafeteria as a cook and kept his daughter well-stocked on a smorgasbord of heavily processed nutrition-free white foods. She sat hunched over her desk and was still the tallest girl in class. Evelin was forced to turn away from the stumps and instead focus on her face.

"What are you perving at cheat?" barked Gertrude in a gruff voice while wielding a large plastic ruler. "I guess Ursula will have one right answer."

"Get stuffed," snapped Ursula.

"One more than you," whispered Evelin while continuing to retrieve her pencils.

"You're lucky I don't hit mental patients."

"Is that under the bully code of conduct?"

"Shut up, it's crazies like you Milk that make mentals look normal," smirked Gertrude.

"You better watch your words then," said Evelin noticing Brackenback's red socks as he crept up behind them.

"Come on girls, if you've finished your test, please sit quietly and respect each other's time, it's not too hard, is it? Just read a book or something, make a list."

"Sorry Sir, Evelin was distracting me again, you know how she is ... unstable," said Gertrude, tapping her head with her ruler.

"What? What does that even mean? I'm sta—" started Evelin before she was cut short.

"Yes Boots, of course, you're stable; solid like a rock. Please keep your pencil case that way, possibly inside your desk in the future," said Brackenback pushing a few pencils gently to Evelin's side with his shoe.

"Yes Sir," said Evelin quietly.

"Yes Sir," mimicked Gertrude.

"Care to repeat yourself Gertrude?" said Brackenback.

"No Sir, just clearing my throat."

Evelin watched as Brackenback leaned in close to Gertrude's ear and whispered loud enough so Evelin could hear.

"Being thirteen means you're no longer twelve and it's time to grow up, that's what 'teen' means. One day you'll probably need Evelin's help." He paused and looked around the class; they were pretending they weren't listening. Evelin left her pencils on the floor and gazed down at her test as he returned to Gertrude.

"But she won't, I know I wouldn't, and as a matter of fact, I doubt anyone here will help. You better make some changes next term because from what I hear you're headed to repeat this year, now won't that be fun?"

The expression on Gertrude's face was enough of an answer.

"Back to your work class, not long to go."

Brackenback returned to his desk.

Evelin's heart was thumping; she could only imagine what Gertrude was plotting. Evelin kept her head down and left her pencils on the floor.

"You and Brackenback are gonna pay; both of you will need help after I tell my dad. You two psychos can drown together."

"Drown?" whispered Evelin.

"Yeah, that's what they do with mental cases, tie 'em to a chair and sink 'em to the bottom of the lake. Let the eels make homes in their heads."

"That's for witches," said Evelin turning her back on her.

"Same thing," scoffed Gertrude. "Any idiot can see you're one of those as well."

"Gertrude Cohne, you're like a dog that bites its owner," barked Brackenback. "Consider that ten percent off your final mark. I wonder if there is anything lower than an F? I'll have to look that up; you might be a school first. Now isn't that an achievement to stick on your fridge?" said Brackenback smiling. He casually flicked a page of his book.

It wasn't just Evelin who didn't know where to look. *What has got into Brackenback? He's ... he's amazing,* she thought. Evelin wanted to smile, even stand up and hug him.

"You're dead meat, you little mental skunk. Skunky two-tone hair! You're a freak Milk," snarled Gertrude.

Evelin's internal happiness fractured in an instant. Once again Gertrude mocked her appearance and her person.

Evelin covered her ears, her eyes hurt, her heart hurt and her stomach hurt. *I'm not mental. Stop saying that!*

Evelin's mind strayed far from the classroom, her thoughts went to an image of her doctor and the clear orange pill canisters appeared in their hundreds. It made her feel sick just thinking about them. It was then that she felt a strange panic ripple over her. A stirring inside and outside that acted all alone as a wave of dizziness hit her head.

"Your wiring is bad," the doctor had informed her, as he wrote out another prescription for her anxiety disorder.

Bad wiring? What wires? I'm not a machine. Inside me or outside? What if someone or something might be pulling them? Why would I pull them? It can't be Gertrude as it also happens when she's nowhere in sight. My mouth is dry. When did I last have a drink of water? Evelin felt nauseous as another wave of anxiety engulfed her from head to toe. She tried her best to ignore it, but it seemed to suffocate her. A swelling built up in her eyes, "I'm not a mental case." The venom inside brought a bite to her choking voice. *No, not again, not here!* she moaned, trying to distract herself by scribbling another character on the back of her test, but her strange drawings began to vibrate out of focus and distort off the paper.

"What's wrong Milk?" said Ursula with a touch of sensitivity in her voice. "Forget to take your pills? You're not going to be sick again are you?" she said as she noisily jumped her seat to the side.

Evelin hid her face within her unruly hair and ignored everyone. She had to control this. She could feel her veins pulsing as if her blood was swelling and gushing with nowhere to escape, pushing at the surface and throbbing at all ends. She threw them down palm up, noticing her pale, pigmented hands and the perturbing blue veins that began to rise along her wrists. Evelin imagined every vein on her face doing the same thing, replicating the road map pattern as her throbbing temples confirmed her thoughts. Small beads of sweat began to push themselves out of leaking pores and dripping from her wrists like clear blood. Saturated with terrible thoughts, panic ricocheted around her head taking over her mind from inside to out. Conflict replaced clarity and thoughts of escape and death took turns in haunting her. Evelin's beating heart punched so furiously she was sure the whole class could hear it.

It won't be long before it breaks inside me, she thought almost crying as she held her shaky hands against her chest.

What's going on? Am I going to faint? I don't want to faint in class; this is crazy, what if I'm dying? I can't die here! Take Gertrude or Ursula, they're the witches!

Evelin's fingers made their way into the desk cavity and found the smooth orange canister. With shaky hands, she twisted the lid off and opened it. Several pills poured out. As quick as a magician, she put them in her mouth. She felt the air in the room beginning to crack her like clay from the inside out. Her tongue, dry and rough, held onto her medication as it released its foul chemical taste. With a screwed up face, she scraped the roof of her mouth for moisture and tried to gulp. Frantically reaching into her bag, she pulled out a bottle of water and downed the tiny blue pills, gulping savagely.

"Let's hope those pills kick in soon Milk, you've gone full mental today," whispered Gertrude. "How they even let you out is beyond me. Aren't you supposed to be tagged or something?"

"Get stuffed, you have no idea," choked Evelin, her voice peaking over her usual monotonous tone.

"Maybe you should have a few more," said Ursula.

Evelin shook her head slowly and with a slight daze, she nestled within her shelter of half blonde fringe and wild dark brown curls, *what's wrong with me? A brain tumour? I have got to get out of here, I can't handle this. Hell, I've done my test, I should just leave my stuff and go.*

Suffocating with emotion, she felt as if she had the uncontrollable capacity to become a monster at any moment, and in a flash she pictured herself screaming at the top of her lungs and throwing her chair through the window. *No, it can't happen!* she told herself furiously. This is what she feared most; her fear had control of her. Whatever it was.

Evelin began to stand up. She pushed back her chair and rose, her movements grounding her to the reality of the classroom and she leaned down across the table, arms spread and head down. She stood locked for what felt like several minutes. *What the hell is going on? Can't they all see me?*

"What are you doing Milk? Have you wet yourself?" asked Gertrude.

"What? No!" spat Evelin as the whole class turned towards her and giggled.

"Girls, what's going on now? This is not very ladylike. Is something wrong, Evelin?" asked Mr Brackenback, removing his glasses.

Evelin thought about it as she looked at her hands and noticed they had stopped shaking and were now limp and warm.

No, it wasn't very ladylike, she thought, taking a long, deep breath.

The wires untangled, one at a time, the pills had kicked in hard and tidal waves of relief washed over her.

Why did I wait so damn long? she sighed, sinking back down.

Brackenback smiled contently and placed his glasses back on after confirming that she was fine. He watched as she sat back in her chair. After a slight pause, he said, "You know Boots, I can't figure out if you're coming or going lately."

"Sorry sir. I just had these thoughts that ... that I couldn't—"

"Don't be sorry, this goes for all of you, try not to let *others* or your emotional thoughts get the better of you. Remember your thoughts seem powerful, but they're not. So don't give them any power. You are always in control. From experience, you may find they can take over even the smartest of minds ... especially the smart ones."

"Yes sir, I guess," said Evelin.

"Don't guess, know there are consequences, not only here, but your actions, thoughts and emotions can impact far beyond the realm of this moment my dear."

I don't understand. What realm? Nottingham? thought Evelin.

"Yes, of course, everything is fine, sorry Sir," she felt her words leave her lips and with a glassy stare she looked across the room. As designed, the monster inside had been silenced. *Brackenback doesn't understand, Gertrude is right, I am a mental case. I'm one hundred percent mental. What would have happened if I didn't have my pills? It's getting worse ... I need help ... I need ... I don't know what I need.*

In a soft circular rhythm, she massaged her temples.

Not long to go now Eve, not long, hang in there now.

Evelin tried to comfort herself with a blurry sense of self-talk. The pills had taken reign, and a hundred-foot quilt of relaxation wrapped itself around her.

"You lost it that time Milk," whispered Gertrude. "Only a fool would try and fool themselves like you do."

After a moment, Evelin turned, gazed up at Gertrude and with a sad light grin said, "I know."

With a huff, the petite Princess turned her back to the woman, walked off towards her bed and left her standing behind the door.

"So, she's sick? Physically sick or mentally?" probed Princess Belleny.

"I beg your pardon? I'm not sure?" said the woman poking her head through the gap in the door. "Miss Snith simply said she wasn't feeling well and probably won't be back."

Unbeknown to Princess Belleny the woman was fully aware of why the teacher Miss Snith had quit as she had remarked, "I refuse to teach such an importunate child, Princess or not."

She couldn't be all that bad, the woman thought and she had leapt at the chance to meet the mysterious Princess Belleny Vera, whom only a handful had ever seen, let alone met in the privacy of her quarters.

In her short and last public appearance at the mere age of nine, Princess Belleny Vera had stood on the sweeping balcony of the castle forecourt and addressed the people of Mare-Marie announcing in a mournful tone: "My mother, The Imperial Majesty Anne Queen Vera of Mare-Marie, Castellan of the Crystalon, Overseer of the Sea of Sorrow travelled to unknown lands. Despite knowing the risk ahead, Mother took it upon herself to leave the safety of the castle to travel deep into the realm seeking out to personally greet each and every one of you. She dared to go forth and brave the extent of Mare-Marie, far into the forbidden lands.

"I am not the Queen; I am not my mother. I shall remain your Princess until the day that I am duly called for and required. Until then you have your beloved ruler, The Emperor of the Known Land, King Vasilis Vera. Good day to you all, my people. May the sea set us free from this eternal sadness."

And that was the last the people heard or saw of her. Personally confined within the castle walls, it had been six years and counting; demanding privacy and detachment from the outside world.

"I presume you're the new substitute teacher?" Belleny whispered to the woman through the door.

"Yes, my name is Miss Stephanie Muscae, lucky number thirteen they tell me."

"They're wrong; it's fourteen. Very well, enter if you must," said Belleny, walking away with her back to the woman.

Muscae pushed the heavy door and took one step inside. She paused in the door frame, holding it tight.

What's in her hand? thought Muscae, squinting as the room was so dimly lit.

Oh my!

Is that?

A head!

A creature's skull hung from Belleny's grip, swaying from its mangled, black fringe. Muscae's eyes quickly adjusted; she could see its feral features, its jaw latched open, caught in its final scream.

Belleny turned around at once, manoeuvring the head with one hand and moving the sharp-toothed jaw so that it mouthed her words, "What are you waiting for woman?"

A mask! ... Oh, Stephanie you fool.

With a wheezing smile, Muscae slouched and let go of the door frame.

"Yes Princess, coming at once."

As she entered the room, she crouched down very low as if expecting bats to swoop down upon her. A gust of air from the stairwell shook the dimly lit room causing the lantern's shadows to waver and the air to fill with the stale scent of potpourri, which was most unwelcoming. With eyes wide open she scanned for familiarity. Apart from the royal four-poster bed, downed and draped in white linen, there was little to be seen. Muscae took three careful steps, as though the floor was booby-trapped and paused by a maid's trolley. Upon it sat a large silver cloche; it reflected her royally flushed face.

"Just one moment my dear Princess, it's not every day one has to climb to the top of a castle. One day they will invent something to whisk us up from the ground. Wouldn't that be nice?"

With no reply and a faint glance the Princess walked off into the vast chamber, past the bed, around a chaise lounge, up a step to an elaborate stone-white, claw-footed bath, past the giant mirror—that made the room look even bigger, past the shelves of ornaments and stepping into the trunk of a tree that grew in the back corner of the room.

Belleny's melancholy voice echoed from within the darkness, "I'll be with you in a moment, please don't touch anything—stay right where you are."

Muscae did as she was told and waited and watched with unease. The gnarled and knotted black tree had roots that crawled steadily and grew out along the walls. Its branches scratched across the roof and its wiry tendrils covered most of the windows.

Oh my! How is that dreadful tree growing in here? What is she doing inside it? Muscae paused and pondered. *Something's not right, and it's not just that spooky tree.* Although she had never been in the Princess' quarters before, she was confident it broke some of the rules of Mare-Marie, but first and foremost, it was truly enormous!

Without a doubt, the tower's a large structure but this is just ridiculous!

She stood upright and rubbed her chin as one does in such situations.

It was hard for her not to be unsettled at the appearance of both the Princess and her questionable chambers. It was completely out of the ordinary and besides the bed and possibly the bathtub, it was not royal in any sense, more of a museum of oddities if anything. Her eyes darted around the room and then up at the roof. She saw her reflection in one of the large panes of onyx that hung eerily from the ceiling.

Darker than the night itself, she thought, *what if it fell? Clearly this part of the castle is lost without a mother's touch.*

She watched the Princess duck between the gold light of the lanterns and from the tree to a cabinet on the opposite side of the room. Muscae couldn't resist; her eyes were drawn straight back to the tree.

"This tree is as terrifying as death itself," she whispered. *Where is she going now?* "Princess? We do have a class remember. If this is some ploy to make me—"

"Hush. One moment woman, I have to remove these shoes before my ankles are rubbed raw," grumbled the Princess.

Princess Belleny pulled at a large door and slipped into another room.

Another doorway? sighed Muscae. "All right, do be quick now, it's getting late," she stretched and leaned across, peering deeply into the room as best she could.

Wait a minute. Is that … no … it can't be true … can it?

The two large pearl doors were left slightly open. Muscae took several steps to the side so she could see clearly.

I don't believe it!

Four mannequins stood inside the doorway, carved identically to Belleny, dressed in dark blue outfits much like the royal guard's uniform. How many more were inside she could not tell, but silhouettes of several others became clear the more she moved around.

The rumours say there are hundreds. That's ridiculous! Could fit a dozen at the most. But the large pearl doors were so large and its frame so regal she knew that it must lead to more than a guarded shoe closet.

The Princess' Change Room, gleamed Muscae. *Although … this looks a lot like magic to me; illegal magic. Who could stop it even if it were? But it is the King's rule.*

Once again, her eyes returned back to the tree. *How can I open a window with all these horrid branches in the way? I could easily snap a few I guess. The balcony looks out of reach.*

All at once Muscae gasped and spun around, "Hey! Who's there?"

But there was no reply.

"Who … who are you? Please, don't hurt me! I'm the substitute teacher, look, my book …" she stammered, but the strange creature of pure white fur, hanging high above the doorway said nothing. Its large frame hung silently from the roof, its thick front paws clawed at the heavy wooden door and pulled its body towards her as the wind pushed through the stairwell.

"Scared the breath out of me!" gasped Muscae, holding the large book to her chest.

It could have been alive if it weren't for its round, dead, white eyes that gave it away. Its mane hung low across the doorway. Muscae stared into the waves of hair; it was soft on the eyes, pure as if it had been killed only hours after bathing. She glanced back to the Change Room. *Good, she's still busy.* With an overwhelming urge to touch it, Muscae reached forward and combed her short round fingers through, with deep, long strokes as if through a lover's mane. She knew a single lock could only bring good luck and fortune. Never had she seen such a creature—but this was not unusual in Mare-Marie.

It would have been a graceful beast, she imagined, but powerful just the same.

"Ahhh! You're ... you're alive!" she gasped as the dead creature moved. She stumbled back, unlatching her fingers with the book she carried now a shield above her head. Nervously she called out to the Princess but there was no reply, only silence; a suffocating silence. After a moment, she cautiously lowered the book, not that it could provide any protection, and to her relief the creature's arms swung lifelessly to a halt. It was still and very much dead.

The solid door had closed and moved the white creature along with it.

The wind, or could it be ... Muscae coiled her face suspiciously towards the Change Room.

Belleny stood in the doorway, her arms crossed.

"Are you finished woman? Or would you like to stroke the dead beast for a little longer?"

"No, no I'm just—" stammered Muscae.

"I know. You're just waiting."

Belleny slid the pearl doors shut and returned, she stood at the end of her bed and faced the woman. The space between them was over twenty paces. The bed dwarfed her petite size, but Muscae concluded the large red costume she wore, which resembled a rose in full bloom, disguised her size the most. Silently they stared at each other for some time, and neither spoke a word. Muscae stood puzzled.

What is she doing? What does she want me to do? Should I say something?

Anxiously she watched as the Princess scanned her from head to toe and then from side to side.

"Have I, have I done something wrong?" asked Muscae. Her eyes returning to the floor, but the Princess ignored her and continued her inspection. Her first subject of the night, it seemed, was Miss Stephanie Muscae.

Interesting, thought Belleny, *not at all like that last skeleton of a teacher who was unpleasant in every manner of the word. Hmm, I wonder if all her family look like giant spinning tops. I bet she looked exactly the same as a child, no difference at all, smaller, of course. She's so weathered though, like an old Mare-Marie sow—the outside will do that to you.*

Belleny stared bleakly into the woman's eyes, her lips held in a thin, tight line and emotionless.

Muscae knew it was impolite to stare back, and the woman lowered her focus towards the floor, every so often looking up, each time a little more confused.

The Princess blinked her eyes, but her gaze was fixed. She noticed first that the woman's hips were wide and grazed both sides of the door frame. The large rimmed woman tapered sharp both ways from her thin black belt. One down towards a pair of white polished shoes and the other up to a small round face that looked on with bewilderment. Her triangular arms, tipped with pie making plump hands, grasped at a large leather bound book. She intrigued the Princess, but it was the satisfaction that she held only one book that pleased her the most so the game of silence could cease.

The Princess pointed to the woman's waist. "Puddings and cakes, I imagine you're quite fond of those comforts."

Muscae gasped and held the book to her chest, *puddings and cakes indeed! If I had known royal insults were to break the silence, I'd prefer the sound of nothing!*

But as the Princess neither grinned, smirked or smiled, it seemed she was somewhat honest. Through Belleny's void expression, the woman considered the possibility. Cautiously she said, "Well, yes, yes I am."

Belleny nodded. "I'm growing fond of them too. I never was before."

The woman lowered the book and relaxed. "Well, it happens. You may have a sweet tooth like me, I tell you it's a curse."

The Princess tilted her head. "Magic? A curse?"

"Well, I may have put it on myself, on purpose," chuckled Muscae.

The Princess sighed unimpressed. "Oh, I see. Do you cook them? Or do you just eat them?"

The woman's face squished into a confused mash. "Well, of course I cook them, what woman with six children doesn't? No one in Mare-Marie makes Mother's Milk Pudding like I do."

Muscae looked on confused as Belleny brought her hand to her mouth, her eyes white and widening.

"What's the matter?" she asked.

Through her fingers, Belleny gagged, "Mother's Milk?"

"Ha—no dear girl! You don't get out much do you. It's not what you think. Eww no ... that's not a nice thought at all. It's merely a reference. You know, when you eat it you feel warm and loved, like when your mother holds you close." Muscae squeezed the book against herself, closed her eyes and hummed a sweet tune.

"I would stop now if I were you!" said Belleny, striking her palm out and carrying a sentencing frown upon her face.

Muscae stepped forward. "I am sorry, I shouldn't have mentioned ..."

The Princess lowered her hand into a clenched fist. "Mentioned what? A cake presumed to be made from breast milk? Or that you favoured to remind me of my dead mother?"

The woman drew back. "I'm sorry, it was an honest mistake. Never would I intentionally bring up such a personal matter my Princess. I adored the Queen, my mother was her friend; I remember her beautiful black curls, like your own."

Belleny leaned up on her bed, surrounded by her garment of petals and kicked out her legs, she looked up at the white creature above Muscae and paused for a moment.

"No, of course, you wouldn't," she said, in a dead voice. Her sad lips returned to a thin line.

With a sigh of relief, Muscae lowered the book from her chest and was reminded to choose her words carefully next time.

"Well then, come closer, you can't teach from that distance," said the Princess, turning from hot to cold. "Let's get this over with, obviously I have better things to do tonight."

"Yes, of course, oh where are my manners. I must say it is a great honour to meet and teach the beautiful and enigmatic Princess Belleny Vera. The one and only daughter of the much revered Vera family, of whom only a handful have ever set eyes upon, let alone have the privilege to—"

"Enough already," snapped Belleny, covering her ears and ceasing the woman from further praise. "When you enter this room you can address me as either, Miss or just plain Belleny."

"Yes Miss, Belleny, Miss Belleny, of course," pipped Muscae and she scuttled forward now eager to start as well.

The teacher recognised this was an unorthodox arrangement with her lack of control of the 'teacher versus student' dynamic. It was commonplace with her other students, she had complete authority, but tonight with this young girl, she had none.

The Princess kicked off her green velvet slippers dropping them to the floor, which revealed her white stockings and petite feet. She pointed at the bed and said, "Go on, be seated then. I can imagine those tiny feet of yours must be exhausted from all your weight."

Muscae smiled through gritted teeth. Her feet ached, but she was more eager to move away from the white creature that hung behind her. Dead or alive it was an unsettling beast.

"You must be extremely fit walking up and down those stairs of yours," huffed Muscae dropping her frame as gently as she could beside Belleny.

"I hardly use them," said the Princess, and she embellished no more. She decided to lay across her bed, her hands propping her head up like a porcelain vase. Now poised, the Princess' languid gaze shifted from the large woman and turned towards an elaborate beaked mask that was sitting on its stand, where it always stood, but just to the side of the teacher.

Muscae took a peek as well. Its dark feathers were oiled and pasted to its skull and looked like no creature she had ever seen or would want to. All the masks spooked her. *What would she want with these? Are they for plays? Who does she play with?*

Muscae stole a glance at the Princess, her inner voice thinking, *Such black hair and so much of it. The poor maid, what a nightmare it must have been to braid it into such an arrangement ... she's much smaller than most twelve-year-old girls, but it may be the giant rose she's wearing? Not an ugly girl though. But peculiar looking just the same. She must be so alone up here.*

What was her father thinking?

As the teacher pondered, without much of a signal, Belleny snapped back into her focus and stared back without a blink. Upon realizing, Muscae withdrew and stammered, "Oh, I hear, I hear you don't like visitors, let alone teachers. But let's trump through tonight's lesson, and I won't annoy you again till next week, how does that sound?"

I should be in bed at this hour anyway, Muscae silently reflected.

Belleny paused. "Very well, go on, but be quick, I have more important things to do than learn about stuff I'll never see and places I'll never go."

Muscae stared on confused. "I'm sure you do, but a Princess must be knowledgeable of her kingdom," she added.

The teacher brushed it aside and began the lesson. She flicked through the large illustrated book. Its front cover held a beautiful ornate frame an in the center it read, *Mare-Marie—Through and Beyond.*

Muscae paused, confused after searching for a bookmark and questioned, "Do you remember what page the last teacher finished up on?"

"I don't think she did."

"Did what?"

"Start ... not many do."

Of course, they don't, thought Muscae.

"Very well, how about we familiarize ourselves with Mare-Marie and its landmarks?"

Belleny sighed out loud. "I know everything there is to know about Mare-Marie, I've had this stupid class for six years woman."

"Yes I know. It's just that Mare-Marie changes all the time. It's a different place than it was even a year ago. A lot different. This book has been recently updated, and it was no easy task let me tell you. Look, we can brush over it and you can let me know if I say anything incorrectly."

"Humor me," sighed the Princess.

Miss Muscae opened the book out before the Princess and a large map of Mare-Marie unfolded revealing itself on weathered parchment. She assertively pointed her finger to the castle in which they sat and began, "The Crystalon Castle is both an architectural and significant cultural masterpiece, it blistered the hands of thousands of workers, took many years of labour and toil and is yet to be completed." The woman paused for a moment then added, "As you've probably seen they're finishing another tower identical to yours on the eastern wing."

At once the Princess sat up and crossed her legs with the rose-like costume ruffling around her, "No they're not!"

"Well, yes they are, how could you have not seen it?"

"Another tower? No, I did not know that. I don't look outside, what proof do you have woman?"

"Open your windows and see," pointed Muscae.

The Princess frowned, "Choose your words carefully."

"Oh yes sorry, well it has been planned from the very beginning, my husband's the Head Foreman," said Muscae quite proud, "I've even seen the plans, even though they're quite hard to follow being so old."

"You or the plans?" questioned Belleny.

"Ha, I meant the plans," chuckled the woman.

"So who is going to live there?"

"I'm not sure, you'll have to ask King Vera. You might have a new neighbour," the teacher answered with an expanded grin, her cheeks pushing her flesh further up around her face.

The Princess suddenly frowned, "Impertinence will not be tolerated, how dare you address the King without his full title."

"My apologies Princess but he is often called by his last name by his people, actually he insists it on most occasions, it's very humble of him."

Belleny sighed and returned, "Humble … yes, you may be right. I know if I were a King I would have everyone call me just that."

Thankfully you're not, thought Muscae as she cleared her throat and continued. She pointed beside the castle drawing her focus to a dark ink splotch on the page that looked more like an accident. After clearing her throat, she began again, "The Crystalon Castle was built in the far west beside of the Pit of Nothingness. Beyond this spot the surrounding lands of Mare-Marie are verdant, rich and fruitful," she pointed out the words and continued to ad lib from the book.

"Don't you think I know this? Why did they draw the Pit so big? You can't expect me to believe it's now the same size as the castle?"

"Well yes, that is a slight exaggeration I must say, but not by much. It has grown in the last six years, that's for sure."

"Of course it has," said Belleny unamused.

"I must say although the Pit looks frightening, and yes the leafless trees that surround it make it no less scary, it's just an exhausted, dead crack in the ground, hence its name. And unless you fall down it, in which first you would have to climb the barrier, it's harmless and nothing to worry about." Muscae took a moment to look across and take in Belleny's thoughts.

"Why the barrier then?" said Belleny unconvinced.

"So curious children and Princesses don't fall in, of course."

"Obviously that is not going to happen, the Pit is harmless, but when the beast that lives inside comes out looking for flesh it will—"

"There's no beast inside the Pit. That's complete nonsense, this is folly, nothing but a children's tale. Have you ever seen such a creature, other than elaborate drawings from fantastical imaginations? No, I did not think so," said the teacher covering her hand over the illustration.

"Fantastical imaginations!" huffed the Princess, "something's down there, without a doubt hibernating. It's only a matter of time before it wakes up and I know how grumpy I am after a long sleep."

I can imagine, thought the teacher. "Either way you will be safe up here. Shall we continue Princess?" she said confidently and began to read aloud. "Unlike the harmless Pit of Nothingness there is the treacherous Sea of Sorrow."

"What child names these godforsaken places? Of course, I know of the Sea."

"I think your parents had a hand in naming them," smirked Muscae.

"Either way it's going to kick us out eventually," said Belleny.

Muscae paused, deep down she felt the same way, "yes, well this could be true. To say the sea is out of control would be an understatement. With its constant rise it has now devoured the entire coastline, not a ship has set sail on its waters in half a decade and its fury gains as it comes head to head with the towering Zale Mountains. It roars against the black rocks, smashing incessantly as if attempting to break into our beloved Mare-Marie." Muscae looked at Belleny with certainty in her eyes, "I've had first-hand experience with the sea and travelled the treacherous path high along the mountain tops, it must be avoided at all costs."

"Why are you telling *me* this?" said Belleny. She frowned down at the map and the enormous section which the ocean had taken over, "You must be more stupid than you look, who in their right mind would even think of such a path. What about this tower then, surely no one lives out there?"

Belleny pointed to the tower on the very edge of the page.

"Every short-cut has its risks," said Muscae, obviously the Princess had touched a soft spot.

"That's Mare-Marie's infamous Eternal Tower," continued Muscae, her body moving in close, "no one's been there, no one returned alive that is. It's further out to sea than this book's map could ever show, just a speck through an eyepiece, but it's out there." She pointed to the illustration of the tower and said, "The map maker placed it there, but it would need to fold out ten times to be even close to scale. Who knows how it got built in such waters is beyond me. Some have tried to fly there; they could have reached it, who knows? No one's returned to tell the tale. It's just too far and too dangerous."

"So no one's there then?"

"Of course not, but there is a rumour, a far-fetched one at that, that a young girl lives in the tower."

"Please, living on seaweed and salt?" mocked Belleny.

"Even from the Zale Mountain's the sea can reach up with its watery fists and rip you from the pathways above, no matter how high up you are. I don't know what's worse, falling into the ocean so it can squeeze every last breath from you or tumbling down the sheer cliff face, no doubt breaking every bone in your body?"

Belleny looked on with distaste, "Are you here to torture me with horrid outside facts?"

"I'm sorry, I got carried away. You can hear the sea's roar, it's quite impossible not to. You could probably see it on a clear day from your balcony?"

"Of course I've heard it, it's like an incessant voice in my head," the Princess paused, "so you've seen it ... up close?"

"Yes, only once and once is enough mind you," Muscae curtly snapped. "Fortunately the mountains are impervious to its fury, keeping us in Mare-Marie safe and sound," she said, moving to the next picture as if that was that.

"Impervious is not indestructible, it's only a matter of time before it overflows or breaks through and drowns all those in Mare-Marie, it's inevitable. Hence the name, Pelagica City of the Drowned."

"Princess it's not called that! That's no way to talk about your land and its people. The mountain stands untouched to the sea's fury so I would say it is indestructible, so please let's leave it at that. And if it does, unfortunately, happen one day, you'll be fine all the way up here."

"Surrounded by an ocean of debris and bloated bodies, it's going to be glorious when that happens."

"Ahem, yes well that isn't going to happen. Why would you think such a thing?"

The Princess shrugged, "seems like a logical outcome, corpses float don't they?"

"You mean illogical, and no corpses don't 'just float', for your information, they float due to the oxygen still in the lungs and as this dissipates, they sink like a stone."

Muscae pointed her finger to the castle once again, "The Crystalon Castle is also indestructible."

"Of course it is," Belleny rolled her eyes, "what isn't indestructible around here?"

"Do you know why it's—"

"Indestructible," sighed Belleny.

"Yes," said Muscae.

"Don't patronise me, I probably know more about the ins and outs of this castle than my father—besides the new tower."

"I don't doubt that," said Muscae.

"The crab's insignia is plastered across every coat of arms," said Belleny.

"Yes the Alphena Crab, it's such a beautiful looking creature."

"Do you find dead things beautiful?"

"Not particularly. Do you know the Alphena Crab left the sea and gathered here to die in the west?"

"What do you mean? That's impossible, they escaped out of the Pit when the creature rolled over," said Belleny.

"They did not. But it is a mystery. Why leave the ocean and climb all the way up the mountain, a feat in itself, then all the way to the West just to die? Sad thought isn't it?"

"I'm sure they were quite happy in the Sea of Sorrow," said Belleny and just as Muscae thought she was interested, she watched as the princess got up and took the strange beaked mask from its stand and began to polish the large eyes on the side of its head.

Muscae scratched at her palms as she did when she was irritated. *Relax,* she told herself, *the Princess is just another student and you've probably taught a lot worse.* After a deep breath, she continued on, "now where were we?"

Belleny placed the mask over her face and turned towards Muscae, "We've done suicidal bugs, destructible castles and mountains, a demented ocean that wants to drown us all and an abyss that homes a sleeping beast that will one day terrorize us all. You're up to flying creatures, dark woods, cursed temples, birds the size of houses and don't forget the invisible giants that steal sleeping children. I'm so glad you came tonight to remind me, I'll sleep well in the morning."

"Oh Princess, the stories you think up, most of those giants are terrified of children," the woman paused and turned her eyes to meet Belleny's, "but you're right, there are some, some creatures that plainly should not exist if you ask me."

The Princess lifted her mask to the top of her head and revealed a worrisome frown.

"Oh, I'm sorry, I don't wish to implant fearful images. But as you already know this is the very reason the kingdom is continuously guarded, day and night. It's a very strange place, temperamental at times, creatures fall from the sky, as it seems, the good and the bad, unfortunately. Keeps it exciting I guess. Sometimes they're helpful—"

"Sometimes they're not. When exactly are they helpful? When they cull the population, so we don't have to ration food?"

"Oh Princess, that's never happened. I mean like the gentle Kylen that flew in from the desert. At first we may have killed a few, but then realised they are as placid as big toes and have been very helpful in the guarding of the castle."

"Kylen, disgusting beasts," huffed Belleny.

"Yes I know, wicked looking creatures, but they can't help it, can they?" said Muscae, "especially with all those blinking yellow eyes following you around and a mouth full of barbs, oh and not to mention those giant thick claws of theirs, tear one of your fathers galloping Rast clean in half if they wanted to, eat it in a few bites. I've seen it happen once, down by—"

The Princess covered her mouth, "Enough already, spare me the gory details."

Muscae shook her head, "I'm sorry Princess, I don't know what came over me," she knew better, but tonight her words had become tainted. "Please don't be afraid of them, they're nothing but playful children, even when they're adults, most things are just games to them. My husband and I had a pet one once, Pepper was quite a character.

"Why would anyone want a pet one?" said Belleny raising a single brow, "so where is it? Out eating a Rast? Did you ride here on the beast tonight?"

"No, he's—" she looked up at the white creature above the door, "gone." Her gaze turned towards the closed curtain as if Pepper flew outside, "He may be gone ... but no, I feel he's alive, I'm sure I would know, he disappeared several years ago. I'm sure he's enjoying himself somewhere."

"Maybe he's been out there all along and ridden by one of those dumb soldiers, they all look the same don't they?"

"Not at all, my Pepper is white."

"White?" questioned Belleny.

The woman turned back, her eyes watery, "Pepper was just a pup."

"A pup?"

"Yes, he had no lights. When they become adults, their wings develop and acquire the ability to project light from underneath."

"Well, I didn't know that. Sounds like magic to me."

"Yes it does, doesn't it?"

"Is that all Muscae? I am rather bored."

Is that all indeed!

The book rose and slapped shut above her head.

"All right Princess, you win, let's call it a night as it's late, well it's late for me. Maybe next time we have the class in the day like normal children or at least downstairs, I wasted half the night just walking up here."

"Normal children? I don't think so, you should have left earlier. Help yourself out and don't touch anything," said Belleny as she turned and walked away into the dressing room.

The teacher sloped, but her walk lead her not entirely in the direction of the front door. She had positioned herself in front of the largest of curtains and beyond the tree's reach. *Ah, the balcony,* she assumed.

With Belleny gone now was her chance. As requested by the King, if the opportunity arose and arise it had. *The handsome bonus will be well worth that awful climb and putting up with that twisted little horror,* she thought, *I should throw her from the balcony head first.* The woman paused and shook her head, *why would I think that? I'm truly not myself up here.* Muscae spoke gently as if Belleny was in the room, "I hear it's a beautiful night outside, imagine the view from your balcony. You could quite possibly touch the roof of the sky from this height," she said.

Like a deer, Belleny's ears twitched in warning. She couldn't see or even hear Muscae but knew in an instant what the woman was attempting. The deer turned into a beast pushing the doors apart with force.

She was too late. Muscae grasped the curtains tight in each hand, "Let me open these up for you a little." She grabbed the thick fabric and pulled them hard and wide apart.

"Don't you dare!" commanded Belleny as the rose-petal fabric exploded from her dress with every thrust forward.

The teacher stood frozen and felt an alarming pain. She looked down at the Princess' strangling grasp, her thin white claws clenched around her swollen wrist. In a flash, the woman thought not of her arm, but of what she saw, *the rumours were true!* Behind the curtains, every single glass panel had been completely masked. Plastered up, pale yellow and opaque to the outside world.

So old ... how long have they been covered up like this? Years? Are they all this way? They must be ...

In an instant the pain brought her back, "Stop it, you're hurting me," she scowled.

Together they looked down at her venomous grasp. The sight was grotesque and the Princess unlatched, dropping the woman's heavy arm, revealing a scattering of raw flecked lacerations.

Between gritted teeth, the Princess hissed, "Get out now!"

Muscae quietly soothed, "Princess, please settle you're overreacting."

The previous teacher was right, she was out of control, but the King insisted she was a good girl.

But the good girl began to growl and with cold fingers ordered the woman towards the door.

"With respect Princess, I will not leave until we find some resolution and work this out" demanded Muscae.

With dead eyes, the white creature looked on. "No," came a faint growl, but it fell on deaf ears.

Belleny reached back and swung her open palm hard and fast slapping the woman square across the face. A glowing handprint welted up at once. The woman stumbled back, completely stunned.

"You're out of your mind!" snapped Muscae in a high-pitched voice. She held the side of her face as the blood rose to meet it. "No wonder the King keeps you locked up here, you poisonous little creature, you're insane, completely insane!"

Belleny barged forward, her spread fingers pushing her with each step, "How dare you come up here, you're just like the rest of them, why can't you just leave me alone, stop interfering with my life!"

Muscae scuffled backwards, tripping on her skirt hem as her weight released a tremendous thud against the doorway. "How dare you treat a teacher like this," said Muscae balancing herself up on one knee and reaching for support. "Just look at my arm, you should be belted—Princess or not."

Muscae's temper had unleashed a beast in the Princess, just as the teacher before her and the ones before her. "And while I'm at it, what sort of life is this?" wavered the woman holding her arms up. "Princess, you're cooped up all day ... all day and night! And what sort of person sleeps during the day and is awake all night? You're completely back to front and upside down, completely lost without a mother's guidance, I do wish I'd never come to this dreadful tower. You're not a Princess, you're a mistake."

Belleny shook from head to toe. Through grey lips, she hissed, "Are you finished woman?"

Muscae pulled herself up. She shook as well. She knew, what was said was said, be it out of fear or anger, but she couldn't believe her own mouth had said them. Instantly she bowed her head.

"Please forgive me, Princess, I have over-stepped the mark ... it's late and I am truly, truly not myself tonight."

Belleny turned on her heel and stormed off, brushing her four-poster bed and slunk off towards a crystal divider. The woman watched as the rose dress fell to the floor and Belleny kicked the petals aside. For a moment, she stood naked with her back to the woman.

"Belleny? Are you all right?"

At that moment there came another growl from behind, its volume was low, but it silenced the woman.

Belleny walked out and knelt next to a mask and withdrew several items from the shelves below it, placing them on the bed. She put them on in several movements; a skin-tight body suit coated her white skin to pitch black. Black gloves pulled tight at her elbows, each arm hung a row of long tassels that fell to her waist, their ends knotted.

"Belleny?" questioned the woman, wondering if she should leave or stay. But her silence continued. So she waited.

The Princess knelt beside the mask and removed a pair of Chopine shoes. She slid each foot into the decorated stilt shoes, their base like black clawed irons stretched up to her knees. When she stood up, she towered thin and shadowed black. The mask was last and placed ceremonially upon her head.

"If you don't mind, I'm leaving now, you're starting to scare me."

The woman reached for the door and glanced back to the creature that was once a Princess.

"Wait," snarled her wild voice from behind the mask.

The woman froze as Belleny turned towards her with stilted movements and moved from behind the bed. Each weighty step held her feet secure, but above her body jerked, as if led by a three-fingered puppeteer. Belleny leant down and grabbed the book on the bed.

Muscae knew it was only the Princess but struggled to reassure and convince herself otherwise. In an instant, she made a connection, turning her head upwards and back to the girl. *Yes, the same, the béte noire.* The Princess resembled the white creature that hung above the door but black with a thin mane that dragged on the floor. Its large wolf-like eyes reflected the lanterns in the room and Muscae huddled against the door.

The teacher joked, "Oh my book, aren't you a good little monster." But the seriousness in the air was suffocating.

Why is she dressed that way? She brings the worst out in me. She must understand this is not normal behaviour? I just had to say something.

Belleny stopped at the end of her bed where earlier she sat like stone and stared at the woman. Silently she held the large white book out in front of her.

Muscae sighed, "Thank you, Princess, I really don't know where I'd be without—"

"No," growled a voice but Muscae wasn't sure if it came from Belleny.

The woman turned up at the white creature and stared into its dead white eyes, "it spoke, it growled ..." she pointed shakily stepping away in shock.

Belleny remained silent as a grimacing curse passed through her lips. The beastly mask she wore unlatched its jaw revealing rows of jagged teeth and out of the silence came—the scream.

The teacher held out her hands, clasping them together, "Stop Princess stop! Please, I beg of you!" Unsure where to turn she fell to her knees. The last thing she wanted was the King to be woken to this sorrowful howl.

With no end in sight the scream continued. It was not a scream of fear or a sobbing cry, but a wild, painful pitch of despair that sent goose bumps across the far planes of Muscae.

But the ordeal was far from over.

Within a clenched black claw, Belleny let the white book hang by its front cover. The woman looked on stunned. How her skinny arm held it with one hand was beyond understanding.

"Careful Princess, that's a—" she paused, watching as Belleny pulled back her other hand, its glove tipped with sharp, black glass nails.

The voice returned, "No!"

But Belleny was far from sound.

"It talked again," jumped the woman, "it said no!" She scuttled below the girl's knees begging and fearing.

With slashing movements, Belleny drove her claws down, deep inside the book tearing out fists full of pages at a time.

"No, Princess! No!" cried the woman, her hands grabbing at the falling pages, "it's the only one!"

Belleny continued till there was not a single page attached. Muscae shook her head, aghast at the scene of scattered parchment her mouth mouthing soundless words. But like the winds, her sweeping fear rose into anger, "You think you'll get away with this, I'll see you're punished, punished in front of all of Mare-Marie!" she shouted with full lungs but her voice held second place to the Princess.

Under no circumstances did the screaming dissipate from the Princess' constricted, broken face and the woman, now white with shock and rage, ran to the door ducking from the beast and wrenched the door wide open, racing down the stairs as fast as one could fall.

"The Pit or the Sea, you'll have by morning to decide!" hailed Belleny, her coarse voice echoing down the stairwell.

The door shut with a thud as Belleny's back slid down against it. The Princess laid her head on her knees, her lungs heaved and her heart pounded.

"How dare he break my rules! He knows better, what's got into him these days? And you!" She looked up, "you're lucky I don't tear you down, rip you up and weave you into a rug," she hissed, spitting through the mask, then closing her eyes.

The creatures hung their heads in silence.

Sitting alone on the muddy bank of the Veelin River, which began deep in the Northern Mare, a young Trickle Fox fed on the blackened flesh of a giant poisonous Glass Fish. The fish itself was now a metaphor for the river. Once a sign of purity and health, it was now opaque and fetid, with oily bloated gills, a horror of itself. The fish quivered helplessly as the fox pinned it's head down onto the muddy bank, nipping and ripping the raw flesh from its spine. The tree stumps, the carrion flying overhead, the rotting fish spines, the haunting willows, everything in this murky and horrid environment was cloaked in black and all that was, had now turned to rot.

The treacherous water raced by in rapid succession, spitting up along the bank as if trying to grab at the fox and take it under. With a ravenous growl, the young fox snatched the fish up in it's jaws and carried it back to its den, which was a fallen tree trunk; dark, dry and safe from the water.

Scoffing up mouthfuls of flesh, oil and scales splattered from the bloated fish cavity and coated his furry muzzle in a rank film. Startled his ears pricked up. The fox bared his teeth and snarled, he was suddenly threatened by an unsettling figure that passed, flecking the sunlight over the entrance hole. The black form had cast a shivering cold shadow and moved without the sound of footsteps.

The fox froze in terror. After what seemed like an eternity, he gulped a quick breath and stole a glance through a small crack in the tree. He could just make out the shadowy figure lumbering towards the river's edge. He watched as it paused, turned back and eerily scanned the land.

Leaving his meal the fox darted towards the rear of the den to make a hasty exit, but soon found it was sealed with a mesh of leaves and branches fused together with clay-like mud. In the darkness he clawed for an escape, but ground to a halt, turned on his heels and listened anxiously—realising the poisonous water had now begun to rise up onto the embankment and pour into the den. All around him the landscape was being slowly digested into the river.

The figure, cloaked in a Necromancer's cloak and heavy hood, begun to move slowly into the water, wading through the tar-like sludge. As it surged forward, the water seemed to break apart and move around it. Its destination, a black shard, a rock that towered from the belly of the river and cursed it's surroundings.

Monstrous shiny black beetles the size of goats, unfurled their wings, writhed and festered at the very top of the sharp rock formation. The figure wafted past and reached out its hand—to stroke and absorb the energy of the rock—revealing its wan and pale clawed fingers. With other-worldly ease, the hooded figure secured itself on the side of the rock and climbed up the jagged planes. It paused again as the water dripped from its cape below. It turned back scanning the rotting land and once satisfied it wasn't followed began the dangerous move upwards and continued the vertical ascent till it reached the very top. There it found a perch and settled silently, it's pale white face emerging from its shroud and shone like an orb in the inky darkness.

After a short while, the figure unfurled it's arms and awoke from its trance in the crevice. It looked to feed and eagerly spied a black resin bleeding from a crack in the rock plate. With sleeves pushed back and cupped hands it leant in and began to drink the oily liquid. Suddenly the figure stumbled backwards, clutching its throat and with violent gasps it collapsed to its knees. It wrenched and jerked on the rock ledge, and as if on long black spider legs, stretched itself up tall. With a harrowing laugh, it threw its arms up and clawed at the air. Violently the river churned and from the rock a massive surge of rapids rose up and tore through the valley.

The fox and it's tree trunk were uprooted and tossed downstream. The fox scurried to the top of the trunk as the water poured in—clawing low and tight— it scanned for the safety of solid ground but gave a low whimper realising there was none in sight. Nervously he glanced back up at the rock.

The hooded creature had now vanished as the landscape descended into oblivion.

Chapter 5 - The Weatherman

*W*here is my mind? thought Evelin. She stared out the classroom window focusing on everything and nothing. Ruegeris Bimatherous had been and gone, so had the monster inside that made her mind spin so wildly.

How could it all vanish just like that? But they've left me behind with nothing. I feel empty.

Evelin pinched her hand, leaving a deep indentation and stared at it.

Nothing ... I wonder what's really worse?

Her eyes caught, what she first perceived were birds, but were just fallen leaves scraping alongside the building. The open window invited them in, and a breeze threw them around the class in a light display of acrobatics.

Birds would never be so entertaining, she sighed.

"I'll get it," said Evelin, standing up as quick as she spoke, which was quite slow. Brackenback gave her a slight thank you nod and continued with his book. She passed Ursula carefully trying her best not to bump the giant, but this was near impossible.

"Watch it Milk," said Ursula, nudging Evelin through the gap between their desks.

Evelin turned her body and head at once and placed her hands on Ursula's desk. Something she had never done before and something Ursula was not expecting.

"Thanks, Ursula," said Evelin apathetically, "I'm going to miss you next year."

"Get off my desk you weirdo, I'm trying to finish my test. Sir!" said Ursula scrunching up her face and pointing at Evelin as if her hand was a handgun.

Brackenback came down heavy from the front, "Boots! Just shut the window already."

"Aye aye, Sir," said Evelin with a sleepy grin, leaving Ursula completely frustrated.

She approached the wall of windows and noticed the clouds behind the school exploding like giant cauliflowers.

Cumulonimbus Calvus, thought Evelin with a grin. *Looks like a storm is brewing Aunt Em.*

Evelin pushed the culprit window across and it slid with a shrieking, metal against metal scrape. As the gap got smaller, the wind let out a howl as if being guillotined in half.

"Sorry," whispered Evelin without turning around. She didn't need to face the firing squad, she could already feel their daggers flung into her back, why would she want them in her chest as well?

Eventually, the window closed with a stabbing click, the finale of her presentation, *how to annoy the class during a math test, By Evelin Boots.*

She crept back into her chair.

"What's wrong with you?" snapped Ursula under her breath.

"What's right with you?" said Evelin, although her reply came out quite dreamy and had little impact.

Ursula did her usual squished up face, shook her head and turned her back to her. There was only enough Evelin Boots she could handle in one day.

Evelin was so relaxed she grinned and glided her hands in front of her face. She was glad she shut the window as now a wonderful cloud of hot air consumed the class. As if underwater she visualized the air moving through her fingers, dispersing into small swirls of currents, which then blended back into the void.

Sitting as still as she could, she tried not to blink, it seemed the only movement in the class came from within the turning hands of time, ticking to its hypnotic beat above the vacant blackboard. Through the coughs and sniffles, Evelin concentrated deeply and listened to its gentle rhythm and stared at the hands with content. Round and round, turned to back and forth, time melting with each second. Then, as if its batteries were about to die it paused.

Tick.

Then the pause again as if time had finally given up.

Not yet ...

Tick.

Could time die? she thought as it began to stretch itself out to a point of nothingness.

Evelin let her imagination free as her head swayed with illusions. Mr Brackenback sank back into the blackboard as another dark shape dove out of the chalky blackness. Quickly it dived in a flash of speckled flesh, its body trailing behind it like a giant eel.

Ruegeris! thought Evelin.

Why is he back? Surely the twins were enough? Is he back for dessert? Could such a creature have a sweet tooth?

She would find out sooner or later. The serpent surfaced in front of Brackenback's desk and stared directly at her.

I mustn't run, she thought, *if it was time, it was time.* And in her mind, she was confident she would be chosen. If anyone were a dessert, her honey addiction would make sure she was the sweetest. Evelin laid out her arms on the desk, closed her eyes and presented herself freely with no regret, *it must be a willing sacrifice,* she told herself. At that moment of surrender, Ruegeris caught her scent of submission and in a wild frenzy made a direct line towards her. Desks meant nothing to him unlike before as he tossed them to the side throwing the girls with them. Even with her eyes closed, she could feel his destructive wave, a wave of ferocious hunger, and in a point of purity she realised, *it wasn't food he was after, it was intrinsic, his hunger was for essence; a spirit.*

Ruegeris appeared before her and she felt honoured. She blinked her eyes open to focus in on his speckled throat that rose before her, presenting himself in full beauty, his jaws gaped wide revealing a deep liquid galaxy within, lit internally by the lights of his now phosphorous eyes. She welcomed him, "Take me," she whispered with consent. Ruegeris overflowed with excitement. His full body towered high above her and with his tremendous weight, plummeted mouth first engulfing her whole as her eyelids simultaneously gave in. Like an anchor thrown to the sea, they drifted down together, deeper and deeper, as they sealed themselves away within dark black lashes.

Like a doll, Evelin slumped forward in silence. Her hair was falling across her face in a pattern of dark curls and a straight blonde fringe. Wherever her dreams had taken her, she was comfortably numb.

Mr. Brackenback stood up from his chair, "That's it people no more writing please, I know some of you have had more than enough time. Please finish what you're doing and place your test on my desk on your way out," he said, looking up at the large black and white clock behind him. "Like I promised you can go fifteen minutes early, just don't disturb the other students," he stared down at Anne, who was notoriously noisy. Anne replied, bending her lips into a slight grin. Austella and Catlan shrugged as he pointed at them, "Don't forget you two, names on top, I don't want to go through that confusion ever again. Thanks girls, have a great weekend, not long till the holidays."

Evelin's mind, like an old bulb slowly flickered. Through squints, her eyes caught enough light to see the class stand up.

Damn, I dozed off again. Finally, it's over ...

From hushed silence came the usual girl chatter, the trample of footsteps, the pushing of chairs and rustling of bags.

"Numbers, good for nuffin," said Veronica with an exhausted grunt, "there you go Brackenback," she said with an obviously fake smile, slamming down her test with an open palm.

"Why thank you, Miss Fein, it's always a pleasure marking your work. It's the centre spread of the class papers. Have a wonderful weekend."

Veronica replied with a raised eyebrow, "Okay—sure? You too."

"Ok girls, move along now, ten to zero."

The girls didn't need to be told twice and before Evelin knew it, she was the only one left.

Last to arrive, last to leave, she smiled.

Mr. Brackenback looked up as he collected the tests and placed them inside his briefcase.

"Earth to Boot's, this is Major Tom do we have contact?"

"Sir?" said Evelin.

Brackenback approached her desk, "I'll take that from you. I see you've had enough time to draw another masterpiece, disrupt the class and have an afternoon siesta," he said with a wise grin.

"I could have handed it in an hour ago," said Evelin.

"I noticed. That's not all I noticed, is something wrong up there on cloud nine?"

"I don't know? What is this place, cloud nine?"

"A happy place, far from problems."

"Why would you think I'm there? And how could something be wrong in a place far from problems?" asked Evelin.

"Personally a place far from problems would drive a mathematician like me insane, although I know it would do me good."

"Maybe you're right, there're problems and then there're problems."

"I'm just hypothesizing. I know you breezed through your test, and then some," he inspected her drawing. "But am I right in saying you've been a little mindless lately?"

"Mindless?" she asked pausing on the thought. "Yes, my mind is less."

"But are you all right Eve?" he questioned.

Evelin paused and let the question hang in the air for a moment before replying, "Yes or no, I'm not really sure where I am at the moment," she said and pointed to her head.

"I see—that's the crux of any old problem right there."

"It is?" she questioned, raising a brow.

"Yes or no is a mathematician's nightmare. It's the absolute that's always going to run you into trouble."

"What else is there?"

"I'm not sure, but I'm going to find out. The truth is you're only human so forgive and forget, and half an egg is better than nothing. Sorry, that's all the advice I have time for," said Brackenback with a grin.

"If that's the truth, I'm confused."

"Great that's it, stay that way if you want to stumble upon any meaningful answers."

"Now, I'm really confused Sir."

"That's the spirit," he said returning to his desk. He placed Evelin's test in his suitcase with the others, "I've got to run to the bathroom. That was a long test for me as well. Take it easy over the weekend Boots, only one week to go."

Evelin gave him a nod as he left and after a second her eyes returned to the open suitcase sitting on his table.

What was all that about? she thought holding her head. *He left his suitcase? Is this the real test? An invitation to Ursula's paper or the detention of a lifetime. She'll probably fail even if I don't touch it. Maybe he wants me to get revenge?*

The thoughts lingered, and Evelin lifted up her desktop. The red lighter up the very back looked back at her. She grabbed it.

Why haven't I thrown you away? Her mind growled as her desk lit up, and a flame danced against the roof of the desk.

Evelin! Control yourself! she scowled as the lighter burnt her. She tossed it back and shut the desk.

I can't be stuffed ... that's my prognosis.

Evelin sighed with a deep yawn and with the comforting thought of being uninterrupted she laid her head down, the new medication seemed to pull her under at any chance it got.

It was moments later, unknown to Evelin that the home bell rang for the rest of the pupils and within minutes the students of Yellow Tree High escaped from every exit. It was not long before they converged along the halls and alleyways and disappeared down leafy streets, leaving the school as silent as a Sunday morning.

Evelin was far from sound. From within a dream inside a dream, she watched the school girls leave from a view high above. Then without flying and more like vanishing, she faded to then reappear beyond the school, thousands of miles straight above. She watched the girls on their bikes, taken away in buses or in their parents' cars. In an instance, she was surrounded by nothing other than the thick white clouds that she previously watched from her classroom window. Unalarmed, she felt in control and with ease she moved through the clouds as if it was foam in a bath. Her body rose effortlessly to stand comfortably on top.

From here the big white continued on forever, in every direction and upon the blanket of mist a very odd man appeared in the distance.

Evelin didn't wonder why either of them wasn't falling to their deaths, and she stood curiously calm as he approached.

Who on, or off Earth, is that man? And what was he doing up here? What am I doing up here?

Evelin stared hard as if she wore glasses and left them back in class. If it wasn't for his shadow skipping along beneath him, she might have missed him all together. He wore a completely pristine white suit, combined with white shoes with white laces, white gloves and, of course, a white top hat that only a magician would wear in broad daylight. With a hop, skip and jump the man approached, gliding effortlessly in the air as if he was a cloud himself. With each step closer he waved, flickering his fingers like butterfly wings and continued to glide in, slowly landing right in front of her. Evelin smiled as the clouds beneath him puffed up in small chunks and several large pieces floated up slowly disappearing around her face.

"Ah-Choo!" she sneezed.

The man stared and looked at her puzzled.

"Ah Choo?" he said, scratching his chin.

"Hello," said Evelin not sure exactly what to say. She noticed he had a bright white smile under his charming silver moustache. She relaxed instantly but just in case she shuffled back a few steps.

"Why—hello?" he said confidently yet a little confused.

"I don't know why, it's just what you say," she said.

"I see, why hello to you as well," he smiled and looked over his shoulders and back to Evelin.

"Am I dreaming?" she asked, realizing this could be nothing else.

"I have no idea what you're talking about," said the man tilting his head. "I haven't seen you around here before. Who are you, what's your name and hmm ... I don't know ... perhaps your favourite colour?"

"My name's Evelin Boots but my friends call me Eve or Boots for short ... I do like white ... but that's a blend of every colour isn't it?" she said, noticing her mind felt wide awake, and her voice was strangely energetic.

"Are you a magician?" she asked.

"Boots? Me a what?" He waved his hands about pointing at nothings. "I'm the Weatherman, of course; people call me lots of things for short, most of it's quite rude—what do they know about the weather?" He shook his head, twisted his moustache at the ends and continued.

"Today is your lucky day Miss Boots, it's going to be hot if you like it, or even hotter if you don't," he said, pointing left with one hand and right with the other, then quickly swapping directions flipping his arms around.

"Oh ... really? I'm not too fond of hot weather? And they're both quite—the same? Maybe you could add something or mix them up?" Replied Evelin, watching the man's moustache curl up tight near his nose then spring back.

"Mix them up? Well, I don't know about that. You can't have hot snow ... or can you? Or can I for that matter? I am the Weatherman, whether I can is another matter," he smiled, turned around and made a tall seat out of the cloud behind him. Without looking, he jumped backwards into the air, landing comfortably in a sitting position with one leg over the other.

"Take a seat then, or make one, up to you, doesn't really matter," he said quite puzzled at his own voice as if he could see the words appear from his mouth in a cloud font.

"Weather is hard work. It might take the two of us to whip this up you know."

"Oh yes, I can imagine," said Evelin as she gathered a large scoop of cloud and pushed it together forming a small mushroom-like seat. It was nothing compared to the Weatherman's, but it worked and cautiously she sank just enough and then it was firm.

"Right! What do you want then? What do I want? I never quite know," he said all muddled, pointing here and there.

Evelin shrugged, not really knowing where to start.

"Look it's all this or that isn't it? Mix it up, mix it down, mix and match the weather round. Making weather is not like baking a cake, young lady. It's experimental, it's elemental, it's all the mentals," he continued with his hands waving in the air, talking to Evelin and himself at the same time.

Realizing the Weatherman was a bit muddled she needed to be more assertive. "Excuse me, Weatherman, I'm ready now."

The Weatherman paused and looked at her with his most confused face, "You're Ready now? Are you trying to confuse me? So you're no longer Boots? Or Eve?"

"Of course I am," said Evelin. "I didn't mean my name's Ready; I'm ready to begin."

"I see, so to be sure ... are you Ready or not?"

"Ahh, not?" Evelin answered carefully.

"Oh, I can wait, I'm quite a patient guy you see. For a second or two anyway. You do know it's most impolite to change your name more than once every hour?"

"Of course," said Evelin.

"Well, I'm still the Weatherman, always have been, always will be. Even if I take the weekend off. Which I do, between you and me, it's doesn't really matter," he said, pointing at the back of his head.

"Shall we begin?" said Evelin.

"Of course, go on we are all waiting," he said.

Evelin looked around to see who he was talking about and realizing there was no one in sight began, "all right, let's start with a clear blue sky and fluffy white cumulus clouds that float gently in the distance. Not too hot, but not too cold. Maybe a light breeze, but not too strong that a hat would fall off, possibly a sea breeze, that's much nicer," said Evelin with a nod.

She looked up expressionless; she could tell the Weatherman was not impressed.

"No good?" asked Evelin, with a slight shrug.

"Are you serious? No good would be a compliment! I've done that before. It just won't do, can't be the same, there must be change, that's the first rule of weather, everyone knows that!" he said, tapping his boot and making puffs of white cloud appear and explode.

"Hey, I'm sorry I didn't know there were any rules," she said.

"Of course there are, well just that one. You do have an imagination don't you?" he asked, patting his hand on her head.

"Yes, that's all I have," she smiled. "Well then ... something a lot different?"

Evelin thought quick and began, "okay if there is going to be sunlight, let it be pink like cherry blossoms, a beautiful sunset that will last the whole day not only for a morning or afternoon."

"Yes, yes, yes, that's more like it, even I need input from outside parties," he said, squeezing his hands together. "Why didn't I think of that?"

His eagerness got Evelin excited as well. "Clouds! Let's make the clouds cover the entire sky and move like hair flowing underwater."

"Underwater? Now I haven't done that before! Who are you Boots?

Go on," said the Weatherman eager for more.

"Really, more? What else haven't I done ... or you ... The wind, let's have the wind change direction every hour."

"Every hour? Someone's going to be working overtime," he said, as his moustache curled up to his nose, "oh well, not my problem. Anything else?"

"Ah let me see—lightning? Yes let's have lightning, but only over the sea, I saw that last week and it was just amazing."

The Weatherman raised and downed an eyebrow, "I did that," he said rubbing his knuckles on his chest, "did and done," he added.

"Oh yes, of course, you have," she smiled.

Evelin dismissed and raised her finger, "fine, but without the thunder, thunder always makes lightning so ... I don't know, scary?"

"No thunder? Oh, they won't like that," said the Weatherman. "Very well, I'll tell them you did it."

"Tell who?" said Evelin.

"Doesn't matter, now Shhh, I need to think."

Fine, thought Evelin and sat back relatively satisfied. She crossed a leg over the other and waited to see how exactly he would conjure up the weather. She watched him with a smile as he thought to himself, muttering a few words, drawing in the air with his finger and moving chunks of cloud into odd shapes. She noticed his silvery white moustache moving into another curling shape all by itself. Then the Weatherman cleared his throat and spoke as he walked oddly around his white cloud chair.

> "I've never had someone ask that of the weather,
> take a heart from a beat, and a bird from a feather;
> If the ocean is sad and the sky is bright,
> the eels will be silent and so will the light;
> Let flamingos dance in a plumage of fire,
> wrapped in zest and cooked in desire;
> All day and all night, let the hummingbird fly,
> only when it stops, will the hummingbird die."

The Weatherman stretched his arms out wide and shut them with thick thuds as he clapped his gloves excitedly, "yes, that will do, that will do!"

"Looks like that hummingbird better keep flapping," said Evelin.

"Do they ever stop? They've got more energy than a ... than a hummingbird? Anyway we're making weather not sand castles," he said, brusquely brushing cloud dust off his jacket.

"I think you did a splendid job," she said.

"Why thank you, Madame, my thoughts exactly. Have you ever thought about being a weather lady?" he asked.

"No, not recently," said Evelin.

"Consider it," he said and took off his tall white hat and bowed as he magically revealed a huge, silky black raven's feather from within. Then after quickly smelling it with a grin, he looked into her eyes and gently tapped it three times against her head.

One.

Two.

Slam!!

Instantly all that was the weather and wonderful had disappeared. Someone had seen to that.

"What no! Wait Weatherman!" gasped Evelin holding her arm out.

Evelin rubbed her starry eyes to a familiar silhouette and surroundings.

"Hello, Milton," she yawned.

Milton shrugged his shoulders, "Who's the Weatherman? I thought this was a math class?"

It wasn't long before Belleny could hear heavy footsteps stomping up the stairwell as the teacher's muffled cries echoed in-between each tread.

"Oh, the drama," she said, kicking off her Chopine shoes. Her face was hidden behind the wildness of her mask. Belleny swung the door open before they could knock or kick it down like they had done once before.

"What's all this racket!?" she demanded, as the soldiers reached her doorstep, out of breath, but committed.

There stood in front of her were two guards. The first was Gustus; who was so generous he made up for four grown men, with his gigantic cranium he had the features of a bear entwined with those of a beetle. The other guard was Kostis, who could be mistaken for a fox if it weren't for the tight black feathers that covered his body. Kostis was an Archer and in a flash he whipped out his reed bow and flint-tipped arrow with a fierce elegance and aimed it at the Princess' masked head.

"Unhand the Princess you fiend, there's no escape!" shouted Kostis.

"Don't yell at me Kostis, I'll have you thrown into the pit from my balcony! Put those away before you hurt someone you fools," said Belleny, hiding behind the door. "What are you doing up here? You're supposed to be guarding my stairwell."

"Princess?" both soldiers asked in unison.

She revealed her face and returned the mask to position once they were satisfied.

"Who else would it be? Unless you let someone get past your watch?"

"Yes, of course, it's you. No one gets past us while were on watch, you can count on us," said Gustus.

"Then why are you up here Gustus?"

"We heard screams from below. And your teacher said—" began Kostis.

"What teacher?" said Belleny, crossing her arms.

The guards looked at each other puzzled, "the one on the stairs? So you're all right then?" asked Gustus.

"Of course I am, why wouldn't I be?" said Belleny.

"Of course, but we could hear a wild shrieking," explained Kostis.

"Shrieking? All the way from the ground?" she said crossing her arms.

"You didn't hear it? It cut through the ocean like a siren. It could have been a Kylen Rider but—are you sure you're all right? Your teacher raced straight past us, I think she was crying, mumbling about a book?" said Kostis.

"She's not a teacher she's a babbling fool. Who let her into the tower? Crying over a book, what nonsense. No doubt woke the whole castle? And the King?"

"We're sure King Vera sleeps soundly," said Kostis, staring nervously at the torn pages covering the floor.

"He could sleep soundly on a sinking ship," she huffed, "thank you for checking up on me and please make sure that woman doesn't place a foot in my stairwell ever again, whoever she is. Goodnight," said Belleny, and closed the door quietly.

The guards were confused, as they were on most occasions, but they were kind as they were dim and turned on their heels pleased that the Princess was safe.

Belleny remained silent, the white creature stared down with dead eyes, hers hidden behind the mask. For a moment, they listened to the huge windmills that circled outside, in some ways they cancelled out the growling voice of the ocean, and it calmed her.

Finally, some peace. The sea is getting louder; it won't be long.

It was then she was reminded of a poem, sung by old Jonah, one of the last Ocean Riders.

> *The gentle voice out of breath,*
> *Not ever to gale;*
> *The gentle ebb and flow,*
> *Soundly set sail;*
> *The gentle dance in the night,*
> *Together at ease;*
> *Sing us a song to sleep,*
> *The gentle ocean and the breeze.*

Belleny had never stepped foot in the ocean and never in her wildest imaginations could imagine it being gentle or calm. She had read the books and seen page after page of its ferocious history, and none of them showed it sleeping or dancing with the breeze, only roaring and fighting with no restraint. It knew of no lullaby's to sing her to sleep, and there were no sailors left alive in Mare-Marie.

To Belleny, the night had just begun. She placed her mask back on its stand; the suit and gloves had been folded and put away neatly, and the tall Chopine shoes were placed back on their shelf.

With her costume set aside, so were her thoughts on the earlier episode. The only one with full recognition was Muscae; her face was still beet-red and her wrist, raw and clawed. Belleny pushed the torn paper into a pile and smiled knowing it would be a while before anyone would be teaching her again.

In the hollow of the black tree, that she named Winta, Belleny sat cross-legged on a large red velvet cushion. Although Winta's gloomy exterior was cold to behold, inside its hollow womb, the tree was warm to the touch, and it radiated a dull heat even on the coldest of days. The tree crawled over her, spreading across the roof with its wild black branches. With a dense claw, it reached across and outwards, covering the white walls in a tangled web of black branches. Belleny never pruned nor snapped a single twig on its head. She would often thank Winta for her warmth and company with light caresses and kind words although she was the only one. Her father, King Vera, was not fond of it at all.

"It's unnatural, a monster, just look what it's done to your roof. How it grows without sun, soil or water is beyond me," grumbled the King.

She replied, "it stopped growing years ago, plus it's holding the roof up if anything. If Winta goes, then so do I."

The roof and the tree remained.

Belleny knew in her mind and felt an unrest in her heart, what lurked outside and beyond the castle gates. She didn't like the sound of it; she didn't like the thought of it, and so she remained within the castle grounds both day and night. Over the years, she blocked the knowledge that she had a balcony and with this the desire to peer outside had vanished. She hated hearing stories about the outside world, with its terrible weather, hideous creatures, cultures and ugly ways.

Being a young Princess with the highest authority, she delivered her first defining rule at the mere age of ten:

"From this day forward, until said otherwise, I wish to remain inside. No one shall mention the outside world to me, or when around me, or they will be thrown without hesitation into the Pit of Nothingness."

By her hand, no one has seen what lies at the bottom of the Pit, but plenty have been scorned by the Princess, and many turned to tears. The Royal Greens Keeper agreed to let the thick verdant ivy climb up her tower and over all her windows as requested. At first he thought no plant could ever grow to such heights but as if by magic it obeyed her wishes.

Born from a desert seed, he mused. The vine was unstoppable, and when it completely covered her balcony windows, as if satisfied with its own sense of achievement, the vine's creeping branches and leaves quietly stopped.

It's true, everything she needed was inside the castle walls, it was safe and nothing from the outside world could cause her harm.

Who in their right mind, in my situation, would ever think of going outside?

The King was confused at first by her request and presumed it was an act for attention. The King realised he could do nothing and say nothing to sway her. She was defiant and stubborn as the seasons are long, and he accepted her ways and with some comfort knew she'd be safe within the castle.

King Vera accepted Belleny's rule but only under certain conditions, this included; private tutoring, all the usual subjects were involved plus an extra class created especially for her called 'Outside World Studies'. Belleny could attend classes on the proviso she had to leave her room once a day. He didn't want an entirely invisible Princess and socially inept daughter, and she happily agreed.

But the weeks turned into months, and even before it turned into years, he understood he'd made a terrible mistake.

It was the old maid Miss Boxtree that took her by the arm one sunny day, refusing to tolerate her fading complexion and unsociable behaviour. She dragged the Princess outside, screaming and kicking down the stairwell and out into the courtyard. It was when Belleny used her molars to remove Boxtree's wedding ring that the King understood she was probably better off inside and put under a watchful eye. The finger had to be removed, and the ring was never found, a gruesome reminder to all.

Belleny had a lot of time to herself, and she utilised this time well. She realised she had fewer distractions if she was up at night and the maids and the teachers couldn't bother her if she slept throughout the day. She kept herself busy on most occasions and not a night went by when she wasn't designing and sewing some decadent and intricate costume.

Although Belleny was starting to wither physically and mentally, due to the years passing faster from her self-imposed solitary confinement. She was borderline obsessive with the creation of her decorative costumes, her creativity and idiosyncrasies increased and she only spoke to her maids sharply and will ill-tempered manners only speaking to the white fluffy listless creature voluntarily, but those conversations were only real in her head. The maids all felt she had become peculiar and abnormal and noticed periods of silence when she was 'talking' to the door frame.

"Your funerals will be held in the Pit!" Belleny screeched at the maids who she caught parading around and wearing her costumes, and to her horror were mocking her in front of her giant mirror.

The King paid off the maids, mainly to keep them quiet and for their troubles, and hoped they understood she was a peculiar young girl.

Despite having no confidants and arguing with the hired help every other day, the Princess did develop a bond with one young maid, her name was Jodin Haire and who was respected like a sister.

Upon developing their friendship Belleny's explosive outbursts were less frequent, yet as a result she became uncomfortably quiet. Sadly over time she noticed it was becoming harder to smile, and rumours spread that she couldn't, even if she tried. It was not only the town's people who talked and gossiped about Belleny but also it was beyond the Mare-Marie kingdom where she was well known and ridiculed. For someone that very few people had ever set eyes upon, her reputation was unparalleled.

"I hear she wears a porcelain mask to cover her sad face," said one.

"I know, and it's painted with a smile because she can't move her mouth," said another.

"Oh, she can move her mouth all right, talks to a dead creature in her room. I hear she killed it with her bare hands."

"She did, it's one of those weird pets she's got. Threw it from her tower, dragged it back up and stuck it on a hook above her door."

"She did not, she can't even lift her feet, sulks in the hollow of a dead tree. Who would have a tree in their room?"

"I would, and I tried, but it wouldn't grow without sunlight."

"Magic I tell you, it's outlawed magic."

Every puppeteer in Mare-Marie had their own 'Princess Belleny' tales to tell as a part of their repertoire. The children would gather in close to watch the marionettes play out fables of the Princess in the tower.

"I don't want to lose my smile!" mimicking a forlorn Princess.

"Then what are you going to do!" roared the King puppet pointing back at the children as the Princes' puppet crouched hiding in the hollow of a black tree, her face masked with a look of sadness.

"Smile! I'm going to smile!" The children would shout back at the King.

The little children of Mare-Marie were joyful and buoyant with their simple lives and alone in the tower, a sorrowful and embittered Princess became more of a recluse.

It had been a short while since the home bell rang, and Milton Carmon stood impatiently inside the front gates of Yellow Tree High. As soon as he stepped on the school grounds he felt nervous, oddly as if attending a funeral for someone he didn't know. Once again, he sat at the large water fountain, faced the main entrance and waited.

He scanned his school blazer jacket, plucked some stray hairs and smiled modestly.

Unlike most boys his own age, he treasured his school uniform. He wasn't particularly fond of his school, nor the teacher's nor students, but the clothing he wore with pride and tended to with great care.

In the beginning, the uniform agitated him. It was bought for him two sizes too large, so it was a very dowdy box shape, and he felt like a poor orphan boy draped in ill-fitting clothes.

Aunty Jean had a hand in tailoring the blazer jacket and trousers and he remembered the moment she began taking his measurements, he froze, his leg stuck out rigid at a 45 degree angle, her tape measure zipping up to his inner thigh, this was truly the definition of awkward.

"These trousers are massive on you child! Are these your dad's pants? Just look at these botched hems, Milton. Did your Mum do this? She's useless at sewing, she's all thumbs!"

Throughout the weekend, his Aunt slaved away mending the clothing and by Sunday afternoon she appeared sat the front door with a dark garment bag hung over her arm. She looked pleased as punch when he answered the door.

"Ta Da!" she said and pushed him back down the hallway. "Let's get this on before you sprout another inch."

Milton unzipped the bag slowly, expecting to see gold frills, white lace, velvet trim or silver buckles.

"Is this, is this my suit?" he said, placing the blazer jacket across his bed.

"Yes child, this is yours."

He realised it was the same uniform from the dark blue woollen fabric, but he had a hard time recognizing it. Where there was a badly over starched mock silk lining inside the wool, now lay a royal blue silk lining that fit the sleeves beautifully. The schools insignia had been appliquéd and was proudly displayed above the jackets breast pocket. Milton touched the silk then moved his fingers along to the dark turquoise buttons and looked up at Jean.

"I hated those gold buttons," he said.

"I know, who do they think you are, toy soldiers?"

"These are nice ... for buttons."

"Let's see how it looks on, shall we?"

Milton kicked off his sneakers at once and grabbed his hardly worn school shoes."

Aunty Jean took a deep breath and left the room.

Milton couldn't believe she actually replaced every ill fitting item on his remodelled school uniform.

Effortlessly his legs slipped into the trousers and caught a glimpse of himself in the mirror. He then removed the crisp white shirt from the hanger and carefully buttoned it up and tucked it neatly into his suit trousers. The jacket went on last, and instantly he realised what it was all about. He moved in front of the mirror, slipping on his shoes and slowly looked up, *she's good, real good.*

The next day at school, Milton felt invigorated and confident. A sense of personal pride welled up inside him. The boy felt he was now a man.

Milton stared across at the Golden Wing School across the road to the untrained eye the school grounds were almost identical to Yellow Tree High, yet one was built to school boys and the other for girls.

"Mr. Carmon, you seem to be a regular fixture to the girls' fountain? Auditioning as a statue?" said Mr. Brackenback.

"Ah, I am waiting for Evelin, Miss ... Evelin Boots."

Brackenback stared at him.

"Have you seen her about? I've been here a while, and I didn't see her come out? I'd call her, but she refuses to use a mobile phone," said Milton.

"Positive, negative, I see. She's still in my class again. Dreaming of algorithms I hope. I was going to wake her, but you know what they say, let sleeping dogs dream."

Milton shook his head, "I think it's, let dying dogs sleep."

"Really?" Squinted Brackenback, an eye turning back for the right answer. "I don't think either of us is right. I'm a numbers man, what's your excuse?" Brackenback smiled and placed his bike on the footpath.

"You better go and grab her. Room forty-five up the back. I don't think she wants to be locked in over the weekend. Although, she could get a lot of studies done—unfortunately, she's the only one that doesn't need it. Good luck with the audition," he said as he rode off.

Inside? Oh, bother.

Milton stood up, adjusted his tie and picked up his brown leather satchel and walked towards the large glass door entrance.

The large front doors swung open effortlessly; he took a left, then a sharp right just below the stairs.

Forty-three ... Forty-four ... room Forty-five.

Milton peered through the small window in the door and as he walked in he whispered "Evelin?, Eve?" he said once again and knelt down next to her. He watched her eyes flickering around underneath her eyelids.

Then Evelin whispered, "lightning over the sea ... no thunder please."

Milton stood up and pulled back Ursula's chair purposely scraping it along the floor. Evelin didn't wake. He slumped down on the desk and stared at her. He felt odd watching her sleep but also felt happy to see her so calm and relaxed for a change.

If only you could wake up this way.

"Evelin! Your hair is on fire!" he snapped but little did she notice him. *Fine, you give me no choice.*

Milton felt a little bad for waking her with a ruler, a metal one at that. But Evelin instantly awoke from her dream.

"Milton? Don't make fun of my hair!" she said letting out a loud yawn. "I told you before; you're not actually allowed in here."

"Eve I—"

"Rule number one, two and three, Miss Boots. No boys allowed," she said sitting up straight with another yawn.

"Boots, this is the third time you've crashed after class this week, besides Brackenback sent me in to get you." He pointed at her furry brown and yellow jumper, "I didn't know bears hibernated this time of year?"

"Hilarious."

"Probably best if you sleep at home, people might think you're afraid of your dad or something."

"Not even."

"Can we go already? This place is creepy with and without girls in it."

"Yeah yeah, I'll just get my things."

Evelin reached deep inside her desk and grabbed her pills, waiting for an opportune moment when Milton glanced away.

"You girls sure do read a lot," said Milton, inspecting Evelins books.

"Most of us do, but not the ones in my class."

"Hey, these library books look burnt?" questioned Milton and inspecting his white shirt for marks.

"Oh sorry. Here put them in this bag."

"From the old library. Can you still read them?"

"The pages are charred, so not really, I guess they're just a keepsake."

"You're a strange one Boots."

The pair rode their bicycles away from the school grounds and took the usual short-cut along the length of the football field to the annoyance of the physical education teacher as it broke the attention of his sports students rep sessions. They rolled through Elden Park, along the perimeter of the woods and down the alleyway between the old antique store, in front of the boarded up and abandoned newspaper printing building and onto Edinburgh Street where Evelin's house appeared right at the top of the street.

During that particular bike road home, Milton couldn't help but notice how his friend was lost in thought. He saw a distant look in her eyes and then when she uttered a few words she looked somewhat sad. He had tried so badly and really wanted to say something to ease her along the ride home but wasn't sure how to find the right words. It wasn't until Evelin claimed she was too tired, and she decided to walk her bike that he spoke, "Hey Eve, you know lately—"

"I was waiting for this ... here it comes," she said in a monotone voice. "I don't know what it is you've heard, but to cut it short I'm in therapy, so what more can I say? Honestly, Milton, I don't know why I went up onto the roof, okay? Let's all move on, I know I have."

"But I wasn't going to ask about the, I was just—" he stammered.

"Honestly I'm fine, I'm just exhausted from studying all the time. Stress, you know?"

"Yeah, I know, you should take it easy these holidays, give yourself a break."

"By 'take it easy' you mean riding my bike, going to school, feeding my fish—"

"Ahh ... okay, I think I'll ride the rest of the way, I've upset you again."

"No, wait, you haven't ... argh, it's complicated. I'm sorry hey."

I want to tell you everything Milton, the damn library fire, the pills, even the incident on the roof ... but not today, I just can't muster the courage.

There was a short, uncomfortable silence, and Evelin looked across at Milton and lied, "sorry the girls wear me out sometimes."

"What? Who? Gertrude the Ogre and her puppet Ursula? You said they didn't bother you anymore. We have to teach them a lesson over the holidays. You shouldn't have to stay back and hide from them in class."

"I don't hide from anyone! What sort of lesson?" said Evelin with a curious look.

"I have a list of things I would love to do to them." She watched as Milton pretended to twist their heads off and then kick them down the street.

"I'm sure you do, but I just can't imagine you locked up in prison!"

"Milton I'm not hiding ... it's peaceful when everyone's left the classroom that's all."

Milton held out his hands, "Sure, Boots. I'm hitting the hill while I have some get go, catch ya later, if not tomorrow," he yelled over this shoulder.

"Fine, see ya, Milton," she said to an empty road, as he was already far away.

Evelin didn't have the energy or the motivation to ride to the top of her street, so she slowly pushed forward, lumbering along with her bike, looking down at her foot steps, in a trance. It was half-way when she looked up and noticed the afternoon sun glowing off her house. The Palace as her father Robin called it was closer to an amusement ride than a house. She had no idea it would end up looking the way it did and wondered if Robin did either. Sure he had plans but they seemed to be for a different house. The Palace was constructed from fixtures that came along as it was built. She could easily spot the hulls of giant boats wrapped around each other, upside down and cut in half. Parts of playground rides weaved in and out, and industrial fridges were used like giant white bricks stacked throughout.

So it would look like less of a freak show, all the structures of the house, big and small, were lacquered in white glossy paint, which Robin saw to while he worked at Yellow Tree's only boat restoration yard.

She gazed at the large white spinning windmills attached to the roof of the house. It whizzed around and looked as if it was preparing to take off.

Was this Robin's master plan? Take me high up into the sky, where I will be far from harm? thought Evelin and continued up the hill. She arrived exhausted, dropped her bike on the front lawn, threw down her school bag and slumped inside.

"Evelin!" shouted Robin.

"Yeah, it's me, in the kitchen getting a drink. Where are you?"

"Basement. Stay there, I'll be up in one sec."

She could hear him squelch around and tip over a few things before bounding up the basement stairs like a giant dog. Evelin watched as he squeezed out a small door; his hands gloved and muddy.

"You're dripping," said Evelin.

"So are you."

"Yeah sweat, not mud."

"Hey, are you well? How did the big test go today?"

"Fine. I finished the thing in twenty-five mins, it was all multiple choice questions, so I was bored out of my mind for the last hour and a half. Can you lose your mind twice?"

"Only if you find it again after the first time," said Robin ripping off his large gloves into the sink and washing his hands with a potent salve. "Multiple choice was it? Nothings multiple choice in the real world."

"I know right? I blame the system," said Evelin, pouring herself a glass of coconut milk.

"I am exhausted, sometimes that hill kills me. I feel like a flat tyre."

"You don't look flat. Esta did say the new medication may take a few weeks to adjust into properly, just give this round time to settle."

"That's what they said about the last ones. And the ones before that. I only hope Milton doesn't think I'm—" she said as Robin's massive arms wrapped around her shoulders "Eww Dad get off, you're covered in, what are you covered in?"

"A certain washing machine has flooded the basement again. Just don't go down there for a few days, it's once again a bottomless pit. Look I lost my shoe in there," he pointed to his feet, one with a soiled shoe and the other barefoot and black as tar.

Evelin raised her hands, "I told you to finish tiling the laundry floor before you do anything else. I'm happy to help you."

"I know, I know. I'll get to it one day, first I have to finish your balcony."

"I told you before, I'd prefer if you left it for a while. I know it's been a while but, I still feel strange out there. I'm afraid I'll have a Humpty Dumpty."

"Why would you do that?"

"I don't think I would, but I might."

"All right Princess, I'll put up a safety barrier first thing in the morning."

"Thanks, at least wait until lunchtime, a girl needs her sleep. Oh, but seriously though you got to pull the plug on that washing machine it's out of control."

"You may be right—but it's part of the family."

"Be a man and pull the plug, now I must go and feed the fish they will be expecting me. Want me to cook tonight?"

"Oh, what's this, does my little lady have an appetite?"

"Possibly, or I want to eat something edible."

"Hilarious. I got some fresh eggs today, not sure if they're chicken eggs though, does it really matter?"

"I'm afraid it does in this state. So omelets then?"

"Boots mystery special," said Robin.

Evelin walked up the strangely constructed stairs to her room on the top floor. Lately, they seemed to go on forever. She stopped halfway to catch her breath, gazed at the small stretch of family photos along the wall and then continued. *I really don't change much do I? It's my hair.*

Evelin's room was big enough to sleep four people. The large four-poster queen size bed looked relatively small up the back; it's sheets and covers sprawled onto the floor like a baroque painting. One wall sank into built-in robes where only a few garments hung and two pairs of shoes. Along another wall, glass cabinets rose to the roof. There was not a thing on display. The only objects in the room were several blocks of books piled up on top of each other, many of them burnt and yellowing. But what attracted the most attention was a magnificent salt water aquarium that towered in the center of the room; an underwater wonderland, as impressive as the house it sat in.

"Oh my, it's good to be back," she said habitually scanning for a creature formerly alive floating on the surface. "Hey, boys. Where are you? I'm sorry I'm late."

Eve shuffled around the aquarium, viewing through the walls of green reeds and bright corals for a flash of white.

Like lightning under water, Evelin caught sight of her paper fish darting towards her. They didn't swim, they flew, weaving through the strange hypnotic reeds and out into the wide open. This sent a burning warmth to Evelin's heart. Gleefully watching as they crossed over the sparkling black ilmenite landscape, twisting over an algae covered skull, changing to a vertical formation and up to her fragmented face looking down at them. She climbed a small ladder and placed the tips of her fingers on the water's surface. Their strange lips bit at her.

"You guys must be hungry," she said pulling back at once, "Sorry I'm a bit late for dinner boys, I slept in." Evelin picked up a jar of fish food, her nose screwed up noticing it was close to empty and mainly from the acrid odour that came out of the jar. "This must taste better in water," she said sprinkling the remaining coloured flakes into the warm aquarium current. Evelin looked within and watched curiously as the food sprung alive, wriggling about as they turned into Sea Monkey baby shrimp and the electric white paper fish forgot their manners and darted to the surface, ripping into the shrimp cloud with such ferocity and disregard to the life.

Evelin climbed back down and inspected the rest of the aquarium. She noticed how big the paper fish had grown since she got them. *Big enough to eat,* she thought. But nowhere as big as the two serpent-like eels that refused to show themselves and lived deep in a ceramic cave that sat under a coral ledge. She noticed its entrance and the new doormat, made from regurgitated shrimp hulls, the poor adventurers that had curiously stumbled in last night. She stared at the eels and tapped gently on the glass with her nail, their mouths as usual gaping and closing in a hypnotic trance. *I'm watching you two.*

She returned to the Paper fish and said in a monotonous tone, "So how was your day? Really isn't that something. Doesn't that sound like fun? Me? Oh, just another day at school. Not really, the test was fine. Yes, only one freak out today, thought I was going to die again. I didn't obviously!" Evelin shook her head, "Yes Gertrude is still alive. I'm glad you guys had a good day."

Evelin wondered around the aquarium and walked over to her bed sat inbetween her stuffed toys.

"Hello, Sergeant Goldberry, how was your day? Is that lipstick on your cheek?" she whispered, pointing to his tabby face. A replaced eye that was different to the other made him look quite intriguing as if winking.

How curious, I thought you and Miss Bodington were just friends

It was then her bedside clock alarm blared four pm.

With a huff, she stared down at its flashing blue lights.

"Already?" she sighed. *I'm already zonked out,* she thought.

Evelin turned off the alarm and reached over to her bedside table, gently she slid open the top drawer and grabbed a small thin cardboard box. She sat back on her bed and read the small red type on its side.

Warning, do not drive heavy machinery.

"Well then, that's lucky I don't drive. What are you looking at?" she said to her stuffed animal friends.

"Goodbye cruel world," she joked, popped a tablet from the metal sealed pack and without water placed it on her tongue and quickly gulped.

"Eww, why don't they make them sweet?" she said to her fluffy cat toy Sergeant Goldberry, who had fallen over onto its side. "Are you laughing at me?"

The taste of the pill made her face screw up, and Evelin vigorously scraped her tongue on the roof of her mouth. She thought of getting some water, but the strange taste had nearly gone as she turned towards the bathroom.

Note to self. Always drink with water.

"Maybe I'll do my homework now so I can have the whole weekend off. Can't sit around all day gossiping like you guys," she yawned.

Evelin melted onto her bedspread, laying between Sergeant Goldberry and Miss Bodington. "Just a little nap," she murmured.

Her toys watched her pull her sheet up over herself and close her eyes.

Through the open curtains, a bright pink sunset rippled over deep blue clouds, as a storm on the horizon silently flashed its electric lights.

Robin called into the speaking tube, "Eve, you awake yet? Dinner is out on the table." The second time he called, it was enough to snap her from a deep slumber. From under her bed sheets, Evelin moved like a re-animated doll and slowly rose from her dreams. The first thing she could hear was the reverberating hum of the aquarium. Its cyclic gurgling was reassurace all was safe inside.

Evelin's eyes caught blackened silhouettes on the balcony. Lined up like suspects she could see four, maybe five large ravens gathered on the sill. They took over her balcony like Watchmen, arriving in the morning and she started to notice they would sit there late into the evening.

One let out a brash call that turned into a tight gurgle till it faded out at the very end; it received a similar reply in the far distance.

"Go away! Go to bed already," huffed Evelin tossing a pillow towards them with a hanging arm but fell short only to nudge the curtain aside. *That's a bright sunset? Wait a minute ... something's not right?*

"Calling Miss Boots. Last shout out for breakfast," called Robin through the speaker tube.

"What the?" said Evelin, sitting up at once and pushing hard against her watch, illuminating its face. *Ten twenty A.M.!*

"Robin, I'll be down in a sec, I'm already dressed."

"Great! See you soon Princess."

What's he so excited about?

Evelin rolled slowly into a standing position; adjusted her uniform, pulled off her socks, and slipped her feet into her usual black ballerina flats. Carefully she moved towards the balcony doors, and when in position rattled them with all her might, which was like a rough handshake, but enough to send the ravens into flight. "Be gone!" she crowed out.

She returned noticing Sergeant Goldberry and Miss Bodington tossed upon the floor, "I'm sorry guys. You would think I'd wake myself up tossing and turning all night. I know Robin is up to something."

She first stopped by her en-suite bathroom and stared at herself in the mirror. Removing a thin black hair tie from her wrist, she tied her wild hair into a less wild birds nest and told herself, *today will be a normal day. Today YOU will be normal.*

Evelin removed a small canister from her bedside draw and as she walked to the bathroom, she caught a reflection in a small mirror of herself swallowing several pills. *Happy Birthday, Evelin.*

Her belly growled.

You can't live off pills Space Cadet.

When she appeared in the kitchen doorway Robin stared at her as if her head was back to front, "why are you ... you do realise there's no school today?"

"Of course I do, don't ask, you already know the answer," she replied slumping down at the table. "So what's all the bubbliness about this morning old man? You got new socks or something?"

"New socks ... I haven't had those in years," said Robin, "toast will be up in a sec."

Evelin curiously watched as he prepared her a plate of scrambled eggs and slid it across the table.

"My favourite," she said.

"I thought roasted grasshoppers were your favourite?"

"You thought wrong. Thanks, Robin, but this better not have anything weird in it."

Robin sipped his coffee and gave a light nod for her to begin.

"You having any? You're making me nervous," she said carefully lifting her fork.

Robin shook his head, "Its all yours, I've already eaten."

She froze and looked up at him, fork in mouth and began to chew.

Robin grinned, "good huh?"

She took several more bites and paused, "this is from chicken eggs right?"

"What do you mean?" said Robin.

"Of course, they're chicken eggs," pointed Robin, "that's the taste of freshness—the hens popped them out at sunrise."

Evelin shook her head and said, "And this is the moment I put my fork down."

"Sorry Princess, Miss Davis brought them round this morning, it seems her chickens are in overdrive."

"I see, Miss Davis," Evelin stabbed in another mouthful and looked up with a gap mouthed grin.

"Are eggs the new path to a man's heart? You can call her Jacqueline; Miss Davis makes me feel downright weird all over."

"Eve, I know she was your teacher, but she wasn't all that bad, one of your favourites if I remember correctly."

"Maybe, I guess, but she had no relative competition, all the other teachers were either sadists or painfully dull. Still once a teacher always a teacher."

"What does that even mean?" said Robin.

Evelin shrugged her shoulders and continued eating only to pause mid-chew.

"What was that?" she said with a mouthful of food, waving her fork behind her. "Can you hear that?"

"The Ravens in the garden again?" said Robin.

"No ... listen, I'm sure it's in the house."

Instantly Evelin gulped away the yellow mush and turned her head to the lounge room. "Something's whining? If you can't hear that, then you've gone deaf."

Evelin looked at him curiously, seeing nothing but guilt in his eyes as they bounced around the room.

"So Jacqueline's eggs aren't what you wanted to show me?"

"Not exactly, they're good though aren't they?"

"Move along, what's out there buster?"

"I was going to surprise you after school ... once you got changed, but you fell asleep before I—just go have a look," said Robin eagerly, waving her into the lounge.

"Really? But—" said Evelin.

"Off you go," he smiled leaning back against the bench.

As Evelin walked into the lounge room, she spotted a box on the coffee table. She read the note written on the lid in marker, '*Take care of me and I'll take care of you.*'

That's not Robin's handwriting, she thought.

Evelin unfolded the box carefully.

"A kitten!" she squealed. It looked up at her with its grey-blue eyes as if it was lost. Instantly it stopped meowing and leant up against the box. Silently they stared at each other. It had been found.

"Hello," she whispered, "don't you worry, I'm not going to eat you, but Robin might."

She turned up towards Robin standing in the doorway, "I can't believe you got me a kitten? He's so—" Evelin wanted to say adorable but after a close inspection she finished with, "odd?"

"I know, but he's special like you," he said.

"What do you mean, special? I don't like that word."

"Fine ... unique then."

Evelin removed the kitten from the box and inspected him entirely. "Unique ... this kid is strange, but cute strange. It's a him right?"

She gave him a sad frown, "You know very well I don't celebrate my birthday today or did Jacqueline also have too many kittens?"

"I know—of course not, he was a gift from a stranger, I couldn't hide him for another month," he said.

He knew full well it was her birthday and sadly the anniversary of his wife's death. After a small pause, he continued, "he's a Peterbald, pretty rare I can imagine."

"Egyptian no doubt, he's a hairless cat right or is he sick?" she asked.

"No you're right, no papers, but I'm told he's healthy ... he doesn't grow much more fur than what he's already wearing, I'm told."

"I like it, it's like peach fuzz. He's got a bat's head doesn't he? Look at the size of his ears. Has he been given another name, other than Peter the Bald?" questioned Evelin.

"No name, call him what you wish."

"Nameless hey," she said holding up the kitten, "I'm not sure? It's got to be unique, something to do with a bat maybe?"

"Batty, Batus, what about Battle-Axe?" said Robin, throwing out names.

"I know it's confusing Robin, but you do realise he's not a Rottweiler."

"Oh right ... yes, well I'll leave it up to you."

Evelin closed her eyes for a quiet moment and upon opening them said, "BC, BC Boots."

"BC Boots, he sounds like a rapper, said Robin."

"Name one rapper? said Evelin.

"Ah, BC ... Ice."

"Quit now. It's M.C. anyway."

"Thanks for making me feel old," he said.

"And forgetful, anyway I have no idea for a name now so from Bat Cat 'BC' will do for now," said Evelin.

"Great. I know my parents must have just jumped in at Robin with both feet. I've always wanted to be called—"

"Robin, you're not changing your name, it's the name of a great villain."

"I know, I know and many girls. Fine, come in the kitchen while I clean up, you won't believe where I found him."

Evelin followed him with BC in one hand and sat back in her place at the kitchen table, "so tell me, who is this mystery donor? Where did you find him? Or did he find you?" asked Evelin.

"As soon as you left for school, it all went south. The belt snapped off our windmill and got snagged, you should have heard it, screaming around on the roof, I've heard nothing like it. I can imagine it made the birds take off for days."

"Don't worry they're back," said Evelin.

"I see. Then I had to take off the propeller to remove it. It's always the last bolt that won't come off."

"You shouldn't do that by yourself, why didn't you ask Oscar to help?"

"I know, I know. He did help the second time round though," Robin smiled.

"Second time?"

"Well, the first time I got it off but it fell, and it crashed into the backyard, luckily the blades were fine but—"

"But?"

"Scarecrow caught him and he's not doing too well."

Evelin rose an eyebrow, "Poor Scarecrow, never was a good catch, he was due for a makeover."

"And as you know the washing machine decided to break free, pulled itself from the wall and sent water everywhere! Flooded downstairs again. Lucky I realised an hour later. Imagine if I went out all day."

"True and BC?" she said.

"Yes, yes, I was on my way to hire a generator to suck out the muck downstairs and I happened to drive past a truck on the side of the road with a flat tire. I noticed this exhausted man crouched on his back kicking at the tire in a huff, so of course I pulled over and offered to help."

"Of course, you would," said Evelin.

"Hiya, buddy! Need a hand? I said. He was on his back kicking at this tire, sweating and greasy from head to toe."

"Damn tire won't budge, I can't get the last bolt off, truck's on too much of a damn lean," said this strangely hunched man.

"It's always the last bolt."

"Yeah, I know! I told him, I had the same thing happen to me earlier!"

"I wished you could have seen him. Said his name was—just wait." Robin reached into his pocket and pulled out a card, "Madchova Namchonka, odd name huh, suited him though, he was a peculiar sort."

"Mad Chova Namchonka?" said Evelin saving BC from the table edge. "That can't be his real name."

"Why would he choose that himself?" said Robin. "When I approached I thought he was wearing a poorly knitted jumper, nope, it was all him," Robin proceeded to pull at his jumper.

"Eww gross, so ... BC?" she continued.

"Well, I asked Madchova, what's the cargo? Maybe if we lighten the load, easier to jack the truck up to levitate the weight distribution."

"He then laughed at me, 'ha, you don't want to do that,' he said in a weird accent, Bulgarian I guess?"

"So I walked back a bit and read the sign on the truck—Robin stretched his arms out at full length—on the side of the truck was a sign written, 'Jo-Jo's Furniture Supplies—Everything and Anything'. Was a great sign, some crazy character painted on the side. Furniture should be okay to move, I don't mind a little hard work," said Robin and presented his muscular arms.

"Let me guess Hercules, there was no furniture inside and the truck was full of pets," said Evelin shooting him several times with her finger and finishing off BC with a single shot to the head.

"You know Jo-Jo? When the traffic died down I could hear them."

"Them? I was right?" said Evelin.

"Exactly."

Robin flicked Madchova's card across the table towards her.

"Looks like he printed this himself," said Evelin.

"No lie, while he checked on the animals, he let me hop inside. It was surreal, not a single ordinary pet. In the corner, what I first thought were dogs, were, but no dog I've ever seen, high as your shoulders with bone thin legs, like miniature giraffes."

"My shoulders? Not even."

"Ah huh, you think BC looks odd, there were snake-faced cats—"

"Snake-faced cats? Now you're telling tales."

I know it sounds that way, but they were white with a black cross pattern on their fur and they wanted nothing more than to get at the upside-down birds. They were vicious as ever."

"Upside-down birds?"

"They were fine, relaxed even, hanging in their cages. Most of them had fantastic feathers; some were hanging upside down with their wings wrapped around like bats while others stood directly above doing exactly the same thing."

"Your story is getting weird."

"Weird but true, and it got even weirder when he showed me these lizards crawling around on the roofs of their cages, dripping this strange honey off their backs, he put his finger in it and tasted it, 'good for your hair,' he said."

"Eww, that's gross," said Evelin.

"I know. So we couldn't empty them out onto the highway, even if they were in cages, Madchova said the daylight would burn half of them."

"Vampires huh?"

"I ended up driving the van against the truck and gently nudged it off the crazy lean it was on. The bolt and the tire came off as smooth as butter." Robin scraped a thick wave of butter across his toast and grinned.

Evelin held BC up in the air at him.

"Okay, Madchova felt fortunate I came along and helped with the tire fixing. I told him about you, your fish tank and possibly today. Then he jumped up into his cabin and gave me little BC and simply replied, I'll tell Jo-Jo he didn't make it, it's a long, hot drive interstate, it happens sometimes."

"That was sweet of him, for a hairy exotic pet smuggler."

Robin stood over her and mockingly clenched his fists impersonating Madchova, "I'm no smuggler, anyway don't judge a book by its woollen cover, maybe that's why no-one stopped?"

"Probably, I know I wouldn't."

"I'm glad you wouldn't. So that's the story, well the start of it. You can keep him in your room if you want. Keep him out of the aquarium," he said poking BC's tiny frame. "Eve, you know your catch-up session is today, you don't have to go but—"

"How long have I got?" she said.

"An hour or so, will be a beautiful day for a ride."

"Sure, I better," she said as her voice lowered, "you know I really lost it yesterday ... scared myself."

"It'll work out Princess, don't worry you're not crazy, just your hair," said Robin, roughing up her wild, brown and blonde, birds nest.

"Hey, Robin ... thanks ... for everything, you know."

"Team Boot's," he replied with a pearly white smile.

"Pull yourselves together, it's just a light breeze ... it's not as if it were a typhoon!" shouted King Vera, trying his best to boost morale for his men. But the truth was, he'd never seen a blizzard so ferocious as if it was pushing them out on purpose.

King Vera's men wore long cloaks, hooded with long sleeves to hide the armour covering their bodies, and their faces were shielded by masks. On the eve of a mission to the desert of Vheen, the men wore bandages of fine leather underneath their metal armour to shield like waterproof skin.

The sand that lay in Mare-Marie was incredibly fine, and sharp, like shards of glass. Even with a light wind it would whip into a frenzy, trying to penetrate the gaps between armour plates, so the leather bandages were always a critical addition. The White Sands of Vheen went far beyond the horizon in all directions and it dispelled into a giant wall of dust where it met the violent sea in a mystic collision known as the Gaze Akarr.

Through squinted eyes, King Vera, could faintly make out the blurred silhouettes of this troop. Each of his men fastened tight to their beast's, the mighty six-legged Rast.

It started off as such a pleasant day, how did it come to this? thought Bernard Chamberlain, a first timer to the desert and the youngest of the troop. *What did I think, we would just ride out to the desert and pick the jewels up, like flowers on the side of the road.*

"Stick together men, we'll find the seeds soon, at any minute!" roared King Vera, towering high upon his rast.

The species of Rast; were a reliable beast, sturdy and robust, towered at twice the size of a race horse. With a streamlined skull with large beetle-like eyes, they had a distinct insect look to them which was emphasised as they strode high across the dessert upon their six bony black legs.

How many more times must we listen to this fat man's orders? thought Bernard and spoke up out of fear, "we must turn back my lord, this is madness!"

"Impossible," shook the King's masked head, "we'll be swept off course, do you want to end up in the jaws of the Gaze Akarr?"

"My Lord, we're in No-Man's land!" cried Bernard.

Commander Vanja DeQuin, the largest of them, pushed his beast up between them and whipped his lizard-like tail into Bernard's beast. "Exhausted! Ha! The creature knows nothing of the word," he shouted.

"Whoa! Careful! He's just—" Began Bernard.

"Careful? It's a Rast, not a baby deer," snarled Vanja, whipping his tail into Bernard's beast. The King shouted "this is not a sandpit, stop playing around and join the others at once!"

Even before Bernard could mutter a word his steed felt Vanja's order and wrenched itself up and out of its sandy foothold. Its black, clawed hooves stabbed into the sliding slope until it stood tall on the crest with the others. Bernard held on like death as it unleashed its front legs, rising higher and higher; bellowing a 'neigh' that no horse could muster. It landed with a dull thud, and it regained its posture, exhaling in explosive sandy breaths.

Vanja had the strength to free his hand from his reins and slap Bernard on the back. "They don't like to be called lazy," he said with a gap-toothed grin, "the storm won't last, if we're lucky, be strong and you shall reap the rewards."

Bernard gathered himself as his rast settled, and he felt a moment of reassurance. He'd heard the tales but never witnessed their power, and now felt fortunate to be riding on one of the King's six-legged powerhouses.

"I'm sorry to doubt you boy," said Bernard, patting the thick muscled neck of his rast before the wind made him grasp on tight.

Vanja pushed himself up close once again, "do you think we'd be out here if we knew we couldn't get ourselves back?" He pointed at Bernard's beast. "They bear two hearts, can kick-start themselves from death, how's that for reliable! King Vera's rast is named Rinn, hell, he's kicked the bucket at least five times, twice in this very desert."

"The rast has done what? Died twice! Out here?" question Bernard, looking across at the battle-scarred Rinn.

"Help!" Screamed Saler as the mighty wind flipped him backwards and drove cement-like punches into his beast. The troop turned back and watched helplessly as the soldier was snatched from his saddle, to dangle high in the air from tight twisting reins.

"Hold on Saler! Wrap the reins around your wrist," roared the King, but it was too late.

Saler's weight wrenched his poor beast backwards, twisting its neck and sending it into choking wails. It leapt up on its hind legs and Saler hit the ground hard rolling inside the sandy rapids below. In a hazardous whirlwind, his rast kicked its four free legs in the air. A single blow from a clawed hoof would puncture through solid steel and pulverise a human skull. Ducking and weaving the troop dodged clear of its anguish, watching as an all-mighty gust flipped the wailing beast head over heels, a sight no one had ever seen before. The troops looked on helplessly as Saler and his rast disappeared in the whirling sand and sunk beneath into the abyss.

The King's Troop stood restless, scanning through the blizzard for any sign of their fallen comrade. Their calls to Saler fell on deaf ears as Vanja roared at the blizzard. As if it heard him the fierce wind and all the sand it carried fell like a giant carpet across the desert. Finally, it had stopped but Bernard's cries continued over the silent scene.

"I told you it would stop!" yelled King Vera, appearing from the peak of a tremendous sand dune now twenty metres away.

"It's Saler!" cried Vanja, pointing him out not far from the king.

King Vera spotting him instantly, half buried in the pure white dune. The fallen soldier appeared as no more than his arms and a head, waving them in the air. His rast was more than half buried but crouched protectively by his side.

"Hold on Saler!" said the King kicking his heels into Rinn. Saler watched through sandblasted eyes, the King like a mirage arrived as a blur coming into a soft focus. He unlatched leather ropes and hooked a clip on the saddled of the buried beast and its beaten soldier. With heavy grunts and wheezing Rinn pulled carefully dragging both of them out the dry river of sand. The sunken rast stood up and shook the sand from its mane, but Saler remained on hands and knees; the grains drained like water from every crevice.

"Next time you'll resist scratching your backside," grinned the King throwing him a flask of water, "save some for your beast, he deserves it."

"I swear this is the last time Vera, these sands are cursed," coughed Saler.

"Hmm, that they are," said King Vera scanning the vast surroundings.

With the wind at bay, his troops gathered themselves and stood tall on a snake-like peak. They unlatched their face guards and removed the fine sand from the pits of their faces. What they could see now was the lonely emptiness surrounding them, travelling off into the distance in vast white dunes with polar shadows as dark as caves.

"I would find it somewhat beautiful if it didn't try to kill me each time," said Vanja spitting out the sand from the back of his throat.

Bernard took out his wooden arcana, which was tied around his neck and played a tune to fill the desert silence. A sorrowful lullaby came, even though he survived the blizzard and the Gaze Akarr was to be seen far beyond the horizon.

Why would the King risk his life a week before his daughter's birthday? thought Bernard.

"Lighten up boy, before that tune brings back the blizzard ten fold," said King Vera.

"Sorry, my Sire,"

"Cheer up, you made it. Not many can claim they survived the wrath of the Desert Vheen."

"Yes, my Sire."

"Yes indeed, you best see to your rast, and then the treasure hunt begins!"

Bernard watched as King Vera pulled at Rinn's reins with a light whip to settle the beast and in turn the creature's anxious claws came to a stabbing halt. "Good boy Rinn," spoke the King softly, clutching its neck and bending it back towards his throat. The creature's skull dwarfed his own. Its face, even with armour, was coarse and raw. Using his finger, he dug away at the sand that collected within Rinn's eyelids. It whipped its tongue, unlatching the King's face guard and it continued lashing at his bearded face, it was coarse but kind.

"King Vera, come quickly!" screeched Vanja.

The raging winds had dropped and what was revealed was a bounty of magnificent glass-like seeds. They glimmered across the desert surface, causing ripples in the sand, each seed radiating their own beautiful spectrum.

Saler held several in the cups of his raw hands and pondered to himself, *were these worth risking my life?*

Bernard pushed a ruby-red seed deep into the side pocket of his boot, *this is the one,* he thought with a devilish grin. He then drove his hands into the sand and raked out another and smiled to himself, *no, this is the one!*

Unlike the others that packed every and any seed they touched, the King held his findings to the sunlight and inspected them one by one, sequentially ditching all of them far across a dune.

"No good my lord?" questioned Bernard.

"I'm only after one," he said.

"I'm sure she'll appreciate even the worst of these beautiful jewels."

"Are you now? You obviously don't know my daughter very well."

"No Sir, she's quite hard to talk to."

"Yes, she's not one for friends I'm afraid, you'll have more chance of catching the wind."

The wind, sighed Bernard.

"Now this is a contender!" cheered Vera, holding his first seed in the air and then deep into his leather pouch.

"Who's that up there?" pointed Bernard.

"Only Vanja could wave a spear that high, could be trouble, get on your rast boy."

Vanja stood tall atop a dune; he held his spear high above; it must have been twenty-foot tall. From it he waved a long flowing flag from side to side; once he had everyone's attention, he lowered the spear and pointed to the North East towards the Gaze Akarr.

"We have company! Everyone off the sand at once," roared Vanja, riding his steed carefully down the dune towards them.

Bernard stood in fright. *Off the sand?*

All eyes turned towards the glassy seeds as they began to roll down the sandy slopes, and it wasn't long before they felt the ground start to tremble.

"Steady men, no movement now, or they'll hear us," said the King as he slowly removed a long spear that was posing as a flag pole behind him.

They could feel the ground shake through their saddles, as what was coming closer rumbled harder.

Instantly Bernard's rast broke from his restraints. Its long black legs whipped down hard at the trembling ground like the foot of a giant typewriter, burning imprints into the sand.

"Control your beast boy! You'll be the death of us all," said Vanja steering up beside Bernard and the King.

"I'm trying! What's beneath us? What's going on?"

Vanja perched himself up high, "hopefully you don't find out."

Bernard held his spear as the others did and watched as Vanja followed the sand with his finger—it was approaching them.

"Wait ... hold on," whispered Vanja, as he watched for the tell-tale signs; it was close but not close enough, but he knew the evil crawled deep and circled them; too deep to strike. Then in an all mighty thrust it took off and pushed a dune apart.

"It passed and fast, quick this way!" said Vanja.

"We're following it!" said Bernard.

"Quick! High ground," said Vanja.

One by one they followed his command and rode carefully to the peak of a dune.

"Not tasty enough are we?" said Saler.

"Tasty enough for what?" said Bernard, who was genuinely shaken.

"Vicious Candar," grumbled King Vera.

"They've gone north, damn fast!" pointed Vanja. "Just when you think they're all dead, the damn things keep returning."

"We should go, my King, we each have what we came for, this is not a good sign."

"What was that noise?" asked Saler as a large weighted boom collapsed in the distance.

"They've found someone else," said the King.

Saler held a telescopic sight to his eye and focused in on a cloud of dust. "There's a carriage of some sort, a lot of dust, the Vicious have hit hard. It doesn't look good."

"What is a Vicious? Who would be out here?" asked Bernard.

Vanja took Saler's sight and had a look for himself. "Hmm looks like a prison cart. We better go see, the driver may be injured or worse, there might be escapees."

A prison cart? Escapees! thought Bernard. "What if the prisoners are dangerous, what about the Vicious Candar?"

"We can deal with the prisoners, but as for the Vicious Candar, they're notorious to hit and run. Come on men let's get this over and done with," said King Vera whipping Rinn and descending at once.

This is just great! sighed Bernard, standing alone and watching the troops power forth. *Fine, I'm not standing around by myself out here.*

"Come on boy!" roared Vanja.

By the time Bernard caught up the dust was settling and the soldiers were circling the cart. It was enormous and something he had never seen before.

How did it get out here? Few, it's still locked.

King Vera circled the cart slowly. Instantly he raised his sword and held it high, the others followed unknown to what he had seen.

"What is it Vera?" shouted Vanja removing his blade.

"Stand back," said King Vera, pointing at the strained leads that came from the cart, they disappeared into the sand. With a single thrust, his sword cut through and like snakes they whipped back at him then vanished into the depths below.

Bernard now realised. "It must have needed more than two Rast's to pull a cart this size."

"Six," replied Vanja, "search the area men, the driver may be alive. You boy, see what's in the cart, it seems to be secure enough."

Bernard swallowed and pointed at the cart, "inside?"

"Don't go inside, just see if it's empty or not."

Bernard looked at the large wooden structure. From its construction, he imagined it held several cells, once used to take witches and warlocks from the kingdom. He rode carefully alongside the cart.

Please be dead, please be dead, he thought peering inside the dark slit-like windows.

Someone's talking? Oh no, they're alive!

Bernard turned towards Vanja and pointed at the cart. "Inside, there's someone inside, I can hear them talking."

"Talking?" said Saler appearing from the other side, "discussing the fine weather no doubt?"

"Don't open it," said Vanja from the top of a dune, "the King has spotted another, possibly the driver, I'm going to investigate, don't touch anything."

Bernard shook his head. He didn't need to be told in the first place.

With sinking strides Vanja descended.

At first glance, what they saw from above resembled a pool of water but on close inspection the water became a blanket of spines in a circling mass.

A soldier jabbed it with his spear and instantly a painful screech came from within.

"Stop that you fool!" Ordered the king waving his hands for them to separate.

From underneath the pile of spikes, two leather gloves reached out and pushed the mass up off the ground.

"At ease men, I know this one, I would stand back if I were you," said Vera. They watched as a shell-white mask appeared from under the sand. With mysticism, it glided across the spiked, blue body. As if connected by magic, it rested where a face would be positioned. Two slits opened across the mask and inside they could see a pair of wet, shinny black marble-like eyes peering back at them. Its spikes lifted around its body in an underwater waving motion. The creature seemed to be alive.

"Calam? Are you alright? It is King Vera."

"Sir," said a soldier pointing to the silent creature's feet or lack of them.

The creature hovered and moved forward as two large gloved hands came out of the sand and reached out, at the same time Vanja moved in.

"Calam! It's King Vera," he commanded.

The creature stopped, and its giant hands lowered.

"King Vera! A thousand apologies my Lord," said Calam in a raw, scabby voice. "It takes me a while to connect with myself these days."

Engulfing the King's hand, he shook it firmly, "tell your men to relax, there's bigger things to be worried about out here."

"Yes, yes there are," said the King.

King Vera knew all too well about the Vicious Candar and on the last full moon of the year ordered their extinction. Sections of the desert Vheen, to this day, are out of bounds by law and laden with deadly traps. *They laugh at them now*, thought the King. He knew they had something to do with the blizzard and the magical seeds but couldn't make a connection. But their trace of destruction was formidable and had to be removed.

Bernard rubbed his eyes as King Vera, Vanja and an overwhelming spikey blue creature stood at the top of the dune.

"I'm glad to see you're alright Calam," said the King.

"Lucky I got thrown off I guess, I'm lighter than I look."

"The Vicious won't get away with this," said Vanja.

"They buried my rasts alive."

"Terrible news Calam, I'm sorry. Let's see what we can do, how many prisoners are in there?" said Vera.

"I'm at the end of my run, just the one in there."

They arrived back at the accident site where a conversation between Bernard, Saler and the prisoner was being held.

"He seems quite nice," said Bernard.

"Nice!" said Calam, "is that a surprise to you soldier? Not all prisoners are violent monsters, even you may end up in here one day," he said banging his fist against the cart.

"I ... I hope not," stammered Bernard standing back from the creature's spikes. "It's all a matter of luck. You alive in there?" said Calam, banging his fist on the back door.

"Calam, I wasn't sure if you were still with us, I'm glad you are and not because you're the only one with a key to this cart of yours. I haven't been that scared since—since I was thrown in here with a dozen criminals."

"You're the criminal here," said Calam.

"Is that so."

"Of course, Bernard informed me what happened, I can't believe they ate all six, for once I'm glad I was in here."

"Yes well—I'm glad you're alright," said Calam.

"I hear the King is here, a real King, I've never seen one of those before. Looking for jewels, in this giant sandpit. It's a pity the Princess couldn't make it. Bernard here tells me she's quite something."

"Did he, Bernard move aside," said the King. "This is King Vera of the Northen Mare, Emperor of the known land and—"

"I get it, you had me at King," said the prisoner.

Vanja stood up to the slit-like windows, "insolent fool, do you want to spend the rest of your days in this cell?"

There was no reply from the prisoner. Vanja shrugged his shoulders.

"Do you want some water?" asked Bernard, who then received a dark look from Vanja.

"No thanks, Bernard, if this is my welcome party I'd rather stay inside."

"We are not your welcome party," said Vanja.

"Now, now, Vanja. It's been a long day for all of us. Calam who is this prisoner?" asked Vera, "what are his crimes?"

"My name is Bateau. I was training with the Great Gonzo Circus when I was—"

"Dumped," said Calam, "left him behind for some reason, they packed up and took off into the night."

The King's eyes lit up at the sound of the Great Gonzo Circus. "And what are your crimes?"

"He's a petty thief my Lord," said Calam, "baked goods."

"A pastry thief? Why is he being dragged all the way out here then?" asked Bernard.

"He didn't get off. His was the first stop, just outside the city. We were going to the Caves of Vheen for supplies and water."

"I see," said the King curiously. "We'll set you up with a couple of rasts so you can continue on if you like. Bateau you're not returning to the circus?"

"I was abandoned. So I'm going on an adventure. I've never gone so deep into the desert before or seen the Gaze Akarr, but I have now. I've also been in a blizzard and met some interesting characters with interesting scents. Calam here said the caves are quite beautiful and up top, there is a good view of the sea."

"There's no good view of the sea, it's a maddening watery beast, you'll do your best to stay away from it ... open this door at once," said the King pointing his sword at the carriage door.

"Yes, of course," said Calam.

They watched Calam as he pushed his gloved hand deep within the shrouds of his cloak and pulled out a large iron looped ring which clanged full of long triangular keys. He placed one inside a battered black lock that was hanging from a chain and without a hitch it unlocked. The thick chain raced through its fasteners and gathered in the sand below, coiling like an iron snake.

"Stand aside," said Calam and with a heave the thick wooden door fell hard.

"Come on out," ordered the King.

Bateau walked forward and paused in the doorway, his two tails flicking in and out of the shadow's curtain. He bowed into the sunlight towards Bernard, who stood nervously.

"It's an honour to meet you, your grace," said Bateau.

"Damn you, this is King Vera," said Vanja, raising his thunderous voice.

Bateau peered across with a grin. "Well of course you are, look at you, you have 'the King' written all over you." Bateau swiftly pointed at Bernard with his tails, "this is clearly an impostor, he's the one that should be in this cart, not me."

"This is why he's not up the front with me," said Calam.

Bateau lowered his head, "I apologize, your grace, I'm not myself out here, the desert makes me, not me."

There was silence as they waited for the King. He tapped his finger slowly on the blunt end of his sword.

Bateau is no beast. He's no taller than my kneecaps. What and who is this curiously strange and talkative creature?

He couldn't keep his eyes off Bateau's two playful tails. The more the King watched them, it seemed the more they amused him. His anger dissipated, even his fear of the Vicious Candar, who he realised were far gone and happily fed.

"It seems you've been through enough and don't even know it. I don't doubt you're guilty of something, but stealing food for hunger is no crime in my book," said Vera.

"I wish you told that to the creature that sentenced me."

The King paused once again.

I wonder what Belleny would think of him and the Orphans? She could hate him, but he could be the type of character she needs to be around, someone with outside experience, unafraid of the unknown even though he's so defenceless.

"Come on then Bateau, I'm quite sure Calam can carry on without. How would you like to return with us and meet the Princess?"

"But Sire!" said Vanja coming in close to a low whisper, "The creature could be dangerous, it looks like Krin, it could harm the Princess."

"Krin was poisoned to the very soul," snarled King Vera. He faced Vanja down to watch as Bateau now played with Bernard. "Can you not feel Bateau's energy, he radiates like the sun, if only my daughter could absorb such a glowing spirit."

"Hmm, he does have a certain something."

And with that King Vera slapped Vanja on the back and shouted, "Come on Bateau we're heading home!"

"Home?" questioned Bateau.

King Vera pointed to a sparkle of light on the sandy horizon and said, proudly, "Castle Crystalon."

The exhilaration Evelin felt from the motorbike ride was met with a rude deflation as Robin pulled into the park opposite Esta Green's beachside house and child therapy headquarters. She removed her helmet, tousled her hair and with a quick goodbye, cautioned towards the front door. The front yard was entirely beach sand, beside a half-hidden cement path that she chose not to take. The dry sand scuffed and moved easily over her shoes. She liked how her boots protected her feet, and she paused watching the grains fall on either side. *Slowest quicksand in the world.*

Evelin dragged her feet towards the house; she had visited so many times before it was beginning to feel like she lived there. In her young age, Evelin felt tired and jaded. She peered through the side window, but there was no sign of Esta's flaming red hair.

The large pale beach house loomed impressively on its own block, acres away from its nearest neighbour. Evelin daydreamed that the house was once a boat; popped out a pair of legs and picked itself up, positioning itself closer to the shelter of the rocky cove and an enclave of a small beach.

It wasn't just the white wooden panels, the porthole windows, the large white sheets that were continually drying on the top and bottom verandas, mimicking sails, but it was the way it swayed up and down, an illusion made by the giant white clouds that continued to roll off the cliff-edge behind it, meeting the deep blue ocean.

Stop procrastinating Evelin huffed to herself and walked slowly towards the house dodging the carcasses of the bleached-white beach snail shells that seemed fixed across the pathway.

As usual the sandy veranda was unswept and from two bare elms, fallen leaves danced around the corner, twisting with the wind. Evelin reached the front door and with a small tight fist raised her arm, but paused, hesitant.

"Oh man," she sighed and her fist hung before dropping like a dead weight falling at her side.

What am I doing? She can't help me, I can't help me, Robin can't help me. What the hell am I doing here? What do I do now? Come on Eve, just knock on the damn door.

Evelin felt like weeping, deep sorrow ached in her, but she refused. *No time for tears*, she told herself.

Evelin turned and peered at her father from under her hair, the kind soul was waiting for her as usual, sitting in the park across the road at the same picnic bench. Esta invited him in repeatedly, but he kindly refused, he preferred the tranquillity of the park; the fountain and its statue, the white swans, reading his paper and watching passers by. She knew he loved the beach, but she also knew he felt it was his duty to be close.

Evelin grabbed the anchor door knocker and rapped it three times. The metal sound sunk deep as if absorbing into the thick pine wooden door. She stood waiting. Looking over her shoulder she shrugged to Robin.

He signalled for her to try again, by rapping his fisted hand in the air.

Two cats were watching her from their sunny saturated positions; one yawned as her presence didn't bother it in the slightest.

Back at the door she decided to knock once again, this time a lot louder.

"Is that you Evelin?" questioned her tainted English voice. Evelin stared at a yellowing plastic security speaker box screwed into the door frame.

"Yeah it's me," she said in a deadpan voice towards the box, wondering if she could hear her.

"Come on in I'm upstairs, the door's open."

"Okay, I'll be there in a sec."

Esta didn't lock her house and said it never had been.

Curiously Evelin inspected along the door's edge and the back of the unlocked door, there were no keyholes or locks and no sign of there ever being one. *She may be telling the truth, I doubt she's ever told a lie in her entire life,* thought Evelin.

Upon entering the house, Evelin noticed a portly ginger Tom cat watching her from within a large porthole window.

"Hello fatty, now you must be Potbelly? Is Esta upstairs? Don't trouble yourself, I'll see myself there," said Evelin.

Evelin passed her fingertips along the width of a large sofa as if exploring the decorative insides. *This place is the complete opposite of my house, it has been lived in, by more than two people anyway,* she thought.

Halfway up the stairs that were covered in white, shag-pile carpet, she could see the door ajar where Esta waited for her.

"Evelin Boots, Hello Sweetheart! Please come in and help yourself to some water," chortled the therapist.

As Evelin entered the room, a blanket of warmth wrapped around her and dove down her throat. She poured herself some water and tried not to stare at Esta or her teeth.

Instantly the voice of her dad followed, *gapped teeth means either good luck or crazy.*

"Evelin, so happy to see you, I was just absorbing this book."

"That's fine, do whatever you need to do," said Evelin, "what are you reading?"

"Oh, it's a beautiful old children's book of verse. I'm channeling the author, hoping he can help me write a children's book one day. It's not as easy as you think."

"I can imagine," said Evelin, wondering if she would survive if she leaped off the balcony.

Behind Esta, the long porch doors of the studio had been opened and folded back, letting the sunlight pour through. The view from the second floor was a complete seascape, stretching from the sandy dunes to the rocky cove, down onto the jetty and out to the glimmering horizon.

"How are you?" said Evelin politely, noticing another cat outside on the balcony. *How many cats does this woman have?* she thought and scanned around for more.

"How am I? Today I'm golden," said Esta, "but more importantly how are you? I'm glad you made it. I won't keep you long on such a glorious day."

Esta didn't force her to answer and gently motioned Evelin close to the long leather seat nearby.

I'm not touching the couch, Evelin thought instantly.

"I'm fine I'll stand for a bit," she said, "I got a kitten today."

"Oh, that's wonderful Evelin, what a lovely gift."

I guess that means I've joined the crazy cat lady group, mused Evelin as she moved away from the couch.

Esta smiled, "I can't live without them, although I have no idea where most of mine come from, fancy cats by the sea," she turned and faced the large ginger tabby on the verandah. "You remember Mr. Barnaby? He appeared last winter, brushed straight past me, jumped up the stairs and claimed the balcony as his. Isn't that right Barnaby?" said Esta, calling him but he was more interested in basking in the sun and kept his eyes shut.

Evelin stepped across the white plush carpet, its thick curling tendrils squeezed up between her toes, slightly tickling her feet and massaging them at the same time.

The fur of a giant dead creature, thought Evelin, *single-handedly hunted and slayed by the calmly spoken, gap-toothed Esta Green.*

"Happy Birthday Evelin, you are now thirteen years old and this is your thirteenth session, oh and I have thirteen cats ... that's quite something don't you think?" said Esta.

Evelin nodded at the floor, gritting her teeth into a false smile. She knew full well there were no prizes, and it was definitely an unlucky number. Her face dropped into a solemn frown. Initially, she was told she would only need a few sessions, and then five came around ever so quickly. Then those were extended and before she knew it she had over ten, and it had continued to thirteen.

What was so lucky about it? Each one of these sessions only confirms the worst.

Hesitantly, Evelin sat down on the very edge of the chair.

"You can lay down if you want, it's very relaxing," said Esta as if she read her mind. She moved a pillow in place for her.

Evelin moved it away. "No thanks, I'll sit, if I lay down, I'm sure I'll fall asleep." Evelin pushed herself back into the chair. It was cold, and its surface moved as if it were padded with gloves, its hands moulding around her. Surprisingly she felt comfortable as if the hands warmed to her. *This is like sitting against a walrus,* she thought.

"So Eve, how did it make you feel?" question Esta, moving in close.

"What? You have to be more precise," said Evelin.

"Your new kitten, how did it make you feel?"

"BC, that's his name, okay I guess? How am I supposed to feel? I presume I'm happy, but I don't feel like running around the room singing about it."

"Of course," said Esta.

"He's odd looking ... like me."

"Odd?"

"Yes odd, the opposite of normal. He's a furless breed with pointy bat ears, and you can see through his odd grey skin."

"Now that is odd, I don't have any hairless cats myself, but my friends do. Do you know if he is a Sphinx, Peterbald, Levcoy, maybe a Donskoy?"

"Yes, a Peterbald. You sure do know your cats."

"I've earned my badge remember," said Esta, "they're a Russian hybrid, keep it out of the sun, they burn quickly."

"Russian? I thought he was Egyptian? I look forward to researching him."

"Indeed a fascinating breed, I can imagine there will be some good books available at your new library.

"Evelin are you alright?"

"I haven't been in there yet," said Evelin.

"I see. I hear it's a vast improvement," said Esta and wrote something down in her notes.

"So Evelin how's Yellow Tree High been treating you?"

"Amazing," said Evelin.

"Really?"

"It's a prison for children."

"Yes, schools are a test of one's spirits. You'll be on holidays soon, and then you can forget all about school. And how are the girls in class behaving?

Esta looked at her notes and read, "Ruth, Ursula, Aniela," she paused, "Gertrude? Are you all getting along lately?"

With each name Evelin squirmed. The last name made her turn away towards the fire.

"Esta, why do you keep bringing them up? Of course, we're not getting along. Arrgh, I'm not going into the dynamics of bullying with you. I was crazy long before I met them, they may be idiots, but they're not the reason. I take these pills, and they're certainly not the reason that I stood on my roof."

"I was wondering that's all. I won't bring them up again unless you want to," said Esta touching Evelin gently on the shoulder.

"It's fine—just stop wondering. Write that down in your notes, it's not of advantage to my well-being."

Evelin turned her back, staring deep into the fire.

A moment of silence had passed between them before either spoke again.

"And what is the reason?" asked Esta.

"Is this a 'Psych 101' question?"

"It's just a question."

"I'm out of order," Evelin sighed, the fire her immediate audience. "I have too many thoughts inside, gathering up and piling into a giant mess, nowhere to go and confusing me even more—sometimes I feel like drilling a hole in my head."

"I've sometimes heard that can work," said Esta twisting her pencil in her hair.

Evelin frowned, "I'm not going to drill a hole in my head."

"I'm glad to hear that."

"This is intrinsic, inherent ... I'm suffering internally. I'm not connecting with myself, and I'm not going to get better by befriending a few horrid school girls, or getting so medicated I talk to strangers in the sky."

"Evelin, that is the most you have spoken in thirteen visits. I told you it was a lucky number."

"I don't think so," said Evelin.

"You're at an age of confusion. Thoughts contradict your feelings, and feelings control your thoughts. Life makes us feel this way on the best of days."

"No not like this, I know what it's like to feel on the best of days, and it's not this."

"I know. You're not the only one that feels this way. I'm here to help you get back to yourself. You'll overcome this."

"Will I ... how am I not myself?"

"It's best not to question this too deeply. You may end up buying another cat on the way home. Accept what is and go from there."

"That's ridiculous," said Evelin, "accept what is? I can't accept this, why am I even here? I should go."

"The choice is yours, but I see a remarkable improvement since day one, don't you?"

"What? Of course, there's an improvement. The previous day I had just been omitted from the hospital."

"Yes, but that's not only why." Esta flicked back to the very first page of her notepad. "Would you like me to remind you?"

"Indulge me."

"You had been administered to me after a very serious ordeal that only a rock could have ignored. Reporting visual and auditory hallucinations, experiencing a de-realization, where you stood on your two-storey roof—and were possibly preparing to jump."

"Jump? Not at all. Well, I didn't did I? I was dreaming that's all, sleep walking," said Evelin.

"You were lucky you were up there so long. Someone had time to call the fire brigade. What if you slipped."

"I don't remember any of it," said Evelin. "Some sleepwalk into the kitchen and eat bars of cheese, I just happen to like views."

"I'm sure it is," added Esta with a grin, "but most importantly your acute anxiety disorder which has been lingering for quite some time, and not to mention a whirlpool of depression and self doubt—all of which are treatable and showing signs of vast improvement. I'm delighted to see the girl I was first introduced to has levelled out to a tolerable conversationalist. Couldn't pry a word out of you in those first few weeks could we?"

"Your scale of vast is questionable," said Evelin.

Esta move from her chair and in a flowing movement, she wrapped her arm around Evelin's shoulder. Her frame was as bony as her arms, but strong and giving.

"The 'accident', has triggered a reflux of emotions and left you quite unbalanced. Hence, that's why you were put on medication."

"Quite unbalanced? Now I'm a zombie, I don't know what's worse?"

"Are they supposed to knock me out? Turn me into a robot?"

"I understand, you're not the only one that's been on them. They are a bit alienating at first. We can always lower your dose, but it's common to feel sleepy and disoriented during the first few weeks as you adjust. I would like to continue the current dose, is that all right with you?

Stopping it may seem beneficial, but it's not."

"I guess ... I don't know what it's doing? But it's doing something, I can't explain."

Esta stood quietly like one of her cats and walked slowly around the room. "Unfortunately, the medication is not a quick fix. You're way too complex. Imagine your 'self' is like a giant jigsaw puzzle, that only you can put back together, especially when it's been thrown around."

Esta glided up behind Evelin spreading her hand out in front of her, "In a sense they're slowing the things down, that like to speed up. Giving you the chance to see for yourself, make unemotional decisions and pick up the pieces so you can move on."

Evelin turned around to face Esta, "What if I'm always asleep? I can't pick up any pieces if I can't see them."

"You don't need to be awake, no doubt you'll do most of the work while you're asleep, and I know when you get accustomed to them, the tiredness will wear off. What happens in our subconscious is much more powerful than our conscious. We need to get through the critical factor and tell it everything is okay, and your conscious mind will work alongside, heal one, heal the other. Although, poison one, poison the other."

"Critical what? How am I supposed to heal something that I can't control? How many minds do I have?"

"Relax Evelin. I'm quite sure you only have one beautiful mind. Too smart for its own sake," Esta let out a light chuckle and squeezed Evelin's shoulder, "I am kidding, but it is the intelligent and creative ones who usually suffer the worst."

"That's great news," slumped Evelin.

"I bet you're tired of thinking the same old negative thoughts. That's what I'm here for. Together we will work on them. How's the anxiety going?" Esta spoke of *it* as if it were a mere pimple.

"It's not going anywhere. That's why I'm here." Evelin frowned, watching her shadow as it danced wildly with the fire.

"Eve, you okay dear?" said Esta noticing her discomfort.

"I'm okay—" Evelin paused and stopped talking. She took a breath and shut her eyes.

"Evelin, I was going to ask. How would you like to try hypnosis next time? Use your vivid imagination to help in the healing process."

"Hypnosis?" Instantly Evelin stood up, "What? No, I may be on this couch but I'm not that crazy!" She crossed her arms. She would have been angry if Esta's damn carpet didn't keep tickling her toes.

Esta looked at her with softness, "Oh Eve, of course, you're not crazy. When you tell me you're a paper plane and jump out the window, I may have to reassess my diagnosis."

"Mmm."

"Yes, it's what psychologists do—on couches like this one. Yes, some of those people are a little confused, and I certainly don't have my balcony doors open when they visit. But sometimes, somehow, deep, deep down an answer is always revealed and together we'll see what's stirring down at the bottom of your basement." Esta returned to her chair and crossed her legs as before. "I've practiced it during the twenty years of my career and I highly recommend it, especially with those with addictions and phobias, like spiders and snakes."

"Spiders ... snakes?" said Evelin unconvinced, these things were real, she was terrified of something unknown that could appear at any moment, not just something you could step on and kill.

Esta paused so Evelin could listen clearly, "It's especially useful for facing your fear and telling it who's boss! And kicking it out."

Evelin had met this 'fear' and it wasn't something that crawled around on eight legs. It was scarier, larger and hiding in every waking minute of her life. Controlling her thoughts and getting stronger each and every time she thought about it.

"You're not going to make me do anything stupid?"

"Not unless you want too."

"Fine—if you think so? We both know I need help. I'm usually asleep anyway, might as well do something while I'm under."

"That's great Eve. I'm quite excited for you."

"Sure," Evelin shrugged and checked her watch again, she didn't want to keep her dad waiting and her session had gone over time.

"I guess I better be going now."

"Goodbye for now Evelin, it's been a good day, we're moving forward, double time," said Esta standing up and grabbing Mr. Barnaby.

Evelin slid into her jacket, graced Esta with a downward smile, and gently closed the door behind her.

Belleny jolted upright and felt her bed sheets drenched in sweat. *Another nightmar*e, she sighed. Her eyes flashed up to the white creature hanging above the door. With her hand pressed against her chest, she gradually caught her breath and watched the motionless creature who was also watching her, its gaze capturing her every move.

She pushed off her thick feather quilt while losing her sheets onto the cold white shell floor. In the darkness she moved to the balcony doors but waited inside and listened from against the wall; the swirl of voices in a myriad of languages, the whimsical tunes, the screeching Kylen overhead and the soldiers who were afoot. Sounds rising up as lost, ricocheting notes, conforming today was the day.

If only I could shut my ears, as my eyes.

I'm not going outside for mere melodies.

"So it has begun," she said directing her voice to the creature hanging above the door, of which even in the darkness of the bedroom chamber, she could make out its snow-white coat. The creature made no reply.

Eerily she stared at the darkness of her room as if looking at a painting for the first time. She returned her attention to the white creature.

"You could have woken me. It must be afternoon by now. Vera will be most upset."

Still no reply.

"You know I must make an appearance, of course, I have to go alone, the Orphans are too afraid to come with me."

The white creature remained silent, reflecting the young Princess in its shiny black eyes.

"Oh well, at least I'm getting one good thing out of today, I'll show you in a minute," she said and disappeared within the enormous doors of her dressing room.

Rows and rows of draped, semi-transparent white silk partitioned the space. It had a sense of endlessness, like a room inside a dream. Inside stood thirty-one upright life-sized white wooden mannequins, tenderly spaced out with visibility from all sides. Each identically modelled as a replication of the Princess in various costumes. Belleny continued inside the silk walls, deep inside until she came to a hand painted sign; on it had a symbol representing the calendar month.

"Good morning Princess," she whispered to one unique little doll. "I have been waiting so long for this day. No, not because it's my birthday, but because I finally get to be you."

Yes, you're my kind of wicked, she thought, caressing the dark, feathered sleeves and circling her prey.

Belleny dropped her dressing gown to the floor. Her ghostly white skin absorbed the streams of sunlight radiating through the open rafters. She paused and closed her eyes as the sunlight warmed her body.

"I'm going to undress you now," she said firmly, "don't worry, you'll have your outfit back tomorrow."

She undressed the mannequin as if it was a real girl, politely removing each section of clothing, placing items on a nearby hanging frame or fitting it to herself in a logical order.

This was more than a costume; this was a perfect disguise—resembling a beautiful, yet dark and malicious bird-like creature. Its overall blue shimmer was as electric and magical to that of a peacock, in swooping feathers it draped close to her skin, from the peak of her head, along her thin structure to cover her feet and trail beyond. It flowed into a delicate and ornate feathered tail, that, with see-through thread, gave the impression it was floating off the ground and curling up and above her head. She pulled on a pair of white satin gloves that ended at her elbows, each finger had been soaked to the third knuckle in black ink and was left to soak freely into the fabric which ghostly crept upwards till it faded. She then royally placed a strange beaked mask upon her head to complete the creature.

"Urgh! Who ever said feathers were light?" she grumbled as the plumage fell behind her, almost pulling her over and backwards. It needed to be connected to one more brace, but once it was attached, she circled around the mannequin as if she was the feathered creature, through and through. Belleny lifted the bustle of frills that flowed around her hips. Underneath she revealed bright red leggings. She dipped her toes into a pair of soft black laceless boots, each with two red talons hooking up at the heel.

When the mannequin stood naked Belleny realised, she was complete.

"You are now the Princess," she said. She was now the creature, she bowed and slipped her dressing gown over the mannequin's head.

They had exchanged not only their outfits, but also themselves. The mannequin now the Princess, the Princess now adopting a pseudo alter-ego.

"Farewell," she said with a light embrace, her voice soft and saddened. It replied with silence and stared into the nothingness as the Princess disappeared through the silk partitions. Her silhouette a stranger amongst strangeness.

The white creature watched her through its unmoving eyelids from above the doorway as the arcane figure moved eerily into Belleny's room coming to a halt in front of a towering mirror. Belleny's smile was hidden underneath the large headdress, and she begun to dance strangely around in a circle, admiring herself. With a sudden thud, she stamped her foot, and it all came to a quick halt, with swirls of feathers flowing around her head. Her black ink tipped fingers pointed at the white creature, hooked high and above the door.

"To you I will be addressed as Queen Kikaan!" she roared.

There was no reply.

"So you're afraid of nothing ... but look where that got you. You're a reminder to us all," she said in a coarse grave voice.

For a second Belleny felt shame and apologised internally, *I'm sorry.*

What are you sorry for Princess? replied the dead creature, sent as a thought in her head.

The Princess crossed her arms and shook her beaked mask, "You know why!" she said, her voice upset and wounded.

Its limbs swayed as she yanked her bedroom door wide open.

"Keep away from Winta!" she snapped and left the room.

There was silence between them, and a whisper came through the gap in the doorway, "Because I don't want anything to happen to you." She then closed the door softly behind her and proceeded down her tower's long winding stairs.

The Royal Ballroom joined directly below her tower and for most of the year it was quiet and empty. Sometimes she would lay in the middle of the expanse, on the white alphena shell flooring, looking deep into the rafters of the echoing room and lose herself in the starlit painting on the ceiling.

The Princess' birthday was an annual public celebration for all citizens of Mare-Marie to enjoy. There was also another poignant note on the calendar; the Zale Mountains celebrated one more triumphant year it held back the violent and troubled Sea of Sorrow.

From far and wide citizens would arrive, each with a traditional dish. The day consisted of three, four, five, and even six courses.

People seated were crammed onto fifty-foot tables, spilling out into the courtyard in the Queen's Royal Gardens, where musician's played, and many danced. The festivities gave people hope, and it was a spectacle of colour, motion and rich diversity of all that lived in the land.

King Vera sat at the head of one magnificent and enormous dining table, entertained by several strange animals—who had discovered his glass of wine—that he carried on most occasions, typically they sat on his broad shoulders. On either side of the table sat his closest guests, each one deep in conversation and eagerly consuming the delicacies of gilt sugar-plums and pomegranate desserts that piled head-high in front of them.

The King was flanked by those that sat by his side and rowed along his table were all familiar and long-term acquaintances. Enjoying the opulence of the ball they let themselves go and ate and drank as much as they could while swapping tales and gossip amongst each other.

"Where's that beautiful daughter of yours Vera?" said the buxom Miss Manor, her voice jiggling around in her soft jelly throat.

"She'll arrive soon enough, from what she's told me her outfit is quite the challenge to put on," said King Vera. The desert sand, resulting in a coarse voice he could not disguise.

"A genuine Queen in the making," remarked one regal guest who fanned her face while stuffing it with her traditional dish, dried Goramor skin.

Madam Nalian Garmus, the wife of Lord Garmus, looked elegant as always, but she had the drawn face of been crying for days. Her husband Lord Garmus was yet to return from an expedition and having planned to travel for one week, and this had stretched into four weeks, so her concern was rife. The tell-tale sign was her bluish skin which ran dark around her large moist, sad eyes. Despite wearing a headdress of curved ivory horns, she was a true beauty of whom people admired but looked the other way to her sadness.

King Vera was also forlorn as he doubted the return of the Lord as he was well aware of the terrain and hazards into which the expedition ventured. The King's gaze turned to the twins Asel and Esla Graver as he knew they were aware of the fate of Lord Garmus, but now at the party this was not the time to be appointing widows, even beautiful ones. The twins made the King wary in their presence. What unnerved him the most, was their grey river-stone eyes. It was with each blink they became wet and reflective. When they were wet, those varnished eyes seemed to conceal hidden emotions, dark secrets and hidden truths.

The king kept an eye on the stairwell, *still no sign of Belleny,* he sighed. He felt the Graver's polished eyes watching him, and he turned to face them, but they seemed to be staring at nothing, deep in a trance-like state. He watched their hands twitching as they murmured to each other. He noticed they had cleaned themselves up quite respectably, their usually stained yellow fur was now snow white and combed. Underneath their armour, the white stripe ran up from their chest, through their throat, up the center of their face and down their backs bridging out into defined rippling ridges.

"Asel you eavesdropper, what's news beyond the Slate Cliff's?" whispered Mand the largest figure at the table.

"You really don't want to know ... or do you?" asked Asel, polishing his eyes with several blinks.

"We do," said Vanja DeQuin taking his seat next to Asel. His long lizard tail curling around Asel's seat.

"Ah Vanja, King Vera tells me you made a little two-tailed friend this week."

"Pardon?" said Vanja.

Mand continued, "As you know we've travelled far from Nibora. We took the eastern route, past the Porcelain Ponds and through Kay Kasa. "It was at night when we camped but even before the morning light we could tell the ponds—"

Esla moved in close and whispered, "The Porcelain Ponds are gone."

Vanja frowned and leaned against Esla, "What do you mean, gone?"

"Gone, dried up, poisoned. It'll need a new name, may I suggest Pungent Ponds."

"Or Perished Ponds," added Esla.

"This is no laughing matter. This is terrible," said Mand, "how long has it been like this? You've been there several times, we've seen your tracks, they're everywhere."

"What of it?" snapped Esla his eyes of stone quickly polished and glistened back at him.

"But the Veelin River runs straight through the ponds," said Mand.

"It runs clear eventually," shrugged Esla.

"This is not going to go away Esla. Have you not informed the King of your findings?"

"Yes, of course, he knows, we've said enough," said Asel.

Mand frowned down at his plate, "I will inform him of our findings tomorrow, I fear there is something deadly serious behind this. Am I right Asel?"

"You may be, but that's not for free," said Asel. He held his black leather pouch from his necklace and shook it lightly before Mand.

"Put that away," snarled Mand.

"Settle down men, this is a time for us to rejoice. There will be plenty of time for discussions tomorrow," said King Vera firmly.

They'll be gone before daybreak, grumbled Mand.

"Is everything all right King Vera?" asked a young voice from behind, "would you like more wine?"

"Yes, thank you Jodin," he replied, holding his glass before her.

As she poured the wine, she noticed his eyes remained fixed on Belleny's stairwell, only attentive once his glass was full.

The King leaned in and whispered in her ear, "could you do me a favour and check on Belleny? She told me strictly to keep away."

"Yes, as I," said Jodin.

"She didn't want me making a fuss on her big day ... but the hours are—"

"I would be glad to if it's an order that is," said Jodin, "I don't want to anger Miss Belleny."

Of the few maids, Jodin loved to see the Princess and quickly turned towards the stairwell.

"Wait!" said the King latching onto her wrist.

"Take this, do not lose it, it will see you past any guards." King Vera secretly placed an object into the palm of her hand, engulfing hers like a giant clam. Instantly she knew what it was. Peeking through her fingers, she saw the ring and held it tight. Jodin smiled discreetly and slipped the ring on.

"Go now, and remember to keep secret what we talked about, the gift for later," he said dismissing her.

"Yes, of course, in the library," she said and vanished into the crowd.

The Gravers held on to every last word. *What gift? What's in the library?* they thought to one another.

Skilfully Jodin manoeuvred through the crowd, untying her apron with a pull of a string, folding it up as she walked and placed it in an old cabinet. She doubted it would be there on her return, nor did she care. She released the bobby pins that held her hair tight to her head and let her lively curls fall to her shoulders, all without losing pace and arrived at the foot of the stairs. There, she noticed a young soldier guarding the entrance. On her arrival, he stood abrasively and rested a hand on the pommel of his sword.

"No admittance sorry, not even for maids," he said. His boyish face was not matching the roughness of his voice.

"How do you know I'm a maid?"

"Lucky guess," he said.

"Hmmf, lucky indeed. Now let me through."

"Not today little one."

"Little one! You look no older than me!" snapped Jodin, becoming frustrated, "I haven't got time for games boy. I have been requested by King Vera himself to tend to his daughter. Let me through at once."

The guard stepped up several steps, moving his hand to the grip of the sword and displaying the silver sheath, "No admittance," he repeated but this time he coughed grabbing at his throat. He looked up with watery eyes and coughed again. Jodin squirmed as if blood had come out and hit her in the face.

"Are you all right?" she asked, "I can fetch you some water on my return."

"No, it's just sand," he said.

Sand? she thought, "Why have you been eating sand?"

"You do what you must for the Princess, now please leave the stairwell," he said palming his hand down at her face.

In a flash Jodin pushed away his hand and punched a tight fist up at the guard's face, the ring sparkled in full presence, "Look boy I respect your solemn duties, but the King will have your head for this incompetence, not to mention the Princess."

The guard looked closer at the ring.

"Where did you get this? Who are you?" asked the soldier.

"Are you thick? Did you just get this job today?" she said furiously. "I am Jodin Clair. I always have, and always will, tend to the Princess and that's all you need to know."

"Stand back! Don't you get it? No one climbs these stairs. A direct order by the King himself."

Through the middle of the spiralling stairwell, a voice roared down from above, "Do as you're told soldier boy! Let her up at once," said Belleny.

"Yes at once!" he gasped.

"Insolent fool!" snapped Jodin and pushed him aside while darting up the stairs with a devilish grin.

"Forgive me," pleaded the guard from behind.

Some ways up Jodin saw Belleny's small black boots, then her bright red stockings that led up to the wild feathers and frills of her outfit. With each spiral, she got a glimpse of more and more of the Princess. She raced up the stairs to meet her.

"Happy Birthday Princess, let me give you a hand, oh don't you look magical," she said all at once. Instantly she held her hand to her mouth, "I mean, not magical, of course ... you know what I mean."

"Thank you Jodin, though I've been stranded up here as these damn stairs are a nightmare to walk down. You would think with all these feathers I could just fly."

Belleny paused and sat herself down, pulling back her mask and resting it on her back, "Let's sit here for a moment. How is it down there? Father? Doom and gloom no doubt."

Jodin smiled, "He's going to be fine now."

Belleny held her hand, "I've been so busy, I just needed some time to myself. I hope you understand."

"As long as you're all right. I must ask, has it anything to do with Miss Muscae?"

Belleny sighed deep and low, "I guess she's told half of Mare-Marie about her visit."

"Half? I don't think there's a soul left that hasn't heard her tales, no one really believes her, thinks she probably slapped herself," laughed Jodin.

Belleny said nothing, her face sullen.

"Is it true?" said Jodin.

"Probably, I wasn't myself that night. Neither of us was."

"Oh, I see. Oh well, one gets what one deserves, one way or another. If there's anything I can do?" said Jodin.

"No, I don't think so, it's just that, well since the teacher came I've had this dreadful nightmare."

"Oh, you poor thing, you must tell me everything, King Vera can wait a few more minutes," she smiled. Belleny looked at Jodin with wide eyes and begun to recall the dream, "I'm standing outside on the balcony, I climb up on the railing of all things to do, meanwhile the white creature is on the ground and out of control, tearing the room apart," she said as she held Jodin's arm.

Jodin flinched, it was tight, and the black dyed fingertips seemed to lock in place, "Go on," said Jodin.

"He smashed the mirror, no, but only after he attacked Winta and she threw him into it. I'm afraid, so I run. He's looking for me, no longer with dead eyes. He tears open the balcony doors and with teeth snarling, he leaps at me, pushing down on my chest with his giant paws. Of course, we fall, and he just stares at me. Never once does he look away. Just as I stop screaming, we hit the ground, that's when I wake up, not in bed, but standing at the doors to my balcony." Belleny took a deep breath, "And to make matters worse, one night I woke up and I had opened the curtains and found my hand on the door handle and a cold breeze blowing my hair."

"Oh no, you must be more careful. You'll need locks put on the doors at once, as soon as possible, inside and out!" said Jodin holding the Princess by her shoulders. "And Esdaile, I'm sorry, the white creature? Must you keep him in your room? An omen like this," Jodin shook her head nervously.

"I know, but I feel I must keep him. He needs me. We need each other."

"Very well, but please be careful."

"He is the one that needs to be careful," grinned Belleny from behind her mask, "come now we best be off."

Together Jodin and the Princess walked one step at a time until Belleny noticed the soldier eagerly waiting at the foot of the stairs and standing as stiff as a board.

"Jodin?" she whispered.

"Yes, Princess?"

"Stay by my side at all times, I'm sure there will be guards, but I won't feel comfortable without you."

"Yes, of course, I won't leave you for a second." Jodin felt a butterfly dancing in her belly.

Belleny nodded, and Jodin could have sworn she smiled. Although unsure as the mask now across her face concealed all.

The young soldier watched eagerly as the Princess descended. Quickly he signalled a guard who had been waiting patiently. He in turn released a lever and the giant chandeliers in the center of the ballroom began to spin slowly, reflecting large shards of light that moved throughout the ballroom. Another guard was waiting for this signal, he responded with his fist high in the air and prepared his bow and arrow. The band changed their tune to a drifting mystical rhythm and the proceedings continued.

All eyes went to the flickering sculpture that spun above. Its shape was combining, moving in angles and prisms. Mechanically it transformed into a mathematical form of pure fractal structure, moving until its angular petals reflected all their light towards the stairwell. Its audience encapsulated by its beauty went from silence to whistles and loud clapping.

Belleny anxiously appeared upon the stairwell, with Jodin by her side. All eyes sat on Belleny, and the audience continued to applaud.

"Stay close," said Belleny.

In an instant, with a clear view of the enormous ballroom, Belleny remembered how it was only a few days ago she laid on its floor and looked at the roof above, when it was completely empty. Today there was no comparison.

There's no escape. This is all for you Vasilis Vera, thought Belleny, staring across at her father, the King. His figure dressed in royal red armour stood out like a cherry in a bowl of vanilla ice cream. She waved to the crowd gracefully and the crystal lights above followed her as she descended to the floor. Jodin went up to assist her. With a tight grasp, she signalled her to stay close.

"Are you okay?" whispered Jodin. "You look amazing, beautiful."

"Thank you. I'll be much happier once I'm off these stairs, can you direct me straight towards my father please?"

"My pleasure." Jodin held out her hand and joined arms with Belleny.

A soldier waiting patiently for a signal had finally received it from the King. He pulled back hard on his bow, shooting an arrow straight into the flower-like chandeliers. It tore apart like cellophane and broke into a thousand pieces. Instead of crashing to the ground like glass it flickered like glitter with large weightless shards falling gently to the ground. From within the explosion, colourful cellophane-winged Lysa spiralled out into the ballroom. They were in their thousands and moved as one lucid body. Glistening in stained glass colours they flashed blazing white in unison, then quickly broke apart and joined back together in rapid formations, like an erratic school of glass fish.

The guests stood speechless, even the band at one point stopped playing, watching in wonder as the Lysa folded into one huge, glass origami-like shape then broke apart and joined back as another abstract angular structure.

"Vera! You've outdone yourself this time!" roared Mand clearly impressed. He stood up from his chair and clapped loudly with approval, slamming his hands together with solid palms. Even the twins agreed and joined in with thunderous claps of approval. It wasn't long before the entire audience gave a standing ovation for the entire event.

The delicate Lysa turned instantly, making haunting shapes and harsh tearing sounds as they scraped against each other. The clapping had triggered an acute fear and panic rose in the flying creatures. Several darted off from the group and tore themselves apart shredding into pieces. In doing so, they lost all their lustre and colour and appeared like ash falling from the sky. Threatened they searched for an exit. The main body of Lysa flung to the edges of the room like water thrown from a bucket, splashing up into the corner. They circled the ballroom looking for a way out, but the doors were all closed, on purpose to keep them inside in the first place.

The young soldier on the staircase ran to Belleny and threw a shield above her head.

"Princess, quick get down, you too maid!" he shouted.

Instantly a whirlwind formation was formed, faster and faster the Lysa spun hitting everything in their path, some instantly crushed on impact as others continued to spin out of control. With the screams of the women and even the men, it echoed throughout the ballroom causing the creatures to move even more erratically, hitting everything from the large pyramid of drinking glasses, full with exploding Firewater, to race down the long dining tables, tossing food and cutlery as they went.

Mand changed his mind about the Lysa as a swarm flew straight into him. His claps turned to more aimed whacks as he squashed them like bugs between his palms. His body was covered in pieces of thin, torn wings.

Tables were now bunkers and those that could fit hid underneath, some picked up large serving trays and held them up like shields as Lysa splattered into them, others ducked and weaved hiding under their hands.

Out of nowhere an arrow fired straight through the middle of them and the spinning whirlwind of Lysa broke apart and back together again. The arrow continued its journey and reached its destination, a small round window. It smashed apart, letting a shimmering beam of light into the ballroom.

The Lysa instantly dove into the light, flashing white with every movement, and like rapids they flowed violently over each other to get out of the broken window.

They had gone as quickly as they appeared.

The soldier removed his shield, "You can come out now, they have gone."

Belleny and Jodin stood in confusion, "What were they?" asked Jodin.

"Crystal Winged Lysa, they come from the Caves of Vheen," said the soldier.

"The Caves of Vheen? Thank you, what is your name?" asked Belleny.

"I am, Bernard, Joseph Bernard," he said in a course voice and bowed down before her.

"This is Jodin Claire. You're advised to address Miss Claire as politely as you would me."

"Yes, of course, Miss Claire, it is a pleasure."

Joseph wanted to tell Belleny how he longed to meet her, ever since a young boy. The ride into the Desert Vheen was a testimony to it all.

"Here please take this Princess, I know it will grow into something beautiful like yourself," said Bernard handing Belleny the glassy red and purple swirled seed he found in the desert.

"Watch your tongue boy," she snapped, but it caught her eye, in an instant she snatched at it, *the tree Winta,* she thought to herself.

"It's beautiful," said Belleny, "where did you get this?"

"It's a seed from the White Sands of Vheen."

"Why would you go to such a place?"

"No, not at all, because I—"Joseph began to cough. Jodin now realised why he had been eating sand.

"I'm sorry I have no time, I must be off," said Belleny as she could see the crowd eagerly watched her every move.

"Good day, Bernard."

"It was an honour," he replied and watched as they disappeared within the hovering guests.

"He sure was something wasn't he?" said Jodin, carefully guiding Belleny up towards the King as the crowd partitioned.

"Such a stupid thing to do," said Belleny, "although admirable."

King Vera looked on eagerly as the crowd shuffled out of the way. These days he couldn't recognize if Belleny were happy or not. She hardly ever smiled but as she clapped her gloves in large sarcastic beats, he grazed a pearly grin.

With a warm welcome, he embraced her with a hug.

"Happy Birthday my darling. You have made my year. Come with me, we'll get this over as quickly and painlessly as possible," he said and pulled her up towards a throne at the top of a flight of stairs. Belleny latched at Jodin and towed her from behind. From here they looked over all. The ballroom had never had such an audience. In a hush the crowd settled. King Vera whispered to the side, peeling a dead Lysa from his chest plate, "They were something, weren't they, I hope you're both all right?"

"We're fine," said Belleny.

"Good," he said and guided her upon her throne. He rose his glass into the air and whispered, "Be strong Belleny, they adore you."

Belleny watched as her father took to the stage and walked from corner to corner. His audience looked on and instantly there was silence.

"It has been another long year, an exceptional year! There were highs, but, of course, there were lows in our little Mare-Marie. We have each other, and we do our best to be strong when our days are fused with constant threats. Yes, I admit that the damn sea hasn't given up," he chuckled into his wine, "but it's only a matter of time before it does. And if not you've all had an extra year to get your houses ready. As you know, it is my darling daughter's birthday, and I'm glad you could make it, most of all, I'm glad she made it! May the year ahead be rich and abundant in life and love."

"Hear ye!" shouted the crowd raising their glasses.

King Vera took Belleny's hand and stood her before the crowd, "May I present the beautiful and ornate Princess Belleny Vera."

The crowd's silence exploded once again into a myriad of claps and whistles. They adorned her as they did the Queen.

Belleny slowly pulled back her mask revealing her silent face. After a moment her captivated audience came to a complete hush. Many puzzled by what stood before them.

What a costume, a creature, a bird of sorts, is this even the Princess?

Belleny gazed out across the ball and chanted, *deep breaths, deep breaths, deep breaths. There is no time for breathing,* she thought and before she knew it, she spoke, her voice firm and royal.

"Thank you for coming today. I understand many of you have travelled from far and wide. May you eat, drink and be merry. May your return be a guided one. But as you wish to live outside, so it is your destiny to die in such darkness. It's only a matter of time before the sea drowns us all, so until then, unite and live as if tomorrow is only a dream."

At first the crowd gasped at such words, but they all took them as praise and blessing.

"Hara! Hara! Hara!" All shouted back in unison, quickly trying to fill a glass that hadn't been knocked over or broken.

The King held her in a warm embrace, and the music once again filled the ballroom.

"Now that was a speech, I knew you could do it," he whispered into her ear.

"Sorry about the Winged Lysa honey, hope you had liked the show before they went a little crazy?" said the King straightening his crown and brushing himself off.

"A little? Yes, it was quite unexpected, I'm guessing ... well, I know you didn't know they did that when they were frightened."

"Guilty, I was told they fluttered around the room like magic paper before your eyes."

"Vera! Did you say magic? I thought you would have learned by now?"

"Well, you can't always know what you're getting until you get it."

Belleny spoke of the variety of creatures that flew away or just disappeared and, of course, the wild Berynic still frozen in the moat.

"That's just a coincidence, anyway no one comes with instructions," said King Vera embarrassed as a torn Lysa flapped beside his feet.

"I am truly blessed with your appearance today. You look as incredible as ever. Are you some sort of bird or a creature that ate too many birds?"

"I'm no wretched bird, I'm Queen Kikaan, and she hates birds, so I guess you're part right."

"Oh, a Queen, well my Queen Kikaan I have a present for you in my library. Please lend me your arm and allow me to walk you through.

"A present for me ... in the library?" inquired Belleny with the slightest of smiles. "A book?"

"Not quite."

It was by chance that Evelin Boots ended up on the rooftop of the Hotel Chandelier, Yellow Tree's most luxurious five-star hotel. Without a doubt, it would have been six if that were credited.

Above the penthouse situated on the forty-fifth floor was a sparkling twenty-five-meter pool, designed in the look and shape of a diamond. Its opulence was completely aesthetic and to swim a lap took little effort for even the weakest of swimmers. Its centre was as deep as it was wide, taking up a whole single floor below, where viewers in the penthouse could watch the swimmers as they frolic. Surrounding the diamond was a highly manicured lawn, there were even worms wriggling in the dirt it grew upon. The garden was kept in pristine condition by Simon Oderve; a professional hairdresser that turned eccentric gardener, who regularly trimmed the grass by hand, with a comb and a pair of grooming scissors.

On one balmy afternoon stroll, Evelin came upon Cavalier Avenue, up the 'Paris' end of town, when she crossed paths with a thin high-heeled lady wrapped in a giant white rabbit fur coat. Her heels caught the leads of her four miniature dogs who seemed to run back at her as if it were a game, tangling themselves around like a troubled maypole. Alarm bells rang when the woman busted Evelin gawking at her. *This is awkward, I better cross the road.*

Evelin turned at once squeezing between two parked limousines.

What? This town is too small. On the opposite side of the road was none other than Ursula, Gertrude and the twins Febe and Rose Listner.

Evelin cringed and hid her face behind her hair. *What's worse, the strange lady or those awful girls?* Unwilling, she returned to the busy foyer of the Hotel Chandelier. From the corner of her eye, Evelin stole a glance. *You're joking. Is she calling me? Come on, really? What about the woman with the pink hair, or that guy standing up against the wall beside you?*

The lady rose her voice and spoke as if she knew Evelin, "Well, are you going to help me or not? You're making me look ridiculous."

Evelin shuddered, turned back several steps and faced the shop window next door. Pretending she still didn't hear or notice her.

"My word! Now your playing games with me," the woman huffed.

What games? Why me? Does crazy attract crazy? What does she want with me?

A young man kindly approached the woman and offered a hand.

"Get away from me! I do not need help from the likes of you!"

Evelin shook her head in disbelief. The woman began to drag herself closer. Towing the dogs as if they were a ball and chain. Evelin sighed, dropping her shoulders, as the woman approached like a ghoul and stood by her. She pointed at the wall of televisions in the shop-front window. The one Evelin was pretending to be focused on.

"Trust me you'll have plenty of time to stare at that box when you're an old vegetable. Who knows, by the time you're my age you can just plug yourself in, stick the damn antennae straight into your head, or wherever."

Evelin had previously met her fair share of crazy people on the streets of Yellow Tree, especially around here, but this one had graced her top ten.

"Look, lady, I'm sorry but the answer's no. I don't know what else you're going to say, but I'm sure I'll still say no, so—"

"Is that right," replied the lady with an almost hissing sound to her voice.

"No," replied Evelin in her own vaporous tone.

The woman stood back nearly piercing one of her dogs with her heel. "With that attitude you must really get pestered down here on the streets. That's why I hardly come down here. Paris end of town, pfft, that's a laugh, street trash riff-raff. More rats scampering around here than a sinking ship."

Maybe she's not completely crazy. Evelin stared at the dogs and said, "Oh, are you lost? If so you've called the wrong person, I forget street names as quick as lightning, funny that ... I don't forget much else though."

After a pause, the woman lowered her dark black glasses revealing her emerald green eyes, and her voice became sultry, "Lost? My dear, that's quite funny from where I'm standing."

Evelin frowned at her inside joke. It was getting hot.

"Aren't you a little something." *Just like your mother.* "I don't forget much either, especially faces and very unique hair styles. How are you with pets then, namely little white dogs?" she said pointing down at the four creatures panting in the shade of her fur coat.

Evelin said nothing, she just looked down at the dogs as if they were loaves of mouldy bread.

Why did she buy them, if she can't even walk them? They're not even dogs are they? Experiments. She probably got them off Madchova. Well, she's obviously not poor but that doesn't discard her being crazy. Who on earth would wear a fur coat? Let alone on a hot day like today.

"Sorry, I would love to help out but I'm just too busy," said Evelin and apologetically shrugged once again. Without losing too much momentum, she stood forward and casually stepped to the side. The woman acted at once piercing her naked leg through the opening of her coat.

"I don't think you understand my dear, clearly I'm not a shell-shocked beggar scavenging for booze money. I'm just asking for your services."

"I don't think you understand; clearly I'm not in this picture and I'm going home. Goodbye."

"I will pay, cash, my dear."

"What for? No thanks, I have plenty of money," said Evelin. *Wait. No I don't. I'm forever window shopping. What services?*

"I've only just turned thirteen," snapped Evelin, "I'm still a—"

It was then that the woman let out a loud cackle as if a witch.

"Oh my, poisoned youth, such a laugh!" the woman continued. "You see I need a break from these—" she paused, held her nose up as she glanced at the dogs, inhaled and rephrased herself, "I need a hand with these beautiful little minkies, that's all. Just a walk in the park so they can do their business. You know what they're like, sniffing other dogs butts—disgusting, not to mention their owners, oh their owners. It's not my duty to be picking up their mess. I'm sure fifty dollars an hour will be adequate, better than slapping burgers for fifty dollars a week and a bonus greasy, low self-esteem to match. Oh, you'll be fed, of course, I'm sure the latter would do you good."

The woman grated a smile and pointed down at Evelin's frame from top to bottom.

"I have a high metabolism, I can eat what I want, whenever I want," snapped Evelin and stood back.

"That's what they all say, then boom, you're all jelly arms and cankles."

Two small pooches sniffed at Evelin's shoe, "See darling, they like you." Evelin flinched and pushed them away gently with her foot.

"I'm sorry thanks for the offer, but I'm not very good with dogs. I'm a cat person, they can probably smell my kitten."

"Fine this is murderous. It's too hot to be standing out in the street quarrelling with my younger self. When I could be swimming in a watery diamond. I'm sure they'll entertain each other in the car while I have a dip," she said and pointed her black nailed fingers at the metallic black sports car parked in front of a limousine.

"But they'll die in this heat! You cannot leave them in a car!" snapped Evelin.

"Well then, that's on your conscience. I did ask nicely, about twenty times and offered you food and money, for a thirteen-year-old you are quite the sadist."

The woman pushed one of the dogs to the side with her heel giving herself space to move. Evelin stood back in disbelief, crossed her arms and frowned up at the woman. She in turn pointed the remote at her face and pressed it down like triggering a detonator. The sound of the automatic door unlocking was like a gun being primed. She watched, disturbed as the lady swung opened the front door of the sports car and proceeded to pull them in by their leashed throats and rake them inside with the length of her heel.

"Fine, one hour! Not a minute more," said Evelin, instantly regretting her decision even if she did save the dog's lives.

"Finally, you do have a heart, somewhere in there," said the woman slamming the door and handing her the leads as if they were attached to rats. "Careful now," she said, firmly placing her hand over Evelin's.

"Of course, I'll be more careful with them than you are."

"No, I mean the leashes, they're real diamonds."

"Real?" said Evelin quite stunned. She stared closely at the rows of sparkling rocks. "Really Real?"

"Of course they are," she replied, so confidently that it had to be fact.

Diamond's on a dog leash? This had Evelin perplexed, having had only seen this many diamonds from behind security glass or on television.

"I won't be long, just a dip and a sun bake, that's all. Such sweltering weather, one needs to soak in something other than sweat."

"You are wearing a fur coat," said Evelin.

"Yes, so I am," she replied as if it was a compliment. Evelin untangled the leads carefully and relaxed the dogs by patting their heads one by one. Their wispy white fur made them seem even bigger than what they were, and their bony skulls felt like walnuts. She honestly didn't like dogs, but up close—not real close—*these ones were quite adorable,* thought Evelin, *unlike their owner.*

"My name's Astina Francis, or plain Astina if you like and you are?"

"Evelin Boots or plain Eve if you like."

"Evelin Boots?" The woman stopped in her tracks, paused and thought for a moment, *Hmm, so it is her daughter.*

"Yes is something wrong with that?" Evelin said tonelessly.

"Not at all. Don't worry maybe one day you'll get married, and you can change it, a few times if you're lucky," said Astina and parted her glossy red lips into a perfect dentist ad smile. "Settle down, I'm only joking. It's a great name."

Evelin rose her brow, "Hilarious. So you're having a swim? I'll just go over to the park then? And meet you back—"

"No, I've already been and taken care of that awful business, you're minding them while I have a dip-n-bake," she said ruffling her jacket.

"A what? Where are you going exactly?" asked Evelin.

"Up. That's the only direction I go. Come on Boots, follow me, and please ... don't talk to anyone. Don't even look at them."

Up? Evelin thought puzzled.

Astina walked quite well considering the height of her heels and now free without the restraints of her dogs. With large struts she took off; straight up into the drive-through foyer, past the limousines and taxis, the guests and their luggage, the busy bell boys—retrieving and stacking suitcases, and through the large glass, sliding doors of the Hotel Chandelier. Evelin followed the best she could but waited, confused. The doors had shut in her face, and there she stood looking at her confused reflection.

The automatic doors slid open as two rather wealthy looking creatures pushed pass on either side of Evelin, each on mobile phones, deep in conversation, Evelin presumed with each other.

Astina stopped, twisted back as if double jointed and pointed at her, "You Boots! Come on! You do know how to use a door don't you?"

"What? What about the dogs?" she asked quietly.

Evelin gasped as the dogs leaped forward yanking the diamond leashes and pulled her into the foyer. They came to a halt as the doors closed swiftly behind her.

Wow, it's beautiful in here.

Within its crumbly exterior, the hotel beamed like the crystal insides of a Geode. The sparkling foyer rose past the top floor and up to the second. It was as if they made a level solely for the crystal chandeliers, which forked back down like an icicle explosion. She now realised why it was naturally called the Hotel Chandelier.

Evelin looked from side to side. There she stood, reflected in its walls. The polished white stone mirrored her every move. It continued, joining the white marble floor that reflected the panting dogs and everything above them.

A large white shell-shaped desk engulfed the tall man behind it. He was in immaculate condition, in his tailored tuxedo, oiled and coiffed hair, shaved, powdered and proper. He tended to several guests as they were checking in or out. Most of the gentlemen sauntered around dressed up like penguins and the ladies all wore dark glasses;

faces crowned in hair, dripping in jewels as they ignored or air-kissed patrons from afar.

Astina walked straight past the large reception desk while the young concierge stood back, bowed and politely spoke, "Good afternoon Miss Francis, everything is in order and to your satisfaction, I hope?"

Not sure what to do, Evelin quickly did a half bow curtsy combination while the tenacious dogs yanked her past. Not only did she feel like a complete idiot, but she stood out like a sore thumb in this grand establishment.

Astina gave the concierge a nod, but mostly ignored him and continued her strut forward as if on a catwalk. Her heels hammered on the marble floor, as she made a bee-line to the elevator. When Evelin caught up, she watched as Astina pressed a button and mouth the word to her at the same time, "Up!"

The large arrowed compass above the elevator lit up as the elevator returned to the foyer. As Evelin caught up, Astina stood poised and calmly wiped her fingers with a handkerchief.

She glanced down towards Evelin. "There's a reason they call them the filthy rich."

This made Evelin grin.

The elevator arrived and after a few moments the doors slowly opened. It was tight, bright red and mirrored inside.

"Wait! Where are we going? Are they coming with us?" asked Evelin.

"Of course they are. Get in we're going up."

After the elevator doors closed there was a pause of silence and Evelin felt a wave a suffocation fall over her.

"Up?"

Oh no! What have I gotten myself into?

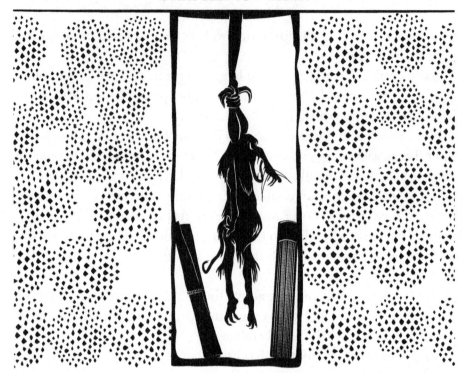

After setting eyes upon Princess Vera entering the grand room dressed in such regalia, the people of Mare-Marie felt strangely blessed by her appearance. Belleny was a peculiar character and some folk whispered in hushed circles she was 'ill' in the head. Despite her idiosyncrasies and odd habits, she was still was adored by the people of Mare-Marie. She was their Princess after all and the majority found her creature-like costume compelling and promptly dismissed the rude comment in her addressing speech, 'that they were all fools for living outside.'

By sundown, the party guests were still rejoicing in the Queen's Royal Garden and continued the festivities late into the night. Throughout the ornate and bizarre gardens and off the winding stone pathways the guests mingled with a chorus of laughter. They admired the garden, the white shell statues and the beautiful Veelin River flowing and pooling inside.

King Vera and Belleny sat quietly watching the antics from inside and he looked softly into his daughter's eyes, "my little Princess has grown up quicker than a Hornet Weed."

"Are you comparing me to a weed?" she asked, antagonizing him.

"No, dear ... it's a beautiful plant really, not a weed at all ... it's hardy, spirited, and no one can get rid of the damn thing," he said digging himself a deeper grave. "Oh Belleny, you know what I mean ... you're as quick and beautiful as ever and my favourite daughter in all of Mare-Marie," he grinned.

"How many daughters do you have exactly?" said Belleny staring into his eyes then up to the two small creatures ferreting throughout his hair.

"Exactly one, no more, no less," he said holding up his finger.

"Then I am also your least favourite of them all," she said, her expression falling between sad and curious.

"Impossible, it doesn't work that way," he stammered. "So my favourite Princess, do you feel any different now you're a year older? You certainly look different."

Belleny paused, placed her bird-like mask back on, clasped her ink-stained gloves and calmly spoke in her Queen Kikaan voice, "Interesting you say that, yes I do feel different."

"Really?" he said intrigued. The small creatures poked their heads up.

"But quite the same, at the same time, so don't get too excited."

"Belleny, please take off that mask for I have something important to tell and show you," he said as he walked her around the room. "I'm proud of you Belleny and I know your mother, bless her soul, is the proudest of all." He placed his hand on her shoulder and together they both looked towards the life-size statue of the Queen that stood at the top of the library stairs.

"I don't know about that," said Belleny lowering her tone.

"You're such a special girl, unique and so creative. You remind me of your mother, she was always the gifted one, I have no idea what she saw in me," he gave a big jubilant grin.

"I'm not sure either," said Belleny. "You miss her a lot don't you?"

"Every day, I have you to remind me. You are so similar, in so many ways."

"The Queen loved to capture life. She would draw everything she saw, so many drawings and notes, of just about anything, be it a hairy bug or a giant scaly Berynic. From the countryside to far beyond, every animal she met to the strange creatures she found under rocks ... not to mention the ones she brought back with her."

Belleny had heard this speech on many occasions and knew where it was headed. *How I have any relation to her is uncanny,* she thought, *she would just hate me. I would no doubt hate her if she pushed her outdoorsy ways upon me.*

"Well, I think it's due time for your presents," he said approaching the statue. The Queen was perched high on the tips of her toes reaching up to the sky, her skirt and hair blowing in the wind. Belleny knew the sculpture well and could be found sitting at the foot of the stairs and admiring it for hours. She touched its smooth surface and glided her fingers along its hand. Crafted impeccably; it was if she had been turned to shell or stone. Made from the shell of an Alphena Crab, its polished surface glistened as if wet.

The plaque at her feet read, *Girl of the Wind.*

"Graceful isn't she?" said the King.

"Yes, she is," said Belleny.

"I can imagine you're going to look just like her one day." He pointed to the small bump in the statue's belly. "You had just begun back then."

Belleny touched her mother's belly and waited for her father to start his speech of the inscription.

"Your mother had Girl of the Wind inscribed to remind you that you're the Girl of the Wind—"

Belleny gave a loud sigh and took over, "I know, I know, not to be shackled by anyone, free like the wind to go and do whatever I please," she said reciting the lines as if reading out her court sentence. "So this is your present, wisdom and motivation?" She looked with inquisitive eyes. "I hope you're not twisting the meaning of this to make me leave the castle, and if so Vasilis Vera, I am complacent, doing and being as free as I want right here," she said firmly.

"Oh Belleny, not at all, it's only as your mother says, you are free to go and do whatever you like, if that means staying inside, so be it and I abide by her wishes." The King moved around so they were both looking side onto the statue.

"Excuse me, does the name Stephanie Muscae ring any bells?" said Belleny.

The King rubbed his beard and smirked, "A bit of fresh air never hurt anyone."

"It seemed to hurt her," said Belleny with a growl.

"Yes, well next time I'll make sure she knows the rules."

"And not how to break them," added Belleny.

King Vera knelt down and pushed hard against the statue.

"What are you doing?" she questioned. "You shouldn't drink so much."

"Just inclining my lady over a little," he said. "Can you keep those terrors out of my hair for a moment."

Belleny snatched the wild looking creatures by their wispy caterpillar hair and placed them on her arm. They ran through her hair immediately and all looked on curiously.

King Vera now changed his position and held the statue in a waltz-like pose. Holding the Queen's hand and another around her waist, and with the weight of his body he gently tipped her backwards. The solid statue silently separated from the floor and exposed a hole carved deep into the stone.

"Why is there a hole in the floor?" asked Belleny her expression slightly interested.

"Reach in there, your presents are inside. Quick now she's a lot heavier than I remembered," said King Vera struggling with the statue's weight and clenching his teeth.

Belleny looked at the dark hole and lifted her eyebrow. "I'm not putting my hand down there."

She hesitated, although the King was close to collapsing, then she saw something poking out of the pitch-black hole.

"Paper?"

"Quick grab it, there should be a book or two."

"A book?" she said and at once knelt down. Belleny reached forward whipping out the roll of paper and with eyes shut drove her hand down once again.

A book about what? she thought as she grasped the spine of one, then several more and lifted them out with a heaving wrench.

"Heavy!" said Belleny.

With a playful nervousness, she reached back down, all the way down to the bottom of the hole. Her delicate fingers froze as they grazed past the sticky fur of something organic at the very bottom. She looked up at King Vera and he frowned for her to go on. Her instincts were to scream, to rip her arm out but instead she waited a second longer. Nothing bit her, nothing clawed into the skin of her hand and with lightning speed she latched her fingers around a strange fur husk of a skeletal body and ripped it out before it could cause any harm. With a yelping scream she threw it onto the ground, "Aghhh what is it?" said Belleny shuffling away. "You can place her back now."

"Don't worry it should be long dead by now."

King Vera brought the statue back to its original position and slid to the floor in a heap. "I'm glad we only had to do that once."

"What is that thing? Why would you or she keep such a hideous dead creature?" Its body was curled up, ghastly thin and vile; its nails grew long and splitting, its large eyes sealed over as the moisture had long dried up. The King picked it up by its long spiny tail and moved it aside. "Welcome back Krin, you don't look too good," he said and placed him on a chair.

"You know that thing?" said Belleny.

"Unfortunately I do, yes."

Belleny put the roll of paper to the side and both sat down cross-legged.

"Diaries?" she questioned, holding what were three rugged looking books.

"Your mother's field notes," groaned King Vera as if they were the cause of all their problems.

Belleny opened the first book. It was parched and smelt of aromatic oils, rich with consistencies of life as the pages spread open before her. Belleny could not believe her eyes. Page after page; detailed drawings, sketches, scribbled notes upon notes and even samples; pressed leaves, delicate flowers and even the strange insects that once lived on them.

"She was obsessive ... the same messy handwriting as me!" said Belleny closing the book and eagerly opening another. King Vera looked on sternly as page after page came illustration of a creature after creature. Small maps where they were found and scribbled notes about their likes and dislikes. Samples of fur, hair and even teeth were attached to the pages.

"Yes, well—this one," said King Vera.

"Yes, well this one is the very reason I don't go outside, just look at the fangs on this bug! No wonder she killed it and stuck it in here." She pointed to a drawing, a creature's jaw and its assortment of expressions. "How she got close enough to draw this is beyond me."

"She had a gift with most you see, they didn't feel threatened, and somehow she saw them all as equal," he said.

Belleny flicked through the pages in disbelief.

She stopped at a double page spread. "Look at this thing! Going by her sketches it's as big as the castle, that can't be true?"

"Yes, that one is very real. Your mother met that creature on several occasions. Trust me I wasn't pleased to find out about her new found friends. You can read about them or not," he said closing the book for her.

"So is that one of her friends?" said Belleny pointing to the small dead creature on the chair.

"This is, or was, Krin ... yes, she named it. It's a Wild Hossla which can be found in the Shell Tree Forest; they can be tamed you know. But your mum found this guy under the Hovering Cliffs. What your mother didn't realise was that this one was sick, he was infected, it lead to her demise and death. What did she expect to find wandering around in such dark places?"

King Vera picked up Krin once again by its tail.

Belleny pushed up her nose, "Krin is that even a name? If it was infected, don't go putting your fingers in its mouth. What are you doing? Vasilis Vera that is disgusting!"

He continued to pry its teeth apart as large dry flakes of tongue—and what Belleny presumed were organs—tumbled and fell out from its throat as he shook it repeatedly.

"A long time ago your mother was waving her locket in front of this thing, working out if it was kind or a killer. She found out soon enough when it swallowed it whole and her hand with it. Days maybe a week later she arrived back here, pale as a ghost, with this Hossla still attached to her arm, you could imagine my horror," said King Vera shaking it.

"I don't believe it, why didn't she cut its throat? Someone must have tried to help rip it off her?" said Belleny.

"No, that's your mother for you, she wouldn't harm a thing, even one chewing on her arm for a week. She wouldn't let go of her locket, nor would Krin. I guess he won in the end, swallowing the locket after she nearly drowned it in the baths, luckily it left her hand attached. But as she wouldn't have it killed, we ended up keeping it in the castle until the locket came out one way or another ... it never did."

"Gross, I would have had its head chopped off. What locket is this?"

"The Queen's Royal Urchin ... you will never see another like it."

"Urchin? From out of the sea?" said Belleny.

"Perhaps, your mother wanted you to inherit the jewellery as it was so important to her. After your mum had passed, Krin was still very much alive and a wild horror possessed it. I had to do something so I threw it in the hole with the other items she wanted you to have. And on this day I would give them to you, as she requested. I was pretty sure it would be dead by now."

"Pretty sure!" Belleny shook her head, her usual sullen expression seemed quite agitated.

"Here it comes, hold out your hands," said King Vera dangling Krin upside down over her unwilling open palms.

"Do I have to? Oh, this is just wrong!" Its eyes seemed to watch her in anticipation. Belleny watched as the Royal Urchin fell out of its mouth and into her grasp.

"There we go," he said dumping Krin on a table. "It's a little dull now, but I'm sure it will be fine with a good spit polish."

"You always said she lost it!"

"She did, inside Krin," grinned King Vera.

"That poor thing infected your mum. It was basically dead when she found it, poisoned by the black waters. Open it," he said with a grin, remembering it quite well.

Belleny looked at the two sides, its surface was a solid and smooth, worn down by the currents of the water. *This came from the ocean.* She found its latch, a simple lever on the side and with a gentle press its dimpled face opened at once.

There, floating inside the locket was a small white baby crab. Belleny stroked the crab gently and effortlessly it spun round.

"It's a real Alphena crab?" said Belleny. "I've never seen one so small and intact before. It spins? Is this a toy?" she asked.

"A toy indeed. Yes, I've never seen such a complete specimen, it's exquisite. It's been in Krin's belly for many years, the encasing has protected it although the outside has had its fair beating. It's gone now but when the lids shut there was a castle your mum carved onto it, the other side, an eye. Open it with the castle on top and the Alphena crab will appear and its front claws will always point home to the castle, no matter where you are. Just like a compass."

Belleny turned the urchin over. She spied a strange mark etched into its surface, that of a ghostly image of an eye.

"An eye? What does it see?" asked Belleny.

"I am to believe it can see what can't be seen; evil, the darkness hiding in shadows or right there in front of you. But mainly it's a pointer of sorts, Anne even stated it knew if someone was going to die."

Belleny kept quiet and looked up at the statue of her mum and returned to the Urchin, afraid to open the lid.

"How would it know this? Anyway I can work this out just by looking at someone, like Miss Muscae for example," said Belleny.

"I know, but maybe you were unsure? A second opinion would always come in handy. Your mum found it very useful."

"Unsure, I don't think so ... what about Krin, he was apparently hiding in the shadows," she said opening the locket. The Alphena Crab was now replaced by flat shards of grey to black triangles. They moved in a whirlpool motion and before her eyes united as one solid black arrowhead. The arrow began to spin, searching for a subject.

"Point it towards Krin," said King Vera.

Belleny scoffed, "Like I said, I can tell if something is dead or alive."

"Can you really?"

Belleny paused, she presumed he was talking about the white creature hanging in her room and did not want to discuss it.

She moved on and aimed the strange Urchin locket towards the corpse of Krin.

The arrowhead pointed at the shrivelled animal and in the centre, the arrow head a symbol of a skull formed, it then broke apart into small triangle shards and formed an image of a white rose, then repeated the arrow, skull and white rose."

"A skull and a white rose?" said Belleny.

"What do you think that means?" asked King Vera.

"Krin's obviously dead ... but he wasn't evil?" she said.

"Possibly, like I said, that's purely up to your interpretation, a second guess," said the King.

Belleny turned towards King Vera and the triangles began to shift into an arrow.

"Don't point that thing at me!" he said jumping behind the statue, the hairy blue ferrets held on tight. "You know very well I'm alive and the best King ever to reign over Mare-Marie."

"I know and this Urchin didn't just wash up on the shore. You must tell me father, who forged this with a dark magic?" her eyes alight for the first time in months.

"Just remember it's probably best that you keep its predictions to yourself, you don't want to cause trouble here in the castle with the M word."

"Of course ... and what is this?" said Belleny holding the rolled up paper. She removed the ribbon, which bound it tightly, but as it had been in that position for so long, it remained curled up. With a book placed on each corner, it became evident that this was no ordinary piece of paper.

"A map ... of the kingdom?" questioned Belleny. "That must be our castle?"

"No another, it's upside down, this is a section of the north far beyond the Slate Cliffs."The King scratched his head with a frown. "She's drawn this map herself you know, this is from far beyond the kingdom. It's not safe there for anyone nowadays. Wasn't too good back then either."

"She really was free as the wind," said Belleny moving the books aside and letting the map roll itself up.

"Yes, yes she definitely was," said King Vera wistfully.

The King remembered laying in his chamber bed alone many nights, wondering where the Queen was, where she was traveling to and where her thoughts took her. Belleny knew how she felt and could easily spend the rest of her days drawing and making clothes in silence.

"Well, there's just enough time for one last gift before I better head out and join Madam Nalian Garmus ... I mean, the guests ... for one last nightcap," he stammered slightly embarrassed by his admission.

"Father you are formidable! But, thank you, now I have everything I will ever need and more."

"You don't have one of these," he said and jingled a silver bell. It's chime rang throughout the room.

"I do have a few bells, although none as piercing as that one."

After a moment, a guard opened the main door.

"Please send her in," said King Vera and together they watched as the maid Jodin walked through the doorway holding Bateau in her arms, then lowered him to the ground.

"Thank you Jodin," he said.

Jodin smiled with a small curtsy and caught a glimmer in Belleny's eyes.

"He's tired but wonderful," added Jodin and gave Bateau a quick pat as he walked on towards the Princess.

"Jodin, who is this?" asked Belleny and she knelt to the ground, her arms outstretched warming Bateau to herself.

"A gift, a friend," said King Vera.

"Really Vasilis, but what is it, not a cat? I already have the Orphans to look after," said Belleny.

"No definitely not a cat, he seems to be able to look after himself just fine."

They watched as Bateau walked towards her casually on all fours, he checked out the huge bookcases and rubbed up against the statue. With a quick jump, he leapt at Belleny making her tip backwards onto her feathered tail as she caught him in her arms.

"He's trained?"

"You could say that," said the King with anticipation, eagerly waiting for Bateau to say something. But he was silent and with a strange meow he stretched out his back like a bridge and curled up on her lap, much like a cat. That was until his two tails unwrapped from each other and gently shook her hand with a kiss.

"Did you just see that? Two tails? He just kissed my hand! He's not like others is he?" said Belleny.

"No, he's not," said the King quietly realizing that Bateau had closed his eyes.

Belleny cuddled him close. "You can't really cuddle the Orphans like this," she said gently stroking her hand along his silvery coat.

"Okay, what is he? Is he going to turn to rock if he touches water?" she said sarcastically.

"His name is Bateau Catealis," said King Vera, "he's quite the character, I'm sure you'll find out when you get to know him better tomorrow."

"Go ahead and use your locket on him if you like?"

Belleny rose an eyebrow, "I have a new locket Jodin, passed on from my mother. This is to be a complete secret OK? Just between the King, you and I."

"Jodin, you must watch this!" Belleny pointed the locket at Bateau and the small whirlpool of triangles forged into an arrow and began to spin as soon as the lid was opened. Belleny and Jodin looked on.

"It's not stopping, oh it can't be broken!" said Belleny in a huff.

The three watched the spinning locket till she snapped the lid closed.

"I'll tell you about it later," said Belleny to Jodin.

"Thanks for everything today father, it was quite an event, and I did enjoy the Lysa and this Bateau fellow is quite a curiosity."

"My pleasure, my little bell," he said squeezing her tightly with Bateau in between.

"Please, father … you're crushing us. What's this?" asked Belleny as he slipped a glistening jewelled seed into her palm.

"One last gift, that's all," he said.

"Oh, how lucky! Belleny it's another desert seed," said Jodin.

"Another seed?" The King shook his head.

"A soldier boy gave me one earlier," said Belleny.

"That little rodent! He knew I went to the desert to get you one! I'll have him thrown in the Pit."

"Calm down that's my job.

"Hmm."

"Thank you for everything Father. I must return to my quarters. I'm so very tired."

"Yes. It was a good day, a great day. Thank you Belleny."

"Thank you."

Together with Jodin and Bateau they began the long journey back to her quarters. Alone in the library the King stared silently into the eyes of his frozen queen.

"She's going to be just like you, and don't you know it."

Evelin zoned out to the slow, easy listening elevator music that reminded her of an old wind-up music box. "Forty-Five Boots, go on then, press the button," said Astina, pointing snottily at the rows of brightly lit diamond-shaped buttons. She then immediately proceeded to pick the stray fluff from her rabbit fur jacket.

Evelin stared at the buttons, there was so many of them, all laid out in diagonal rows. She skipped her finger along the numbers until she reached the very last button number forty-four. She was puzzled, was Astina toying with her again? There was no forty-five, just a red diamond button.

Evelin paused, *Should I press it? It's red.*

"What are you doing Boots, you do know how a button works? Just press it, girl, it's always on red, stops children from annoying the adults." Astina glanced sidewards art her, "You'll understand one day."

Evelin tentatively pushed the red 'forty-five' and the elevator proceeded to lumber upwards after a sharp jolt. She hadn't ridden in an elevator in a very long time. There were very few buildings in Yellow Tree with them. Here she was in close confines with four very hyperactive and spoilt miniature dogs with her new employer, the eccentric and strange Miss Astina Francis.

The wires and cables rattled as the lights and numbers of each floor slowly shone through a small diamond shaped window in the door. The elevator certainly was an antique, perhaps built during the Industrial Revolution.

Come on, so damn slow. It wasn't only slow but along the way it seemed to scrape on each floor. Evelin looked up at Astina with worry in her eyes.

At the seventeenth floor, the elevator slowed down even more, and once it reached the twentieth floor, it stopped with an elastic jolt.

Good, we're here, Evelin thought but looked up at Astina, who was nodding negatively. *Oh no,* she now realised it had stopped to pick up more passengers. *How are we all going to cram in here?* She shuffled the dogs aside the best she could as the odd figures entered the tight quarters.

A long-faced man with high cheekbones and a gravity defying black moustache entered first. He wore a crisp white short-sleeve shirt, black belted white shorts and was adorned with sailor tattoos, even on his neck and finger knuckles. But all Evelin could look at was his doll-pink, plastic prosthetic leg. He smiled down at Evelin, "You're not like most kids are ya," he said, pointing to her hair.

Evelin shrugged her shoulders, "No, I guess not.""

He was followed by a short barrel-shaped man wearing a bright red military jacket, adorned with golden tassels and shiny brass buttons. He gave Astina and Evelin a light nod and then swivelled around on one foot. He held his hand up high to escort a towering and delicately thin oriental lady inside.

"My lady," he said and brought her into the lift as if boarding a ship. She ducked low and remained bent inside. Evelin glanced up at her powder-white and brightly painted face. She glowed in the elevator light.

Evelin tried not to stare at her, or the man's leg. The little red-coated man looked like he could explode at any moment, holding a tight Cheshire Cat grin across his face.

Astina greeted them with a strained toothy smile.

"Good day, Miss Francis," said the one-legged sailor.

"Good afternoon to you."

Evelin watched as Astina ended the conversation abruptly. The guests all face outwards and the elevator door closed and it slowly rose upwards.

What if this door doesn't open and we're stuck for hours? I can't be trapped in here! Something's wrong it's going too slow. My mouth's dry, I've got to get out! Evelin squeezed her eyes shut, it was better than looking at Astina or any of the strangers around her, but it made no difference with her rising anxiety. The sound of the scraping metal began to overpower the music inside. Her head started to spin. With nowhere to move and no sign of escape she snapped.

"I've got to get out," Evelin muttered.

"Out?" said Astina biting into the thick air. "Have some patience girl."

"I can't breathe, I don't feel—here take these," said Evelin handing Astina the leashes.

"Boots! Get a hold of yourself," said Astina as she folded her arms.

The leashes dropped to the floor as Evelin squeezed past the short man and the plastic-legged sailor. With a fist clenched she hammered the buttons on the elevator hoping it would stop on the next floor. But it didn't, and the dogs began to dart around among the human legs, barking as if it was a game.

"I've got to get out of here!" winced Evelin, her head in her hands.

The oriental lady knelt down comforting her with her big painted smile, "You'll be okay little lady, pretend it's a ride, you see?"

"Only a few more to go," said the plastic-legged man, his leg pushing up against her.

The elevator arrived at the next floor with a jolt. The doors slid open revealing a window of bright light and Evelin ran out at once.

What the hell was that? I'm not going back in that metal piece of crap ever again! I've got to get out of here.

"Here we are, see that wasn't too bad was it?" smiled the painted lady patting her on the head. "Next time you will be less worried."

"Have a nice swim," said the lady and the three strangers hopped back in the elevator and rode it back down.

Swim? thought Evelin, then she realised why she was there in the first place.

"Welcome to the top floor Boots, make yourself comfortable, but please don't drop the leashes again." Astina dropped her jacket on the floor and unveiled a white, full piece swimsuit underneath. Graceful & elegant, like a ballerina, she glided towards the pool.

"Be a darling, put my jacket on one of the deckchairs Boots. I'll be in the pool."

Evelin did as she was told and scooped up the fur jacket in both arms and pulled the dogs alongside her.

I can't believe she was only wearing a bathing suit under this fur!

As Astina stepped elegantly into the rooftop swimming pool, her pets pulled forward on their leashes, and together they peered like Meerkats. Astina's head came into view, popping through the surface of the clear blue water as steam was rising from the surface and then proceed to swim breaststroke with her head above the water.

What am I doing here? I should just go. Evelin slipped her shoes back on. Astina's jacket was hot and cumbersome, Evelin threw it over the back of a chair, she was glad to be rid of it.

From the top of Hotel Chandelier, the view of the Yellow Tree was indeed breathtaking, and Evelin fought her vertigo as it inched towards her.

Feeling uneasy she walked the dogs over to a clear patch of grass and sat down. All she wanted to do was tie the dogs to a table and run down the stairs, all forty-five floors of them. *What have I gotten myself into? ... I'm such an idiot.* The dogs curled up on her lap the best they could, even though, there was only enough room for two. The others sat their heads on her legs and stared up at her.

You guys, what's got into you? *The little dogs made Evelin smile for the first time that day.*

As she fumbled through her purse, she looked at the contents and wished she had looked earlier. *So much for my anxiety in the lift! Weren't you supposed to stop that little Pill?* she thought irritated. Evelin painted her lips and looked at the small canisters once again. *Mad if you do, mad if you don't.*

"Boots, please be careful up here, I don't want you falling off onto some unfortunate bystander," said Astina sitting against several water jets that foamed up around her back. "Go and see Royal around the corner and help yourself to the buffet, take the nippets with you, he should have prepared something for them."

Evelin knew if anything could make her feel better, without letting Astina know, it would be food. "Did you hear me, a buffet?" *I wonder if you guys have been fed today? Or ever?* She squeezed one of the dogs as she moved him off her lap. *You're no bigger than my cat BC.*

Astina watched as Evelin walked them one after another along the side of the pool.

"Evelin?"

"Yes?"

"I thought you weren't a dog person? I've never seen them so obedient."

"I'm not," Evelin wanted to smile but kept poised.

Is she being nice? That's one less brick in the Francis Fortress.

As a reward, the poolside buffet was all that she imagined from a five-star hotel. It was small with shiny chrome domes bursting with a variety of rainbow salads and super foods, fragrant rices, bright seasonal fruits and jugs of pressed juices. Evelin drooled as she watched a young chef plate up grilled prawns, squeeze a massive lemon over the top, crack some pepper and place onto a tray.

"Good afternoon Mademoiselle?" the young man said politely.

"I've been better, but this may change things," said Evelin. "Are you Royal?"

He stared back at her with a grin, "I guess I am to some people."

"So you're Astina's ... niece?

"Not even, I'm a hostage; I was captured on the sidewalk and forced to look after these guys."

"Ah, I see, she chose well, they're usually running around up here like—"

"Like mice after eating a bag of candy floss?" she chuckled.

Royal appeared from behind the counter. "Here ya go," he said placing two white, fine bone china plates in Evelin's hands with two large portions of thick slices of lasagne with fresh parsley onto each plate.

"Are you kidding me?" said Evelin.

"But it's lasagne, you can't feed them that?"

Royal shrugged. "So it is." He took the plates back off her.

"Best if they eat over there, Astina has had complaints about the dogs eating lasagne near the buffet as you can imagine."

"I can think of worse things they could do."

Astina approached casually in her white one-piece swimming costume, Evelin was impressed by her lithe figure. Astina patted her dark wet curls and coiled them up in a towel.

"Afternoon Royal, I see you have met my new assistant? I'll have the usual, let Boots get what she wants; I'm going to work on my tan while the sun's still out. Bring the dogs over once they're done, which shouldn't be long, they're like piranhas. Oh and Royal?"

"Yes, Miss?"

"Please wash your hands."

"Very good, Miss."

Astina turned and took off. She was like no woman Evelin had ever met. *Assistant?* she thought.

Royal washed his hands and returned. "So Boots what will it be today? Astina did call you Boots didn't she?"

"Yeah, that's my last name."

"Figures, I like it. It's tough, like a gangster 'toughie's name. My name is Eric, Eric King, Astina calls me Royal."

Evelin grinned, "Royal works. Plate me up like the dogs please ... you don't get to say that every day."

"Good choice, I'll bring it over to you."

Miss Francis had dragged a deck chair away from the rest and laid outstretched with a large white hat over her head, dark glasses on and an ice-filled large water underneath the deckchair.

"Boots there's a drink there for you, let the dogs loose for now, no guests are up here."

Evelin let the dogs off their leashes, instantly they ran up to Astina.

"Go away," she hissed.

The steam was floating up from the surface of the pool, it captured Evelin's attention and she gazed at it with such intensity that she could have been watching television. It danced on the surface in a hypnotic rhythm, moving as one then breaking apart in swirls.

Astina spoke, "You've always lived in Yellow Tree haven't you?"

"Yes, how do you know?"

"I know everything," said Astina. "Plus, how many girls do you know walking around that have both natural dark brown curls and a straight blonde fringe?"

"Oh God, I know. I hate it."

"I know you do dear. There's no other explanation for it," said Astina with a lipstick red grin.

Evelin pushed her blonde fringe back behind her ear, "It's always been like this."

"Can you cover a curse with hair dye? What would you do? Are you more a blonde or a brunette?"

"Not sure, I tried blue last time."

"Of course you did, mine's grey all over these days, I'd look like a haggard old witch without my saviour Mr. Hair Dye, the colour is 'Raven's Wing.'"

"I'll be happy when mine's grey all over," said Evelin.

"Look, as long as you don't go bald. It's all right for men, they look distinguished, but even the slightest bald spot on a woman, well that's never a good look."

"Never," added Evelin, patting the dogs to sleep.

"Do you come to the Chandelier Hotel often?" asked Evelin.

"I should do, I don't just live here dear, I own the hotel and this block including four streets that surround it."

Evelin was stunned.

"If you want to continue working for me I'll see if I can get that curse lifted from that hair of yours."

"I don't understand—"

"But don't start taking advantage of the buffet, once a fatty always a fatty." Without looking, Astina pointed haphazardly across at Evelin's legs.

Evelin couldn't imagine how someone could own a hotel, let alone a block with several streets, she couldn't fathom that wealth.

"I'm guessing by the odd look on your face you're saying Yes, thank you, Miss Francis," she said peering over her dark pointy sunglasses.

"Oh yes, sorry, thank you, Miss Francis. May I ask, how did you afford this hotel, it must have cost a fortune?"

"Boots have some manners, that's none of your business," said Astina tight-lipped. "I like it up here, it's nice don't you think?" said Astina calmly.

"I don't like heights; I have to argue constantly with myself that I won't jump," said Evelin and thought of the time she stood on her roof.

Astina laughed, "I thought the exact same thing when I first bought the place, had a barrier put up, can you imagine that, a barrier. Why have a view if you don't see anything but a solid wall? So after a while I said to myself, if I jump, I jump, so I removed the solid barrier, at least I won't have to look at that ugly view again. I had in place, forty rose bushes in plant pots, so the rose thorns keep me from the edge."

"Yes Astina, they're so beautiful, roses are my favourite. I dreamt I wore a dress that looked like a rose the other day, if I could, I'd have cut roses in my bedroom every day," gushed Evelin.

"In your bedroom?" questioned Astina.

"I couldn't bear to have them only growing outside, there's so much to watch as they bloom, their petals and their exquisite beauty, such life and death … I dry the flowers, hanging them up by their stems too."

"You're a classy girl Boots, despite a bit strange," Astina remarked warmly.

Royal arrived and placed a plate of hot lasagne in front of Evelin with a garnish of fresh salad and olives.

"Bon appetite, Miss Boots," he said.

"Thank you, Royal, it looks delicious."

Astina held out her hand without looking up at Royal and pointed downwards at the small side table beside her.

"And one garden salad," said Royal placing a plate of green leaves on her table that was garnished with a combination of shredded radishes, onions and coriander.

A moment ago I could have died, now I feel like a movie star, Evelin mused.

"Is there anything else?" asked Royal.

"No, thank you, as you were," said Evelin cheekily.

"As you wish," Royal smiled, as his dimples appeared on both cheeks.

Evelin dove into her lasagne, an all-time favourite dish. The hot creamy béchamel sauce melted in her mouth and it tasted equally as good as it looked under the sunlight.

"Please don't stop breathing Boots," said Astina.

Evelin paused, her mouth gulped the food down then smiled.

Astina positioned herself on her towel, laid back on her deckchair and closed her eyes beneath her sunglasses. Neither said a word and for close to an hour they both rested.

"Oh no!" exclaimed Astina sitting up at once.

Evelin jolted up and the dogs as well.

"What? What's wrong?"

"My hat, the wind has taken it!"

"What? Where is it?" Evelin turned to see that Astina's broad-brimmed hat had whisked along the grass by a stray gust of wind and tumbled through the air hooking within the rose bushes.

"It's okay the rose bush caught it," said Evelin, "I'll get it."

The roses swayed in the breeze, and the clear edge looked ever so daunting. She reached out and held the hat in her fingertips. But as she turned she was hit by another gust of wind, it pulled the hat from her reach and it vanished straight over the rooftop edge. Evelin gasped and watched it tumble all the way down. It fell against the building several times, then out onto the street below.

"I'm so sorry, I had it, but the wind—"

"The wind? I clearly saw you throw it off the edge, here I thought I had made a friend with someone normal."

"What? No, I am normal," Evelin's heart began to pound.

"Yes of course you're normal," Astina said sarcastically. "Most people find joy in throwing people's very expensive hats from rooftops!" Astina glared at Evelin and stood up. Her glasses glaring back bright daggers from the sun, with large struts she came straight over staring deep down at her, "Have you any idea how much that hat cost?"

"But ... it was the wind," stammered Evelin.

"But the wind what? Picked up your arm and made you toss it?" Astina towered over her looking down into the abyss where her hat had fallen.

"I'll go down and get it," said Evelin, he mouth dry and coarse.

Evelin noticed a dizzy wave come over her. She felt so faint and her balance became unstable. This made her thoughts take flight, and her heart began to beat against her chest, *what the hell is going on? I've got to get out of here!* Quickly she pushed Astina aside and ran for the elevator. The dogs woke from their nap and chased close behind barking at her feet.

"Boots! Where are you going?" shouted Astina at full volume as if ordering her to stop.

But Evelin was now running, and she didn't look back once. She reached the elevator and pressed the down button repeatedly as if it was an arcade game. She looked up at the diamond display devastated; the elevator was still on the ground floor. *I've got to get out, got to get off this roof. Where the hell is the stairwell?* She wanted to scream. Reaching into her purse she grabbed her orange canister and poured the pills across her shaky palms. *She's crazy,* she thought to herself and swallowed several white pills.

"Evelin dear, what are you doing? Here quick drink this."

Evelin looked up and saw Miss Francis holding out her glass of red wine. With eyes watering, she felt the pills sticking to her dry throat making her cough. She grabbed the glass, spilling wine down herself and with a gulp washed the strange taste from her mouth and added another on top with the red wine.

"God, I was only joking Evelin," She smiled kneeling down and putting her hands on Evelin's shoulders. But Evelin looked at her with a frown,

"That as so mean. The cruellest joke I've ever—" It was then a wave of relaxation flowed throughout her entire body from head to toe.

Evelin spoke gently, "You frightened the hell out of me Astina, on a roof of all places, I shouldn't be up here."

"I am very sorry darling Boots, I have a wicked sense of humour ... but I did notice you frightened yourself a bit there."

"It's complicated," she said, noticing Royal watching her from behind the buffet. She moved behind Astina.

"Is that why you take those pills? I'm sorry, I didn't know you were so anxious."

"We'll there's a lot you don't know."

"Come on dear, let's go downstairs then. I think you have had enough excitement for one afternoon. Here take this before I forget," Astina removed a wet fifty dollar note from her bathers and pushed it into Evelin's jacket pocket and then gently placed it over her shoulders.

The elevator reached the top and with a light tune its doors opened up.

"Royal, look after my dogs, I'm just walking Evelin to the car," said Astina as she grabbed a white towel robe to cover up with and gently began guiding Evelin towards the elevator.

"Darling, I'll have a driver take you home, to Edinburgh Street."

"I'm okay Astina, thanks. But there's a tram that goes straight—hang on a sec, how'd you know I live on Edinburgh Street?"

Astina clicked her fingers and waved a white limousine forward. It pulled up beside them lowering the passenger window.

"Hi Robert, please drive Miss Boots home she lives are Forty-Five Edinburgh Street."

"Yes, as always Miss," said Robert tipping his cap.

"I'll see you next time, when you're ready?" said Astina.

"Bye," said Evelin sinking into the warm leather.

Astina held Evelin's hand and gave it a squeeze, "Goodbye Evelin, I'm glad we met, you'll be all right, remember, tough as Boot's."

"Bye."

"Next stop Edinburgh Street," said Robert looking back through his rearview mirror.

"Forty-five," she smiled.

Number Forty-five.

Seen through the steaming mist, the languid, dark shadows moved and concealed a figure of immense stature and otherworldliness.

What creature could make such a piercing, gurgling, bubbling gargle? A demon? questioned Evelin. *No, it was a Banshee,* she was sure. Through its wail and a mysterious veiling mist, it appeared once again. Through the haze, an arm reached out and its hand was clawed, snatching at the air as if it was trying to pull itself back inside. Then to the right its other arm appeared and to Evelin's confusion she noticed its hand was shaped like a spoon. *What demon has a spoon for a hand?*

Then she realised, *it must be the Last Supper Banshee.*

"Nearly there Eve, ready in one more minute!" said Robin shouting through the billowing steam as he slaved over four pots on boil and fry.

Evelin didn't answer Robin, she was tired and thankful the Banshee had vanished. Her focus had moved and she stared at a silver spoon intently before bending it with her hands and haphazardly threw it on the table with the rest of the cutlery.

One day spoon, one day.

"There you go Eve; spicy red cabbage, baby carrots, matsutake mushrooms, egg noodles and my 'Mystery' dumplings," said Robin taking off his apron.

"Thanks, do you need a hand?"

"You do realise you ask that before someone has made dinner? Help yourself, get them while they're hot," he said picking out a fork and the bent spoon from the pile of silver cutlery. "I didn't know you could bend spoons? Such a powerful mind, a gifted Princess I have, or a little witch?"

"I can also read minds, you're thinking about a certain teacher."

"Hilarious. You know this town is quite famous for witches and their eradication, especially children."

"Yeah, yeah, I know, and for some reason they stopped and now I have a classroom full of them."

"Well, you can always join them."

"Is that what you did?"

Evelin reached for her habitual jar of honey and with a fork drowned her plate with the golden syrup. Robin quite used to her eating habits, eagerly sucked a whole dumpling into his mouth.

"Hot ... hot, hot!" he sputtered as it burnt his taste buds from his tongue.

Evelin waited; she could see the hot steam firing out of the dumplings as her fork stabbed into their weak, pale skin. The last thing she wanted was a burnt tongue.

"Can I have some of that?" said Robin pointing at the jar of honey.

"Sure," said Evelin and slid the jar towards him. "Hey, what sort of dumplings are these anyway? These aren't vegetarian, and they're not prawn or chicken? They look more like jellyfish?"

"You honestly can't smell it?" said Robin still bemused that her sense of smell had completely faded away to nothing.

"No? Tell me, what is it?"

"They're fish dumplings with garlic and herbs."

"Fish? What sort of fish, jellyfish?"

"I'm not sure what kind? It's just the eyes you see, I bought a whole bag of them for literally nothing!"

Suddenly Evelin's face was a little paler than before, and her mouth began to tremble. "Eww! I don't feel so good," she coughed dribbling the dumpling back onto her plate. The eye rolled out from its flesh.

Robin still chewing on his replied, "They sell them at the markets, rich in vitamins I'm told and good luck."

There was a short silence as they stared at each other.

Appalled, Evelin continued, "Who buys a bag of fish eyes? Honestly, who makes fish eye and garlic dumplings? Let's, please eat something normal one day Robin? No wonder BC has been upstairs all afternoon, did you force on him some of your delicacies?"

Robin finally gulped down his eye, "I did, but he didn't touch them, look they're still in his bowl, maybe he would like them cooked?"

Evelin turned to the cat bowl and there they were, a bowl of eyes looking this way and that. "That is seriously messed up Robin; you *are* the Last Supper Banshee. I want them gone next time I look at that bowl."

"Dinner time is my favourite, such a bonding session," said Robin stabbing into another dumpling, "I like em, they're chewy!"

"Hmm, you're lucky you cooked vegetables ... I did notice BC has a thing for the paper fish you know, I think they're old friends. He's still up in my room staring at them now, couldn't pry him away, cries like a little monkey."

"Make sure you keep the top secure on that aquarium, cats can't swim."

"When was the last time you looked at that aquarium, I need a step ladder to even feed them."

"All I'm saying, curiosity killed the—"

"Don't say it. Anyway, of course, they can swim. Just because they haven't got a stroke named after them, they're probably better swimmers than most dogs I've met lately." In a flash, Evelin was reminded of Astina's small white dogs and paused holding her fork in the air.

"Earth to Eve? You okay? Your batteries dead again?"

"Probably. No, I was thinking about today."

"Yes, of course, I want the whole story. It was one thing seeing a limousine pull into the driveway, having you stumble out of it was another, only to sleep all afternoon leaving me in suspense."

"It wasn't very glamorous, I stared the whole way blankly. I did meet probably one of the strangest ladies in Yellow Tree. She threw herself in front of me, practically begged me to look after her dogs while she had a dip-n-bake or whatever she called her type of swimming."

"Swimming?" asked Robin, "you went to the beach?"

"No at a hotel in town. On the roof in a diamond-shaped pool. I made a complete fool of myself and freaked out, once in the elevator and then again on the roof. But the weird thing is she didn't help me, probably because she was the main reason. I don't think these things are working Robin."

Robin swallowed and asked all at once, "She has a pool on her roof?"

"Yes the ... Chandelier Hotel?"

Robin shook his head and whispered with excitement, "No way!"

"Way," mimicked Evelin. "I'm fine now, but earlier I really flipped out. I don't think I'll go back there or ride in an elevator ever again. It wasn't a joy ride," she said turning down on her plate.

"Don't if you don't want to, but it's probably not the place that was bad, perhaps your thoughts at the time made it seem that way."

"Thanks, Professor Boots for your situational diagnosis but you weren't in the elevator, it was a wire away from free-falling and Astina belongs in a hospital, she has 'crazy rich lady' syndrome. But the food was good. Cheesy thick Lasagne, oh you would have loved it."

Evelin grinned as the whites of Robin's eyes grew.

"Remember Eve you can always ring me, I'll come and pick you up any time on my bike, maybe get a bite while I'm there."

"Yeah right, I was going to run at first, but I changed my mind when I had a plate of lasagne in front of me."

"A cure for many an ailment."

"Francis. You know her? Astina Francis."

"Yes, Astina Francis, of course. Who else has a pool on their roof. We haven't spoken for a long time. Your mum once worked with her actually. Looks like we all have now, she's one of Yellow Tree's well-known moguls, a gold digger, so the rumours run."

"Mum worked with her?"

"Yep, real-estate tycoons the both of them, sell a leaky garage to a blind man. This is getting weird. You remember Goliath?"

"Who? What? The Cyclops?" said Evelin.

"I don't think Goliath was a Cyclops, wasn't he a just a huge giant?" said Robin chewing on another dumpling.

"Isn't a giant huge already? Or is Goliath bigger than most giants?" asked Evelin, watching bemused as Robin chewed away.

"He's probably bigger. Anyway, that's the name of the last luxury yacht my team painted for two months, maybe three in the end."

"Yes, how could I forget, you wouldn't stop talking about it forever, it had a speedboat on it called David, I liked that. Do you know David cut off Goliath's head to prove he was dead? Ever heard of a pulse David? Hey, have you switched the subject as my story is not finished?"

"Not at all, David and Goliath was owned by Astina's late billionaire husband Ethan Convey, she probably owns it now, what a dream boat."

"She must have more money than the Elden Park wishing well."

"Possibly, although she spent more time in court than a judge, front page stuff over the years. Her wealthy string of ex-husbands kept dying on her, I guess they never got her in the end, guilty or innocent, only she will know, you might find out though?"

"Ooh a mystery. I could totally see her pushing them off that roof of hers. I did ask how she got to own such a building, and she snapped at me. I never know if she's going to bite me or pat me. I don't know ... she isn't all that bad, lonely I guess, a lonely witch, maybe I should take her some eyes. I suppose it couldn't hurt to walk her dogs every once in a while. Poor little pups."

"Just don't lose them, especially in the restaurant district."

"You're not funny."

Evelin looked at her watch and pushed her dumplings aside, she could see the eyes watching her through their jelly white bodies.

"Lucky I had that lasagne today, you can definitely have the rest of mine. After a disturbingly weird dinner and afternoon, I think it's best that I go to my quarter's captain."

"Okay, I think I've had one too many myself."

"One is too many," said Evelin squishing up her nose.

"You may be right, I'll catch you tomorrow."

Evelin pointed at BC's bowl, the eyes and frowned back at Robin before climbing the stairs. At the top, she turned straight into the bathroom to clean her teeth and rinse the fish eye from her mouth.

A mirror filled most of the bathroom wall, and its slight warps and buckles made the room and its viewer seem quite surreal in particular sections. Evelin reached forward, pushed back her blonde hair into the brown curls and pinned her hair on top of her head.

Fish eyes ... idiot. Hmm, I look like more like a badger, not a skunk.

"I am the Badger Princess," she said royally. Although she couldn't remember exactly what they looked like and pictured, they were either black striped with white bodies or vice versa. As she scrubbed her teeth, she stared at herself vaguely. *Do I need a haircut?* She was reminded of Astina's brown curls. *Or maybe I should try dying it again?*

Evelin inspected her watch, it was only seconds before the alarm would chime. Probing around in her pocket she grabbed her pills and with a spearmint gulp she swished them down trying not to let them touch her tongue.

Tip-toeing softly into her bedroom the dark curtains blocked out the light outside and the aquarium lit the way. Evelin spotted BC as she had left him, he was curled up on the end of her bed in awe of the paper fish and their underwater world. She joined him and gently laid down beside him, curling in close around his thin shell. He was warm and as if he had a small motor in him, he vibrated with each purr.

BC awoke, meowed and together they stared deeply into the aquarium, the automatic lighting had dimmed down low and the fish, half asleep, drifted around hypnotized with their eyes open.

Life inside the tank flowed with the rhythm of the whirring filter. Although she knew it wasn't perfect, many of her gilled friends had been replaced. Their watery world demonstrated much that encompassed hers. On the day Robin poured in the first bucket of water he said, "The sea is an endless cycle of birth and death." Evelin could never forget. She thought about death habitually. The original plan was to put Ghost Crabs in before the fish, but they all died after the filter malfunctioned and turned off.

Peeking past a bright yellow, coral ledge she caught the two eels poking their dark blueish-green heads out of their den. The eels jaws were wired in a constant screaming shape, only to shut their mouths every once in a while to scream out again. Their rows of barbed white teeth were always on display. With deep black pupils ringed with a golden yellow iris, they stared in all directions and none, waiting and watching. Unfortunately for Evelin they didn't eat fish flakes or frozen brine like the others and she had to always top up the aquarium with live shrimp. It was at night the eels would escort them inside and in the morning sweep their empty coats onto the doorstep.

Evelin noticed BC's purring had calmed down to a gentle rhythm and he had fallen into a deep sleep. She closed her eyes as well and it wasn't long before the hum and ambient light of the aquarium had put them both to sleep.

What's this dust? Sand? She rubbed her eyes and sat up confused. She pushed her hand into the pillow, and it dispersed into an unfiltered mist floating in the air. *Something tells me this isn't air,* she thought and then realised her hair was now suspended around her head. *What's going on!* In a panic, she stood up quickly trying to take in a deep breath but took in nothing but water. She held it in, afraid to take another breath and covered her mouth with both hands. *No, no, no, no!* She panicked and when she couldn't hold on any longer she screamed out like the eels, but her scream was more like a muffled whisper and the water disguised it.

"What are you quietly screaming about?" said a curious voice. "I haven't heard anyone scream in ages, can't remember the last time I screamed, tell you the truth ... I don't think I ever have."

Evelin spun around opening her eyes, her mouth was still wide open. There in front of her sat a giant shrimp the size of a man and he wore a shiny silver suit of armour. He sat in the middle of a cup of golden yellow coral spiralling out its many tentacles around him.

"I, I can breathe?" said Evelin taking in cautious breaths of water.

"You're screaming because you can breathe? Interesting, you must be the new town fool," said the shrimp, he sat up and licked his long thin antennae back, staring at her continuously with his beady black round eyes.

"I am certainly not a fool, I should be put up a level if anything, who are you?" said Evelin.

"What do you mean, who am I? You must be the town fool. What about now?" The shrimp moved its many legs into another cross-legged pose and rested its head on its dozen clenched fists.

"Ahh?" Evelin really didn't know what to say.

The shrimp shook its head and with all his hands pointed to the golden cup coral he was perched upon, "I'm sitting on a ... throne and who usually sits on a throne?"

"A ... King?" Evelin assumed.

"Well done fool, finally, took you long enough. I'm King Henry the MMDCCLI," said the shrimp fluttering his little swimmers.

"King Henry the ... MMDCCLI?" said Evelin trying to pronounce it as King Henry did.

"Roman Numerals, it's the way of the future, better than repeating King Henry the twenty-seventh thousand five hundred and fifty-first!"

"I can imagine, that's a lot of Kings."

Before he could answer three other shrimps climbed over the coral shelf to greet the King. They looked identical to the King, but their shells were translucent and they wore no armour. The shrimp at the front spoke first.

"Greetings Your Majesty, how is this glorious night treating you?"

"Fine, fine. I'm admiring the view and teaching this screaming fool a thing or two about Roman Numerals, thrones and all things Kingly. You'll find out all about it when you're King tomorrow," said King Henry.

"She looks strangely familiar? That hair is particularly familiar? You fool—have we met before?" questioned another shrimp.

"I ... I don't think so? Not like this."

The shrimps shook their heads at each other confused.

"Like talking to a starfish," scoffed King Henry.

Evelin ignored their remarks and turned around to see more of the view. On the other side of the coral ledge was an enormous cavernous pit and to her horror four dish-size, yellow beading eyes glared back at her.

"There's—giant eels over there!" screamed Evelin pointing at the cave. She quickly climbed to the back of the coral throne, nervously hiding behind King Henry as the coral wrapped its tentacles around her.

"What are you doing back there fool? Why, of course, there's eels over there, that's where they live. Tonight they're having me around for dinner as their royal guest, every King dines with the eels on their first night, it's tradition."

"Are you mad! Tradition? Are all the Kings around here shrimps?" asked Evelin.

"Of course, who else? A starfish!"

They all laughed.

"All shrimps are King for a day," replied King Henry re-aligning his crown to the comity of shrimp who nodded in time with each other as a general consensus.

Evelin felt a scratching on her face like that of a nail file. It stroked her cheek several times and then it stopped.

"Why are you flinching? What's wrong with you fool?" asked the King.

"I'm not sure, something is poking at my face."

Evelin felt her cheek, and despite being underwater, the 'poking' sensation made her more in tune with her senses and she felt the water around her. In a whir and a blur, her eyes opened to see the dim glow of the fish tank, she was awake and back in her bedroom curled alongside BC.

"BC," she yawned. "Looks like we both nodded off," she said nudging him with her nose.

BC started to give himself a bath with quick repetitions of his tongue. Then he reached forward giving Evelin's face several long swipes before she pulled back quickly.

"Thank you for waking me, but your tongue feels like a worker's boot. For someone with very little hair you sure do clean yourself a lot, they have pills for that you know."

Night time. I must have drifted off? Strangest dreams...

Evelin starred into the tank and watched as a shiny shelled shrimp sat up upon the golden coral cup and another disappeared inside the Eels' cave.

Goodbye, King Henry.

Chapter 16 - Behind Closed Doors

As Bateau awoke from his slumber, it took him a while to adjust and realise where he was and exactly who was whispering to him. The ground was softer that marshmallow and he was completely engulfed by giant cotton-puff walls. Belleny sat down on the edge of his bed, watching him curiously and noticing his gentle to near-fearful quiver.

"Hello, I hope you're not having nightmares, you were quivering," she said standing up gently. She wandered off, kicking her feet through the torn paper that still covered the floor, "I'm sorry about this mess, I'll clean it up sooner or later."

He watched her curiously and silently. She seemed to embellish the strange made-up character whole-heartedly. Belleny walked ever so oddly around her enormous room; kicking the torn sheets into nest-like piles, touching her strange oddities on her shelves like she hadn't seen them in years and conversing quietly with Winta as she sauntered past.

"You must have been exhausted Bateau, to sleep through the party with all that commotion, you know it's still going and will be for hours I imagine," she said as she returned to his bedside. With gentle strokes, she patted his head as if he was a cat. Silently Bateau closed his eyes once again.

The noise from the full-bellied guests billowed up from the Queen's Garden and through the chamber windows. Belleny found the sounds a pleasant change from the ocean's constant roar and as long as she wasn't required to be present, she was content.

She took the opportunity while Bateau slept, to gaze at her locket and study the mysterious map as there was some familiarity with several landmarks that she knew the names and rough terrain. It intrigued her to see exactly where about they were and how far he had travelled, and most incredibly, her adventurous mother.

Bateau's ears pricked and turned towards the glass windows and the doors of the balcony as if there was someone calling him and he got up on all fours and began to meow in vowels. Belleny had never heard him meow, but assumed this was a normal sound he made to communicate.

"Don't worry, it's just the wind. Unfortunately it's like that up here, imagine how bad it is out there?" she said approaching the balcony doors. She drew the curtains aside revealing the boarded windows. *Maybe I can have a quick look at the Queen's Royal Garden, I'm sure it's lit up beautifully. No! I can't ! What am I thinking?* The wind blew ferociously just as Belleny leant down to turn the latch and the force pushed through the double doors and threw her aside like a doll. The sight of the door wide open sent shivers across her skin as the heavy curtains began to blow wildly like torn sails on a ship and they whipped around from their brass rings.

"No stop!" she shouted at the wind. As if the wind was listening, it died down at the direction of her stern words.

"What a nightmare!" she said getting to her feet and quickly returning to shut the door.

"See, nothing but vines and a wild zephyr," she said turning towards him and pointing to the open balcony covered by a thick green leafed creeper. "I must close it now, it's done enough damage."

It was then that Bateau leapt from the bed, bounced off several pieces of furniture and like an acrobat jumped through the vines quicker than Belleny's eyes could follow.

"Wait no! Get back inside now! We're not on the ground floor!" she shouted.

To her relief, she noticed one of his tails curling back through the vines. In a heartbeat grasped at it with an open claw, but the tail disappeared just as quick, leaving her with a handful of torn leaves.

"Get back inside now! I demand you!" she shouted through the faint gaps in the vines but Bateau was nowhere to be seen.

In anger, she clawed at the vines, again and again until her fists hung by her side exhausted.

This is intolerable! She snarled up at the white beast hanging above the door for support.

What was I thinking?

I have to close these doors, I'm sorry Bateau, she said to herself and shut the first side securing it back into place.

"No!" Came a deep voice from behind, instantly Belleny turned up to the white creature hanging above the doorway.

She shrugged, "He shouldn't have gone out there! It's not my fault, I'll open it when he comes back to the door."

"He won't—jump, will he? The poor thing, no he wouldn't ... Arghh I'll go get him, but I swear this is the last time these doors ever open for as long as I live."

"Bateau get back in here now!" she shouted.

One by one, she yanked the leafy vines apart. She was surprised at how they fell away and for the first time in years she peered out. She felt as if it looked back into her with such force, with all the years' combined light and energy. From behind the mountains and against the rooftop of clouds, the descending sun gave its all, screaming out at her as if it would never rise again.

"Oh my, it's too much," said Belleny as a wave of light shook through her entire body. Through the glare, she could see the silhouette of Bateau on the very edge of the balcony.

"Bateau! I'm so glad, please come back inside, it's too dangerous out here." In a panic, she flung herself through the vines and held him within her arms. Belleny's mouth fell ajar, she stood shocked at the overwhelming landscape which was ablaze in a golden vision of light and unimaginable beauty. Belleny loosened her tight grip on Bateau and he jumped back nimbly to the ledge. She whispered aloud in a teary voice, "The outside, it's ... staggeringly beautiful."

All across Mare-Marie the shock wave of the Princess's heart let a deep undercurrent of vibrations which was felt by all living things in Mare-Marie, a sign of which a life force had been reignited.

Belleny realised she had missed out on so much. The fauna and flora, the seasons, life and death, rebirth and the life force of her land ... and this pendulous weight of remorse, pulled her head down.

Belleny stared down into the glowing garden. A wave of vertigo forced her eyes closed, but she held on. *I must see,* she thought and pushed herself to look once again.

Glowing lanterns floated in the wind, anchored to the myriad of plants, moving as one, illuminating the party as if it was a creature from the deep blue sea. The music also had a life of its own, and the guests danced round and round like falling pine seeds while the water fountains flowed up towards her continuously crying with happiness.

Within the enormous garden walls, which were mostly an overgrown hedge, Belleny scanned for familiarity. It all looked so different since the last time she saw, which she couldn't remember when that was ... it was so long ago.

Bateau listened but didn't look at the town for long; he was completely affixed with somewhere else.

Belleny stared at the Pit of Nothingness, which was a gigantic cavern that tore into the ground sinking into darkness, it hadn't changed since the last time she saw it. The same sparse forest of crooked trees surrounded the entrance and struck out like frozen black lightning tearing through its surface. Never once had they grown leaves, and if they did, no one had ever seen them.

"You're probably looking at the white things flapping about in the trees," said Belleny, pointing out the strange white creatures perched along the branches. "At least someone is putting that hole to use. Of all the things outside it scares me the most. Such a deep fear, it claws in so tight. It has no purpose and no reason other than to haunt me. We should go back inside now, I've seen more than enough."

Bateau slipped from her embrace and walked along the balcony to the other side.

"Where are you going? You do realise how high up we are?" she said and grabbed him once again holding him back from the edge.

"Oh, I see," she pointed out far into the distance. "They're the infamous Zale Mountains that do an excellent job of protecting us all from the sea on the other side. My mother travelled beyond the mountains but no one's gone beyond the sea," she said pointing out at the clouds above it.

To the East conquering and dividing the main lands, all the way to the distant Slate Cliffs, the mountain range rose up into the sky in some places as high as Belleny's tower only giving a glimpse of the ocean's turbulence. Nothing grew on the solid Tonerae Mountains, it had rose from the dead and stayed that way, like a scar. But the mountainous wall was a blessing, it held back the Sea Of Sorrow. Without the mountain range, Mare-Marie would drown.

"What was that?" said Belleny as a shadow of darkness raced past her tower, disappearing around to the other side. Then it reappeared, this time slightly slower, its body black as coal, moving in even closer. With a skull full of marble eyes they reflected back at her, her heart took flight and quickly she grasped Bateau and dove through the vines, slamming the door shut with her hands and feet.

"What was that thing? Did you see that? A winged demon!" said Belleny panting heavily with her back to the door. "Maybe it has something to do with the party, one of father's strange pets, I hope so," said Belleny turning around to peek through a hole in the plastered window, but it had gone.

Silently she listened. The party continued for several minutes without any screams and she sighed, "Of course it's one of those disgusting Kylen beasts, I'm glad I never have to see that again," she said making sure she pulled the door shut and pulled the curtains back across.

Belleny sat down on her chair and wrung her hands. *Is this what thirteen feels like?* she thought sarcastically.

Belleny paused, looked up from her hands and slowly crossed her arms with a frown, Bateau started to talk with a plummy pronunciation "Yes it is for you Belleny" he gently whispered.

Belleny stared down at him raising her eyebrow, "You do know I *am* the Princess Belleny Vera?"

"Yes the most famous of all Princesses, to be Queen of Mare-Marie one day I'm sure."

"Then address me like one! Why haven't you spoken till now? Why didn't you come back inside when I ordered you! What are you exactly? And explain yourself thoroughly!" said Belleny in a huff.

"Exactly?" asked Bateau with his tails shrugging either side of him. "My name's Bateau Catealis and I've never met anyone like me; I'm an Orphan.

Another Orphan? thought Belleny.

"I'm sorry Princess, it seems like I'm misbehaving, but I'm only able to speak when—I'm not sure really, once I start I'm usually fine but sometimes I don't talk for days, not that I don't want to—I just can't."

Belleny stared at Bateau her voice slightly alive compared to before, "You can call me Belleny if you want, my friends do, well Jodin and the Orphans. You must tired; I watched you sleep through the noise of the ball. Where are you from Bateau?"

"I'm not from anywhere. I travel a lot. I had been on the desert road for days with very little sleep. Your father, King Vera, rescued me from an awful situation."

"You'll be looked after here, there's no safer place that inside the Crystalon Castle," she said patting him on the head. "Oh I'm sorry, do you liked to be patted? It's quite strange now that I know you talk."

"Of course you can, it's warming, it's been quite difficult lately—on my own and all."

"I can imagine, you're very brave," said Belleny.

"Shall we finish watching the sunset before it goes? I've never seen one quite like it."

"No! I thought you were brave but now I think you're just stupid," she said instantly.

"Stupid? Why? Ah! The winged demon. It's not out there to hurt you, it's there to protect you. I'm quite fond of them," said Bateau.

"Sorry, still no. It's not that I don't want to, I just don't want to."

"What does that mean?" he said curling his tails up.

"I'm not sure what I was thinking tonight," said Belleny looking back at her hands.

"Oh, I understand, you're bored of sunsets. I guess you've seen a hundred different types, you must love clouds though? I love them, but then again who doesn't?" said Bateau winding his tails together.

"I'm not bored of them, it's complicated," Belleny paused and her hands tingled again. She tightened her fists.

"You're free," came a voice and Belleny turned slightly eyeing the white creature.

"Who's that!" said Bateau standing behind Belleny.

"His name was Esdaile, but now he is 'The White Creature.'"

"Is ... is he dead?" questioned Bateau.

"No he's not, he hangs up there, limp, he is just an unanimated version of himself."

With Bateau in her arms, Belleny mustered the desire to stand out on the balcony. The sun had completely disappeared, but the clouds were lined with golden hues. Together they stood speechless absorbing the sites and sounds for some time.

"Near the northern edge of the Zale Mountain sat the very end of the desert, just before the sea meets the white sands, that's where I was found," he said pointing with his tails.

Belleny looked out into the distance.

"But that's the Gaze Akarr?" said Belleny, remembering back to her studies. "It's dangerous and so very far away from anywhere." She couldn't fathom the thought of it, especially for someone like Bateau to endure as he is so small.

"I was in a cart and quite safe." *She doesn't need to know the gritty details,* he thought. "I've never been so frightened as when we travelled along the top the Zale Mountains, the sea constantly smashing against the wall and clawing up at us, that scared me half to death," said Bateau pointing along the ridge in the distance.

"You went along the Zale Mountains? I just can't believe a word you're saying!"

"Believe it," said Bateau.

"Outside sounds awful, you've been through such an ordeal. How you survived outside is beyond me, you will be safe here from now on."

"Well ... you learn the ropes as you exist and live in it Princess."

The sun dipped, and the sky had become dark. Small twinkling lights filled the land below and smoke drifted from the glass chimneys that scattered across the tile rooftops.

"Shall we return? I'm not dressed for the night air," said Belleny, and together they returned to the comfort of her room.

I can't believe I stood out there and I felt nothing, Belleny thought as she pulled the curtains shut behind her. She laid down on her bed with her arms behind her head and sighed.

"Oh, listen to that racket," said Belleny covering her ears as a new band began to play in the gardens below.

"Shall we join them or do something else?" Bateau asked inquisitively.

"Oh no! I'm not going out there, day or night and I'm definitely not going to bed. I never sleep at night, I prefer to sleep during the day," she said arrogantly. "We must go to the other side of the castle and visit my friends; they'll be expecting me. I'll introduce you, to the Orphans, they live in The Jungle Room," said Belleny over her shoulder.

"You have a jungle inside the castle?" said Bateau inquisitively.

"Of course!"

"What do you mean? Don't ever leave?" he lightly questioned.

Belleny rolled her eyes as she began to recite her lines she had always said,

"Outside is not for me. I'm a Princess, and it's dangerous, so why would I go outside into the wild? What if I get lost and never make it back to the castle? What if I faint and no one is there to help me and creatures take me underground? What if I go outside and forget my name? What if I get attacked by one of those giant black creatures out there and taken away to its nest where I'm fed leg by leg to its children? What if I—"

"No more!" cried Bateau. "What if that all doesn't happen?"

Belleny frowned straight into Bateau's eyes and took a deep breath.

"I've travelled with the circus from the White Sands of Veehn to Nibora and back, I've never forgotten my name or been attacked by giant birds, most of them are quite friendly, maybe a bit too friendly and I'm sure if I was lost, lots of people would help me back home, some way or another." Bateau said looking up at her genuinely. "But are you telling me you haven't even wandered through the Queen's Royal Gardens? I spent the morning there today, mostly sleeping, but it was like another world, it's as big as the whole castle," said Bateau as his tails hugged tightly to his body.

Belleny frowned at the thought and said quickly, "No of course not, I don't think that's a good idea!"

"I think you should say, 'I do think that's a good idea' and have a stroll around, even a picnic, it's perfectly safe in there, you do know the Queen planted nearly all those plants herself, so it's written on a plaque," said Bateau.

"Come on you, let's go and I'll hear no more," she said, but as she stroked his fur she felt that strange, comforting feeling once again, and even though he was talking of the forbidden there was something that made her feel warm inside. Her eyes took to the White Creature as they began to leave.

"Are you happy now?" she questioned the beast.

"Very," he said through his limpid eyes.

It took them a while to get the bottom of the stairwell. It was a long walk through the corridors to get to the other side of the castle.

Belleny looked straight ahead and quietly walked down a never-ending hallway, decorated with paintings that seemed from another world.

"Who are those paintings of? They're beautiful," asked Bateau.

"I don't really know?" said Belleny shrugging her shoulders.

"But there's so many of that little girl?"

"It's not me, obviously I don't have hair like that," she said in nonchalant way.

"So no one knows—"

"No one knows who she is or who painted them, there's no signature on any of them, maybe that's why they're down here, why have a castle full of pictures of someone you don't even know?" she said and continued down the hall.

Bateau noticed the sound of Belleny's shoes went from a constant tap to a more scuffled resonance. Looking down he noticed the smooth white polished floor had slowly faded into a dull and quite dusty covering. The walls too, bit by bit it began to change, now resembling the outside of an old weathered building, with the shell-white walls flaking off in patches and splitting with cracks.

They walked for some time until they reached the end of the hall and faced an empty wall.

"It's a dead end? Did we take a wrong turn?" said Bateau.

"No, we go through here," she said tapping on the wall with her fingernail.

"A handle? What does it do?" he said.

"What do you mean? What do most handles do on a door?" she said lowering him down to the ground.

"What do you mean, a door? This is a wall ... isn't it?"

Belleny knocked gently as if the inhabitants were sleeping and turned the handle gently. The door unlocked and opened effortlessly with the slightest push.

She picked up Bateau and stood inside, "Welcome to the Jungle Room."

"Hello?" she called out just louder than her usual tone. She stepped forward now holding Bateau tighter to her chest.

He felt her unease and was speechless himself, the room, was only a room because of the walls but it was like stepping outside. The roof was so high it was hard to tell if there was a roof at all.

Did they remove all the floors from the castle? thought Bateau.

In the centre was a large pool of water with creeping plants searching high above twisting around and covering every surface.

There were several huge windows but like Belleny's room they too were completely covered up by vines and drapes.

"Hello, Orphans?" Belleny called out.

"Palia, Dillon—Monté, Agarus?"

"Strange, where could they be?" she huffed but that turned quickly into worry. She looked at Bateau and shrugged her shoulders, her heart began to trigger instantly.

"What do they look like?"

"Well, they're different; they're not like most."

Bateau was silent.

Pretty big place for imaginary friends? he thought.

Thinking the worst, she scuffed quickly through the leafy floor to the edge of the lagoon, but thankfully they weren't there.

She looked up. "Something's wrong, I have to go up there," she said pointing up to a large cubby house of sorts. She placed Bateau down on the ground and started to awkwardly climb a thin wooden staircase. Bateau followed and put his tails to work grabbing at the bars and branches like a monkey.

Out of the corner of her eye, Belleny saw a skinny, yellowish, pale white tail flickering side to side.

"Dillon!" She shouted. "Don't worry I'm coming."

Nervously she raced up towards the cubby house.

For someone that's afraid of heights, she's a pretty good climber? thought Bateau.

"SURPRISE! HAPPY BIRTHDAY!" sang a chorus of off notes and screeches from the darkened depths of the wooden structure.

They are real? thought Bateau covering his ears from the noise.

Belleny crossed her arms and gripped her hands into tightened fists.

One by one they stopped until there was silence, then all at once they started to apologize in a cacophony of unnerving voices.

The noise was unbearable and Bateau squeezed his paws and tails over his ears.

"No more!" he meowed shaking his head to the ground. Quickly Belleny picked him up caressing him close.

"Quiet! All of you at once!" she ordered, raising her voice like never before.

The creatures in the dark went silent once again.

"Really sorry," said one, adding in one last apology.

Bateau looked up at Belleny, her fuming face, her posture unchanged, her brow digging hard.

"Hey, it's all right Belleny, they meant well. Whoever is in there."

"Well, if you're going to surprise someone, you do it without frightening them, what's the idea of hiding all the way up here? I thought you had disappeared at the bottom of that lagoon," she said in a snap.

"I told you this was a bad idea," said one pushing another into the dim light coming from a slit in the window. "It's not my fault! It's is the only place we could hide your huge head," squawked another.

One by one they appeared from the shadows, their sweet mangy faces pooled with forgiveness. A twitch hit her eye and she gritted it away with her teeth.

Belleny scanned across them and noticed the last one was holding a small round cake, with a single candle on it.

She felt strange and she swallowed the lump in her throat.

"Thank you for the surprise," she said, "I'm sorry for my anger."

Bateau curled a tail around her arm tightly and with the other tapped her shoulder.

"Oh yes, I would like to introduce you to my friends The Orphans, Orphans this is our new friend Bateau, he's come to stay with us at the castle."

After a lengthy pause they awkwardly spoke together, "Hello Bateau," Their voices were weak, unnatural and fractured.

Bateau forced his frightened expression into a shaky smile.

"Hello, it's nice to meet you all."

What in the world are they?!

CHAPTER 17 - GOODBYE

goodbye & good luck

All throughout the year Yellow Tree flourished with many golden Elm trees which grew hardy and abundant like contorted Bonsai bushes. Footpaths cracked like wafer biscuits from the puzzle of root systems underground and birds were always flush with an array of nesting branches to pick and choose from. During Winter, when the leaves had fallen and the branches were black and stark, the streets looked cold and felt as if every road led to a devil's lair. Edinburgh Street paved a crooked obstacle course to Yellow Tree High, which had its own fair share of demons and unsavoury types.

Evelin was on her way to school, dawdling, as she preferred to wander alongside the footpath and onto the front lawns of the pedestrian strip. With each step she stared down at her boots and watched the patchwork of grass types and colours change, ever-changing front yards and imagined she was far away, looking down on a topographical map if she were a giant.

The old elm trees were shedding their golden and rust coloured leaves, covering the ground below with a yellow carpet. She stopped and picked up a golden-brown leaf that had started to dance out from her hand in the wind. It was bigger than both of her hands combined and with her delicate fingers she tore the leafy flesh from its leafy vertebrae.

It wasn't long before something special caught her attention.

Cicada! She cheered inside as she pinched a golden insect husk from the bark of a tree, marvelling its semitransparent shell and its robust and alien body shape.

"There you are," she said noticing one insect, was in mid shed, she watched intently as the cicada peeling itself out of a shell revealing massive green and yellow jewelled body and bright green wing tips.

The morning school bell sounded in the distance.

Let it ring, she huffed before hurriedly the plucked several more shells from the tree trunk and placed them carefully inside her lunch box.

I'll take care of you.

She arrived at the school fifteen minutes later and approached her first class, which was math, "Ah Miss Boots, glad you could join us today, I won't be a moment and you can all be on your way," said Mr. Brackenback, who was surrounded by cardboard boxes.

"Morning," she said with a smile noticing Gertrude and Ursula were nowhere in sight. *Of course they're not here,* she thought and sat down noticing last week's test paper on her desk.

She smiled, its appearance brought back memories of an old treasure map she once made, although this one before her was made with ink and drool. Flicking through she noticed the distinctive red marker boldly correcting her answers. *Thankfully some part of my brain is working,* she thought and curiously watched her teacher once again.

The class session went by in delightful tedium that came about at the end of term. Students were cleaning out their desks, sharpening pencils and on hands and knees fishing out pencils, loose change that had rolled under cupboards that lined the windowsills.

Mr. Brackenback was doing his own spot of tidying up, his desk was piling high with strange cell-like prisms, his ancient yellowing computer and its keyboard hung from the side, books were removed from his shelf and his famous square globe had been moved from the window sill to his desk.

What is he doing? Spring cleaning for next year I guess? She turned around wondering if any of the others knew the answer.

Evelin watched as he finally finished stacking items and replaced them neatly into a cardboard box and proceeded to stand. He turned towards the blackboard and in large, looping cursive handwriting wrote,

'Goodbye and Good luck!'

He then signed it down the bottom, Mr. B.

"What do you mean goodbye?" said Evelin at once, "You're leaving?"

Mr. Brackenback walked around to the front of his table and leaned against it, moving aside a box, picking up his square globe as it spun around oddly in his hands.

"Today is not only your last day of books and numbers. It is also mine, this old mathematician has recently calculated that it's time to move on."

Nobody said a word and there was a long silence, then Carley said, "So we can go then?"

"Yes, go on, get out and keep your voices to a minimum," he said shaking his head at them.

Evelin was slightly stunned at the very notion that her teacher was leaving. She stared again at her test sheet, on the last page she noticed the comments he had written, Congratulations Evelin, you have shown through high hurdles and immovable obstructions a way to subtract difficulties and multiply effort! All the best, Mr. Brackenback.

It wasn't long before the class was empty and Mr. Brackenback watched his students leave for the last time. Soaking up the moment he remained leaning against his table, looking out at the empty desks for the last time in his life. Being a teacher had been everything for his last thirty-three years. Then with a smile through his glasses he returned to Evelin.

"Miss Boots, you're staying in?"

"Do you mind?"

"Not at all, I'm sorry to have to leave you like this Eve. Maths, teaching, students, this school ... you know it's been my whole life."

"What happens to it now?"

"Good question? I guess a new chapter begins ... I hope it begins."

"A part of it ends for me," said Evelin.

"I know," he looked at the floor. He knew she would be upset by his departure, he was not only a teacher but a mentor and most importantly a friend.

"Any advice then? Any last words other than goodbye and good luck?"

"You're on the right track Evelin, you don't need the good luck, although most of the others do," he turned and rubbed the words out with his duster.

"Learn the fine art of being punctual, don't try turning up fifteen minutes late with your next lecturer."

"Miss Boots, please take this." He held out his large square globe. It was Brackenback's world.

"I can't take it with me while I'm floating down the Amazon. I'll keep in touch now and then, anonymous postcards to the class, you can pinpoint where I am," he pointed to the globe and gave it a light spin.

"Goodbye Mr. Brackenback, thank you for everything."

Evelin couldn't get out of there quick enough. She walked as fast as she could down the empty hallways, scraping her footsteps in time with her heavy heart. Tears welled in the corners of her eyes only to be drawn back inside. She pictured Mr. Brackenback wiping down his blackboard, dusting his dusters and filling his lungs with the powdery white chalk for the very last time.

Evelin disobeyed all the rules and ran straight across the road to the boy's school. She remembered Milton's first class was Archery and went straight to the oval where upon arriving she noticed him sitting on the bench. Quietly she sat down beside him.

"Hello Milton," she said softly.

"Boots what are you doing here?" he said.

She shrugged, "Why aren't you playing Robin Hood?"

Milton pushed her head down so the coach wouldn't see her. "What's going on? Where did you get that globe? Are your classes over already?"

"No," she said quietly.

A guilty grin came across Milton's face. "I got sent off by old Randerhall. Actually you're not far off, I'm in quite a bit of trouble, but good news there's now a handful of arrows on the roof of the sports shed. We can come back and get them on the weekend."

Evelin shook her head, "But you don't have a bow?"

"That's next on my list. Hey, are you all right? You look like you're going to cry."

"Well, I'm not. Mr. Brackenback is finishing today."

"What do you mean? We're all finishing today."

"No, he retired. He's packing up his things as we speak."

"I just don't like it when ... when people leave me, you know?"

"Brackenback lives four blocks from us. Anyway he ain't going anywhere, he just bought that giant satellite dish and had it installed in his backyard, we can see it from your balcony. He's probably a spy for all we know, a life of undercover espionage, disguised as an eccentric maths teacher!"

"MILTON CORMAN! Move yourself out here and help Eddie pack away the sports equipment," shouted Mr. Randerhall.

"I told you Eve. I gotta go, but I'll see you later today, I can't skip any classes, I'm on my last warning."

Evelin sniffed the afternoon air and sat on the grass under an elm tree. She grabbed her school bag and dug out the lunch box which protected the cicada shells she adoringly placed in it earlier and started to attach them onto her blazer jacket like Royal badges. These insect shells, gave her hope and a bit of courage when all seem a little lost and sad in her tiny world.

Chapter 18 - The Orphans

King Vera had a reputation as a collector, like the Queen he also worshipped exotic and rare animals and studied the biology of all living creatures and kept some as pets. It was a commonplace to see him with several sitting by the throne, being walked on tiny leads in the Royal Garden and he adoringly had the little creatures perched on his jacket lapels and in his hair.

Queen Vera designated a wing of the castle as an animal sanctuary ward to care for the wounded or the orphaned and later some would be released back into nature or they would seek out a happy life in the garden grounds, the Jungle Room or the sanctuary.

Those creatures belong outside the castle walls, why mend them if there only going to come back and poison us?

Belleny stayed well away from the animal ward.

The Orphans arrived on a morning of electricity and noise; a storm was raging twisting in a wild lighting sky.

The towns watchman, Yuka Nake, pointed his thick clawed fingers to the menacing cloud and shouted down below, "I tell you people this is it! It's going to overflow! You're doomed if you stay outside. Get to your homes! This is what we've been waiting for! I told you so!" He rang the gigantic brass warning bell five times and the echo sung sounds into the deepest nooks of Marie-Marie valley and he slid down the ladder of the tower lookout and landed on a tin roof with a thud.

"It will overflow I just know it," said Gustus on watch at the castle gates. He shook his large beetle-like face nervously as his towering body stood solid as a rock.

"Well, if it does we'll have a great view from here," said Kostis trying to cheer him up. He noticed for the first time in a long time a real fear rising in Gustus's black beetle-like eyes.

"There's no great view of a tidal wave Kostis."

"At least we're not out there. Think about how scared that poor girl is right now, trapped in the middle of the ocean."

"Kostis, you can't really believe there's a girl out there. The Eternal Tower is as empty as our pantry, anyway like I've said before, there's no way to get out there."

Gustus stared out into the sea his eyes reflecting the lightning as it cascaded across the waves. The sound of thunder compressing the land under it's bellowing roar. He turned down to Kostis and said, "The townsfolk must be petrified, for I know I am."

A dark, black and pendulous storm cloud, surged swiftly and lightning shattering the sky, hitting the land in a tremendous shock wave.

"Now that was a sign!" said Kostis looking for cracks in the giant Zale Mountain as the sea crashed hard and sprayed foamy white mist miles high into the sky.

"Can you hear horses? I swear I can hear horses?" said Gustus.

"It's called thunder my friend," said Kostis shaking his head.

"I know that, listen over that way," Gustus pointed with his giant fingers outwards towards the trees dividing the main entrance.

Under the dense roar of the sea he heard a thunderous gallop, "You're right, I can hear horses—no they're too heavy, mega Rast's if anything."

Something was in a hurry and although the thunder was threatening from afar, whatever was connected to those hooves were getting closer and closer, heading straight towards the castle at a relentless and breakneck speed.

"I told you, look at the size of those, what are they?" shrugged Gustus.

"They're not horses or rast's," gasped Kostis.

Eight giant creatures, black as pitch all snarling and gnashing their cavernous mouths roared up the white cobblestone road at full speed, their hooves smashing heavily at the stones and destroying the path as they went.

"There pulling a carriage," said Gustus.

"Gustus get away from the gate! It's not slowing down! There going to ram the castle!"

"Stop or I'll shoot!" shouted Kostis pulling back his bow and searching in his sights for the driver, then realising short after, there was no driver at all and the wild beasts were driving themselves. Gustus latched on to Kostis as he hung over the edge and fired several arrows. The black creatures turned viciously slamming the entire carriage against the drawbridge and in turn released a large wooden crate at the castle gates.

In full flight, they continued onwards dragging the completely destroyed carriage behind them.

"What the snuff?" said Kostis as he got to his feet.

"Did you see that? They smashed right into the gates and took off?"

"They seem to have delivered a huge wooden box."

"A box? A box of what? You call that a delivery service? said Gustus trying to look straight down but having a difficult time with such a massive frame and no neck.

"Let's have a closer look," he smiled excitedly directing him to a large wooden wheel with spokes on it.

In unison, they turned the spoked wheel. A thick metal chain lowered the hanging weights and slowly the solid gate lifted, made from the shell of a single Alphena Crab.

"How exciting," whispered Kostis, swiftly climbing down a rope ladder, "come on Gustus!"

When Kostis landed on the wooden bridge below, the early morning sun had begun to appear but remained completely hidden behind the crate. A strange silhouette formed in the light. He noticed several arms and legs extending from each side. It was if the box could stand up and walk away at any moment.

Gustus arrived with a loud thud as he hit the floor with both feet.

"There you are, I was worried you forgot your way down," smiled Kostis.

"You shouldn't make fun of a Slog, I'm at least five times bigger than you," grunted Gustus adjusting his eyes to the glaring sun and approached cautiously.

"Kostis are you forgetting something? You should turn around already," said Gustus pointing over him.

"Oh yes, the box, where would I be without you, my giant conscience. Wow, it stinks, like swamp water."

"Swamp water is a compliment," said Gustus screwing up his giant beetle-bear face. "What is it? How many legs does this thing have? We should call for backup."

"Backup? Nonsense it's clearly dead just by the smell. Maybe they were on the way to the Pit, that's where this belongs."

Kostis approached with his knife out wide, tossing it from hand to hand. The box rose to head height and on the tips of his toes he looked inside a splintered crack in the side.

"Poke it with your knife, is it alive?" said Gustus striding round to the other side. He stopped confused at the strange body parts sticking out from the broken panels.

"Yes I would feel safer if I knew for sure if it were dead or alive."

Slowly Kostis pushed his blade into the box. There was nothing. He turned and shrugged.

"Harder," said Gustus motioning him to jab the blade right in.

Instantly the form within the box let out a blood-curdling screech as if he had stabbed it in the eye.

"It's alive! I'm turning on the alarm—it must be a trap!"

Kostis moved quick on his feet, darting inside the gates, throwing his shield and chest plate along the way. Arriving at a weapons stand he grabbed a long bow twice the size of himself and carefully chose a black feathered tipped arrow from the assortment. In several perfected movements, his front foot slid to the right as he crouched low and locked his knee into the dirt. He kissed the tail feathers, paused for a split second, took a breath in and exhaled a light whistle. With a flick of his wrist and the surrender of his thumb and forefinger, the arrow vanished whistling through the air.

*

Princess Belleny had been wide awake watching the menacing storm. Safely from her balcony, she witnessed the clouds grow, explode into the sea with a violent downpour and dissipate.

It wasn't long after the cloud gave up when the alarm screamed within the castle walls. The King took off downstairs with a group of riders and headed towards the outer gates.

On their arrival, Kostis and Gustus saluted and said, "King Vera, just before sunrise a cart pulled by eight black beasts and no driver raced by smashing against the gates and leaving this large wooden crate. I warn you Sire, please do not come any closer as there's dark magic here and we fear a dark beast, some kind of creature that smells like a fetid and rotting ditch" Kostis pointed at the box with his blade, "As you can see, there is a tail and over this side a clawed paw, and over here another and a wing, I think?"

King Vera moved in cautiously, "A beast has darkened on our doorstep. A wagon was towed by beasts, with no driver you say? Most unsettling," he said noticing the debris of smashed carriage covering the floor and trailing off along the pathway.

"Look there, a note, see?" King Vera pointed hard at the box.

Gustus looked over and shrugged his shoulders at Kostis.

"It's written in a forgotten language; the ancients would use this," King Vera mumbled out a few lines to himself and then began to repeat it louder.

"Here are five, from a far away place,
I wish I could raise them, but that's not the case,
I hope you find it, deep in your heart,
To keep them together till death do they part."

The King paused and turned back the band of soldiers, "It's not one creature, there's five of them, orphans you see, left at my doorstep."

He pointed to Gustus, "You there, Gustus, bring the box inside."

Although Gustus was nearly twice as big as the box, it was surprisingly heavy and the smell seemed to be getting worse. With slow, careful steps he began to move forward, each step turning into a steady plod. The heavy gate closed behind with a thud clawing deep into the ground behind them.

"Where do you want it? It's starting to move King Vera," said Gustus.

"That's far enough, place it down here, we should be fine. Now let's see what we have inside," said the King signalling them both to open it up.

"Give me a hand up Gustus," said Kostis as he pounced on the top of the box and swiftly wedged his blade into the groove and pulled back hard. Gustus squeezed his fingers beneath the lid, and together they shook it free.

One by one, the sides fell to the floor exposing the confusing contents. Kostis stayed on top of the lid held in Gustus's hands and from above they both looked down with curiosity.

King Vera stood back and covered his mouth, the smell that escaped was more than ill. Before them sat a squashed pile of creatures; limbs, tails, wings, mangy fur and snouts were entwined with each other. From within a loud monstrous moan escaped as they lifelessly tumbled apart like stuffed animals from a tipped over toy box. As each one slowly emerged, they sat, slouched or stood awkwardly in a delirious daze.

The King tilted his head, "What creatures in the seven lands are they?"

From head to toe, they were drenched in a dull, squalid grey tone, like the soiled water left in a wash basin. Their fur was tattered or in oily clumps, and where there was no fur bare grey patches were exposed.

The King could see they were no harm. They could barely stand up. With their strange, beaten down but innocent faces hit a chord with him for he lowered his sword.

"King Vera, there's something in that ones claw," pointed Kostis at the large shiny black object.

"A seed? From the White Sands of Vheen possibly? Take them to the shelter, I don't want to see their bony ribs ever again."

He turned up and waved at Belleny watching from her balcony. He just knew she would like them, and she did, looking after the Orphans as if they were part of the Vera family. He promised to keep them together as the note requested and from that day they stayed in the castle, as did the black seed, and eventually it grew into the tree named Winta.

*

Many years had passed since that day and the Orphans had grown up. Although they were washed, fed and cared for, their fur or feathers had never developed, and they remained in the same tatty state they were found in.

The Orphans now consisted of four individual characters, the fifth Esdaile, *The White Creature*, now hung above Belleny's door in a lifeless state.

Back in their giant cubby house Belleny introduced the strange bird-like creature to Bateau, "This fine feathered soul is Palia," she said stroking Palia's raw and bony skull as she bowed down before them.

Bateau stared at her without trying to stare.

Fine feathered soul? What is she? Can you call them feathers? he thought nervously.

Palia looked like a prehistoric vulture, with the strangest wild beak, matted feathers and black rings circling around her eyes. He couldn't help but notice she had the sharpest pointy grey teeth rowed along her beak. *What sort of bird have teeth? I never thought of anyone eating me till now,* he thought. Her wing-like arms were tatty and flicked out to the side as if broken. He couldn't possibly see her flying with those, and she never had.

"Greeting Bateau," she said in a long drawn out conspicuous tone, "yes I'm Palia, Belleny gave me this name," she boasted, "don't stare at me like that, I mean look but not for so long, I don't trust those eye's of yours. What are you anyway? Who has two tails? I don't trust anything with two tails? Do those ears of yours get in the way? They look like a nuisance, I'm glad I don't have big ears," she said, changing her frequency like a possessed radio.

"Hello Palia, nice to meet you, not everyone has two tails and big ears, I was just unlucky I guess but trust me you can trust me," said Bateau trying his best to hide his worried face behind a smile.

"That's what they all say," whispered another voice in the shadows.

Belleny placed Bateau on the ground and walked over to where the voice appeared and pulled a creature into the light. Bateau stood back a few steps and watched as she held the creature by the scruff of its neck and yanked it forward. From it's strange stretched alligator shaped face a worn long body continued. It's thin long legs were joined to thick black claws, each paw as large as Bateau.

Belleny held up the creatures head upon her shoulder, "And this jubilant fellow is Agarus, he has the most beautiful smile you'll ever see although it only appears when he's sleeping, but that's better than never."

It was true, like Belleny he smiled very little and if there was anyone one to blame it on, he blamed himself.

"Sorry, I hope we didn't frighten you?" he said, as he revealed a jaw full of jagged, broken and grey teeth.

Bateau looked at Agarus and once again tried his best to smile, "It's okay Agarus, I like surprises."

Agarus was like no other, to the untrained eye he looked like a legged serpent, but his head was long like Palia's, and he resembled something of a scale-less reptile. As he stood in the light, he revealed his jagged spine that poked against the skin of his back and into a thick wolf-like tail that he always kept between his legs. He approached Bateau and crouched low on all fours. Bateau stood back once again, but Belleny held him close, "Don't be frightened," she whispered, "there probably more afraid of you."

"Welcome to the Jungle Room," said Agarus holding out his clawed hand. Bateau grabbed one of his thick, black, pointy nails and shook it nervously while staring at his open mouth and up into his round black eyes that sat nearly at the side's of his head.

"Montë, are you hiding back there too?" said Belleny.

"Yes Princess," he replied in a sad wilting voice as he squeezed out between the others. He was always hiding behind one of them. A fragile and timid figure who only stood as tall as Belleny. His fur was tattered and bare in many places, he had long white whiskers that pointed straight outwards until they touched the ground, and on most occasions he was only to be seen by these long white hairs.

"I'm Montë."

Montë pointed at Bateau and directed his questions to Belleny, "Why is he here?" he whispered, "What does he want from us? We're not moving are we? Oh is he moving in? He leaned in close to her ear, "You look nervous Princess ... what's going on? Has he got you hostage? Is he a spy?"

Belleny raised her voice, "Montë you know it's rude to ask more than one question at a time and of course he's not a spy," she huffed.

"And last but not least, come forward Dillon," said Belleny.

"Aghhh, do I have to?" a voice moaned in the shadows.

As the others shuffled around Dillon slouched forward. Bateau looked to the last creature in awe. Dillon was stranger than strange, Bateau had seen his fair share of wild and bizarre animals in the circus, but here stood a beast so odd that he seemed to be a combination of five strange creatures. Confined to the room's height he crawled forward on all fours like a caged lion. His breathing rattled in his chest and with each exhale hot wet saliva hung from his chin.

"Welcome to the Jungle Room, yes, my name is Dillon," he said in an apathetic tone, "make yourself at home."

"Now I want you all to relax," Belleny said, "clearly Bateau is not a spy, and honestly you have nothing to be spied upon. He's come a very long way to be here on my birthday and I feel quite happy he did."

"Happy?" said Palia suspiciously, "are you sure? This could be his plan; we're only looking out for you Princess."

"I have no plan? I was brought here by King Vera himself," said Bateau.

"He still looks suspicious," whispered Monté from behind Agarus.

"We've already lost one, I don't want to be next said Dillon."

"Now be seated. I have something to tell you all," the Princess said calmly and knowing the full repercussions of such a statement held out her hand to silence them before they could start. "You all very well know how I feel about this matter."

"What matter? What's the matter?" said Agarus.

"I don't like the matter," said Monté.

Palia leapt forward in a squawk, "Oh no! We're being moved outside, I knew it, the King wants us out."

"Of course he doesn't," said Belleny, "it's more complicated than that."

"It's already complicated, if only Esdaile were here, he would know what to do."

"But he's not! I haven't even told you what it is?" said Belleny.

"It has something to do with, you know, him doesn't it?" said Dillon frowning at Bateau.

"Quiet, I will say this only once! I'm going outside into the Queens Gardens and I would very much like you all to join me."

The short silence was full of wheezing, short breaths and a general sense of overwhelming disbelief.

"You're joking aren't you? said Monté.

"Oh very funny Princess, you're tricking us on your birthday, you sure gave us a scare," said Palia, "outside indeed, and this Bateau is your jester, of course it all make sense now," she crowed a cackling laugh.

Belleny crossed her arms and waited till there was silence, "When was the last time I told a joke?" she said sternly, "of course I'm not joking!"

"What's wrong with staying right here?" said Agarus.

"Belleny you've been brainwashed," huffed Palia directing her sharp eyes at Bateau, "obviously he's been filling you with tall tales and wild lies. Anyway you know how you burn, even under candle light, just imagine what the horrid sun would do to your fair skin, you'll be instantly turned to charcoal."

Agarus moved in like an eel and stared down hard at Bateau, "You're a bad influence, she's never had these thoughts, not in a long, long time."

Instead of being afraid Bateau was more shocked and it gave him the venom to stand up for himself, "What do you mean tall tales? Haven't you been outside all this time either? Not even into the Queens Gardens? This talk is absurd."

"Absurd indeed. Of course not and why would we? Look out there, as you said yourself, we have our own private jungle, but nothing can harm us in here," snapped Palia.

"The Jungle Room pales in comparison to the Queens Gardens. They're known throughout the land as the most beautiful place in all of Mare-Marie, full of rare and exotic plants that are native to nowhere else on Mare-Marie," said Bateau, holding himself in his tails.

"Exactly, you just said it in one word! Creatures, dangerous creatures, no doubt poisonous flowers, giant Princess eating birds, one hundred toothed weasels, venomous trap door spider monkeys, to name just a few, we're not idiots," said Dillon, counting them off on the nails of his claws.

Belleny's sullen face dropped even lower and she looked down at Bateau, "I'm sorry Bateau, I think there right. I'm every so confused, I'm not sure now?" She continued to spiral, "I don't know why I even considered the idea."

"Listen to yourself, you must go outside. To see the garden's at least, then you will see, your mother grew it on behalf of you," he turned to the strange and now furious Orphans, "can you not hear the celebrations outside in the garden now, there obviously outside and having fun, outside and not being eaten by the dark."

Bateau stood speechless, "Your all mad," he huffed and jumped from the cubby house, swung along the jungle gym and up to the one of the large arching windows and began to yank at the windows handle.

"What are you doing?" shouted Belleny, "I order you to get back here now!"

But Bateau didn't care for her command, crossed his arms at her and undid the latch with his tails.

He shouted across, "Look here, you've all been cooped up in this castle way too long, being outside is a zillion times better than being inside, you're all your own prisoners in my eyes," Bateau shouted, while pulling the windows wide open. "More vines!" he grumbled shaking his head and like a cat he clawed them away.

He could feel the Orphans approaching and pictured Palia ripping him down with her horrid teeth and Agarus tearing him with his long nails. *I better act quick,* he thought and turned back at once, but they were too afraid of the open window and remained in the cubby house.

Finally, he got through to the other side, and the garden from this angle could be seen in full glory. It was a magical sight with giant blue luminous lanterns lighting up the garden.

"See!" shouted Bateau to the disbelievers, "there are no giant Princess eating birds or one hundred toothed weasels!" He proclaimed pointing into the air, "Look at everyone dancing and laughing out there. If there were they wouldn't be out there at all, obviously!"

"It's only a matter of time, there all goners," muffled one of the Orphans.

"We have seen enough of your show and tell, shut that window at once," said Palia.

"What about the giant trap door spider monkeys?" Called the faint voice of Montë hiding behind Agarus.

"What? No of course not!" said Bateau slapping his head with his tails, "I don't even know if they exist?"

"Oh, they do," said Montë to the others.

"Of course they do!" huffed Palia, "no one in their right mind would make up such a paralysing creature."

Bateau listened to the complaints and slapped his face with his tails, "What? You're not supposed to look at it, it's the sun? Stay there I'll be back in a second," he said as he jumped from the window ledge and onto a hedge below.

CHAPTER 18 - THE ORPHANS

Belleny couldn't believe her eyes, "He just jumped," she said in disbelief.

"He's a goner, shut the window quickly before anything crawls in Dillon," said Palia.

Belleny frowned unamused, "He is not a goner. Bateau come right back this instance! That's an order!" she shouted at the open window.

But there was no reply.

Dillon took off at once leaping across the monkey bars towards the window. He stood on his hind legs and slammed the window shut, "Too bad, I was beginning to like him," he smirked back at the others.

"Nice work Dillon! Make sure it's locked tight," crowed Palia.

"Not yet, can you see him?" asked Montë.

"Can you see him?" shouted Agarus.

"All I see is darkness, and strange blue lights," said Dillon.

"Don't worry Princess, it's for his own good, he belongs out there and we belong in here," said Palia.

"Do we?" sighed Belleny, her face resentful of their actions, "he is my friend."

Tap!

Tap!

Tap!

"Oh no, he's back!" said Palia.

"Should I open it?" Shrugged Dillon.

Belleny stomped her foot and pointed, "Of course, open it at once!"

"What if it's not him? We don't want anything in here, from out there!" he replied.

"Just let me in already," Bateau shouted.

Dillon unlatched the window, and there stood an unamused Bateau, "Thank you Dillon I have something to show you and the Princess, please follow me," he said as he swung back towards the others.

Instantly Dillon slammed the window shut.

The Orphans circled Bateau with their sad, angry faces looking in.

"What were you trying to prove by going out there, it's really no great feat, let's see you spend the whole night out there in your magnificent garden," said Palia, "actually spend an entire year out there for I care."

Belleny ignored Palia as she was fixated on the objects Bateau revealed in each of his tails. In one was a strange spongy flower with iridescent, coral-like petals and on the other, a fragile, translucent blue clawed porcelain mouse.

Belleny continued to stare and Bateau noticed her dazed expression as if looking into a fire, "Isn't he just wonderful Princess, don't worry he won't bite, he has no teeth," smiled Bateau.

"Of course he has teeth, he just bit that cherry clean in half, don't get your fingers too close," snapped Palia.

Bateau ignored her and the Orphans and passed the flower to Belleny. At first she resisted, then she tentatively reached out and touched it with her fingertips. Although they had flowers throughout the castle, there was none as exotic as this one.

"Flowers like these need moonlight to bloom, there's a patch of them just outside your window."

"Moonlight?" said Belleny.

"Be careful Belleny you might be allergic to it," said Montë stepping out from the shadows to get a clearer look. It lit up Belleny's face with a bright yellow glow.

"It's beautiful," she said, her eyes did not believe what she could see.

The Orphans watched her hypnotically as the flower glowed even brighter as if was enjoying itself. They also noticed Belleny's face, it was unlike any expression she had ever held before.

"Stop that at once Princess! You might set it off or something," said Palia.

Bateau took the flower from her, "Palia it's just a flower, here Belleny take him," Bateau let the porcelain mouse sit in her palm but it was quick on its feet and jumped up her arm, to her shoulder and with a short quick pounce it landed sniffing at her skin, then proceeded to stroke either side of its face against her neck.

"It likes your perfume," smiled Bateau.

It then proceeded to run through the back of her hair to the other side of her neck and repeated rubbing its face on the other side.

"I can't watch, he's just preparing to bite you I just know it," said Dillon.

Belleny paused and looked up at him with a slight frown.

"There are probably more mites in here than out there," whispered Bateau. "There're beauty and wonder outside, don't try and tell me it didn't make you feel wonderful ... if this little porcelain mouse can live outside, I'm sure you can at least have the courage to take a walk out there."

For the first-time, none of them said a single word. They wanted to, but they just couldn't, something deep inside each and everyone knew he was speaking true sense.

"Thank you Bateau, these are both very beautiful," she whispered to the floor, "I would like to see more but—" she sighed then clenched her fist, "I don't know why, it started off as nothing and then ... well, now I don't know ... it's easier to just stay inside."

Dillon shook his wild head and stood forward, "That's settled then, we'll get rid of the mouse and the flower and never speak of it again."

"Agreed, this is all to much for our Princess, look at the confused state she's in, she'll be bed ridden for weeks I just know it," said Palia.

Belleny said not a word and stared at the flower and for some time the room went quiet.

Bateau held her free hand with his tails and she continued to stare in deep in thought.

"Fine," said Belleny, "tomorrow we shall have a very, very quick look."

The Orphans gasped in unison, a most disturbing noise at that.

"I've felt so strange for so long, but something happened tonight, maybe I've grown up? Maybe this is what I need to do. I don't want to be the crazy Princess anymore, my people deserve better."

"You're not crazy, there all crazy," said Palia, hearing her words she now went quiet.

Belleny held out her hands and caressed the Orphans one by one as if they were her very own children, "Palia, Dillon, Agarus and my dear little Montë. Bateau may be very well right, or very, very wrong. It's time we go outside and confirm it for ourselves. We shall go to the Queen's Garden and no further. I'm so tired of this prison of my mind, enduring this battle of voice in my head ... ignoring my gut instincts that tell me to seek new truths from outside. I know you all mean well, but if this fragile little mouse can be happy playing outside then maybe so can we."

"You'll like our backyard garden BC, it's overgrown with vegetables, weeds and rambling roses, a real jungle out there," said Evelin holding BC's paws like an animated doll.

What's Robin up to? Her father's heavy footsteps moved about upstairs and proceeded to make their way down the staircase towards her room.

"Morning Robin," she said calmly as he appeared by her doorway.

"Hey kiddo, good morning BC, you're looking as strange as ever. It's a beautiful day out there, let me get this window open."

"Whatcha you up to?" she said pointing at the spanner in his hand.

"Tinkering on the roof ... putting together a strategy for world peace, this and that."

"Why don't you tinker in the basement?" she said pulling herself into a burnt grey woollen jumper.

"Yeah yeah, in due time, it's still a swamp, it's a bit on the nose with the smell ... so I'll press on with fixing the cracked tiles on the roof."

Evelin stared up at him with a furrowed brow, "OK, but just be careful up there."

"I will kiddo, Oh and I saw Milton hanging around like a bad smell outside this morning, he's out front."

"I'm sure he was. OK, I'll see you later Robin."

As Evelin was applying lip gloss in the bathroom mirror, BC sat at the foot of the bed and stared at the watery world, continuously following the paper fish as they swam around in their tight, rhythmic formations.

"I guess you've never seen fish before," said Evelin, "bet you'd like to gobble them up."

What is going through your mind BC

Slowly she walked him around the aquarium and the fish followed. BC let out a slight meow. Wriggling slightly he pulled out his paw and Evelin moved in closer as he pushed it against the glass. The fish swam closer and one by one, gently rolled their bodies against the glass like white-gloved fingers.

Evelin's eyes opened wide, am I dreaming?

"Have you all met before?" she whispered to the fish and into BC's large transparent ears. Without notice, she shed single tear which edged it's way down her cheek. It felt so foreign and softly she closed her eyes and felt her lashes moisten together. It was the first time she had shed a tear of happiness, even a tear, in a very long time.

Evelin carried on pottering about, tinkering with cleaning the gunk out of the filtration system and applying de-chlorinate. *What on earth's that sound?* she thought but also knew intuitively that the clambering around was BC even though she had never heard him make a noise outside of her bedroom before.

"BC where are you? BC?" She looked back at her open door, *he wouldn't have gone downstairs would he?*

Evelin flicked the switch the start up the filters in the aquarium and took off downstairs nearly crashing into a large potted fern on a bamboo frame. She scanned the kitchen and fear welled up inside her as the back fly screen was left wide open.

"Puss, puss! Where are you BC?" she started to despair and dropped to the grass out front of the patio, ignoring how hard her heart was beating.

Get it together Eve, it's the back door to the backyard, not the front door to the street. But she imagined how easy it would be to crawl under the house. There were so many ways under and through.

"BC, BC!" she called, looking under the house for a movement, inside the bushes and fishing through the tall reeds in an overgrown flower bed.

To make things worse, the old elm tree that they built the house around had dropped its leaves and the entire back yard was covered in a rusty orange blanket. The backyard was quite a scene with is wild plants, dark leafy ponds, grape vine sculptures and overgrown pumpkin vines, dumped pot plants and a rusted tin shed.

Evelin raced over to the elm tree where it sat on a raised mound and like the other trees ripped its roots high above the ground. BC was not there.

"BC, come on, stop playing with me, puss, puss, puss!" she called getting louder and louder.

Oh no! Evelin ran to a small wooden bridge.

Laying down she stared into the clear water checking either side, she didn't want to see him sitting on the bottom, but she looked just in case.

Is that him? She stared close as several fat carp raced to the surface.

"Move aside you're in the way!" she shouted but the fish didn't listen and continued to blow bubbles at her.

"No!" Evelin kept digging her hand into the water, pushing the fish aside and grabbing at BC, the thick reeds twisted and turned around her hand as her fingers grasped at the cold body.

"A rock?" she gasped.

"That's one way to piss off a fish," said a voice from the back door.

Evelin looked back in a panic as if guilty and there standing in the doorway was Milton, completely unaware, holding BC in his arms.

"Don't you ever run off on me again!" she pointed her finger at his nose. BC played with it like it was a game. She looked up at Milton with sad eyes.

"Where the hell was he?"

"Right here? On the doorstep ... this is a cat right? Where's his fur?"

"No, he's not sick, he's a hairless cat," she said, holding BC up at him.

"BC meet Milton, Milton meet BC the disappearing cat."

Belleny scooped up BC and walked towards the house with Milton trailing her. Closing the fly-screen and slamming the front door, she placed BC on the table. "You little terror, you're not allowed outside without me, or we'll think about putting you in reigns like wearing a harness."

"Maybe take a photo of him too, remember when we lost Quick Draw, went to put up a missing dog poster and realised we had no pictures of him, I ended up drawing him from memory, people brought round some of the ugliest dogs I've ever seen."

"Poor Quick Draw, I'm sure he's still chasing seagulls down the beach," said Evelin.

"Yeah ... did we even look down there?" Milton began peering into the fridge smelling plates of food and peering at condiment jar labels, "Why do you have so much cake in the fridge? It's not your birthday for ages? Is it Robins? Why wasn't I invited?" He inquired continuously picking at the pink frosting.

"No, it's not. Help yourself Miss Davis dropped them off and the eggs."

"Miss Davis? Why does that name sound familiar?"

"Maybe because I've been talking about her for the last two months."

"I know," he said with a cheeky grin, "is she trying to squeeze into some big boots."

"Don't weird me out."

"She's all right though, will do your dad good to have a teacher whip him into shape."

"Did you not hear my last comment?"

"You know what I mean Eve."

"Sure. Now she works at Bandit Bakery in Claremint."

"No, really? I love that place," he said biting into a handful of cake.

"Do you want a plate?" asked Evelin with a shake of her head.

"Nah, I'm OK I'll probably finish it before I put it down."

"She said it got damaged and couldn't sell it, so she brought it round here, it's the third *damaged* cake over the last few weeks."

"That's keen, I bet she drops them on purpose. Nice technique to visit your old man."

"She also dropped off that wicker basket and keeps leaving cartons of eggs on our doorstep, said she had too many eggs and couldn't possibly eat them all, take some if you want, I doubt we could eat that many."

"So what's the plan? Do we get BC a collar or something," Milton enquired helpfully.

"Yes, so we bike it?" she asked, "I'll go lock this escapee up first."

"Done deal, I'll meet you out the front."

Evelin shot up the stairs with BC and placed him on her bed. He stared into the aquarium.

Like babysitting a kitten with an aquarium television, she thought, "I'll be back soon my furless friend."

Milton moved out the front and rode his bike in circles at the top of the hill. Evelin quietly grabbed her bike and whizzed past.

"Hey wait up!" he shouted and took off after her.

"Hey, wait up!" he shouted and took off after her. "What's a cat like BC eat? You know my friend Mikey Ross feeds his cat jelly, it loves the stuff, although it has no idea how to eat it, it's a blast."

"Jelly? I don't know about that? We haven't bought any food for him yet, Robin fed him an omelette and fish eyes but he didn't like them of course, anyway that's why were going to the pet store, they'll know."

The pet store was easily recognisable by the piles of junk hanging out the front. Dog kennels, carpet covered cat scratching stumps, bags of dog food piled up like manure, bird cages full of budgies squawking out like soccer fans, and enormous plastic Saint Bernard dog statue that was graffitied and cross-eyed.

Evelin leant her bike against the plastic dog, "That's a good boy, anyone touch our bikes, go for their throats," she said, patting its hollow head.

"Their throats? I'm glad you got a weird cat and not a Doberman," said Milton adjusting his tie, "hey look there having a closing down sale, but they haven't even been opened long?"

"Oh, that's sad, what will happen to the pets?" asked Evelin.

"Party pies probably," smiled Milton.

"You're not funny."

Evelin inspected and spreads the rows of dog leads hanging down from the entrance and Milton followed close behind. The leads reminded her of the diamond leashes Astina had her dogs on, *I wonder if I can get them anything in here?*

"This place is huge," said Evelin standing on the tips of her toes and looking up to the very back.

"I know right, sure smells like a pet store, let's have a quick look around first," said Milton.

"I'm going that way," she pointed wandering towards the aquariums.

The tanks were positioned side by side, but there was more than just an air of neglect surrounding them. The glass sides were foggy with creeping tank scum and clumps of water reed floating on the surface while the water gurgled and gulped as the filters recycled the soiled water. The fish barely moved, while others swelled up floating to the top or sunk heavily on the bottom.

Milton had ventured straight to the Reptile section as he had an innate knack and desire to annoy critters and adults alike and today it was to be a Black-tailed Rattlesnake. *Oh, I see,* realised Milton and moved his tie back and forth. The snake moved its head the same while hissing and rattling its tail furiously.

"Boy! ... What the hell do you think you're doing?" said a man in a coarse voice then coughing hoarsely as he held his chest.

Milton turned and saw the large employee wearing a tightly fitting apron, stomping towards him while pushing several cages aside. "I said what do ya think you're doing? I'm sick of you kids coming in here, this ain't no petting zoo. Don't ya know these snakes are poisonous? I'm yet to get the venom out of em! Put one of them down your trousers and you'll know all about it." He coughed again and pushed his fingers deep into his mouth removing a palate of pet hair from his tongue and wiped it on his apron.

"Ewe," said Milton taking a step back and bumping the snake aquariums. The snake continued to hiss and rattle its tail, "Anyway I wouldn't steal this one, he's a bit edgy isn't he, you should try patting him," said Milton.

"Why you little—"The man pushed his body forward, cornering Milton against the glass wall of snakes. He gripped Milton's shirt with one hand, twisting it in his fist, as several buttons tore off and fell to the ground.

"You're crazy! What do you think you're doing! You'll pay for this." Milton squealed again as the man grabbed a chunk of his clothing.

Milton wriggled as the rattlesnake was yanked out of its tank. Its anger was nothing short of the man's fuming rage. He pushed the snake up against Milton's face, "Get it off, get it off!" screamed Milton.

"Milton? What's going on!" said Evelin.

The man turned at her with a devilish grin, "Your Milton is busy, so scram!"

"Get out of here Eve, this guy has gone full mental!," said Milton.

"Leave him alone! Get that snake away from him!" shrieked Milton Adrenalin surged and fear gave Milton the strength to grab the snake's scaly body."

"That's my rattler, let go of him!" said the man pulling the snake back.

But Milton refused and pulled the snake from the man's clasp. He then realised he was holding a snake and threw it to the floor at once.

The man jumped aside and let go of Milton's shirt. With this opportunity, Milton dove beneath his thick arms and took for the door. The man swung down hard hooking his claws tightly into Milton's backpack. Evelin watched as he hung inches off the ground like a puppet.

"Go! Just Go!" shouted Milton.

She didn't know what to do, but she knew she wasn't leaving him. The commotion had sent the birds into a frenzy of feathers and wild squawks. She looked into the cages of flashing bright yellows and green's and without hesitation she stood forward. In an instant, she unlatched the cage doors, swinging them completely open and kicked hard against the wire cage.

"Go you're free, get out!" she screamed and turned back looking straight into the horned frown of the pet store worker.

The birds didn't need to be told twice and from behind her they flew out in all directions. Some flew towards the man as if seeking revenge while others flapped in and around the fans looking for a way out while others went for the daylight and flew straight out the doorway.

"You little witch!" roared the man as he pulled Milton backwards. Like fluorescent darts of light, the birds flew above them at high speed. The man let a hand free to grasp at the birds, like a monster swatting fairies he had no chance, but Milton saw his and seized the moment wrenching himself out of his grip.

"Go, Go!" he panted, grabbing her by the arm on the way out.

"You'll pay for this!" he snorted, but all they could hear were their thumping hearts. Never before had they jumped on their bikes so quickly, tipping the plastic Saint Bernard over in a massive crash as they took off down the street.

"You'll pay for this! I know your name Milton and your little witch of a girlfriend!"

"Woo Hoo! That was incredible Eve! Did you see those birds! You are unbelievable," he laughed into the air.

But Evelin's face was pale, straight focused and cold.

"Evelin? You okay? Eve we got away, it's all good, there was nothing in my bag, he'll never find us, Eve?"

"I'm freaking out," she said, holding her throat.

"Evelin you okay? Do you want some water?"

" Water. Tablets. So dizzy, I've got to slow down ... stop."

Milton followed her as she rode into a park and rolled deep into a crowd of elms. She dropped her bike in the leaves and snatched at her bag and ripped it open, diving in and pulling out her pill container.

"Eve you OK?" said Milton.

Evelin poured several pills in her palm, looked into Milton's eyes and swallowed them dry. She squinting as the bitter taste coughed up in her throat.

Evelin closed her eyes and squeezed her fists into a tight ball. When they opened she looked back into his eyes, "I'm sorry Milton," she sighed.

They didn't quite know what to say and said nothing the whole ride back until once again they reached Edinburgh Street and Milton spoke up.

"You want to walk up?" asked Milton hopping of his bike.

"Yeah," she whispered and kept her focus towards the ground, "Milton?"

"Yeah?"

"Sorry, back there, I hope I didn't weird you out too much."

"Hey, I'm sorry for antagonising that nuts snake charmer back there.

"What happened back there? she asked, "I can't believe you touched that snake."

"I know right, I have no idea? But I want to get one now."

"Now you're talking crazy, oh no we didn't get any pet food or a collar."

"Does BC like cake?"

"No. You're as bad as Robin."

Milton shrugged, "Strange food for a strange cat."

"And an even stranger owner," smiled Evelin.

Belleny, Bateau and the Orphans rose early, but shabbily after a lousy night's sleep. The exploratory trip outside, beyond the castle and into the Queens Gardens, gave way to restless slumber for all, their dreams were filled with foreboding nightmares and premonitions. Alone with Bateau Belleny paced around her room collecting items for the trip and constantly reconsidering her decision.

As the Orphans climbed up Belleny's towering stairway Dillon asked, "We're not really going outside—are we?"

Palia huffed, "I know I'm not. It's all Bateau's fault. I say we throw him head first from the balcony, now that will put a thorn in today's event."

"Palia! That would only make things worse," said Montë riding on top of Agarus.

"What's worse than going outside?" moaned Agarus.

His question was met with silence. Exhausted they continued to drag themselves up in a wheezing, coughing and whining cacophony. Dillon listened to their disturbing and echoing sounds and said, "Maybe we pretend we're sick? We definitely sound sick."

"I do feel sick," said Palia, "I don't need to pretend and these damn stairs aren't helping. Whose idea was this, Bateau no doubt."

"Well, we better act sick quick, we're nearly there," said Montë.

All looked up at the Princesses majestic, carved alphena shell door.

Before they could knock, Belleny opened the door wide open. It was then she witnessed a poorly timed and acted scene of dismay. In unison, the Orphans began to moan and groan and hold their bellies.

"Orphans! Oh my, you all look so terribly ill," said Belleny.

"We are, very ill, so very ill," said Agarus shaking his long bony frame around the others.

"The sickness, we have the sickness, I just can't possibly go outside today," said Dillon.

"Oh, you poor things, how did you manage to climb these stairs in this condition, you should have stayed in the Jungle Room."

Palia crowed, "We did it for you Princess, we had to—"

"Had to what? Lie and pretend that you were gravely ill?" said Belleny shaking her head.

The Orphans' act went quiet.

"We could hear you in the stairwell you morons," grumbled Bateau.

"I'm sure you could with those big ears of yours," snapped Palia.

"Settle! I had a feeling you would come up with something, pretending to be sick was on the top of my list," said Belleny. "I thought the walk up here would take the event off your minds. You can stop acting and wait over by Winta; I won't be too long. I've cleared a patch in the balcony window, if you would like to see where we are going."

"That's the last thing I want to see," said Montë sulking over to Winta and slouching himself down beneath its black wiry branches.

"Suit yourself," said Belleny. "I have no time to entertain children."

"We're not children," huffed Dillon as he slumped next to Montë.

"Well, stop acting like it, don't you know how hard this is for me?" "You're supposed to be on my team."

"We don't like who's on your team," snarled Palia under her breath.

"Palia! Truly, I've never seen you act this rotten," said Belleny. "If you're all going to be so gloomy, you might as well wait downstairs."

"But we just climbed all the way up here!" exclaimed Dillon.

"Then sit there and be good. You should be excited to be in my quarters it's been such a long time," she huffed.

The Princess stopped inviting them up some time ago. They weren't to know she still kept Esdaile, the white creature, who now lay hidden in the Change Room.

"Do you like my outfit?" she said, as she threw a cape around her neck and let its black scales drape around her.

"You look ready for a battle," said Bateau.

"What sort of creature are you today?" moaned Agarus.

The dark outfit she was referring to was prepared to be worn during the annual Black Knight's Tournament, one which she did not attend, but she felt it would be perfect for exploring the garden. The suit looked like it was torn from the back of a deadly night crawler. From the inside out it consisted of the finest black chainmail and woven leathers that hugged her frame. Scales wrapped around her arms and jagged thorns lined in a row, up past her elbows and continued to horned shoulder pads woven together with threads of black silver. A high-neck collar rose straight up and wrapped around her head. It was a royal outfit, one of power and intimidation. But beneath the costume she was scared. Her skin felt like it was peeling, her mouth was bone dry, and her head was splitting, but this only seemed to make her decision even stronger. She questioned her feelings: Such a reaction. *Why would I feel so ill, yet so strongly about this? Do I honestly believe the outside is bad? What if I am wrong? Is today the day I die? I must stop this nonsense talk at once!*

Belleny moved on and noticed shiny black rock that was encrusted with white crystals. "What about this?" she asked Bateau.

"Are you serious?"

"It's pretty."

"Pretty heavy. Why would you take a rock outside? There's more than enough out there—oh sorry is it your pet rock?"

"Of course it's not! I give up! I need a break," she snapped stomping past the Orphans to flop exhausted inside Winta.

There was a light tap on the door. It opened slowly held by several jewelled fingers. Belleny noticed and sighed at once.

"Good morning," said King Vera poking his head inside the dark quarters. He scanned the room and found movement, "Oh there you are, all up here, it must be a special occasion," he said, his teeth beaming through his beard. "Ah! Hello Bateau, have you settled in nicely, I hope you've found your voice today?"

"Oh, he's found his voice all right," grumbled Palia.

"King Vera! Yes, I have thank you. What a marvellous castle you

have, and the Princess, such a delightful girl and her friends are most …
entertaining," said Bateau.

"Why thank you and where is my favourite Princess hiding?" He then
lowered his voice to a whisper, "Oh is she asleep, not under that pile?" he
asked, peering over her bed.

From within the dark cavity of Winta, Belleny withdrew her hand
from her temple. "What brings you all the way up here Vasilis? Since
you know very well I sleep during the day?"

"Who me? Well, I heard a certain Princess and her friends were going
a certain somewhere today?"

"I haven't the slightest idea what you're on about?" said Belleny.

"Interesting? The Orphans were quite adamant I intervened. See if I
could change your mind?"

"Oh really! Did they just?" she said leaping out of Winta and stomping
in front of them.

"We just thought King Vera should know. He's with us, he doesn't
want you to go outside either," said Dillon.

"What? Is this true?" asked Belleny.

"Of course. Not unless you want to. Do you?"

"Possibly. I have no idea what's come over me. It all happened out on
the balcony. A change."

"You were out on your balcony?" asked the King, pleasantly shocked.

"Yes, I was retrieving Bateau when something happened, I felt so—"

"I knew it! It was Bateau all along!" snarled Palia.

"Yes and so be it Palia. I feel have to see for myself once again," said
Belleny, "and yes these grumpy sacks are all coming along with me, even
if I have to tie them together and drag them. I didn't want to say anything
till I was downstairs because—well you know very well why, I may change
my mind."

"I completely understand," said King Vera, trying his best not to jump
for joy, "you picked a great day to go outside, nothing but blue skies ahead.
I also wanted you know the head chef's put together a royal-sized picnic
for you all and it will be waiting downstairs. You might need to saddle
up Agarus."

Like a weed, Belleny twisted up at him. "See this is exactly why I said
nothing to you, look what you've done, now what if we don't—"

"No pressure Princess, if you change your mind you can eat it inside, or I will." King Vera held up his hands and slowly stepped back into the stairwell. "I'll let you get ready, or not! Up to you and I may meet you downstairs in a bit, no pressure, stay here all day if you want, it's also a beautiful day inside."

Belleny nodded and graced a kindling of a smile. "Thank you father, we'll all be down sooner or later, don't tell anyone else please," she said, gently pushing him out and closing the door behind him. She glanced up at the vacant space where Esdaile usually resides and returned.

"I have a few things to gather, then we can go. Agarus, fathers right, can you carry the food and provisions for us?" she asked, pointing to a riding saddle and its side bags.

"But that means I *have* to go."

"Of course you do!" said Belleny.

"Orphans can you help Agarus I have a few more things to get then we can go." Belleny looked through several drawers and revealed a dark leather pouch. It made that indistinguishable marble sound that only marbles can make and she tied the small black bag to her belt.

I don't want to ask, thought Bateau.

"Go on ask me? I know you're dying to," said Belleny as if reading his mind.

"Are we going to play marbles?"

"Of course not, I don't play games."

"Oh, then—"

"Have you ever been hit in the face with one of these?" she asked.

"Not recently," said Bateau.

"Pity," grumbled Palia.

"It hurts—a lot," said Belleny pulling out a delicately carved white slingshot from her top draw. After pulling back the elastic and aiming it at the Orphans, she secured it to her belt.

"That was not funny Princess," whimpered Dillon.

"Cheer up, as if I would hurt you."

"Do you know how to use that?" asked Bateau.

"I do indeed, not all Princesses just sip tea and sew napkins."

"No, I see they don't."

"Next a mirror," she said, grabbing a small oval mirror with a carved shell handle. "Yes, this will do nicely, if the marbles don't blind them their hideous reflection will," she said placing it in a loose black leather bag.

Belleny moved to the back of the room and slipped her feet into a pair of tall brown boots, folded them down at the knees and pulled the laces tight. "Now these are boots," she said, and like an officer strutted across the room to face head on with the Orphans.

"Attention!" she roared.

"Belleny stop it please, you're frightening us," said Montë shivering behind Agarus.

The Princess smiled as she turned up her leather boots to reveal knife handles protruding out on either side.

"Knives! Are they real?" said Dillon.

"Of course, you can't very well cut out a creature's tongue with a wooden spoon." She pulled the knife out enough so a blade could be seen.

"Let's hope they're small tongues," said Bateau inspecting them.

"Very funny. Remember when I said my costume wasn't finished? Orphans you better prepare yourselves."

Belleny walked beyond her bed and into the mysterious Change Room. The Orphans waited nervously.

"One moment," she muffled as she pulled a mask down across her face. The mask's wild mane blended with her hair and fell across her chest and shoulders. Its face feminine, yet purely animistic and wild. As she appeared from behind the drapes, from within the shadows, she crouched and raised her head, sniffing and staring at each of them one by one.

"Which one of you should I eat first?" she snarled through its jagged teeth. The Orphans huddled against Winta

"Yes you look tasty Dillon."

"No Belleny! Not me!" said Dillon.

With a pounce, she ran towards them, as they cried she leapt upon Dillon and saddled her legs across his bony frame.

"Be still! If you're coming with me, you'll need to be brave!"

"But I don't want to go," whimpered Dillon.

"You're weak, all of you!" Show me your inner beast! Show me!" she roared sitting up straight and pulling back at Dillon's scruffy mane.

"Now!" she demanded

In a cacophony of roars and screams, the Princess got what she demanded as the Orphans brought her quarters into a wild zoo. Dillon arched his back and snarled his long daggered teeth and with a haunting roar it filled the room. It sent fear up Belleny's spine.

"Enough! Enough!" shouted Belleny, jumping off him.

"I'm sorry Princess! I don't know what got into me, I'll never do it again."

"No—you did well Dillon, all of you," she said in a strange dark voice. "You can come back Bateau, sorry we scared you."

"I liked how he scampered away," smirked Palia.

"Very funny. I'm fine way over here," said Bateau.

"Your mask has turned you into someone—something else," said Dillon.

The strange creature's head gazed at the floor. "I thought this up in a dream ... a nightmare actually."

"You look terrifying," said Montë peering from behind Agarus. "Are you going to wear it outside?"

"Of course, I'm quite fond of it, it fits like a second skin," she said, staring at them through the dark pits of the mask. "You know very well it's me and if we do meet any nasties, then maybe I can frighten them off."

"Them?" quipped Montë.

"I wouldn't wear it all the time, the guards might put an arrow through your head," said Bateau.

"Don't speak to the Princess like that!" squawked Palia.

"Oh my! I never thought of that! Do I look that scary?"

Bateau nodded and pointed across the room with his tails, "Have a look in the mirror."

Belleny moved towards the large mirror and from under her mask a gasp could be heard, *I am the creature from my nightmare.*

She quivered, "You're right, I am frightening."

No wonder Miss Muscae was so afraid.

There in her reflection stood a beast incomparable to any other. The mask held a formidable stare that unnervingly frowned back at her. Its wolf-like snout held an open snarl, full of pointed teeth that she had carved from shell. Its forehead was pierced with three black horns, parting through a wild, untamed mane. With the full outfit on, including clawed gloves, the beast was now alive.

The Princess removed the mask, revealing her pale face. "I didn't realise. I won't wear the mask all the time, I just wanted to blend in out there.

Just remember it's still me," she said pushing the mask backwards and into her hood. "Well, I'm ready if you are?" she continued picking up her bag and Bateau in her arms. Without turning back, she walked towards the door, "Come on Orphans, you'll never be ready."

"Yes let's see what the chef put together," said Bateau.

Dillon shook his head. "This is a bad idea ... she's gone bonkers."

"That may be true, but our Princess cannot do this alone. Come on we have to look after her," said Agarus rising to his feet.

"I doubt she'll go through with it anyway," said Montë.

"Oh, she's going through with it, she's changed, one way or another. Don't blame me if we come back without our heads," huffed Palia.

"Oh Palia, nothing is going to eat your head, it's too bony," said Agarus, and together with Montë riding on his back they left the dark limbs of Winta and descended.

King Vera waited patiently downstairs. Next to him were four kitchen maids, five guards, the head chef, his assistant cook. A strange ferreting creature played on the King's shoulders and through his beard. He jolted around as he heard Belleny approach.

"With such an audience, I can't change my mind now!" she said, passing Bateau to her father and ramming the mask down across her face.

"Oh my! Are you as furious as you look?" he asked.

Belleny sighed, "No. Let's get this over and done with. The Orphans are on their way." Belleny grabbed Bateau back off him and began to step into the courtyard. King Vera held his breath as she paused with one foot on the sunlit grass and one on the shadowed pavement.

What am I doing? Just take a step why don't you? But I can't? What's wrong with me? Oh, mother please help me.

But there was only silence in return. *Well, what did I expect.*

King Vera looked on anxiously as Belleny removed her mask and wiped her face.

"Just don't think about it, let's go, I have your back," whispered Bateau held tight in her arms, "we're going to have so much fun."

"Fun? I don't know the meaning of the word," she sighed and commenced to strut outside as if she had done it every day.

Bateau rolled his tails around her arm and gave her a gentle hug.

"Thank you," she said as she noticed it was a beautiful day. The courtyard was still decorated for the recent celebration and looked as beautiful as in the night.

For a second, her worries and fears were in another place and for a moment she felt like never before. One step after another she took off towards the giant hedge and the enormous gates of the Queen's Gardens. Belleny paused as the sunlight warmed her face. She looked at her arms and huffed, "I just knew I wouldn't turn to charcoal."

"I hate to say it but aren't we forgetting someone?" said Bateau.

"Oh, I haven't forgotten. I wanted them to see I didn't turn to dust or get eaten as soon as we walked out here."

"I'm glad you didn't, that would have been quite embarrassing."

Oh no, she's turning back, she's not gonna do it, thought King Vera as Belleny stopped and turned towards him. Belleny paused and looked up at the castle which in the morning light was a truly magnificent sight, towering over her and rising up into the clouds.

"Where are they! Better hurry up before I change my mind," she said placing Bateau on the ground and tying her hair away from her face.

The Orphans appeared one by one. They were muttering discontentedly amongst themselves as several soldiers secured their provisions inside Agarus's side-saddles. At once King Vera turned to the Orphans, "Quick off you go now before she changes her mind. Do it for the Princess, do it for Esdaile, and do it for yourselves. Go now, that is an order!"

There was nothing they could say and there was no going back to the Jungle Room now. The King took off his crown and waved them on. One by one each stood nervously in the sunlight.

They're a lot bigger, but they haven't changed much over the years, thought the King, looking at their mangy appearance.

Belleny watched as they came out into the open. One by one they shivered forward as if the sunlight was icy and the soft breeze a blizzard. She was so proud of them and knew how difficult it was. But they were doing it and so was she. It was then that the purest and the sweetest smile appeared across Belleny's face.

King Vera's bottom lip trembled, his fingers fumbled and he dropped his crown. "Do you see that? She's smiling," he said nudging the soldier beside him.

"It's a great day of many my King," he replied, holding his helmet to his chest.

"A great day indeed, I great day," he sniffed.

"Don't let me turn back Bateau, tell me I'm doing fine!"

"You are doing fine, it's these guys we have to worry about," he said as the Orphans came to rest by her side. "What took you so long?" Bateau smiled swinging up onto Agarus.

"Get off me!" grumbled Agarus.

"Oh Orphans, your outside! Thank you," said Belleny.

"Are you all right? What's wrong with your face?" said Palia.

"Palia don't be silly, I'm smiling,"

"You don't smile? No, you're worried! We should turn straight back before—oh my the castle is overwhelming!" said Dillon.

"It sure is," said Bateau, "we should stay well away from it, at least for the rest of the day."

"Stop playing with our heads," snapped Palia.

"Settle down you two, I have important things to organize," said Belleny reaching into her jacket and retrieving her mother's amulet. Once opened the alphena crab spun around and around and stopped suddenly pointing back at the castle.

"What is it?" said Agarus as the Orphans circled her.

"A compass," she said, showing the others. "No matter where we go this will point us home." Belleny spun around in a circle and no matter which way she faced the crab's delicate claws pointed towards the castle.

"Forbidden magic?" said Palia. The Orphans nodded in agreement.

"Keep that to yourselves," said Belleny. "Doesn't it make you feel a little safer though?"

"No," said Dillon, "What if you lose it? What if it breaks?"

"That's not going happen," said Belleny scuffing up his wispy mane. But before I forget let's tie ourselves together with this white ribbon. I don't want to lose anyone on my first outing."

"Loose one of us! I don't want to be lost, not out here!" said Monte.

"Then tie yourself together, It will be night before you're ready," sighed Belleny.

The Orphans were hesitant at first, but Belleny insisted and once they were all attached they continued towards the giant hedge wall.

"Is that so they don't run away?" whispered Bateau.

"Of course it is," said Belleny.

— PART TWO —

Together Apart

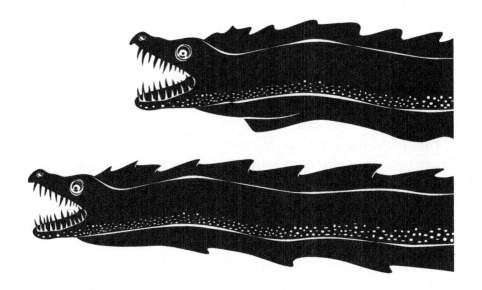

Evelin awoke in the night and stared at the illuminated pattern reflected by her swirling aquarium. BC purred beside her and for a moment she felt unsure if he was asleep or awake. From the stillness, he whipped his head back and licked himself with some serious focus. She grinned without much thought and left her arms by her side, closed her eyes and waited to fall back asleep. *Why do I feel so awake? Have I finally had enough sleep? Something's different? My head space ... seems clear.*

She stroked BC, he outstretched and curled up beside her, always returning to face the aquarium.

"Hello, sweet BC, sorry if I woke you ... or are you as awake as me? What have the paper fish been up too?" she asked and stared at the enormous wall of the aquarium in front of her.

"Eels!" She gasped spotting the large black snake-like figures swimming in the middle of the aquarium. Quickly she ducked under her rugs to appear quite hidden at the end of her bed. With her hand, she guided BC up with her and together they spied.

"The eel's are out! It's been years since they last appeared," she whispered.

Their large, thick tubular forms defied their liquid environment, moving with ease and elegance. Their bodies entwined, they swam with caressing movements as the reeds flowed round them in a green and mysterious veil.

Evelin felt unnerved. She was used to seeing just their slow motion gnashing teeth from deep inside their hidden cave dwelling, but now their neon green speckles stood out on their fine scaly black flesh and were in stark contrast against the tanks illumination. The pattern continued down their throats to cover a layer of dark purple tiger marks that lined their pure oily black bellies.

Evelin was transfixed, as they began to curl around each other in a frenzy, then released, they were tightening, swirling, twisting into strange and sporadic knots then releasing their hold.

The eels hooked and snapped as they bumped against the tank walls, a 'bump' sound escaping through the thick glass. The paper fish darted back and forth trying to find safety as both eels charged at once at least six hundred volts that looked like a fork being stuck into a power socket.

"What the hell ... they're electric!" she spluttered, as the sliver of light flashed when they recoiled.

In an instant, they repelled from each other, only to be magnetised back at full force, twisting violently and landing hard on a patch of black silty sand. A dark mist exploded around them as the water enveloped their swirling bodies and everything in between. It wasn't long before they were completely gone, hidden in a dark, stormy haze. The eels now only to be seen by flashes of electric lights.

"Incredible," she said as she jumped out of bed and circled the aquarium with BC in her arms. For some time, she sat at the end of her bed and stared into the dark waters.

"You know BC, that is just like how my head feels most days. A whirlpool of sand and electricity.

As Belleny, Bateau and the Orphans walked towards the gates of the Queen's Gardens they were spotted by several winged creatures circling high like buzzards. Belleny watched them nervously through the eyes of her mask and then down to Bateau seeking his reassurance.

"Don't worry Princess, they are royal guards on patrol," said Bateau, "King Vera will have a hundred eyes on watch today," he smiled.

Belleny took a deep breath and nodded, "I hope so."

"Have you ever seen an eight-legged Wompig? They're very rare, I spotted one in the garden. Hopefully today we will be just as lucky," said Bateau, with a yawn stretching out his arms and tails.

Belleny froze at once, "What's a wompig? I don't want to see anything with eight legs!" she squirmed.

"Did you just say wompig!" exclaimed Dillon.

"Oh no, a wompig! What's going on up there? I knew it, I knew it!" said Palia as she was squawking and flapping her wings about.

"Settle down back there, for someone without ears you sure have an acute sense of hearing!" remarked Bateau. "You have nothing to fear from a wompig. They're as small as a mouse and covered in white wispy fur like a cotton ball and have eight fluffy legs," said Bateau.

"Why did you stretch out your tails implying it was enormous?"

"Princess I was yawning. Talk about a wild imagination."

"My imagination is not wild!" retorted Belleny.

Bateau pointed at each of the Orphans with his tails stopping at Palia.

"You know I once heard some sound advice, it went 'Your head battles with the difference between what's real and what's imaginary, so if you want to be scared you're better off being afraid of the actual real stuff.' So the fact here is, we're all going for a walk into a contained beautiful garden, not climbing into the Pit of Nothingness."

"You should be thrown in the Pit," said Palia as she brushed past him.

As they approached the giant hedge wall, the shrub loomed high above them and quickly blocked rays of sunlight casting an icy shadow which sent shivers through all of them. Bateau noticed the stark shadows and soothed, "It won't be long before we'll be back in the sun again."

"A shadow I can handle," the Princess muttered.

"Is there another way in? I don't like the look of these gates," said Agarus.

"This hedge goes around the whole garden. The only way inside is through this gate unless you fly in from above ... but I don't think any of us can do that," said Bateau.

"Don't look at me when you say that, I can fly, I just don't," snapped Palia and pointed her beak in the air.

"Of course you can Palia," Belleny whispered in a warming voice.

The gate was a large wrought-iron, fourteen foot high and double fronted garden master adorned with fawns playing throughout the bars. It was as old as it was grand and seems to exude a personality as if it was the selector into the garden domain. The vines that wove and intertwined through the giant hedge, ducked and weaved into the gate's decorative design. Along the vines grew graceful white petalled flowers that waved together, back and forth, in smooth undulations as if underwater.

"Look!" whispered Agarus pointing his long snout inside one.

"Looks like you found your first porcelain mouse," said Bateau.

Monté ran up Agarus and looked down from his neck, "Oh no. It's not moving, you found a dead one!"

"Dead!" cried Palia. "Who would kill a porcelain mouse? This place is just awful, we shouldn't be out here!"

"Oh Palia, please control yourself, you're making me anxious," Belleny said impatiently, pulling down the branch to inspect the mouse. She stared at it as if it was a star in the sky and felt a wave of sorrow. "So sad, he's still so beautiful," she sighed.

"Dead?" questioned Bateau taking a closer look. "Not at all, they're nocturnal like you Belleny, asleep and as still as stone or porcelain."

And with that said the polished smooth white mouse curled around inside the flower and continued to sleep, thankfully ignoring the strange wild faces watching it.

Bateau smiled up at Belleny but noticed she wasn't looking, her arms were crossed and her wild mask was staring back towards the castle.

"Take one more step, I dare you!" said Belleny furiously. It was then her costumes persona became alive and horrifyingly real.

"Wait here Orphans!"

The Princess stomped up and around to face the frozen Palia. Belleny pulled back her mask and together they looked into each others saddened eyes.

Palia dropped her jagged beak and said, "It's all too much, I can't do this, I'm no part of a team that thinks being out here is normal, just look at the size of this hedge, who knows what lurks inside those gates? I can't even breathe out here, the air isn't moist or heavy, I don't even know if there is any air in this air!"

"Enough of this talk!" slammed Belleny.

The others watched from the gate as Belleny placed her palms in front of Palia. "This is not a final order, it is a plea. We must go on together. I feel a strange strength with each step I take. I want to know why others are out here and why we are not, what's wrong with us? Don't you question it too?"

Palia shook her head slowly at the ground.

Belleny retained herself and spoke calmly, "Listen, you're overreacting, the mouse, it wasn't dead Palia, it was sleeping. It is hot, but none of us are on fire. I can't believe I'm saying this, but I have a feeling we may have been wrong."

"I can't believe it either, who are you? You're not the Princess I know. She's the one who told us there is nothing but evil in every direction outside."

"I'm sorry but don't think I believe that anymore."

Palia's sad feathered face rose with a faint smile, "You and the Orphans are my family. I'm only trying to protect you."

"Protect us only when we are in danger. Please let's go."

As Palia returned quietly to the group, she met with silent nods and pats of approval. Dillon passed her the ribbon and she tied it back around herself to rejoin the throng both figuratively and literally.

The tunnel ahead cut straight through the hedge wall, an immense, ever-growing barrier that surrounded the Queen's Garden and continued growing above and thicker than the castle walls.

Belleny shook her head, "I never realised how big the hedge had grown., I was a young girl when I was here last."

"It's also repairs quickly," said Bateau snapping a small branch. "Look close, you can see it grow before your eyes."

"Incredible," said Belleny and the Orphans agreed.

And so it was, the hedge was forever growing, building itself around the castle and bordering the Queen's Garden, making itself thicker and stronger each day.

"Okay, everyone this is it," said Belleny pulling the gates apart and revealing a long dark leafy tunnel. At the end of the archway, a bright window of daylight shone through and a constant sound rumbled towards them.

"What's that noise?" asked Dillon.

"It's the stream," said Bateau. "It runs through the centre of the garden and then forms into the Veelin River. It journeys far from the peaks of the Northern Mare, the Veelin River is the life force of Mare-Marie and it ends right here in the Queen's Garden in a beautiful crystal clear pool."

Belleny stood impatiently as the woven branch walls began to unwind and reach out towards her.

"Be ... behind you!" shouted Monté.

Belleny froze. She could hear the creaking and twitching of the branches unwinding and the leaves rustling against each other.

"Who's there?" she cried and from the corner of her eyes, she saw a long, leafy tendril only inches from her face.

"Relax they're just saying hello. They're here to help us," said Bateau and as he spoke the vine seemed to caress her cheek.

"What? Plants don't say hello," she said, jumping forward and slapping it aside. As she hit the vine, it instantly lit up as if it was electric and a small group of globe-like flowers blossomed brightly along its branches lighting up the tunnel.

"Like I said, it wants to help us through," said Bateau squeezing one of the branches with his tail and lighting it even brighter.

"But how?" asked Belleny reaching out and lighting up another.

"I'm sure the garden has many more inside like this, but you'll have to wait until night to see them," said Bateau. "It was quite smart of your mum to plant these in here."

"We are not staying out here until night! Are we Belleny?" said Montë with a shiver.

"Of course we're not."

"Why didn't you tell us about the vine?" snapped Palia.

"Because the Princess needs to explore for herself, it's part of being outside, and I knew she would love them."

"Enough! I know what he's up to, and he's right, I have to find out for myself." Belleny stood vacant for several seconds, illuminated by the glowing branches before ordering them, "Come on you lot before its nightfall." Into the darkness of the leafy tunnel, she lit the way behind her. She ignored their moans and for a moment grinned silently to herself.

With each step, the group made, the stream called to them and beckoned them closer. A soothing cascade that echoed throughout the tunnel. The Orphans held an eerie glow around them, and Bateau tried not to look back at them but kept an eye on Palia, who he could hear wheezing close behind. To his relief, it wasn't long before they needn't light the branches, and the exit was filled with sunlight.

"Move aside Bateau, if this is a trap," snarled Palia thrusting herself past, her weathered feathers felt like a branch of swamp-drowned leaves. "Stand back Princess, you don't know what's out here ... oh my."

"Palia what is it, should we run back!" said Agarus trying to turn back around.

"No Agarus wait ... it's ... beautiful," she whispered and then stumbled forward as if hypnotized, in a trance by the paradise in front of her. One by one they followed and stood in awe, Dillon gasped, Montë let out a low moan as if his heart was deflating. The Queen's Garden flowed out before them in a rolling carpet of mystical nature and utmost beauty, a paradise held within the confines and safety of the towering hedge walls. The crystal clear stream glistened before them as it ran into a shimmering oasis and continued winding its way into the far distance.

Belleny stood frozen. She watched the Orphans untie the ribbon and one by one they separated. Anxiously they moved cautiously like kittens in a park.

"This can't be outside?" said Montë as if the gardens were an illusion.

"I can't look up," said Dillon shaking his head at the ground, "it's too much."

"Don't trust your eyes Orphans," snapped Palia. "I just know we're being fooled some way or another, keep close Princess, this is no place to be lost."

"Don't be absurd Palia, this is the best place to get lost," said Bateau hovering inches off the ground with his arms crossed, "stop fooling yourself and give in to what's around you."

"Bateau! You're floating again!" said Belleny running up and waving her boot across his shadow.

"So I am," he said, looking down with a cheery grin.

"Show off," said Palia in a huff before moving away towards the others by the pooling water.

Belleny grabbed hold of him and held him close. "How do you do that?" she asked, moving him gently around like a balloon.

Bateau shrugged, "I catch myself floating on the strangest of occasions. But sometimes it just stops and I end up falling flat on my face. I think that's why Gonzo left me, I'm not a reliable circus act."

"You're a walking nuisance, that's why," said Palia under breath.

The Orphans moved forward and gathered by the pooling waters. They drank as if they were back in the Jungle Room. It's clear icy waters were like none they had drunk before. Above them spinach red lily pads rose up and out of the pool like giant umbrellas as their soft white flowers peeled opened up and took to the air like lanterns, only to be held back by their long thin purple tendrils. The Orphans watched with some delight, but their sad faces returned to the water. Dillon held his strange squalid face only inches from the surface and sighed, staring down at his reflection as if it teased him. The others had followed and for a moment they waited silently for the water to return and be still like glass. Montë frowned at the sight of himself, he knew what he looked like, but today it hurt him deeply. Agarus looked inquisitively as if his reflection was not his and silently questioned what he even was. Palia seemed to be crying, although her eyes were still stuck in a menacing frown and she refused to let it go.

"Guys, I feel awful, my head feels strange," said Montë as a wave of dizziness rushed over him.

"Montë are you alright? You look really ill," said Agarus.

Dillon tried to lift his head as it fell lifelessly under the water's surface with a weighty splash, as it rose, water gushed from his mangy face like a drenched lion being pulled from a river. "I think you may be right Palia ... this place is ... I feel ... so sick," he said, peering to the side, then stumbling forward like a tired mule collapsed onto his bent forelegs. With sickly coughs, he heaved a black tar-like ooze and covered his mouth with his hand as it seeped through his claws. Teary-eyed, he looked up at the frightened Orphans as the blackness dripped from his mouth and down his chest.

"Dillon! What is that stuff?" said Agarus holding his stomach.

"I'm going to be sick too," crowed Palia as a thick line of black liquid dripped from her toothed beak splashing into the water. "It's happening ... I told you Princess," she crowed, "this is the end, no one listens to Palia! No one listens to me, you're the death of us Bateau! Outside will kill us!" she cried, dropping her head hard against the edge of the grassy embankment. Her bleak black eyes stared into nothingness.

A distraught Princess ran to their assistance. The painful moans of the Orphans were as bad as the vile looking oil that poured out of them.

"No, it can't be! What's wrong! Please get up!" cried Belleny. "Don't drink any more water!" she said, pulling Agarus out of his curled up ball, and now lying in a pool of black tar.

Bateau held Palia's bony beak and wiped the oil from her mouth she lay lifeless. "Palia can you hear me?" said Bateau.

In a violent fit, she wrenched her head up and said, "Get away from me, this is all your fault!" she spluttered as her head fell back splashing at the water's edge. Violently she coughed again and shook her head as the water poured into her beak and black ooze dripped in and out with each breath.

"Bateau!" coughed Montë.

Instantly Bateau left Palia on the edge and leaped towards Montë.

"I got you, come this way," he said and dragged his head to the water's edge. "Drink some water Montë, I'm sure it's not the water, did you eat something in the tunnel?"

"No, nothing all day," he coughed, drooling a black tar.

Belleny wept as she crouched in the water and held Palia's oily head in her lap. "This is all my fault Palia. I'm so sorry, I should have listened to you. I'm such a fool. I'll never go outside again. I promise."

"I told you! This place is poisonous, the air, it's rotting us from the inside," snarled Palia.

For some time the Orphans lay motionless by the water's edge, their pale bodies quivering in the sunlight as the black oil continued to seep from their mouths.

Bateau raced over to Dillon. He sat upright with his feet in the water, his head hung low.

"Are you feeling better? Please say yes," said Bateau.

Dillon lifted his head and Bateau was greeted with a snarl that turned into a smile, "Yes better ... actually I feel like I've had a hot bath," smiled Dillon, "although I haven't had one of those in a long time.

"That's tremendous! Really? What about the black stuff?"

"Well, it's all out now, whatever it was?" He continued his gnarled smile and stared across at the others with his strange wet wild face.

"Bateau!" called Belleny as she stood tall next to Palia who was also up on her feet. Agarus stretched his back and towered as he stood up on his hind legs and stretched his long body and tail.

"Palia thank goodness you're alright!" said Belleny hugging her bony frame.

"Please forgive the mess Princess. I have no idea what just happened," said Palia wiping her beak and wringing out her mangled black feathers.

"We must go back at once!" said Belleny.

"No wait," said Palia, I" would have thought I was very ill, but now I feel fine? I feel alive."

Agarus said from above, "I don't know what it was, but I feel so much better. I don't want to go back at all."

Montë wiped his mouth and slicked back his whiskers, "I've never felt worse, and now I've never felt better. What just happened?"

"Oh, I'm so glad you're all right, no something is wrong, we should go straight back at once," said Belleny. "Why has no one come to our rescue? I'll have someone thrown into the Pit for this!"

Palia squawked, "No Princess it's fine, we're better now. No one is to blame. We only just got here, let's have a look around, this place is like a dream!"

"Are you feeling all right Palia?" Bateau said cautiously, peering across at Belleny and shrugging his shoulders.

"Of course I am? Never felt better. I think I'll go for a walk over there, this place is just beautiful isn't it? Who's coming with me?"

Belleny looked back at Bateau and shrugged her shoulders again.

"Wait up we're all coming!" they said and took off with Palia as if nothing had happened.

"Are they alright? We should probably return," said Bateau.

"They seem fine now. Better than ever really ... we should go up there and keep an eye on them."

Belleny took a stepping stone pathway to the top of a sloping hill which looked down across part of the garden. Even from this height they could not see over the giant hedge.

"I see you," said Belleny pointing at a statue of a strange little girl hiding in an entrance made of fanning ferns.

"Turn around, looks like her friend caught you," said Bateau pointing at another statue of a girl hidden in the bushes.

"They're so happy, of course they are, playing hide and seek all day."

"Want to play too? Well, see if you can find me!" said Bateau skipping off along the path and disappearing into the garden beds.

"Please Bateau, don't go!" she called out, but he had vanished. As she ran to find him, there before her on the other side of the hill was the most picturesque garden scenes, including a beautiful white lattice pergola. She removed her mask stared at it like a painting. It was like something out of a dream. Although faint memories knew that she had been here before. From the pooling oasis, the water flowed up the hill, gently around her, and down to the pergola in small gullies. It divided several sculptures and led a watery pathway around the pergola.

Oh we must have our picnic in there! she thought turning back to the others. "Orphans come up here! You must see this!"

The Orphans appeared out of the exotic scenery one by one, their haggard faces glowing a vision Belleny had never seen before. *Were they not gravely sick only moments ago?*

As they greeted her, she asked, "Is everything all right? Are you feeling better? Wait ... are you smiling Palia?"

"Of course I am, look where we are?" she replied.

"We found a tree that laughs!" said Dillon waving his tail about.

Belleny stared at his tail, never had she seen it out, let alone waving.

"Please be careful up there Monté what if you fall? But yes isn't it, look at that pergola, we would be fools not to have our picnic in there."

"Well, we better not eat anywhere else then," said Agarus.

"I've never been so ravenous in my entire life, let's eat!" said Monté.

The others agreed and down through the gardens they went towards the pergola. Along the way, they had never seen such playful sculptures. From Winged Lysa catchers with nets to small children riding giant flying bugs with their wings out wide. Belleny placed her mask back on at once. "I nearly forgot, I've got to conceal my identity, who knows who's watching us? Has anyone seen anyone? I haven't even seen a gardener," she wondered, looking about.

"You won't, like the hedge, many of the plants in here don't need looking after, they look after themselves, so I read on a plaque back there, and King Vera has kept it empty for our eyes only, I doubt you'll need to wear that mask in here," said Bateau.

"I found you Bateau," said Belleny.

"That's not fair."

"Oh no, giant bees!" pointed Monté noticing several circling around the pergola. Busily the bees picked up the stray vines and threaded them around one another. Their long dangling white legs weaved the vines like rope.

"They're not bees," said Bateau, "They're Beedle Birds, quite harmless, too busy weaving vines, they're all over Mare-Marie," said Bateau.

Beedle birds? No doubt one's squashed within my mother's diaries, thought Belleny.

One by one they walked inside the pergola and dropped themselves in a circle. The pergola had never seen such an odd group. Eagerly Dillon poked his head in and untied the saddle baskets from Agarus. "I hope there will be enough for all of us!" he said, inspecting the assortment of fruits, cakes and savouries. He placed the baskets within the circle and Belleny unlatched the sides to reveal the contents before them all.

"I'm sure it will be, but first things first," said Belleny reaching out for a Thermos. She placed white carved cups in front of them all and poured a drink for each of them and said, "I would like to make a toast."

They each picked up a cup and nodded somewhat proudly to each other. "To my brave, adventurous friends the Orphans and of course Bateau, having the wisdom, courage and strength to come on this uncertain and unknown journey with me ... a small step but a step in the right direction. You are now free from your fears, free from your misguided thoughts and free to go and do whatever you want, inside or out."

"Hear hear!" they cheered in their wild harsh tones and then guzzled down their drinks.

All of a sudden the sunlight had turned off and an ominous shadow covered the pergola, as a gale like wind blew through the vines. There was a strangling silence as Bateau signalled everyone to be quiet. They all felt the presence of a foreboding creature. Its breathing, thick and harsh, its shadow moving side to side of the pergola, they could see it stepping closer and closer. Agarus ducked his head low and Monté put his hands over his eyes. Dillon scurried away from the shadow and Palia put her claws around her jagged beak. No one breathed a word. At once Belleny stood up. Her fists hung by her side clenching her daggers. She turned towards the figure and roared from behind her mask, "Who's there! I demand you show yourself. We don't take lightly to intruders!"

Her heart thumped fast and hard.

"Ah, excuse me, I don't wish to intervene," came an intense and weighty voice, "I was just so excited to hear that you're out and about. It is I, Garon the Quick, commander and guardian of the Mare-Marie Kingdom."

Belleny peered outside the pergola but couldn't see who was talking. She knew his name well from her father's tales, but she couldn't remember what he looked like other than being a giant bird-like creature. Nervously she stepped outside. "Show yourself!" she said with a light growl.

"I'm sorry it's just that I can't fit in the pergola, and I've been warned to keep off the flowers," he said apologetically.

From between two large trees, Garon stood towering as high as the pergola.

There standing before her was an enormous black raven. The eight foot high birds legs were trussed up with leather bands and strapped with dark brown leather armour. He was saddled like a horse and wore a leather and steel helmet which a protective T-strip ran the length of his face and shielded his beak. Belleny stared at his legs, for they were like no bird's she had ever seen. They were extremely long and scaly like an ostrich. He crouched down towards her and looked at her from side to side then proceeded to walk around like birds do, with their back-to-front knees. With his giant wing across his chest, he bowed down to the Princess and her friends.

"It's alright Orphans, Bateau," she signalled as she flipped her mask back into her hood. She gazed up at him in disbelief. *How could I forget such a creature? I have been inside way too long ...*

Garon bowed once again, "So it is you Princess, for a second there I thought about shooting an arrow through your head," he said.

"Hello, Mr. Quick, my name is Dillon, you said you're a guard, but what do you guard against?"

Garon leant down low and poked his head deep into the pergola, "Why hello Dillon, I haven't seen you since you arrived. You're looking much the same. Been inside for some time I was to think you didn't even exist. Please don't be alarmed, I'm here to keep the peace and move everyone along at the end of the day, especially those damn giant Larch Snides, they don't know when to go home, even after they've eaten and destroyed half the place."

"Giant Larch Snides!" quivered Belleny.

"Oh I'm sorry, they're harmless, mostly, just extremely pungent that's all, they belong in the sea, but the ocean is not as it used to be, so we're stuck with them up here on land, a true stench," moaned Garon. "I didn't mean to frighten you, I'm told I say the wrong thing at the wrong time." He knelt down closer. "But never fear, I will always be here to look out for you, I'm on your side."

"How many sides are there?" said Bateau.

"Now that is a good question," he winked, "I'm guessing you're the new addition to the gang."

"I guess I am," said Bateau turning around to the others, "my name is Bateau."

"Welcome my friend."

"You dropped something?" said Belleny picking up one of Garon's large black feathers.

"Oh dear, there goes another one," said Garon.

"I'm sure another will grow back," said Belleny as she placed it in her hair.

"That reminds me, I have something for you," he reached into the leather satchel strapped to one of his towering legs and pulled out a small wooden whistle.

"This is for you Princess. When played it will alert the nearest guard, beyond the sight of eyes you see. It is not a toy so don't go playing it when you're bored."

Garon put his wings to his ears and shook his head, "Speak of the devil, I must be off. Have a wonderful afternoon Princess and my new friends, I hope to see you soon."

Then with two giant flaps he rose off the ground and took off towards the castle.

"We sure have nothing to worry about with him around," said Montë.

*

Time slipped through the afternoon and the sun was sitting low. It sparkled off a bug who watched them all curiously. Dillon noticed the snail creature and shuffled out of its way. He could see where it had been from the trail of black tar splattered footsteps and it seemed to have followed all of them. But it wasn't the only one who was watching them.

"What's this I see?" A harsh voice pondered while staring into an oily, tar-filled cauldron. On the surface, the glimmering oil-slick pattern formed into shapes and movement and revealed the bug's view in a black oily vision.

"Now isn't this interesting? This is your doing witch," said the shadowing creature twisting the oil with her long nails, poking at the tar and taunting the surface. "Look here woman, your cursed rats have finally escaped their cage, although they're still disgusting as ever." She continued to prod at its oily surface. "Not a bad curse Lucretia you should be proud of yourself," the creature cackled, "but wait ... does this entail the Princess has left as well? Let's hope not for your sake. She will be angry."

The bug, as if controlled by the drag of the claw in the cauldron, moved towards Belleny and Bateau as the hooded creature watched from far, far away. Its trail of tar began to build up, as it paused in position, salivating stringy black drips below.

"Eww gross, look out, that bug on the roof is sick as we were, it's dripping everywhere," said Dillon and dragged away from the drop zone.

It was then that Belleny stood back from the oily drips and removed her mask as to see better.

"You're right Dillon, it is disgusting," said Belleny stepping aside and out of the pergola. The bug followed her every move and hung from the entrance.

"Why are you following me? Shoo! What are you looking at?" she asked as it looked straight into her eyes.

"Princess Belleny Vera!" snarled the hooded creature as it clawed at the oily liquid. "I don't like the looks of this, she's trouble ... for the both of us," it snarled, "This is not good."

Belleny flicked her fingers at the bug, "Go on shoo!"

The bug coughed at her and scattered to the top of the roof. Without a second thought, it jumped head first and from its hard-shelled back, several wings flicked out and it buzzed slowly into the distance.

"Oh well, I did try," shrugged Belleny. "On that note, are we ready to return home? I know we haven't been out that long, but I don't think it's going to be the last time we step outside again—agreed?" said Belleny.

The Orphans looked at each other, and although they didn't want to admit it, they thoroughly enjoyed themselves, and humbly signalled in agreement they would return.

"Before we head back is there something you would all like to say to Bateau?" said Belleny picking him up in her arms.

"Thank you Bateau, you were right," they said in unison.

It was then that Bateau let out a strange vowel-like meow and curled his tails around themselves.

"The day just gets better and better," smiled Palia.

Little did they know what tomorrow would bring.

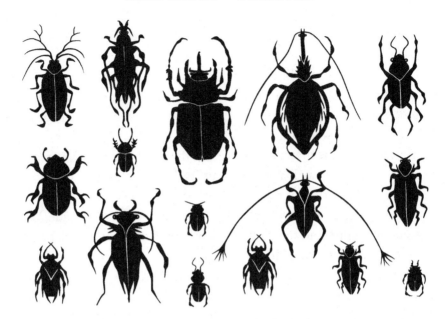

A flock of Blackbirds danced overhead in a self-organised and dynamic group of blue-black feathers and choreography. They were engaged in a wild dance where their tireless wings broke the morning sunlight as it streamed through Evelin's window casting patterns across her sleeping face. After the exposure of the eels and their late night theatrics, Evelin returned to bed and slept soundly until a momentary surge of adrenaline woke her. "Electric eels!" she cried and in a flash and whipped off her bed sheets and snatched at a disorientated BC before leaping off the bed.

"Where are they BC?" she asked, scanning the enormous wall of water aquarium glass. The aquarium water seemed surprisingly settled and clear as if last nights turmoil didn't occur at all. The paper fish instantly swam towards them and displayed their usual liveliness.

"Good morning, I'm so glad to see my little acrobats are alive ... two, three, four ... are accounted for and well," she huffed.

Evelin's face went from an expression of glee to glumness as she noticed the eels who had returned to wallow deep inside their blackened cave.

"Well, what have you got to say for yourselves?" she said as one stared out of the darkness, its mouth constantly unlatched revealing its unnervingly sharp teeth.

"I ought to have you evicted, you don't even belong in here," she snarled, and as if it understood, it coiled around and disappeared into the shadows of its cave.

"Yeah, you know what I'm talking about, you think you know everything," she said, pressing her finger against the glass and leaning in close. After a moment, the eel returned and poked its head back out.

Wait a minute? she thought.

"Are you alone in there?" she asked, somewhat foolishly, but realising it had to be by the way it moved about in the small cave so freely.

"Where is the other one BC?"

Intrigued, she quickly walked around the tank to the other side. Where the sand was white and the land baron besides a cracked porcelain teapot which had been placed inside years ago.

Evelin shook her head, "We'll that wasn't hard? What are you doing out here?"

On this rare occasion the eel was out in the open, on the far east side, its dark tubular trunk contrasted boldly on the intensely white sand.

Evelin stood silently and watched as the eel snapped haphazardly at a group of small Neon fish passing by in a triangular formation before coiling itself around the teapot like a snake.

"Are you all right?" she asked, kneeling down to its level, its eyes eerily staring back as it twitched it head.

On inspection, she saw no visual injuries and thought, *Can an electric eel be electrocuted? Maybe? It's about time they got some shock therapy.* She secretly grinned and tapped the glass with her nail, although she knew it was wrong. Like a frightened dog, it began to wriggle backwards, tipping the teapot over as it jerked its body from side to side.

"Sorry, but you deserve it, I hope you're going to put that back," she said pointing to the teapot.

The eel's had always stared at her as if they knew her deepest secrets, in a flash she was reminded of yesterday's adventure, before and after the pet store antics, then as usual a the continuous flash of memories followed one another.

Just leave me alone, you know nothing and I don't care anymore, she thought. The paper fish also kept their distance from the eel's and rushed pass them. She watched with starry eyes and grinned, then through the sparkling water to BC, who had returned to the edge of the bed. She walked over to be by his side and stroked him softly. Together they stared at the aquarium until her light reflection came into view.

"How are you this morning my little friend? she asked. "You're very quiet, are you tired? I feel different ... alert and quite awake."

And it was true, something was different. Trying to analyse it, she came to the conclusion she may have adjusted to her pills, or at least had a good night's sleep.

Finally, she thought.

"You awake Princess? Want to come down to the King Brown?" asked Robin, his voice echoing up through the hollow tube fastened to the wall.

Instantly she moved to the pipe and spoke into the receiver, "Why? I don't think so."

"Rubbish," he replied, "sure you do."

"Oh, I get it, the tip, yes, of course, I'll be down in a sec."

"Great!" said Robin.

"Do you know your disturbed eels are electric?" she added.

"Electric? Really?"

"Yes, dead certain they are," she said flatly and moved to her wardrobe.

Evelin dressed automatically knowing exactly what she was going to wear. She pulled on her black jeans and pushed her feet into her beaten up fourteen hole boots, slipped into a large black t-shirt that hung like a smock and grabbed her dark green leather jacket that was completely weathered and patched in all the usual places. The leather jacket was like a second skin that warmed to her, the soft leathery material coated her own with a strange protectiveness. It was her mothers, and although Evelin was shorter, it fit well enough.

Evelin left BC on the bed and moved to the bathroom, he followed and rubbed his face against her leg until she finished brushing her teeth.

"Right, so you want to come for the drive? Cheeky cat. OK fine, but you're going in my bag and there's no leaving the car. Don't make me regret this."

Evelin grabbed a large red sports bag and filled it with a soft chequered shirt. The bag had a large wheeled big-foot car printed in metallic sparkle ink on each side. It was one of her great finds at the tip, and she always took it along hoping to fill it with something special. This time it was already full before leaving. BC sat inside sniffing around and carefully she zipped it up so he could poke his head out just enough. He sat comfortably, disappearing into the bag and then re-appearing contently.

"You're not like any cat I've ever known," she smiled.

Evelin tiptoed down the stairs with BC in her arms and seated in the kitchen was Robin dressed for the 'Tip Trip', wearing his usual rubbish outing attire; consisting of eighteen hole dark army boots, camouflaged army pants and flat cap, chequered flannel shirt and on top, he wore an apricot coloured hand knitted woollen jumper with an orange cat face featured on the front. Evelin liked this look a lot.

"Morning Captain Chaos," she said, looking him up and down, "I'm ready to be dazzled."

Together the trio walked through the front door to where the truck was parked on the lawn. Its tray was near empty.

"Robin do you even have anything to throw out?" Evelin crinkled up her nose as she inspected the back tray that was near empty.

"Not really, just some old rags, empty paint tins and scraps from the side of the house ... anyway it's not what we take, it's what we bring back.

*

The King Brown Rubbish Tip sat next to an old Peppermint mill, in the adjacent six hectares of disused shrub-land and it was more like a county bazaar, chock full of weird and wonderful oddities, furniture items, broken neon lighting and signposts, miscellaneous bric-a-brac, toys, random pot plants and electronic goods. The entrance sign was kitsch and paid homage to the 1960's DIY with painted signage in odd, unwanted colours, on disused fridge doors, hulls of broken dinghies, school lockers, just about anything that wasn't a sign.

Just as Robin, Evelin and BC were about to head off, Milton appeared casually from behind the truck and leaned against the bonnet, his blue suit complementary to the bright orange truck, "What's going on here Boots? he coyly questioned like a movie star from the silver screen.

"Well, if it isn't the snake charmer," said Evelin.

"Mr Corman what can we do for you today," said Robin.

"The usual, provide lunch, companionship and wisdom. I noticed the Boots Bat Mobile was out front ready for an expedition, is it that time of the month already?"

"You can't really say that about going to the tip, but yes we're going, go get your crap," said Evelin feebly pointing to his place across the road.

"Great! I do have an old push bike or two my aunt's been nagging me to get rid off, got much room in the back?"

"Funny you should mention it, we've actually got plenty of room," smiled Evelin, her eyes gazing up at Robin.

"Nice, I'll be back in a second, don't go anywhere without me," said Milton as he darted across the road.

"Milton!" called Robin.

"Yeah."

"You might want to change out of your suit for this one, remember last time, your run in with the can of house paint."

Milton shrugged, "Oh yeah ... I better wear my tweed, Ha!"

"Run along, just get your bike," said Robin and looked down at a starry-eyed Evelin.

"Hey kiddo, you okay?"

"Yeah what?" she said looking up at him with cheeky grin, "I'm good, just thinking."

"Thinking! You know what I told you about doing that."

"It will rot my brain like paint stripper?"

"Exactly. Hey Eve, I want to talk to you ... I hope you're happy with my new friendship with Jacqueline. It's good for a loan ranger like me to have new friends."

"Pardon? Yeah, I know, I'm cool Robin, I may go on about it, but I'm cool if you're—"

"I'm ice cold Eve. I better go help Milton with those bikes," said Robin.

"I'm going back inside for a sec... I forgot something."

"OK Princess."

*

Boys will be boys, thought Evelin—having returned and now sitting in the pickup-truck—as Robin and Milton wrestled a rusty and very broken bike frame into the back of the truck. Both of them squeezed in either side and buckled up.

The truck started without a hitch and Robin took off down the street. All in all the roads were empty, he seemed to get green, after green light, which he drove through at top speed.

Milton turned to Evelin, who was making small snoring sounds, "Hey you brought BC?" he said, giving BC a pat as he poked his head out.

"Evelin," groaned Robin, "what if he runs off?"

"She's asleep," whispered Milton.

"Oh," said Robin.

"What's up with her?"

"I've heard it's a rare condition called sleeping," said Robin.

Milton rolled his eyes and whispered, "You know what I mean Mr Boots. She's been acting pretty strange lately ... actually a lot of strangers lately."

"Pretty strange? She is a teenage girl Milton, is there no other way they act."

"True," said Milton and he went silent for a moment. "It's narcolepsy isn't it."

Robin smiled as he kept his eyes on the road.

"Look at her? She's spends more time asleep than awake these days and the pills."

Robin peered across to Milton and back to the road.

"Has she mentioned anything?"

"Nothing ... I tried ... she looks placid, but she has bite."

"That she does. It's complicated Milton. But so you know—"

"Go on," said Milton, watching Evelin continuously.

"She's going through a rough patch. Every once in a while her head can't keep up with her thoughts, she wears herself out you see," said Robin.

"She does think a lot, a lot more than the girls in her class ... so she's alright though?"

"She will be."

Milton moved back as Evelin gave a light cough. Robin looked across at him and touched the side of his nose.

"Yes Sir, I understand, I'm her man, I mean not her man, just a man, the man, you know what I mean."

"Sure I do," smiled Robin.

"So, Eve tells me you fancy Miss Davis hey," winked Milton.

The large ceiling windows in the Jungle Room were flung wide open for the first time in many years. The thick wall of creepers and vines outside let through a filtered fresh breeze that shifted the musty closet smells and the morning sunlight reached every corner of the room bathing the room with its warming touch. Belleny and the Orphans slept calmly in the enormous cabin high above near the rafters.

Dillon was the first to surface. Sleepily he stood, carefully minding the myriad of bodies laying next to him and stretched his arms out wide, they felt light but supple and strong. He began to yawn and then it happened. From the depths of his lungs came a thunderous gust that rose louder and louder, turning into a menacing growl that he could only imagine making.

Instantly Belleny woke and let out a stifled and confused scream barging through the bodies of the Orphans from the rear of the room.

"Get out! Orphans run!" she shrieked snatching Bateau by the scruff of his neck before running outside. With a yelp, she froze at the edge and stared at the ground far below and quickly pushed her back against the outside wall.

"Careful Princess! What's going on?" said Bateau squeezing himself from her grips.

"We shouldn't have left the windows open, wild beasts have got in, they've—the poor Orphans," she slid her back down and crouched into a ball. *There's no use running,* she quivered.

"Wild beasts?" said Bateau peering inside the doorway and whipping his head back. "You're right but who are they? What are they ... where are the Orphans?"

"I don't know! Eaten obviously! You're the expert!" shrieked Belleny.

"Princess Belleny," a resonant voice echoed from inside, "there's no need to be afraid."

The heavy pads of its clawed footsteps thumped down on the wooden floor as it approached and paused only inches from the doorway. Its breath a coarse growl-like purr.

It knows me? trembled Belleny, her eyes could not get any wider as her skin became even whiter.

"I demand answers! Who are you and what have you done with the Orphans?" cried Belleny.

"You've always known me, but not who I am," said the creature.

"Is ... is that you Dillon?" said Bateau. He realised his words made no sense, but the beast held such similarities.

The white creature lowered its head even closer, "Yes Bateau it is me, but my birth name is Aelios," said Dillon.

"Lies! What have you done with my Dillon?" said Belleny crawling backwards as the creature peered its giant head outside.

Bateau stood in awe, even though, its mouth was big enough to engulf him whole.

"You look like Dillon but—"

"I am more than Dillon," said Dillon.

He lowered his head to Belleny, "please come back inside Princess, I will cause you no harm."

"What ... I don't recognise you, what happened to you?" she asked."

He turned back inside the cubby house and escorted Belleny by the hand, "Knights, quiet down now," he said as a commotion had started to fill the room.

"Orphans? Are you all ... still you?" said Belleny, trembling in disbelief.

"Yes, it is us," said the elegant winged one. Belleny presumed it was Palia, but she stood quite speechless, in a bewildered awe at the sight of her glorious appearance.

"Yes my Princess, it's me Palia but I am also known as Oliv."

Bateau looked on curiously, "I'm sure I've seen her before."

Gone were their dry, grey, mangy patches of fur and crimped oily feathers, now each was replaced with a slick, white shiny coat and radiant plumage. They all shone with magnificence and Dillon sat proudly with his head held high, whereas before he was resting his chin on the floor, his ribs pushing against his thin layer of skin, he had a full coat of fur that shined like white silk from his head to the very tip of his tail.

"Belleny, it's me! I'm me again!" said one of the figures looking down at its clawed hands in delight. "It's me Monté, I'm back to my old self!" He laughed, running up to her and into the light.

"Ha ha!" laughed Dillon. "Why look at you Roli Poli!"

"Roli Poli?" said Belleny.

"My actual name is Roli. But I like Monté just as much."

Monté stood straight up on his hind legs and walked like it was the way he had always walked. He had the same slick white fur as the rest and a dark black ring inches from his marble black eyes.

"I hope I change into something," smiled Bateau as they all turned towards Palia, who was flapping against both sides of the cubby house, trying to open out her wings.

"There's not enough room for us in here anymore, we belong outside," said Dillon.

"I guess by the commotion I'm not the only one with a makeover?" said Agarus as his dragon-like head poked through the entrance.

All eyes turned towards the doorway and a cheer escaped from the Orphans.

"Gormus! Good old Gormus!" shouted Dillon.

"I'm only a month older than you Aelios," he rolled his eyes and smiled with a mouth full of sharp white teeth.

"Agarus? Gormus?" questioned Belleny in total bewilderment.

"Yes Princess it's me. Once I was known as Gormus but I feel I've been Agarus for my entire life," he smiled.

"You are—" mumbled Belleny.

"Enormous!" said Bateau.

Belleny peered from the entrance and looked at Agarus from the top of his head all the way down to his tail that hovered off the floor. He clawed along the jungle gym with ease like a lizard in a tree.

"Well isn't this something," he said in a smooth and husky voice, "I don't know about you kids, but I'm feeling pretty fantastic right now. I'll be down by the pool, I have a ravenous thirst."

From the tree house, the group descended swiftly, diving with acrobatics, grabbing at tree branches and contorting their bodies around like forest nymphs. Palia launched with outstretched wings and demonstrated dynamic soaring, "Look at me!" she laughed as she effortlessly flew up towards the ceiling and descended again in a spiral.

In full light the Orphans fur shone.

"I feel like I haven't thought of anything in years," said Dillon crouching down into the emerald pool and looking at his bright reflection.

"Nothing positive anyway," said Montë.

"But I sure can remember one creature in particular," said Dillon.

"Lucretia," said Agarus with distaste in his voice.

"That witch!" said Palia her beauty concealing a strain of hidden pain and anger.

"What witch?" said Belleny. "There are no witches left in the kingdom."

"She is not inside the kingdom," said Agarus.

"She is not even a witch," said Montë. "She's something much worse."

Agarus leant down to Belleny with a sharp-toothed grin, "but we are now released from her evil curse."

"What about the old Orphans?" said Belleny quietly.

"I'm sorry Princess," said Dillon, "we will no longer be the Orphans you have always known, we have returned back to our true forms."

"Goodbye old scruffy bunch," she sighed and looked at how each of them shimmered in the light, their faces immaculate, but ultimately they were happy.

"I miss you, I feel lonesome … I'm confused, happy and sad, nostalgic almost," said Belleny.

Dillon sniffled and lowered his head as tears dripped from his black polished eyes.

"Please don't cry," said Belleny looking down at their sad reflections.

"So sad … with what happened to Barera," said Palia.

"Who?" said Belleny.

"Esdaile," added Dillon.

Belleny froze.

Dillon remembered Esdaile staring at the windows of the Jungle Room, day after day, never to be opened, unsure why he hated the outside so much.

"He was strong, but not strong enough, the curse was all too much for him," said Dillon.

"Where is he now, what happened to him?" asked Bateau, then as he spoke, he realised instantly that Esdaile was the creature hanging above Belleny's doorway.

She stared down at him with a wild stare that cut him in half.

Esdaile was her secret, thought Bateau.

It was then that Belleny said, "he fell from my balcony."

"He was not one to fall," said Dillon, "he jumped, this was no way to live."

Belleny knelt and picked up Bateau, she held him tight, "yes ... it's true. I couldn't stop him."

Palia clawed at the ground and said, "I remember when we were in Shell Forest, the witch wandered through the trees to the Sealess Shore where we were resting, she was beautiful, enchanting, dressed in white, I remember she had been crying."

"It was our funeral," huffed Agarus.

Palia continued, "She never spoke, but whistled a haunting tune, do you remember? She dragged her staff around us, dragging it through the shells, such a sound, I remember watching Monté collapse as if he was dead, then Agarus fell, then Dillon, then—I must have been next or Esdaile."

Agarus screwed up his face, "Then we woke up, trapped in her prison of a castle."

"Oh, you poor things," said Belleny.

Monté shrugged, "But it was as if she cared for us at the same time, always feeding us and caring, it was so strange Belleny."

"Not as strange as losing my feathers!" said Palia.

"Or my strength," said Dillon.

"Or my will," said Agarus. "It could have been weeks, months, I can't remember, but eventually we were in a wooden box and taken here."

"I don't believe it!" said Bateau whipping his tails in the air as a moment of clarity embraced him, "I know who you are! I had a feeling we'd meet somewhere and now I remember. You've travelled with The Great Gonzo Circus! I've seen posters of you all over his caravan, missing person posters, the artwork was so old, they must have been taken years ago, before I even met Gonzo and yet now I know the mystery of why you were never found, despite the promise of that enormous reward!"

"Oh my Gonzo, my golden Gonzo," said Palia.

Golden Gonzo? He wasn't all that golden to me, thought Bateau.

"Tell me he's still alive?" pleaded Palia.

"Yes he's fighting fit, he and his circus are fine," said Bateau looking at the ground.

"I'm so glad. The good old days!" said Dillon.

"It's been so long, we must find him," said Agarus.

"Thank you again Bateau, without you, we would all still be under that curse," said Palia.

"You certainly got rid of it in the Queen's Garden, it came out of us like poison. The water seemed to drive it out of us?"

"We knew something had happen, but I didn't want to jinx it. Afterwards, you were entirely different in the pergola," said Bateau.

"Oh no, remember that bug on the roof? said Dillon.

"How could I forget, it splashed muck all over my outfit," said Belleny.

"Ones like that crawl all over Lucretia's castle, I just know it's a spy, I'm sure we were being watched. She doesn't know we've changed back, but she knows we were outside and the Princess."

"It's been so long, would she even care," said Palia.

"What would she want with the Princess?" said Dillon as he stood up tall. "Let her come here, I've got something to say to her."

"Looks like we have visitors," said Belleny. The clashing sounds of metal plated soldiers could be heard running throughout the castle, down the corridors and were forming a line of attack at the Jungle Room entrance.

Belleny, Bateau and the Orphans watched as the doors were smashed open and over forty guards came thundering in. Row after row, they surrounded them against the water's edge and nervously pointed their long spears at the Orphans. King Vera came storming in behind them.

"What's going on!" he roared, pushing the soldiers aside. He took one look at Belleny surrounded by the Orphans and pulled out his sword swinging it up at Dillon. "Let her go you silky ... white beasts, or die where you stand!"

"No father stop!" said Belleny stomping in front of Dillon with her arms out wide.

Secondary soldiers now aligned their bow and arrows at the newly transformed Orphans. Belleny shouted, "I demand you to lower your weapons, or each and every one of you will be thrown into the Pit!"

King Vera held out his hand and motioned them to lower their weapons a little.

"Father, look closer, can't you see? There's been a metamorphosis, a transformation! They're the Orphans."

"What are you talking about Belleny? If this is some game of yours it's not very funny, who are they and what are they doing in the Jungle Room ... and where are the Orphans?" said the King.

"But I'm telling the truth. They are the Orphans Dad," sighed Belleny, she hung her arms by her side exhausted. "They were under a witches' curse; somehow the river broke it when we went outside into the gardens."

"Lies! A curse! There are no witches in Mare-Marie I removed every last one of them myself and magic along with them," he said.

"It is true. It was a time long ago and beyond the kingdom of Mare-Marie," said Dillon, his voice sending fear into the soldiers who nervously raised their weapons. Dillon roared, "Get back before you get hurt," and at that moment the short silvery white hairs that covered his body flicked forward and he went from white to pitch black in an instant.

"Dillon, you're changing again!" said Bateau.

Belleny looked on stunned, "Dillon, are you alright? What's happening?"

Instantly the Orphans recalled their abilities and one by one they changed their silky white coats to black and Agarus rose up towering over them, "Listen to her," he growled, his jaws clashing with every word.

Belleny stood towards the soldiers and King Vera.

"Stop it all of you! The witch is called Lucretia!"

It was then that King Vera dropped the point of his heavy sword to the ground, he held with both hands as his throat knotted with a lump brought on by guilt. Without further interrogation, he ordered the soldiers to lower their weapons and step back.

The Orphans, one at a time, returned their coats to a pure white.

"That's incredible guys, truly remarkable they're Shifters," said Bateau as he shook his head in disbelief.

The rest of the morning, the fragments of memories came back to the Orphans and turned into stories and explanations. They sat in the King's domain, he upon his throne, his head sunk in his hands.

"I knew someday she would return to haunt me, but I never knew that she had been tormenting me and my daughter all along," he sighed, "it's all my fault."

"What do you mean your fault?" said Belleny.

"I banished Lucretia and many others when I banned magic from within the Royal Kingdom, from here to the Slate Cliffs. I was so furious, I had such a temper back then."

"But you never really said why?" said Belleny.

He reached out and held Belleny's hand. "Your mother had passed, I was so upset, my thoughts plagued me with sadness. One night many weeks after her death, your beautiful mother, Anne, re-appeared from the shadow of death and walked into the castle and sat down at the end of the dining table. I knew in my heart it wasn't her, it couldn't be, but to see her once again I just fell back in my chair in awe. We ate and drank, and she told me she didn't want to see me this way, said she had to go, but she was fine, she loved me and to look after you Belleny," he sniffed. "Then after some time of silence she left, I couldn't move from my seat ... another spell, I wanted to run after her. I knew it couldn't be her, but I also didn't want the lie to end."

"You've never spoken of this," said Belleny.

"I have not," the King shook his head. "Afterwards I felt even worse, letting that impostor take me for a fool, concealed behind a cheap spell."

"She's some sort of shape shifter, I guess," he sighed.

"The witch vanished into thin air and I sent the spies to the Wandering Gravers who were Asel and Esla, but when they finally reached her beyond the Slate Walls they returned with nothing but bad news."

"What did she say to them?" asked Belleny.

King Vera looked up at her with deep sorrowful eyes, "I will take your daughter, as you have taken my son."

"Oh no!" said Dillon under his breath.

Belleny remained in silence.

"She had a son?" said Bateau.

"Yes a young boy, I didn't expect them to go and live in the Shell Forest, then again, there are not too many places to live safely beyond the Slate Wall. I can't imagine how they managed alone, even if she was a witch.

"Asel and Esla brought back news of a creature, a dark sorceress, and an ever-growing darkness that surrounds the North East. An area once as fruitful as the Queen's Gardens, but now we simply call it the Dark Lands and it remains strictly out of bounds to all of my people, it's just not safe there ... anywhere beyond the Slate Cliffs."

"So this is what she has become, some demented sorceress?" said Belleny, "Fuelled on years of hatred. We're not safe here, not even inside the castle."

"Now don't worry Belleny, she's far from here," said Palia.

"How do you know? She could be heading here right now with her army."

"We are aware something has taken over Castle Morne at the very edge of the North. It was built long ago, upon the remains of the last fallen giant called Goramon Morne."

"How do you know? How long have you known this?" said Belleny.

"Long enough, but there is nothing I can do. The Gravers have seen unsightly figures coming and going from the castle and spreading through the nearby forest, they say she may be growing an army," the King sunk his hands into his fists, "and seeks to bring them here."

Belleny shook her head, "This can't be happening ... why haven't you stopped her? What about the King of the North?"

"I have not spoken to or heard from King Macer in years. The lands are unpredictable, changing like the weather from one moment to the next.

Dillon approached slowly, "King Vera, the witch must have had a reason to fuel her malice. This may have festered over time and it could be a far more powerful entity now."

"We must go and stop her," said Agarus, towering over them as he stood up on his back legs. "It's true, it's only a matter of time before she forms an army to strong to repel."

The King shook his head, "Thank you my friends, but the land beyond the kingdom is not what it once was. If she's turning the animals and creatures into her own beastly army ... well I really don't know, I'm afraid."

"I knew it was bad outside, but not this bad," said Belleny.

"You realise hiding here and waiting for her to show up on your doorstep is not the answer, she will take over the kingdom if she is not stopped, and that will be the end of Mare-Marie," said Dillon circling the throne.

"Of course I know!" slammed King Vera. "I've lost more men than I can bear, we're just not fighters, we're the peace of the land."

Palia ruffled her feathers, "gather a handful of your best and we'll stop her, I feel removing this curse has rejuvenated me tenfold."

"We'd still have Esdaile by our side if it weren't for her," said Agarus.

The King sat up straight and adjusted his crown, "I commend you on your bravery, you are the opposite of the Orphans I once knew."

"They sure are," said Bateau.

"You met Garon the Quick yesterday?" said King Vera.

"Of course, how could we forget," said Belleny.

"Good. I know he's planning an attack and has several skilled men to help him. But I refuse to let him go, the kingdom can't afford to lose him."

"You must make a move King Vera before it's too late," said Dillon.

"We would make a good team and I would be honoured to go with him. Set him free," said Dillon.

"I know I wouldn't go without him, he probably knows more than the Gravers combined. You will have to prepare. Armour and weapons I'm sure, anything you desire is at your dispense," said King Vera.

"Father don't encourage them! Are you serious Orphans? You have only just returned to your former selves? You're clearly not thinking straight, give yourselves time. Bateau tell them!"

"Looks like that curse still lingers in one of us," said Agarus.

"It does not!" slammed Belleny. "I'll lead the way, I have a map of the land and a compass."

"Amusing Princess, you'll be going nowhere," laughed King Vera quite seriously.

"The King is right Belleny, but I can't think of anything more exciting after being trapped in this castle for all these years, the sooner we go, the better!" said Montë.

"I'm with you Montë! Imagine what's outside, after all, this time," said Palia.

"I'll advise the Commander Quick at once!" announced King Vera.

The trio putted along on the pick-up truck and after a few kilometre's the engine had warmed up and was travelling steadily down Riverside Drive. Evelin sat comfortably between Robin and Milton. Every once in a while she stole the occasional glance, peeking down at BC as he slept in her bag. The dashing white lines appeared and disappeared along the main road and eventually blurred into one, wandering off and leading them down a series of twists and turns that gave them glimpses of the river through the leaves of the bright orange trees.

When they arrived the faded bitumen road turned into a sandy dirt track full of limestone and pebbles that followed along the town's infamous King Brown River. The current and lower rapids surged like wild horses and looked as murky as pea soup.

Robin slowed down to a light roll and gently approached the sandstone road; otherwise he was sure the van would fall apart like several guttered wrecks that lined the roadside.

"Come on baby keep it together," said Robin grinding the truck into second gear. The vehicle shook like a paint mixer, and they looked across at one another with nervous grins.

Evelin kept one hand in her bag and comforted BC as he tried to push his head out. Robin drove on and took aim for the worn tyre tracks to make a smoother commute. Milton pointed out several people fishing along the banks; it didn't seem to worry them that the water was mostly mud or that the rubbish tip was nearby.

"What can you catch in there besides a virus?" asked Milton.

"Mud," murmured Evelin.

"I've caught Catfish, Yellow Bellies, Pigmy Perch, Hairy Backs, the odd Flounder and of course the King Brown Cod," said Robin.

"So you caught the King?" said Milton. "And now you're cursed to look like one."

"Very funny, I bet you'll grow a beard like mine one day, you're already on your way."

"Ah, you noticed," said Milton gracing the stray fluff on his chin.

"BC has more than you, and he's hairless," said Evelin.

"Speaking of BC," grinned Milton.

Evelin ignored him and turned to Robin, "hey I can't remember the last time we went fishing?"

"I stopped taking you when you started complaining about the fish's feelings, it ended up being an ethical discussion and I couldn't relax."

"Sorry … but it's scientifically proven they feel pain and a whole array of emotions, especially fear. Even those eels of mine aren't as stone cold as I thought."

"You were saying they're electric?" asked Robin.

"They were out last night and messed up the whole aquarium; it was like looking into a sandy thunder cloud, flashes of lightning."

"The paper fish seem happy enough. One eel is a little shocked but nothing he doesn't deserve."

"Those eels are amazing," said Milton.

Evelin shook her head in disagreement.

They continued to drive for some time and the cheerful scenery changed from open picturesque riverside views to a dismal close up of the brown river, mounds of motley grey sand that had danger written all over them and razor wire fencing that sectioned off the rubbish tip desert wasteland.

Mothman's main entrance could be seen not too far ahead. Behind it, the landscape was nothing short of a post-apocalyptic film set, where all machines have broken down. Out of a furnace and brick smokestacks, belched thick grey plumes of smoke, which pushed up into the sky and joined the clouds forming one mega cloud. Circling seagulls littered the sky and several dusty yellow Bull Dozer's gripped the terrain as they climbed the waste mountains, pushing the rubbish higher and higher.

"Can you see Mothman or Madame Tipanthea?" asked Evelin.

"Not yet, but we did notice your little stowaway," said Robin his eyes watching the road ahead.

Evelin shrugged, "What stowaway? Oh ... I couldn't just leave him."

"You know what we do with stowaways?" joked Milton, pretending to cut his throat from side to side with his finger.

Robin approached the entrance with caution. It was like entering the site of a demolished mall, no two materials came from the same world, piled on top of one another like the worst game of Tetris.

Within the fort-like entrance, two massive wire gates confronted the with hand-painted metal signage that was wired into its facade. Macabre human form mannequins, a one-armed mother and her headless daughter stood on either side holding toy plastic machine guns. A metal booth fashioned from a caravan sat out the front and was held together with scraps of metal and various coloured car bonnets.

Evelin looked up at the mannequins that stood inside it, one holding binoculars looking down at them.

"The weird mannequins are new," said Evelin.

"Mothman's army is growing every day," said Milton.

"It's quite a fortress of junk. I would want to protect it too," said Robin.

"You would," she said.

"It's to keep what's lurking inside from escaping," said Robin.

Instantly she imagined an enormous fat baby-like creature feeding on the endless scraps and hiding in a cave deep within a mountain of rubbish, Mothman could be hiding anything in there, she thought.

Slowly the truck came to a halt, and Robin had steered the vehicle one metre away from the entry gate where a pair of beady staring eyes greeted him. They belonged to the proprietor Madame Tipanthea. The

Madame was as a woman in her late fifties. She wore rainbow makeup and looked like a thick impasto portrait. Both her ears were pierced like curtains to the very top and stuck out through her thick, pale blue crown of hair that stood up in a strange vertical wave. Robin watched as she tapped her fingers against the counter, revealing the assortment of glass rings she wore. Madame Tipanthea hunched forward leaning her chest against the counter and eyeing Robin up close.

"The Queen of Detritus," mumbled Evelin.

"Hello, there handsome. Just dropping trash off and asking me to dinner on your way out?" she said in a gravelled cigarette voice. Her eyes locked unwaveringly onto Robins, completely ignoring that Evelin or Milton were in the truck.

Robin found himself unable to articulate a sentence and was tongue-tied having nowhere to divert his eyes and nowhere else to look.

"Well then, that's a ten a for you, fifteen dollars if you got any tyres back there, hmm?" she said, peering into the tray on the back of the truck and pointing to a never-ending pyramid of burning tires in the distance.

"No rubber tyres, thank you." Robin handed her a wrinkled ten dollar note. Madame Tipanthea placed her hand on top as quick as a croupier and held it admiring his fingers.

"A handyman I'm sure," she said, "is this for later," she grinned and dragged the note away slowly between two fingers before pushing it between her cleavage.

"Later?" Robin's eyes open as if startled and he quickly retrieved his hand out of her grip.

The Madame changed her tone, "You know the rules?" She pointed at the signs on the fence, and her gaze still locked onto Robin.

"Ah yes." Robin turned towards the signs and quickly read, "Keep to the baths, no fluorescent light-bulbs, no batteries, no bodies, no motors, no fires and no chemicals."

"Handsome and can read. Go right down the back, to the left, anywhere in section C-3 is fine, there's a sign you can't miss it. Stick to the paths! And for god's sake you two, don't eat anything in there. Already had an ambulance up here this week." She faced Robin and cupped her hand to her mouth, "kids will put anything in their mouths these days. I'm a bit like that if you know what I mean," and with a wink the corners of her mouth raised slowly into a small bite. A loud device buzzed and an electric mechanism jolted the gates apart, as soon as there was just enough room Robin took off.

Without a word he looked across at his two passengers, his expressionless face said it all.

The trio proceed along in the truck. There was a minute of silence brought on by the inappropriate innuendos of the Madams words that lingered like her perfume.

Hey look, out on the river," said Robin changing the vibe and pointing to four large barges joined to one another by a taught tow-rope. Each had a mountain of bagged garbage on their backs. The white gulls circled and dove down inside, screaming at each other over the scraps.

"Now that's a river cruise," said Evelin.

"Maybe you can take Miss Davis on a cruise like that," smiled Milton with Evelin grinning by his side.

"Maybe I can put you two on it and drive off home."

"Go left! Left!" shouted Evelin, pointing at the sign C-3 and the path to take. Robin quickly swerved and followed it down into a valley of despair and debris.

"I got a good feeling there's something down there for us today."

"How can you tell?" said Milton

"I can smell it," said Robin with a deep breath.

"Okay. Evelin you know the drill, you and your sidekick are on the roof, sweep the area for hostile and you know who," said Robin.

"Yes sir." Evelin opened the glove box and removed a plastic film camera and a handmade slingshot. "Hold on BC, we're heading out."

"What's that for?" said Milton.

"Crows, rogue Hyenas and to keep you on your toes," she said.

On the side of the truck, Robin had welded a foot ladder to the metal and some metal trunks.. Evelin slung her bag over her shoulder and climbed to the roof of the truck. She'd left a dent in the center, and dirty footprints marked where she had walked many times before. The roof warped and contracted with her weight, but formed a nice spot for her and BC to sit comfortably.

"Great view from up here BC," she said scanning the territory.

Together they watched Robin diving into the rubbish. He held up a huge round birdcage with the base missing and presented it up to her.

"What do you think Princess? Want some birds?"

"I don't think so, I've had my fair share of birds this week, we could always keep Milton in it?"

Robin pulled the cage over his head, "Let me out, I'm innocent, I was framed!"

"Hold it there!" she said reaching into her bag and pulling the camera up to her eye. "You're guilty Robin, you and your stinky partner in crime!"

Evelin wound on the 35mm film inside the point and shoot camera and took a photo and gave them a 'Thumb's Up' signal.

"Guys, look its Mothman!" she whispered as loud as she could.

Evelin zipped up the sides of her jacket to the neck and put her hand underneath it gently holding BC in place.

Milton was on the other side of the truck where he had found a teacup with a dead rat lying in it. It looked like it was having a spa bath and now with a carefully placed piece of newspaper it looked like it was also reading the paper. Behind it, he noticed a cardboard box.

"Whoa! Check this out!" He removed the two sheets of cracked glass and held up the frame so Evelin could see. Inside the frame was a collection of large and strange looking beetles, pinned down onto a whiteboard, individually tagged, each with their relative names.

"That is pretty cool," said Evelin.

"They look clean, they'll go great with the rest of your weird stuff," he said, returning the bugs to the truck and closing the door.

"Whatcha got there, sonny?" An old voice coughed from behind him. Quick as a flash Milton turned around and tilted his head back. There was Mothman wearing his usual tall rubbish tip stilts he had fashioned together from various discarded objects and strapped around his old but muscular legs.

"Nothing, just some of my beetles, I've decided not to throw them out. Sentimental."

"I see ... you're a bit dressed up for the tip aren't ya? You're not some snoop are ya'?" said the man eyeing him off.

"Snoop? No, I like to look sharp even in dumps like this," smiled Milton.

"Hey, you two, hope you're not annoying anyone," said Robin, waving to Mothman.

"They're being good," said Mothman, waving Robin off and crouching down to Milton's height.

"So boy, whatcha throwing out today?"

Milton shrugged, "old bikes and crap."

"Bikes ... hmm ... what about toys huh? Records, stamps, dolls, brooches, glasses, jewellery, watches, cameras, old books and maps, clocks, old stuff your grandparents used to play with?" he said as his hunched back extended out over the van's tray peeling back the blue tarpaulin with his pinching bony fingers.

"Not today but last week we threw out some real old stuff my granddad gave me, mostly boring stamps, few clocks and a box of my grandma's dolls she had as a kid. I don't need them."

"Really? boring stamps you say? Grandmother's dolls?"

"Yeah, way over there, near Tyre Mountain."

"Stamps! You crazy kids know nothin! Let's hope the gulls ain't shat all over them!" said Mothman, and in giant stilt steps he raced off.

"Milton. That wasn't very nice, funny, but not nice," said Evelin.

"You're supposed to find the treasure, not ask for it."

He returned to Robin and left Evelin, who seemed to be in her own world, shortly after she began firing marbles in all directions with her slingshot. If only I could do this all day, she thought. One after another, she smiled as the marbles flew through the air to be either silently engulfed by the rubbish or exploded shattering pottery or the face of an old T.V. "Oy! Enough of that!" said Robin, shaking his head and followed by a smile.

When the marbles had run out, and a cool breeze picked up, she decided it was time to sit back inside and listen to the radio.

"Okay coast is clear for miles, we're going back inside," she yawned out loud and awkwardly climbed into the ladder.

Milton stood underneath, his hands out ready to catch her.

"What are you doing Milton?"

"I saw you yawning and I ... ah ... I thought you might fall?"

"Ah ... okay." Evelin smiled graciously and swung open the passenger door, climbed inside the cabin and wound up the window waving to Milton to go away with a flicker of her fingers.

It wasn't long before her watch alarm had gone off and she was going through her usual routine, counting out two pills, swallowing the tiny shapes and sipping a mouthful of bottled water, scrunching up her nose and shaking her head.

About fifty metres ahead she noticed Robin tugging at a large clear shielding in the distance.

Part of a boat? Or the canopy of a plane? she thought.

Robin waved Milton over, and she watched them pull the structure from the wreckage. She imagined it was from a plane, one that crashed into the towering mountain of rubbish eventually finding its way to the bottom of the rubbish pile.

Yellow Tree's very own Bermuda Triangle, she thought. After several lengthy blinks she leaned back and watched through squinted eyes, the seagulls that circled in the sky, then she languidly gazed at the smoke that poured from the furnace chimney towards the clouds that had turned dark grey. *Looks like a storm is coming?* she thought and closed her eyes. It could have been minutes or hours, but eventually she found herself back inside a familiar dream.

"Why hello again," said a voice.

Evelin recognised it instantly and turned to see the white-suited man sitting on a grey seat of cloud with his top hat in his hands. He glanced up under his fringe that was usually slicked back and gave a saddened smile.

"Weatherman!" she said, kneeling down to him. "How are you? You look upset. What's wrong? It's rather stormy up here. Did you do this?"

"Do I have to answer all of those questions? Or can I just choose one?"

"None if you like?" she said putting her hand on his shoulder.

"No I didn't do this, although at the same time I did."

"What do you mean?" she asked.

"I've made a mistake and not a common one either."

"A mistake?"

"I don't want to go into it ... but I would like to get out of it, I have a feeling I might lose my job."

"Lose your job? But you're the Weatherman? What happened?"

"Well, if you must know, I took yesterday off and left someone else in charge, I don't know if you noticed how nice it was yesterday?"

"I did actually; it was a perfect day. What's wrong with that?"

"Only that I didn't do it. Nor would I."

"Oh ... why not?"

"I don't think you seem to understand."

"No, I don't think I do," said Evelin.

"Look what you're sitting on."

Evelin looked down at the grey swirling clouds that seemed to be getting thicker and darker as they spoke.

"Oh, I think I see, the nice day is the calm before—"

"The storm," said the Weatherman as he stood up. "It's not just bad news for those down there; it's bad news for us up here as well."

"Who would want this?"

"The Eels, it's when they come out to play," said the Weatherman as his moustache curled up towards his nose.

"The eels?" she said confusedly.

The Weatherman looked down at his feet and lifted one up off the cloud below. "You don't want to be up here much longer; they'll be here soon."

Evelin began to look around for the eels as the clouds got denser and denser, darker and darker. "Should I go? What about you?"

"Oh, course you should, or could, or can," he said looking upwards.

It was at that moment Evelin looked up and saw the great swirling ocean above. Then from behind the Weatherman a bolt of lightning flashed as bright as day and a giant crack of thunder exploded beneath them. Instantly Evelin woke up with a jolt.

"Look who's joined us in the land of the living," smirked Milton.

Evelin's ears caught the sound of the truck grinding it' s gears up towards Edinburgh Street as heavy sheet rain started to hit the windshield.

"Quick inside Eve it's going to pour down any second," said Robin, pulling into the driveway and parking the truck.

"I'll catch you guys later, my shirts are on the line!" said Milton darting off across the road.

Evelin stared up at the thick wall of cloud as it engulfed the last of the blue sky and lightning flashed in the distance.

The eels are out...

O ver the course of the next few days, a dark and pendulous murmur could be heard amongst the citizens of Mare-Marie. The looming and whispered battle against the dark witch spread a gripping fear and the course of action was to be a tentative one. Belleny and Bateau stood quietly by the excited Orphans, surround by the vast expanse of the castle courtyard. They were waiting at the proposed meeting place for those few brave volunteers who had planned to go north, but the turn-out was dire, not a single volunteer showed up.

King Vera approached and with each step his head seemed to droop lower and lower to the ground. With a dispirited sigh, he slowly looked up and said, "I fear that both the Royal Comity and the small army that's left of Mare-Marie have spoken, they refuse to fight a witch. I cannot conscript them, none have returned in the past. What shall I do?"

"So be it, we go on our own then," said Dillon.

"We're not alone," said Palia as she pointed to the sky. Garon the Quick circled and wheeled in the air overhead.

King Vera waved up at Garon and all eyes watched as the circling black figure descended to the ground in an effortless spiral. It wasn't long before he was clearly visible and with talons outstretched, he clawed the ground for a safe landing. Astride the towering bird, a figure held on, shrouded in a warriors outfit as inky as Garon's feathers.

Garon turned towards the gatekeepers at the far castle drawbridge and sung out a long sharp whistle. All eyes watched as it began to open and slowly revealed a silhouette of a colossal creature on all fours.

"King Vera why so glum," said Garon, "for here comes my comrades."

"You're not letting that creature in here are you?" questioned Belleny. Anxiously she grabbed Bateau and hid behind Agarus.

"Of course, that is our good friend Raveene the Verill and its rider, Danté," said Garon.

Bateau looked to the top of Raveene as a flock of small birds scuttled above and returned perched along its mountainous body.

Belleny watched in bewildered awe, the gigantic creature lumbered forward and stopped only a few feet from them. High on its back, the rider Danté gave it a short pat and threw its reins to the side. As the beast knelt it lowered its enormous head towards them and the long slender figure, Danté, launched into the air and landed low on the ground. Silently and slowly he rose before them as if pulled up by invisible strings. Belleny noticed his long pointy black boots first and admired their ornate and delicate leather work, with mystical swirling patterns that wound up and around his long slender legs and covered his knees.

He looks like a warlock? questioned Belleny. *Father will not be pleased.*

She tried to get a glimpse of his face, but it was concealed behind a high collar and headgear that only revealed his deeply shadowed eyes. Although completely hidden she was impressed with his outfit. It covered his body, head to toe in a layered mix of mystical black woven fabric and cross-quilted leather armour. Only his long, pale, bony ringed fingers could be seen dangling by his side.

"Thank you for coming my friends," said the King, "I'm afraid no one else has volunteered. With Garon joining you, I need at least my second in command, Vanja DeQuin, to stay and take his place. We are not an army built for battle, our forces are mostly for defence and protection."

"We understand, Vanja will be as vigilant and forceful as I, if it is needed," said Garon. "You can't blame them, it takes a brave step forward to face the unknown, let alone a sorceress in the treacherous north."

"Yes, what is it princess?" asked Raveene.

"Nothing! I mean what, what are you, a Verill?" asked Belleny, hidden under the brim of her hat.

Without turning its head, the creature's ears flicked and it's giant moist black eyes focused on her. "Yes Verill, born in the golden sands of Royalin," said Raveene in a monstrous, abrasive tone, his breath as dry and hot as the sands he was delivered in.

Garon added, "You may venture there one day Princess, hot it may be, but a beautiful place it is."

Raveene blocked out the sun as he leant in, his foreboding skull frightened Belleny to the point she could not move. He sniffed back with his raw wet snout and said, "No Garon. Royalin was beautiful ... once, but as the North spreads its poisonous death, it won't be long before it's golden sands turn black and kill everything in it."

"I'm so sorry Raveene," stammered Belleny looking into the infinite depths of the creature's jaws. She could see right into his engulfing bite where flecks of golden sand lined his throat.

"And if there's anyone that hates black sand, it's me," said the mysterious thin figure that rode Raveene.

Garon outstretched his wings and said, "Princess, King Vera and friends, may I introduce Danté Vakares, I wouldn't be going on this mission without him. He is one of only a few living beings who resides in the ghost town of Kay Kasa. He will see us through to the nearby Valley of Illusion safely enough."

"It is the least I can do," spoke Danté from behind his veil in a calm and reassuring voice, "plus a short break from the valley will do me good."

Garon turned his beak up to face the silent rider upon his back, "And last but not least is Kale Saalen."

Kale politely tipped his peak, and like Danté he wore a dark suit of leather from head to toe, his face masked behind a devilish horned and adorned peaked hood. A velveteen cape draped over his frame and wrapped around him, his body hidden completely.

"Kale lives beyond the valley in the Temple of Thought, well known for its height, which has views far out over the north. He's witnessed society slip from bad to worse and feels it won't be long before the temple is taken over by the darkness in the nearby forests. We can not allow this to happen," stressed Garon.

"Thank you Kale, all of you," said King Vera, "the witch must be stopped. I want her head for what she's done!"

Kale cleared his throat and stared at King Vera in silence. An awkward pause fell over them.

"Father," said Belleny.

"Fine, not just her head, on her body too. But she will be punished for her ways!"

"And what ways are they?" defensively snapped Kale, "magic ways?"

"Of course! We wouldn't be in this mess if it weren't for magic," growled the red-faced King.

Danté quickly stepped in.

"We'll do our best, but don't forget she's not the witch you once knew," said Danté as he unlatched the hard leathery face plate from his headgear. From underneath, he gave a sharp tooth grin. Belleny had seen many a strange character at the castle ball's but never the likes of Danté Vakares. Even with his face coated in black dust, like his feet, she imagined he was like few in Mare-Marie.

"Garon informed us of your friends and the wicked curse you have endured, I also know of such a vice. I commend you Bateau for your encouragement and of course Princess Belleny for your courage."

Danté turned towards the Orphans, "It is my pleasure to be riding along side you, am I right in presuming you are the famous Gonzo Circus's White Knights? You are hardly mistakable my friends."

"Of course, the White Knights? Yes, that was your name on the wanted posters!" said Bateau.

"This would be correct," said Dillon.

"White Knights?" said Belleny.

"A mere stage name Princess, you can still call us the Orphans if you wish?" said Palia.

"A stage name? Hardly!" said Danté, "your acrobats were more than well known for their abilities."

"Abilities?" questioned Belleny.

"Yes, our act would require us to confront large guests that Gonzo would find wandering in the Gaze Akarr, teamwork is our speciality," said Dillon.

"Confront indeed!" added Danté and knelt down before the Princess, "to have finally met the actual Princess of Mare-Marie, the hidden gem within the infamous Vera family," he continued as he peeked up and winked, "Princess Belleny Vera it is with a great honour, I never imagined you would look so radiant for someone who has been concealed from the sun for so many years." Danté paused and shuffled through a small satchel, "Kindly accept this humble gift, please disregard its flaws as I carved it on the journey here. Raveene may look as steady as a rock, but he sways about like a boat at sea."

Belleny reached out and accepted his gift, "you are too kind." She inspected the small carved object; a hand with a snake that wound itself around each finger.

"Oh my, how did you do this? It's beautiful," she said showing Bateau.

"I'm quite one with the blade. It is the hand of courage, grasping the serpent of fear, just as you have done."

"Let me see that, hmm, for a second I thought it was glowing?" said the King.

"The sun will play the best of tricks," added Danté with another hidden wink towards Belleny.

But Belleny was deep in thought about her fear and pictured it as a serpent, and how it once ruled her. She tightened her fist around the amulet and said, "Fear! I now feel nothing of the sort," she said calmly, "I could stay out here all night if I wished."

Garon returned to the Orphans, "Well if this is it, then this is it."

"I'm sure others will arrive later, it is still early, although it's strange not even the Graver twins have shown themselves?" said the King.

"They have until tomorrow noon," said Danté.

"Orphans, you will need armour to disguise yourselves, as my ghostly white friend Danté and Kale have," said Garon. "Where we are going, the land is a shade of black and you will stick out like the moon."

"Not to worry, it seems they were born prepared," said Belleny.

Dillon signalled the Orphans and together their fur coats shimmered and iridescent metallic sheen, changing and morphing from silky white fibres into charcoal black versions of themselves.

"Impressive!" clapped Danté.

"So are you white or are you black?" asked Garon.

"Good question," said Palia as she changed one of her wings to white and left the other black.

"You'll still need armour," said Kale bluntly, rising from his silence.

"Don't worry we can organise that, said King Vera. He approached Garon and questioned, "So what are you to do with Lucretia, do you have a plan?"

"Yes we have discussed it, although I'm sure Danté can provide a small example. Danté, the salt."

"Salt?" questioned King Vera.

Danté walked up to him and from his jacket pulled out a small leather pouch, "Have you by chance ever seen Scissor Salt before?"

"Scissor Salt? No, I've never heard of it? Don't tell me you're going to cook the witch?"

"More or less," said Danté. His dark red lips turned up into a crooked smile revealing his sharp whitish-blue teeth.

"Depends on if she's even a witch anymore," said Garon.

"How's salt going to do anything? Is she allergic to it?" asked Dillon.

Danté opened a pouch and poured the white shard-like grains into his glove, they glistened against the dark brown leather. He knelt down beside a flourishing flower bed and returned with a large maroon snail upon the edge of his black blade.

"Now watch and learn," he said as he spread the salt across his palm and nudged the snail across with his blade. Instantly the snail convulsed and recoiled back inside its shell, as expanding bubbles frothed from underneath. As if being cooked the shell turned white before their eyes and the snail began to wail a high pitch scream that all could hear. Then it stopped. Between thumb and forefinger, Danté held up the shell before the others and poured out the powdery remains of the once slimy snail, "And this is how you remove a witch from its home."

"That poor snail!" said Belleny.

"I apologise my princess but come moonlight he would have removed every last one of these royal orchids, a nasty pest in all parts of Mare-Marie," said Danté.

"Impressive," said Bateau.

The King gasped, "Scissor Salt, well I never! For all I know, I could've been sprinkling it on my dinner."

"I guess you're not a witch," said Danté.

"Although she didn't have snail-like skin when we last saw her?" said Agarus, "She was quite beautiful."

"A sorceress has many an appearance, but the salt will reveal her true form or even destroy it," noted Kale.

Danté swung high up top of Raveene, "The salt is being prepared and will be delivered here tonight. We shall saddle up and leave by noon tomorrow.

"Very well, drop your gear off at the gates and I will send for the maid to show you your quarters, you shall feast and drink with me tonight."

The voyagers took off towards the gates of the Queens Gardens as the Orphans played about in the courtyard as if the journey was a walk in the park.

"They have no idea do they? What are you thinking about Vera?" asked Belleny, observing him stroke his beard.

"Yes I hope they'll be all right. Hopefully Garon can talk with Lucretia, or they can come to some reasoning."

"I'm worried about the Orphans, they're going beyond the Slate Cliffs, to stop a witch, she may put up a fight."

"The White Knights sound like they can handle the situation on their own," he turned back to the Orphans and shouted, "Orphans! Come with me to the armoury, we'll have you suited up by the end of the day."

Belleny waved goodbye, "I will leave you to it, Bateau and I are going to retire, all this daylight is making me light headed."

"Are you all right?" asked King Vera peering under the brim of her hat. She looked as sad as she always had.

"I know the Orphans have had a recent metamorphosis, but look how happy they are. Underneath they are still the Orphans. You can find out all about them when they return. Go lie down, I'll have Jodin bring you both something to eat."

"If they return," she whispered quietly and slowly walked off.

King Vera unlatched a large brass bolt, pulled open a ten foot wooden door and led the Orphans into the armoury. The building in its history had been used as a grain silo and over the centuries, the cement rendering had faded into a smooth white shell with small arched windows peppered on the facade that only a cat could squeeze through. As they entered into the darkness, the light of the lanterns danced and bounced over the metal-work, carved white alphena shell weapons and ornate armour that hung on the interior walls.

"Help yourselves my friends, I'm not sure what you need. However, you're welcome to test the items out. You don't want to upset Kale. The Rast armour is made from the finest leathers and plated with the hardest of shell, you'll find it over there," said King Vera.

"You're very kind, thank you King Vera," said Palia.

"You're welcome and thank you for being by Belleny's side all these years, even if you were under a curse, you still loved and protected my daughter, I consider you family."

King Vera left the Orphans and they spent the rest of the afternoon until nightfall preparing themselves for the long journey ahead. They were like kids playing dress up and choosing the right armour was like a game. Never had they been so excited.

The following morning the corrosive Scissor Salt had been delivered and lay in a pile, far away from the Queen's Garden as requested by the Princess. The Orphans woke early and after suiting up in their battle regalia went off t find the salt pile. Garon and his troop had already prepared themselves and were studying a topography map with the King and discussing last night's plans. Salt poured from the large leather saddlebags on either side of Raveene. Garon wore the salt in small suede pouches, tied like water bombs around his waist and ankles and Danté and Kale fastened tiny bags of salt behind arrowheads to act as a poisoned tipped dart, as when fired, they were hoping to get the salt shards deep into the witch's heart.

The Orphans arrived solemnly, their fur was now black and they were armoured from head to toe and behind them, Agarus wore a saddle and Montë sat high upon him like a noble rider. When they arrived, they needn't say any more than good morning and Garon greeted the Orphans with a confident nod. They also got a nod of approval from Kale, and Danté signalled them to the remaining bags of salt.

Small leather satchels of all shapes and sizes leant against each other. Two large bags were placed either side of Agarus and although they were heavy, it was nothing for him to carry in his renewed body. Kale held on tight as Garon rose tall from his crouched position and announced, "If you are ready, we best be off White Knights. We've decided we can't wait until noon, as time is of the essence. If we leave later, we won't reach the Temple till night and we can't have that. If any more are to join us the King knows our route and they can always meet us along the way."

"Garon is right, it should take us six suns to reach the Slate Cliffs, and we will be out of the Royal Kingdom. Hopefully we'll reach the safety of the temple by final sundown. There is nowhere safe to wander at night beyond the cliffs," said Danté.

"We are ready," said Dillon.

"What about the Princess? Should we not say goodbye?" said Palia.

"I don't think I can," said Montë, "it would be too sad."

"Up there," pointed Garon, "she's been watching us from her balcony all morning. She looks quite sad indeed. I don't think she can bear to see you go either."

The Orphans squinted up at the Princess's tower, unable to see as far or as clear as Garon, but they could see her long white silk scarf as it flowed over the balcony.

With heartfelt waves, they said their goodbyes from a distance and watched as the scarf drifted off gracefully, flowing over the giant hedge and into the Queen's Gardens.

"Let us go my friends," said Garon looking away from the balcony, "she has gone now and so should we. Look after yourself King Vera and take care of our Princess."

The voyagers began their journey through the Queen's Gardens. As Raveene was too big to fit through the gates, and would destroy half the plants, he climbed along the towering hedge wall and graced along it as if a cat on the edge of a fence. The Orphans were amazed by such a sight and never imagined the hedge could hold his weight, it was truly a structure of immense power and magic.

The garden seemed to be carved from pure imagination and manifested into physical form. Nowhere else grew plant life like here, it was if it belonged underwater or born on another planet. The plants moved ever so gently as if welcoming them, changing colour with the morning light, and even flowering or revealing themselves as they approached.

"Look up there Montë, hold on tight," said Agarus as he stood tall and towered over the others like a giant lizard of the past. Montë reached forward and grabbed Belleny's fallen scarf from the branch of a spiralling tree. He realised it was the one she had tied them together with, on their very first outing. He folded it up neatly and placed it inside his pack.

"She will always be with us," he said.

"Yes, always," said Agarus.

"We are not the only ones who have changed and by the time we return I feel she will be a completely new person," said Montë.

They watched as Palia took to the sky. She felt as if her wings were those of angels and she flew straight up as high as she could. The Orphans and Kale, who rode sternly upon Garon looked up and watched in awe as she flashed her feathers white, beaming in the sunlight and descending in spirals and then back again, soaring through the sky like the acrobat she was. Below in the myriad of colours and shapes of fauna she noticed the watery path dividing the enormous garden in half, and continued, flowing off into the far distance, *Ahh the beautiful Veelin River, the lifeline of Mare-Marie,* she thought as a wave of happiness rolled through her.

After circling the garden, she descended, swooping past Raveene as fast as lightning and returning to the group in complete elegance as if it was the ending to her perfect routine.

At the end of the Queen's Gardens, Garon lowered Kale to the ground while Raveene watched the activity from above, turning his enormous head and slowly frowned as he stared out into the distance. The Orphans could only imagine what lay on the other side now and their excitement grew with every heartbeat. Before them a similar metal gate to the entrance stood shut, but this one was solid, yet by their feet it stopped short and let the stream continue to flow underneath to the other side. Kale held its handles and turned back to the Orphans.

"White Knights welcome back to Mare-Marie," he said and pulled the doors wide open before them.

Garon stood to one side as Danté held out his hand and ushered them through. Dillon raced by with Agarus and Monté close behind. Stepping through those gates was like diving into a cool pool on a fiery hot day. It was now the Orphans knew how free they really were and the adventure before them, they wanted to run like children and roll down the blue, grassy hillside and toss themselves weightlessly into the brilliant yellow Canola field flowers. The Orphans ran as fast as they could, never had they felt the muscles in their legs and their hearts beat so wildly. With joyous laughter they cheered and the further they ran the higher the blue grass grew, taller and taller until Agarus wound through like a serpent of the wind and only Monté could be seen high up on his back.

Eventually, they came to a break in the field and Mare-Marie unfolded even further before them. Palia swooped through the blades and in a gush of wind settled beside them on the crest of the hill.

"If only Belleny could see this," said Dillon.

"It's truly beautiful," said Palia.

"We must bring her here on our return," said Monté.

"That is a good thought to take with me," said Dillon.

The group reunited and embarked on their quest in a stoic manner. They trekked high up into the clouded mountain tops, travelling for stretches that lasted from dusk to dawn, Kale always pushing them to move at a constant pace and when they tired took turns riding upon Raveene, Agarus and even Palia took Danté on a short flight.

It was a little trickle of a stream of water which had now widened into the beautiful flowing Veelin River was way their true guide on the route. Dillon looked back and a heartfelt memory of the Princess alone in her room remained. The castle, although once so prominent in the skyline was now nowhere to be seen, hidden far beyond the horizon and their new horizon was constantly changing.

Today the sun hovered above like a heat lamp. It felt as if it beamed down in a single stream. The Orphans absorbed it the best they could and stuck to the shade of the trees at any chance. Even Garon was hot and exhausted, his black feathers had warmed up and he felt his body drained with each and every step.

"Kale I suggest we take a short break in the shade ahead," said Danté, "I'm starting to smell Garon being cooked alive and it's making me hungry."

Garon gave a light grunting chuckle, although Kale did not answer.

"Kale are you alright up there?" said Garon, giving him a nudge.

Deep in a trance, he woke unsettled, "Garon? What's going on? Is there a problem?" he said, sitting up straight and reaching for his blade.

"Everything is fine. Sorry to wake you but we have to stop, the sun's got bite and we need to drink and bathe while the water is still clean."

"Yes, of course, I'm sorry, I was miles away."

"Is everything alright?" asked Garon.

"Between you and me, I don't think it is. But rest up we'll need more than our strength beyond the Slate Cliffs."

The adventurers set camp in a quiet gully beside the river. The shade of an arching Welloa tree gave instant relief and was mesmerising as its pale green umbrella-shaped leaves spun weightlessly to the ground.

"How are you going Agarus? I guess this is the heat Belleny always warned us about or did we warn her?" said Monté.

"I think we persuaded each other, looks like we haven't burnt to a crisp as we once thought we would."

"It's alright once you get used to it. That river looks inviting though," said Monté dropping his bags.

"Sure does, it makes you laugh at the things we once said to each other, although it wasn't that funny."

"No. We've gone so far, it's been nearly a week. I hope she is okay, I miss her terribly."

Palia listened on as she dipped herself into the water and gracefully spread out her wings, "Belleny is on all our minds, but I am confident Bateau will keep her company. I just know she'll be a different person when we return, you could see the change in her even after a few days and it was her energy that was radiant."

"We have to keep moving soon," said Kale. "Fill all your water bottles as you won't find water as clean as this from here on. The land it flows over in the north is ill."

"Listen? What's that beautiful sound?" said Montë.

"Song Reeds," said Garon diving into the water. He rose pointing at the long, thin plants along the river's edge. Their tops waved in an explosion of wispy blonde hair.

Garon pulled one down towards them, "As a flute, they grow hollow and under each leaf is a hole that plays a note when the wind blows. With the right breeze, you could be fooled a band was hiding within them."

And now as the light breeze pressed on an off against the leaves, they sang a soft and enchanting melody, as they waved their golden tops from side to side.

"Hmm, I don't like whistling tunes anymore," grumbled Dillon, "they remind me of Lucretia."

Agarus weaved out of the water and up onto the embankment. He leant up against his saddlebags like pillows and laid back soaking up the sun. It was then that he felt the salt in the bags move against him, possibly even kick the back of his head, and he swore he heard the bags yelp as he tried to make them more comfortable.

But it was when Montë returned, he noticed Agarus staring at the bags and holding up his finger to be quiet, they both looked on perplexed. The salt bags twitched by themselves and when he caught Garon's eye, he signalled him over. Garon approached dripping wet, tall and inquisitive as the water drained from him.

At the sight of the bag twitching, Garon moved in, "Hold it right there! Show yourself!" he shouted. "Sabotaging our salt!"

"No wait!" shouted a muffled voice.

Danté ripped the bag open and grabbed horid little beast by a leg.

"Let go of me!" It demanded and kicked free from his grip. "I can get out myself," it growled.

"Witch's spawn, we should tie you up and throw you in the river," snarled Dillon.

From within the salt bag, the beast began to crawl out backwards. They watched as a wild and evil looking creature looked up at them snarling on its hands and knees. Instantly Garon slammed it down into the dirt with his claw.

"Don't even think about it!" he said, reaching down and flinging its knife to the side.

"Please you're crushing me, just let me wash this awful stuff off," It said.

"You're not going anywhere without answers!" said Garon caging it down face first within the grips of his giant claws.

"I demand you to let me go at once!" It wriggled violently in the mud.

"Yes, please Garon you're standing on my favourite tail," said another voice as a dark grey tail poked out through the bag then another.

"Bateau? What are you—" said Garon lifting his claws off at once and pinching him out onto the embankment.

"Thanks, Garon, you better let that one go too," said Bateau brushing the salt off.

"Bateau! What are you doing here? Who is this beast you stowed away with?"

Bateau looked up at the others and squinted with a light grin.

"Garon your anger has clearly blinded you. You probably shouldn't squeeze that beast too hard, her father will be even more upset if you disembowel her," said Kale, who hadn't moved from the trunk of the tree and sat back casually.

"Who's father? Do you know this beast? Who is—oh no, no, no, no!" Garon quickly removed his claws and the creature stood up and took off its mask by unbuckling a latch hidden under its scraggly mane. The mask dropped to the ground and revealed a dirty, wild-haired waif who resembled their Princess Belleny.

"Belleny!?" sung the Orphans as they helped her up.

Garon unimpressed rose towering over them, his wings out wide in a violent mixture of rage and worry. "My Marie! Oh no! How could you do this? You have jeopardized the whole mission! King Vera will hang me for sure, stew me with carrots and beets," he dropped to his knees and placed his feathered hands across his eyes. "Someone tell me this is all a dream? I have heat stroke, yes that's it, heat stroke."

Slowly he removed a feathered finger one at a time.

"Oh no! How could you let her do such a thing?" Garon roared down on Bateau.

"She's a Princess, I can't tell her what to do, no one can," he said hiding behind Dillon.

"We've been travelling for five and a half days, how you managed to hide this long is beyond me. What did you eat? Where did you sleep? Wait ... who else knew?" said Garon, eyeing off the Orphans viciously and then Danté.

Danté shrugged, "Not me."

Belleny looked up, "No one, well possibly my maid Jodin."

"So that's who we waved goodbye to?" said Agarus.

"Yes. Thanks for saying all those nice things about me. We got out at night, I brought supplies and slept most of the day, as I do, it's quite surprising how comfortable a few silk sheets sewn into a sack can be, besides the remaining salt."

"You hopped out at night! I'm going to faint," said Garon, who was clearly about to.

Kale pulled down the tip of his hood, "Don't worry Garon, I had an eye on her."

It was then that Garon twisted around and stared down at Kale as if he could eat him there and then, "You knew?!"

Danté grinned but was as surprised as Garon.

"Of course, that's why I was on watch ... every night."

"But why? What have you to gain? She's practically never been outside before, she's not coming with us to the north!"

"Of course she is," he said and he stood up slowly and stretching "we best be off soon, looks like rain is coming."

"No, no, no, she is not my cloaked friend," frowned Garon.

Danté stepped in and said calmly, "And why is she coming, may I ask? Not that I mind, I'm just curious."

"Arrgh you're as bad as each other," cried Garon as feathers fell from his shaking fists.

"She's going to kill the witch. She may even save her from herself. One or the other. I've seen it happen, several versions actually ... in my visions, ultimately it's up to her," said Kale.

There was something about Garon's wild raven laughter that made the others question his mental condition and once he stopped, he shook his head and said, "You're telling me you let the King's one and only daughter, the one who's lived more days inside than out, who knows nothing of the outside world ... let alone killing, stow away because you had a dream she destroys, no possibly saves the poisonous witch that threatens to destroy her kingdom and everyone in it?"

"Yes," he said calmly.

Garon let out a short, snorting huff, "Or you will turn back?" he added.

"That is correct, so too will Raveene and Danté I'm sure, possibly the White Knights?"

"I don't want to turn back," said Dillon, "the adventure has only just begun."

"Dillon, we have to think of the Princess's safety," said Palia.

"Thank you Palia, at least one of us has some sense," said Garon.

"But I'm sure we could all keep an eye on her, she's done quite well with just Kale's supervision. If she keeps her mask on, who would know?" added Palia.

"She's been hiding in a sack!" roared Garon.

Garon knew Kale had visions and many, if not all came true enough. As an informer, he had helped stop many from threatening the kingdom, but ultimately Kale was the one who knew weeks beforehand when the Slate Cliffs would rise and divide the North from the South. Giving Garon time to warn many ... although, unfortunately, some wouldn't listen and died as the land tore apart. He knew he had to listen to Kale but knew the King would never understand.

Garon knelt down and looked at Belleny, "So my Princess what is your decision? Do you feel you're ready to kill this witch Lucretia with your bare hands?"

"I ... I don't know?" she said nervously.

"There is your answer," huffed Garon.

"Let her finish," said Kale.

Belleny stood back from Garon's temper and said, "Well of course not with my bare hands ... but together we could stop her. I wouldn't have come if I didn't think otherwise."

"Oh, I am sure. This is not a school play my dear. We're not using paper swords and masks, the creatures are real and their bite is real. And what do I tell your father? He will have my head! Even if you did slay this woman," said Garon.

"He will understand. I have my strengths Garon and I'm also superb with a slingshot," Belleny continued ignoring his snide laughter, "Father will never know I'm gone as long as Jodin pretends to be me, she's a magnificent impersonator, I've been teaching her for years. I need this as much as the Orphans, adventure is in my blood as it was for my mother," she said confidently.

Garon paused and shook his head, "You really are the Queen's daughter."

"We must make tracks, we have many more miles to gain today," said Kale.

"Wait. Let me think," said Garon. He sat on the water's edge and held his hands to his head. The reeds beside him sang a soft, sad melody and soothed his temper. He felt her approach alone but didn't turn around. After a moment, he spoke towards the river, "Belleny you have put yourself and Bateau in grave danger and what makes it worse I've never doubted Kale and his visions."

He turned and stood tall towering over her as the reeds played and the others looked on. Bateau came forward and sat by her side.

"The Mare-Marie Kingdom is a beautiful place and you deserve to see it like your mother would have always wanted, and who no better than this motley crew being by your side. Beyond the Slate Cliffs though is another story, you're right we can take you no further than the Temple of Thought where you will be safe and we can pick you up on our return ... unless you wish to continue, which I doubt you will. And if your father ever, I mean ever finds out ... you will all be at the bottom of the Pit of Nothingness before I'm clipped, boiled and thrown head-first inside."

"Thank you, Garon," said Belleny squeezing him tight, "I will always be in disguise and never in your way, isn't that right Bateau?"

"I'm staying in your backpack the whole way," said Bateau, who had slowly begun to levitate.

"You never know, the Princess may come in useful as bait or be used as a lure, was that in your vision Kale?" said Danté.

"Useful! As bait!? This is not a joking matter. I don't think you all realise how serious this is, she is all our responsibility now," Garon shook his fist and pointed down at them. "We're already delayed because of you two, Bateau go and wash that salt from out of your ears before it sends you deaf."

"I need to relax," said Garon as he flapped up onto a large pointy rock. With a wooden flute, he played a haunting tune into the sky. He played in harmony with the reeds.

"Welcome to the team," grinned the giant Raveene.

Belleny looked at Bateau nervously as Garon growled and stared down at them, "Go on you two, go and wash that salt off, I'm amazed you're not burning red. You have five minutes."

With her head down Belleny went to the water's edge and knelt behind the singing reeds.

"He's not as furious as I thought?" whispered Belleny.

"What?" said Bateau.

"Well, he didn't hit us."

"For a second there I thought he was going to peck my head off."

"I know," smiled Belleny.

"Why are you smiling?"

"I'm sorry I can't help it, I can't believe I'm outside Bateau, not just in the Queen's Gardens but really outside! Look at me," she said, staring at her reflection, "I'm free."

"How does that feel?" asked Bateau.

"Wild, exciting, scary and I feel really nauseous ... but alive."

"Let's hope we stay that way."

Garon played his flute and tapped his thick talons against the rock. He watched and waited for her to climb back into her outfit and place her mask back on.

"Where did you get that outfit Princess?"

"It's a costume I made a long time ago," he voice trailing off.

"Your imagination really got the better of you ... I doubt we'll see anything as wild as you Princess," said Danté.

Garon grunted, "You know very well we will."

"It needed some alterations, armour padding here and there, the fur and feathers are real though, I carved the teeth and claws from shell, quite sharp. I lined most of it with silk and chain-mail."

"Silk," said Danté.

"I am a still a Princess."

"Shh ... not out here you're not," said Garon.

Garon put away his flute and huffed silently, he turned to the others who were ready to go, "Well I hope you're all happy! Come on you two, you're lucky I wear this thing ... should put you back in the sacks," he said, kneeling down low and helping Belleny and Bateau onto his saddle.

"Are you ready?" he asked as his frame rose higher and higher.

"I better be."

By noon, the following day, an endless formation of strange luminous, cerulean blue clouds had taken over the sky. They seemed to move as if alive, morphing into one another and pushing steadily across a dark marine backdrop. The sun was developing into an eerie glowing orb that hung behind the floating cloud masses, its silver rays illuminating shards of geometric light for the travellers. Belleny had never seen anything like this great vastness of the sky, nor had her companions, and this was one of the unpredictable and beautiful wonders of Mare-Marie. The group watched in bewilderment as the clouds chugged along like a giant jellyfish, quietly filling the sky and bobbing along in a strange parallel ocean high above. Some clouds drifted low enough for Palia to fly alongside and through, and she danced in the air with the swirling winds that headed west towards the Sea of Sorrow. Her gaze drifted down as she approached a valley with thousands of shimmering pools that stemmed off elliptically into the distance.

It was here the voyagers continued their journey.

"The water looks as beautiful as the sky above," said Belleny as she trekked beside Garon. His giant claws stepping over and dodging each and every puddle.

"I guess," he muttered, "when they behave themselves."

Garon stared into one with a dark frown and turned away with a huff.

"What do you mean? Behave themselves?" she asked.

"Nothing," he replied and continued on at the same pace. Belleny stopped puzzled and watched as the giant bird walked off. The others were close behind and for as far as she could see there was nothing in all directions but them. Quickly she caught up to Garon as the wide open emptiness gave her the chills.

"Garon?" she said.

"Mmm, what is it? You want to return home?" he said, knowing full well she didn't. He peered down at her with one eye.

Behind her mask, Belleny held a soured expression, "Of course not, you know nothing, once I make a decision, my decision is final."

"The whole kingdom knows about your decisions," said Garon as he stepped over a puddle as if it were a trap, "what is it then?" he groaned.

"Are they rain clouds? They don't look like rain clouds," she asked.

"No?" he said firmly then pointed down at a puddle, "they're not from the sky."

"What do you mean, not from the sky?"

"I mean they're not rain clouds, and this is not water."

"Of course it's water! You can't fool me with such a ridiculous notion. I suppose then you're not wet?" Belleny jumped feet first into a puddle splashing Garon's giant dusty talons. He let out a slight groan, paused and waited for the others to catch up.

"Coming down!" called Bateau as he leapt off Garon and landed beside Belleny.

"Be careful Bateau," she said. "I don't think Garon wants to carry you the entire way."

Garon leant down close and grunted, "That goes for both of you."

"Understood, it's just these puddles are making me thirsty," said Bateau and he began to drink from the nearest pool.

Instantly Garon stomped his claws into the puddle, splashing Bateau and Belleny. "I wouldn't drink from the pool, they're not as pure and clear as they seem."

"Garon that's not funny! I'm wet now!" spat Belleny.

"You'll dry."

"He's not wrong!" retorted Bateau. "Tastes worse than the slop in the circus troughs."

"Oh Bateau, here drink this," said Belleny, handing him her flask.

"Thanks, I don't think it is rainwater Princess," said Bateau.

"Really?"

"Of course it's not," grumbled Garon, "don't you two listen to anything I say?"

"Of course we do, but Garon's right Bateau, you don't want to be coughing up black slime like the poor Orphans did, do you?"

Garon halted mid-step, "What black slime? When was this?"

"In the Queen's Gardens, they were terribly ill. An awful black liquid came out of their mouths. Montë and Dillon collapsed straight in the water; it was terrible and disturbing, I thought they were dying."

"But they seemed alright in the pergola? A little unwell, but then they often did, before they were cured."

Garon rubbed his feathered chin, "The blackness may have been the curse itself, the poison that lived deep inside them. The Veelin River might have cleansed them, even the mist around it has healing properties, that's probably why Kale and Danté insist we stick to it," said Garon.

"It was awful, only a curse could look so vile, it bubbled like black, but then it disappeared," said Bateau.

"I've seen a similar rot in others, I must warn you many more have this beyond the Slate Cliffs, the Orphans are not the only ones with such a curse."

"No! Others ... that witch!" said Belleny.

"Too many to count. Not all are as strong as the Orphans though. Hundreds of smaller creatures lie dead in sticky black pools. The bad news is that they are now showing up inside the kingdom, I've found a dozen this month, even pulled some from the Veelin River, but some are just too heavy, so I had to cut off parts of their—"

"Garon you can stop now, you're frightening her," said Bateau noticing Belleny holding herself in a silent quiver.

"Apologies my Princess, sometimes I forget who I'm talking to with that horrid outfit on."

Belleny composed herself and said, "It's fine, I can handle your outside stories, I've heard them all before and then some. Fables if you ask me and I've probably made most of them up."

Garon began to scoff, "You know nothing."

"I know more than you think I do, of course, I'm not blind, one look at Raveene and I can imagine what's out there."

"Be happy he's on our side ... we're going to need him."

"Actually he's a lot cuter than I first thought."

"Cute! You were scared stiff! Oh, Belleny you truly have no idea, don't let him hear that he'll crush you in half with one bite," said Garon, leaning in close. "Don't worry, you'll be scared, it's only a matter of time once we cross the Slate Cliffs, then you'll be begging me to turn back, then what? A wasted mission."

"Then what? Then you'll come to my rescue, I am a Princess aren't I?"

"Not out here! Just keep your mask on and your head low, who knows where the witch's spies are lurking. In one of these pools? Maybe one is a pool? I wouldn't put it past her to curse even the water," said Garon as he clawed over one.

"Are you trying to scare me back home? It's not working, I'm not letting my fears decide a fate for me," she said and jumped feet first into several pools of water. "Well, those ones weren't spies Garon, only a million more to stomp in."

"They taste like spies," said Bateau. "There must have been a big storm, we're lucky we missed it."

"Storm! Like I told you before, there was never a storm, not today, not this month, or any before it," said Garon waving his wings about.

"Liar, it must have rained," said Belleny as she spun round and crossed her arms. "So they just appeared out of nowhere? Or is the ground leaking?"

"No, it's not leaking. The water around here never absorbs or comes up through the ground. It doesn't evaporate, it doesn't shift, not even in this heat. It's a strange place as any in Mare-Marie, I've never seen it rain here, the season here is ... fixed."

"Never ever?" said Bateau.

Garon shrugged, "Think yourself lucky Bateau, you'd be swimming if it did."

"Well, I don't swim," said Belleny. "I can paddle well enough in Castle Baths."

"Castle Baths? Paddle?" said Garon. "You better not jump into too many puddles then, who knows how deep they might be?" Then for goodness sake keep your distance from the river."

"Yes sir..."

Throughout the afternoon, the breeze had rippled the pools as if they shivered in the shadows of the luminous clouds. Garon noticed the wind drop first, a silence fell that was unnatural. He turned back and pointed to the side and nodded.

Danté and Kale acknowledged him and he continued on.

"What was that all about?" asked Bateau.

"I'm not sure?" said Belleny. "Just informing each other I'm still here. Obviously I can't get lost, even if I tried."

Belleny could see the horizon beginning to move as the heat bent the ground into waves of unfocused land. The pools of water lay undisturbed and each looked as if they were made of solid mirror.

"Can I remove my mask? I'm going to faint in this thing, there's no one around," said Belleny.

"I guess so," said Garon looking back at the others, "would be good to see something other than that creepy mask of yours."

Belleny pulled off her mask, revealing a worn and weathered young teenager. "So hot outside, I knew it was awful in the sun," she said in the same detached tone as she felt before. She drank from her flask and spat out the water, "gross, it's full of sand."

"You'll be praying for it when we hit the caves."

"Caves? I'm not going into any caves!" she snapped.

"Then you can turn around and start walking the other way," groaned Garon.

Garon watched eagerly as she poured the rest of the water over her head and shook it through her hair. He turned back at Danté and Kale and winked as she checked herself in one of the pools.

"Oh no! The sun's destroyed me! I knew it! It's turned me into an old lady," she screamed.

"What are you talking about, you look okay, a little haggard but fine," said Bateau.

"Is this what you call a little haggard?" she said as she pointed at her head.

Belleny held her shaky hands to her face and to her relief felt her smooth and youthful skin. She looked back down and her reflection moved as she did, "That's entirely wrong!" she said.

"What's the matter?" asked Bateau. "I think the heat's got to her Garon."

Angrily she folded her arms, watching her reflection do the same thing. Puzzled she paused and so did her reflection. Then she jiggled about and paused in mid pose.

"Do still have salt in your pants?" asked Bateau.

"No! Yes ... probably. Look Bateau, who is that person in the water,? If that's me, it looks nothing like me!"

Raveene approached with thunderous steps and paused. He peered down into her pool of water with a giant toothed grin. His enormous head filled the sky's reflection behind her.

"Raveene you look the same ... scary," she said.

"Haha, an old lady," coughed Garon. "That's you all right, don't you worry about that."

She stared up at a laughing Garon, who had tears in his eyes, "What are you up to bird? What's this witchcraft!" she demanded and pointed at her reflection as the old version pointed back.

Danté came up alongside, "Don't listen to him, he's just jealous because he usually looks like a grumpy wet old seabird."

"I do not!" huffed Garon.

"Don't worry you're still a beautiful Princess. The reflections reveal how you are seen through the eyes of someone else, usually someone close by," said Danté.

"What do you mean? Someone else? Which fool sees me like this? I'll have them thrown in the Pit," Belleny looked back into the water. "I look at least thirty years older. I look like my mother."

"What are you complaining about then?" said Danté.

Belleny paused for a moment and said, "I guess I'm not, but—"

"The reflections are up to you to interpret. Maybe someone sees you've grown up in your boots, wiser in your ways."

"Maybe they see me as a grumpy old hag," she said.

"Ha! That too," chuckled Garon.

"Hey! How come you all look exactly the same?" asked Belleny pointing into Danté's reflection and Garon's nearby.

"Because it only works when you see yourself through someone else's eyes. When you see my reflection, there is no difference as they're through your own. I never see myself the same, today I'm nearly transparent ... quite peculiar," said Danté.

"Nearly transparent? Most interesting, I guess you don't show all your cards do you?" said Belleny.

"Kale must be invisible then," said Bateau.

"Quite the contrary, he mentioned he was made out of light itself," said Danté.

"Light? Incredible. So what do you see Garon?" asked Bateau.

"Me? I prefer not to look these days, it's usually the same ... a soldier, is a soldier, is a soldier," he grumbled.

"Oh, I see. Sorry. You are a good one at that."

At that moment, Garon stole a glance into a pool beside him and to his astonishment saw something he had never seen before. His reflection was glittering like a golden trophy as if he had been dipped in liquid gold. His eyes were giant red rubies and his armour was like new with silver embossing on an ornate and gilded mould. He looked down at Belleny and she smiled up at his glowing expression, "Still a soldier?" she asked and pulled her wild mask back upon her head.

"I can only imagine what the Orphans can see," said Danté as they all turned to watch the Orphans who were pointing and laughing in hysterics.

The voyagers continued along the flat planes noticing the further they walked the wider the river grew and its waters now moved with gusto.

"Forest ahead and it's huge," said Palia as she swooped down around the group.

"Finally some shade," said Belleny sitting back in Garon's saddle with her feet in the air. "Where are we now? What is this forest?" she asked.

"This is the beginning of the Veelin River and the start of the Woven Woods," replied Garon.

"The beginning? The beginning is the start my feathered friend," said Belleny.

"It begins when the Woven Woods begins to grow and hook, in this case."

"Hook?" said Belleny as she clawed her fingers together.

"Look here," said Danté. He knelt down and pointed at a row of small boot high plants poking through the soil.

"I can't see a thing from up here. Garon can you lower me, please?"

"Gladly," he said before kneeling down.

With an awkward plunge, she jumped, landing clumsily into a fall. Danté moved fast and with a quick grasp he held her body only inches from the ground.

"Steady there! You're still a Princess remember? We can't return you bruised and broken."

Belleny ignored them and wove her fingers through the plants, "They hook," she whispered.

From here she could see how each and every seedling leant low and hooked itself around the larger one in front, winding themselves around one another, forming a weave as the next in line did that to the next and so on.

Belleny tilted her head and looked up at the tier of twisted trees before her, rising high up into the far distance.

"So the whole forest is holding on to each other?" said Belleny.

"From the smallest to the tallest," replied Garon.

"Like a family ... I guess the little ones hold on the tightest?"

Garon nodded, "I don't know about that. But they trip me up like little brats."

"It gets very dark in there, they weave a dense formation," said Danté.

"I can see through the darkest shadows," said Belleny. "Is it darker than the Baroque Woods?"

"No, not that dark," he sighed looking at the ground.

"But then there is the Thorned Woods, always dark be it day or night," said Garon.

"Thorned Woods? Are you making that up bird? I didn't see that on my map," said Belleny.

"It was once the Yellow Tree Woods, but nothings yellow there anymore, nothing but shades of black."

"We're not going through it are we?" asked Belleny.

"Not even the wind goes through the Thorned Woods, but you never know, we might be," said Danté.

As the Woven Woods grew thicker and taller, it wasn't long before the sun, and the strange luminous clouds were out of sight. Palia took to the air before the trees could capture her, and the others went through the giant pathways paved between the leaning trunks. The Orphans at this time were deep in conversation with Bateau; they wanted to know more about Gonzo and the circus and they couldn't wait to see him again. Bateau, on the other hand, wished he felt the same.

"Don't worry Bateau," said Dillon. "I'm sure there's an explanation, he would never leave you or anyone on purpose. He's a good one, our Gonzo."

"He's right Bateau," said Agarus. "I'm sure you did nothing wrong and even if you did Gonzo wouldn't abandon you ... unless you did something really wrong ... you didn't did you?"

"No of course not! I don't think I did? What do you mean by really wrong?"

"Set a Horgon on fire?"

"Wobble him while he was on the flying fox?" said Dillon with a smile.

"Touch his wine?" said Agarus.

"No, nothing of the sort ... I just hang about mostly, I don't even have a real job there, other than floating by his side while he conducts the show ... although recently I just sat there. He knows fair well I can't float on command."

"I see, I doubt it's that, it's not in his nature to throw anyone out no matter what they do, the circus is full of casualties he's taken on," said Dillon.

"Don't I know it. No, he got that scowling Garivin to do his dirty work, I gave that low life something to remember before he shoved me into a sack and ditched me though," said Bateau.

"I think we need to find this Garivin character before you point any more tails at Gonzo, my friend," said Agarus peering right down at him.

"But Garivin does all the dirty jobs around the circus, and I mean dirty, he cleans up after the animals and some dirty work on the side. Gonzo always told me to keep clear of him," said Bateau.

"Hmm, Agarus is right, I don't like the sound of this Garivin at all," said Monté. "We'll get to the bottom of this Bateau don't you worry."

"Thanks, guys ... I hope you're right."

"What?" said Dillon looking on inquisitively.

"I ... I still can't believe you were once the Orphans, especially Palia."

"Yes I can imagine it's quite a shock, especially for the Princess. She has kept her distance from us. I feel like we're strangers to her now."

"In a way you are. Not only do you look different, your personalities are completely opposite. I think she just needs time to adjust. I can tell she misses the Orphans, which honestly I don't understand at all," said Bateau.

"Yes, well we're going to make sure we'll never be that pathetic again," said Dillon.

"Hey guys I'm going to climb up top and see where Palia is," said Monté.

"I'll race you, come on Bateau I'll take you up top," said Dillon as he leapt onto a horizontal trunk and pierced his claws into it.

"I'll be alright, there is a limit to my landing trick."

"Be careful Dillon this is not the Jungle Room," said Agarus.

Monté climbed up onto another trunk and stretched his back as the tree arched up into the sky. The trunks were as solid as rocks and wound themselves around like giant ropes.

"Go!" shouted Dillon and without any hesitation he took off. Bateau watched as Monté leapt forward with several bounces and caught up to Dillon in a flash. Like a tightrope walker, he held his hands out and effortlessly ran up the tree, both disappearing into the thick green canopy.

"We're nearly there!" Monté shouted down from above, hopping skilfully from limb to limb.

"I can see the ocean!" he called down again, but they were so high up that not a word could be heard by the travellers, although Agarus felt he could hear every word within.

"Dillon and Monté can see the sea," he shouted up front.

"The Sea of Sadness," grumbled Garon. "Tell them to get back down, we're here."

"Keep your head low Princess," said Garon as he stopped in his tracks.

"We're here? Why, what's happening?" she whispered, but Garon watched cautiously as Danté signalled them and continued on, disappearing into the thick green bushes up front. Silently they gathered. Raveene leant up against a giant trunk and scratched himself. The leaves fell like rain and the trunk swayed, opening up the canopy for a moment to reveal an enormous smooth stone wall in front of them.

"Did you see that?" said Belleny in a whisper. "I think we're here Bateau, at the edge of the kingdom."

Danté signalled everyone to continue waiting where they were. He took out his blade and went back towards the wall.

Garon knelt down. Holding his wing out to cease the Orphans and Raveene from moving any further.

"Tell me what's happening?" said Belleny.

"You have surpassed many, we have reached the edge of the kingdom, where only some have dreamt about," said Garon peering through the gaps between the trees.

"So it is the edge?" said Belleny nervously, reminded of how far away from home she was.

"The Slate Cliffs," said Garon moving his head from side to side. "It's from when Mare-Marie broke in half."

"I've been told about it, the stories of the land tearing apart and rising up to the clouds. I've seen it on my map, but it's no more than a line."

"A line that soars high and takes the north with it. The only entrance is where the cliff has been split by the river, we shall climb its stone stairway. Mare-Marie is surrounded by this impossible barrier, it would be easier to climb the Zale Mountains."

"The river split the cliff?"

"Water is stronger than any rock," said Garon.

"So it's true the sea is going to destroy the Zale Mountains?" said Belleny.

"Possibly ... one day."

"What's Danté doing?" asked Bateau.

"Talking," said Garon.

"Talking to who?" said Belleny.

"Didn't I tell you two to be quiet?"

Silently they waited and it wasn't long before Danté returned, this timeless cautious but approaching with his head low. Kale looked down from upon the giant Raveene as if he knew exactly what news Danté brought.

Sullenly he looked up at Kale and across to Garon and spoke, "Poskar won't let us pass through the gates, he said no one can leave the safety of the kingdom and to return, he's not even allowed to venture through."

"What? Not even you? But you and Kale live on the other side? What about your homes? The Temple of Thought?" said Garon.

"He said to leave them ... let them rot if they must."

"Subtle," scoffed Kale.

"Poskar has strict orders, but given to him, not from King Vera. If we must return, he said take the desert and walk around through the Gaze Akarr, knowing full well we would never consider it."

"Go through the desert indeed! Does he know how far we've come and what we're doing?" roared Garon.

"Keep it down Garon, he may or may not know you are even here with us, I said Kale was not far behind and I would inform him."

"I'm sure he knows full well we are here, and I'm sure this is exactly why he said no," piped Garon.

"Who does he think he is? Clearly on the witch's side," snapped Belleny.

"He doesn't take sides, he lives on the edge of both," said Kale.

"He's also big enough to sit on both sides," added Danté.

"Let me talk to him, I'll tell him who he's dealing—" started Belleny on an uproar.

"You shall do no such thing!" roared Garon. He twisted his head back towards her, his eyes scanning into her mask as if looking to poke her eyes out.

Belleny held her tongue and squeezed onto Bateau like a stuffed toy.

"Garon meant not to be so harsh, did you Garon?" he held his hand up to her. "To those familiar, Poskar is otherwise known as The Leech King, although he is no king, but he has been waiting for such a young and spirited shadow," he pointed down to the Orphans' shadows, "any of you really, but he would especially like yours Princess," he said.

"My shadow? What for? It doesn't do anything ... does it?"

Danté shook his head, "If Poskar sees you, he can and will take your shadow. Born without one he takes them and feeds on them for years. He says they all taste different, the younger the purer, and they give him strength and immortality ... as long as he has one, even if the original owner is long gone."

"He can have mine, it does nothing but follow me around," said Bateau jokingly.

"He can't have mine!" said Belleny kneeling down and touching hers as if it was a pet. Belleny froze. She stared at Danté's feet.

"Where ... where's your shadow?" said Belleny looking up at him.

Danté held out his hand and rose the Princess to her feet, "Poskar's got mine, I made a careless bet, but it doesn't matter," he said turning back towards Poskar's gate.

Belleny froze.

"It doesn't matter that he took and cannibalised your shadow? But it's your—" said Belleny but Danté had left and walked off back towards the wall.

Kale placed his hand gently on Belleny's shoulder, "Best not talk about it, he'll be all right."

*

While Garon and Kale discussed, the situation Monté and Dillon sat at the peak of one of the highest woven trees. It stopped short only metres from the cliff, the sands of the north and a mighty fall. Together they stared into the distance. They could see far across Mare-Marie, past the misty haze of the Gaze Akarr, across to the Zale Mountains and into the wild waters and darkness of the Sea of Sorrow.

"No sign of Palia," said Dillon. "Look over there, the ground is so high up, and there is more of the Woven Woods."

"They got separated when the north and the south tore apart," said

Montë. "Palia could be anywhere." He scanned and stopped short as the Sea of Sorrow took all his attention. Its wild, chunky whitewash and misty explosions filled the sky for miles as it repeatedly smashed against the mountains.

"The sea looks furious," said Montë.

"It looks sad," added Dillon, "They both do."

"Who?"

"The sea and the mountains, neither of them have given up after all this time," said Dillon. "They're as strong willed as each other. One will have to give up eventually and then ... I just hope it's the sea."

"I feel it has only gotten stronger, the water has risen so high since we last saw it."

"Yes I know, I've got shivers just looking at it from here. So much water."

"Look over there," said Montë, who pointed across the river.

On the top of the Slate Cliffs, the land changed into the Highland Forest and the river continued on throughout it. As the woven trees dissipated on one side of the river the trees grew tall with each and every branch pointing straight up into the sky like a mighty Poplar, many twisted around each other in pairs as they covered the land. The other side of the river was treeless with smooth rounded rocks that seemed to have fallen from the sky. The longer they looked it seemed as if they were moving.

"Can you hear Agarus?" asked Dillon.

"I think so," said Monté. He flicked up his ears, although he only heard Agarus' voice inside his head. "He's calling us to come back."

"We're getting our telepathy back. I hope everything is all right. Let's go at once," said Dillon and they descended as fast as they ran up. Within a few minutes, they spotted the giant Raveene and their companions.

Kale met them first and said, "Do any of these trees reach up to the very top of the cliff?"

Dillon nodded, "Some of the larger ones do, they're trying to grab the trees on the other side. Why is there a problem? Isn't there a staircase in the river?"

"Some shadow eater won't let us through," said Belleny.

"Shadow eater?" said Montë.

"But if we got up there could we jump across the gap?" asked Kale.

"But the Princess, she's not going up there!" said Garon.

"It's possible, we thought about it jokingly ... but you wouldn't want to misjudge your jump, it's a significant drop," said Dillon, "but what about Raveene?"

"Don't worry about me, I'm a born climber," he said as his mouth peeled up into a wide toothed grin.

Bateau remembered Raveene climbing up and along the giant hedge wall like a cat but couldn't imagine such a feat as this.

"You would need a running jump, there's not much of a solid surface up there. If you slipped or didn't jump far enough, well ... you know what would happen," said Montë.

Belleny gazed upwards, the trees by this stage blocked out nearly all visible light and towered so high into the sky it seemed too unreal. She didn't mind climbing to the cubby house in the Jungle Room but this was incomparable. Alternatively she didn't want to lose her shadow to Poskar, who could appear at any moment. Both frightened her tremendously, but thoughts of falling to her death and hitting the many branches on the way down were terrifying.

"I'm sorry Garon, I can't do it, there must be another way, some other stairs? A ladder? Can't we just tie him up?" asked Belleny.

"I'd like to see that," said Danté, "Poskar can sink into his shadow and he's a tricky bastard at that. Too risky."

Garon stared up at the trees, "We could go back to the beginning of the woods and fly over as Palia did, but not all of us can do that. We go as one or not at all. I like our odds. You two can ride with me, Kale and Danté on Raveene and I'm sure our high flying acrobats are just dying to swing around up there, how does that sound?"

"It's high, but the circus had a flying fox even taller, it's just mind over matter really, just don't look down," said Dillon.

"Are you sure Garon, there are only tales of victims falling to their deaths here, never the victors?" said Kale.

"We must move either way, Poskar knows we won't give up this easily," said Danté.

"Fine, just make it quick!" said Belleny.

"We'll follow you just in case," said Kale.

"Yes," said Garon, as he scratched his talons back and forth across a rock to sharpen them.

Kale and Danté swung up onto Raveene, "Are you ready Verill?" said Kale into the giant's ear.

"Of course," said Raveene as he flicked his ears.

"This is the path we take," said Danté. The tree trunk Dillon stood next to was enormous. Its width was so wide a bus could drive up it. It twisted out of the ground and turned so tightly in on itself, it looked like it could unwind at the touch of their claws.

"This one looks thick enough for Raveene to climb, I was a little worried," said Dillon.

"Don't you worry about me," said Raveene as he rippled his spine to tail like a wave cracking every bone as it went. Several small birds who had continued the journey from the very beginning flew off his back and returned as they were.

"This tree goes quite close to the edge, you must follow this one and only this one otherwise you may not get close enough," he paused and flicked his fur. "Follow me," he said as he changed his coat to white so they could see him before he started to climb. "Wait, was this the one?" he said, looking back with a smile, "Let's go."

Garon looked up at Belleny, "Do you trust this guy?"

The Orphans went first, they climbed up the tree with agility and speed, their claws digging deep into the trunk. Garon watched precisely and when they were out of sight he took his first step clawing tight into the trunk claws sinking deep into the slick bark.

"Hold on tight and keep your head down you two, don't look up until I say so, the quicker I get up and out the better," said Garon, trying to balance with just his wing tips and clawing the start of the nearest vertical twisting trunk. The tree seemed to stretch on and on, it was so much longer than it was tall and it was very tall indeed.

Garon kept his eyes ahead and never down, watching as the path got thinner at the very top, You can do it, thought Garon as he picked up speed. Higher and higher he rushed through the leaves, skilfully snapping away branches with his beak, and clawing on without slowing down a beat.

The Orphans grabbed at the branches and the trunk as if it was growing in their Jungle Room. They had no trouble at all and could see patches of light shine through the canopy. They blasted through the surface one at a time. It was if they were being shot out of a canon, running so fast that they saw the cliff top in an instant and leapt straight into the air calculating the feat as they went. One at a time they landed with a thud, clawing hard into the black sandy surface.

Garon saw the Orphans disappear, each one flashing their fur white. With giant strides, he clawed forward, but with little room for his wings to open he wrapped them in close, streamlining them to his body. The closer he got, the more the branches seemed to whip at his face and the louder he growled. Until at last the canopy sparkled above. Like a diver gasping for air Garon burst through the treetops leaping high into the open, exploding thousands of tiny green leaves into a swirling dance around him.

Belleny couldn't help but open her eyes as the sunlight hit her and just as she did Garon unwrapped his giant black wings. In slow motion, she watched as the bright green leaves flickered around them and disappeared revealing the gap to the other side as they flew right across. Garon landed with a clawing thud as the fine black sand took their weight.

"Ha, ha! That's how it's done!" Garon shouted.

Belleny's heart had thumped so hard against her chest; she didn't have time to panic or take in the new scenery around her.

"You can stop pulling out my feathers you two ... we made it," said Garon.

"Oh my, we're so high up," said Belleny.

"You'll forget about it once we are away from the cliff, which is now," said Garon as he moved away from the edge and felt the warm black sand sink between his claws.

The group waited and watched the canopy as the torn leaves settled, then back to each other. There was no sign of Raveene or his riders.

"Did anyone see Raveene take off?" said Dillon.

"No, I didn't look back, I assumed they were right behind me," said Garon.

"What will we do if they don't make it up? We're stuck up here!" said Belleny.

"Settle down Princess, there's always an option," said Agarus.

"But what if—" began Belleny but stopped mid sentence as a giant pointy wet nose poked through the tree top and sniffed at the cool air, bit by bit the huge beast poked its head out of the canopy and with his giant black eyes peered over at them and winked.

As Raveene clawed out, Danté appeared on his back with Kale holding on behind him. It was a sight to behold as the giant creature balanced on the tips of the branches as if his weight meant nothing to them. It seemed he didn't even run up the trunk and took his merry time strolling.

"Well, I never?" said Bateau and watched as Raveene wriggled his hips like a cat about to pounce and that's exactly what he did. With an outstretched leap with no run-up, he kicked his back legs and dived. From his mouth bellowed an enormous growl. It looked as if Raveene was flying.

Belleny looked straight above as he leapt right over her on top of Garon and past the White Knights landing on the other side of them with a tremendous thud that shook the cliff like an earthquake. Pieces of rock began to crack off and fall.

"Quick get away from the edge!" said Kale to Garon, but Garon already had his wings out as he flew to a safe distance.

"That was quite a comfy ride, bit of a bumpy landing but on the all quite pleasant, thanks, Raveene," said Danté jumping to his feet.

"Poskar won't like this at all," said Kale knowing they had crossed the line.

"The Shadow King can rot," replied Garon.

"We are now in the land of Lemane, we follow the river into the Tonerae Mountains, the temple is on the other side, always stick to the river, it will lead us there," said Kale leading Raveene along the river's edge. He stared back at them, and beyond the travellers, they turned and noticed the Sea of Sorrow in the distance.

"The sea!" said Belleny dreamily.

"We have no time for it, we must move on," said Garon. "Look there's Palia!" pointed Garon at a speck in the sky.

"Your eyesight is truly amazing Garon," said Bateau.

"Thank you, come on she'll be down with us soon enough," he said and took off along the river. The Orphans followed, and Raveene and his free-loading birds continued forward one step at a time.

The surroundings were all new and interesting to Belleny, but she couldn't keep her eyes off Raveene.

"How did Raveene just do that?" she asked Bateau.

"Beats me. I've never seen anything like it; Gonzo would just love to have him in the circus."

"He sure is strange. Does Gonzo have creatures as big as Raveene?"

"Bigger, the whole circus rides on the back of three creatures a hundred times larger than Raveene."

"Lies!" she snapped.

"It's true. Horgons," said Garon as he listened.

"I'll believe it when I see it."

"The river is quite alive up here Garon; it's as if it's running away from itself," said Bateau.

Belleny watched with him and the more she looked she couldn't tell if it was coming or going even though it was racing on such an angle. She turned and looked back as the water fell and rose up in between the stepping-stones that paved the way up.

"Let's hope we can use those steps on the way back," said Belleny.

"That won't be an option I'm afraid," said Danté as he and Raveene took the lead.

Belleny frowned, "How else are we getting down?" she asked, to no reply.

From up on the highland surface, they could see far into the Mare-Marie Kingdom. For the first time, Belleny could see over the Zale Mountains and could not only hear the Sea of Sorrow but now see it, revealing its true face of horror. This was as close as she ever wanted to get. It smashed against the mountain as if its life relied on breaking through. Whitewash exploded above its peaks and sprayed an icy halo into the air that continued on for miles. In the distance, the water vanished into a mist of sandy yellow wind that formed as the empty and never-ending Sandlands.

Belleny eagerly removed her map and compass from inside a soft furry leather sporran and gently begun unrolling the map so she could see exactly where they were.

"Look Kale, my mother left me this map of the north for my birthday," she said hoping to spark more than a one-way conversation.

Kale nodded, "The Queen's map?"

"Look it starts here at the Woven Woods, The Slate Cliffs, and there is Poskar's Gate, The Sea of Sadness, the Sandlands, and here look your Temple of Thought," Belleny pointed at each with enthusiasm.

"We follow the Veelin River through the Tonerae Mountains to the Valley of Illusion. Yes, my temple lies over the far edge. Remember we are out of the Kingdom, please, if anything happens always stick to the river."

Belleny took out her mother's locket and eagerly opened it to see the direction home. The shards of dark grey triangles moved about in their circle chamber forming into a large arrowhead, but instead of spinning back from where they came from it pointed straight ahead and followed Raveene. She flicked the triangle about with her finger, and the triangles broke apart only to return and point in the same direction.

"Great it's busted," she mumbled, but to her further dismay she saw the triangles merge into a haunting black skull.

Oh no, the skull! she thought and quickly slammed the lid shut. The eye her mother once carved into the lid stared back at her.

"I had the urchin upside down!" she sighed. Curiously she opened it up and watched on as the dark triangles returned, they pointed forward and once again followed Raveene as he crossed through the water and on the other side of the river. Then she realised it was not only Raveene it pointed at but Danté who rode high up upon him.

"Oh my!" said Belleny, covering her mouth.

"What's wrong Princess?" said Garon, coming to an abrupt stop.

"It's just that—it's nothing, keep going, my compass is playing up," she lied not wanting to alarm anyone.

But it clearly is working, she thought, that means either Raveene or Danté are evil? Or at worse ... going to die. She looked down again and the skull flashed into an arrowhead and followed them once again, "the skull of death," she whispered.

Danté turned back and called out, "Looks like we're in the clear from Poskar. It's possible he may follow us, but I doubt he would ever stray far from his post. He rarely does."

Bateau looked behind along the black sandy grounds and into its shadows. "What does Poskar even look like?" he said aloud. "No don't tell me Garon, I really don't want to know."

Bateau swung around Belleny to capture her smile, but instead noticed her sad eyes shining through her mask.

"Are you all right? It looks like it's working to me?" said Bateau. Together they watched as the arrow pointed towards him, then changed into a rose, and back to the arrow again.

"Yes it does," she replied with a light smile and closed the lid.

CHAPTER 30 - THE LAST DAY

End of term schedules and repetition had worn Evelin out. Several days of this, while others, like Gertrude Cohn, who roamed free outside, made the last week of school quite unbearable.

Two hours and twenty-four minutes till freedom, she thought as she pulled at a thread that unravelled her school jumper.

Good timing, she thought.

Evelin stood alone as she emptied her locker.

Why is the last class of the term also my worst subject? It's not even a subject. This is a sad joke, I'm not going, stuff it, she thought as she tore down the daily schedule from the back of her locker door.

I should just go home. I wonder what's the best way out? The back door and across the school oval, I'll be out in the open, but there's less risk than the front door. But the—

"God! You scared me!" snapped Evelin as she held her chest.

The reticent Miss White didn't speak at first, just acknowledged Evelin's presence and murmured, "I see."

Evelin's anxiousness subsided as she downed a frown, "Can I help you?"

"I doubt it, maybe you can help yourself. You do know you're supposed to be preparing for my class right now; most of the girls are already on the court."

"I'm not in your class," said Evelin, "not willingly."

"If you participate at least once, I might not fail you. I've never failed a single student, and I don't wish to start now. What do you think Miss Boots? You don't want to be the first and only girl in Yellow Tree High to fail at physical education. Even Monica Rhodes passed last year and all she did was roll about."

Who the hell is Monica Rhodes? thought Evelin as she dodged eye contact.

Evelin shrugged her shoulders and put her head deep inside her locker, "Just go away," she muttered, yet it echoed out behind her twice fold. She froze with a light wave of panic as Miss White's gritting teeth could be heard gnawing behind her neck.

"I thought just as much, so be it Boots!" said Miss White and with a sharp click of her calloused fingers she left. Evelin exhaled and listened to the distinct echoing clack of Miss White's heels as she stomped off down the hallway. She imagined her latching onto the lockers and crawling eerily along the roof like a spider.

I can't believe I told her to go away? But it worked, smiled Evelin. *I should say what I feel more often.*

Quickly she closed her locker, swung her bag across her back and followed the sharp footsteps, hoping to gain access to the back door and dodge Miss White from behind. Corridor by corridor, she followed her closely and watched as she disappeared inside the doors of the main basketball courts. Evelin found herself standing by the girls' change room doors.

"This is ridiculous! I'm not going in," muttered Evelin.

"What's ridiculous?" questioned a strangled whistling voice from behind her.

Evelin spun around to face Selma Gerra, the only girl in school who found it fun to ride her mountain bike up and down stairwells. Eventually, it wasn't fun when she slipped and fell head first down a flight of stairs and broke both her legs. But even with two broken legs, she still participated in netball as a rookie coach. This irritated Evelin to no end.

"Hey Sel, you're running late," said Evelin.

Selma leant into her crutches and shook her head slowly.

"Hysterical Evelin. This is not as fun as it looks."

"It's a good look on you."

Selma scrunched up her face and said, "Hey you're in this class right? Aren't you?"

Evelin shrugged, "Not really, it's complicated."

"Me either, not really, not with these broken legs and all."

Evelin's sombre tone neither rose nor held sympathy for her, "It's a pity Sel, you could have really made a difference."

Selma stared down at her legs in solid white casts and sighed, "Yeah I know, we could have made state finals."

"Every girl's dream, 'them's the breaks', pardon the pun," said Evelin as she looked over her shoulder for Miss White.

"Yeah, I know ... hey Eve can you get the door for me?"

"Sure."

Evelin stood forward and pushed the swinging doors slowly, hoping Miss White wasn't inside.

"Thanks, the coast is clear Eve," said Selma as she pushed her way through.

Evelin exhaled with relief; it seemed the other girls had already hit the courts. She stood by the doors and watched Selma hobble around on her crutches, ponder a spot then dump her bag amongst the others. Selma glanced back with a smile and continued through to the courts. Evelin forced herself to grin back for a moment, but her face returned to a stony and pensive expression. She couldn't help but listen to the distinct and unnatural sounds coming from the direction of the court. The high treble pitch of synthetic soles squeaking against the polished basketball courts, followed by an erratic dense rhythm of basketballs repeatedly thrown against the hard and unforgiving surface. But it was the chorus of out of pitch schoolgirls, calling one another, that annoyed Evelin the most.

What am I doing here? I'm not doing this! She told herself and threw her bag against the others. She sat down in a slump and stared at the ground.

Samantha Goldblume ran in as if she was missing out on the fun and quickly got changed. Evelin shook her head as Samantha proceeded to do several stretches, a few small jumps, then rise on the points of her toes. She stretched her calf muscles along the bench towards Evelin and then skipped out to the courts as if there was a crowd awaiting her. She saw but ignored Evelin completely.

"Watch it Goldbum!" snapped a familiar voice and through the open doorway came the reliably late Cory Tamiya. She threw her sports bag against the lockers, and it fell in a bulging heap on top of the others.

Evelin sat silently and curiously watched, *she simply doesn't care,* thought Evelin.

As if at home on a couch Cory pushed the other girls' bags like cushions clearing space along the bench. With the heels of her black school shoes, she forced them against several bags and kicked them off, making a terrible amount of noise as several fell to the floor. She then removed and put on her runners while continuously drinking a can of soda through a straw. Cory paused, noticing Evelin in the corner blending in with the school jackets hanging from the hooks above her.

"I knew I was being watched. Same time, same place I see."

"Hi Cory, you're later than usual?"

"Yeah, didn't realise I had so much junk in my locker. I'll get a quick escape after class you know."

"Better late than never though. If I miss this class, I may fail the year or something ridiculous like that. They're playing with our lives, cause theirs are so messed up. You're not shooting any three-pointers today I'm guessing. Like why start now huh? That would blow the witch away, imagine that you got out there and never missed a shot, which would be gold."

"It's not going to happen," said Evelin.

Cory grinned back, "Seen the spider yet?"

"Spider? What spider?" said Evelin, raising her feet up to the bench, then realizing her foolishness said, "Oh Whitetail, I saw her before, but not in here, she's probably not too far away."

"God she is a pain," said Cory.

"To put it mildly," said Evelin.

"True, you should just go, not as if you need to pass Phys Ed."

"I was trying to; somehow I ended up back in here?"

"She weaves a sticky web," grinned Cory, puzzled at Evelin's posture just sitting on the floor like a small child, her hands wrapped around her knees.

"Oh well, I better get out there, the Whitetail spider won't be far."

Whitetail was commonly known as Miss Andezia Camperia White, but the students had decided that Miss was her first name as they were forced to repeat it so often. Just like the notorious and deadly Whitetail Spider, Miss White had venom in her walk and her talk. Her wardrobe consisted of black and garnished with black, as long as it vacuumed around her bony frame. Her hair was bleached bone white and sat high upon her head in a tightly wound beehive, even in the strongest winds it did not move an inch. The hive sat firmly upon her skull, which was angular as if it had fused with several irons. Somehow placed within it sat two beautiful big blue eyes, if it wasn't for her sour red lips, which were pulled down at the corners by invisible hooks, she might have looked ... pretty? But she didn't. And with it came a scratchy, deep, hoarse voice brought on by the large amount of cigarettes that she sucked down, which frightened not only the students but even her colleagues. She belched smoke.

Cory approached Evelin and placed her hand on her shoulder. Evelin froze and stared at her black and silver painted fingernails.

"Are you okay?" said Cory. "I mean like we haven't spoken since—"

"What? I'm all right, don't worry."

"Okay well, if you want to talk that would be cool but I understand if you don't. It's over anyway."

"You better go."

"Yeah sorry, do you want me to tell Whitetail an excuse for you?"

"There are no excuses left."

"Might need to break a bone or two like Selma, think about it, for next year," smiled Cory revealing her prominent incisors.

"Maybe I *should* break a finger?" said Evelin looking at her hands. "What one do you think I would need the least? I guess it's too late now, but you're right, I could do it next year."

"Honestly Evelin you're the strangest girl I've ever met, don't go breaking any fingers for Whitetail."

Evelin rose her chin up and pushed aside her blonde fringe. She always thought Cory was the strangest girl she had ever met, and for a second thought, *how strange am I, if the strangest girl in school thinks I'm the strangest girl in school?*

Cory returned to her bag and slipped on a ragged black shirt. It had a pirate gun on it. Evelin remembered it from the day of the fire. Above the pistol read in large jagged words, *Arrrrr!* And below it read, *Pillage the*

Village! Evelin noticed it was singed across the shoulder and had several holes across the front. It was far from any sports uniform, but she got in less trouble than not playing at all.

"I better go, see ya soon Evelin, maybe we can catch up over the holidays? Good luck," she said and curtsied down to Evelin as if she was royalty. "My lady," she said, trying her best to impersonate a posh man's voice before continuing out onto the courts.

Evelin gave a curt wave goodbye, and then like usual, she waited for Whitetail to crawl habitually in and find her. Then the lecture would begin, a recital about sport and its benefits including team spirit, self-esteem, self-confidence, and the joys of being healthy. She spent more time lecturing Evelin in that locker that teaching her students.

Evelin looked at her watch, *I better take my pills,* she thought. She took them from her jacket pocket and walked across to the other side where the sinks and mirrors were.

"Evelin Boots what a surprise. I was under the impression you were on your way home? So here you are. Are you joining us today? Or are you becoming the first in the great hall of fame for failures?" said a painfully familiar voice.

Whitetail! gasped Evelin as a sharp stab of panic poked inside her stomach. For a second she flinched like a scared dog, but slowly turned back to stare into Whitetail's deceivingly clear blue eyes and down to her sour red lips.

"I was going to take my medication, and then I was going to write out a list of things to do other than play basketball," said Evelin calmly, so calmly that it surprised even herself.

"Evelin if you are given a class, you have to take it, like it or not, it's in your curriculum. What medication? Are you sick? You don't look sick to me. If this is another excuse you will need to provide a doctor's certificate—for the whole year," Miss White caught her breath and hunched forward, waiting impatiently for a response.

"Am I sick? I am five foot tall, I have the energy and coordination of a baby deer, and I am the last person any one of those half-wit girls would ever pass too!" Evelin walked towards Miss White; it made her heart thump with every step.

"You haven't given it a go once Evelin, and the last term is over, everyone out there had a tough start in the beginning, but they're giving it a go and are all winners."

"Winners? A tough start? You have no idea. Anyway, I'm here aren't I?"

"You may have attended but you're wrong in thinking you're going to pass by sitting in this change room young lady."

"Why did I even bother?" Evelin slumped her bag on her back. "Honestly no one will care if I fail, I don't care if I'm an A' level student. You're only doing this because you don't want to fail. Get over it."

"It's not all about throwing a ball young lady, it's about being part of a team, using not only your body, but your head to outsmart the competition, feel the glory of what it's like to win and just as important to deal with the disappointment of losing."

Evelin knew all too well about the disappointment of losing and scowled back at Miss White.

"Deal with disappointment such as losing? You have no idea how disappointed I am and winning or losing a stupid game of basketball is not going to change a single thing."

"Now Evelin," said Whitetail lowering her tone.

"I hate every one of those girls out there, why on earth would I want to play any game other than Russian roulette with them? Don't ever put me in a class with you next year or I swear I'll—aarghh you make me so mad! I'll be going now."

Evelin's heart was beating in its cage. Miss White said nothing more, she just stood there with her red-lipped mouth gaped open and watched as Evelin stormed through the swinging doors and straight out of the change rooms. It was then that Miss White realised the courts were dead silent, and the whole class had been listening by the door.

"What are you all looking at?" Miss White whipped her hand up at them, "Get back out there and wipe that grin off your face Tamiya, or I'll fail you too!"

Evelin didn't care if it was still school hours. *There are probably more kids on the streets than in school,* she thought. *She can tell the Principal, I don't care anymore. I can't get expelled on the last day, can I? Of course not!*

Evelin pushed straight through the front doors and by the time she had reached her bike and rode to the end of the street she realised what she had said and done.

"What has got into me?" she said out loud, "I'm out of control."

She felt like a prison escapee with nowhere to hide, nowhere to run, *What should I do now? I can't go home yet, and I can't be out here.* Then for some strange reason she thought of someone, *Astina.*

Without a second thought, she pedalled off towards the city, towards the Chandelier Hotel and the lady of the house Astina Francis. *If anyone, maybe she would understand,* she thought.

It didn't take long to reach the river separating the city and the northern suburbs. She stopped in the center of the main King Brown Bridge. The long wooden boats elegantly rowed down the river's mirrored surface and something caught her eye. Each one was disappearing under the bridge and appearing quickly on the other side. She looked up and on the hill saw the school watching her through Yellow Tree Park, even from here it still looked like a jail, with its bare cement walls and barred up windows. She stared out into the distance and back down at the murky waters, *Come on Eve there's no time for this.*

Riding at full speed and ignoring several red lights she arrived at The Chandelier Hotel. The same man as before peered down from the service counter and asked, "Can I help you?"

"Astina, I mean Miss Francis, is she in?"

With a slight pause, he said, "And you are?"

"Evelin Boots."

"Is she expecting you?" he added.

Evelin thought about lying and said, "No but—"

"One moment please," he said.

The man turned to the side and spoke gently, "Sorry to bother you madam but there's a Miss Boots in the foyer."

"Yes, Boots, indeed like the shoe, I'm quite sure," continued the man, "Yes miss, very well."

Evelin looked up with deep wet eyes.

"Miss Francis says it's all right if you go up and see her by the pool, just take the elevator to level forty-five, the red button," he smiled and held his palm up towards the elevator.

Evelin nodded, she knew the torture device quite well and on arrival reached out to press the button but then paused. She reasoned with herself that it wasn't a good idea, *What if it happened again? I could take the stairs?*

Level forty-five though? I'll show Whitetail, she thought.

Evelin took to the staircase. It was coated in a rich rose motif that seemed to go on forever. With every floor, the carpet appeared to move beneath her. The vines seemed to be real, and she could see deep down into the thick thorn bush as the bright red roses held up every step.

It wasn't long before Evelin was dizzy and out of breath, *Maybe I should do some sports,* she smirked. She paused with a heavy sigh and slumped herself down.

What the hell am I doing going up forty-five stories? Why am I even here? Evelin put her hand against her heart. She looked up at the never-ending rose garden stairwell. *This is crazy, how do I get out of here?* she thought, pushing through a red fire-escape door. She felt that her head had switched back on and with her heart coming to a comfortable beat she let go of her chest. Once through the exit door she approached the elevator and pressed the up button. She could hear it taking off and see the moving cables as the numbers above the doors glowed consecutively with each floor.

Damn I didn't get to take my pills, she thought and reached into her bag. "Thanks for nothing Whitetail," she said and swallowed one as if it was a sweet.

It wasn't long before the elevator found her and opened its doors. She stepped in without a twitch of anxiety.

"Hurry up," she said, pushing the red button several times and waited as the doors slowly closed her in.

The inside of the elevator was panelled with mirrors and curiously looking up Evelin could see herself looking down at herself. For a moment she gazed at the roof then down, deep into the mirror ahead, *Not too shabby for an escapee,* she thought.

She gingerly admired herself from both sides, "You're okay Eve, nothing to worry about, although you are talking to yourself," she smiled. Part of her felt it was all a dream, one she had had many times before, and was relieved she finally found some common sense even if it was artificial. The elevator arrived with a jolt, and the doors proceeded to open, revealing the blue afternoon sky above. She stepped out as if the ride was nothing.

Just as before there was no one in sight. Royal was not behind the portable chrome buffet, no dogs on diamond leashes or strange circus folk.

She found Astina Francis in the same position, stretched out on a deck chair, wearing her white bathers, dark shades and large white brimmed hat.

"Damn hat," grumbled Evelin and proceeded towards her.

She passed the stand of hats, snatched one for herself and approached Astina hesitantly.

"Don't drag your feet Miss Boots; it's not proper. I thought I was dreaming you were on your way, did you take the stairs or something?" she said, and in her strange way of being humorous she was half right.

Astina peered up and a glimpse of a lipstick smile could be seen, "I didn't think I would be seeing you so soon? But I'm glad I am."

"Thanks. Where are the pups?" asked Evelin.

"Royal's taken them to the park. Hopefully, he leaves them there."

"I'm joking Boots; I would at least try and sell them first. So what's new, school finished already has it? Can't be three thirty can it?" Astina tilted her glasses; it was as if the school had called her and told her everything.

"Not for some of us. I had an argument with a teacher and stormed off. I can't believe I did it ... and on the last day of school but I'm not myself these days."

"Better than on your first day?" said Astina, sitting up further. "Not yourself?"

"Is that even a sentence? Well, I'm not going to tell you who you are or were or will be. Actually I may. Although last time you were a lot different. A little—"

"Crazy?" said Evelin.

"I was going to say anxious, but—"

"I am. It's alright, I know I am, I think of doing crazy things all the time ... but I don't, not really. You're right though, I was afraid to get on the elevator and took the stairs but then I felt fine, so I caught he elevator the rest of the way. Anyway you probably figured me out from last time, I am crazy."

"Yes you are a little aren't you? You better sit down Boots you're making me nervous."

Evelin liked when Astina smiled, but this was not what she was expecting. She laid down on the deck chair beside her and in the shade of the umbrella closed her eyes.

"Astina, with respect I don't think you understand. I'm not right, madness happens to the best of us. You see crazy people all the time, I bet they thought it could never happen to them. Now they're walking around with radios taped to their heads and talking to themselves. I've read about it, age is not a factor."

"These radio people are not crazy, they're just idiots Boots, there is a difference, and you are clearly not an idiot."

"No, you're wrong, it's the smart ones that go crazy, their minds can't control all the thoughts and processing. Idiots have very little to go crazy about, other than what channel to turn to."

"You may be right, although I've never known a sane teenager, not when I was one, not when I was in high school and definitely not as a woman, you're all completely mad," she said calmly, "tell me, how crazy do you feel right now?"

Evelin paused and thought about it, "I can't really put it on a scale."

"Fine from zero to ten? Ten being I better get off the roof and I'm taking the invisible stairwell."

"Right now? Zero, I guess."

"Of course you do. See it's all in your head, we all feel crazy every once in a while, it's personality shining through."

"Of course it's all in my head. That's what I've been saying. If it's not faulty wires, it's an over-imaginative mind. It still doesn't help me. Of course I have a lot in my head, who doesn't," said Evelin with a deep sigh.

"You're right we all do, but you've got at least a billion and one things. Don't worry they fade away. By the time you're my age, you'll probably have a handful—if that."

"You and my shrink are as confusing as each other."

"False emotions appearing real," said Astina whipping her words.

"What?" Evelin shrugged her shoulders.

"I don't want to spell it out for you Evelin as it's quite a nasty little word, and little it is ... fear," said Astina boldly.

Evelin's face saddened. It was a nasty word and she didn't like associating herself with it.

"I know but, it's not just that," said Evelin her eyes still closed.

"I'm no psychologist Evelin, but I've lived long enough to have my fair share of ups and downs, and I've got the scars to prove it. Describe Astina Francis when you first met me?"

Evelin paused, "Nice."

"Nice! Don't lie Boots, it's not going to get you anywhere."

"Fine, I thought you were cold and mean, but I know you're not ... not always," she smiled.

Astina breathed in and let out a long slow breath.

"Do you know why I seem that way?"

"Because you're afraid as well?"

"It's a wall Evelin, a protective barrier, nothing out and nothing in. It works on many levels, but ultimately it's good to let it down," she shielded her hands across her chest and brought them apart, "do you understand what I'm saying?"

Evelin knew and gently nodded. She felt she had lived with a wall her entire life. She started to get teary but held it back as she always did.

Astina leaned over and said, "It's good to cry Boots, let it out if you want, you'll feel much better. If it helps, go for a swim and cry in the pool. I'm sure it needs topping up."

Evelin's sad face curved up into a grin and she thought; *this was a lesson only a mother could give.*

Giant Cicada husks lay scattered across the scorched and arid surface of the Tonerae Mountains. High above the tallest peak, flying forms wheeled and circled in dark vaporous shadow of formidable beasts, moving in a hypnotic frenzy of claws, gnashing fangs, sweat and spittle and arching barbed backbones. Some of the beasts soared high in the clouds and flapped their leathery bat wings, some beat their wings like an egg-beater and some creatures hovered without the need of flapping their wings at all.

As the voyagers continued their arduous journey, Belleny and Bateau rode high in the saddle upon Garon and they scanned the sparse Highland Forest where the trees grew tall, but the hard sandy land was actually very flat. The great romantic Selt Trees courted off in pairs, their rhubarb red trunks twisted around each other, trunks and branches arm in arm, and kept their distance from the other 'tree couples'. The trees were peppered quite densely across the terrain, but the foliage line drew to a distinct end at the foot of the Tonerae Mountains where it's presence would be menacing and the sensation of foreboding doubled with the cyclic cloud-like whirlpool that spun relentlessly above the highest peak.

The rock face is so craggy and scarred, thought Belleny, her eyes following the mountain as it tore upwards at the sky like a stairway built by demons from the underworld to the gates of the afterlife. "That's not good," grumbled Garon as he stopped a tune short. He turned back to Danté, who approached on Raveene.

"What? What's not good? Tell me at once!" snapped Belleny leaning forward and staring into one of Garon's shiny, wet black eyes that were squinting on the side of his head.

"No, it's nothing, just sit back down, be quiet and keep your mask on Princess."

"I'm not even thing of taking it off. Why did you turn back and look at Danté? What's not good?"

"Where not lost are we? Following a river is not exactly a great plan. What if it dries up or floods?" said Bateau.

"What are you looking at? What can you see up ahead? Oh no, it's not a Larch Snide is it?" said Belleny.

Garon paused, holding his feathered hands over his temples, "Please be quiet you two, you're starting to give me the worst headache. I'll let you know, what you need to know, when you need to know."

"Princess," soothed Danté shaking his head, "what Garon means is that the big bad black cloud circling the mountain is not a cloud as you probably presumed."

"Of course it's a cloud! A storm cloud, of course! I don't care, I'm not afraid of a little rain, this outfit is practically watertight," snapped Belleny.

"It's not a cloud," whispered Garon as he turned back at her pensively.

Behind the mask, Belleny looked up at the cloud puzzled, "What is it then? Smoke? Oh no! The mountains are on fire! Is that why it's so stinking hot?"

"It's a swarm," said Danté as he mounted on top of Raveene who lumbered forward.

"Come back, Danté? A swarm of what?"

The creatures drifted around the mountain organically, in and out like a swarm of locusts, a vicious circle of hunger that moved wildly around each other. Although the travellers were too far away to see the small creatures that snapped and snarled at each other, they could now make out the giant ones, the ones that looked like storm clouds themselves, just drifting along like ghastly black silhouettes blotting out patches of the sky.

Belleny shook all over, not from the cold as it was sweltering on this side of the Slate Cliffs as if the mountain was volcanic, but because she was terrified. *Several wild beasts and a witch*, she imagined the group could handle, *Raveene could probably do the job all by himself*, she thought, *but not this, this is a swarm of pure evil*. She couldn't last much longer and Garon could feel her unease rattling her frame.

"I'm sorry, but you were going to find out sooner or later," he said softly.

"I demand an answer," ordered Belleny."

"Shhh look!" hushed Garon his eyes fixated on a dark figure silently hovering in the distance. With its face covered with beady black eyes, it silently watched them and continued on towards the mountain.

"What was that thing? It saw us! Oh my, it could have swallowed us all in one bite! Garon!" she cried.

Garon turned back and shrugged, "Princess control yourself, luckily it's not interested in us ... but no I don't know what it was."

"I've never seen anything like it before. We must talk to Kale or Danté again unless the river decides to go uphill, we won't be following it for long. Don't worry we're still a long way away."

Garon leant forward and let out a sharp whistle.

Raveene's ham hock thighs stopped lumbering and grinding into the dry ground, his giant skull turned almost 180degrees towards them as he repeatedly sniffed at the air. Danté turned back as Garon moored up beside him.

So hot, thought Belleny as an immense heat radiated off Raveene, *I hope he's not sick? Or evil*, she was reminded of her compass and the skull that pointed his way.

"This is unusual," said Danté. His eyes fixated on the swirling mass above the mountain.

"This is more than unusual," said Garon as he outstretched his wings and pointed in the direction of the creatures, "we should leave the river, find cover in the shrubs immediately."

"What?" scoffed Garon. "We have the safety of the Princess to consider, haven't you seen what's in front of us?"

"I for one think Garon is right for once," said Belleny, "I'm afraid something terrible is going to happen—to all of us."

"What are they waiting for? The cicadas?"

"We have arrived on quite an occasion Princess, these young nymphs are on the eve of impending adulthood. I'm not sure why but they're stirring quite a commotion. Can you see the golden husks?"

"Those little specks?" Bateau questioned innocently.

"Those specks are about the size of Agarus, head to tail," said Danté.

"I've witnessed this once before. Never was there such a swarm of this capacity," said Garon.

"They don't have a chance, it will be a massacre," added Danté.

Behind the mask, Belleny took a terrified breath, "A massacre! They're going to eat them? This is madness, we must keep well away, we'll also be eaten alive, even before we get half way!"

"They must taste good?" said Bateau.

"Revolting, though could be just to your fancy" smiled Danté.

Reluctantly, Garon followed Raveene broke through a thicket of branches on the perimeter of the last cluster of the sheltering trees. The long plateau stretched out towards the mountain like a arid virgin battlefield.

Belleny kept her eyes fixed on the mountain and the shapes that crawled upon it. The closer they travelled towards the mountains, the clearer the outline of the golden cicadas stood out from the rocks. The glassy cocoons absorbed the sunlight like polished amber, each one a translucent moulding as solid as Garon's talons. Suddenly a small pack of swooping monsters made a break from their circle and aimed fire at the cicada shells, clawing at the husks and clasping on tightly, trying in vain to peck and gnaw with ferocity. The husks were impenetrable from the outside, even to the largest of the creatures that chewed on them with giant jaws as if they were pieces of toffee.

Garon tightened the saddle from underneath and said, "Belleny buckle yourself in up there and make sure it's tight, you too Bateau I don't want to lose you."

"Let's ride!" bellowed Garon in a tone that roared like the ocean.

The others were swiftly left in a cloud of dust and hastily shuffled to catch up to him.

"If you didn't walk so fast you wouldn't have to keep stopping

"Do not turn around," said Garon as the sound of his talons scratched at the ground.

"Why? What is it?" said Belleny. She turned around at once and cupped her mouth from screaming.

What madness have I got us into? she thought.

Standing out in the open they watched the forest trees bend and buckle in the distance as another ominous creature appeared floating low from behind the Orphans. The sound of its heavy breathing echoed like a wind tunnel through horizontal gills and each gill flap shimmied like a ribbon fin of the Knife Fish. Its heavy eyes looked down upon them, ever-watching and with a groaning roar, black oily liquid dripped from its facial cavities. It hit the dry dirt around them and splashed into the river. It continued leaving a trail of black tar as it went.

"What was that? Ewe! What is that stuff?" cried Belleny. Never had she moved so quickly. She reached down and latched her boots into the stirrups. If Garon was going to run, she was going with him. She pulled the thick saddle straps across her thighs, it latched tight, it hurt, but a notch looser and she was sure she'd slip out if he had to bolt.

"Bateau get in my rucksack—now!"

Like a fox, he disappeared into her bag before she could speak another word.

Garon kept his eye on the beast as it flew off towards the mountain and pointed, "Look there are creatures on top of it hitching a ride. Don't worry it's gone."

Garon's large black eyes seldom blinked. His eyesight was incomparable, most things he saw took the others an hour's walk before they could see what he was talking about. He could see the cicadas in their golden shells wriggling and squirming about. He could distinguish between the varieties of creatures, in horrid detail as if they were two feet in front of him. They flew in from many directions, yet prominently from behind the mountain. He noticed that there were some as large as houses, not only in the sky but also climbing the steep mountain. *What if they're also in the mountain?* he thought. *What evil must the witch be brooding on the other side? Will Kale's temple even be standing?*

"You better keep away from the swarm Palia," said Garon as she returned from her travels with Raveene and Danté.

"I'm not intending to go anywhere near them, that thing was enormous and foul. Danté said we're going through the mountain, a cave of sorts, I hope he knows where he's taking us."

"What does Kale say?" asked Garon.

Kale who they presumed was asleep had jumped from Agarus' back and knelt on the ground holding his hands to his temples, "Everyone stop! It's happening!"

"Speak of the devil," said Bateau. "He wants us to cover our ears?"

"What for? Apart from Garons moaning, it's dead quiet," said Belleny.

"They're hatching early! Cover your ears now!" repeated Kale as he ran past the Orphans and up to Garon and Belleny.

"Hatching? said Garon scanning the mountain, "But Danté said—"

"How can he tell?" said Belleny.

"They can't be? Most of them are still pupae?" said Garon.

"They're scared, they're going to make a run for it! Everyone block your ears now!" shouted Kale pointing up to the mountain as the squalling cloud began to surge into a thick mass and descend before their eyes. It was as if the mountain sucked them in like a vacuum. The sound was a whining roar like a thousand howling hounds.

This can't be happening! Belleny's eyes were immovable from the dark scene before her. Through the screams of panic and cries of a birthing freedom, the cicadas smashed through their golden husks each shell releasing a catastrophic explosion that sent a shock-wave which reverberated physically and audibly across the plains.

Instantly they all covered their ears as a new wave of cicadas smashed through their husks. The roaring voices of the flying beasts rose to match as the mountain's surface screamed out in a glass cacophony. With both hands pressed tight against her ears, it seemed to make little difference and the Princess began to scream just as wildly.

"Stop! I can't take it anymore it's unbearable!" She made a tight ball with her fist and beat down at him. He knelt to the ground and wrapped the group in a protective tent of feathers. With great speed, the cicadas took to the sky in all directions, knowing full well what circled above and with each exploding exit they unwound their ripe transparent wings and took to the falling sky.

As the last of the cicadas broke free from their encasing, the glass-shattering sounds diffused, but now the screams of the insects only got louder.

"Quick we must go now! To the mountain at once!" yelled Kale, who jumped up on Raveene with Danté.

"Remember if anything happens, you must follow the river!" said Danté.

"Hold on!" he snapped as he unfolded his wings exposing Belleny and Bateau to witness the nightmarish actions above. She stared at the nightmare and felt a tear roll down her face.

"Let's go White Knights!" called out Garon as they released their hands from their ears and took off behind him.

"Go Garon go!" screamed Belleny and he too took off with a thrust of his giant wings. Belleny jolted back and Bateau poked his head out of her bag, wrapping his arms tight around her. They watched as Raveene went from a steady pace to an unstoppable bolt, powering on ahead at full force, the faster he galloped the less his front legs seemed to touch the ground, then to their surprise they left altogether and swung by his sides.

"Raveene's running!" shouted Belleny as Raveene towered, using his hind legs to stand upright. Danté and Kale held on either side as if it was the natural way to ride him.

"Keep going, do not stop!" shouted Kale turning back and thrusting his arm forward.

"Look out Orphans!" Garon squawked as two spiralling cicadas came crashing down. One spun out of control right in front of Garon and one with wings torn from its body dive-bombed straight behind. Both were covered with ravenous creatures tearing into them while others swooped by. Belleny let out a scream as Garon dodged a near collision and jumped into the air, stepping over a rolling cicada, barely missing it as the relentless school of creatures snapped behind.

The Orphans watched as Garon flew up into the air, his wings in full spread, while his claws grabbed at the falling cicadas, he jumped up and over as they fell around him.

The sky exploded with black feathers as Garon swooped and turned in near acrobatics. Belleny and Bateau held on for their lives, gripping the saddle which was saving them from a near fatal fall.

"Hold on!" Garon yelled as he spotted Raveene near the stream, and dove at full force. Feathers clumped and puffed from the force of the dive from Garon's wings as he passed through gaps of creatures, skimming the shrubs and rocks on the ground with his wing tips.

More and more cicadas fell from the skies, out of control like gunned down war planes. The impact levelled and took out the twisting trees in the forest and they smashed hard against the dry land. The creatures continued to cling on, all the way through impact and only let go to seize a tighter grip. Black tar blood pour from the cicadas as they lay motionless, the lucky ones died on impact as the creatures tore off their wings and lapped at the pooling black blood.

"Watch out!" cried Dillon as the enormous creature returned and hovered above them. Its body was as wide as a house, its mouth the same width. It continued to poured greasy black saliva down around them as it unlatched its jaw opening up a giant gully within. It swallowed the cicadas like flies and the wild creatures flew inside without haste eating from within even as the beast chewed. Blackness poured from its mouth and covered the sandy ground below.

"It's awful Garon!" cried Belleny, she drew her leather hood over her mask just as another shower of blood splashed against Garon and her side.

She kept her eyes closed, white-knuckled fists clenching around Garon's saddle as it shook about wildly with each jump, leap and step.

"Hold on Princess!" he shouted as he hit the ground clawing into a hurdling run. Belleny shook about with her eyes clenched tight as Bateau, in the bottom of her bag, held himself with both tails. As her heart continued to thump, Garon slowed down to an even pace and gradually came to a halt. *Why is he stopping? He can't stop, they're everywhere!* She panicked but then heard laughter, *Kale and Danté ... they seem to be laughing?*

"Belleny you can come out now, we've made it," said a breathless Garon.

"We made it where?" said Belleny.

It was then she noticed the cicadas' screams, the glass husks and the creatures' vulgar cries of terror had diminished to a distant wail and all she could really hear was the beautiful sound of the river.

Garon reached back and lifted off her hooded cover.

"Are we ... we're inside the mountain!"

She turned at once as the Orphans darted inside a giant split in the mountain, gasping and cheering as they came.

It was as if a giant had sliced the mountain in half to let the river flow through. In places it was wide enough for Raveene to squeeze past, yet in others it bellowed out, glistening wall to wall with fragments of blue and majestic white crystals. At the top, it closed to no less than a slight split only wide enough to let a splinter of light flicker inside.

"Well done everyone, we will be safe in here," said Danté.

"Raveene, you were amazing!" said Belleny.

"Thank you, Princess," growled Raveene with a large toothed grin. "I do like to go running every once in a while, it's good for the heart."

"Have I got something on my face?" said Dillon his entire head dripping black with cicada blood.

"I think you better wash up Dillon, who knows what's in that stuff, cicadas don't usually bleed black blood," said Kale.

"It went straight in my mouth," said Montë who spat out chunks of it and took large gulps from the river.

"Has this always been here? Why wouldn't I have known about it?" said Garon looking at his fragmented reflection in the crystal walls.

"The Tonerae Mountain has a broken heart, for as long as I can remember. From above it's a slight crack, you probably flew straight over. Luckily it's our way through to the other side," said Danté.

"You could have told us from the beginning," said Belleny.

"I did, where's your sense of adventure girl?" smiled Danté.

"When you reach the bottom of the Pit of Nothingness I'll tell you."

"That was madness out there," said Palia. "Have you seen it before?" She turned to Kale and Danté.

"Yes, but nothing like that," said Danté.

"They were after the cicadas' blood," said Dillon.

"Blood is not black," snapped Palia.

Belleny took off her mask, "Garon can you let me down? I've got to wash this stuff off, I'm covered in it."

Belleny spat on the ground, it was black and coated her teeth. The blood had passed through the eyes and mouth holes of her mask and slowly dripped down her face.

"Disgusting! I've swallowed it!" she said, looking at her scattered reflection and running to the river's edge.

"You're not the only one," said Garon wiping his beak and flicking the black tar aside.

"The witch is to blame," said Danté bluntly, "the cicadas have never been prayed on like this before."

"It's freezing!" shouted Belleny her hands ripping out of the water.

"Yes, the river runs like ice inside the mountain; a cold heart. It's frozen in the center," said Danté pointing up to the eerie darkness ahead.

"Frozen, a frozen river?" she said fascinated by the notion. "But what about the fish?" Never before had she thought such a thing possible.

Once cleaned and renewed it wasn't long before they continued. The crevice wasn't wide enough for all of them to walk side by side so the Orphans took lead, with Belleny and Bateau, who rode upon Garon next and behind them Kale and Danté rode on Raveene.

It wasn't long before Belleny felt the icy shadows of the subterranean world tearing into her bones and she felt helpless. The fur of her suit gave her extra durability and warmth, but most of it was wet and she wasn't prepared for this sort of temperature. She didn't realise it was possible for it to be so cold, it bit through her clothes and into her skin. Shivering, she trembled violently until she became numb and her limbs no longer resisted. She noticed that it was unnervingly quiet and only their footsteps and Raveene's heavy breathing could be heard. *The river!* she thought and looked down at the water, it had now turned to solid ice.

"Look, the river is frozen," she said to Bateau with a touch of fear in her voice.

"That's nice tell me when it's running again," said Bateau hidden under several layers of Garon's feathers.

Garon could feel Belleny's knees rattling on either side. "Won't be long. I thought we would be out by now, this mountain is bigger than it looks."

"What do you mean? It's the biggest thing I've ever seen!" said Belleny.

"True, it probably is," Garon chuckled to himself.

"Garon," she said a little hesitant.

"Mmm, don't worry if there is anything in here they don't stand a chance. We're pretty safe, for now."

"Oh, I know, we can hardly fit let alone those giants, but can, can I have some of your down feathers? It's so cold in here, I have no padding like the Orphans."

He reached deep into his chest and pulled out a handful of small, wispy black feathers.

"Here you go, should be plenty. We must be at least halfway by now," he said, passing the feathers to Belleny while keeping a steady pace. His claws creating an unnerving sound as his talons carved into the frozen river.

The Orphans who lead the way up ahead had transformed once again from dark silhouettes to shimmering white furry coats. Each hair was transparent that reflected all visible light, taking on the appearance of the caves, ice and snow.

"Hold on you two, let's get out of here before my beak snaps off."

Belleny turned to see how far the others were behind them and to her surprise Raveene was right behind them as silent as a fox.

"Princess? That is you up there, isn't it?" shouted Danté.

"Raahh! From now on you'll call me Queen Kikaan!" roared Belleny as she held up both her hands quickly clawing at the air, then grasping back at her saddle.

"Yes you are, we should all remember to address you as Kikaan from now on," said Danté, "It's a different place beyond the Black Mountain."

"Yes Kikaan," added Garon.

The Orphans stood along a ridge that looked over the valley and the imminent darkness on the other side. The Temple of Thought although some ways away was the first structure in sight. The main housing perched high on top of a long brick chimney-like pillar.

Garon busted through the opening, his last few icy breaths disintegrating into the light.

"Sunlight!" growled Garon as he stretched his wings out wide. A wave of stained water gushed off him, pooling on the ground.

Instantly they turned up to the mountain and watched as several stray creatures circled the peak.

"They must be feasting in the plateau, it's not going to look pretty," said Dillon.

"Let's hope they take a nap afterwards," said Monté.

"Off you hop stowaways," said Garon kneeling down.

"Thanks, Garon," said Belleny as she unlatched the harness and splashed boots first into the pool of water below.

Raveene approached pushing them all to the side with his head, sniffing up at the sunlight. Both its riders jumped to the ground and stared up at the temple.

"Oh my," said Belleny looking out into the distance, "was there a fire? Did the blue trees not burn?"

"A fire, no, colour doesn't seem to grow on much out here, but you will see it is quite beautiful, you will be surprised, one way or another," said Danté.

"We best be off, darkness is approaching," said Kale, "I'm afraid there's no time to stop by your place Danté. We must get to the temple before the night and its creatures emerge."

"Creatures of the night!" coughed Belleny.

"You are far from home Princess, the nocturnal thrive in the north."

The grain of tiny rocks that made up trillions of particles in the Black Sands were a type of Crystal Quartz and would ignite when sparked by a combination of sulphur and sunlight, crackling as an effective natural fire starter. The land was a dry and scorched Luna landscape, completely void of living creatures. The trees were silhouetted and clung to the grainy surface with raised uprooted claws, each with their wiry branches preying up into the sky like the Devil's Poplar. The only real colour that made them seem alive came from the small green leaves that began to sprout along their branches.

Feeling quite moved by such a sight the Princess reached out to touch one. With an open-handed slap, Danté swung down towards her. He was too late and she pulled back from the tree with a yelp, finding out quickly for herself.

"Princ—Kikaan!" squawked Garon.

"Are you alright Princess?" whispered Danté, "I wouldn't touch any of these trees."

He inspected her hand. In shock, Belleny stared at her glove and the black scorch marks on her fingertips. She looked up at him with wide eyes and then back at the tree.

"It burnt me?" she whispered quietly from behind her mask of horrors.

"Are they sick?" she asked. "Have they dried up and split? No, it can't be, they're wet? It's as if they have a fever?" she said, pointing at the small droplets of water that beaded off the bark.

"Very sick," said Danté, "they're nearly all in this condition. They were once beautiful, and bone white as the Alphena crab but the insides have been bled and lie below on this blackened soil," he kicked his foot through the layers of ash and sand and sighed. "Although not all the trees are like this, the blue ones not far up ahead, the Hyde trees, seem to be quite unaffected, they're actually thriving in the valley."

Belleny returned high upon Garon and sat with Bateau. As Garon moved forward large patches of sandy blue grass appeared which brought more colour to the landscape. As the strange Hyde trees came into view they took over the sulfura's five to one, they were of all sizes and roughly spaced in groups of five. Together they set the remaining landscape towards the tower.

"What is this place? What goes on here?" asked Belleny to Garon, but he just shrugged and said, "Illusions ... dark ones."

"What? That's just a name; it doesn't mean anything does it?" she said to Garon whose silence mimicked the land, not a breath of wind moved throughout, nor did a bird sing. Not even the river that dwindled down to a stream had much to say.

"Fine! What sort of dark illusions?" she said.

"You'll see soon enough."

"What, like the mirror pools? Just tell me in advance, I don't like surprises!"

"Enough now Kikaan," huffed Garon, adding quietly, "we must not bring attention to ourselves."

Danté, who rode upon Raveene, pointed up ahead, "The land is not as it seems, stay close and always follow the river! It knows the way."

And so it was with no more questions asked they diligently followed the river, turning and weaving their eyes fixed on the long and winding path ahead. For a while, they continued through the black sands making sure not to touch the sulfura trees, but it wasn't long before the Princess sat up and removed her mask.

"Put that back on girl," said Garon scowling up at her. But Belleny just squinted ahead and rubbed her eyes, unable to believe what she saw.

"What do you think Kikaan?" said Danté as Raveene turned his massive head up towards her and hummed a light tune.

"Is this possible?" she said, "Bateau get up you lazy thing!" said Belleny as she watched the trees and even the very land beneath them begin to move.

"Are we there?" said Bateau.

"I don't know if we're here or there?" she said, and together they looked across the moving land with starry eyes.

"It's not wise to wander off," reminded Danté, "it's extremely unstable, stick to the river ... remember it's our only true path."

Belleny pointed at a group of blue trees as they moved away slowly, and the sand beneath them poured uphill. Some trees looked like they followed four orbiting suns, twisting one way, then another. It wasn't just the trees Belleny noticed, sometimes it was the ground, one minute it was in their path the next it was a pooling hole with its fine black sand pouring out and then pouring back inside. To make things worse, the river was changing as well, it had dwindled away to no more than a trickling stream.

"Something's up ahead, it disappeared, but it was coming this way!" gasped Belleny.

Raveene pounced forward with Danté jumping from his back, and he pointed outwards, "Everyone hide, don't go too far though," he said while staying visible in the open.

"Who is it?" whispered Belleny.

"Quiet little one. I think it's Tjaman," said Garon, trying to spy on the figure and keep out of sight. This was rather difficult as the sand and trees they hid behind continually moved into different positions as if they were trying to expose them. Through Garon's feathers and moving foliage, Belleny and Bateau watched intensely.

"Yes...I see you," whispered Garon.

"Where, who is he?" asked Belleny.

"There, right in front of Danté," he pointed as it slowly revealed itself.

It was near invisible until it removed its pitch-dark hooded cloak. Eerily it stood perfectly still only metres from Danté.

Beneath its cape its body was strikingly white, a sharp contrast against the black surroundings. It stood tall and straight like a man, but it was clearly no man as it stood as if on stilts and overshadowed Danté. With defined features, as if carved with a wood plane, its mask-like face held a void expression.

He looks like a royal guard, thought Belleny, observing its uniform which was made of white panels of armour that contoured around its main limbs and chest and when it walked gradients of flesh darted through the panels exposing heavily pigmented orange skin.

"What a marvellous costume," whispered Belleny.

"Shh!" shook Garon with a heavy frown. The figure's head moved an inch towards them, then returned to Danté.

Bateau was intrigued by the stranger but was fixated by the bird by his side, a most angelic creature; he stared admiring its poise. It sat quietly perched on a round stone. *But it can't be stone, it can float like me?* pondered Bateau as it defied gravity and floated chest height beside the figure. A delicate leash joined them from the figure's wrist to the bird and it occasionally sparkled in the dim light.

Raveene leant down and forward as the figure placed its hand on Raveene's forehead and rested it there for a moment. Raveene overshadowed the figure, but it stood confident and strong, its bird didn't flinch either. Danté knelt down in the soft black sand and bowed.

"Tjaman, Palice, it's good to see you both, how's home?" said Danté.

He kept quiet as Tjaman seemed to be in conversation with Palice, although no audible words were being spoken. Danté looked at Palice; up close she was beautiful, elegant and hypnotic.

Tjaman's harsh voice broke the trance, "Home is scared," he said.

Tjaman then moved. He leant around Raveene as if expecting there to be others and then returned to his position. He skipped the formalities and spoke as if very little air could escape, "You have returned—with guests?"

"It may be vast, but you can't hide in my ocean unless you're made of water or sand," said Tjaman, patting Palice. The eyes that formed in Tjaman's mask read—I know your secrets.

The tone of Tjaman's voice was foreboding, and Garon kept Belleny and Bateau blanketed under his dark wings while Kale and the Orphans remained silent hidden in the background.

Tjaman moved up close to Danté, Palice floated forward with him, "Are you—all right?" he continued to look into Danté's eyes, "Palice says you're afraid, why would that be? Did you witness the massacre on the Black Mountain? A slaughter from any angle, I doubt any survived, the creatures have peculiar tastes, although it's more than that."

"Yes. We saw," said Danté, "it was awful, why would they do such a thing? They had black oily blood, is this the witch's curse?"

Tjaman looked at Palice then turned back, "The answers are known, but will be kept silent, as you are hiding something from me."

"Creatures hiding, reveal yourselves now!" Rose Tjaman as he pointed to where the Orphans were hiding, his fingers long and moulded like white plastic.

"It's all right, Knights you can come out," said Danté facing his attention away from Garon, Bateau and especially Belleny.

Kale came out from his hiding spot too, "They are the White Knights from the Great Gonzo Circus," said Kale.

"So it is true you're out of your nest Kale, probably a good decision, although you need not hide from me. I don't care that you're out; it's not me who's interested in your doings," Tjaman said and looked back down at Palice, "Most interesting ... Palice here says the White Knights are all but dead, died long ago. Who are these impostors then? Uninvited and contaminating the valley, you both know the rules!"

"We are not impostors, we are The White Knights," said Dillon.

"They were put under a curse and transformed into horrid beasts by the witch Lucretia. They have returned," said Kale.

"A curse?" Tjaman turned to Palice and paused. His mask-like face moved into a sad expression, "How unfortunate—revenge is on the cards."

"Tjaman we mean no disrespect, but we must get to the temple before nightfall," said Kale. "It's hard enough walking through the valley in daylight."

Tjaman shook his head, "Oh really. I wouldn't be in such a hurry."

"What do you mean Tjaman? Is something wrong? What's happened to the temple?" said Kale.

"It's still there—obviously, but someone doesn't want you as its tenant any more; you may have to move into the valley with Danté, Palice and I."

"What are you talking about?"

"When you finally left, there became new occupants in the Temple of Thought. You have been evicted."

"Evicted! Impossible, by whom? No one owns the temple; it's sacred," said Kale, looking up at the tower in the distance.

"Who or what indeed?" Tjaman's blank shell-like face revealed no feelings towards Kale while his bird Palice continued to stare silently at the Orphans.

"I recommend you turn back to where you wandered from, there is no safety in the temple, you have left and it is yours no more," said Tjaman pointing from where they came.

Danté stood forward, "You know this won't stop at the temple, the witch will destroy the valley too, you and Palice will be next."

"The witch is confusing true, but she knows not to disrupt the valley for consequences will follow. Palice can't work out her ways, she seems to be not who she once was. The Wandering Gravers say she's quite the manifestation, although sadly they wander no more."

"The Gravers, what's happened to them?" said Kale.

"Gone, and they too were told by Poskar to stay away. Palice feared for them and many others, your King sent them to their graves it seems," said Tjaman.

Raveene stretched and stood up, "Tjaman we don't have time for this, we best be off," he growled softly.

Tjaman bowed, "You're right Raveene you probably should be. Poskar's not stupid he knows full well you've returned," he said, waving his finger across at Kale, the Orphans and then straight over to where Garon, Bateau and Belleny hid.

"Tsk, tsk, Danté you really disappoint me, you know how I hate visitors disturbing the valley," Tjaman's mask-like face returned towards Garon and added slowly, "interesting even the valiant Garon the Quick has left his King to join you. You will need his assistance I'm sure boy."

Garon slowly rose with Belleny and Bateau hidden beneath his giant wings. He bowed towards Tjaman and held his ground.

"I apologise, I know how you hate strangers in the valley. We have not strayed from the river, nor shall we," said Danté.

Tjaman shook his head, "I can't believe you would disobey Poskar. Do you not know the position you put me in. If it weren't for me, he would dispose of you child, like a flame of a candle."

"Why would Poskar not let us through? Is he working for the witch?" asked Kale.

"He works for no one. He has a job to do as do you. The sooner you go, the sooner you'll see for yourself. I have a job to do as you very well know; time is of the essence." Tjaman stood aside with Palice floating alongside him. With a swaying hand gesture, he allowed them to continue then wrapped himself back in his black cape.

"Thank you Tjaman, Palice, I live by our agreement, I will be back soon enough, but this evil must end, for the longevity of both of us," said Danté as he bowed down to Tjaman's hand.

"I shall hope so, a promise is a promise," said Tjaman as he and Palice slowly turned and walked off down into a misshaped dune that then started to pour upwards into a hill. He disappeared over it as it changed once again.

Garon sighed with relief and whispered, "He's gone."

"How can you tell with that cloak?" said Bateau.

"Stay under my wings, he could still be anywhere," said Garon spying through the strange ever-changing scenery.

Danté rode on Raveene with Garon walking by his side; Belleny and Bateau sat low on his back, sheathed under her cape. The Orphans quickly circled them with a multitude of questions.

"Whose side is he on? What was he? That bird was so elegant! Did he know Belleny was there?"

We best be off, I'll inform you all as we go, said Danté walking towards the stream and continuing on, "Tjaman is worried, the last thing he would ever want is his valley disrupted. Palice can't work out the witch's ways, but together they both know more than enough, and they know something terrible is about to happen, but the key is more important to them," said Danté, "They're linked you know, not just Tjaman to Palice but also to this valley, I'm not sure what it would do without them."

"Yes, I'm sure he saw her but I don't think he knows who she is with that outfit on. I was hoping we would not have crossed paths today, although we are old friends of sorts."

"Your agreement sounds impossible? How could anyone find a key in a place that doesn't know how to stand still for a second?" said Kale.

"What key? What promise?" asked Bateau.

"Shh, Bateau have you ever heard of the word privacy?" said Belleny tapping his head.

"No, it is alright, this is my duty. There's a key to free Palice from its silver chain, but it's lost somewhere in the Valley of Illusion and no the chain can't be broken or Palice will shatter into a thousand pieces."

"A curse! Was it the witch? Only she would do such a terrible thing!" said Belleny.

"No—Tjaman did it, he captured Palice."

"What! Why would he do that?"

"But they're so connected, they spoke like one," said Bateau.

"They are. Capture bonding is very powerful, it's a strange situation but Tjaman only lives now to set her free."

"That's a strange kind of beautiful," said Belleny.

"Yes, I feel for them. This place is always changing so it's yet to be found if ever. To make things worse for Tjaman he doesn't see like you or I. I don't know exactly how he does? Maybe through Palice. We have an agreement, I will search for the key in exchange for the stone orb that Palice rests upon, but more importantly, he will exchange his shadow for mine and free me, his shadow is one Poskar would die for," said Danté.

"Shadow swapping! But why the orb? How long have you been looking?" said Belleny infatuated by the dilemma.

"Over ten years, for half of those he still had his shadow," said Kale.

"You're joking!" exclaimed Belleny.

"This may be true, but it's no different than staying cooped up in that tower of yours. The orb is more important to me than my shadow," said Danté.

Kale shrugged.

"I don't understand? Why, what is it?" asked Belleny.

"Transportation," said Danté.

"How? Doesn't he just float there?" asked Bateau waving his tails.

"No, Palice said it can go where ever it likes, with a single thought, I've built a harness to go over it, Mare-Marie will hold no boundaries for me. Show me your map. It may not be on it, but—"

"Yes here," Belleny pulled it from her backpack like a sword and held it out.

"Look out in the Sea of Sorrow, way out in the middle of the ocean, there may be a structure?"

"The Eternal Tower?" said Belleny finding it easily, and she knew there was no other landmark in the ocean.

"The Untouched Tower," scoffed Garon.

"Yes that is it. They say way out there, floating high above it, is a similar orb but much, much larger. Palice's may have come from it, I don't know, no one does, no one can get there."

"There's a small symbol of it here, it looks like an orb," said Belleny.

"Tall tales, nothing can survive out at sea if there was anything it would be in ruins by now," said Kale.

Raveene let out a light roar and shook his head.

"You may be right. But I have seen it from up on the peaks of the Zale Mountains, it glistens like a star when the sunlight reaches it," said Garon, "No one has been there in my lifetime, no one's crazy enough to try. That ocean is possessed."

"The sea will tear any boat apart. Yes, you can try and fly above it, but eventually it will wear you down with its wild electrical storms," said Danté.

"I wonder what's out there?" whispered Belleny.

"I think the ocean is protecting something ... someone. I hear voices calling me and not only in my dreams. I'll tell you when I find out, I must find that key."

Evelin scanned the kitchen with dismay. Tiptoeing across the wet floor, the space was sparse, smelt of bleach and resembled something from a display home.

This is creepy clean, where is everything? Where's the microwave, the coffee machine?

Both of the fridge doors had been left ajar and the inside racks were completely empty with the exception of one large pickle jar on the middle shelf. Evelin distinctly remembered the gherkin pickle that had been an amusing topic as it sadly floated in the brine over the course of several weeks. Carefully she inspected and removed the small Post-it note taped to the side of the glass, *I can't believe Robin ate it.*

Through the kitchen window, in matching white singlets, Robin and her Uncle, Oscar, stood out amongst the decaying vegetable plants. The tomato vines towered over both men although their time were up. She watched as Robin drove his shovel repeatedly into their roots and Oscar tore them from the ground. Their bright red and shrivelled fruit covered the dug up dirt.

Uncle Oscar wasn't by true definition, Evelin's Uncle. An unusually tall man; poised, stoic and strong, without being covered in muscles. His face was drawn as he was now in his early fifties, but his characteristics still displayed a noticeably large jaw, balanced by the outer tips of his thick dark eyebrows, which had turned a whitish grey.

Once a head chef, he worked at the Green Yum restaurant, a small but humble vegetarian establishment that he owned and cooked at for many years before hanging up his apron after one crazy night. This was the night Evelin was born.

It was a lot different from any other evening. The usual busy kitchen was run singularly by Oscar. Most of the employees were stuck on the other side of the King Brown River; after an accident involving circus convoy and Yellow Tree's familiar tourist horse and cart. An incident which caused the immediate deaths of the horses and the escape of five ferocious circus lions.

"Don't worry Miss Butternut I'll make this as quick and clean as possible," he said and rocked his knife over the pumpkin's buxom form. Oscar then paused as he heard a woman's high pitch laugh and the overall volume of the restaurant rose several decibels. *Gee whiz what a cackle? One lucky guy caught that one. What could be so funny?* he thought and shook his head. *If I were her man, I'd stick to dull topics like the weather.*

As Oscar sliced the butternut a woman's wail, like a half scream, filled the entire kitchen.

Now that's not laughing!

Oscar stabbed his knife into the table and left immediately. It didn't take him long to reach the dining room, and he needn't look hard. Clawed to the armrests was Evelin's mum laying on her chair like a ghost had entered her body. Several women were circling around her and their male partners huddled together as if a sport's strategy was being planned.

"What's going on in my restaurant?" said Oscar.

The waitress at the time, a young Spanish girl named Manta, waved him over. But before he could take a single step he was approached by a panting, skinny man with thick black hair and a matching beard, his pupils exaggerated behind his large-framed glasses. "I'm so sorry to do this to you, and in your restaurant, but it just happened—"

"But what just happened? Was it the food? What's wrong with her?" asked Oscar.

"Robin! The baby, she's coming! Call the doctor!"

"Baby?" said Oscar.

"Yes, my baby," said Robin, pointing over to his wife.

Oscar shook his head, "What here? Now? No, no, no this is not right, take her to the hospital at once! Call an ambulance!"

"I did but they said there's been an accident, they can't get across the bridge."

"What? There's got to be more than one way across? What about uptown?"

"She said she can't wait, I made laugh and her water broke all of a sudden and my little girl's already coming!"

"Fine, let's get her into the kitchen. Use the phone, get a doctor here. I'll deal with these people."

Oscar paced to the front door and flipped the open sign around. He turned to the patrons, some sitting and staring while others gathered around.

"Excuse me everyone, I'm Chef Garamond, is there a doctor in the house?"

The situation was starting to look dire. Between the heavy shrugs and vacant nods, there didn't seem to be any customers with medical skills. Oscar, taking the situation in hand, headed toward the panting woman.

"Hello, little lady, do you think you can stand up, with help? We'll get you into the kitchen where it's warm and get you comfy while we wait for the doctor."

With watery eyes, she looked up and panted, "Are you a doctor?"

"Me a doctor? Sorry no, I only operate on vegetables, your doctor's on his way. How about we get you into the kitchen where it's a lot cleaner than out here. Just a joke people," he said, looking up with a broad pearly grin.

Just as Oscar was about to lead the heavily pregnant woman into the kitchen a friendly face appeared.

"Hello, my name's Ruby, I'm a nurse—well I'm training to be one. Please let me help."

The pregnant woman said nervously, "Thank you dear. When are we going to the hospital?"

"We're just going to make you comfortable till the doctor or the ambulance comes, in this situation, he said if your water's broken and—"

"Robin!" she cried.

It was then the baby began to move, it wanted out.

Ruby cleared the kitchen bench in a swoop and threw down a tablecloth.

"Robin grab the seat cushions from the bar, we'll make her as comfortable as we can," said Oscar.

Robin ran out and into the eatery, most of the restaurant patrons were still waiting. He grabbed a cushion from every stool at the bar. A young lady standing next to her boyfriend clapped and others joined in with a cheer. Robin grinned with a clenched jaw, his arms full before returning. He threw the cushions down on the bench like overlapping petals.

"Ruby let's get her up onto the table. She'll need support as well."

"Okay, on three. One. Two. Three!"

"There you go, now that was easy wasn't it miss … I totally forgot to ask, what's your name young lady?"

"Eva, Eva Boots," she said as her voice trailed.

"Such a beautiful name," said Ruby.

"Named after her mother," said Robin from the other side of the room with the phone against his ear.

Eva made several loud, tight breaths and seized the edge of the table, "The baby, she's coming!"

"Robin, you better tell him to put his foot down," said Oscar.

Robin held one hand to his forehead head and strangled the receiver with the other,

"Where are you?

"You're where?"

"How long?"

"Do what?"

"I don't care about the damn lions!

Oscar put his hand on Ruby's shoulder and whispered into her ear, "Have you ever given birth to a baby?"

"Me? No, I don't have kids," she said.

Oscar laughed, "No Ruby, I meant help someone as a Midwife."

"Oh no, not exactly? I've just enrolled as a nurse, we're up to week four."

"You'll get a crash course in Midwifery tonight."

Eva followed with wide eyes as Robin paced back and forth and angrily hung up on the doctor, "Honey? Don't get mad, it's going to be alright, but it'll be another 30 minutes till they open the bridge, until then he said, hang tight and keep up with the breathing. He said you might be in labour for hours after your water breaks. Just hang tight honey."

Eva trembled, "She's coming Robin."

Oscar grabbed a box of kitchen gloves, "Ruby put these on!"

"Guys if we have to—we're going to do this here and now. You're going to be okay and so is your little one. Would you like a stiff drink from the bar? Robin go get yourself one, you look terrible," Oscar smiled, "and be quick, she's coming."

"Now?" said Robin.

"Now!" she cried.

"OK, we're ready, you do what you've got to do Eva," said Oscar, standing at her feet.

"What? But you're a chef Oscar not a doctor," said Robin.

"I've seen this done a hundred times on television, it's the Eva who needs to do all the work," said Oscar, "I've just got to catch the baby."

"Robin squeeze my hand, it's going to be alright," said Eva.

Ruby wiped the sweat flooding from Eva. Her pale skin was turning a translucent white.

On the other end Oscar was getting excited, "That's it Eva you're doing it, keep pushing, here she comes!"

Oscar pointed with his jaw, "Ruby, there should be a clean tablecloth in that drawer over there. Towels too!"

"We're nearly there! Keep pushing, that's it! One more push!"

Eva ground her teeth as she let out one last squeeze. Robin comforted her as she collapsed exhausted into the cushions, let her tight grip go and dropped her legs by her sides.

"On behalf of The Green Yum restaurant I would like to present you with—a baby girl!" said Oscar.

Cheers could be heard from the restaurant as they listened to the whole event. He was so pleased with himself and held the baby in the air for all to see. Ruby wrapped the baby in the tablecloth. Robin's exhausted face showed off the happiest moment of his life. Eva gracefully smiled up at her baby, her lips closed with a heavenly grin. Oscar brought the baby in close to her. Silent and exhausted she mouthed, "She's beautiful."

Eva caressed her baby girl with loving fingertips and like iron bars dropped her arms as her eyes fell back.

"Eva? Eva! Eva!!" shouted Robin as he cradled her lifeless body.

Baby Eve began her first cry, her sorrow filling the room.

Eva Boots died that night and Evelin Boots was born.

It wasn't long after the birth that Oscar sold his restaurant. Delivering a baby had changed him. He realised running a restaurant and slaving away in a kitchen all night was no way to live a life. Oscar and Ruby met on the zany and electronic night and years later were still solid and happily married. They moved only a few streets away from Robin and became close friends, helping Robin gather up the pieces, build his towering white palace to commemorate his wife, and raise his daughter Evelin.

Evelin never brought up her birthday and moved it ahead by several months, refusing to acknowledge that sorrowful day.

Kale stood with fists clenched and poised with anger as he stared up at the mystic Temple of Thought. The weary travellers were pleased to arrive before nightfall, but the entrance two enormous barn-like wooden doors, had been vandalized with a large oily black X splashed across them. Like stale blood, it also tarnished the pale sandy bricks as they towered towards the wooden roost high above.

"We're not alone," said Kale as his fingertips scraped through the oily X.

"Tjaman was right," said Danté, "someone has been here."

"No, someone is inside," added Kale. He placed his open palm against the door and said, "Look it's unlocked ... I'm going in."

"What? Wait! We can't just walk in!" said Garon.

But it was too late, Kale had signalled Raveene and the giant creature bulldozed the doors wide open with a nudge of his snout. The doors hit either side with an echoing slam.

Belleny and Bateau held on as Garon stood tall and spied inside. From what he could see there was no one in sight. It was sparse inside the echoing temple with only several pieces of furniture on a large square of red carpet.With the sun down it was getting darker by the minute. Kale lit the ornate lamps spread around the furniture, instantly they revealed the enormous room. He waved them in.

The Orphans took the lead, followed by Danté.

"Come on Garon, Kikaan will be safer in here than out there tonight," whispered Danté.

"You don't know that," said Garon.

"There's no one in there?" said Belleny.

"No one? Of course there is. This is nothing but a trap," groaned Garon as he stepped inside.

Raveene waited for him to enter, then like a giant cat, he squeezed through the doorway effortlessly. Able to rear up and stand on hind legs, it was with a deafening thud he closed both doors behind him.

"Raveene lock the door," ordered Kale.

Raveene lifted the large piece of wood nearby and dropped it into position to prevent the doors opening from outside or from within.

"What if something happens to Raveene? Then no one's getting out!" said Garon.

"Thank you, finally someone with common sense around here," said Garon

I've been wondering that myself, thought Belleny.

The Orphans wove together and formed a ring in the room, like a single unit they were the eyes and ears of one another. They looked up into the roof rafters above.

"It's a bit like the Jungle Room in here," said Belleny, "but abstract and oddly empty."

The temple rose above them endlessly, it towered and swirled in an enchanting pattern of bricks. At the very top Garon could make out the inside of a room.

"If someone is here, they're waiting at the top, upstairs," pointed Kale.

"Of course we're coming with you," said Danté as he sat down on a large couch and crossed one leg over the other. "Come on, take a seat Orphans, you'll love this."

"How do you get upstairs with no stairs?" said Bateau.

"I'm confused, is it just me or has no one noticed there's no floor up there to the temple," said Palia.

"The only way up or down is by this elevator lift in the middle of the floor."

The Orphans moved onto the carpet. "Whoever is upstairs, they won't be expecting the likes of us!" puffed Dillon.

"Welcome aboard the elevator platform White Knights," said Danté. "Come on Raveene, you can squeeze on."

Raveene tiptoed onto the carpeted platform, dodging the furniture, turned about face and sat down slowly.

Belleny grinned at the big lump as he looked like a stuffed toy.

"This platform isn't going anywhere quickly," said Bateau nudging Belleny with his tails, "nothing can lift Raveene, he must weigh at least a one hundred tonnes. No offence big guy."

"None taken," bellowed Raveene as he took a deep breath and held it.

"Ready Raveene?" said Kale.

With a silent agreement from all, he whispered a few words and pulled back on a lever attached to the wooden floor. Instantly it began to creak and they felt it rise.

"I don't believe it, we're … moving!" stammered Bateau poking his head under the carpet.

"Sit down," ordered Garon.

"We're floating!" gasped Bateau.

"Black magic," whispered Belleny.

"We're not in your kingdom anymore Kikaan," said Kale.

"If there's ever been a trap, this has got to be the biggest one I've ever walked … flown into. Stand close Kikaan. Who knows what's up there waiting," huffed Garon.

"You're right, we don't know, but we're going to find out," said Kale calmly.

"Personally I can't wait for Kale to cook up a cauldron of his famous beet soup and soak my feet in some hot soapy water," said Danté.

Beet Soup? thought Belleny as she and Bateau grinned at each other.

Bateau held his tails out baffled, "Raveene how are you so heavy and light at the same time? Isn't anyone else confused? How did he stand on the tips of those branches back in the Woven Woods? And balanced on the Queen's Garden hedge?"

Raveene continued his frown and shook his enormous skull down at Bateau.

"Settle Rav, it's just a simple question?" said Bateau his tails flicking side to side.

"Now is not the time to disturb Raveene," said Danté.

"Why?" asked Bateau.

"We've arrived," said Kale pointing with his blade outstretched, "everyone keep low."

The wooden floor locked into position with a dull thud. They were all amazed that the lift was now the floor of a huge house. Surrounding them were walls of framed oil paintings, towering bookcases, a fireplace and a bounty of nicks and knacks of a well-lived house.

Agarus curved his long body up and around the furniture, "I can't see anyone?"

"Oh my, the fireplace is a light," said Belleny.

"No, it's always on, night or day," said Kale.

"What do you mean, always on?"

"Magic," nodded Bateau.

Incredible, thought Belleny.

"Get down you two," said Garon scanning the area frantically.

"This is strange? Who was Tjaman talking about?" said Danté.

"Shh someone's here!" said Kale, raising his blade.

Belleny ducked dropping behind a large ornate sofa as Garon threw his wing over her and Bateau.

"There's two of them, in the kitchen!" said Kale. Instantly they flocked to all corners of the house, hiding where they could. Raveene let out a deep growl and stared down at the figures.

Kale held up his hand for all to wait.

There was an uncomfortable silence as they watched. The sound of the crackling fire filled the room.

Who are they? Why are they just sitting there?

"Friends of yours, acquaintances?" questioned Garon.

"No, not friends," replied Kale, feeling a wave of unease from the silent visitors.

Raveene went from being cautious and timid to confrontational. His mannerisms were akin to a frightened dog and he snapped, exposing his black gums and rows of jagged teeth. The building echoed as he bellowed a growl that unnerved his comrades. But whatever lurked in the kitchen did not move an inch.

Oh no! Raveene, please be careful! What could be out there? thought Belleny as she held Bateau hidden under Garon's wing. She couldn't resist. Slowly she poked her head through his feathers and up over the couch.

"Get down!" snapped Garon, covering her with a face full of feathers.

"What's out there? What did you see?" said Bateau.

With her mouth aghast, Belleny stood frozen with confusion and terror. What sat ahead was a gigantic sixteen foot dining table, covered with marble tiles, brass legs and candelabra the size of a small car. At the head of the table, at either, side sat two identical figures, each with weathered leathery yellow and orange skin. Similar to Tjaman, the figures wore blank faceless white masks and were cloaked in panelled armour spread across their limbs. The pair sat motionlessly, their chins resting on tightened fists, elbows perched on the table and mirroring each other.

"Your move," whispered Danté pulling back his bow and aiming at the angular face of one of the characters.

"Wait … look, up there," whispered Garon, pointing with his beak.

Above the two figures hovered a large solid black, glass-like object. Its shape was something similar to an octahedron. Danté removed his sights from the figures and pointed his arrow directly at it.

As if the glass was watching them it now began to spin, rotating on no particular axis. One by one its sides lit up illuminating the strange figures below.

"Oh my!" squeaked Belleny.

"I said keep down!" roared Garon.

Belleny tried to speak but couldn't. Instead, she pointed to her boots and with shaky eyes mouthed the words, "Nothing!"

Their feet, which were missing sunk into dark shadowy pits.

Kale pointed his blades at the figures, "Who are you? What are you doing in the temple?"

Instantly the kitchen lit up in a blinding flash as all eight sides of the spinning object began to flash from within, its sides emanating a lucid glow. Hypnotically Danté stared into the light and lowered his bow as the giant Raveene ceased his growl and held a blank empty stare.

"Don't look at it!" squawked Garon as he covered his eyes in a blanket of black feathers.

The object returned to black and with it extinguished the flames in the fireplace leaving everyone in pitch-black darkness.

Garon watched as the Orphans changed their fur from black to their iridescent white coats. They appeared in the darkness and scattered around the room like a pack of hyenas, ready to attack.

"We are the Occupants. We are employed to stand guard of the Temple. You have been evicted from the Temple, eradicate yourselves!" they said in a coarse static voice. Simultaneously the strange black object began to spike its angular sides, bob about in-sync to their words.

"You're the ones who are leaving, this is my tower!" shouted Kale.

"No longer. Eradicate yourselves!" repeated the Occupants.

Raveene snapped at the creatures and with a deep growl shook the building.

Belleny gasped as Kale launched himself into the kitchen wielding his daggers high overhead. The hovering object lit up at once rapidly rotating and disfiguring itself in violent, juddering angles. Suddenly it froze and a blast of continuous white light struck Kale directly in the face immobilizing him and with an electric current, plucked him off the ground.

"Let him go!" screamed Belleny.

"Kikaan! I said get down!" roared Garon, watching as the object held Kale lifelessly by a wire of light. He turned to Danté who seemed to be still stuck in a trance, "Damn it! Shoot Danté!"

With rapid precision, Danté fired several arrows. Two at the figures and one at the object above them. In a flash, it spun and shot back several electric beams, destroying the arrows with one hitting Danté in the face. It proceeded to lift both he and Kale effortlessly off the ground.

The whole time the Occupants sat motionless as if paralysed or desensitised in a dream state. Collectively they spoke, "Eradicate yourselves!" They demanded in unison, "or die by the Gajaban Eye."

"Meeooowwww!" cried Bateau from under the couch.

The table shook as their leathery yellow fists slammed down on the table, "Eradication is nigh!"

In a single move, Garon launched over Belleny and Bateau, and from behind a shielded wing, drove a hand full of daggers towards the Occupants.

Belleny squeezed her eyes shut as a flash of light exploded inside the room and the sound of Garon's blades clashed against the floor. The room returned to pitch black.

"Garon!" cried Belleny just as the room flashed again and as if Garon had fallen from the sky he crashed, slamming into a hypnotic Raveene.

"Damn it!" roared Garon getting to his feet and scurrying back to Belleny and Bateau.

"Are you alright?" said Belleny.

"I've been better," he grumbled.

Raveene woke from the bump and growled wildly, scraping his claws at the wooden floorboards like a wild bull. The glass object spun and drew a line of beams across his face.

Raveene clenched his jaw and launched, racing towards The Occupants with all his strength, but after a few steps he let out a groan and stumbled heavily on his forelegs, collapsing on the ground with an enormous thud. The dark glass-like object above the Occupants, the Gajaban Eye, had brought him down like a Tazer, paralysing every muscle in his body. All without once releasing its lighting hold on Kale and Danté. The Occupants were yet to move a muscle, they remained fixed and void of movement.

The Gajaban Eye redirected a beam of light at the lever and instantly the elevated floor began to lower itself back down to the ground.

"No!" shouted Monté, he leapt onto the lever and pulled it back as the Gajaban Eye fired beams of crackling electric light at him. Each blast lit up the room as if it was daylight, yet each time, it did nothing but radiate Monté's sparkling white coat.

In a flash, the Orphans leapt out bravely with Dillon holding Kale, trying to pull him away but with no success. His body lifeless as a doll as the light held him up by his head. Agarus had the same problem with Danté and felt he was doing more harm than good tugging at his body.

"Look out!" squawked Garon as he kept an eye on the Gajaban Eye. Triangle shapes spiked and darted, light and shapes slid around erratically. It froze again revealing a large evil face that screamed in a muted form in front of them. It fired a beam of light at Dillon connecting head on. Dillon howled as his eyes were engulfed with light. He held up his hand and blocked the electric beam, but the effect was as if it was nothing more than a beam of a torchlight.

Again the Gajaban Eye spiked and turned into another angular face, it also screamed with no sound at them.

It looks like a woman? The witch! thought Garon as the Gajaban Eye furiously fired another beam to no avail. It contorted into another face and shot at both Dillon and Agarus and together they laughed as the light only radiated and bounced off them.

Palia flew up to the pinnacle roof and with a wild squawk dove head first towards The Occupants. The Gajaban Eye spun firing light at her, she swung her claws out connecting with one of the creatures, tearing off its mask.

Instantly the fireplace ignited furiously and the room filled with blue light. The Occupants revealed a dark blue shadow-like face and to Palia's shock it seemed to float out at her like oil leaking from a damaged boat. Simultaneously they began to move towards each other slamming their fists down on the table in a drumming tribal beat. As a duo, their forms were re-animated and reacted by glitching back and forth, turning towards each other, their mouths arching in a silent scream.

The bright beams of light projected from the hovering shape suddenly stopped and Kale and Danté dropped to the ground like puppets cut from a string. The Gajaban Eye fell as if it weighed one hundred ton. Crashing hard upon the table and fracturing into several glass shards.

Palia returned landing behind Garon, Belleny and Bateau. The Occupant's mask still held within her claws. Kale and Danté slowly woke in a daze, as did Raveene, opening his eyes and lifting his jaw off the ground.

The remaining masked Occupant let out a fearful shriek and pulled his twin forward as it flipped over and slammed its back onto the glass covered table. Everyone stood back and stared as it began to thrash about as if electrocuted and the unveiled twin proceeded to drive itself inside the other face first. Its leathery yellow skin stretched and contorted. It wasn't long before it devoured its twin from the inside out and its mask now sat in place where the other's once was. Slowly it regained its posture, cracked its back and stood before them. Even with its feet sinking within shadowed holes it towered. It stared down at the shattered remains of the dark glass object and screamed viciously, scraping up the broken shards with long clawed dark blue fingers.

Danté, now revived and fresh, pointed his bow and arrow at the creature. It stopped screaming, turned and peered down at him with a menacing frown. Effortlessly Danté lets go, piercing the creature through the neck.

It sounded like he shot the arrow through a leather cushion and the creature snarled back at him, snapping the shaft with the twist of its neck. It turned back to the pile of shards. With a hand over its face, it removed the mask and proceeded to push handfuls of glass deep inside its faceless void, returning to the table for every last piece. As it placed the mask back on its face, it turned and said one last time, "Eradicate!"

"Never," said Kale as he reached forward and from his clawed hand fired a shard of black light hitting the creature in its chest as it smashed backwards through the window and into the darkness.

Magic! Black Magic, thought Belleny in awe of his forbidden powers.

Garon ran to the window and stared down into the darkness. Scanning for signs of the Occupant.

"You did it!" said Bateau, who levitated off the ground.

"Yes! Well done everyone!" cheered Dillon.

"We are lucky we had you here White Knights," said an exhausted Kale as he collapsed in a chair. With his eyes closed, he removed his gloves and let them fall to the floor.

"Are you all right? Your hand, it's burnt!" said Belleny.

"I'll be fine, I shouldn't have been caught off guard."

"Magic?" she whispered.

"It can have its repercussions," sighed Kale, rubbing the tarnished and cindered skin from his fingers.

"Those light beams had no effect on the Orphans," said Garon.

"Most interesting," said Danté, "and most fortunate for us."

"A memento for your mantle piece Kale," said Palia dropping an Occupant's mask by his feet.

Kale reached forward and with disgust, threw it to the back of the fireplace, smashing it into pieces.

"I don't want a memento, I want answers."

Oscar lead an almost nocturnal life, his night time hours dictated by his job which covered a graveyard shift and were juxtaposed with day hours of sleeping in the morning and spending his afternoons in the garden at the Boots' property.

"If only I had a garden like yours Robin," said Oscar wiping dirt across his brow, "I would give you a run for your money, I've grown some of the biggest pumpkins you've ever seen. The sort of thing you see in cartoons."

"Oscar this is your garden, you've spent more time in here than me, even that scarecrow resembles you," quipped Robin.

"I probably should have checked before moving onto that dried up limestone infested property of mine, but it was worth it. I'm practically your neighbour! Say, Eve hasn't been over in a while, she used to love digging around in the limestone."

"It's a jungle of rocks and towering weeds Oscar, I'm amazed she hasn't been bitten by something."

"That's why she likes it. Speak of the devil, here's your little monster now," smiled Oscar.

Evelin gave a small wave as she approached with BC.

Oscar's attention was fixed on the kitten cradling in her arms.

"So this must be the newest member of the Boots clan. He looks like something from the future. Does he have a pair of antennas or do they only come out when he beams his spaceship?"

"Possibly," said Evelin, "BC meet Oscar, he's also from another time … and place."

"Gee whizz it's hairless! You can see right through its skin—far out! Just look at the size of those ears, cor it's tail is so bony!"

"I get the picture Oscar … I know, I know, he's a weird looking cat."

"Don't get me wrong I like the little guy, please don't put no Egyptian curse on me."

"You best watch your words then. Hey, thanks for cleaning up the kitchen Robin, it's never looked so … empty. Did you actually eat that last pickle?"

"Maybe. Speaking of pickles, are you interested in doing some food shopping later?"

"Erm, we have plenty of eggs to live off don't we?" said Evelin angling her body towards Oscar, "please help yourself Uncle Oscar, I have a feeling we'll have a constant supply."

Oscar nodded, "Yes I've heard all about her … I mean them."

"Well then looks like you two have your afternoon set," smiled Robin, "I would join you, but I have to do a few things around the house."

"Robin, you're not coming?" Evelin's voice started to rise and she found herself staring at him anxiously.

"I'm coming darling, it's all okay, all right?"

"Of course … I'll go get ready."

*

As the car pulled out of the driveway, Evelin felt a wave of sickness engulf her. *I don't think I can face the crowds in the shopping centre. Why does the car park have to go so deep underground? What if there's a fire, how will we escape? What will Oscar think if I panic here in the car? Get a grip girl. This is the reason you're on medication, you're going to be fine … but what if it doesn't work!*

The thoughts continued as they pulled into the shopping centre car park. From the outside, it looked relatively quiet, but she knew if the car park was full it would be packed with hundreds of random strangers inside.

"Okay, Team Boots. Fist things first. I'm going to find some coffee. I'm sure I'll bump into you along the way," said Oscar, grabbing and spinning a trolley like a toy.

"I'm sure you'll bump into a lot of things," said Evelin and they took off in the opposite direction.

"Earth to Robin, Earth to Robin are you receiving? What are you looking for?"

"Nothing. Oh, what are those?"

"They're corn chips, you don't need a fancy logo to spice them up."

"But what about these ones? They have extra cheese!"

"The box is the extra cheese."

"Hey—is that who I think it is ... it is!

"Did you plan this?" said Evelin folding her arms.

"Plan what? Who? She's here!" said Robin.

In the aisle ahead stood Miss Jacqueline Davis. Evelin scanned her up and down. She was no different from her school days, her hair had grown longer and it looked as though she still tied it up in a bun the same as before.

"Go on, go and say hi then," said Evelin nudging her father forward.

"What? What do I say?"

"Just be friendly, just go and say hi, tell her we're now living off her eggs."

"I can't say that! She'll think I'm nuts."

"She's going to find out sooner or later."

It was then that Jacqueline spun her trolley towards them.

"Robin Boots?" she said in an excitedly warm French accent, which sounded more like *Vobin Bwoots*.

"Miss Davis ... ehm Jacqueline."

"Twice in one day, I'm so lucky."

"Twice today, already?" quizzed Evelin.

"Hello Evelin. Oh, your hair has blossomed into something quite magical hasn't it?"

"That's one way to put it," muttered Evelin.

"I must be the only woman who hates shopping, although you can't live off eggs, although you can try," she said with a wink.

She also hates shopping? Five points for Miss D, thought Evelin.

"Oh look at me, I must look like a mess!"

"You look fine Jacqueline, look at us, we're practically in our pyjamas too," blurted Robin.

Evelin looked up at him with her usual stunned, raised eyebrow look, "Speak for yourself. But thanks for the eggs, it's good to eat something fresh."

"You ate them! That's great news, my chickens just don't know when to stop. They hide them you know, I found one inside the house, can you believe it, six eggs laid on my couch?"

"Lucky you didn't sit down," Robin blurted.

"Weren't you saying you wanted to invite Miss Davis around for dinner to show her your appreciation?"

Before Robin had a chance to respond, Jacqueline answered, "That would be superb, when shall we set this date?"

Robin stammered, "Date, um this Wednesday, is that too soon?"

"What about Sunday?" said Evelin.

"Magnifique!" exclaimed Jacqueline.

"Terrific stuff, okay bye bye Jacqueline, we best be off we have a lot of shopping to do," said Evelin and left, pulling Robin by their trolley down the aisle.

"Nice going Mr. Boots, got yourself a date."

Evelin and her father sauntered off down isle four in search for cereal. Despite the minimal conversation, both their minds were spinning and they revelled in each others company and the general hum of the possibility of the unknown, new friendships or a new romance with a lovely woman entering both their lives within varying degrees. Of course Evelin did not share her thoughts with her father, she simply smiled quietly to herself.

"Hello strangers, fancy meeting you two here!" Oscar beamed, pushing an overflowing trolley of cans.

"Expecting a disaster?" asked Evelin.

"It's best to be prepared. That reminds me, I better get some garlic," said Oscar. "Hey, you won't believe who I just saw," he then whispered into Robin's ear.

"Miss Davis?" said Evelin without intonation.

Oscar looked down at her, "How long have you been psychic?"

"Long enough, He's cooking her dinner Sunday night."

"Well, well, well," said Oscar patting Robin firmly on the back, "French lady, you'll need to make something special, I know just the dish, but I don't think you can buy snails here."

"Oscar, she's lived in Yellow Tree most of her life," said Robin.

"Anyway she's quite the catch, she looks a bit like Lexie Luve, from Channel Two's Romance Roulette, teach you a thing or two about ... cleaning," said Oscar pausing slowly and peeking back over his shoulder at Evelin.

But there she stood, a million miles away, staring into a shelf of hair dyes.

Darkness fell quickly upon the night sky surrounding the Temple of Thought. Belleny and her exhausted comrades found little comfort as they rested. Strange and foreign noises carried through the night. It wasn't until Kale had prepared a hearty broth for the group did their nerves settle down and they started to relax. The soup soothed them instantly; it was blended together with a variety of unfamiliar spices and vegetables found in the ornate kitchen. As the remainder simmered inside a giant cauldron, the delicious aroma filled the temple with a sense of comfort, even after the confronting episode with the Occupants only a few harrowing hours before.

Belleny and Bateau lay slumped on a Chaise Lounge, with tired eyes, she watched Danté in the kitchen as he poured himself a fourth helping and downed the soup with plentiful gulps. He stumbled over to Raveene, who was asleep and had spread himself out like a giant dog, curling around the outer walls and taking up most of the floor. Danté slumped down deep within his thick white furry underbelly and fell asleep instantly in his boots and all.

Garon and Kale stood outside on the balcony staring into the darkness. A sea of trees took over the scene from here and they watched as scattered patches were set ablaze, flickering and crackling across the dark domain. The unnerving sounds of breaking branches came from afar, but also cracked and snapped from directly below on the woodland floor. They listened to the grimy, savage voices, snickering and quarrelling, darting up at them like knives through the still wind.

"What are we going to do about the Princess?" sighed Garon. "I planned for her safety here, maybe the Orphans can stay behind and guard her?" He turned back towards her and watched as she slept. "I still can't believe she stowed away. King Vera will have my head if the witch doesn't chop it off first."

Kale scraped his boot against the balcony. Chunks of dried mud fell far below. When they finally hit the ground, he said, "You may be right, but after today I think the Orphans are destined to join us, not stay cooped up forever."

"You said that about Belleny as well," grumbled Garon. "She's a young girl, not a warrior. What a mess, why didn't I just turn back when we found her?"

"She is much more than a warrior my friend."

After a moment of silence, Garon suggested, "What about upstairs, can we lock her up there?"

"Lock me up where?" said Belleny. She stood behind him with arms crossed and a heavy frown.

"Belleny!" squawked Garon. "We're considering our options."

"So you're going to lock me up like a prisoner?" she said, getting a glimpse of the dark emptiness beyond.

"You are a stowaway are you not?" said Kale.

"No one's locking you anywhere," he added looking outwards. Kale lowered his voice, "no one's turning back, you're coming with us."

Garon gasped, speechless at the decision, "You shouldn't have gambled your life so hastily, you hadn't even been outside for over a week," said Garon.

Kale turned and put his hand on her shoulder, "You're a lot like your mother, she too had such desires for adventure. She journeyed here to the temple on several occasions."

"Queen Vera, came here?" said Garon.

"So far from home," whispered Belleny.

"She didn't need a castle or a place called home, she had it in her heart where ever she went," said Kale.

"She came to learn and to forget, to clear away everything, cleanse and control her thoughts."

"How do you know all this?" she said.

"It's written in many books here."

A heavy noise rustled below and Kale turned to the balcony and scanned below.

"What was that?" said Belleny.

"I don't know," said Garon slowly. He peered down into the darkness and pointed in the direction of the sound.

"The temple will fall, if the witch doesn't first," said Kale.

"What, no, she wouldn't, anyway there's nothing here, the place it's empty," said Belleny.

"Not quite, it's never been so full," said Kale. "The temple walls hold the largest collection of books this side of the Slate Cliffs."

"Books? What sort of books? I didn't see any, and what kind of books would a witch want?"

"Books of Magic," said Kale.

"Magic!" blurted Belleny, covering her mouth.

"She didn't really need to know that," said Garon.

"Quiet you two. Where are these books? Upstairs? I can't see them."

"When your father expelled magic from the kingdom, the books found their way here and lined the temple walls. You can't see them as they've been hidden from prying eyes, but trust me, there is not a gap left for an envelope to slide in."

"So my mother sat in the library, she read these books?"

"She did. From what I've read she too learnt to see the unseen, commune with the parted and see into the future."

"A fortune teller?" whispered Belleny.

"Yes she had the insight. I have seen things too", admitted Kale.

"Here we go ... story time and now it's time for bed," grumbled Garon.

Kale took one last look into the distance and returned to the kitchen.

"Looks like the decision is made for both of us," said Garon, his eyes were bleak, he felt his stomach twist in knots. 'I'm sorry, but this is how it is, Kale's in command from here on. We don't have a choice."

Belleny frowned up at Garon, "Of course we have a choice. We both know I'm not a warrior or a witch killer. Kale's obviously having nightmares, all these absurd vision's he's seeing."

"He seemed quite adamant it was you and unfortunately he's been right many times before."

Belleny unfolded her arms and hung them lifelessly, "Goodnight then."

She turned and walked back into the lounge room, crawled up onto the couch and pulled a large white fur over Bateau and herself.

"Is everything okay?" said Bateau half asleep.

Belleny's mouth trembled and she choked, "No everything's not okay."

Exhausted, Bateau fell back to sleep. Belleny laid back on as well. She didn't have the strength to tell him the journey didn't end for him here either.

She stared at the fire until it too seemed to be sleeping and the embers of a twisted stump glowed peacefully. She tried her best to turn off her mind, as her mother once could but couldn't stop the spiralling fearful thoughts, even though she was exhausted and had little strength.

Kale returned to the balcony and gave Garon a bowl of steaming soup. They talked so quietly she could only hear heightened words, like Witch and Castle Mourn.

Kale said goodnight once again. Belleny shut her eyes quickly and pretended to be asleep. Through her dark lashes, she watched as he unlocked a wooden door. She noticed a stairwell as he lit a lantern and disappeared, closing the door behind him. She listened to his gentle footsteps, *he walks so quietly,* she thought. *He's so peculiar, he must be a warlock. Oh Mother, such secrets you held.*

"It will be all right," said Garon catching her staring into the fire. He turned and placed a large branch on the dwindling flames and instantly the fire woke up and lit the darkened room.

Garon's black-feathered coat glowed against the fire embers in a rich orange gradient, "Sorry," he whispered, turning back and making sure the others were still asleep. There was a big long silence as they watched the flames dance. It mesmerized them both and they willingly let it, anything was better than their wild and haunting thoughts.

With a long yawn, Garon stretched out his giant wings, wrapped them up tight and squeezed himself into the kitchen.

The Princess watched as he proceeded to curl up into a ball of black feathers.

"Goodnight Garon," she whispered.

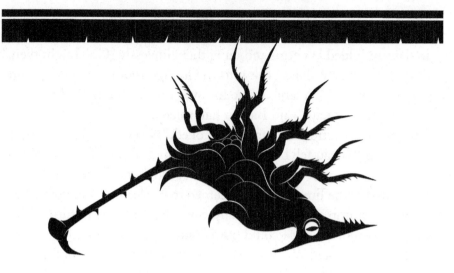

ragmented images of wild creatures with black oily blood plagued Belleny's dreams. The Occupants moved towards her, chasing her through the darkness while the floating glass Gajaban Eye spun above wildly above them. Belleny was thrusted from her slumber and sat bolt upright. She threw off her bedding and turned to face the kitchen, scanning the table and chairs and then across to Garon, who was still fast asleep. She held her beating chest and sighed with relief. The room was filled with the peaceful sleeping noises of her friends. The Occupants had not returned as she envisioned in her dreams.

Lucky I can't see into the future, she thought. She stood up and made her way over to the fireplace which was now embers. It seemed to reignite and grow with her presence. *Can you believe where we are Orphans? You're so different now, although you're not really the Orphans anymore are you? I miss you so very much ... I can't believe the Queen came here, was she really a witch? Father would never believe me ... I wonder if he knew?*

"What is that?" Belleny crouched down low and moved behind the couch. She noticed a small creature perched outside, facing out into the darkness. She pulled on her mask and reached for her blade. Quickly she let go of its handle and dug her hand into her jacket to retrieve her urchin-shaped compass.

What is it? It must be a spy. But why would it sit directly under the light of the lantern? Belleny watched her compass carefully as the triangle shards began to move into an arrow and point directly at the creature. *Come on, tell me ... friend or foe? A Rose! What a relief.*

The shards formed into a rose and repeated the sequence, an arrow and back into a rose again. Belleny closed the puzzling locket and placed it back around her neck.

"Then who are you?" she questioned.

Its coat fluttered in the light breeze. *It looks like it's made from black rose petals.* Slowly it turned towards her. It didn't bark out, cower or attack. The creature sat comfortably perched on the railing. Curiously it flipped upside down and the petals that were lying flat across its body peeled open to reveal a deep rich magenta interior. Its insect thin legs were now its arms and from underneath several black limbs extended out from a crossed legged position. Belleny was gob-smacked, she had no idea what it was.

"Are you a friend of Kale's?" it asked in an enticing voice. Its white teeth flashed through the petals.

"What? Who are you?" she said, her voice gravelly as Kikaan.

"What and who are you?" It replied scanning Belleny from head to toe, "and where did those strangers come from?"

"I'm Kikaan. We're Kale's friends. We've come from far South, beyond the Slate Cliffs."

"Kikaan? Interesting," it said slowly, "from the far South? But Kale doesn't have any friends unless you count me."

"He doesn't? You? Well, he does now, we're his friends," said Belleny.

"Most interesting," it replied.

"What are you doing out there?" she pointed.

"Night watching, what are you doing?" asked the creature, "you can remove that mask, I'm sure it's neither comfortable nor flattering. You are the Princess. Don't be alarmed. I am Rel. Kale had informed me earlier of our royal visitor before he took sleep."

"Rel that is a secret, please keep it that way.

"But, of course."

"So you are Kale's friend?" she said timidly removing her wild mask.

Rel let go of the railing and from out of its body two more pairs of legs poked from its side as it walked along the balcony wall. It pushed a small window open and climbed inside.

"I just told you he had no friends, I'm his Familiar."

"What's a Familiar?"

"It's a spiritual guide or spirit animal. A being that attends to and assists a higher Being. For me, I assist Kale," he added.

Rel crawled across to the fireplace and stood on the mantelpiece. His thorny hooked tail looked like a rose stem and he used it to latch around a large nail to dangle his body in front of the fire.

"Be careful," she whispered, shuffling quickly to the fireplace where she watched as he breathed in the smoke as if it was fresh air, expanding his body twice in size.

"Kale had unwelcome guests—he said as smoke billowed out of him—were they your friends as well?"

"No! Of course not!" she gasped, trying not to wake the others, "They were the witch's aides."

Rel proceeded to crawl along the wall towards Kale's door. He made a deep tapping sound with each footstep. Belleny realised the trailing patterns scattered across the entire temple walls were actually indents left behind from Rel's claws, and like a worn house carpet she could see where he had travelled most. It looked like he had been here a very long time.

"Good night Rel," she said as it squeezed through the gap in Kale's doorway, its tail pulled the door shut quietly leaving her standing by the fire trying to contemplate what just happened.

*

Morning sunlight woke the others with its lilac and welcoming glow, and all were awake and in preparation for the long and unknown day ahead. Belleny had finally fallen asleep and lay wrapped in the white fur. Kale boiled another concoction for breakfast while Garon returned to the same spot on the balcony and stood alone.

"The woods were alive last night. Some of the trees were set on fire. We could also hear them around the temple," said Kale to the others.

"What about Belleny? She won't be safe here," said Monté.

"That's why she's coming with us, she will be quite useful," said Kale stirring the cauldron slowly and looking deep inside.

The Orphans kept quiet, they felt oddly strange that this was true.

"The temple is not safe anymore, the sooner we leave the better," said Kale.

"We shall guard her with our lives," said Dillon.

"Mmm, we shall," said Kale as he served out each a steaming bowl of broth.

"She looks like one of us in that white fur," said Agarus.

"She is one of us," said Montë.

"What are you all gawking at?" yawned Belleny.

"Kikaan wakes, just in time for breakfast," said Danté.

"Mmm ... something sure smells good. Good morning my White Knights, did you sleep well?"

"As if we were in the Jungle Room," said Agarus, crawling along the beams in the roof.

Belleny sat down at the kitchen table where the Occupants once sat, "I had nightmares about those creatures, I feel exhausted from the barrage of abstract dreams I had."

Belleny spotted Rel hanging above Kale, its petal-like feathers rustled in the steam of the broth.

"Good, good morning Rel," said Belleny, "for a moment I thought I dreamt you up."

"Good morning—Princess Vera," he said in his peculiar voice.

"Now Rel we have to keep that knowledge to ourselves," said Kale, extending his arm towards him.

Rel squinted his eyes, "It's common knowledge, everyone knows what a morning is."

Rel stepped onto Kale's arm and crawled up onto his shoulder. Belleny now realised why his large shoulder pads were so cut up and worn.

"Rel and I have known each other since I was very young, this is his home as much as mine, he will also be joining us on our journey as he too is no longer safe here alone."

Belleny stared at the odd creature, it made the masked Kale seem even stranger.

At that moment, Palia flew inside. She overlapped her white feathers with black ones and glided in like a shadow, coming to a rest on the edge of the couch.

Garon entered in a flash of feathers, "What's your report Palia?"

"Good news. There're no insidious beings in sight. A few trees are smouldering, burnt down overnight, some were even pushed over, but there's no sign of anyone," said Palia.

Rel laughed as a puff of dark grey smoke escaped from his mouth, "Nothing indeed."

"Rel?" Kale asked staring into his eyes.

"Oh, there's something out there, you just can't see it."

"Why didn't you warn us?" said Kale.

"You needed to rest. He's not a bother unless he wakes up."

"He?" asked Dillon.

"Come follow me," Rel leaped off Kale, latched onto the wall and crawled along the fireplace. He dropped himself over the edge and breathed in a lung full of smoke as his petals rustled. Once full he held his breath and continued to the balcony, "come close and look through, you shall see," he mumbled and breathed out a fine cloud of smoke and through the tiny grey particles a grey misty scene displayed an enormous creature. It was asleep.

"Oh, my! What is it? Is it really out there?" said Belleny covering her mouth.

"Gretn Maramon," said Kale with distaste in his mouth.

"Tiss tiss, Gretn is no harm. If we let him be, he shall let us be," said Rel.

As the smoke dissipated, the giant creature became invisible once again.

"Is that thing really out there?" said Bateau rubbing his eyes.

"Did you not just see him?" said Rel. "Of course he is, but the question is why?"

"It looks like a dirty Larch Snide, I swore I could hear it scratching away last night."

"Close. Gretn is a Nighdorax, he's invisible while asleep but once awake, well then he's clearly visible."

"It can't be, they're all dead," said Garon.

"And who told you that lie?" said Rel. "Nighdorax can sleep for months, some can be dormant for years at a time, although they do prefer ocean caves, not so much out here in the open. It's been a long time since we've seen Gretn around here, hasn't it Kale?"

"I don't particularly want to wake him to ask why," said Kale.

"Ocean caves?" said Belleny. "It's a sea monster?"

"How long has it been out there?" asked Garon.

"He arrived the day after Kale left. I was going to say something to him, but we had uninvited guests who kept me quite occupied. I suggest we go soon before the sun heats up the sand and the mites, they're bound to make him restless."

It wasn't long before the travellers were gathered in the centre of the room and waiting to journey back down via the elevating platform to continue on their quest.

Kale clicked his fingers over the lever and in an instant the floor began to creak and groan, descending back down towards the ground floor.

Belleny tracked Rel's footprints, as they covered the towering curved walls in a criss-cross pattern. Just before halfway, Kale leant over to Belleny, "Kikaan."

"Yes?" she whispered.

"Please repeat these words aloud, 'Aparen Vooloice Monaire'."

"Why?" she asked curiously, "Is this a trick?"

"No questions, please do it quickly," he said and eased the lever back. The lift slowed down.

"Aparen Vooloice Monaire!"

To their amazement, the walls of the temple transformed before their eyes revealing a spiralling assortment of racks. The walls revealed hundreds of wooden shelves and hundreds of thousands of books, all archived into a tone according to the colour of their spines.

"Unbelievable!" said Bateau.

"Did I just do that?" asked Belleny.

"Hmm, magic words for magic books," grumbled Garon.

"You're welcome to read them on your return," said Kale.

He then whispered some inaudible few words and the books with their shelves vanished.

"Magic is no crime in the North Garon," said Kale and with a start, he waved his hand and pushed the lever forward, continuing downwards again.

Everyone was bewitched and silent, in particular, Bateau. He was amazed by the magic books and was still perplexed as to how Raveene could be so robust and massive yet as light as a pot plant when on the elevator platform. The floor came to a rest and Raveene took an enormous breath, stood up on his hind legs and walked off the platform towards the door with thunderous steps. They all watched as he removed the heavy wooden bar that secured the entrance door. With a push of his paw, a hot, dry breeze blew inside and with it came an assortment of bugs, leaves, and spicy smells of the lands strange fauna and flora. There was also the waft of another scent, that spelt danger.

"Eww bugs!" roared Dillon, swatting at them with his palms.

"What's that stench!" said Garon, "Larch Snide!"

"No it's Gretn," said Kale, "quick we must get out and shut the door."

Everyone followed cautiously outside. They could hear the river nearby and the breaths of the sleeping creature.

Kale pointed out to a row of assorted boulders that looked as if they had rained down from the sky. They formed a ring around the temple and consisted of various colours and shapes, some were as tall as Garon and others were small and seemed upside-down. They weaved through to the rocks towards the river and hid within them knowing the giant Nighdorax wasn't too far away.

"These are ancient rocks, brought from far corners of the land, they protect the Temple of Thought," said Kale.

"Not doing a very good job," said Garon.

"Hush," snapped Belleny,

"Look at this one," said Agarus pointing to a large opalescent rock that had been cracked completely in half as if it had been hit by a bolt of lightning.

"It was not like this before I left, the Occupants may have done this or the Nighdorax—or something else," Kale looked at Rel who was silently perched on his shoulder snapping at bugs as they flew past.

"Shh, you'll wake Gretn," said Rel blowing smoke into the air. The grey cloud fell slowly and through the vapour they could see the outline of the huge creature Gretn Maramon. Belleny didn't want to look, but she couldn't keep her eyes from staring at its coat hanger skeleton covered in thin drapes of white, grey skin.

"Ah bugs, they're on me!" Belleny shrieked as they latched on to her leather shoulder lapels. With several slaps, they continued to hook on and she hit even harder smothering their black tar-like blood against her suit. "Ah! Garon, help! They're everywhere!"

"Quiet now Kikaan, just squash them," said Garon.

"I'm trying, I hate bugs!"

Kale turned to where Gretn lay, "It's Gretn, they can smell him out in the open, they'll feed off him while he sleeps, some will get so full they'll die drinking his blood but I've never seen so many in such large numbers. We're protected here in the rocks, but we better get moving as they will wake him. Go now, quickly stay down and follow the river."

Behind the mask Belleny's face grew sad and she stared back, she didn't know what Gretn was doing, or if he was a friend or foe but being covered in blood sucking bugs seemed no way to sleep. She watched as the shape of Gretn became outlined, slowly becoming more and more visible as the bugs grew in numbers.

"The poor thing," she said, raising her locket towards Gretn's invisible body. The grey shards in her locket reformed into an arrow and started spinning as it followed a swarm of bugs as they raced by, it then settled into a skull shape. As the bugs latched on and gnawed into Gretn's head, the compass arrow started changing from skull to rose.

"I don't think he's bad," she said to Bateau.

"I don't think I want to find out."

Clawing through the fine black sand, he pushed forward, clearing Gretn as the bugs multiplied in number. The White Knights seemed unaffected by the bugs and once past Gretn continued to pick up the pace, not wanting to leave Belleny out of sight.

Kale and Danté walked beside Raveene and left the safety of the rocks. The closer they got to Gretn the more the bugs seemed to realise their presence, or taste it, and the mites began to jump onto Raveene in droves, crawling around his face and burrowing into his skin. It all happened so quickly. He wanted to growl but kept quiet not wanting to wake the beast. But he couldn't take it and viciously snapped at the air. Kale and Danté wrapped in leather armour were somewhat protected, but Raveene was only wearing his thin fur and had nothing.

"Go Raveene, get to the river now!" said Kale and with a flick of his blade he slashed the heavy salt bags hanging from his side. Raveene leapt forward trying to be as quiet as he could while jumping over one rock and perching onto another. With a giant splash, he landed rolling his back and digging his snout into the moist soil in the river bed. In a matter of seconds, the mites flew out of the riverbed clay and gnawed deeply into his skin burrowing past the first, second and third layers of the dermis.

Danté felt the bugs crawling over his back and rolled over the salt trail left by Raveene, it poured into the black sand.

Gretn Maramon's grey leg had become clearly visible as it began to scratch at its body revealing raw red marks.

"Go! Get out of here," shouted Kale running as fast as he could after turning back to see the skull of the giant creature snarling into its hind leg like a dog gnawing at its fleas.

Danté bolted up to Raveene, who was clearly in distress.

"Close your eyes!" Danté shouted at Raveene and poured his entire bag of salt over Raveene's face only barely covering his enormous skull. He yelped and quivered, snarling his lips as the salt burned and the vicious bugs all gave one last bite before falling from his skin onto the ground.

Belleny heard Raveene sobbing and turned back to face him.

"Raveene?"

Garon came to a halt, turning sharply, he saw another problem. Gretn rose to his feet and stood up, brushing the bugs off his body like dry beach sand. He was now completely visible and upon his hind legs he was as tall as a church tower.

"Fly Garon, fly!" said Belleny.

Garon turned up to Belleny, "Strap yourselves in, we are in big trouble."

The White Knights watched as Gretn continued to dust the bugs off with his thin dagger-like nails. He was frighteningly ill-looking, his pallid complexion showcased his veins against his transparent grey skin, his organs squelched and gurgled and he was covered in a waspy down of aged white hairs. Lolling his long face from the side to side, his solid black eyes were slowly scanning trying to hold their gaze. With a throaty howl, he lunged forward, each step enough to uproot trees from the ground. It didn't matter how fast the White Knights ran or how Danté dodged through the crooked trees, Gretn towered straight over them.

"Keep moving, he can't focus on all of us," said Dillon.

"He's big, but he looks weak," claimed Agarus staring up at the creature's bony frame.

"Keep away from its mouth!" shouted Montë as Palia flew up and circled the creature.

"Stop!" growled Gretn blowing Palia away with his thunderous voice.

Kale jumped up several rocks to stand on the peak of the tallest one and shouted, "Why are you here? What do you want Gretn?"

Gretn leant down, his enormous skull resting only metres from Kale, "I have come to warn you," he said, his deep voice full of sadness.

"Warn us?"

The Nighdorax paused, taking a long, deep breath, his nostrils circulating a vacuum of air pulling Kale in towards them.

Kale latched on tightly to the rock face and held Rel with one hand to save him from being sucked into the giant breaths.

"What have you seen Gretn Maramon?" said Kale.

"Death," he said slowly, "it grows beyond the Baroque Woods. You must not go, even I don't stand a chance."

"Death? Against who?"

"The witch."

"But why is she doing this? What has happened in the north?"

"The mites infestation in the north rots all living structures with decay. Her darkness grows."

Gretn leant back up and looked around, "I care not. I'm traveling further beyond the known lands ... following the ice."

"You're a fool, you'll die," said Kale.

"There is no other choice, I belong in the sea—and that is death itself. These lands are falling into shadows. Mare-Marie is beyond help," Gretn paused and scratched the burrowing mites off his face.

"Gretn we must go! Please let us pass," said Kale.

"He won't be going anywhere," said Gretn pointing to Raveene, "the black mites, they are the witch's doing. Their poison runs deep. This one must come with me, he will die without soaking in the clear mountain water of Veehn. The river is nothing but poisonous mud from here onwards."

Danté jumped aside as the giant reached down with its bony claws and scooped at the sandy ground. He picked up Raveene like a rag doll as the black sand beneath him poured below. Raveene moaned, looked up and dropped his head, too weak to resist.

"Raveene!" cried Danté, reaching out to him as the dark sand poured around him like black rain.

"I will look after your friend, we must go at once," said Gretn. "Travellers, go as you wish, but your fate is in your own hands. You have been warned."

The Weatherman shook his head and said, "You can't lead a faithful and fulfilling life, merely by existing in this one. You cannot be real if you think you are just you. Aspiring to be something else does not do your true self any justice."

"What do you mean? Who am I if I am not my true self? That's just ridiculous," said Evelin.

"You tell me?" said the Weatherman. "Now she is something, you on the other hand are—"

"I am me, Evelin Boots! There is no other! Well, there is a chance there is but she just has the same name."

"Yes that's who I'm talking about!"

"Oooooh ...you know what I mean!"

Evelin slumped her shoulders and stared at the palms of her hands, "I am me ... I exist because I just do."

"You do? Honestly kerfuffle can muddle and cause confusion to the best of us. You'll know who you are when the time is right. Sometimes you just need a little time. Magic, they say it gets better with age, you know."

"Oh Weatherman, you are too cryptic."

"Hmm, come to think of it maybe you are her?"

"Of course I am and even if I had temporary amnesia that lead me to forget, eventually my memory would return and I would still be Evelin Boots," she paused and looked up at him slowly, "who else could I be?"

"I have got it!" he said and adjusted his tall white hat, "Evelin Boots is not herself when she is someone else!"

Evelin slumped back into the soft cloudy floor, "Is that even an answer?" she quietly moaned, "I don't even know what the question is anymore? You're exhausting," she huffed.

"Shh, girl this is important," said the Weatherman and continued, "Evelin Boots was someone else, but she is now herself!" he said with a light clap. "No wonder I didn't recognise you!"

"But I'm always myself," she whispered sadly.

"Always? Try telling that to a butterfly," he scoffed.

Chapter 40 - Dark Swamp Kind

Gretn Maramon scooped Raveene up in his enormous bony arms and strode into the distance. It was some time before he left the traveller's sights and they watched mournfully as the giant's towering silhouette vanished beyond the distant mountains with their critically ill friend in his arms.

These creatures in the north were peculiar, confusing and troubling to Belleny. Her thoughts were conflicted with the 'hows' and the 'whys' such beings could exist and she thought they could only be born from a wild and troubled imagination. She scanned the sky and felt uneasy as the sun displayed a new dawn, it still looked like early morning, even though they had been travelling for many hours. The sun refused to reveal itself and remained hidden behind the hazy clouds and decaying forest that surrounded them. When the sun disappeared yesterday, so did the last few ounces of her fleeting courage.

If only I could wake up, back in the safety of the castle. Father must be furious and worried sick about me. I'm no witch killer.

"Kikaan?" she heard Garon's deep voice breaking through her concentration.

She paused, looked up and said, "What? Are we finally stopping?"

"No dear, I am just checking on you, see if you're okay. You look miles away in thought."

"I am miles away."

With each giant stride, Belleny rocked upon Garon's shoulders like a small boat set adrift at sea. From high above she had seen the river and its land change from towering forests, to mystic black sand, to the rocky mountainous terrain, and now, a swampy darkness and a barrage of decaying trees as far as the eye could see.

The river looks so terribly ill, thought Belleny. She wasn't the only one as she watched Danté stir the muddy waters with a large twisted branch. A putrid rotting scent seeped from the muddy banks. Bubbles spat out of the thick mud and the Blue Mangrave trees had sprouted barbed vines which coiled back into the ground and sucked up all the bottom dwelling shrubbery.

"Garon?"

"Mmm," he said, continuing on through the marsh.

"I guess this is the swamp lands you talked about or is this the Baroque Woods?"

"It is difficult to say exactly where the swamp starts and the woods end," he groaned, "I don't have to tell you we have to be careful in here, just keep your mask on and be alert as best you can."

"This muck is atrocious! Hold on," said Garon, as he flapped up onto a large coarse rock to scrape the mud off his filthy talons. The smooth pebbles that had been shimmering along the riverside had now been replaced by sharp stones which were cold, coarse and jagged. Small grey and twisted creatures noticed their movements and gathered along branches, like barnacles clinging under an old jetty. Other oddities watched from blackened cobweb holes and thick murky puddles.

"Look! Over there, something watching us!" said Garon.

Danté removed his bow and aimed his arrow in one smooth move.

Garon had found his sights on a heavy boned creature with an oily leathery skin that wrapped tight around its bulbous stomach. Its eyes were a milky green colour, opalescent, the creature looked as though it was blind.

"Leave him, it's just an old Moraa, poor thing has barely any vision," said Danté, "not many that can escape the rot when it's in their food and water."

"Oh my! What a monster!" said Belleny. "He looks dead."

"You would too if your diet were nothing but ... mud," said Garon.

The Moraa sank slowly in the dark waters, gazing ahead at nothing as it disappeared into the watery abyss.

Little did they know the witch was using the Moraa's cursed eyes as a looking glass, she has seen all, peering from a hundred miles away.

Garon was worried about Kale's mood. He moved nimbly and with a few flaps of his giant wings, he approached his sullen looking comrade. He stood at a barrier made of twisted woody spines. "Kale, you haven't spoken all day, do you care to share your thoughts?"

"It's a dead end. In all directions but backwards, the river was our true guide," muttered Kale. He pointed skyward in the direction of a swarm of silent black figures that hovered high above, "they've been following us for some time now."

"Yes ... I see you noticed them too—spies," said Garon.

"Garon! You can't keep that information to yourself!" snapped Belleny, saddled upon his back.

"Quite you two."

"Hey, I didn't say anything!" said Bateau.

"Hmm, we can evade them, there is always another route, off the river road," said Garon, pointing to the right, "what do you think Danté?"

"What is this muddy slop, the river shouldn't be this way! This is very, very bad news," said Danté as the White Knights caught up. "The river is a metaphor for the lifestream of all that is living, both good and evil in Mare-Marie, darkness is upon all living creatures when the river dies."

"Damn it!" squawked Garon, kicking a tree stump and completely uprooting it.

"What do you think you're doing ya big dumb bird?! That's my house you just kicked over!" shouted a raspy voice as the stump rolled and slowly sank into the swampy embankment.

Everyone turned to see a short, grubby, big-mouth gremlin who had smeared a thick white stripe down his broad chest and bulbous belly. He crossed his arms and thumped his three thick round fingers

Garon knelt down and said, "My apologies I didn't realise."

He returned the tree stump upright and awkwardly wiped the dirty mud from its bark.

"You can stop Garon," said Kale shaking his head.

"Why you! This can't be your home it's solid," said Garon pushing the trunk back down and deep into the mud with his mighty claws.

"Haha, bird brain," it laughed slapping its slippery palms over its muddy belly.

"You picked a bad day to mock me," said Garon stomping in close.

"Get back beast, I'll have you cooked alive," he spat, "and that goes for every last one of you," he cursed swaying his fists up at them.

Garon let out a roaring laugh as Belleny and Bateau held on, "Finally some humour on this forsaken journey. Do you know any other jokes besides pushing out that painted belly of yours and wiggling your slimy arms about?" said Garon stabbing his beak up close.

"What? You'll be sorry you spoke to me that way, I'm not what you think I am!"

"And what are you little one? Besides fat, vulgar and short? Oh and, of course, a liar. You couldn't live in a tree trunk, let alone fit in one."

"Stop this at once!" shouted Belleny wildly pulling back on Garon's reins, "we're very sorry, he doesn't know what he's saying, let alone doing. We have been travelling for some time, we are all weary and a little agitated, my name is Kikaan."

The creature stood back, picked up its stick and pointed it up at Garon's face, "Control your beast, he looks like he's already tarred and feathered, next time I recommend you turn him into soup." The creature finished his speech by slamming his stick into the mud.

Garon chuckled to himself as it snapped in two.

Belleny composed herself, cleared her throat and in her scratchy voice declared, "My name is Kikaan, and these are my friends, can you help—"

The creature shook his stick up at Belleny cutting her short, "Odger is my name and I don't care who you lot are, you're just like the rest of 'em, so go and bother someone else." He turned in a splash of mud and plodded off in a huff.

"Wait! Please don't go we just need directions," begged Belleny, "I have sweets," she added lowering her tone.

With a heavy snort Odger started to laugh, "You think you can win me over with sweets, you'll need to try better than that."

"What do you want?" said Belleny, "please wait!" yelled Belleny but Odger stomped off grumbling into a thicket.

Kale's patience had worn thin. He ripped off his gloves and marched through the sticky mud, straight up to Odger, twisting him around by his shoulders and drove his knife up against his side.

"What is wrong with you Odger? We're here to stop the evil that seeps through these woods; it can be returned to how it once was."

"Erm, how about you put that blade away ... what's this evil you speak of?" he said twisting himself free of Kale's grip.

"You know very well of the evil that's spreading," said Danté with a sly half-smile.

"The witch won't be stopped by the likes of you," blurted Odger, "she's won the North and next will be the Mare-Marie kingdom."

"Where is her lair? Is she still at Castle Morne?" asked Kale.

"Castle Morne? Most call it Castle Fall around here," snorted Odger.

Garon poked his sharp black beak and wet black eyes only inches away from Odger's face.

"No Garon! Let him speak," said Belleny holding on tightly.

"Go on," said Kale as he loosened his grip and returned his blade.

"I haven't been back in a long while, shouldn't have gone there in the first place, I'm pretty much stuck here now," he said, shrugging his shoulders, "but if anyone knows the direct way Mune the Worm will know, he used to work there, you'll find him down the road," said Odger pointing behind him and there they noticed a broken fence and a gate that lay flat half submerged in the mud.

"Ha, a fence!" said Danté.

"It'll be a tight squeeze for you through those first trees, but beyond them there is a path of sorts, best stick to the path if I was you."

"But it's heading back from where we came?" said Dillon.

"So what?" said Odger, "it circles around the river, follow that and only a fool couldn't find the castle. Now where's that candy you were talking about?"

"Thank you Odger," said Belleny and she untied a leather satchel and threw it down to him.

"You had candy smuggled with you all this time?" said Bateau.

Odger ran off and dove, squeezing his belly down a muddy crack within a large tree stump.

"So he does live in a dirty tree stump, after all," said Garon.

The group took the path suggested by Odger; it was comforting to see the broken gate and fallen fence, proof that this was once a trail. Once through the thicket of trees that grew wildly across its entrance a pathway soon revealed itself. Deep in thought Kale chose to walk silently by himself; Belleny watched him curiously. He surprised her with his threatening outburst at Odger, such a change from before. She noticed when he removed his gloves his hands were clean and waxy white as if they had never seen the sun. His skin glowed against the dark scenery and decaying textures. She also noticed he only took off his mouth guard to drink and eat, leaving the rest of his face hidden under his hood. Kale was so unlike Danté, who along the way unashamedly stripped off his protective garments, close to nakedness, to bathe in the river.

The path circled as Odger said and rolled down a steep hill, deeper and deeper until a row of fence posts appeared upright, this was a good sign, thought Belleny until the path and the fence began to split up and go in several directions.

"Oh, this is just great, now which way is the river?" said Garon, standing at the crossroads.

"Guys quickly come over here," shouted Montë, "I found a worm." Montë had spotted an iridescent blue worm on top of a charcoal rock.

"Hello, my name is Montë, are you Mune?" he asked.

"This is ridiculous," said Garon approaching with a huff, "Odger was playing with us, I've never met a worm that could talk and I've met my fair share of worms."

Everyone gathered around the worm, it didn't do much, every once in a while it would twitch but, for the most part, would lay still.

"Let me try," said Palia who strangely remembered a worm at the circus that could talk, "Hello? Are you Mune the Worm?" she said and they all waited silently for an answer.

"This is embarrassing," said Garon.

It was then that a light snicker could be heard in the trees above.

"Who goes there?" roared Garon.

"Who goes there?" replied someone imitating him, "And who talks to worms on this fine day?"

"Names are not important," said Garon removing his blade.

"Put it away, Mr. No Name," the voice said, "you'll find it quite difficult to stab me my friend," said the voice as a creature climbed out from behind a dead tree branch no thicker than an arm. He was very strange indeed, his face long and thin, made his eyes squint long ways and up close together.

It seemed he had an extra set of elbows and knees resulting in extremely long arms and legs, which he could extend ever so far moving like a Preying Mantis.

Belleny was not frightened, as she felt even she could snap him like a twig if the situation arose.

"I am Mune," he said.

"We were told you were a worm?" said Garon.

"What are you supposed to be?" he replied, "they call me the Worm because I'm thin and I love eating dirt," said Mune as he continued to move back and forth from the branches, spying on each of them.

The group fell quiet as they realised the joke Odger had played on them. He had them all speaking to a worm.

Danté spoke first, "Can you direct us out of here and towards—"

"Castle Fall?" asked Mune abruptly.

Without breaking eye contact, Danté grasped the handle of his blade. Blinking, Mune stared at Danté's threatening gesture and his expression soured and turned to a frown.

"You are a fool. Many have been looking for the castle and it's beyond me as to why it cannot be found. It's not as if it's easy to miss. It's built within the skull of a fallen giant!"

"Which one of these roads leads to the castle?" questioned Danté.

"Follow the fence until the trees start to grow leaves, you can't miss the river, but you must cross the old wooden bridge or you'll never get across.

All other paths across have been destroyed, although you two could just fly over," he pointed to Garon and Palia. Kale tilted the peak of his hood and said thank you.

Silently Mune whispered, "I hope you find what you're looking for before it finds you."

The weary travellers took heed with the directions provided by the creature Mune. Obeying, they followed the picket fence for hours and hours, silently walking into the unknown. Kale glancing at Danté who's edgy expression reflected his own slight misgivings about the exactness of the path they were taking. One by one, they all started to feel more confident as the scenery began to unfurl and change. Belleny sat up as she noticed that the empty black branches began to sprout tiny lemon green leaves. The sprouts reminded her of the tree Winta, which grew in her room, clawing its branches across her roof and walls.

"I can hear the river!" said Bateau.

"It's like thunder!" added Belleny excitedly as Garon sped up.

The White Knights took off climbing from branch to branch and together they sat high upon the canopy of a towering wall of trees. Open mouthed, the group stared at the epic scale of the horizon and the terrain ahead, through the branches a sliver of sunlight beamed through the swirling grey clouds revealing a savage mountainside covered with shrubs, harrowed trees and giant dry white stones. The river tore around the mountains and roared off into the distance.

"I'm flying next time," grumbled Garon.

"Next time?" said Danté.

"That doesn't look good," said Kale pointing ahead, "what's happened to the Veelin River? It looks furious!"

"I don't think it is the Veelin if I'm reading this map right. They look like the five grey mountains don't they Bateau?" said Belleny.

"That's the Veelin River," Kale pointed to a dark and muddy river running into the forest behind them, "then that monstrosity in front of us is the Cassan River," said Kale.

"It can't be? What happened to it? It's supposed to be a trickle compared to the Veelin," said Garon.

"Looks as if something's blocking the Veelin on the other side of the mountain, a dam maybe? Splitting its waters down into the Cassan," said Kale.

"Nice move witch," grumbled Dillon.

"We at least know where we are. Come on we'll have to cross it," said Danté.

"I ... I ... can't swim in that," blurted Belleny.

"I'm not too good with water either," added Bateau.

"I could fly you over, but I can't lift half of the White Knights," added Garon.

"Perhaps we use the bridge that dirt eating worm recommended," said Dillon.

"That could be it up there," pointed Belleny.

"I'll go scout the situation," informed Palia.

"Please be discreet, we'll wait for you here," added Garon and with that she flew, her feathers a charcoal black mirroring her shadow beneath. When Palia returned, they could see she brought bad news.

"The bridge has been sabotaged, it has completely collapsed into the river."

Unimpressed they ventured forward, the bridge submerged, sunken into the river as wild muddy rapids smashed hard against it.

Garon stared into the distance, "Look," he pointed to a clearing of torn out trees forming a pathway up the mountain, "I have a good feeling the castle is right over there."

"Is it on the map Belleny?" asked Bateau.

"No, but there is a drawing of a sleeping giant on the other side. Going off this map it's enormous!"

"The giant is long dead," said Kale.

"From what I'm told the castle was built within its skull," said Danté.

"Bridge or no bridge we have to get across this river," said Garon.

"I'll go and find this castle. Hopefully, I'll find a way for you to cross, you should lay low here and rest," said Palia.

"Hmm, are you sure?" said Garon.

"Please be careful," said Belleny.

"There is room for us to hide under here," said Kale as he crawled beneath the broken bridge. "Palia's right we need rest. We have been walking for some time, now would be a good time to eat."

Agreed they sat in the cold beneath the bridge and refuelled, watching the wild rapids surging below.

"What's that?" said Garon noticing something large coming down the river, "some sort of a boat?"

"A boat in these waters?" said Kale,"

"It looks big," said Danté.

"It's not a boat! It's a bug," said Garon.

As the giant form revealed itself, though the crashing rapids, it appeared as a gigantic beetle the size of a bus using its hard shell and long stabbing legs to stride through the muddy water. On its back, it was carrying a family of Laramok's, strapped into a balcony type scaffold erected on its back.

The beetle walked through the currents on ten-meter tall barbed legs, steering through the muddy waters as it gushed underneath. The largest Laramok with a face housing more than enough pairs of eyes sat at the front of the scaffolding in a strapped down rocking chair. He pointed at Garon with the handle of his long leather braided whip.

"Bridge won't let you pass eh? Yep ... they will do that," he said as his face full of eyes blinked randomly at them.

Puzzled, the travellers paused and looked at each other.

Danté spoke first, "We need to get across can you give us a hand?"

"Why doesn't he take you over, feathers not what they used to be old man?" he mocked at Garon.

"The river's too dangerous, we can't risk anyone falling in," explained Kale.

"Okay then. Wait! Before you step foot onto my sweet bug mobile ... show me your mark."

"What mark?" said Garon, looking at the others puzzled, "what mark?" he shrugged.

"What do you mean what mark? The witch's mark, you know how she is these days?" he said squishing up his face. "No mark, not gettin across the river," he flashed them his wrist. A crude symbol was burnt into his skin.

"Well no, I didn't know we needed one," replied Garon.

"Not need a mark, 'ear dat kids," he turned slightly shouting over his shoulder, "not need a mark he's sayin."

The laramok kids burst out laughing in unison like baby goats.

"That's enough you little buggers! Look no one crosses the Cassan without one, it's the rules, its be the law of laws. Don't want to be caught on the other side without one, you'll be anyone's free dinner."

"Where do we get this mark?" inquired Kale.

Belleny stared down at Bateau, behind her mask he could see the whites of her eyes. He held her hand tight with his tails.

"At the castle, of course," he flicked his whip up at the last of the five mountains and they imagined it sat just on the other side. "First timers 'eh, well you don't want to miss out tonight then? Rumours are it's going to be quite the event, plenty of helpings if you know what I mean," he slapped his hands against his pot belly. The small children playing on the back of the beetle began to cheer.

"But if the castle is on the other side of the river, how does anyone get across to get this mark?" said Kale.

"Well that's the thing isn't it, she don't want too many outsiders coming this way anymore, there's only just enough for us, many mouths to feed, it's demanding work I can imagine, I should know I have six of the buggers, not six hundred."

"Six hundred!" gasped Belleny.

"Enough what?" asked Garon.

"Ah, you're funny big guy, you should go easy on the stuff," he said and whipped the giant bug. Slowly it crept off the embankment.

"Ya' gut no mark, I can't help ya'," he shouted, "I got a job to do, it's going to be a long day, try the bridge again, they need a good poking," he laughed, pointing at the broken bridge with his thumb and with several hard whips the bug began to stride off through the muddy rapids. Belleny watched as the strange insect-like children poked their tongues out at them. She crossed her arms angrily.

"Use the bridge!" griped Garon, he picked up the nearest thing, which happened to be a large white rock and with all his frustration threw it at the bridge. It smashed across several planks, before disappearing into the water.

Like thunder underwater a thick bubbly growl came from within the river.

"What was that?" said Belleny.

"I'll tell you in a minute, everyone out!" yelled Garon.

Quickly they climbed up to the surface as the two sides of the bridge began to creak and move out of the rapids, heavily and slowly they wrenched themselves out of the river.

They watched in disbelief as the two sides of the bridge pulled themselves out of the water and as they did the large planks of wood formed themselves into the shape of two giant figures, one an old man on their side and another an old woman on the other side of the river. Dripping with mud, reeds and barnacles, their large wooden hands removed the reeds and scratched away the mussels. The closest one, resembling the old man, had his legs buried deep in the ground.

"Damn barnacles, get in all the wrong places," he growled and once finished picking them off, he turned to the travellers, eyeing off Garon, who looked rather guilty.

"What's the big idea, throwing rocks at me and my wife?" he growled and leant down at Garon as much as his body allowed.

"How rude! Don't you dare let them across!" huffed the woman on the other side, "how would you like me to drop a rock on your head. There's no way we're letting you across," she continued, "people these days have an inflated sense of entitlement, trying to take advantage of any situation," she said thumping herself down on the embankment.

"Yes dear, but I can handle this situation from here," said the old man.

Garon stepped forward, "I am sorry, I didn't realise, I didn't know—" his voice continued to fumble.

"Stop stammering, just show us your marks and you will be on your way," the old man said in a huff.

"I'm afraid we have no marks," Belleny said politely.

"Well then little one, you better make yourself comfortable over this side. Anyway you're all better off here, what would your mother think?" he said, crossing his arms with a heavy wooden thud.

Bateau was confused and asked, "Forgive me if I'm wrong but have you always been … a bridge?" he asked.

"Of course not!" he grunted, "No one's born a bridge," he slammed his fist into the muddy embankment flinging mud in all directions.

"Are you under a curse?" questioned Kale abruptly.

The planks in the old man's face began to quiver.

"Of course we are," he answered with a rumbling sigh.

"What's going on over there?" shouted the bridges wooden wife.

He turned and shouted back, "Hold on to your britches woman!"

"Are they crossing or not husband?"

"Patience please wife! I'm talking to them," he said and leant in closer to the group.

"Sorry about that she gets agitated quite easy these days, with the barnacles n' all."

"Who is she?" asked Belleny.

"My love, my light, my dearest wife. We're doomed so spend the rest of our lives together as wooden structures in this surging wet mud," he lowered his head, "we're damned, thanks to that wicked creature. We both lived, worked and even got married in the castle. Our surname is Bridges. After that creature had taken over she thought, it would be quite humorous to turn us into actual bridges. It's been so long now ... I can remember when we once walked along the riverbanks and watched the fish in the stream below ... bah!"

Belleny's heart tightened, "Oh my that is terrible, we too had been cursed by her," she pointed across to the Orphans.

"And we broke it," said Dillon proudly.

"What? You broke it!" said the old man nearly ripping himself from the ground, "I can't believe it, how? You must tell me!" He began to crawl forward until he became stuck.

Kale stood forward and put his hand on the old man, "We need to get across this river, the witch alone can lift the curse and we're the ones that will make her do it," said Kale.

"You're too late. Maybe a year ago you could have had a chance. Do you even know what you're up against?"

"We do. We are prepared," said Kale.

"We've seen this place go from sadness to madness and now beyond. We've sent others away just to save them and the ones that we thought might have a chance, we let through and never saw them again, not a single one."

"You have nothing to lose," said Kale.

The old man rubbed his wooden chin and stood up on his rickety legs and turned to his wife.

"Please stand up my dear, I'm allowing them to cross."

Slowly the bridges met in the middle and held hands. Belleny watched in amazement.

"Quickly cross now," said the old man "this is not as easy as it looks."

Excited they raced across. Halfway Belleny told Garon to stop and she leant over touching both sides of the bridge, "Thank you, I will do all my power to release you from this curse."

"This is not your destiny to be stuck like this, this is my destiny to free you," said Belleny.

"Just keep out of her cauldron and don't go near her shadow," said the old man."

"Did you hear the young girl my love? Did you hear, we're going to be set free?"

"Yes I heard, another destiny," she sighed.

From the stony hillside, the voyagers watched as the old couple released hands and unlocked their wooden embrace. With a thick muddy splash, they sank below the rapid surface, deep beneath the water to the silent depths and out of sight.

— PART THREE —

Lost & Found

If experiencing the dating scene was a tricky business, then getting back into the game was bordering on gruesome for Robin Boots.

Evelin watched her father flit back and forth around the kitchen as he re-wiped surfaces in an already spotless room. Intermittently she tried to start a light conversation to restart his overloaded sensory switchboard of a brain, but it was no use. Robin's nervous pacing and mono-syllabic answers it was near impossible.

Maybe I've inherited his nervous gene? Ha, but definitely not the Boots 'cleaning' gene.

With a fine-line marker pen, Evelin distracted herself and carefully began to draw a top hat on an image of a white cat in a hardcover book.

Robin paused mid wipe, "Hey! You can't do that. Isn't that a library book?"

"Yes they all are," said Evelin calmly patting the small pile, "I'm a reader Robin."

"And a vandal! Give me that pen Evelin!" he firmly said and smiled.

"I wonder if BC would look good in a little top hat?" she asked.

Robin circled closer, "Actually, that's not bad, that's a fine looking cat and a finer looking top hat! Hey isn't that the same breed as BC, a Peterbald?"

At a start, Evelin began to tear the page from the library book.

Robin snatched the book from her, "Evelin Boots the book destroyer, well I never."

He turned around to see that Evelin's face had dropped into a pale and sorrowful expression.

"Oh Eve, I was only kidding around."

Evelin stared down at the silky white cat image and spoke quietly, "I'm not a book destroyer Dad, please don't call me that."

Robin crouched beside her and said, "Hey I know, I was just playing with you, it's not as if you burnt down your school library."

Evelin froze for a second, her heart beating against her chest.

"Pardon? ... of ... of course I didn't," she stammered.

In one swooping motion, she slammed the book closed and stood up.

Try to change the energy in the room and change the subject, Evelin began, "No wonder she's fallen for you Robin. I don't see why you're so worried? She's a school teacher, not the Boogey Man."

Ignoring her veiled compliment, Robin began opening and closing and re-opening the pantry for the one-hundredth time, "should I start cooking now?"

"Robin! It's not even three in the afternoon, what are you cooking, a Jacobean banquet?"

"Not tonight. I'm baking a quiche. I thought I'd use her eggs, it would be the right thing to do."

"She's probably sick of eggs, but yeah, it's a good choice. I can pick some greens from the garden and make a salad for you. You try your 'special' salad dressing. It will give you something to do while you're figuring out how to string a sentence together."

"Speaking of the hairless devil," said Robin pointing behind her.

BC sauntered triumphantly into the kitchen as if he had lived there all his life. Without a second thought, he sprang onto the kitchen table.

"Hello, Mr. BC, they say we have to keep you out of the sun," said Robin.

"Yes, a Vampire cat. Let me look at those fangs of yours," said Evelin, pushing up BC's top lip to reveal his pointy white incisors, "you may be right Robin ... hey the phone's ringing, your turn."

"What if it's Jacqueline?" gasped Robin.

"So what if it is?"

Robin cleared his throat and took the receiver, "Hello this is Robin

Boots speaking."

"Oh ... Hi Milton ... You're where? Does your mother know this? Oh is she? ... Yes Evelin is here, I'll put her on."

"Why doesn't he just come over?" asked Evelin

"He's not home, he had to go to Southington Prison, he's actually ringing from inside!" exclaimed Robin.

"What? Southington Prison?" she gasped. Evelin took the handset, "Milton?"

"Eve! Guess where I am? I'm inside the big house, I'm using the wall phone."

"So—you are in Southington?" Evelin whispered in disbelief..

"Yeah, Aunty Jean and I got news about my parents last night, they're being moved to another prison, eight hours drive away in the middle of the desert. Mum also wants me to go live there as well because she misses me, don't worry I'm not, it's supposed to be some alternative rehabilitation programme where we can all hangout or something. Good for them I guess, I wouldn't want to be locked up with a bunch of nut jobs if I were only a thief."

"Only a thief? Your folks were bank robbers Milton. So you're coming back soon, right? It's the holidays." Evelin walked towards the back door with the phone in her hand and stared into the garden.

"Well, probably be away for a week, there're a few things that need to be sorted out and my aunt has organised to see another lawyer, he's got a nice white suit too. They're working on getting an early release date for good behaviour."

"A week Milton," Evelin went silent and her voice crackled when she began to speak, "but—"

"This is good news Eve, I thought you would be happy. I'll bring back a prison souvenir for you. Chin up Boots, you'll be okay, I'll see you next week. Sure it's the holidays but it's about time you had one all by yourself, without me hanging around screwing it up. Go on your own adventure. Eve—you there?"

"Yeah," she replied, her voice barely audible.

The payphone made a few alarms and Milton dug his hands into his pockets, "Damn, sorry Eve, I don't have enough coins, stupid pay phone, I'll ring you when I get—"

Click.

The phone line went dead. Evelin put the phone down and turned up at Robin.

"Prison," she said quietly.

Robin saw that familiar sadness in her eyes, so he quickly comforted her with his hand on her head and scuffed her hair.

"Don't worry Princess, he'll be back before you know it. We can hang out these holidays, okay?"

It was then her watch alarm went off. Shaking her head, she shrugged and grabbed BC and went upstairs to her room. BC, not quite sure what was going on was squished tight within her grip.

"What's going on?" she grumbled, "I've had enough of this!" she said reaching for her pills. The container slipped from her hands and the small white pills came tumbling out and bounced like hailstones across her jewellery box and dressing table top.

"Eve, are you all right?" said Robin from outside her door.

Quickly she swallowed one.

Robin peered in, "You okay Eve?"

She looked up at him as if she had been caught stealing, embarrassed she put her head into her pillows.

"Evelin, you're going to be back on track in no time." He walked up beside her bed. "I'm here, I'm not going anywhere and I'm always going to look after you."

"Yeah, I know, I just wanted to hang out with him. It's the holidays, you know," she said, picking up the framed bugs Milton gave her ... I just ... he keeps my mind away from my thoughts."

"Your thoughts? Are they bad?"

"Sometimes."

Robin noticed her dresser and the snow white pills sprawled across it.

"It was a bad one, hey?" he said in a comforting tone, "would you like to visit Esta? She did say to go anytime something came up. Or not, it's up to you, but I'm happy to take you."

Evelin paused for a moment and stroked BC.

"Maybe, do you mind? I think I need to see her."

"Of course. I'll give her a call and book you in."

"Hey wait! Jacqueline's coming over, your dinner date remember?"

"We'll be back in time, if not, she'll understand," he smiled.

Evelin listened to Robin talking downstairs on the phone, she couldn't work out if he was talking to Esta or Jacqueline. She was feeling quite drowsy and placed her head on her pillow. Robin's deep voice rose and fell like rolling waves and before she knew it she had fallen asleep.

"Where am I? Weatherman is that you?"

She rubbed her eyes, adjusting to the glare of the soft white surroundings. The Weatherman appeared although somewhat different than his usual perky self, he sat forward, slouching on a large cloud chair with his face cupped in his hands.

"Oh it's you Boots," he sighed, "you've come at a bad time I'm afraid."

"Oh no! What is it? What's the matter?" she asked stepping carefully across the spongy clouds.

His moustache quivered as he slowly looked up at her.

"I'm expecting the worst Boots. Something that's truly worse than worse, but this is much worse."

"That sounds awful Weatherman, what should we do?"

"Oh, Boots you are a living, breathing questionnaire aren't you.

"A questionnaire?"

"A person that asks a million questions at once!" he bleated.

The Weatherman looked back over his shoulder, "Stay sharp Boots, it could come at any moment," he whispered, hoping it couldn't hear him. "I don't know exactly when, could be now, or even then."

"Oh no," whispered Evelin. She too looked behind her as well but there was nothing but white clouds to be seen. "Do you think we can hide from it? Inside a cloud?" she asked, crouching down and looking up at his sorry face.

"No. There's nowhere to hide up here, everyone knows only clouds can hide in clouds. Don't go climbing inside one, you'll fall straight through."

"Straight through?" she gulped.

"Of course straight through the clouds. Didn't I mention that?"

"Well, you know now. Better late than never, but never later than never."

It was then Evelin was reminded how the Weatherman at times made little to no sense, at least in her mind. She stood up, composed herself and asked politely, "May I ask what exactly we are hiding from?"

"I don't know what it is. I've never even seen it. I don't think you can?"

he replied shrugging his shoulders.

"So how do you know when it's here?" asked Evelin.

"I can feel it in my bones, cold as ice, it gives me the chills all over."

"So it is real?"

"Of course it's real, as real as you and I are both standing here."

Chapter 44 - The Tunnel

The Cassan River surged forward at great speed. Large rocks in the river bed broke the flow of the muddy water, creating massive rapids from which the water tore at the river bank. It brought with it broken branches and uprooted debris, splitting the banks further apart. But there was one species of creature which saw the waves as small obstacles, this was the black Double Decker Bus-sized Goramor beetle who used the waterway as a highway. These gargantuan beetles remained in the violent waters unfazed, they were the public transport systems of the wild North. Upon their backs, they would carry numerous passengers, loan warriors, creatures doing their daily shopping, rogue oddities and general ruffians all sitting up high on makeshift scaffolding aligned like bus seats all in a row.

Kale led the travellers down into the wild shrubbery beside the riverbank. As they huddled down low, nestled within a clay crevice that cut deep within the embankment, the exposed wiry tree roots helped give them camouflage as they were metres from the watery slurry of the river.

"Sit low you two," advised Garon, shielding his wings across Belleny and Bateau creating a protective wall of feathers.

"Look at these monsters. Those creatures in the water! They're ... they're enormous!" Belleny stammered.

"Shhh, sit back down," said Bateau, tugging at her with his tails.

"There's no way we can pass them," she whimpered, "this reaffirms that my fears of the outside world were valid ones. This situation is even worse than anything I could have ever imagined."

Upon the giant beetles, a horde of terrifying sub-creatures with wild yellowing eyes and a taste for violence argued and pushed each other about. Their leader was the deformed and grotesque Badgabar, who sat up front steering the beast from a towering high chair. With a violent crack of his long whip, his barbed fingers clutched the leather baton whip up high. Badgabar yelled at the winged creature standing behind him, "If you bump my chair one more time I'll—"

"You'll what?" roared one winged hideous beast as it launched up from the platform, swooped and soared past him. The winged creatures main delight was to antagonise. It flew a circle and plunged back down towards Badgabar, "You don't want to know what I'll do!"

Badgabar hissed, unnerved by the open threat. He brought his arm down hard missing the creature's face by several inches and continued down whipping the goramor across its bulbous eyes. The giant bug halted and jolted its massive frame, knocking many of its passengers into the murky depths of the rapids twenty metres below.

The dark blue beast opened its winged arms out wide and scraped its claws along the goramor's hard shell, leaving a mark of victory, "Nice try," it snarled.

"Move back I said!" Badgabar roared over his shoulder. "Or I'll chuck you overboard!"

"Sink or swim! Sink or swim!" the Spit Goblins began to chant in unison, sounding like a booger chewing cacophony.

Like a possessed rugby scrum, the rowdy passengers pushed forward. Bedazzled, the blue, winged beast known as Lord Verious, had little time to secure his footing, and he received the full force of their grunt, knocking him off balance. Flapping wildly he clawed forward, but Badgabar raised his whip and flashed it down latching onto Lord Verious's ankle. As the creatures surged forward again, Lord Verious swiped his bony claws at Badgabar, only to latch onto two other victims by their throats. Lord Verious plunged overboard with two screaming Spit Goblins.

"You will pay for this!" howled Lord Verious as he swallowed gallons of muddy water and tried in vain to clamber back onto the two squealing goblins before all three were sucked into the dark depths disappearing into the swirling cold darkness.

Frightened by how close they were, Garon held his breath and covered Belleny and Bateau behind his outstretched wings. He felt as if the creatures removed their focus from Lord Verious and across to the river's edge they would surely be spotted.

"Sink or Swim! Sink or swim!" the rowdy passengers continued to heckle as everyone moved to the side of the goramor and watched, entertained as Lord Verious returned to the surface. Many cheered and clapped at the spectacle of his anguish. With a gurgling roar, Lord Verious raised his fist into the air. Their cheers came to a gasping halt as one pointed out an enormous spiralling tree trunk flooding down the rapids directly towards Lord Verious. The howling and chorus chanting increased.

"Nooo!" screamed Lord Various as the tree appeared above him as it swung sideways like a brick door, slamming straight into his face. It continued on at full speed and like a dead moth in a storm water drain Lord Various floated lifelessly downstream and into the distance.

"Now that's entertainment!" sniffed a hooked nose Boz Hrog.

"One less mouth to feed," grinned one razor tooth Crakheth.

"You can talk fatty, move over or you're next," one snarled, pushing him into the others.

"What? You move over! You Stinky Larch Snide."

"Who you calling stinky? Hog-face!"

And with this, Badgabar drove his giant beetle forward and once again the quarrelling began.

"Quick! Now is our time to go," said Kale. He signalled the travellers and without discussion took off uphill, weaving through the bramble and strange white rocks to the wall of grey trees that circled up the mountain-top incline.

"Just great, look at this," said Garon smashing his feathered fist through the bone-dry branches, "this will take us forever to get through, maybe never," he grumbled.

"Come on Garon, we've been through worse, we'll clear a path," said Danté.

"You do know where we stand Danté?" said Garon.

"Is this ... the Yellow Tree Woods?" said Belleny after studying her map while high upon Garon.

Garon nodded, "It was once called that ... but now this hellish place is known as the Thorned Woods, it's as if overnight the river and surrounding lands were poisoned.

"No witch could do this to a forest. The forests hold their own barrier. Something much stronger has taken hold of the north," said Kale.

"Not the witch you say?" said Garon, "bah! Of course, she did this. Look around this place is all her doing, it's the result of pure evil."

Monté leant down low to the ground and closed his eyes, "I can sense how sad the forest is. Even the soil feels scorched, it's in tremendous pain."

Garon reached forward and snapped a branch letting it fall to the ground, "Pain or not, these trees have more roots above ground than underneath. It will take us days to climb through ... and exactly what direction would we go?"

"You're right," said Kale, "I think we've all had our fair share of thorned branches. We'll have to find another way if there is one."

"Of course we have," mused Rel stirring from his slumber.

"Rel, how nice of you to join us. Any advice before you doze off again for you third sleep for today?" asked Kale.

"Fourth, the bugs woke me. You know very well I'm nocturnal. The goramor always take the quickest watery path, I suggest taking their lead."

"Or there is an alternative route," said Rel pointing into the Thorned Woods."

Danté nodded, "If we stick to the path along the river we should have adequate time to hide for cover, but any sight of us hiding could arouse suspicion and could spell disaster for the princess. I don't think we have seen what we're up against just yet."

"That large white rock in the distance would be a safe destination," said Garon.

"Yes, we must be quick then, follow me," said Kale. He tilted his hood and scanned the devoured landscape below. Like a fox, he darted and ducked through fallen tree trunks, passing through small bushes and weaving through strange ornamental gardens of flat white rocks that seemed to be sporadically thrown across the hillside. In a flash, he ripped off his glove and signalled the travellers, his pale white palm illuminated by the scorched soil and stark surroundings.

One at a time each as skilful as the next climbed back down the jagged slope arriving unseen by the water beasts .The river curved around the mountain, the muddy slush made noises like a giant's ravenous stomach, belching, bubbling and burping as it went.

"Garon!" gasped Belleny, "What's that in the water?"

A fat waterlogged creature bobbed pass, cold and lifeless.

"It's nothing," said Garon lifting his wing, "don't look Kikaan."

Like a pack of protective wolves, the Orphans surrounded Garon, Belleny and Bateau and they led them along a winding path safe from the river's edge. From here they noticed the goramor bugs had arrived at a docking station and they saw hordes of creatures ascending the mountain, not only from the river but many approached from across the terrain as well. An extensive pathway of trees had been removed from the earth, brutally snapped and yanked up from their roots by their base.

Like Cockroaches, the mass horde of goramor climbed the steep mountain as a row of buses, their enormous bodies dripping barrels of oily river mud and painting a slippery path for those stuck behind them.

"We should be safe here for a while," said Danté.

"Safe?" scoffed Garon, "Nowhere in the north is safe."

"Can you hear that?" said Montë as his ears twitched back and forth.

"I can, it's been getting louder and louder," said Bateau.

"An endless waterfall," said Belleny, "it's here on my map. Unfortunately there is nothing more drawn on it, we'll have to add it ourselves."

"What do you mean, the drawing on the map just ... stops?" asked Bateau.

"There is nothing on the edge of something," said Rel. He leapt from Kale's shoulder and stabbed his black nails into the side of the chalky white rock. With a small puff of smoke, he let the travellers look into the smoke vision.

"From the endless waterfall to the great cliffs of Azare, there is nothing, but nothing is something waiting to happen is it not? Such fertile grounds have Mare-Marie. The Endless Waterfall began as once a trickle of a stream. What is it now?"

"I have no idea what he is on about," whispered Bateau into Belleny's ear.

"Rel is right, there will be no correct map for Mare-Marie," said Danté, "Tjaman and Palice have also been here before. Palice once drifted out into the endless nothing attached to Tjaman by its unbreakable chain, and as far as the eye could see was emptiness in all directions."

Rel scattered upside-down and paused, he looked up again and curled his spiked tail towards the top of the rock.

"What is it?" whispered Kale.

Rel smirked and replied, "A beating heart of scales and spikes. Not a danger unless it bites."

"Rel the poet. Danté pass me that stick, we are not alone," said Kale taking it and stabbing it into the ground. Magically he removed his cloak and without changing his stance placed it on the sick mimicking himself. With a silent nod, he disappeared into the shrubs surrounding the rock.

While the travellers were pondering their surroundings and formulating a strategy, unbeknownst to them, a scaly green figure was watching them in silence. The creature lay flat against a chalk white rock and like an animal stalking its prey, was peering over the edge and eyeing them with its bullet point pupils.

"What have we here? One, two, three, four ... creatures as black as night, a giant raven and its beastly rider, many strange ones indeed. Why do they hide? How very peculiar," it whispered, its voice clear yet tainted like its patchy green face.

"You're quite peculiar," said Kale as he crept up from behind, pressing his knife against its throat and his hand grasping it's shoulder tightly.

Like a cricket with a torn leg, it flicked its body wildly, but Kale continued and pushed his blade deeper into its scaly neck.

"Don't even dream of making a move," Kale growled.

"Please put your blade away, I'm just looking, just looking," it moved its jaw out of sync with the words that were tumbling from its mouth, revealing rows a snake teeth and a forked black tongue.

"Couldn't help but notice such strange strangers, different sorts all around these days, none like you though." Its head hung over the edge, turning downwards at the others bellow and back to Kale and his blade. The curious creature grinned wildly, "Not seen you before, or have I?"

"No, you haven't," said Kale inspecting the creature's strange reptilian features. It's human form seemed to be fused together with those of a lizard, although he hid them behind a well-kept outfit of woven thread and leather.

Kale removed his blade only slightly, "It's a slippery steep climb to the castle, why do you not ride the goramor? Dangerous I suppose, but you don't look like you fear danger or is it because you have no mark?"

inquired the scaly creature.

Ignoring his question Kale said, "You're hiding aren't you? I sense a deep sadness in you."

"Sad? Of course, everyone is sad. Why would I be hiding? I've been redeemed, I have the mark, I hail the witch," it said, but Kale could hear the resentment in its voice loud and clear.

"Redeemed?" said Kale.

"You don't know? Wait, what side of the river are you from? First time is it, hmm but if you don't have the hunger yet? You must turn back, you must not try," it said.

"The hunger?" asked Kale.

"Yes the hunger! You must turn back."

"Kale? What's happening up there?" called Garon.

Instantly the green creature kicked its legs towards Kale, the blade pushing through his scales and slicing his tough leathery skin. The lizard creature now hanging precariously from the edge of the rock face, it then proceeded to kick again, forcing himself off the edge.

"Wait!" shouted Kale as he leapt forward. He watched as the creature fell, but instead of splattering on the floor, he extended thin lime green wings from the underside of his arms and landed skilfully on the ground, right behind Danté.

"Ahh! Danté look out behind you," screamed Belleny.

In a flash, the creature grabbed Danté and from behind began to strangle his throat. Piercing barbs could be seen rising from his arms and legs, poking through his thick woven outfit.

"Stand back! You're not taking me to the castle, I'd rather die!" it snarled as it squeezed Danté with fervour.

"Let go of me!" Danté chocked.

"We're here to stop the witch, release him or die," ordered Garon removing his blade. The Orphans circled. Snarling, baring their teeth as a sign of aggression.

The creature's reptilian eyes dilated as he watched Garon stand up tall and tower over him, "I wonder if I will put this blade between your eyes before my friends will pull you apart with their teeth."

"Wait!" shouted Kale arriving at the scene, "Garon lower your weapon, White Knights I order you to step back."

"Grrrr ... as you command," said Garon stabbing his blade into the mud, "but I don't need a blade to peck off his arms and legs."

"We are here to stop the witch," said Kale.

"Stop the sorceress? You are mad!" it gasped.

The creature looked down at Danté and instantly unlocked his grip. With a giant leap, he jumped over them and latched himself against the white rock face. Rel quickly scattered away from him.

"You're also blind, have you not seen what travels the river, climbs the mountain and what flies the skies?" it said pointing outwards.

"We have seen," said Danté coughing as blood trickled from the sides of his mouth.

"Sincerely, I apologise, I will mend you."

"It's just a scratch," said Danté.

"Not just a scratch, I'm poisoned, you will die if you reject my help," it said, crawling down the rock and into the nearby bushes searching for something in the undergrowth.

They watched as he crouched down low dusting the ground with his claws. He uncovered two large metal rings and with both hands pulled with much force, "We will have to open both doors," he said moving to the other side and doing the same. From upon Garon, Belleny stared deep down into a stairwell that faded into darkness.

"I'm not going down there!" said Belleny.

"Oh, but you must, you must, not safe out here, they'll catch you, spies everywhere. Hopefully, you haven't been seen. Lucky I found you first."

Belleny opened her royal urchin locket and watched as the black and grey triangles moved into an arrow and pointed at the lizard-like creature, her eyes widened as they then merged into a skull. *Death!* she thought nervously. Then it changed again and the triangles formed into a white rose and repeated back to the skull.

Just like Krin who bit my mum ... maybe he isn't evil, just poisoned?

Rel, who at this time had been ever so quiet, leapt from the wall and fluttered down past the creature and into the stairwell lighting the lanterns as he went with bursts of his fiery breath.

"Yes, that's good, follow your little friend," it pointed, "Don't worry, you will fit, you will, plenty of space down there even for you two," he pointed at Garon and Agarus.

"I'm not fond of being six feet underground," said Garon.

"Come on, Rel knows best," said Kale and helped Danté down the stairwell.

"Those that fly are not meant to go underground," huffed Garon and continued his decent.

The Orphans followed into the dark tunnel, but remained on high alert. The stairs led them down to several rooms with impeccably designed high ceilings, carved deep into the large white rock. The rooms were clean and organised, lit by small candles that were rowed along wooden oars that hung along the white tiled walls. It felt like a kitchen more than a living room, filled with pots and pans, wine bottles, crates of vegetables and jars of preserves, bags of herbs and strange bottles of potions and strange oddities.

"Welcome, please sit down," it pointed to many a seat and cleared its throat, "you can call me Sharpie, I was once known as John Edward Sharp, but sadly he is long gone now."

Sharpie scurried in and out of the underground rooms, cleaning as he went, "Don't mind the mess, it's hard to organise all these things in such a space, I was meaning to burrow out another room, but I'm afraid to get too close to the river or the emptiness on the other side. I won't be long my friend, heal you good as new."

Belleny spoke in her eerie voice to match her disguise, "So much food. Do you live alone?"

"Just me, much safer on my own," he said moving a metal lever, which opened up a burrowed hole in the wall. He then proceeded to light the fireplace below and a current of air sucked the smoke away with a wheezing sound as if it was inhaling.

"Here, you must place this on your cut," said Sharpie handing Danté a metal container.

Danté inspected the white milky liquid that sloshed over a sponge.

"Wring it out and let it soak on your wound," said Sharpie.

On touch, Danté realised that it wasn't a sponge, but a cut of leather with its long white fur still attached. He looked up at Sharpie unsure.

"You must, you will soon be infected without, please use."

Everyone watched as Danté drained the fur sponge of its milk and patted it against the weeping cuts on his neck. His red blood glowing on the white fur made Belleny and even Garon feel nauseous.

"Feels good yes? Hold it there for a moment, it will absorb the poison," he said and watched in glee as Danté looked up gratefully "Thank you, it's soothing."

"Where does that hole go?" asked Garon, as he peered and shuddered from a chill that wound it's way back up through the clay walled tunnel.

"Out to the emptiness beyond the cliff," I sent a Rubel Mouse down there once—it never returned, pity, he was my last friend."

"Sharpie why do you hide here? What's happening in the castle tonight? What have you seen and what is this hunger you speak of?" asked Kale.

"Questions, questions, I'm guessing to get to this side of the river you must have met the Bridges, unless you flew over?"

"Yes we met them. So sad," said Belleny.

"Yes a terrible curse indeed. I too worked at the castle, but as a chef," Sharpie pointed to an old picture of himself where he was once a man. He held a rake and a giant yellow fruit with blue stripes. He continued to throw herbs into a large pot on boil. "After killing King Mourne and taking over, the Sorceress made me her assistant, cooking for her and her unsightly guests—and the potions, those awful poisonous potions. In the beginning, no one would touch it. Drink from the cauldron! She screamed at us. Many were unable to, it came straight out most of the time, it was so disgusting even diluted and mixed with honey couldn't remove its awful taste.

"Potions? Spells? These are things of the past," said Garon.

"Poisons are very present," said Sharpie, "just look at me, it changes you in one way or another. Some get strength, some move faster, grow taller, leathery skin, some even sprout wings, but all get violent at some stage, rude, greedy and the more I am on my own the better. Keeps me calm, I keep me safe. She calls it your calling, your true form and a chance to *redeem* yourself. I call it revolting."

He stirred the cauldron and noticed his captivated audience and continued, "But not at first though, no, it takes many small helpings to get quality changes and those with greed," he smiled showing off his sharp fangs, "those that have too much, too soon, end up losing control. I've seen small creatures turn into savage beasts. One even tore out its own heart, smashed it on the ground, before it died, because its hearing became so heightened it was the only way to silence the drumming heartbeats."

"This is all madness," said Garon.

"But so many are coming back, they know a small helping will be just enough. To get another taste, change a little more, they'll always be coming back wanting more."

"This is terrible and tonight there is a feast of some sort?" asked Danté.

"Yes, tonight she returns."

"Returns from where? Where does she go?" asked Kale.

"Don't know. I've even seen her disappear, out there, into the emptiness sometimes."

"Did you drink the potion, is that what happened to you?" asked Belleny.

"Oh, you noticed," it smiled sadly. "Yes, of course, I drank it. I had no choice. I was the potion tester."

"Oh no," whispered Belleny.

Sharpie stared thoughtfully into the fire, the flames licked and danced, the light illuminated his green scaly skin. Belleny mused at how gracefully he wrapped his very long clawed hands around the fine bone china as he sipped his tea as if the cup were the most precious thing in the world.

"Not long after my last and painful transformation, these teeth of mine, I sought revenge. I scaled vertically up the castle walls and crept through an open window into her room. As planned, my knife sunk deeply into her flesh. But her wails were short lived, they rose high at first but switched into a most horrifying laugh. She then snatched my arm with one hand and throttled me with the other. Her skin shifted and bubbled from the knife wound, but she seemed unaffected as she pulled the seven inch blade from her chest. With the strength of a Gladiator, she tossed me head first over the top of her towering balcony." Garon shook his head, "And you survived this how?"

"The potion made me like this, but with it also came these," said Sharpie lifting his top and revealing his thin transparent wings.

"Incredible," said Bateau.

"They helped me land and escape without being caught by even her fastest of fiends. Subsequently I have been down here hiding out in the dark ever since. Tonight the castle doors are left open and welcome those with the special mark, if they behave which is near impossible for some, they will be invited to the feast and drink the witch's toxic potion."

Sharpie revealed the strange black markings burnt into his arm, "Those without this, line up outside at the castle gates and get branded and their first taste, only a spoonful but it's all they need. They will be transformed into hybrid beasts, all different though, all terrible."

"Hybrid beasts? Yes, we've seen a few," said Garon. "Do most of them end up looking like you? No offence, I want to know what I'm up against," asked Garon.

"None taken. No, none are the same, but it's never good. She's building herself quite the mutant army. As the feast is tonight, we must stop others before they're branded with the mark and poisoned. Many will die in the process but even more will become her slaves," said Sharpie.

"Are we really doing this?" said Garon, looking into the flames.

"I don't understand, how is such evil coming from her, what does she want from this? Revenge?" asked Kale.

"Possibly, she has never mentioned a foe other than the king of Mare-Marie for banishing her from the South," said Sharpie.

Belleny gasped.

Garon moved away from the fire, "We're bound to run into trouble if we just walk up to the gates, and I'm sure not getting branded, I have enough scars on my legs. There must be another way in Sharpie?"

"You're right, there is a tunnel. One entrance is under the waterfall which carries onwards and uphill towards the castle, it's the one I use to get these supplies."

"Damn tunnels," grumbled Garon, "traps, that's all they are."

"Under the waterfall?" quizzed Dillon.

Yes, the tunnel is unoccupied and the safest route to take. You will blend in with the shadows, but I feel the witch's spies will be on the lookout for the likes of a giant bird and even strange ones as yourselves."

"So you will take us? Do you really want to go against her again?" asked Danté.

"Of course not, but you won't know the way without me, the tunnel spreads off into many directions, some lead back to the emptiness and the next thing you know you'll fall endlessly into the nothing, not to mention the Wompigs that feed on the waste in the tunnel mud."

"Wompigs!" gasped Belleny.

Garon had heard enough and said, "This is all very well, but if this is some trap, I promise I will kill you."

Belleny remembered the first instance when she pulled out her mother's locket, Sharpie landed on the death skull and the white rose. *Was Garon to kill him?*

"We have no choice but to trust him, a secret tunnel and a guide helpful or not is better than what gathers above," said Kale.

Meanwhile, high above Palia had found the castle, its immense size and jagged construction emitted evil from every harrowing tower. She could see the castle had been built within a skull of a colossal creature born of long ago. She noticed its bones scattered all across the hillside and what they once thought were stale course rocks were clearly not.

The ground surrounding the skull swelled up with oily black dirt and continued upwards, covering most of the skull and castle walls. Across its surface were giant burnt trees, all charred to a sharp point and jarring up into the sky as if lightning had struck each one.

Palia flew fast, higher and higher and from her great height, the minions climbing the hillside looked like a possessed shadow forcing onwards uniting as a single body. She was worried about the safety of her friends and especially now that she knew more of what they were up against.

Palia flew onwards and couldn't shake a dreadful feeling that this was no place to get lost. On her return, she could see the waterfall cascading mud and she noticed the familiar figures of Garon, Belleny and Bateau, Kale, Danté and the White Knights taking a path along the cliff. One by one they walked into a cave behind the waterfall.

"Belleny! Dillon-Aelios! Garon!" shouted Palia, but they had disappeared and the thunderous sounds of the waterfall veiled her calls.

Evelin woke early. She enjoyed mornings although sleeping had become the norm for quite some time. With no destination planned she took off down the street. Although she had lost her sense of smell, some years ago, she caught the faint aroma of Mr Cabley's freshly mowed lawn, then the familiar scent of someone's hot waffles wafting through the air, and with delight even her own body odour, which wasn't too bad.

I can't believe it? I'm starting to smell things again? At least something's changing for the better, she thought. Evelin continued on mindlessly heading towards Elden Park, letting her subconscious lead her and made a bee-line towards Yellow Tree High despite it being the first day of the school holidays. She arrived at the school hall and as she stepped onto the kurb, she snapped out of her trance.

I'm not normal, she thought, looking up at the front of the sparkling new school library glass doors. She stared at her reflection, *What am I doing here? My thoughts and behaviour are getting worse, I've got to tell someone before I burst.* It was then her reflection lurched to the side as a glass door swung open and nearly collected her.

"Evelin Boots? What are you doing here today? Returning overdue books perhaps?" asked the head librarian and Cory's father, Mr Tamiya.

"I was just—"

"Evelin, if you want to come in you are welcome to have the whole library to yourself. I have some archival work to do and as it's the holidays it will be quiet. Though kids your age should be outside enjoying the freedom of vacation."

"Oh ... really?" Evelin's glum face transformed into a smile, "I guess if it's okay with you. I wouldn't mind researching cats, you see I have a new kitten, he is a Peterbald, have you heard of it?"

"What a majestic feline, a very fine specimen. Have you tried researching over the Internet? You'll find limitless information there."

"No, I don't really use computers. I prefer the feel and smell of books. Plus we're having problems with our phone line."

"I see," he paused and tried to change the subject as he sensed Evelin's awkwardness.

"I'm doing book restorations, ones we salvaged from the fire."

Evelin hesitated, "Oh I see. Did they catch and charge the arsonist?"

"No," he sighed, "the Police say it could've been an electrical fault ... why, I never would've thought ... an arsonist you say? That's a very bleak theory Evelin. I don't believe Yellow Tree would harbour such unsavoury types."

Politely side-stepping Mr Tamiya, Evelin sought immediate relief as she stepped into the cool open foyer, a wall of air-conditioning lessened her anxieties of the recent trauma of watching the old library burn to the ground. Her eyes scanned across the multitude of coloured spines that were lined up like soldiers, saluting her with their paper-rich bodies. Each book was new and crisp, they stood noble in their organised shelving. She hung her head as she walked the length of the main floor, mourning the old library and feeling very guilty and ashamed of a recent event that by default she was accountable for.

Evelin sighed at the memory of Mr Tamiya, how he raced in and out of the burning building, covered in soot and clutching bundles of books, rescuing the precious cargo.

'Don't just stand there people!' he wheezed frantically.

Evelin had watched the building from outside standing among the gathering bystanders. She was also standing very close to Cory Tamiya, who looked on like a child watching a show ground ride. Cory gripped Evelin's jacket arm, keeping her still and in place, 'Don't run off Eve, it will look suspect,' she whispered and smiled to herself in the most discreet way. Sensing Evelin's urgency and after a few faltering attempts, she let her turn away from the burning building. Cory ran up to a garden hose and thought to herself, *well this will look like I actually give a damn about the place. But if the books weren't burning I can destroy what's left with water.*

Hot coals glowed in the rubble for several days. A waft of blue smoke, spiralled and danced in the breeze, lifting ash fine bits of parchment into the sky littering the streets and some towards Evelin's house.

"Evelin Boots what may I ask are you doing here?" A strange voice struck through her. Evelin's body flinched, dropping her book to the soft carpeted floor.

"Cory! What are you doing in here?" she whispered, "you scared me to death."

"Um ... you do realise you're in the school library and it's the holidays."

"So are you," Evelin snapped back.

"Yes ... so I am. Have you seen Tamiya?"

"Yes he let me in," said Evelin, "I went for a walk in the park and somehow ... I just ended up here?"

"Did you now ... I see," said Cory.

There was a silence that lasted a good ten seconds.

"Feels pretty weird to be in here, huh?" stated Cory as a rhetorical question to break the awkward moment.

"Yep," said Evelin staring down at her books.

"The last I saw of you, you were telling Whitetail to shove it."

"Oh, you saw that?" said Evelin.

You don't have to be embarrassed, "Who didn't see your little outburst! Nice work though, you've got spunk girl, you can let the verbals rip when you need to." Cory placed her hand on Evelin's shoulder. "In all seriousness, you're okay right?"

"Yeah, I'm fine. I'd actually forgotten the whole thing. So did you pass her class?" asked Evelin inquisitively.

"Of course I did, anything higher than a D grade is passable in my book."

How does a librarian's daughter run from knowledge? thought Evelin.

"So what ya' got there? Nice cats," said Cory tapping the hardcover.

"Yes I got a kitten. Sort of like this one, less fur?" pointed Evelin to a Sphinx on the books cover.

"No friken way. Oh, you're so lucky, I always wanted a cat, but Dad's allergic to them and everything else under the sun. Is it Egyptian? It must be, it looks like something Cleopatra owned. You know they treated their cats like gods, they even had a cat god ... Baset, Basil? No it was female—"

"Bastet," said Evelin.

"Yeah, that's it. I'm sure they even sacrificed humans for her. When I say her, she had a human body with a cat's head. I wish I was a cat, I really do, with a cat's body though. Do you? You would make a great cat."

"I guess?" said Evelin.

"Well then, you can't hang out here all day, want to do something with me?"

"Maybe?" said Evelin knowing exactly what Cory was capable of.

"Show me this cat of yours? Hey, you eaten? I still haven't been around your fancy house yet, it must be amazing inside? It's finished, right? Didn't you say you could see my house from your balcony?" asked Cory in her usual manner of firing a round of questions.

"Yeah, no, I haven't eaten, not yet but—" stumbled Evelin trying to catch up with her.

Evelin stood silently as Cory skipped off in her own strange way to find her father restoring books and ask him for some spending money.

It had been a few weeks since the new carpet had been laid on the second floor and it held on to its chemical clean scent, its toe-tickling tendrils and ocean blue sparkle as if it was imbued with magic. In the far corner of the floor, a temporary restoration depot had been created to restore fire and water damaged books.

Cory's father Mr Tamiya was the book surgeon, dressed in a white lab coat taking his painstaking repair job very seriously. Upon her approach, Cory shook her head as she saw his bony cheeks were smeared sooty fingerprints as he delicately held the books with white-gloved hands and searched for survivors.

"Don't worry dad, that one has gone to a better place, maybe reincarnated into a dictionary?" joked Cory.

"Cory! You startled me."

"You forgot your phone charger," said Cory, raising her hand to her head.

"You're sweeter than a Carabao mango," smiled Mr Tamiya.

"Thanks, I think? Dad, do you want some lunch? I'm pretty hungry. Are you ready to take a break? Evelin said she's quite hungry too."

"Good, yes, of course. Well, I thought today would be a good day to talk to her. She seems a lot more stable than a few weeks ago. Acquired a new cat I hear, a Peterbald, quite the specimen, although I'm highly allergic to hairless cats," said Mr Tamiya as he stood up and looked behind him at the mountain of burnt books. "Well, I would come with you, but I have—"

"It's fine, you stay here then, I'll bring you a bite back," said Cory firmly.

Preoccupied with books Mr Tamiya quickly noticed a possible survivor hidden within the pile in front of him and reached forward pulling it out carefully with a smile, gently wiping its bright glossy cover clean.

"Ah, this one survived unscathed, the title is *The History of the Machine Age*," said Mr Tamiya.

Cory rolled her eyes at his dorky comment and quickly held onto a crisp twenty dollar note in her hands. Without him noticing she left him to his work. The brand new elevator stayed on the second floor and once she was in she pressed all the buttons at once in a very precocious way and the machine floated down to the ground floor as if it was carried by clouds. Cory looked out for Evelin and picked out her strange dark curly hair and straight blonde fringe immediately. Evelin was checking her books out at the front counter.

"Are you checking yourself out? How do you even know how to use that?" said Cory sneaking up behind her.

"Oh, yes I'm done," said Evelin pushing the books into her bag.

"Okay Evelin, it's Tamiya's shout, let's eat!"

Cory flashed the money in front of Evelin.

"You're not vegetarian are you? Matter of fact, I know little to nothing about the real Evelin Boots other than what I've seen and heard."

"What have you seen?"

"Everything," said Cory sternly. "Only joking, I know enough to know you're one of us."

"Us?"

"Yeah, you know? Anyway I'm not a vegan but I don't eat pig's bits, horse bits, cow or chickens bits, you know; feet, or brains unless they're raw. But I love fish, do you?" said Cory pushing open the door for Evelin.

"I love fish," said Evelin, "especially as pets, as best friends even."

"You're dating a fish? I knew it! I am too, there I've said it world! We're dating fish," shouted Cory as she immediately went silent and walked in front of Evelin, spinning around and looking at her from head to toe as if she was a detective.

"Rice then?" said Evelin, shrugging her shoulders.

"Done, Japanese it is, we were going there anyway," said Cory. "I love Japanese food more than anything but don't tell my boyfriend."

"You have a boyfriend?" said Evelin.

"Of course not, nor a pet fish for that matter," clapped Cory.

Cripes she is highly charged. Did she have a coffee back at the library? Evelin mused to herself.

"So Evelin Boots, day one and you're already banging down the door of the library. Nice work. You're as bad as Tamiya, you sure *you're* not his daughter?"

"How come you call your dad 'Tamiya', what's his first name?" asked Evelin.

"Cameron, but I don't like calling him by his first name, and Mr Tamiya sounds like a teacher and he's not a teacher. He's a librarian."

"I call my dad by his first name, Robin," said Evelin, "always have, he thinks he hates it, but it's a good name."

"It is. Most people don't like their name as they don't get to choose them. Maybe we should be a number till the day you give yourself a name?"

Evelin had a flash of the dream she had of the shrimp king, King Henry the MMDCCLI and said, "Like Roman numerals?"

"Exactly," said Cory.

"I know a girl that got hers changed to Miriam Manhattan, but that's cheating, don't you think? What if you changed your name every day? Who would you really be? You would have to make up a new signature every day, I guess that would be fun?"

Evelin said nothing and thought of all the answers to all Cory's questions in her head.

"Anyway, Dad is so old fashioned," said Cory, pulling out a packet of gum from her jeans. "Gum?" she asked, passing it to Evelin. "But I guess Mum is okay, I doubt I could call my mum Carol, it's just too weird. Like Tamiya calls mum Carol and if I did as well, it's more of a friend-down-the-street name. Mum is—" Cory paused in mid sentence and looked at

Evelin, "Oh I'm so sorry, I shouldn't mention the M word."

"The M word?" said Evelin. She raised a brow and smiled awkwardly, "It's fine, I never really had one so I don't have the problem of what to call her."

They had arrived at The One Armed Samurai, one of the more reputable Japanese restaurants in Yellow Tree. Cory entered and walked up to the counter as if she lived there.

Evelin waited patiently as Cory habitually ordered several dishes, pronouncing them correctly and confidently.

"What would you like Evelin?" she turned back with a serious face, "I've already ordered you some sushi with String Ray flaps, fried Axolotl, fish eyes ... care for anything else?"

Evelin's eyes widened and she shook her head hoping she was just joking. *Of course she was,* she thought. They took a seat and Cory slumped down in front of her.

"So, have you planned anything for your few weeks of freedom?" said Cory playing with her necklace. "Boots are you in there?" said Cory lifting back Evelin's blonde stripe with a pair of chopsticks.

"Sorry, I'm a little tired," she said reminded of yesterday's panic attack and then Esta's overwhelming hypnosis session.

"Oh yeah? I only get tired between 4am and 5am."

"No, you don't say? You do have a lot of energy. I used to before I got put on—" Evelin paused.

"Put on ... what Eve? You can talk about it," said Cory, reaching out her hand tenderly.

"I have a few problems and I had to go see someone. Now I'm even worse I think," said Evelin letting Cory into her vaulted world.

"Tell me about it," said Cory shuffling through her bag and pulling out a small silver container. Evelin watched wide-eyed as Cory placed three different pills on the table and one at a time swallowed them.

Evelin sat speechless.

"Yeah, I got to take them as well, keeps me level, you know, no one can keep up with me otherwise, not even myself," said Cory while balancing a chopstick on her finger.

"At least you know yourself, replied Evelin, "I feel as though I am dissolving away like an aspirin in a glass of water."

Chapter 46 - Unlucky or Not

In the north, the Cassan River roared through the canals, a once narrow gorge was ripped apart like a gaping wound, descending rapidly between enormous boulders and towering cliffs. It tore at the land as it surged outwards and straight off the cliff face like projectile vomit, up and out into the void of the great Azare. Sharpie led the group along a crevice that extended out from the cliff face. He continually smiled, reaffirming the nervous glances between the travellers as he swore he would lead them to a secret tunnel that lead straight to the castle. The jagged path was a premium view of the great Azare and the cosmic edge of Mare-Marie. From here the expansion of the emptiness continued on for what seemed an eternity.

Sharpie pointed ahead, his cloak sleeves fell back revealing his mutant teal green arms and scales, "Not far now," he said with a sharp tooth grin.

"You've been saying that for ages," grumbled Garon.

Hmm this is no place for a Princess.

"Not far, just around that edge, then straight up to the castle, I promise."

"Please be careful Garon, I can't see the ground! whispered Belleny.

"I can't see anything out there," added Bateau.

"Did you see that? Lightning! But no thunder," said Belleny as she pointed with one hand and strangled Garon with the other.

"Yes, it's the endless storm, raging on for all eternity. What does he want now?" questioned Garon.

"Look Garon! See, your friends have found it," said Sharpie, pointing to a rocky ledge towards Kale and Danté not far up ahead.

"Finally! I gave them strict orders to wait for us," muttered Garon poking his head cautiously around a ledge. With a gasp, he paused, witnessing the waterfall which only previously he could hear gnarring louder and louder. He watched in disbelief as a torrent of mud relentlessly spilled off the edge of the cliff.

"Where are they? Can you see the waterfall yet?" said Belleny as she leant forward.

"Get back down, this is no waterfall I've ever seen. Hold on," said Garon, waving the Orphans forward and continued.

"Oh my!" gulped Belleny, "we're not going near that are we?"

Sharpie shook his head and blinked his bulbous eyes, "but we must. Don't be afraid, it's safe if you keep your distance. A lookout up ahead. See look, your friends have found it."

Kale and Danté sat deep in conversation, their legs dangling over the rocky lookout. A scene of emptiness stretching far and beyond. Their conversation cut short as the others arrived.

"Thanks for waiting," fussed Garon.

"Is something wrong Garon?" asked Kale getting to his feet.

"Not at all. On the contrary, everything is just dandy. Look around us, it's like a stroll in the Queens Garden. A picture of paradise."

Sharpie helped Danté to his feet, "Good my friends, I will go forward and prepare the lanterns, quite dark inside the tunnel, quite dark."

"Are you all right Kikaan? You look a little shaken," asked Danté gently touching her leg.

"I ... I am not to good with heights. Especially when I can't see the bottom."

"Don't worry Kikaan, if Garon slips he can always fly down and pick you straight back up. He's got all the time in the world if there's no ground to hit."

"I knew this would happen!" inflamed Garon. "This is not a joke. See here Kale, you know nothing of the danger you've put Kikaan in! The Azare is no place for anyone, not to mention the Endless Waterfall!" Garon twisted down at Kale with a heavy frown. "I insisted she stay at Sharpie's, but you refuse to leave her, where it would be safe and on solid ground!"

"Of course, why would I leave behind our secret weapon?" said Kale, crossing his arms and staring out into the ghostly Azare.

"Secret weapon!" scoffed Garon.

"I feel Kikaan has brought us much luck on this journey," said Danté.

"Luck?" questioned Belleny, "I have nothing of the sort! Kale, you don't know me that well. No one does. Garon I think you're right. I've taken this too far. I've put us in danger. Kale you're wrong. I order you to return me at once Garon."

"You don't have to order me, it would be my honor," said Garon.

"What?" asked Bateau and Danté simultaneously.

"Fine. Start flying in that direction," said Kale as he pointed out into the bleak Azare

All eyes turned up to the towering bird, his confused wings out either side, the masked princess at the helm.

"What's … going on?" questioned Dillon as the White Knight's arrive.

"This doesn't look good," whispered Montë.

"I'm going back," said Belleny. "Turn around at once Garon!"

"Stop jumping around up there, we might fall!" said Garon.

"So what? If I'm so lucky we'll be fine, we might as well leave everyone here, fly straight to the castle, kill the witch and get this whole escapade over and done with!"

"It's not that easy Kikaan," said Kale calmly. He stood back to give them room. "This journey is not only yours, nor does it lie solely on your shoulders. We shall all seek justice together."

"This is madness, we won't be victorious together, I know more than you think, I have seen things as well. I knew something would happen to Raveene, and I know he's not the only one in trouble," said Belleny crossing her arms. "Victorious or not, those creatures aren't going to let us inside that fortress, not without our heads cut off and impaled on a lance!"

"I see," said Kale, "your mother guided you well."

"From day one!" she huffed and quietened as Danté stood forward.

He reached up, held her tight-fisted hand and said, "You're right, from what we've seen it's going to be crowded, more monsters than any of us have ever seen before. But this may work in our favour."

"And why would that work in our favour?" she asked.

"If you keep your disguise on and zip that royal mouth of yours, we should be fine. In and out. Just look at us, we're a motley crew of monsters as any, we'll blend right in."

"Speak for yourself, I'm nothing of the sort," said Bateau.

Sharpie ran back quickly and said, "I have the lanterns ready, we must keep going, the witch won't wait for us."

"Sorry, we were just coming, weren't we Kikaan?" said Kale.

Upon Garon, Belleny stared silently into the swirling darkness of the Azare. *What am I doing? I can't do this? But I can't let them down, we've come too far.*

"I'm ready to turn back when you are," said Garon.

"Turn back? Get a hold of yourself Commander Quick," growled a boisterous Kikaan, "straight ahead, we have a witch's head to bring home!"

"As you wish," groaned Garon, "I'm a fool amongst fools."

"Thank you," said Kale as he humbly led Garon towards the ferocious mud fall and the hidden tunnel inside it.

The Orphans all looked perplexed with the recent outburst, they all knew the risks they were taking, but understood their duty and forged ahead.

"Watch your step! We're here!" said Sharpie pointing to the burrowed out hole in the cliff face. A slurry of green discharge oozed out of the tunnel and pooled at its entrance before dipping off.

"Damn it, it's no more than a Grick Slug's lair," whined Garon.

"This is the exit, not far inside the tunnel is much wider and taller, enough room for the two of you," nodded Sharpie.

"I hate tunnels. You sure you don't want to turn around, it's not too late," asked Garon, facing up towards Belleny and Bateau.

"I don't think we have a choice Garon," said Belleny.

Sharpie approached with a glowing lantern in his claws and said to all, "The light will guide us." He lowered his lamp revealing several more lanterns hanging from a hook and across to other items such as shovels and a pickaxe. "Oh and here is a treat or two," he smiled. Swiftly Sharpie knelt inside the weeds growing out of the tunnel. A large wooden chest unlatched and he waved them in close. His lantern revealed several compartments, each full of an assortment of goods; preserved fruit, handfuls of nuts and seeds, smoked fish and lizards with their tails stretched out, thick black Pill Bugs curled up tight black balls and plenty of oddities that remained nameless to all.

"Thanks, Sharpie, I was getting tired of chewing Sap reeds."

"Wake up Rel, you have work to do," said Kale grabbing a lantern. He woke up intermittently to light the lamps and fell back to sleep.

"Sharpie they're not, no they can't be, Arpintine seeds?" gasped Garon.

"Yes, yes they are. Eat up, I insist! Magnificent for stamina and helps with vision in the dark," said Sharpie. "Go ahead plenty more."

"More? But there can't be. I haven't had these since I was a child … I thought Arpintine plants vanished years ago? They were always my favourite. Made me who I am today."

"So that's how you grew so tall," said Bateau.

"I see. Yes, so very true, all gone but here. Look near the waterfall, they grow like weeds, take as many as you like. Plant them back home in your garden."

"I don't believe it, a living treasure. Thank you, Sharpie."

"Maybe you're the lucky one Garon," said Kale.

Sharpie continued into the tunnel as his lantern radiated around him. He turned back, his skin emanating an emerald green glow, "Come this way, don't be afraid."

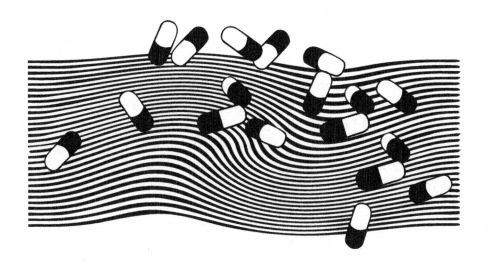

Evelin turned to Cory and sighed.

"Spit it out Evelin. Don't bottle it up. You're making me feel weird."

"I'm the one who's weird. Some days I don't even know what's real anymore, it's like I'm swimming through vapour. I really think I'm going crazy."

"You know what I think?"

"Tell me what you think."

"I think 'Crazy' is the name of an android with emotions."

"So you think I'm a machine?"

"We are all just machines Eve. Whatever medication our Doctors have prescribed us, I am convinced is in no doubt doing a major reboot of our sensory switchboards, switching off channels in our heads like a technician does to a T.V. Imagine a remote control changing the channels and reprogramming our irrational, over-sensitive and over-processing, doubtful and repetitive minds off and turning on, the Primetime News."

"Good analogy! Yes, yes I've heard brains can be like television sets, some broken and in need of an electrician," eagerly said Evelin.

"Precisely!" shouted Cory as she sprung up standing, "but there are one billion switches up there, how do they know what they're turning on and off? That's got to make you feel a little crazy. Your mind's not a computer they can simply reboot with chemicals."

"You think so?"

"Maybe," shrugged Cory, "you're the smart one, I guess you'll figure it out before me."

"I don't think I can outsmart myself," sighed Evelin.

"Hey, cheer up Eve, when is the last time you had a good laugh?"

"I don't know? I don't really find things that funny anymore."

"No way Eve, you're not quite 100% at the moment, think of it just like another TV switch that's probably turned off, when you're on these pills your mind's turning switches off and others on and you don't know what going to be on TV tonight, whether it's your favourite show like an animal documentary or some sweet cartoons."

Cory paused and put her hand on Evelin's shoulder and looked at her friend and gave her a reassuring smile. After a few seconds, they both picked up their bags which had dropped onto the pavement and they continued back silently to the library. Mr. Tamiya was still whiling away at the book restoration where Cory had left him, surrounded by the piles of damaged books.

"Cory, you're an angel, thanks for delivering my lunch."

Cory rolled her eyes and gave Evelin the side-eye stare at his comment.

"Hi Mr. Tamiya," said Evelin.

"Hello, young Evelin, hoping all is well? Now, before we continue pleasantries, please call me Tamiya, this is insisted by Cory. I'm not a teacher, I'm a librarian," he smiled and pushed his hair back with his round frame spectacles.

Evelin had never seen him without his specs off before and she could see the resemblance of shared features in Cory. They shared the same triangular shaped head, but more obvious when he moved his spectacles were the shared mysterious and uniquely aligned pale green eyes.

"Do you want to come sit out in the sun with us Tamiya?

"Don't mind if I do. I don't want the books smelling like wasabi or raw salmon now do I," he joked and Cory smiled back at her father at the geeky comment.

Once outside, they moved to a grassy knoll that was verdant and green tended to by the school gardener. Around its perimeter ran a circle of fiery yellow roses with bright orange tips. The knoll was one of Evelin's favourite spots in the school and during Spring she could sit in her special place nestled in the ring of rose bushes, the brambles and green foliage protected her with their tight tearing thorns.

"And here we are, Evelin's little hideaway," said Cory taking a seat on the dry grass.

Evelin looked across a little stunned and snapped, "Hideaway? Have you been following me all year?"

"Maybe I did follow you around a bit, I mean what else is there to do at school —study?" grinned Cory. Her father looked at her over his glasses which had slid down the bridge of his nose as Cory's grade average at been nothing short of abysmal.

As the trio sat in the middle of the grass circle, Evelin noticed that Cory not only had Tamiya's eyes, but she had his motor mouth as well. *It must be hard for him being quiet all day*, she thought.

It was then that Evelin's watch began to alarm for her to take her medication This still embarrassed her greatly.

"Forgot to sleep-in today?" said Tamiya hovering his chopsticks over the assorted sushi.

"Ahh—" Evelin looked at Cory, her wide eyes pleading to keep it a secret.

"Evelin's on medication Tamiya, that's her alarm to take them, she's self-diagnosed herself as 'Crazy,' said Cory ignoring all of Evelin's pleading silent expressions.

"That makes three of us then," he nodded passively.

Evelin stared at them both as this topic was anything but a joking matter.

"It's true! I may be crazy and sometimes I feel like I'm about to die from this wretched anxiety. It comes and then appears out of nowhere, then I feel fine a moment later. I am constantly battling with irrational and the loudest thoughts it's as if I've got an evil twin inside me trying to break me down! I might be psychotic, have multiple personalities, schizophrenia or all of them, the medical professionals are still unsure."

Evelin was exhausted and slumped down over her food. She took out her pill box and swallowed one, sorrowfully sipping it down with a splash of salty Miso soup.

"Sorry Evelin," said Tamiya, "Cory already told me you had a little problem some time ago, I hope you don't mind. You know I once had a similar anxious condition like yourself, back before I met Cory's mother and it hasn't really gone away of which I feel it never will, but you will get support and treatment, and you learn to make the most of what could be an enjoyable and fulfilling life. No one's ever died from anxiety even though you may feel like you could be sucked into a Black Hole."

"I don't think we're talking about the same thing? It might kill me, or I might lose control and kill someone else. My brain could be deteriorating away by some black fungus, there might have been others with this, but I'll probably be the first to die from it," said Evelin.

There was a little silence. Cory looked across at her dad. And together they watched Evelin staring down at her food, not eating, but pushing it around like a child.

"You're not going to lose control, no more than me or Cory."

"Why me? Why is it happening to me? I've been cursed from the day I was born," said Evelin. "I can't live with it, I just can't, it's going to take over my life until I die in my room, too afraid to go outside. Unable to get into a lift or buy food from the shops."

Cory moved in close and put her arm around Evelin, feeling her body's light tremble.

"You won't be like this forever Eve, Tamiya meant he took control of it, as you will, we're here to help," said Cory.

"That's right. It didn't happen straight away, but gradually I taught myself, nothing can make me feel a certain way, my feelings are mine, I'm in control ... I don't need to be a false victim. My own mind is only over-protecting me from something that's not even there!"

"That's what I am, a false victim, ever since I was born," said Evelin miserably.

"Oh Evelin, you can't think that way anymore," said Cory.

"What am I making stronger?"

"Evelin I know it hurts. Trust me, crap like this, it happens to the best of us," said Tamiya. "But over time it went away when I stopped thinking about it, and when it reappears I don't give it the time of day."

"It's always there, I can't escape it," said Evelin, her head still down.

"You're exhausted Eve. You have to take power back from your incessant thoughts, the continuous scanning searching for shadows behind trees even in broad daylight, I bet you're always wondering when the fear will strike again."

"I know!" Evelin began to raise her voice, but when she looked up Tamiya held out his hand and passed her a sushi roll, stabbed through the centre with his chopstick.

Evelin smiled through her misery and grabbed thankfully at the sesame seeded inside-out roll.

"You planned this whole sushi intervention didn't you Cory?"

"Well I—" she began, but Evelin cut her short, "Thank you, I'll try my best to think less and I'm glad I have someone else to talk to, it's been bottling up."

"That's my girl," said Cory and swallowed a whole piece of sushi in one gulp.

Tamiya pushed back his hair and stabbed another sushi roll. "Well, I'll leave you girls to it, I'm going to rescue some more books. If you need to talk Evelin, you know where I am."

It wasn't long before the breeze blew through the bare stems and they decided to move on and together ventured towards Evelin's place.

As they walked through the back door, Evelin wondered how Milton was doing and hoped he would come back soon. She realised now keeping her secret from him was hurting their friendship and her immeasurable sense of irrational guilt by not telling him about her medication and condition, but she knew he would understand and not judge her.

Cory lit a cigarette. She coughed after her first inhale and Evelin went to take it from her hand to give it a try. Cory pulled away and lightly slapped her hand back.

"You don't want this Eve," said Cory her frown was heavy.

"You must let me have a go," said Evelin reaching back and taking the cigarette from her. Evelin inhaled slowly lighting up the fiery embers. She blew it out and her mouth felt dry and coarse. Her tongue licked for moisture, but there was none.

"Evelin are you alright? I warned you about smoking!" said Cory a little worried.

Evelin looked up from the cigarette and said, "It's a similar feeling!"

"Similar as what?" said Cory swiping back the burning cigarette.

"A wave of swirls came over me and my mouth is dry and I'm choking—but in this instance I'm fine with it."

"Are you sure? I don't get it."

"No, this is really interesting. My mind doesn't know the difference. You can keep that, it's not for me."

"I'm glad to help out," said Cory with a cheeky grin, "I think."

The school in the distance from any angle still looked like a prison, especially so without the hustle and bustle of students and commotion of activity. The girls walked back to the library in silence. As they neared the edge of the garden, a familiar white tiny dog ran over to Evelin and circled her feet smelling and yapping as if to say Hello.

"Evelin? Is that you?" Evelin didn't recognise the young man until he lifted up the brim of his Fedora hat and smiled.

"Royal?"

"Hello Eve, it's so nice to see you. Are you well?"

"Yeah, I guess, thank you for asking."

Evelin knelt down and the dogs instantly ran from Cory's feet to her, licking and folding themselves into the palms of her hands.

"Hello, my name is Royal," he said, holding his free hand out to Cory.

"Cory, Cory Tamiya," she said confidently.

"I haven't seen you in ages, um ... how's Astina?" asked Evelin.

"Astina is terrific, she does bring you up in conversation all the time Evelin, I'm sure she would like to see you again."

Evelin turned to Cory, "Royal works at the Hotel Chandelier and Astina is the woman that owns it."

"Right, nice place is it?" said Cory.

"From the outside it looks pretty old but inside it's basically made out of crystals and mirrors, and there's a rooftop pool and restaurant up there, that's where Royal is, I looked after these fluff balls for her once, well sort of."

"You could come today, nice day for it," Royal asked rhetorically.

Cory instantly said yes in her head, but it took a few seconds before she realised it was in the city and said quite firmly, "No, I don't go to the city that often, public transport is a drag, I would bike it I guess? But there's no way I'm walking."

"That's okay, if you like Astina's chauffeur can take us? He's waiting in the car over there, he can drop you off back home as well," said Royal.

"Today?" said Evelin. "It's a bit short notice, I mean Astina doesn't know we're coming?"

"The surprise will be good for her," said Royal.

Evelin took the diamond leashes from Royal. He took off his hat, slicked back his black hair and placed it on Evelin's head, and she wore it the rest of the way.

To Evelin's comfort, the drive to the hotel was brief. The white hotel shone like a bleached pebble in the daylight and stood out from the palm trees and grey cement and orange brick bland buildings surrounding it.

"Okay, this will do nicely, I would want a job here," said Cory staring up at the front entrance.

Royal lead the way with Evelin and Cory trotting behind him, both girls doing nimble half jumps to dodge the dog leads as they darted about excitedly.

"Ahh good, you're back Royal," said the man behind the front desk. "The sun lotion and Air freight magazines Madame Francis ordered have just arrived, can you take this up for me?"

"Of course, can you let Astina know Evelin Boots is here."

"Right. Boots," said the man, looking at Evelin and then Cory up and down.

"And..." he paused.

"And her school friend," said Royal.

"Very well."

"Okay let's go. You okay Eve?" said Royal, looking at her staring at the elevator while the dogs chased around her feet.

Evelin was busy thinking over and over about the lift that she didn't even hear Royal. Cory noticed and took her by the arm, walking her forward, "She's going to be just fine."

As she did, Evelin took a sharp breath in as she watched the elevator doors open.

"Don't let it have an effect on you Eve, think of it as a ride at a fair, it's fun, remember you're in control," she whispered.

Cory squeezed Evelin's hand and her sad pout lifted into a smile.

After the elevator door closes, the lift shot upwards quickly, and it wasn't that bad as it was before. Before Eve knew it, they had arrived at the top floor.

"Ta da," said Cory, patting Evelin on the back and letting her through to the roof.

"Maybe you can get a job as a lift attendant," said Evelin.

"Erm that's not the job I was thinking of. Up here though, this is the life," said Cory stepping out onto the grass. Her toenails were painted a light blue and the colour matched the sky.

Evelin, Cory and the dogs walked past the pool to the deck area.

"What can I say Evelin, there is nothing to be afraid of up here but having too much of a good time."

"I guess," said Evelin watching the dogs lap up the water from their glass bowl and sitting down in the shade of a towel covered chair.

"Check out all those hats," said Cory.

"Yeah, I know about the hats, take one if you like," Evelin smiled.

"What does Royal think I'm going to do, pee in the pool?" said Cory.

"No, he's just looking out for you, Astina can be a little bit abrasive."

Cory began to lay down on a deckchair when a voice came from the end of the pool.

"Don't even think about it," said Astina appearing from the patio, her voice sending the dogs into a quiet yelp, presuming they were being told off.

Cory stood quickly, and they turned to see Astina approaching casually along the pool. The water reflected her tall, thin body. She was dressed in a large 1980's power jacket, replete with shoulder pads, a drop waisted garment hung open with her swimming costume underneath.

"Boots, if it isn't my little panic station, did you bring your bathers this time?" She fluttered her long fake eyelashes and gave Evelin a smile and a quick hug hello

"Hi Astina, it's been a long week."

"I bet it has, it's been rather tedious for Royal and I, Royal won't stop talking about you, hormones running rampant at his age."

Cory's eyes widened.

"So what have we here?"

"I hope you don't mind, this is my friend Cory Tamiya, we bumped into Royal and he offered us a ride."

"I bet he did," Astina looked at Cory while Evelin continued then paused.

"Hello Miss," said Cory straightening her posture.

"Hello. I'm guessing you're older than Boots, or is it just the cigarettes that are sucking away your youthful glow? Either way, that's my chair, and that's my Martini," she pointed to Royal, who was walking along the poolside towards them. "Your drink is the juice."

Cory, speechless took the glass from Royal and watched as Astina placed her towel across her deck chair, grabbed the sun cream off Royal and positioned herself facing the sun, masking it across her long arms and legs.

Royal left them a plate of grapes. "Seedless," he whispered and walked back to the kitchen.

"Thank you," said Cory, still a little stunned.

"So Boots, how's the roller coaster ride? Did you notice I got the elevator fixed or did you walk up the stairs again?"

"Oh, I see, I did notice, it was a lot better."

"And the music," Astina added.

"Yeah, I liked it, but I'm ready to get off my roller coaster ride if that's what you wanted to know," said Evelin.

"I can imagine. What do you think Miss Tamiya?"

Cory paused and looked at Evelin, then at the lady, her dark black glasses shading her eyes.

"Or do you not think?" said Astina impatiently. "Or are you one of those girls who feels she can get by in life just on the basis of her looks?"

"No, of course, I think," said Cory putting down her glass. "I think Evelin's working things out one step at a time, and she's going to be just fine." Cory bumped Evelin's foot.

Evelin felt the tension in the air, *why did Astina have to be this way?*

"I've thought about your problem Evelin, it's distressing me," said Astina breaking the silence, "Royal tells me you need a good feed, but he also says the pool water's fine to drink."

"Please don't stress over me, although it's very kind of you," said Evelin.

"Well, it happens to the best of us," said Astina, her unchanged expression shaded under her glasses and a broad-brimmed hat.

How can this lady care for anything? thought Cory. She kept silent and controlled herself by watching the water glisten across the pool.

It wasn't until Evelin's watch started to beep that the silence was broken.

"Looks like it's that time again," said Astina making Evelin feel quite insecure.

"What do you mean? Looks like it's that time again?" said Cory.

"Boots knows what I mean," said Astina sipping her Martini.

Evelin sat there quite unsure what to do. Her hair was blowing around in the wind, matching her thoughts and before she knew it, she was walking off away from both Astina and Cory.

"Are you leaving Evelin?" said Cory starting to stand up.

"I just need a moment," said Evelin while reaching for her pills and feeling relieved when they rattled in her bag.

"I'm going to the bathroom, I'll be back in a minute," she said.

"Why are you so rude to her?" said Cory standing up.

"Quiet child. What would you know? You're probably on them as well," said Astina, who guessed the correctly.

"So what! She needs them at the moment."

"She does not, Boots is a lot stronger than she looks, the last thing a child needs is a dependency."

"Just leave her alone, she doesn't need any more negative advice than she gives herself."

Evelin walked out of the bathroom and back along the grass beside the pool. She could see that Cory and Astina had obviously had an argument by their body language.

"Evelin, please show me what you have been taking?" said Astina holding out her long white arms, her bony fingers peeling out towards her.

Cory spun around on her chair, looking at Evelin with a frown.

"Why?"

"Why? I have been on more of these than I've had varieties of tea. I'm curious that's all."

"Play Astina nicely, I know you mean well," said Evelin.

Astina took the small canister and read the labelling to herself, "Hmmm, I see, are you taking anything else?" she inquired.

"Well, I have other pills, for other times when I need them," Evelin passed her more tablets.

"I see," said Astina clawing at the plastic container, "you don't need these."

"How would you know what she needs?" said Cory.

"What happens when you forget to take a dose? What happens to you then?"

"That's why she has her watch," said Cory defiantly.

"Hush you little Snapdragon!" Astina exclaimed.

Astina shook the canister, "This is just another problem," she said, and in one swift jerk of her wrist, she twisted the cap off the container and threw the lot into the pool.

"What are you doing?" yelled Cory as the dogs began to bark at the commotion.

Evelin's reactions were very slow, her medication had taken effect and she couldn't raise an alarm in her head. She just stared at the canister as it bobbed around on the surface as the pills drifted down in slow motion. The dogs continued to yelp.

"Bitch!" said Cory snatching the remainder back off her.

"Such a sweet talk you have Cory. Now, Boots please trust me, you don't need those ones, she pointed at the empty container floating in the pool. You can have the others back, but I would like to see you wean yourself off these for good and just be yourself."

Astina stood up, finished her drink and walked off, "One day you will understand and recognise what is going on."

Evelin looked up in a daze, she was taken aback by the passive aggression of Astina, but then she didn't feel it was necessary and watched as Astina disappeared around the corner.

It was commonplace for Gonzo Victori to have premonitions, and when he was about to experience a vision, he body would have a series of rapid and very physical effects. Gonzo's two dark purple and forked tongues which would flap and twitch, then he would feel as he would explode from a simultaneous sneeze, cough and burp, coupled with the rapid blinking of his four bulbous eyes. No one in the circus, not even Gonzo understood why he was gifted. There was a running joke among the circus folk that was he was able to smell money and used his sensitive premonitions to sniff out the next village to travel too. Some said he was being followed by something much darker and far more sinister. Whatever the truth was, it was not an easy task to manage, and it was after one particular tricky episode, that Bateau went missing.

"Good day to you, Mr String, I wonder, have you seen Bateau?" asked Gonzo as he was rushing around the corner.

String stared blankly and with a frown, then quickly realising who was calling his name he smiled "Gonzo!" and grinned back at him.

"Sorry, oh sorry to interrupt, please continue," insisted Gonzo as he realised his colleague String the Beast Tamer was in the middle of a precarious session wrangling a group of frisky Borgawoots. String would keep cracking his whip across a barred circus cage perched on top of wooden wheels that housed five Borgawoots that hissed, spat and paced up and down within the confounds of the small enclosure.

"Their bark is worse than their bite, but they're tired and they're ready to be moved to Augustus," said String lashing his whip with a deafening crack.

"String, I can't find Bateau. I did a thorough head count of all Circus staff before we left Atlas, he was accounted for, but now he's been missing over two days. It's a bit of a worry," said Gonzo earnestly.

"Gonzo, I'm sure all will be right soon. You know, despite his odd behaviours he's a sensible little thing really," soothed String.

"I hope you're right, I hope he hasn't found himself in trouble."

"Gonzo, the last time I saw him was yesterday when he was napping up top on Kabela the Fortune mistress' caravan. I have a feeling if anyone knows his whereabouts, she will."

"She's not a real psychic String she's in the Circus for a novelty only! I highly doubt she will be able to locate him. I don't have a good feeling about this, actually my right little finger is tingling ... never a good sign."

The Great Gonzo Circus travelled the lands on the backs of a mega species called the Horgan. These were humongous shell backed creatures, the size of a football stadium with two solid horned antennae protruding from their heads like a Stag Beetle. These were monsters from the great unknown.

The family of four Horgan giants arrived in Mare-Marie after appearing from deep inside the realm of the Gaze Akarr after a night of thunder and lightning caused by a mystic collision of sea and sand. Gonzo discovered the four creatures while he was taking in a private moment of reflection and saw them lumbering along the desert in a very slow and linear way. He was scared, but instantly he saw the financial opportunity that the giant beasts offered. He managed to climb the beasts and attach make-shift reins to the horns of the first creature and a pulley system joining all four creatures into one stable transportation unit.

Each has its own circus real-estate the first in line is Atlas, he carried most of the living quarters and audience tent gear, the second creature named Auress carried the amusement rides and a giant Ferris Wheel. The main tent was pitched on top of Aesar, and it was on top of Augustus—the last of all four—who carried all the weird and wonderful creatures the circus had to offer. He was surrounded by a huge perimeter fence that enclosed animals as large as dinosaurs, as this was no ordinary circus.

Gonzo resumed his search for Bateau and climbed a towering ladder high into the sky towards a flying-fox platform held in place by an assortment of wires. Without hesitation, he swiftly jumped into the air with both feet and held on tight. String watched awe as Gonzo sped towards Atalas. As he descended along the wire, he focused on the bright signage painted in red and yellow and written in flowing cursive font 'Cosmic Kabela—Psychic, Taro, Fortune Teller.'

"Bateau are you up on that roof?" he yelled out, but there was no answer.

Gonzo walked up Kabela's wooden stairs and knocked heavily on her door. There was no answer so he got on the tips of his toes and peered through her window. What he noticed first were the taro cards thrown across the table and covering the floor, then second a large potted plant had been tipped on its side with dirt splayed across the wooden floor.

This was nothing too peculiar as when the horgans walked the carriages rocked back and forth like a giant ship out at sea and cards were destined to be scattered and a few pot plants as well.

"Kabela are you in there?"

Gonzo wasn't giving up on Bateau yet, he was still very upset about losing the White Knights those many years ago and he hadn't lost a member of the circus since.

Garivin the animal cleaner had returned to Kabela's carriage.

Ahh, not Gonzo! He panicked and hid behind a nearby wagon watching him as he sat on the stairs of Kabela's doorway.

The cleaner didn't want to be seen today, especially by Gonzo, as he touched the still bleeding scratches across his long weasel-like face. He hid nervously behind the carriage of the Siamese twin Geldan—who had two heads of the same name. Geldan stepped out of his cabin bumping Garivin out into the spotlight.

"Sorry about that Garivin, I usually look both ways," his heads laughed two entirely different laughs as he pulled Garivin up, "are you all right?" he asked.

"Yes I'm fine," grumbled Garivin.

"You don't sound fine, does he sound fine to you Geldan?"

"No Geldan not at all, the opposite of fine, rough even."

"I said I'm fine! Quick move aside you imbeciles," said Garivin impatiently trying to escape.

Gonzo noticed the commotion at once, "What's going on? Is that you Bateau?"

"Sorry Gonzo, just us and Garivin."

"Ahh hi Geldan, Garivin, have any of you seen Bateau?"

Geldan's heads looked at each other, "We haven't seen him today, yesterday yes, today no."

Gonzo approached Garivin and said, "What about you Garivin? What happened to your face, you're bleeding."

"Who me? No ... no, no, no. This is nothing, a few scratches while cleaning the animals. I've been busy, busy cleaning; I better get going, what goes in must come out."

"Nonsense, talk with me, have you seen Kabela then?"

"Yes, no, I don't know where she is."

"Those scratches—" said Gonzo peering in close.

Garivin quickly held his hands up, "All part of the job, not all the animals like bath."

"Hmm, they look nasty, you'll need something on those, what animal exactly did this?"

"Oh, it was ... the Morac, yes the morac's, sharp claws they have. I must be more careful next time. They'll heal, I'm fine, honestly."

"Morac?" questioned Geldan. "But we don't have them anymore, remember last weeks show they were stepped on by the dancing Don-Don's?"

"Hmm, they look like fresh cuts to me," said Gonzo firmly.

"Not fresh, old, no I pick the scabs, I can't help it."

"Nasty habit, come back to my cabin and we'll get you cleaned up."

Meanwhile, Kabela watched from the shadows, and once they were gone, she snuck inside her caravan and quietly closed the door.

"Would you like a drink Garivin? You know I have been collecting these bottles from every corner of our travels, some of them hold quite the potion. Black or White Garivin?" said Gonzo pointing to two bottles out of the many ornate glass bottles that stood along the shelves within his cabin.

"You're too kind Gonzo," said Garivin pretending that sampling the drink was a rare thing when really he wanted the black liquid more than all the coloured bottles combined. He had sampled it once before and how it made him feel, alive, unstoppable, although he felt he was never the same again. *Oh no! How it makes me talk,* he remembered, *but taste I must.*

"Please the black one," he said as calmly and patiently as he could.

"Cake?" said Gonzo taking the cover off a large glass display. The cake had only a slice missing. As the lid was removed it released its freshly baked aroma into the air.

"Yes, how kind of you," his dirt-black nails, dark with stains, grabbed the cake knife and began to cut himself a slice.

"That's a nasty shake you have there," said Gonzo watching the knife jitter in his grips.

"Oh yes, comes and goes," he said, holding his arm down against the table.

Gonzo slammed a glass of black liquid beside him and in a fright Garivin jumped back and then relaxed as the liquid pulled him in. Garivin ignored the cake completely and put down the knife, swapping it for the glass, "Thank you Gonzo, it's not often I get to taste the finer things."

"Personally I don't touch the stuff, I'm just a bottle collector you see, here let me help you with that," said Gonzo and he took the knife, slicing the cake ever so slowly. He then served a slice on a small round plate and put the lid back over the cake. By this time, Garivin had finished his drink and placed it back on the table.

"Another?" said Gonzo, holding up the bottle. Garivin looked at the liquid as if it was his own soul swishing about and he joyously nodded, "Yes another, yes please," he said while his thoughts screamed, *Give it to me! Give me the bottle!*

Gonzo poured the drink and put the bottle back on the shelf. Garivin sighed internally, he knew there would be no more and sadly he knew what Gonzo was doing, he wasn't that stupid but if he was going down he might as well do it right. He gulped it down in one swill. Gonzo watched as Garivin's eyes began to change colour, a yellow tinge; it didn't take long for the potion to take effect.

"Garivin, you know, I know, what you've been up to, don't you?"

"What? What do you mean? Lies! It wasn't me!" Garivin covered the scratches on his hands fumbling the cake on the table, then grabbed at the crumbling pieces once again. Licking his fingertips. The sweet taste, the conflicting thoughts and senses. He shut his eyes and licked his lips, he just wanted to stay in this sweet swirling world. But Gonzo would see that they opened with a slam of his fist against the table.

Gonzo pointed up at the glassy black bottle sitting on the shelf, "Tell me everything and the bottle is yours. Where is Bateau?"

"Kabela, it was all Kabela, she wants the keys," Garivin pointed at the large ring of keys that swung around Gonzo's neck.

"These keys?" He held them up.

"Yes ... those keys."

"The keys to the circus safe?"

"Yes ... the safe," he said, looking up like a child caught stealing, as the cake hung in patches from his stubbly face.

"Kabela said I had a future if I got the keys, a good one, not this one," he whined. "No more animals, no more mess, she saw it in her crystal ball. I knew it was wrong, but the future didn't have me in it scooping dung. I was somebody ... not a nothing." His eyes welled with tears that pooled, then stung as they poured down against his scratches.

"Garivin ... you are somebody, you don't need deceit and thievery, both of these things make you a nobody."

"I didn't want to leave Bateau but Kabela said—"

"What have you done with Bateau?!" Gonzo's heart pounded at the sound of Bateau's name. He had heard enough to kick Garivin head first from Atalas.

Garivin shook and stumbled back into the corner, "Bateau was on Kabela's roof, she thought he heard her plan. Just in case she told me to get rid of him."

"WHAT?"

"I put him in a bag and I left him in an alley, right before we moved on, I didn't lay a finger on him, I swear, I'm the one that got hurt."

"Don't move!" said Gonzo and picked up an old wire phone. Garivin squirmed as Gonzo's finger reached the name Eddie.

"No, not Eddie, please keep him out of this."

Gonzo shook his head and pressed the button next to Eddie's name, it lit up. Several seconds later a scaly thick voice answered.

"What's up Boss?"

"We have a problem. Go get Kabela and bring her to me. Put the word out, she has nowhere to hide."

"Right thing boss, over and out."

Eddie was an escape artist, famous for his circus act where he dived from the dizzying height of the big top, chained in a straight jacket and into a giant pool of quicksand where Gonzo's prized Vicious Candar was enclosed. He was also Gonzo's right-hand man. He wasn't one to be messed with and conveniently his carriage was only three behind Kabela's.

He acted quickly but not fast enough. Kabela's caravan was empty, she had fled and her possessions were strewn over the floor and set on fire. Several others outside had noticed the smoke billowing from the window's and when Eddie saw out of the corner of his eye a silvery figure floating in the air. There she was, climbing the flying fox ladder. He took off after her in hot pursuit.

Kabela felt the sudden shock of the ladder shaking. Damn! Eddie that snake. Taking off her backpack she decided to unpack and empty her goods onto his head as they were all stolen. She had successfully reached the top, grabbed hold of the Zip-line handles and unlatched each one, and sabotaged any chase by throwing both onto the ground leaving herself one. She held on and jumped, shut her eyes and sped down the wire towards Auress.

After a few minutes, Eddie regained his speed and reached the top of the ladder. He couldn't see Kabela, either she fell off or had landed on Auress. Before jumping, he grabbed the telescope fastened to the side of the platform. It was hard to see anything from this height, but with a little adjustment, he picked out Kabela darting through the amusement rides. Eddie reached out to grab a Zip-line handle, but there was nothing to grab. The chase was foiled!

"Kabela you hag! You will have nowhere to hide!" he shouted.

Eddie took off his leather jacket, and slowly he stood back sizing up the jump. With no time to lose he took off and like a hawk diving on its prey, he leapt into the air, flicking his jacket around the wire and latched onto it on the other side, the leather slid fast and he flew along the cable, straight across to Auress.

The chase continued from Auress, back to Aesar, through the Big

Top and all the way to Augustus where the circus creatures resided. When Eddie arrived, there was chaos on Augustus. Kabela had sabotaged several cages and let the surly bizarre creatures free. Walking, slurping and crawling around, screeching and gargling at each other. A distraction, which hopefully would delay him while she ran to her escape vehicle that was on the back of Yeena.

Yeena was one of the main attractions she had wings similar to a Manta Ray but with the ability to fly, it could be the only safe way off the moving horgon. Not that anyone had tried.

"There you are Yeena, looks who's here, it's me Kabela," she said wielding a blade and grinding her blade against her ropes, "I'm going to set you free Yeena."

"Jump if you want to leave but Yeena stays!" roared Eddie.

Kabela looked up with poison eyes, "Come any closer, and I swear I'll stab her to death!"

"Do that and you're as good as dead yourself."

"Back off! I mean it!" shouted Kabela cutting through the last of the ropes. She crawled up onto Yeena and yanked Yeena's reins, "Rise Yeena, rise!" she cried but Yeena, although cut free, stayed put and flapped her wings gently hovering a foot off the ground. Furious Kabela held the blade in both her hands and raised it above her head, "Come a step closer, and I'll kill her, I swear I'll do it!"

"No Kabela! Leave Yeena out of this."

"Get back then, go on, back off!" shouted Kabela scanning around and looking for an exit.

"You haven't seen the last of me!" she snarled, jumping off Yeena and onto the barrier fence.

"What are you doing?" said Eddie as Kabela climbed to the very top, bit her blade between her teeth and then dove into the dusty darkness below.

It was a while before Eddie returned to Atalas, exhausted and empty-handed. He knocked on Gonzo's door.

"Eddie! Come in, I guess you can't find her either?"

"No Gonzo, I found her all right. I don't know what got into her—she jumped!"

"From Augustus. I gave chase across the whole circus, she tried to steal Yeena and fly off, but Yeena wouldn't budge, so she climbed and jumped off the barrier fence. So what's going on? Garivin?"

Garivin shook nervously in the corner; the potion was wearing off.

"She must have been up to something pretty bad," said Eddie directing his voice at Garivin.

"She tricked me, a trick; that's what it was, just like the White Knights! I never got anything out of that either!"

Gonzo felt a lightning bolt tear through his heart at the mention of his friends. With four wild eyes ablaze, he launched onto Garivin, "What did you say? What do you know about the White Knights?!"

"Don't hurt me! You promised the bottle," he squirmed.

Eddie walked up to Garivin and stabbed his knife into the table, with one hand he picked up Garivin from Gonzo's grips and drove him back down into the chair.

"You have a lot of explaining to do. Start talking!"

"Don't hurt me, please! Kabela promised me change, a new life but I only got worse, sick on her potions."

"What of the White Knights!" roared Eddie.

"I led them away from camp to the Shell Forrest, there was a lady who sung and put them in a trance, she gave me potions to give to Kabela. I swore I wouldn't tell, I guess it doesn't matter, she can't hurt me now."

"But I can," said Eddie.

"What lady? Why would she want them?!" said Gonzo, "I can't believe you withheld this from me!"

"Not just a lady, a witch. I wanted to tell you, and get the reward, but the sorceress said she would kill me if I spoke a word of it."

"Oh Garivin," cried Gonzo, "you fool ... where in Mare-Marie could they be?"

"I know," said Garivin smugly, realizing his tone brought frowns upon Garon and Eddie he held up his hands and said, "she spoke to the White Knights and I heard her say she was taking them far north all the way to Castle Morne."

"Castle Morne? Cripes that is the last place someone would look. We don't dare venture to the North anymore," said Gonzo to Eddie, "especially the North East."

Gonzo grabbed the receiver and dragged his finger down the list of buttons till it reached the name Denkar. He pressed it hard and Denkar answered straight away.

"Dankar turn us round, we're heading north."

"What! But we only just made it across the Zale Mountains Gonzo."

"Well we're going back.

"But the sea, it's out of control, we can't do it Gonzo. We'll all drown if any one of the horgans gets dragged in, we'll be done for. Is everything all right? What's going on?" asked Dankar.

"The White Knights, we've found their tracks."

"The White Knights!"

"Exactly. Fine we'll take the desert Vheen. We'll have to go through the Gaze Akarr!"

"But it's just as unpredictable?!"

"Do we have a choice? asked Gonzo."

"I guess not."

"Head towards the Crystalon Castle, we'll need help."

"Yes sir, I'll let everyone know to hold on, we're turning round!"

Chapter 49 - Into the dark light

The wind howled and raced through the tunnel sending shivers up Belleny's spine and for a brief minute, a flurry of wind would drown out the fetid smells of rotting plant matter, dank mud and mould. Kale walked quietly alongside the Princess as they wandered deeper underground towards Castle Morne. Dodging the wiry roots that dangled down like fingering claws, the tunnel made disgusting gurgling noises as if it was drowning on its own vomit. A thin layer of sludge oozed downwards towards the direction of the great Azare.

Like Belleny in her decadent and scary masks, Kale seldom removed his headgear but today, as he stared across at her he unlatched his chin guard and revealed the lower half of his face.

"Kikaan, I know how hard this must be for you, here you must drink," he said passing her his flask.

He's so young, just a boy? She stared at his mouth as the water cleansed the dry crust caked in the corner of his mouth. Underneath the grime his teeth were porcelain white, as was his skin and he seemed to radiate in the darkness.

"Please drink, it will revitalise you."

"Thank you, Kale." She lifted her mask to drink. He watched as the water washed her lips and removed the black tarry blood that had splashed off the butchered cicadas. Belleny sighed and said, "I've not stepped a single foot outside in years ... I still can't believe this is happening. I've gone from a royal fool to ... I think I've reached new limits of foolishness. I can only imagine the state my father is in right now, let alone what is in store for us. I don't understand why I would go against his wishes, to be here of all places."

"I do and I'm sure your father's pain will be washed away on your return," said Kale calmly.

"And I'm sure I'll feel his pain when he kicks me from one side of the castle to the other," said Belleny.

"We all have a purpose in Mare-Marie. More than just title or a name that has no meaning."

"Even the sea?" asked Belleny.

"Especially the sea."

"What about Raveene? Was he to be attacked by a swarm of sand lice and carried away by the giant Gretn Maramon?"

"Unfortunately yes."

"Did you know that was going to happen?"

There was a short silence and Kale replied, "No, I did not. Mare-Marie, from the Sea of Sorrow to the Shell Forrest and beyond, and all of us here, even the darkness are part of something much, much, bigger."

"Something else?"

"Someone else, a child. This place, Mare-Marie, is built on a foundation beyond magic, more than I can understand. The Temple of Thought and its books hold all of our answers."

"I don't understand? Someone else? What child?" said Belleny.

"I will teach you all I know one day, as your mother once did. Do you trust me?"

"I ... I do, that's why I'm here, I trust all of you, the Orphans were my only real friends. I couldn't just let them leave or leave me. Otherwise, I would have stayed at home."

"You sound just like your mother."

Belleny looked at her locket that sparkled in the lantern light.

"She had made it this far ... hadn't she? She fought on and each step made her stronger. I will strive to do the same."

Kale put his palm on her shoulder, "That's the spirit. Not only will you become stronger, but with each step Mare-Marie will change for the better with you. We are all its life force, as it in turn is another's far away. Together we will grow and help each other."

Danté pushed his head between them and said, "You're not going on about that girl are you Kale? Watch out Kikaan he'll have you locked up in his temple reading old dusty books about far away places and stories of a very mysterious girl named Evelin.

"What are you on about Danté, you've read most of those books and always ask for more," smiled Kale.

"True, I can't get enough of her!" laughed Danté out loud as his voice bounced through the tunnel.

"Quiet down back there!" grumbled Garon, who walked hunched over and ahead with Sharpie.

"I'm glad you can find room to laugh ... aren't you both scared?" asked Belleny.

"Of course I'm scared," said Kale, "traveling into the unknown to capture a confused witch amongst her minions has got to be a little daunting."

"Daunting! You have such a way with words—when you do speak. Now what do you mean capture? I distinctly heard you say that before to Danté? I don't understand? You swore I would be her demise. Otherwise, I don't need to be here!"

Instantly Belleny and Danté's eyes stopped blinking.

I've never seen him smile ... beautiful amongst this decaying place, she thought.

I wonder if they have any good food at the castle? thought Danté.

"Forgive me I've completely forgotten what we were talking about?" said Belleny shaking the flock of hair fashioned as a horse's mane attached to her wild mask.

"Something about ... I can't remember either? We must be getting hungry," said Danté. "I'm going back to the White Knights, I hear they still have plenty of rations."

"Stay alert Danté, don't forget we are not alone down here," said Kale.

Kale looked up at Garon, made sure he wasn't looking and then passed Belleny one of his blades, "Here take this, be careful now it is not a toy. You will look more the part, at least make those creatures think twice before challenging the mighty Kikaan."

"Mighty indeed," she sighed. "Thank you, I hope I don't have to actually use it."

A black blade how strange. "I can hardly see it down here, I won't be needing this then," she said removing her kitchen knife from the side of her boot and stabbing it into the tunnel wall.

At that moment, Rel sprung awake and clawed into Kale's leather bound shoulder.

"Rel you're hurting me," said Kale.

"Rel are you alright?" said Belleny.

"We have visitors, approaching fast," snarled Rel.

Sharpie heard Rel and threw his hands on the grimy floor, "Oh dear he's big!"

Kale secured his faceguard and said, "No, there are three."

Sharpie turned back to Garon then to the others, his eyes darting about, "Remember heads down, no eye contact and let me do the talking."

Immediately Garon pushed his shoulders against the roof and spread his wings out wide, blocking the entire tunnel with a solid wall of feathers, "I'll be the judge of that, sorry Kale, watch Kikaan till it's safe."

"Garon? Don't be a fool. Let me through!" shouted Kale left in the dark.

"This better not be a trap Sharpie or you'll be the first to go down," snarled Garon.

Chapter 50 - Whirlpool and few Demons

Esta Green placed her hand on Evelin's arm gently, pointed up and said, "I want you to look into the corner of the room Evelin, where the walls and roof meet and listen to my voice, let it guide you."

"Now raise your left arm slowly and point to the corner."

Evelin felt awfully strange and embarrassed, but lifted her arm and stared at the corner of the room. She noticed how the walls and the roof merged together, seamlessly, and at its axis she felt her eyes had locked deeply onto that point.

"Let the sound of my voice feel heavy on your eyelids, with each and every word I say feel them getting heavier and heavier until they close on their own. Take a long, deep breath and hold it for a few seconds and when you're ready, let it out softly through your mouth, and back in … and out … in … and out, smooth and comfortable. That's it Evelin, doesn't it feel good to relax?"

Evelin didn't reply, she heard Esta loud and clear, but said yes, in her head, rather than with her mouth. She had drifted off at the sound of Esta Green's voice, she didn't need to continue with the induction and Esta could have been reading from a shopping list and she would have drifted away; carrots, onions, bar of soap … and so on.

Evelin felt loose and limp all over and fell back into the leather recliner with her arm still held high in the air. It was now that Esta felt that she had the complete attention of Evelin's subconscious and needn't deepen her any further.

"Evelin I want you to imagine you are sitting in a small wooden boat which is floating down a sparkling and calm river. On either side of the banks are verdant green meadows and the sun is just in the right place for you. Yes that's it, and let your body feel warm all over."

"Mmm," Evelin replied quietly.

"I know you can do anything with your wonderful imagination and I would like you to remove the boat and sit on the surface of the water like a fairy, can you do that Eve?"

Evelin felt like stone and said, "Of course not, I'm too heavy."

"It's up to you, you can be as light as a feather if you want, can you not?" asked Esta knowing the answer.

Evelin nodded ever so gently and removed the boat from her imagination and for a little while she sat on the water's surface as if she was a plastic cup.

"I have no reflection?" whispered Evelin, searching through the glassy water. "I can see the clouds though. Looks like a storm is coming." Esta silently wrote down several notes and let Evelin discover herself and her new surroundings. But before she could focus she realised the water was rising around her, but she couldn't feel a thing, "I'm sinking, but I don't feel wet?"

Esta spoke calmly yet firmly, "That's fine Evelin let it be, I want you to drift slowly into the water and like a wet cloth I want you to drift down and let the water guide you, it's okay, of course you can still breathe. Down you go, the water is fine, deeper and deeper, deeper, relaxed. Tell me when you reach the bottom, okay?"

Twenty silent seconds went by and Evelin's eyes moved rapidly under her lids. She could hear Esta scratching her leg against the wooden chair leg, the ocean and the waves crashing on the shore, the breeze whistling around the house and even her beating heart, but somehow all of this existed in a different place, a channel she chose not to tune into any longer.

It was then that an ocean reef appeared, hesitantly Evelin pulled back as it flashed in several abstract and bright colours, dotting about in fractals then fixing in a hue of yellow and orange. She settled in a patch of warming coral that extended their tentacles and embraced her.

"Coral, a rock covered in coral, they're touching, holding me."

"You are safe, let them hold you and tell me what you see?"

"Deep blue in every direction, there's nothing else. I'm alone."

Evelin said nothing more, she felt nothing, it was as if the coral numbed her with every touch. Squirming she pushed down and away, but the more she moved the more the coral seemed to attach themselves. In a state of anaesthesia, her senses deactivated and lifelessly she watched as her body moved forward, taken by the coral to hang above a sinking ocean ledge.

Evelin gasped and quickly Esta moved forward, "Eve, you always have control over the coral, over anything in this beautiful dream-like state, remember you are always in control."

"But the coral has me."

"That's fine, move with it, I think it wants to show you something."

Evelin felt her body moving as the coral's tentacles took her even further from the edge and she looked deep into the endless blue, "What are they showing me? There's nothing, nothing but—wait—the water's changing, darker, swirling. Oh my!"

"What can you see Eve? Remember nothing can harm you, you are in control."

"I know but there's a whirlpool down there. It's getting bigger! It's pulling me! What if the coral lets go?"

"Evelin don't fight the whirlpool, let it get bigger and bigger until there's nothing left for it to swallow. It can't hurt you, give in to the whirlpool."

"I can't, I don't want to, it's pulling me!"

"You're in control Eve, it's okay, now take a deep breath in—that's it. Now you tell it, I am Evelin Boots and I am not afraid of you and I never will be again."

Evelin repeated the words to herself.

"Now say it again Eve, louder and stronger!"

This time Evelin spoke up, "I am Evelin Boots and I am not afraid of you and I never will be again!"

"And again!" said Esta.

This time Evelin shouted the words and each and every time the whirlpool got smaller and smaller. Even the coral had pulled her back to the soft membrane ledge. There was little water to be seen and it now came up to her ankles.

"Well done Evelin, where is the whirlpool now?" said Esta quite enthusiastically.

In her dream state, Evelin walked to the edge of the coral rock and watched the whirlpool. It was nothing more than a bathtub plughole, dissipating and twisting back into itself. "It's gone? So is most of the water, but it's gone," said Evelin quietly.

"Good girl, it's time to come back now, so as I count back to one, with each number I want you to drop your arm and when your arm reaches the chair you will wake up feeling refreshed and better than ever before."

Esta began and counted back from five.

"Five ... four ... three."

But then Evelin began to squirm once again, "It's back!" she shouted. "It's in the sky! And it's pouring all the water back out, but now it's black."

"Evelin the whirlpool knows you're winning, it's giving all it's got. Take a deep breath now and when you exhale I want you to let the black water cover you whole. Give in, and as it does the coral will set you free."

"What? I can't do that. Then what?"

"Whatever you like, you can float to the surface like a bottle out at sea, where you can float comfortably on the water once again."

Evelin thought this was crazy and she resisted, but the opaque water kept flowing and it was rising fast, pushing her hair up. She took a deep breath as it covered her face entirely, still the coral had not let go.

Back inside the therapy room Evelin panicked and squirmed in the chair, struggling, she reached out latching onto Esta.

By this time Esta had realised this was doing more harm than good and continued the countdown, "Four, three and two and one. You can open your eyes Evelin, wake up now."

Evelin jolted up and stared her own hand turning white as she was gripping tightly around Esta's bony wrist. Esta remained calm and touched Evelin's fingers gently.

Evelin stared down at her hand and unlatched it instantly, "I'm sorry. That was so scary, it was trying to drown me!" said Evelin, her chest heaving in and out.

"But you didn't though," said Esta, "you did really well my dear."

"I've got to get some air," said Evelin.

She walked outside onto the balcony and looked out over the ocean cove. Esta gave her a moment, then appeared beside her.

"Eve?" she said lightly, "sometimes when we need to get away from it all, from reality, memories, our mind can create a door to escape. In some ways, we are then safe, yet it is still a facade, and we find ourselves unpleasantly trapped on the other side and in this state it can create anxieties, depression and illness. Not only that, some say this is where your inner demons dwell."

Evelin sighed, "I'm sick of them, I feel cursed."

"You showed them today though, I'm proud of you. Next time will be even better."

"Next time? You're joking right?"

"Like it or not Eve, you must return, you've got more courage and determination than ever before. You knocked about what you're up against and you'll be ready for round two on Friday."

"Robin's going to laugh."

"But you're not, are you?"

Evelin paused at first then said, "No, it's not funny. I guess I'll see you Friday then."

"You are ingenious and a very brave girl, please remember this. I'm so glad you came today," said Esta.

Evelin gave Esta a light hug, said nothing more and left.

Like clockwork, Robin waited for her across the road, leaning against his old motorbike. With an underarm swing, he threw her helmet across to her.

"You dork," she grinned and stared at the weird smiley face he had drawn on the back of her helmet with white chalk.

"Everything all right?" he asked.

"Just a bit of light talking, a chat with a whirlpool and a few demons," she replied.

"Good good, nothing serious then."

Kale's estimation was correct. Three creatures were lumbering through the cave. The largest were Bagger and Buildar, competing to be the meanest and ugliest of the trio. Jasic darted at the front and kept his distance from the their dirty clawed feet behind him. He was knee height, had an extended weasel-like snout and like Bagger and Buildar also had clawed bare feet splashing into the caves sewer trail. He was scrapping with the other two and before he launched into another rant, paused mid-sentence as his eyes focused on Garon and Sharpie through the low-level lighting emanating from their lanterns. Jasic pointed at them, "I knew it, I knew it you idiots, I told you so! I could smell them from a mile away."

"Yeah, little Jasic, you're right as usual. I can smell him now ... yum they smell delicious."

"But where is he? Can't be that old bird?" said Buildar as he scratched his balding tufts on his head.

Jasic tapped his foot on the slimy tunnel floor and stated in a horrible snotty voice, "So what have we here, a giant rat with wings and a walking weed? Who else you got back there then? Where'd you crawl from exactly?" He then proceeded to remove a significant amount of snotty mucus from his nose and smear it on the tunnel wall.

"A rat with wings!" growled Garon, but Sharpie held up his arm and stopped him from going any further.

"Greetings, I am Sharpie, the humble guide and this is my travelling companion and we've been down to the waterfall this morning, a bit of sightseeing you see, just to enjoy before the big night at the castle."

"A guide? Sightseeing? Are you all stupid? There's nothing but falling mud and a whole heap of nothing," scoffed Bagger.

"Yes you're right, they didn't believe me that there was nothing beyond the cliff face either, a whole heap of nothing."

"You're damn right," snarled Jasic, "nothing but nothing and if you do find anything it's ours, you hear me!"

"Ah yes ... righteo," said Sharpie holding up his hands in defence, "we best be on our way, we don't want to miss out on a good seat tonight."

Jasic folded his arms and slowly shook his head, his weasly long nose slid with it, "Not so fast bug boy."

"Don't tell me what to do. Move aside you little twerp," said Garon in a low growl.

Jasic grinned, "Where did your manners go? Though I would not expect much more from a feathered rat. Ain't you heard of a bird bath? What have you guys been doing, bathing under the mud fall?" Jasic's smirk was drowned in a snot bubbling laugh that echoed down the tunnel and it stopped before Garon' completely lost his temper.

"Nah, come on, drop the long face ratty, I was only messing with ya', but honestly why you not flying hmm?"

"I prefer tunnels," grunted Garon preparing to whack Jasic back from where he once came.

"Let me tell you this," began Jasic, "I know my nose ain't pretty, but my nose knows when it knows a liar and you my friend is a liar. Now tell me what's a flying rat and his little bugs doing, crawling, hiding, deep down in trash alley? You can't fly can ya'?"

"Of course I can fly! Stop calling me a rat damn it! I have a beak!" snapped Garon as Jasic began his snot-filled laughter once again, this time Bagger and Buildar joined in until Jasic snarled back at them. "Okay, that's enough! We have pressing matters to discuss with our new acquaintances ... don't we?"

Bagger dropped his enormous bag of rubbish and clapped his hands with deafening thuds and cheered, "Yes we do, two tail stew!"

"Two tail stew!" gasped Bateau as he had heard of the dish before.

Belleny looked down realising she held Kale in a vice-like grip. She let go and he turned back, holding his finger to his lips, he pointed to her and Bateau to move far back with the Orphans. She agreed and nervously she scurried behind Dillon with Bateau shaking even more nervously in her backpack.

Sharpie stepped forward with arms out wide, "Please forgive my friend, he's had a stressful day. We're looking forward to tonight like everyone else; we'll see you there I'm sure. Plenty of stews there for all no doubt. Now we'll be on our way."

"Squeak, squeak, squeak! Noisy green bug aren't you?" said Jasic as he began to sniff at Sharpie then up at Garon. He lifted his long snivelling nose up and around him, "I was right boys, the fear is making it smell even sweeter."

"What are you sniffing at? Everything stinks like vomit down here!" snapped Garon.

"Not everything," said Buildar, "we smells it back there. Two tail treat, two tail treat!"

"Yeah, give us the little critter!" said Bagger impulsively.

"Two tail treat? What? Who Bateau?" said Garon picturing Bateau's lively tails.

Sharpie looked up at Garon and shook his head disappointedly.

"Oh dear," mumbled Garon realizing he spoke out loud.

"Yes Bateau! Tasty little Bateau!" said Buildar.

"I think you're mistaken, Bateau is anything but tasty," said Garon with a light chuckle.

"Tell that to my belly," snarled Jasic.

Bateau peered out of Belleny's backpack and cried out, "I'm not a tasty treat, honest!"

"Oh yes, you are!" called out Bagger in a girly voice which made all three burst out in laughter again.

Bateau began to cry a deep undulating howl.

"Now look what they've done! Don't worry Bateau no one's going to eat you." Belleny gripped her new blade and in a menacing cry shouted, "Never! You'll die first!"

Garon turned and thrust his beak forward, "Quiet back there, are you trying to get yourself killed?"

Jasic peered through the gap in Garon's feathered wall and said, "I see you back there, come here Bateau, come on now or I'll have my boys come back there and yank you out screaming."

"I would like to see you try," said Garon pushing out his wings and sealing the tunnel.

"Oh, would you now?" snarled Jasic as he scratched at the oily ground with his bare and unsightly nailed feet.

"Nice move birdy!" said Buildar, "But what ya' going to fight with now?"

"You'll see," growled Garon tapping his talon's like fingers on a table.

With wild eyes and surprising speed, Jasic sprung forward and with his nails he latched onto Sharpie's shoulders, puncturing his jacket and sunk into his green flesh. Without losing momentum he continued his attack and launched like a thrown cat towards Garon. In less than a heartbeat Jasic had brought Sharpie to his knees and now clawed his arms and legs tight around Garon's throat.

"Aagghhh!" howled Sharpie.

Buildar and Bagger began to point and laugh.

"Garon!" shouted Kale. Unable to see or help, they listened helplessly to the fight as Garon's wall of feathers scraped against the tunnel walls, back and forth.

Unable to speak, Garon let out a low and grasping growl, yet he continued to hold his ground, wings out wide as Jasic continued his stranglehold.

Sharpie glanced at his bleeding shoulders and what oozed out which wasn't red blood but a tarry black oil and like a wasp he flicked out his wings, sprung from the ground and darted towards Jasic.

A sound like several pens being pushed through a cardboard box could then be heard. It was then that Jasic's face changed from wild and manic to stone cold and sombre. Sharpie slowly removed his fist and several scalpel-sharp prongs from Jasic's temple. A black ooze trickled out as the lifeless snotty creature fell to the floor with a wet splash. Garon stomped hard on Jasic's chest and leant forward looking not at Jasic but the dumbfounded two behind him. The sound of Jasic's chest being punctured made even Buildar and Bagger feel sick.

"Little Jasic?" said Bagger but Little Jasic was not getting up.

"You killed him! Bagger, they killed Jasic!"

"You'll pay for this!" growled Buildar, removing a giant axe from his back holster.

"Garon let us help you!" yelled Kale, "Enough is enough!"

"Cover your eyes!" said Sharpie as he revealed a small bottle to Garon. The liquid inside made the whole tunnel glow an eerie green and lit up Garon's marble black eyes. He couldn't help but stare at it. The group watched as Garon began to glow green as the light radiated all around and through the tips of his feathers.

"Stop staring Garon!" yelled Sharpie and in one swift manoeuvre Garon retracted his wings and turned his back to the giant creatures pushing them back out leaving Sharpie alone with them. In the instant that Garon turned around and dropped his wings, they watched as Buildar roared forward with his axe in hand.

"No! Garon behind you!" cried Belleny.

The mere sound of glass smashing tinkled in the tunnel. Garon gasped as he fell down on one knee and shut his eyes. Then there was silence. Belleny held his face and caressed his long grey scarred beak. His black eyes squinted open and closed once again, "Garon!" cried Belleny.

"I'm sorry!" he gasped.

"Come on Garon, before he crushes you to death," said Sharpie.

Everyone looked up at the sight in amazement.

"What just happened?" asked Garon opening up his eyes puzzled and feeling behind him where the fat beast Buildar was laying out cold against him.

Bagger remained floppy and his head tilted downwards, slumping in a deep sleep-like trance.

"Quick now we have little time, a sleeping potion that's all, it's quite old so I don't know how long it will last. Please help me get this beast off him, before he's crushed," said Sharpie pulling Buildar's trunk-like arm.

With a deep sigh, Garon rubbed his neck, "Thanks, Sharpie."

"You're bleeding!" cried Belleny, her hands covered in a mixture of his red and black blood splattered from Jasic.

"Just a scratch and I'm missing a few feathers," he said rolling Jasic face first into the dirt as he stood up.

"Next time let us help you Garon, you're no help to us wounded," said Kale.

"Or dead," muttered Dillon.

"Yes sorry, I thought the little weasely one would be a push over."

Belleny took the satchel from Sharpie, removed the white fur and wrung out the milky liquid it soaked in. She placed it on Garon's neck. "You'll be alright, it doesn't look too bad," she said. But she couldn't really tell underneath such thick feathers.

"What about you Sharpie?" asked Danté.

"The poisoned heal differently, I will be as fine as I can be," said Sharpie wrapping his wound taut as he returned his jacket.

"Thank you," said Bateau appearing from Belleny's backpack with his voice returned, "I thought that was it for me."

"Well let's hope for your sake we don't run out of food, this two-tailed stew sounds pretty good to me," said Danté scuffing Bateau's head.

Kale took Sharpie by the arm and said, "You're a warlock?"

"Well, more a thief," he replied with a grin, "there are always a few fringe benefits to be gained from working alongside unsavoury types."

"Oh, I see," said Kale.

Sharpie raised the filament on his lantern and lit up the travellers, all the way back to the Orphans. Their black eyes glistened off the light. "I suggest we move fast my friends, we have a little while to go and I only have two of these sleep potions left."

Belleny walked closely beside Garon as the roof dripped oil and rank mud from the tunnel roof. At times they both looked across at each other in silence and she knew in a fight raining fire and walking through Brimstone, he would be there to protect her. *Brave old fool,* she thought, after witnessing the first real fight with the dark creatures of the North.

At various stages the tunnel widened, then rose twice as tall as Garon, then it contracted tightly and squashed him to down, so he shuffled along his knees. Every once in a while it split off into several directions, but Sharpie, who they hoped led them to safety, seemed to know exactly where to take them. For every path they didn't take, Belleny imagined what lay watching in the darkness. Nervously she turned back to reassure herself the Orphans were safe. Bateau kept quiet and more to himself. Their shared stories of the Great Gonzo Circus only made him regress into himself. He preferred to be within Belleny's arms or asleep in Garon's feathers high above and away from their tales. Up ahead the silent Kale and his dormant familiar Rel, Danté the energetic voyager, and Sharpie the strange green poisoned character, had talked between one another for some time.

"What's that sound?" squeaked Bateau. His long ears striking into the air as did his tails pointing at the roof. Garon stopped instantly jolting the Orphans behind him. Everyone faced the roof together, squinting as the soil crumbled down like dry, dirty rain.

"All those creatures, the giant bugs! They're walking right above us!" gasped Belleny.

"This tunnel won't hold them much longer," said Danté waving them on.

"There are so many of them, they seem to be wearing down the mountain, we must hurry, quick, run now!" said Sharpie.

"Come on Kikaan get a move on! Orphans move it!" said Garon as he picked up speed, and together the group ran until the footsteps and voices above became a low rumble.

"Bateau are you all right?" asked Belleny. "He's lost his voice again," she said to Garon, "it happens when he's scared, when I met him he couldn't talk and then he couldn't stop, then it goes, and he can only make strange noises."

"He's weirder than the Orphans, no offence," said Garon, "at least they were under a curse," he chuckled.

"Garon don't be mean, Bateau is a hero," said Belleny.

"Indeed," added Danté.

"Garon?" said Belleny.

"What now?"

"I would like to talk to the Orphans, please. I'll be back in a moment, please entertain Bateau for me," said Belleny.

Garon turned towards her at such speed, his beak nearly knocked her to the ground. "You ride up on Dillon! You hear me, it's quiet now, but trust me, this place is dangerous."

"Understood," she said as she stood still, turned and waited for the Orphans to catch up. They too were quite large and between them filled the tunnel from head to toe. Dillon and Montë were at the front while Agarus could be seen trailing at the end and she was reminded of their first adventure walking through the leafy tunnel to the Queen's Garden where Agarus fleetingly ran away from a butterfly. She smiled as they approached and kicked aside an old basket of mouldy potatoes that rolled through a weak hole in the tunnel. Within seconds, the crunching sounds of them being chopped in pieces echoed out, followed by a snorting and sniffing sound. Belleny didn't run at first, or point or yell for help, she curiously looked down the hole. The Orphans watched as a giant snout covered in barbs pushed through the hole and began sniffing at the Princess, who had become completely frozen.

"Belleny move!" cried Dillon, but she couldn't, her mind said run but her legs didn't listen.

The creature pushed out its long, pimply marked tongue and stroked it up and across her chest. With small bite-sized pecks, it bit out towards her trying to snatch, but its immense size kept its body wedged in its burrow. It was then that Belleny snapped wide awake and fell back against the greasy tunnel floor, slipping as her hands searched for grip amongst the chunky slime.

"Wompig!" screamed Belleny knowing precisely what it was.

Garon turned sharply tossing Bateau into the air, "No!" he cried realising he could not reach her in time. For each step, the wompig pushed itself closer and in moments she would incur a bone-crushing bite. Like a flash of lightning, the tunnel lit up for a split second, and the horrific features of the wompig glowed revealing all its hideous glory. Belleny saw Kale's blade drive deep into the wompig's eyeball and with a wild squeal it clawed and squirmed back inside its burrow. To Belleny, there was complete silence, but all around her the Orphans, Garon, Danté and Bateau shouted for her to get up, still in shock she stared into the dark hole. It wasn't until Kale yanked her arm and pulled her to her feet, did all her senses come back, and tenfold.

"Are you all right?" said Dillon letting her stand by herself.

Her heart pounded and she found it hard to stand on wobbly knees.

"That was a wompig, right?" stuttered Belleny in the circling light of their lanterns.

"Yes, a big one too," said Danté.

"Everyone one get well away from its nest, it won't give up so easily!" said Sharpie, waving his clawed hands in the air.

"Disgusting!" said Belleny wiping thick wads of the wompig's saliva from her outfit.

"Come on you heard him, get away from there! Before it—" said Garon stomping towards her.

But then it happened too quickly, the wompig returned ramming its horned skull and ripping at the dirt like dry bread. Belleny slipped back down again and her legs dipped into its burrow, kicking at its salivating and whiskey mouth as it pushed forward.

Belleny couldn't remember what happened next as it was all too fast, but she watched herself rising to the roof as Garon yanked her up like a toy doll. The next moment she was back on the slimy ground as the wompig flung Garon aside, releasing a confetti of torn black feathers up into the air. The Orphans drove their claws into its side, but it shook them off like flies. Danté moved to attack, but Kale held him back. "Wait," he said firmly.

"She'll die!" replied Danté but Kale refused to let him go and squeezed his shoulder. Danté looked up mournfully and watched as Belleny pulled herself onto one knee and the creature rose to its feet and heaved a heavy breath down onto her. Its one good eye stared deep and reflected the young girl. But the girl was also Kikaan, she was projecting her inner beast and with a roaring frightening scream she raised and swung her blade with both hands. "Leave me alone!!"

With a downwards plunge the tip of the blade sliced through the base of the wompig's snout, a greasy black blood sprayed out like a broken hose from its tap, splashing all over her. The creature screeched; it bucked and bayed, throwing its head about as the tunnel walls began to breach. Belleny stood up as Agarus slithered as fast as a serpent, up the side of the tunnel wall and came down, driving his claws into the top of the wompig's head. It bucked Agarus up and down like a rodeo rider and then it stopped as Belleny swung her blade once again, cutting the air in half. Garon looked on speechless as the wompig's hideous tongue fell at its feet, flicking side to side while the creature continuously squealed, squirted and spat as it wriggled on the floor. Agarus jumped off its neck and crawled over it on the roof as the creature gave one last attempt, biting up at him like a dog snapping at flies.

"Finish him off!" roared Garon getting to his feet.

Belleny heard his words and without a second thought she lunged forward and drove her blade deep into the wompig's bony skull. Now both of Kale's black daggers sat deep in its head. Like a tranquillized rhino stumbling to its knees, the wompig dropped lifelessly before her in a heaving mass. Garon looked on stunned; his beak fell wide open. The Orphans looked at each other in disbelief. Kikaan heaved her every breath with the wompig's oily black blood dripping from her hands. In her wild mask, which seemed to be more real than ever, she stared back at them as if she had wanted to do this her whole life.

"I meant for Agarus to finish him!" roared Garon shaking, "Get away from that thing now!"

Kale patted Danté on the back, passed the disgruntled Garon and retrieved the blades from the creature. The second one, secured deep in its skull, needed the levering of his boot and two swift kicks with his heel. Wiping the blades clean on the wompig's hairy cheek he passed hers back.

Kale leant into her ear, "You see mighty Kikaan, you are a lot stronger than you think."

She pulled back her soiled mask, shook the tarry blood from it and looked across at the dead creature.

"It wanted me to do it," she said, "my first."

"Not your last," said Kale swiftly as Garon approached.

Garon turned to Kale, "She is not your toy to play with—Kikaan is a—"

"Yes," said Kale calmly, "I know very well."

"Good work little one!" cheered Sharpie jumping between them all. "Never in my life have I seen such ... courage! I'm glad to have you on my side." Sharpie turned to the wompig and gulped, "Let's keep moving, it might have parents. Quick now." He then took off with his lantern glowing brightly in hand.

It was a precarious climb before they reached the exit. It seemed to be getting colder, the wind howled through, which was good as it took the vomit smell with it, but more and more often the creatures could be heard once again, scampering above.

Words were few until Sharpie turned around and said, "Good, it's not blocked."

"What? You fool get out of the way," said Garon pushing him aside. "This way Kikaan!"

"Take cover, the witch has spies," said Sharpie getting to his feet. One by one, they ventured out of the tunnel which was hidden in a thicket, close to the castle. The surroundings were bleak, leafless trees, thorny bushes and bone-white rocks stuck out of the ground in every direction.

"Giant..." whispered Monté.

"We wait here and go over our plan," said Garon standing under the ancient bone claw of the fallen giant's hand.

"Yes, he must have been huge. We've made it ... Castle Morne," said Belleny, nervously pointing through the trees and up at the giant's half buried skull and the castle built within it. The draw bridge which was built out of the giant's mouth lit the entrance. Flames torched and created a pathway of amber light illuminating a continuous flow of creatures of all shapes and sizes.

"It's worse than I thought," said Sharpie, "but we're in luck as it hasn't begun, there's way too many outside."

"That is lucky," grumbled Garon.

"Are you sure about our strategy?" said Kale.

"I don't like to split up, but I know it's in our favour," said Garon.

"A wise move," said Sharpie, "we'll have two chances then, attack her from both sides if we're lucky."

"And if we're not lucky?" asked Dillon.

"If we split up into groups we're less likely to be noticed, and we'll double our chances," said Garon.

"Of getting caught," said Danté.

"The decision has been made," said Kale and he crossed his arms.

Sharpie pointed up at the castle and said, "The central kitchen is on this side and an easy entrance, and the boiler room, around the back, is another. I know of other ways to enter, underneath the drawbridge and through a drain by the moat, but honestly I'd rather walk through the front gate with those beasts. If we keep low, blend in and don't talk to anyone we'll get to the main ballroom. The destination is in the center of the castle, all paths lead you straight to it—what was that?"

"Who's there?" said Garon turning up and raising his blade at the shadowy figure.

"I finally found you!" cried Palia from above. "What happened to you down there, are you all right?"

"Palia!" waved Belleny "are you okay? What happened to you?"

"Yes I am fine. I saw you enter the tunnel near the waterfall but as I prefer the sky I flew."

"Wise move," said Garon.

"And yes I could sense the White Knights, even when you were deep underground. Happy to see you my friends."

Sharpie moved forward and pointed at a skull-shaped bone sticking out of the soil, "So the boiler room or the kitchen are our two best options, here and here. Who goes where then?"

Kale put his hand on Danté's shoulder, "Sharpie, Danté, you will come with Rel and I, we'll go the basement tunnel via the boiler room. Garon and the Orphans, you're going through the kitchen."

"What about us?" said Belleny with Bateau in her arms.

"You're coming with me, of course," said Garon shaking his head at the ground.

Kale produced a very fine silver whistle with engraved markings of a leaf on one side. "Garon listen out for this sound and you'll find us." He blew the whistle gently. There was no sound that Belleny could hear, but clearly Garon could hear it by the way he shook his head.

"Are you done? Stop that blasted noise!" he growled.

"Oooh can I have one of those?" said Bateau.

"Quiet you or I'll throw you into a hot pot when we return for dinner," huffed Garon.

The teams agreed and positioned themselves in their allocated groups. Sharpie gave Garon a small parting gift, one of his bottles containing the green glowing freeze potion, "Here my friend take this, be careful not to drop it."

"Sorry, I don't do magic," frowned Garon.

"I'll take it," growled Belleny in the tone of Kikaan.

"Well then, we go that way to the boiler room, it should take your group around the same time to get to the ballroom more or less. Once inside lay low and quickly find somewhere to hide, there are plenty of places even for you Agarus. I don't recommend the ballroom itself, as it will be too dangerous. Ultimately you will reach the witch, she sits high upon her throne, you will spot her, seated at a distance from the creatures."

"What's the best way to the kitchen?" asked Dillon.

Sharpie pointed, "Either continue along the edge of the forest or continue close to the castle wall until you see a large wooden door, there are only a few doors, most are boarded up shut, you won't miss it, it's got a white chef's hat painted on it. The cooks are overweight idiots, you will have no problem getting past them."

"Oh ... what ... is that above?" squawked Palia, a blackened leathery beast was flying and flapping its giant bat wings high above the castle steeple.

"It's huge, a monster," said Agarus.

"Is it a Kylen Rider?" asked Belleny.

"No kylen could grow that big," droned Garon.

"We're not in the kingdom anymore Garon, this is a witch's world," she added.

"Let me see. Damn it's her, we must go at once!" said Sharpie.

All eyes watched the winged creature as it swooped around the castle. Like a bird of prey, it hovered on the spot and with wings pulled back it dove, disappearing within the giant's skull and castle.

Belleny held her black blade in white-knuckled claws, "This is it then. No turning back."

"Speaking of backs," said Garon crouching beside her, "you two get back on top."

"Goodbye," said Kale, "we must go." He pulled down his hood, low across his eyes, and ventured towards the castle.

"Wait up! See you on the inside my friends. Let's go Sharpie," said Danté and like the night they disappeared into the shadows.

"Farewell," said Belleny as a tear-soaked into her mask.

"Let us go then," said Garon and together with the brave and transformed Orphans left the safety of the giant's claw.

Palia's feathers shimmered and changed to jet black as she flew towards the castle. Sharpie ducked and weaved through the white bone rocks before he disappeared completely from sight. Garon and the Orphans had different terrain to navigate through the forest that circled the castle. It was brittle, jagged bent in every direction and peppered with impenetrable bushes.

"We have to get out of here, let's go close to the wall and follow it that way. This forest will slow us down," said Dillon.

"I'm with you," said Agarus, looking through the trees to the castle, "it seems clear and the shadows are deep along the wall, we would be safe from peering eyes."

"No wait, there's someone over there," said Garon. He pointed to a few shapes huddling by a large fallen tree.

"If it's only those few, I'll distract them while you guys move up and onwards, I can handle myself," said Agarus.

"Hmm, no we shouldn't split up," said Garon.

"Garon's right Agarus," said Montë, "we can wait till they go inside."

"That may be hours, I fit in well enough with the best of them here, I may even find out some information."

It was then they heard grumbling and cursing in the trees behind them. Belleny stood high up on Garon and peered back, "I can't see them yet.

It's coming from over near the cave. Do you think it's Buildar and Bagger, the ones that attacked us?"

"I don't want to find out!" said Bateau.

"If it is, they'll soon have Bateau's scent," sighed Garon. "I guess that's a sign, we can't wait here much longer."

"Don't worry I'll meet you inside. Don't forget to look up Belleny, I'll probably be on the ceiling," said Agarus and he took off into the open.

"Goodbye Agarus, please be safe! This is not a game!" said Belleny.

"Let's get moving, they're getting closer," said Garon.

Agarus climbed the hill and walked in the dark shadows of the castle. He turned back towards the entrance, never before had he seen so many creatures. As he moved on and closer to the fallen tree trunk, one of the small gang noticed him.

"Oy Greb!" he called out at Agarus.

Agarus stood tall on his hind legs and walked towards him.

"Hey, you're not Greb? My mistake big fella you look just like him in the dark. Hey whatcha' doing past the fence? You know no one's allowed back here but workers."

Agarus stood tall and imitated his voice slightly, "I don't like the crowds or the company."

"I hear ya', half of them chew ya' face off for a swill of the good old black stuff. I don't blame 'em."

"Who, is ya' then?"

"I'm—" Agarus thought quickly, "Edgar."

"Edgar? You can call me Four Eyes, everyone else does, four eyes you see," he pointed to the four slitted eyes on his face. They opened up one at a time, then blinked simultaneously. Agarus was taken aback and politely didn't know which one to look at.

"We be relaxing before the big night," said Four Eyes.

"Yes, the big night," said Agarus slowly, as he was disturbed by Four Eyes' strange bestial features. His silhouette was shaped by an adult man, but up close revealed his four black eyes, thick-clawed hands and a grey-blue complexion with chalky skin.

"Come on, you should hang with us. Don't worry, I gots a table reserved for us, I'm one of the witch's favourites. We all are."

"Really? That would be wonderful," said Agarus thinking of how perfect his plan could be and how close he could get to the witch. But also now the others would have a smooth journey to the kitchen if he could keep their attention.

There were three others standing around an enormous tree trunk. The tree formed a thick muddy trench that tore through the soil as it had been pulled uphill from within the forest. Half of the tree trunk had been hand cut into large sections and a fresh blanket of sawdust covered the ground, others were axed and piled up wall to wall as firewood, filling an enormous stable. Agarus realised they were the witch's woodsmen.

"All right then, these be me mates, look here fellas he ain't Greb, which is probably a good thing."

This made them all laugh. "This here is Edgar, don't any of you mess with him, he's all right," said Four Eyes while pointing a claw at them like a teacher's ruler.

"Greetings, I am Baron Von Hudwig the Third, but you can call me Baron," he said proudly. The Baron was dressed in an aviator outfit similar to what the Kylen Riders wore back in Mare-Marie. His forehead was barbed with thorns akin to a rose stem and they poked through his slick black hair. His ghastly features looked as if he had been in a mid-air collision and somehow survived.

"Baron," said Agarus and shook his hand.

"And this piece of work is Nails, don't shake his hand," Four Eyes quickly added.

Agarus looked at the creature's hands, his fingernails were long, more like talons, bandaged and dried hard with black blood.

"Hi. It's going be a good night yes?" said Nails. His voice was scratchy and harsh as if he had been eating nails.

"Yes, I look forward to it," said Agarus.

"You must have been here quite a few times, like me," said Nails.

"Uhuh," said Agarus.

The Baron pulled forward a creature that hung in the shadows of the castle, "And this little fellow is Shovel you can shake his hand but I don't recommend that either."

The huge creature stood forward and was as silent as a tree with fists the size of barrels that hung like demolition balls. He looked down at Agarus curiously and said in a deep voice, "You're covered in blood."

Agarus looked down at himself, he had forgotten about the sticky blood that fired out from the Wompig's head and wiped his chest, "Wompig, got in the way."

"Nosey bastards," said Shovel thumping his fists together.

Not this one, thought Agarus picturing Belleny slicing off its snout.

"They taste good though," said Nails. "Did you eat it?"

Eat it? thought Agarus, "Not this time, it ran away with an eye short."

"Enough small talk ladies, who's got fire as I would like to enjoy my pipe?"

In spite of being cannibals they are a civilized bunch, Aragus smiled to himself.

Meanwhile Garon and his posse had made their navigation to the castle triumphantly. They took the path along the castle wall and found a series of doors along the way, many of them boarded up but after much inspecting they found one which had the symbol of a chef's hat.

"Do we go in?" asked Dillon.

Bateau carefully peered through the door "No one's in there? Yum smells good!" he said and stepped inside.

"Wait," said Kikaan.

Bateau ignored the order and went further inside following the pastry scent and the warmth of the hearth. The room was solid, no windows or fixtures, with dry cardboard brown walls. Above where the lanterns sat, large burn marks rose up to the roof. In the corner sat an enormous oven for baking, *or cremating*, thought Garon, as it roared from its grills, crackling full of life and pushing flames through its vents.

"Come now, the coast is clear," whispered Bateau, but he spoke too soon as just inside the pantry door lumbered a soiled, wrinkly, wide-mouthed, almond coloured creature in an apron. He held a large flat pizza board on a wooden handle which was stacked with fresh pies. Not only was the chef round, but he was also tall and each limb was as round as a car tire. "Oy you!" he shouted, "I thought I could smell something pretty. What are you doing in here? Ya' stinking thief!"

He snarled down at Bateau and his wrinkles made him resemble a monstrous Shar-Pei dog.

"I can't believe my luck, you're going to make a delicious pie, come here now, come to Chef Barbadoa."

"Beellaannyy!" cried Bateau in a yowl as he scampered back into Garon, who pushed himself into the doorway. One at a time the White Knights, who were transformed as the Black Knights, raced into the kitchen.

Belleny peered around the doorway and stared nervously at the chef. *Nothing less than a monster in an apron,* she thought. "Come here Bateau!" she said kneeling on the ground and receiving him in her arms.

"Don't cry it will be all right," she said but then realised it was not Bateau who was crying. "Who's crying then?" She looked up at the chef and for a ghastly moment she thought, *is it coming from him? From his belly? It can't be ...*

Belleny peered across at the chef's pastries and as she did a paw punched through the lid of a pie, "Oh my! The pies are crying! He's going to cook them alive," Belleny shrieked.

Barbadoa stomped to the side and peered over Dillon.

"So what! Get over here with my two-tailed treat!"

"Not again," sighed Garon as he pushed Belleny and Bateau behind his wing. "Watch them Montë."

Dillon stood as tall as Barbadoa and stood forward and snarled up at him.

"Fresh pies tell no lies!" mocked Barbadoa as his pies began to wriggle and cry even more.

"Put the pies down," said Garon shaking his head.

"You don't tell Chef Barbadoa what to do in his kitchen."

"You're a monster!" shouted Belleny.

"Quiet!" snapped Garon.

"You're right though, they're even better raw," smirked Barbadoa, "I love when they cry in my belly. You'll be next little one!"

"Montë!" screamed Belleny as he yelped and flew head first into the kitchen wall near Chef Barbadoa. Belleny turned around to face two hairy round trunks, and a gut that hung at its knees. Shock made Belleny's heart beat faster so she clutched Bateau hard against her chest.

A similar looking, slightly smaller but fatter chef wearing an apron appeared outside at the doorway dusting flour from his hands.

"Ya' can't even have a break without someone sneaking in trying to steal our pies," he said spitting horrendously to the side, "and they always end up in them, don't they boss?"

Garon turned sideways and pushed Belleny around with him. The chef held Palia by her neck, "Look who else I found sneaking around, looks like one of this mob?" He then threw Palia inside and straight into Montë's chest.

Garon pointed toward the inside door, "Get out now!" he crowed at them. Montë and Palia stood up in a daze and then realised he was shouting at them.

"Get out and go!" roared Garon.

"But—" said Palia.

"Now!" said Garon, for he knew they would only get hurt.

"Quick Palia do as he says. This way!" Montë pulled Palia as they ran out into the unknown. Quickly they slammed the door behind them.

Chef Barbadoa ripped the door open and shouted, "You can run, but you can't hide!"

Belleny and Garon sat tight and held each other in the darkness. Then with the dreaded sound of a heavy latch clicking closed, they realised Barbadoa had locked the door.

"A lock down is it!" said the apprentice from the other side. He reached back pulling the outside door shut with a heavy slam, he also locked the door with a heavy wooden latch.

"No one else is escaping now, especially the tasty treats you got there bird," said Barbadoa pointing down at Belleny and Bateau, who's shaking tails could be seen under Garon's wing.

"Smells good, I'm starving," said the apprentice slapping his belly.

"You'll die hungry," said Dillon as a ferocious roar came deep from within revealing a row of jagged teeth all the way to the back of his neck.

"Oh, don't worry, you'll be an excellent stew, soften up that tough meat of yours," laughed Barbadoa.

Garon's eyes frantically searched the area and noticed a small door and he scooped up Belleny and Bateau with one wing, leant forward and kicked back with all his might nailing the chef's assistant against the door with a giant clawed foot.

"I'm sorry. I'll come get you soon. Stay put!" he said frantically.

"No Garon! Don't leave us," said Belleny.

The assistant got up fast and pulled hard at Garon's neck, ripping out a handful of feathers.

Bateau stared into the dark chute, the tunnel wound down into a vortex of darkness.

"Please, please," wailed Belleny.

And before she knew it she was tumbling head first down the chute, with Bateau meowing close behind with a gush of feathers. The small door then slammed behind them and suddenly it was pitch black.

"You'll pay for this! That was my dinner," said Barbadoa as the pies he once held slid onto the floor landing in a soft pastry splat and a dozen creatures covered in gravy proceeded to climb out. "Now I'm really mad. I'm going to pluck you bird and make you into a big pie!"

The small creature's bit at Barbadoa's ankles and with a kick, two were flung against the wall. Dillon pounced with lightning speed, but Barbadoa swung a heavy hand, backhanding him with a deafening slap, knocking him to the other side of the room. Without pause, he sprung back, ran up and across the wall and pounced, teeth in razor mode, digging deep into the chef's neck, dropping him to the floor with all his weight.

"Get him off me!" growled Barbadoa.

"I'm coming!" said the apprentice as he hammered Garon in the chest with both hands and pushed him back against the door. He thudded towards a strangled Dillon and with his chubby thick fingers he squeezed Dillon's tail.

"Never squeeze my tail," said Dillon as he flipped himself free into a wild kick, pushing the apprentice against the fiery oven. His sausage-like fingers slid across the hot top and sizzled as they burned.

Garon returned and watched as the apprentice yanked his hands off the stove and looked down at his skin still sizzling and sticking on the surface of the hob, "I'm going to break your neck!" he roared. Now the apprentice was running towards Garon, who stabbed deep into his chest with his claws and pushed him back into Barbadoa like a Domino. The two chefs helped themselves up and laughed.

"Is that it? My mum hits me better than that!" said Barbadoa, even though an oily black blood oozed from the puncture wounds on his neck.

The chefs stood next to each other, ready for round two.

"Just you and me then," said the apprentice pointing at Dillon as he climbed to the rafters. "Fine you can wait up there and watch your friend get torn in half."

"You're mine then birdy prepare to be flattened!" said Barbadoa pointing at Garon with one hand and slapping his belly with the other.

"Be careful Garon," said Dillon.

"Careful, don't worry, I'm only afraid if we hit them too hard they'll explode all over us."

"There's only one way to find out," replied Dillon.

Barbadoa and his apprentice launched their fat bodies forward. Garon held his position in front of the small chute door. Barbadoa stomped forward and with full force shouldered Garon against the door in with a deafening thud. But Garon had dug a claw into the chef's stomach, and with his long legs pushed the chef back into his apprentice, who was trying feverishly to grab hold of the energetic and acrobatic Dillon.

Barbadoa might have been big, but he was also strong enough to carry all his weight. He turned on one leg and stomped down with the other. The solid floor cracked beneath him. "Nice try Mr. Garon, but you see I got thick padding," Barbadoa mocked.

"Thick all over from what I can tell," said Garon.

In a super move, Dillon launched from the rafters and dug his claws deep into the apprentice's back. The apprentice fell backwards into the pots and pans as the room exploded with noise. With a wrestling Half Nelson floor move, the apprentice ripped his arms in the air, tossing Dillon back up towards the roof, being so nimble as a cat, Dillon latched onto a rafter and looked down at the fuming red chef.

"That was fun," said Dillon, "let's do that again, no wait, watch out Garon, he's behind you!"

Garon felt like he had been hit by a fallen tree as the apprentice stepped out of the pots and drove a fist hard into his back. Garon dropped to his knees and landed in Barbadoa's fatty grasp. In one move, Barbadoa lifted Garon up and over his head and spun him only inches from Dillon, crashing him hard against the hot, fiery oven.

Garon screamed as his feathers singed together and filled the room with a horrid smell of burnt feathers.

"A bit too hot for you birdy" mocked Barbadoa grabbing Garon by the neck and digging his elbow into his flank.

Garon used all his might to lift his head as the hot plate sizzled. "I'll break your fat—"

"No!" cried Dillon as Barbadoa knocked the words out of Garon's beak, knocking him unconscious with a thrust of his fist. Dillon watched helplessly as the apprentice stood beneath him and swung a kitchen knife at him.

"Keep him there! This won't take long," said Barbadoa and with all his weight he knelt down on Garon's neck.

"That's it boss, break it!" cheered the apprentice.

But Barbadoa couldn't as much as he tried, "I'm trying?" he mumbled.

"Put some elbow grease into it," egged on the apprentice.

Dillon watched in fear as Barbadoa's shadow began to move up and away from him. Like a mould, it filled up with an oily darkness, forming and resembling the shape of a creature unknown to them.

Then it spoke, "Don't kill him!" it snarled and lashed at Barbadoa.

"I'm sorry my master, I didn't realise you—" began the chef, but the shadow-like creature held his face and pushed it like putty within its dark, oily fingers.

"Where are the others?" the shadow screamed at him.

"Oh? They ran away like little rats," said Barbadoa.

"Fools! How dare you let them get away. Tie them up and find the others, I want them for tonight!"

"Yes, of course, that will be no problem at all," stuttered Barbadoa.

"What would the witch want with you then?" Barbadoa asked Garon, pulling up his head like a rag doll.

"A sacrifice no doubt," said the apprentice waving his knife up at Dillon. "Now stop playing around and get down here already!"

CHAPTER 54 - DOWNWARDS SPIRAL

The aggressive whirlpool was twisting into a black vortex, constantly spinning and sucking into a liquid oblivion. It was if young Evelin was made of tin foil and her new boss or therapist Astina Francis had managed to knock a dent in her side. Evelin woke up in pain, feeling fractured and more vulnerable than ever before. From her negative experiences caused by her hypnotherapy sessions with Esta and the stress of the new job with Astina, her thoughts were flooded with images of the whirlpool and her medication being thrown into the hotel pool which made her feel redundant and helpless.

Three days after the hotel incident Evelin remained in her bedroom, tucked away and accompanied by BC, the paper fish and her loyal dolls. *You are all I need, I'm never anxious when I'm here with you,* she thought.

Evelin frowned at the noise from her wrist alarm that blared and only reinforced her anxiety. She grabbed her medication, swallowed her dosage and recalled with a muddled memory of whether she took them yesterday. *Of course I did,* she thought irritably. She stumbled into the bathroom and stared into the long buckled mirror. Her hair was tied up on top and teased out at the sides, it hung just like Cory's. Yesterday's makeup was smudged, and her lipstick smeared onto her chin, her clothes were layered on like a walking wardrobe, sleeves pushed back with elbow length gloves, fake feathers and sequin patches.

"Who am I?" she said to herself only inches from the mirror, "What have I done to deserve this?"

After a long silence BC watched as she returned to the room, a ghostly dormant Evelin flopped down beside him sinking back into the bed like a heavy book.

"Hello BC," she whispered, her eyes at half-mast, "I'm better now, no more thoughts."

She knew instantly when the medication got hold of her. She stared at the roof as her eyelids grew heavy. The afternoon sun coated her with warmth, the aquarium's hum filled the room, as did BC's repetitive and soothing purring.

"Might as well call it a day," she sighed and it wasn't long before she fell into a deep afternoon slumber.

"Well, well, look at you?" said the Weatherman, who was sitting on his usual throne shaped cloud.

Evelin turned and stared curiously as he lit a single match, then flicked it to the side. She watched as it spun in slow motion, its flame grasping onto the matchstick as it rotated and fell through the cloud with a light sizzle. She then came to some clarity and realised she was on a cloud miles above the ground. She dropped to the damp floor and grasped the soft, spongy surface.

"What are you doing?! You shouldn't play with matches!" said Evelin.

"What may I ask are you doing?" said the Weatherman, quite bemused.

"I'm afraid of heights," said Evelin in a snap and closed her eyes tight.

"What are you doing way up here then?" said the Weatherman, scratching his head.

"I have no idea," squirmed Evelin.

"But you weren't scared before if I remember correctly? But I can't remember, correctly that is."

"I wasn't scared before. Of anything! What's wrong with me Weatherman?"

"Obviously you've been talking to the wrong people, or not listening to the right people, or was that talking to the right people but—"

"You're not helping," said Evelin.

"Really? I'm sure I was. Try looking upwards, that might help? Although the ground is probably closer than the moon, and it could take you years to fall onto that. Imagine that, falling for years, now that's a thought."

Evelin opened her eyes and grumbled, "No it's not, it would be boring. Anyway you can't fall upwards."

"Why not?" he shrugged.

"I don't know?"

Although he didn't make one hundred percent sense most of the time, Evelin felt that he might know something she didn't and turned her head towards the sky further above.

Speechless she gasped. What she thought would be the sky above was quite the opposite, there were more clouds, but through them she could see a shimmery wet surface.

"Water? An ocean?" she whispered.

"Of course where do you think the rain comes from?" said the Weatherman.

"Precipitation?"

"Pre-sipping? Sipping before or after has nothing to do with rain Boot's."

As the clouds slurped along Evelin could see a beautiful blue ocean rolling above her. She noticed huge bone white clouds dipping themselves into it and soaking up the water like enormous sponges and then continuing on sinking slowly through the cloud they stood on.

"There's ... there is an ocean above us, for the rain clouds?" said Evelin positively stunned.

"Well, of course, don't tell me you're afraid of oceans as well?"

"Of course I'm not, but ... maybe I am now. What if it falls?"

"Why would it possibly do that? You make no sense at all young lady, no wonder you're afraid of everything, don't you have any common sense ... or is that uncommon sense?"

"I can't believe my eyes, Weatherman did you just see that! Flying fish ... Flying fish!" Evelin watched on, stunned, as a school of flying fish leapt out of the sea, raced by and splashed back up into the water above.

"Better watch out for them, nothing worse than flying fish in your face, oh—besides them," the Weatherman's moustache went limp and he shook his head.

"Besides what? What's wrong?" She turned around and noticed a dripping wet cloud soaking up the ocean and turning an awful doomsday grey. But it wasn't the cloud that scared the Weatherman, it was the two giant eels, the size of rainforest trees, which twisted around each other and were now heading their way.

With a shaky hand, Evelin pointed up and turned back at the Weatherman, "They're eels! Giant eels! They're coming here! We have to hide!"

"We can't, that's never an option around here unless you're a cloud."

It wasn't long before the two giant eels were circling around them both, intertwining around each other as one. Both were a as black as each other, but as the sunlight reflected off them one shimmered silvery blue, the other a emerald green. They spoke no words and with memorising movements, spiralled down into the cloud beneath, disappearing completely.

"They're below us! I know what they're up to ... they're going to eat us. Weatherman I'm so afraid," said Evelin holding his arm.

"Still afraid huh? So forwards, down and upwards didn't work ... hmm ... Try looking behind you? Or are you afraid of behinds as well?" he smiled.

"Don't be stupid, this is not a time for jokes!" said Evelin crossing her arms and turning around in a huff. There facing her were the two giant eels staring at them with enormous round eyes. Evelin was too frightened to scream. They lay along the endless white surface of clouds, eerily silent they then spoke simultaneously, "The girl, she's here?"

They stared at Evelin, who ran behind the Weatherman's chair. Like snakes, they rose up on their long speckled underbellies and stared down at her.

"What are you looking at? said Evelin, "Please don't eat me!"

"I think you better leave," said the Weatherman in a heavy tone.

"Me?" said Evelin.

"No them."

The eels slithered back and continued to entwine around each other. Like monsters of the deep they opened their mouths wide open, flaring their barbed teeth.

"This isn't over," spoke the eels and together they raced off, up towards the ocean above and dove deep inside.

"You did it Weatherman! You just told them to go, and they did? I was sure we were dinner."

"That's right Boot's that's the power of being assertive and the fact they can't breath for very long out of water.

"What do you mean? Oh, in the ocean."

"They can also swim in the storm clouds, nice and wet in there. Like that one," said the Weatherman pointing up at a huge lumbering dark grey cloud, "see look there they are."

Evelin watched as the eels moved within the clouds and from the dark grey mist a flash of lightning exploded from within and shattered out in all directions.

"Ahh! I can't see!" cried Evelin.

"Show-offs, they're not allowed to do that up here," said the Weatherman pulling an umbrella from within his coat and opening it out, "you better step under here ... oh and cover your ears."

"Why?" asked Evelin, rubbing her eyes, but it was too late.

It was then the loudest deafening thunder roared across the clouds and shook the ocean above. In an instant water fell from the sea in thick apple size droplets. Evelin was drenched.

"Not up here! That's it! It's Summer from now on you here!" shouted the Weatherman.

Evelin removed her hands from her ears, and from her dripping wet face said, "Eels make the lightning and thunder?"

"Of course, as disobedient as they are they do a pretty good job. Anyway I can't do everything I'm a busy man. Hmm looks like they've gone."

"I'm glad," said Evelin, "What did they mean when they said, the girl she's here?"

"Well, it's obvious isn't it? Eels are blatantly observant, oh good I found it," he said pulling out a red lighter.

A Lighter? That's ... that's my lighter? thought Evelin and she asked nervously, "Where did you get that lighter?"

"This? I found it, and it still works! Look, see?" The Weatherman flashed the lighter before her.

"No, don't!"

"Eve, Evelin are you there?" said Robin from outside her door waking her simultaneously.

"What, lighter, eels, Robin? What? No ... I guess, what is it?"

"You have a visitor, a Miss Cory?"

There was silence for a second as Evelin rose and sat up against her bed-head.

"Really? Cory here? Okay thanks, can you send her up? Thank you."

"Sure thing, you need anything? I can fix something up, no worries."

"Ahh no, I'm okay, thanks Robin."

Cory here? Evelin wiped the warm sweat from her head, she felt awkward and quickly got out of bed. With one move, she pulled the covers back over, placed her stuffed friends in the corner and upon looking up Cory was there.

"Evelin Boots," said Cory. She shook her head and crossed her arms.

"What? Hi ... sorry, what did I do?"

"Oh Evelin, nothing you little fool," smiled Cory. In a warm embrace she held her close, "I missed you these few days."

"You did?"

"Of course I did, I hate eating alone," she grinned, "what an aquarium! It's surreal, like another world in there. Oh, you have eels, wicked city!"

Eels thought Evelin as an image of the giant eels flashed in her mind.

"Yeah, I know, they are always watching me," said Evelin. "Oh, I'm sorry this room is a mess," she said and quickly picked up her stuffed toys placing them on a shelf.

"You don't have to put them away for me," said Cory softly picking up Sargent Goldberry and placing him back on her bed, "I like him, had them long?" she added.

"They were my mum's," Evelin said softly.

"Oh, they're beautiful."

Cory sat down on the bed and noticed how warm it was, "Have you been in bed all day? It's so nice outside, even for me."

Evelin shrugged and said, "I don't mind, it could be raining money for all I care."

"Eve...Ahhh it's alive!" yelped Cory as BC began to lick her hand. "What and where did you come from?" Cory picked him up in her arms.

"So this is the famous cat of yours?"

"Yes BC."

"BC huh, he's so pure."

Pure? thought Evelin. She had never thought of him as pure. She stood quietly as Cory held him in her arms and stroked him into a deep purr.

"You look like an Egyptian Queen," said Evelin.

"You can call me Cleo from now on," said Cory in one of her many voices.

Evelin tried to smile, but she had never felt so sad in so long. *You might as well have him,* she thought.

"Evelin what's wrong?" said Cory, her voice ever so caring.

"I'm not right. I thought I was getting better. I feel terrible, trapped ... I don't know anymore. I thought I was finding my way, but I'm lost ... so lost."

Chef Barbadoa opened the small wooden door and roared down the chute, "There's no escape for little rats! Run all you want, but we'll find you!"

"Go Belleny!" screamed Bateau, finding his voice once again. He pushed up against her as the bulbous head of Barbadoa blocked the opening of the chute.

"I can smell you both down there!" Barbadoa grumbled and slammed the door behind them.

"Come on let's go!" said Bateau.

"Poor Garon!" whimpered Belleny, "do you think ... he's dead?"

"No, did you hear? Someone was up there, said the witch wanted us alive for tonight?"

"Oh no, this is madness. What is she going to do to us?"

"She is not going to do anything to us, we're getting out of here," said Bateau.

On both hands and knees, Belleny waited nervously as Bateau squeezed past, his tails patting her on the shoulder attentively. Belleny dropped her head, "What have I done Bateau? I'm so sorry, I want to go home, I want to go back to the castle now."

"There's no time for defeatism! This is just a hurdle, we'll help each other out and get through this together."

It was then they heard Dillon cry out in a plea for mercy, his howls rose to a deafening cry as the chef's heckling laughter took over.

"That was Dillon!" said Belleny.

"I know, I know. Come on we must keep going."

The small chute that was now some distance behind them was wrenched open. "Ready or not, here we come!" roared Barbadoa and then slammed the door shut. "They're trapped now, let's go downstairs and fish 'em out."

"Let's get out of here," said Bateau and he pushed against the small exit door. It wouldn't budge. He tried again this time with all his strength. "Princess, it won't open."

"What?" cried Belleny. "We're stuck here forever? No! Let's go back, when the chef's leave the room, we'll run out of the kitchen and into the forest."

"We can't go back Belleny! They'll be waiting."

"No! We have to get out of here!" Belleny shouted, her fears turning into anger. Belleny kicked the door furiously, the door shook and lifted them up inches off the ground.

"It's underneath us as well!" said Belleny. "Bateau we have to jump up as we push."

"Of course. Ready, one two three!" counted Bateau and together they jumped forward and pushed all their weight against it and the door fell forward, scooping them up from underneath and throwing them head first deep into a pile of hessian sacks.

"I thought it was flour," coughed Bateau as he crawled out of a sack. Belleny wanted to laugh at Bateau, covered from head to toe in flour but, instead scurried to her feet and scanned the room in a frenzied panic.

"No one's here!" said Belleny as she ran to the main door and locked it with a solid wooden latch.

"It's a pantry, look at all this food!" said Bateau taking a handful of nuts and eating them. "Sort of fresh. Actually I wouldn't eat any of this."

In a low voice, Belleny growled, "I swear I'll kill him, I'll push my blade through his fat ugly neck."

"You may get your chance sooner rather than later," said Bateau, his ears turned towards the door. "Get over here now! Someone's coming!"

"They're in there, I can smell 'em," echoed a horrible voice.

The sound of the door being rattled echoed throughout the room as the creature paused and said, "I knew it, the dirty rats have locked the door."

"Not for long, move aside," said another.

It only took them one go, and the thick wooden lock snapped like spaghetti. The door flung open, slamming hard against the wall and hung on a single latch.

There stood a gangly silhouette with three pairs of arms and a forked tail. The room was silent, "Bring them to me!" echoed the witch's voice, and the creature began by tossing aside huge sacks of flour and mouldy vegetables as it scavenged for them.

Belleny and Bateau scrambled quickly into the small chute away from the ripping arms and flying sacks.

One after another, strange and curious creatures stepped into the room, "They've got to be in here," one snarled.

"Watch the door. You two look over there. I'll go check over here, tear this place apart!"

"Looks like they're not here?" said one scratching its monstrous head.

"Who locked the door from the inside then stupid?" said another who looked much like the offspring of a Pug and a Yak.

"I dunno? The wind?"

"What wind you idiot?" he snarled and lifted the creature off the ground by its neck. With its arms wailing he threw it, screaming across the room. Belleny cried out as the body slammed against the chute door. Bateau held her tight and hushed her down.

But it was too late, someone heard her.

One creature unlocked the door above and ever so quietly, moved it's tentacles down slowly and silently from above and with lighting speed it wrapped its boneless limbs around Belleny and Bateau and with force ripped them out of their hiding place.

"Well done Zaeble, you got 'em!"

Belleny and Bateau screamed and shouted as they hung upside down by a creature that had tendrils extending from its arms and legs.

"I did, didn't I?" it said with glee. "They look delicious, no wonder she wants them," it snickered.

Quickly it peeled itself forward and out of the empty kitchen. Garon and Dillon were nowhere to be seen.

The Princess wailed, "Let us go! I order you to put us down at once!"

"I don't think so little one, you obviously don't know what sort of reward you have on your heads."

"I'll double it, whatever she's offering!"

"Endless helpings of the tonic, the Royal Blackness?" it said.

"Endless? It will kill you, it's poison!" said Bateau.

"You have no idea—be quiet will you!" it shouted down at Bateau as it yanked at his tails.

The creatures followed Zaeble as he moved forward at a steady pace, weaving through corridors and up a long stairwell as if he was floating. With every step, a constant squelching sound oozed from its limbs as they sucked at the ground and twisted around each other.

It pushed open two large doors and entered with Belleny and Bateau hanging high up in front, "I have them, look at me, I have them!" it shouted as Belleny kicked back as she passed hideous face, one after another. The room was enormous, twice as big as her own ballroom and full of evil with a stench of rotting flesh. Side by side the creatures sat along picnic-sized tables that had been shoved together in three dozen rows. A figure clapped its hands three times from upon the high altar and the creatures of all shapes and sizes came to a sudden silence. They watched Zaeble climb the stairs and approach the throne.

No, not Belleny! And Bateau! panicked Agarus. He sat at a table of monsters; with Four Eyes, The Baron, Nails and Shovel. He wanted to tear off Zaeble's arms, but all he could do was look on helplessly. He stood up to see clearer over the eager minions who began to shout out with excitement.

"What a devilish looking beast?" said The Baron.

Agarus gulped, "Yes devilish."

"Now have you ever had two-tailed soup?" said Four Eyes licking his lips.

"I can't say that I have," said Agarus trying to keep calm. *What can I do Belleny? What has happened to Garon? The Orphans? Kale and Danté where are you?*

Zaeble stood puzzled and turned to the crowd, "Where is she?" The throne was empty and in its place was a thick cloth cloak. As if being moulded by an invisible force, a shape from under the fabric began to emerge, and darkness began to surface. Several creatures pointed behind him as the hooded cloak rose from the throne, and an oily black shadow manifested before him. Belleny screamed for help as the creature of darkness emerged. She strode forward, stabbing her black ankles deep into her shadow. Zaeble stood back in fear; the sorceress's shadow moved towards him as if it was alive and sniffed at his limbs like a ravenous dog.

"Your Majesty," said Zaeble dropping them to the floor and whipping its arms around their throats.

"Take it," the witch croaked through parched lips and tossed a golden chalice into the air. Zaeble whipped a tentacle around the cup and hugged it close.

"Tonight your feed is limitless," she said and flicked her fingers at him. "Let them go, they're not going anywhere."

"You are too kind, too kind my Majesty," replied Zaeble and released his grip on the Princess and Bateau. They fell to the floor with a hard thump as the witch's shadow latched around them and secured them down. The tentacled beast, Zaeble, shook the golden cup into the air as the room roared into a hackling cheer.

"Silence!" the witch screamed so ferociously that parts of her shadow seemed to tear out at them and claw at their throats.

"Let us go!" said Bateau flicking his tails in the air as the shadow chased them and pulled them to the floor.

What has happened to her, she's not a witch, a poisoned monster. "Please don't ... no!" cried Belleny.

Belleny felt her head rise as the oily shadow pulled her close, up to face the witch, it then paraded her around in front of no less than five hundred creatures.

The witch's yellow teeth glowed through the darkness of her skin as she pierced a sickening smile. Belleny felt her feet become unstuck as the witch's shadow returned to her frightening figure. Bateau leaped out and watched as Belleny looked down at her blade hidden in her boot and back at him. Bateau shook his head slowly as Belleny became Kikaan once again. The gangly audience began to crow out loud as the witch looked up from beneath her hood and felt the blade only inches from her yellow grin.

There is no laugh like that of a harrowed witch. Belleny snarled as she pushed the metal in deep.

But the witch shook her head and grabbed Belleny's wrist like a whip lashing a tree branch.

Belleny felt pain. She stood paralysed by the witch's shadow. The darkness was coiling up around her legs and pulling at her hands, prying her fingers apart. The blade dropped into the witch's clawed fingers.

"I see you have more than just a bark Princess," she said looking at the knife curiously. "Feisty little thing, aren't you? The darkness seeps deep into your skin. You're as cursed as all of them ... not that it is a bad thing."

Belleny looked down at her hands as the creature's oily black blood stained her fingers and under her disguise dripping down to her elbows.

"Feeling a little different I can imagine," she said and laughed out loud as the creatures joined her, filling the room with snickers and snorts. With a flash, the witch threw the blade at Bateau.

"No! Bateau!" cried Belleny.

It stabbed into the stone only inches from his tails and the witch growled through clenched teeth, "You better stay put Bateau, or next time I'll aim for your head." With one hand, she held Belleny by her mask's wild hair and with the other pushed Belleny backwards against the hard stone floor. The crowd roared as the witch held the severed head of Kikaan and revealed a dirty-faced and messy-haired Belleny.

She tossed the savage mask down at her, "I don't know which head is more disgusting to look at?"

This got the crowd in hysterics and once again the witch silenced them.

"You're a long way from home Princess Belleny Vera, or should I say Queen Vera, how sweet your mother once was."

"Let me go witch!" screamed Belleny.

"Let you go? Why in Mare-Marie would I do a stupid thing like that? Not after you've come all this way. You must at least stay for dinner."

"I'd rather starve," spat Belleny.

"Oh, would you now? I hear Chef Barbadoa is cooking up quite the dish. Once he's finished plucking that giant bird."

"I'll kill you! All of you!" cried Belleny.

The witch stepped around Belleny taunting her with her shadow.

"So here you are, you've made your way into the world. Good for you. Now, with all your friend's dying, was it all worth it?" She twisted down at Belleny, her sharp yellow teeth piercing her every word.

"No! No thanks to you! You should be cursed! Turned into a bug and crushed. How dare you ruin our lives! What have the Orphans ever done to you? Where are they?" demanded Belleny.

"I don't think you understand little one, I have nothing to do with your ugly little Orphans or should I say, White Knights. But I do feel it's all been rather entertaining," said the witch curling her fingers into a fist.

"Lies! You are Lucretia the Witch aren't you?" said Belleny getting to her feet and slapping away the witch's ravenous shadow.

With a distorted twist of her body, the witch snarled down at Belleny, "A witch yes—but Lucretia the Witch, don't insult me child! I am a Sorceress of the darkest dominion."

Then through her cloak she raised a wet, black arm with a blue oily tinge and pointed behind the Princess. She turned around at once and there was a large ornate bier with an old crystal stone coffin upon it. *Is Lucretia in there, dead?* thought Belleny, *Then who is she?*

"Go on take a look," spoke the Sorceress.

Through the crystal, Belleny could see a figure and nervously she moved towards it. She looked in close as a palm hit hard inside the coffin lid, but not a sound could be heard. *Lucretia! She's alive in there! But why?* thought Belleny. Lucretia stared up at her with teary blue eyes. Her hand fell back down. Belleny could see she was weak and thin, her hair was ghostly white and her skin the same.

"That's your Lucretia the Witch," snarled the hooded creature.

"Then who, who are you?"

"I am Varin Eel, I am what darkness hides from."

As Varin Eel spoke her name a vile black poison dripped from her mouth, and after letting it drool and pool before Belleny, she villainously licked it from her yellow fangs, "And these beautiful creatures are the redeemed," she said and spread her arms out and let their horrid voices fill the room with howls and cheering.

"So you see I've already caught Lucretia for you, you should be thanking me—no wait, the pleasure was all mine. Go on take your blade and kill her, you wanted her dead didn't you?"

Belleny turned back with a heavy frown and shook her head, "No."

"No? The Princess is a liar," said Varin and walked towards Belleny and Lucretia trapped inside the coffin. With each step, her long spidery legs could be seen as they poked out of her cloak and sank into her shadow with each step. "We asked to move in so very nicely, didn't we Lucretia? But you declined ... such a pity, such a big place with so many rooms going to waste, it's quite full now though isn't it? That's why we're taking yours next Princess, I hear you have plenty of rooms free since your father kicked out half the kingdom. All because he couldn't handle a little magic," said Varin, her shadow flickering around her as if yanked by wires.

"I know all about you," said Varin. She held up a long bony arm into the air and from the back of the room flew a large black-eyed bug that landed on her inky wrist, "Why you and your friends came here is beyond me? You are so very confused," she said, "but don't worry, you weren't the only ones." She pointed along the wall to the black statues that circled the ballroom. They looked as if they were carved from charcoal not stone. Belleny stared closely at the ones nearby and realised it was the twins, Asel and Esla Graver.

"What have you done to them? You killed them!"

"They killed themselves, just like your friends did when you crossed the Cassan River and stepped onto my land. Wouldn't your father have done the same? Possibly a punishment, not so permanent, but the castle needed a few statues after so many were destroyed taking this place.

"Come now, where is the entertainment?" said Varin and pushed Belleny back towards the throne. Belleny took Bateau in her arms and put her mask back on.

A ant faced creature climbed the stairs, bowed and said, "They're ready your majesty."

"Play some music and bring them in," shouted Varin as she sat down and pulled her cloak over her legs. Her shadow continuously moved like blown ink across the ground.

Several creatures played instruments and hollered a short horrid tune as several large figures entered and walked down the aisle.

Belleny wanted to run, but Varin's shadow held her legs, "Oh Garon what have they done to you? Dillon oh my Dillon!" she cried as Chef Barbadoa and his apprentice entered, one dragged Dillon by his tail and lifted him up for all to see and Barbadoa had Garon over his shoulder. His legs chained, his beak and wings were bound with rope. Handfuls of his beautiful black feathers were torn from his wings and body leaving him patchy, bald and bleeding.

"Good, here comes appetizers, I hope you like your food raw?" said Varin to the crowd of highly entertained creatures.

No, Dillon! Garon! I'll get you out of this! thought Agarus, but he was clearly unable to help by himself. I must wait for an opportunity. Where are the others?

"Wake them up!" said Varin.

The apprentice eagerly slapped Dillon across the face, back and forth, harder and harder until Dillon began to cough and as he woke he smelt the beasts and began to howl a wild and menacing growl.

"Let me go!" he roared slashing his claws back at the chef.

Garon woke with a growling scream as Barbadoa began to tear out handfuls of feathers from Garon's neck. Garon's eyes instantly flashed open as the room came into focus. First, he saw the roof ablaze with fiery chandeliers, then the red curtains and down to the tables and the creatures that pointed at him and yelled.

"Belleny!" he shouted, scanning the room as Barbadoa pointed up at her next to Varin Eel.

With a burst of rage, he drove his beak hard into the apprentice's chest as thick black oily blood fired out across Dillon and Garon. Soiled and bound, Dillon fell to the floor trying hopelessly to run.

"Are you finished?" shouted Varin, "There is no escape in here!"

"You'll pay for this!" cried Barbadoa, who held Garon by the throat.

"Not so 'Garon the Quick' are you now?" croaked Varin Eel. "Barbadoa stop that, I want him alive."

Varin turned to a towering creature in the corner and held up three oily clawed fingers, "Crackler my dear, drop me three cages. And be careful I don't want their new homes damaged."

Crackler nodded, unlatched and released three chains one at a time, as three huge metal barred cells were lowered to the foot of the stairs.

Varin snarled at Belleny and Bateau, "In you get!"

"No!" said Belleny.

"Come on Belleny, do as she says," said Bateau.

"Yes listed to Bateau, or I'll throw you in myself."

Varin turned to Barbadoa, "And throw those two in separate cages."

Belleny and Bateau walked down the stairs and entered the cell untouched, but Garon and Dillon were thrown head first like rag dolls. With the doors slammed shut, Varin signalled Crackler and the cages rose back towards the ceiling and hung between the chandeliers.

"Don't spoil your appetite my children, I'll be back with the main course," she spoke over her shoulder as she walked down the staircase, sinking into her own shadow and disappearing before them.

The creatures went wild, gobbling food and throwing bones and scraps at the cages.

"Don't worry, Kale and Danté will be here soon," said Bateau.

"Not if Varin Eel is after them," said Belleny, staring helplessly at a lifeless Garon and Dillon. A giant wooden spoon, full of porridge hit their cage and splattered across both of them.

"How dare you! You awful things! Don't you know we have come here to save you?"

"Save this!" said one throwing a meat-torn bone at her.

"We're unstoppable, Varin Eel has saved us!" scoffed Four Eyes.

"Don't you see, each time you drink her poison you get worse not better? Look at yourselves, you're all sick! What would your mothers think?"

"Your mum is a trash eating wompig!" shouted Agarus.

"How dare you!" roared Belleny poking her head out of the bars and tossing a bone down at him.

"Princess, control yourself, please ignore them," said Bateau as he pulled her back with his tails. "Save your energy. They're not worth it."

"And she smelt like one too!" shouted Agarus as the room filled with laughter.

Belleny leapt against the cage and pointed, "I'll have you thrown into the pit!"

It was then she realised who she was pointing at. Belleny couldn't believe her eyes and stumbled back next to Bateau.

"Bateau, it's Agarus!"

CHAPTER 56 - FATE

There was silence between the two friends as they sat and stared deeply into the aquarium at the foot of Evelin's bed. The record that was idly spinning on the record player was a sombre melody of cello and violin. BC purred as Cory stroked him on her lap and once again offered to pass him across. Evelin rose her hand slightly and mouthed, "No thanks, you keep him."

The silence continued as they watched the paper fish somewhat dance from one end of the aquarium to the other. Evelin imagined they enjoyed the music, and it annoyed the eels; it amused her. They had returned to one another and lay in their cave screaming back out at her just as before.

The musicians seemed to take an endless and unpredictable path but had come to an end with a climactic crescendo. Evelin moved to get up and turn the record over, but Cory placed her hand on Eve's.

"Wait," said Cory, looking into Evelin's sad eyes, "I am sorry, I really am."

Evelin knew what she was talking about, and she had wanted to hear those words for a very long time, "You know we could have gone to jail for what we did. It was libricide. One step away from burning down a church."

"Libra what?" said Cory, "anyway Evelin, I did it."

"I'm the one that gave you the lighter, then I just stood there and watched—at first I thought you were joking, it just lit up so quickly."

"No one got hurt though," shrugged Cory.

"Your dad got hurt, he still is, I got hurt, half the town thought we were under attack by aliens. People are still suspicious, talking quietly. No one thinks it was an accident."

"Shh Eve, keep your voice down. You were in the wrong place at the wrong time."

"I get that a lot, my conscience is killing me."

"Just think of the new library and how neat it is, and all those new books, five times as many as before."

"It's not that easy for me," said Evelin staring at the beady-eyed eels; it was if they knew everything.

"I know it's hard, thank you for not saying anything. You won't will you?"

"I haven't yet. We never spoke about it till now, and I don't even know why you did it?"

Cory stood up and ventured around the aquarium returning from the other side.

"I was furious, those idiot teachers put me back a year at school. Can you imagine how awful I felt knowing I would have to repeat another whole year of school? Let alone with girls below me—they were lucky I didn't burn down the whole school."

"You nearly did, but why the library? That's where your dad works?"

"I don't know. I was just hanging out the back one day after school wondering how I was going to tell Tamiya how I'd flunked a whole year. I went to light up a smoke and realised I had no lighter. You turned up; God knows why I asked you for a lighter, and for some bizarre reason, call it a stroke of fate, you had one ... and you don't even smoke?"

"I found it on the ground," said Evelin.

"See it WAS fate and the next thing I know we're watching a building go up in flames. Who would have thought books burn so well?" smiled Cory.

"It went up pretty fast didn't it?" said Evelin, holding a little grin.

"It was great, I could have told Tamiya anything that night, flunking didn't amount anywhere close to the library burning down,
now he's just happy I'm happy."

"Are you happy?" asked Evelin.

"Sure why not? It worked out in the end."

"Mr. Tamiya took it pretty bad."

"True. I don't think he'll ever forget that day."

"And night, it burned for nearly two days," added Evelin.

"Well, he comes home now, it seemed to kick him into gear, he has clear priorities—me," said Cory pointing at herself.

"He does seem happier. Besides the being covered in sooty book blood."

"He now runs a state-of-the-art library, better than the town library. Of course, he's happy."

"But if he ever found out, if anyone did," said Evelin.

"I won't tell if you don't."

Evelin shrugged, "No point is there?" She got up and turned the record over.

"Do you feel better we talked?" said Cory.

"I guess, I'm glad I now know why you did it, I thought you were a pyro."

"A pyro!" laughed Cory, "Not at all, just your everyday wickedly spontaneous teenager."

Evelin dropped the needle on the record. After a moment, the music began to play.

"Let's go out on your balcony, I want to see my place from here," said Cory.

"Alright, no doubt it's a mess out there. The birds seem to have made it their home."

Together they climbed the stairwell to the roof. The day was clear and for once the wind wasn't racing up and around the hill.

"This is amazing Evelin; I'm amazed you haven't invited me to your place earlier."

"I was afraid you might burn it down," said Evelin with a giggle,. "The Plastic Palace wouldn't burn, it would melt," smiled Cory.

"Where did you live before this place?" asked Cory looking out into the distance.

"We've always lived here. Robin demolished the old house not long after I was born; he was dealing with things in his own way."

"With your mum you mean?"

"Yeah, said he couldn't stand being in the house without her, but at the same time loved it up here on the hill."

"I bet."

"But I feel I'm not making things any better."

"Don't say that, he would see her in your eyes."

"Exactly, a constant reminder. Anyway, I don't want to put him through all of this as well," said Evelin pointing at her head.

"Put him through what? Every teenager does something or another to their parents. I do it to Tamiya, he doesn't understand me most of the time, we're changing from kids into teenagers, and it's fine because they did it to their parents," said Cory.

They both listened as the song on the record finished, and after a pause the next track began. They listened and after some time Evelin said, "Do you know I stood out here from dusk to dawn."

"What do you mean? When?"

"Before the school year started, last holidays. One night I got out of bed, climbed up here and stood on the railing—I've been on medication ever since."

"But why?"

"My neighbours across the road rang the fire department, then they rang the police, can you imagine?"

"Why didn't you just go inside? Were you sleepwalking?" asked Cory.

Evelin chuckled, "No, I was waiting for the sun to rise, I wanted to see it one last time."

"Oh Evelin," said Cory putting her arm around her and holding her in close.

"I was in a bad place, don't worry, I haven't thought like that in a long while. Probably these pills, although I haven't really thought of anything."

"Eve you crazy kid! You're talking like you've had a mid-life crisis!" Cory grabbed Evelin by the shoulders and shook her gently, "Come on let's go and have some fun! Let's wake up that inner child of yours!"

Evelin sighed, "I'm sorry, but I have a feeling she's dead."

It took the strength of all three individuals to lift the wedge of dense timber and drop it into position, securing the entrance to the boiler room and also their exit.

"I'm sorry, but we can't afford to be ambushed down here," whispered Kale making sure the door was secure.

"I understand, but no one comes down here, it's out of bounds," added Sharpie.

"And why would that be?" questioned Danté as he lit his lantern and let the flame shrink to a blaze of amber.

"The witch insists it's out of bounds, no questions asked," said Sharpie.

On entering the room, the trio were taken by the grandiose architecture and the enormity of the underground vault. The ceiling towered overhead and sections let light through distant floorboards. The creatures shadows could be seen converging above. The walls were made of blue granite masses and adorned with fiery lanterns allowing illumination to show the subtle detail of the stone masonry, carvings which were macabre and gruesome, faces grimacing from the stonework. Cautiously they stepped into the near darkness as a wave of warm, saturated air enveloped them in a suffocating vapor. A few metres into the room, they paused, eyes darting as a heat swelled and curled around them, held for a few seconds and released as if the room were breathing.

"It's nothing," said Danté, he felt the need to explain despite unsure of what the strange breathing sensation was.

"Sharpie?" questioned Kale.

"I'm not sure, probably just residual heat escaping from the beasts above us, through the wooden panels of the ceiling."

"Hmm, I hope your right," added Kale.

"What happened during the fall of the King"? asked Danté to allay the sense of foreboding and change the subject.

Sharpie leant up close and blinked.

"The witch had her way with, King 'Morne' Macer and he was then cindered and turned into a statue. This treatment wasn't exclusive to Royalty, most of his people were turned to charcoal too. She sought pleasure from filling the ballroom with hundreds of burnt statues, she crushed many of them for entertainment."

"She crushed them, after burning them?" said Kale.

"She smashed them into a thousand pieces," said Sharpie. "Although she has room filled with many, many more."

The trio had a collective silence.

"It's getting darker, come this way, not long," said Sharpie and motioned them onwards. Moving forward and deeper into the bowels of the castle they appeared in the mechanics of the Boiler room. Their lanterns flashed light against a maze of pipes, many of them pearling with dewy beads of evaporation. Large turnpike machines lay dormant and only a faint sign of life existed with the scurry of bugs and small critters who were startled at the sight of them.

"Look at all these pipes. You sure this boiler isn't operational?" said Danté knuckling his fist against the boiler and pulling a lever to no effect.

"Shh, don't touch anything," said Kale as the pipes cracked and echoed outwards rattling along the wall and waking Rel from his trance-like sleep.

Sharpie replied, "It was once a great heating system for the entire castle, but when the River Cassan turned to mud, then so did the water in the moat, and so did all of this."

"But the pipes are warm?" said Danté, "everything in here is warm?"

"Why and how is a Centacean living down here?" gasped Rel.

"Good afternoon Rel," said Danté, "glad you could join us."

"Exactly what is so good about it? Can you not see the giant in front of you?" asked Rel.

"Rel, stop playing games ... what giant?" whispered Kale. Rel crawled from Kale's shoulder to his wrist and pointed ahead.

"A game of life and death. A Centacean sleeps nearby, can you not feel its presence? It's overwhelming."

"Down here? A Centacean? But they belong in the sea? Or at least did," said Kale.

"Nothing belongs in the sea," said Danté.

"This one does. Look in front of us," said Rel.

"But it can't be? Are we safe?" asked Kale.

"Not in the slightest! A living nightmare, so much darkness. We must turn back before—"

"Sharpie! What is this trap?" snapped Kale.

"What? Never! This is a shortcut I promise, there's nothing allowed down here."

"If there's nothing down here I suggest you go on ahead and make sure while we wait," said Danté.

"Don't wait, we must leave!" said Rel.

"I don't even know what a Centacean is?" said Sharpie.

"One of the ancients, a water creature from the ocean, a giant at that, it doesn't belong down here," said Kale.

Sharpie shook his head, "A water creature? There are no water creatures alive ... oh no ... but what if? I was told he was dead."

"Who was dead?" said Danté.

"The witch's pet, Drokura."

Through the darkness, in the corner of the room, the giant called Drokura rolled over. With thumping hearts, they hid, finding cover in the maze of pipes.

"We must leave," said Rel, "you can't hide from it."

"There is no exit Rel, we locked the door," said Danté.

"Permanently," added Kale.

"You are idiots. I will show you your fate," said Rel sucking in the candle's flame until it went out.

"Now I can't see anything!" said Danté.

"Shh, show us Rel," said Kale.

Rel breathed out an ash grey cloud of smoke and through the hazy mist the giant could be seen.

"Are you kidding me?" said Danté, "Is that your Drokura, Sharpie?"

"Yes that's him, but bigger, much, much bigger," he replied.

"What is a Centacean doing down here? They belong in the water, not caged underground," said Kale pointing at the creature's thick, swirling tentacles and enormous clawed limbs of a crustacean.

"The witch has bred a monster," said Rel.

"And to think, he was once the witch's pet," said Sharpie.

"A pet? Never," said Kale.

"Yes it's true," whispered Sharpie, "I heard Drokura once lived in a lake, within the Shell Forest, but when that dried up it was exposed, dying in the dry air. I understand they need to be kept moist or they dry up and crack. I guess that's why it's still alive down here. The witch took the king's men and together dragged it to the castle. She put it in the moat to keep as her own, somehow it survived the ordeal; called it Drokura. When the trench turned to mud I thought it died, honest, it was never seen again."

"No wonder she doesn't want anyone down here anymore," said Danté.

"It's probably too big to get out, not without destroying the castle," said Kale.

"What do we do then?" said Danté nervously.

"The entrance is not far. Unfortunately—" said Sharpie

"What?" said Danté.

"It seems Drokura sits in front of the doorway."

"Aren't you always the bearer of good news," said Kale sarcastically. "There is no other way?"

"No, there's only one door, but it leads straight up and around to the throne room, a great shortcut as we bypass the whole ballroom, just as I promised. Belleny and the others will be arriving soon if not already there," said Sharpie.

"A great shortcut? I don't care if it leads straight to the witch's treasure chest. We're going to have to find another way," said Danté.

"We could wake it and lure it away from the door?" said Kale.

"Wake it! Are you mad?" said Danté.

"It's only a matter of time before he wakes I'm afraid," said Rel sucking in the last of the disappearing grey dust and licking his lips.

Danté rose the flame on his lantern into a blaring light and held it to the floor.

"What are you doing? He'll see us," said Sharpie.

"I want to know what we're up against."

"Wait!" said Kale but it was too late.

With a sweeping kick, Danté swept the lantern across the floor.

In disbelief Drokura still slept as the lantern glowed below its oily grey body. Like a sleeping dog, he began to whimper and grunt noises and as if in a dream, his tremendous paws clawed at the ground in jolts.

"You have got to be joking," said Danté.

"That's him all right," gulped Sharpie, "looks like he's having a nightmare."

"How can a nightmare have a nightmare?" said Danté.

"Shh, listen," said Kale as Drokura started to take deep wheezing breaths. It rolled onto its side crushing the lantern beneath its black lobster shelled leg. Darkness hid the beast and all was silent. Then one at a time Drokura opened his eyes, and there were many, and the evil yellow glow that curdled within them was a fearful sight.

Drokura had risen.

Drokura blinked lazily and with a laboured yawn it crouched low sniffing at its leg where it had rolled on Danté's lantern. Instantly he snorted into the air and smelt their scent. Like a threatened dog, he let out a growl that filled the boiler room and rattled the pipes against their brackets into the stone.

Drokura moved heavily out of his corner. The strange debauched creature appeared in the faint light from the cracks in the roof.

"He is a big boy isn't he?" whispered Danté.

"What is he doing?" said Sharpie.

"What are we doing? We're supposed to be going the other way," said Rel holding on tight as Kale ducked and weaved through the pipes.

"Look out!" cried Sharpie, "He's coming our way!"

"Quick, up high!" said Kale, "To the roof!" The sound of their hands and feet clawing up the pipes caught Drokura's attention and he lunged forward unable to stand up swiping at the air in front like he was swatting flies. A thick wave of oily black liquid splattered against the wall and dripped from the pipes below them. Drokura hooked his strange crab-like limbs in between the pipes and furiously he returned with nothing in his grasp. Opening up his lungs he bellowed and hammered his forearms into the ground and whipped his slimy tentacles from around the back, curling them around several pipes and crushing them tight.

"He's seen us. He's found us!" said Danté as he quickly used his strong feet and legs to climb himself up across the pipes while removing his bow and black glass tipped arrows ready to attack.

"Both of you, when I say go, just run straight for the door. I'm going to slow it down and light your way, you'll need time to kick in the door if it's locked," said Sharpie.

"Locked?" said Danté.

"Sharpie? Wait!" whispered Kale.

Sharpie removed a bottled potion and held it high, the green glowing liquid splashed about as if it was alive. At the sight of Sharpie illuminating off the glowing liquid, Drokura made a small whimpering noise and turned its head, puzzled. Sharpie spread his insect wings from under his arms and slid down the oily pipes. The Centacean shuffled forward unable to lift its enormous legs. The closer it got to Sharpie's glowing potion, the clearer it could be seen. Its head was a bizarre mixture of a microscopic insect, magnified and blown up in all its horrific glory and mixed with the monstrosity and strangeness of a deep sea creature. Above and below its clawed arms grew tentacled limbs, thick and scaly, that continuously curled around each other. It pulled itself forward, dragging and clawing its hooked hind legs behind it. Black saliva-like poison dripped from swollen sacks across its back and inside human-sized larvae could be seen wriggling inside.

"Sharpie!" said Kale as he slid down beside him and snatched the potion from his hands, instantly he hid it beneath his cloak and darkness returned. "Go that way!" said Kale pushing Sharpie and forcing him back inside the mechanics of the boiler. "It can't stand up, we'll use that to our advantage."

Drokura stopped and moaned and threw his arms forward smashing the pipes tearing the brackets from the wall. Danté leaped from one to another as his pipe bent down and hovered over Drokura. Its swollen sacks squelched as it sniffed the moist air for their scent.

Danté watched in fear as the Centacean looked up and opened its mouth revealing rows of needle-sharp teeth. As if possessed it dropped its head to the ground and yanked it back up towards him, repeating the movements again and again.

"Quick go!" cried Danté, "what's it doing?"

"It's going to be sick," said Rel, "take cover!"

"Quick!" Kale shouted. He ducked and weaved through torn out pipes. Splashing on the oily floor as Drokura's heavy breath pushed him backwards.

"Take cover!" shouted Rel. Kale held Rel tight and ducked behind a pillar, just as the giant Drokura heaved violently across the room. A wave of thick, oily chunks and black watery liquid flew from its mouth. The floor was plastered in a thick greasy blanket. Drokura held its body tight and shook. Danté climbed as high as he could watching as Drokura moaned and coughed in bouts of dry retching. *It was time to go,* he thought and made his way to the oily ground.

"Talk about discussing!" said Danté as he slid towards them and clawed against the pillar. "What is this black stuff? Stinks! Is it dying?"

"No, not dying, poisoned," said Rel. "It will feel a lot better once it's purged, we should hope to be gone by then."

"Why don't we kill it? While it's down and out," asked Sharpie.

"No!" said Rel. "The Centacean is cursed, it would bring ruinous misfortune to those who bring down an ancient."

"That's just great, hey I can handle a little misfortune if you can?"

"Can you handle never finding Tjaman's key?" asked Kale.

Danté frowned, "So what's your plan?"

"We'll have to get in close, stun its eyes, that's its weak point, that and it can't manoeuvre down here. Sharpie you didn't throw that potion of yours did you?"

"No, it'll do little on Drokura."

"I'm sure a little will go a long way in its eyes. Enough to get us out of here."

"It's all yours, but how are you going to do that?"

"Rel, we need your assistance," said Kale.

"Fine, but it's not going to be happy."

Kale gave the misty green potion to Rel. "I'm counting on you Rel, you know what to do once I get close."

"Of course master. You don't have to worry about me. You be careful."

Drokura dragged its slippery arms back and forth across its mouth and up over its eyes. He stood silent for a second as oily drool splashed below it. One by one his eyes caught the eerie glowing green light emanating from the potion as Rel fluttered with it in his grips.

"Guys, he's looking this way. Scrap that, he's coming!" said Danté.

"When I say go, go," said Kale.

"Fine," said Danté, "just meet us on the other side all right?"

"Go!" shouted Kale as Drokura's head launched forward and snapped at the green light. Kale took off with Rel holding the potion in his thorny grips. With a giant leap, he landed on Drokura's beak-like top lip and continued upwards with each step.

Danté and Sharpie bolted for the door. Each step a hazardous splash as they witnessed the immensity of Drokura from mere meters away.

Drokura swiped at Kale with each leaping step, missing and slapping itself hard against its face. Facing a forehead of eyes, Kale leaped into the air as each and every eye followed him. He threw Rel up towards the roof and away from the twisting arms. He continued towards its bony seahorse coronet on the top of Drokura's head. Rel's petal-like body fluttered in the air as his feet locked into the roof, potion in hand. Drokura ignored Kale and paused, staring up at Rel and the green glowing light.

"Now Rel!" shouted Kale.

Rel understood and bit the cork off the bottle and poured the glowing liquid over Drokura's ever-watching eyes. Drokura made a strange trumpeting sound like a fish out of water and wiped his eyes vigorously. Like a child in a rage, he swung his arms furiously in the air and along the ground hoping to connect. In unison Sharpie and Danté jumped its fatal attack and continued at full speed, navigating through discarded play toys, unlucky creatures left in its wake.

"That should do it, he's slowing down," said Rel as he darted downwards and latched onto Kale's shoulder.

"Well done Rel, let's go," said Kale.

"Wait!" said Rel, "Cut those sacks, the poison breeds within it."

"Understood," said Kale, he leaped from its thorny skull and slid to the ground digging his blade out wide and into Drokura's sack-lined back, slashing into them one after another. Black oozing blood shot out and across the giant's dusty back as it flung its arms from side to side. The creature roared out in pain, pulling its tentacles down along its back like logs tumbling off a swerving truck. Drokura turned its head around and saw Danté and Sharpie running for the door. He nudged his body around scraping his back on the roof.

In a belting whack an arm connected, hitting Danté hard as Sharpie dodged, jumping high into the air.

"No!" cried Kale, watching from above as Danté was flung along the oily ground and slammed hard against the wall.

Drokura then closed his eyes and stared at the floor.

"Better late than never," said Rel holding on tightly to Kale's leather bound shoulder.

Half in shock, half unconscious, Danté got to his knees and wiped the black ooze from his eyes. In a faint, blurry outline he could see Sharpie running towards him, waving his bright green palms up at Kale and Rel as they ran down along the creature's back and along a wall of spiny, dark blue dorsal fins.

"He's back!" said Rel watching as Drokura's tail began to rise. A monstrous pronged tail uncurled and slid out from the darkness.

"Look out!!" called Kale as he leapt high into the air and dodged an awakening Drokura.

Drokura's tail, too big and confined to see all of it, whipped across the ground from wall to wall. Sharpie jumped in time, but a ready arm took him down with brute force. A sharp cry pierced the room and from the corner of Kale's eye he could see Sharpie bent completely backwards like a snapped straw and then rolling lifelessly along the floor.

"Keep going!" said Rel, they needn't go back and check. They both knew nothing could survive that and their guide Sharpie was dead.

"Run Kale, run!" screamed Danté as Kale splashed forward at full speed and Rel held on tight with his petals ruffling.

"Stuff this, we can't kill the witch if we don't even make it!" said Danté firing arrow after arrow at Drokura's head as he crawled towards them with all his might. Danté looked across at Sharpie's still body, face down in the creature's black ooze. "Damn you!" he cried and pulled back another arrow. He paused and remembered Sharpie's words, *If the door is locked.* Instantly Danté turned to the door, *there's no handle!* He panicked and pushed the door hard. It didn't budge. Drokura roared towards him and Rel shouted, "Open the door!"

Kale shouted, "Quick!"

Danté removed his blade and shoved it in the gap between the frame and the door and pulled it upwards, screaming with all his might. The heavy latch on the other side was raised and fell loudly on the other side.

Kale slammed into the doorway with his shoulder and it swung wide open. He, Danté and Rel scurried through.

Drokura sped up, lashing out his tendril-like arms and making noises as if he was crying, screaming for them to stay.

"Not today ugly," said Danté as he slammed the door shut and Kale wedged the heavy lock back into position. Instantly heavy punching tentacles slammed against the door and shock waves sent them back against the stairwell.

Drokura arrived and slumped his body weight against the door with a moaning growl.

Danté gave a grinning smile to Kale and Rel, "That thing needs to be walked!"

"These walls won't hold it for long," said Kale.

Unnervingly they listened as Drokura moved away from the door. *No doubt to find Sharpie,* thought Danté.

"Such a wicked beast," said Kale.

"That's the strange thing, Centacean's are usually extremely placid creatures," said Rel

"Extremely placid! I guess you didn't see it snap Sharpie's back and throw me fifty meters onto my head?"

"Oh, I saw that. You need to practise your landings," said Rel.

"Ha ha, glad you made it too little buddy ... so where are we?" said Danté.

"Looks like we go up," said Kale, looking at an old wooden door at the very top of the stone staircase.

"I guess so. I'm not going back in there," said Danté pointing down at the pooling black ooze seeping beneath the door. They stepped up a step before it reached their feet.

"We're lucky Belleny didn't come this way," said Kale.

"We're lucky, she's lucky. Could you imagine her poor little face?" smiled Danté.

"Covered head to toe in black muck like always," smiled Kale, "come on, we best go find them."

Milton sat up in the front passenger seat with his aunt as they drove back together from the Interstate Prison in Drobura County. He was emotionally exhausted and silent for most of the long journey home after visiting his incarcerated parents. With flashbacks of the inmates tattooed necks and faces, with their bright orange smocks covering the rest of their ink-stained canvas. The barred cement cells and high-walled razor wire fence, his mother's tears and his dad telling him how everything was 'fine and dandy,' he couldn't help shake the fact that his parents were criminals and they were in jail. *How dandy could that be to a young boy?*

Evelin stood up from her silence on the balcony, "Milton!" she gasped, watching as they pulled up into his driveway across the road and a few doors down.

"Milton?" said Cory standing up beside her. "Do you want me to whistle? I have a pretty mean whistle, it's probably because I have—"

"Yes, whistle," blurted Evelin.

"Yes Maam, you should cover your ears," replied Cory and placed her fingers into her mouth. She wasn't kidding, she could whistle louder than a police siren. It sent birds from trees, dogs hidden behind fences began to bark at one another and even a car alarm started.

"I told you," said Cory.

Evelin waved down at Milton as he waved back. She watched him as he dropped his bags, said goodbye to his aunt and walked towards her Plastic Palace front door.

"Coming right up!" he shouted up and over the house.

"So is he your boyfriend?" asked Cory.

"Cory Tamiya!" said Evelin. "No, he's not. He's been away, look don't say anything, but he's been visiting his parents ... in prison."

"Prison? Who's parents are in prison?"

"I just said Milton's. They were transferred to another prison, even further away. It sucks, I really feel for him, but he puts on a brave face."

"You mean like prison, prison prinson? asked Cory still not believing her entirely. "Not the Slammer, the Clink, the Big Hou—"

"Yes the Big House, they're the ones who robbed the Tower Bank."

"Nooo, the Tower. Get out! Are they mad? That place is a fortress."

"They were the cleaners," said Evelin. "They pulled it off, but the money was traced back to them, it wouldn't have been hard. Milton's lucky they got to keep their house, his aunt lives there with him now. Cleaned him up a bit too. Quite the snappy dresser."

Evelin stared down the stairwell.

"Hey Boots! Back n bader then ever," called Milton as he climbed up the stairwell. He paused at the entrance and eyeing off a silent Cory.

Who is she?

"Milton!" she said quietly and greeted him with a tight hug.

"Eve, you're up on the balcony again? Are things improving in the old head tank then?" questioned Milton.

"Ha hardly. Are you all right, how are your parents?"

Milton held Eve by her shoulders, he didn't answer any of her questions. He knew her long enough to see she was really upset and the running mascara across her cheeks didn't help, "What's wrong Eve, is BC all right? You can tell me. I'm sorry I had to go on short notice, it might be the last time I see them for a while, they're in the middle of the desert. Not even public buses go there."

"I know, I understand. BC's fine he's watching the paper fish," Evelin paused, "no I'm not really—"

Cory cleared her throat and blew out a cigarette puff of smoke to the side.

Milton and Evelin both turned towards her.

"Sorry Cory, this is Milton, Milton Carmon."

"I know," said Cory.

Milton looked at Cory and the trailing cigarette smoke that crept around her face.

"You know, me?" said Milton.

"I know everyone in this town," said Cory.

Evelin shook her head, "She doesn't really know you Milton, I just told her your name then. Cory put that thing out, you're not impressing anyone."

Cory held out her hand, "Fine, pleased to meet you Milton."

"I hope you don't mind I told Cory about your parents."

"That's fine, I'm sure she already knew," said Milton with a cute grin.

"So how are they?

"They're as good as they can be I guess, they have their own cell, it's like a lounge room with a bed, which is bizarre, but cool, they seem to have adjusted or accepted their fate."

"Their own cell, that's good," said Evelin.

"Cell, I hate that word," said Milton.

"Sorry."

"No, it's alright, they treat them like animals you know, in cages. I don't think I'm going back again."

"But what about—" asked Evelin faintly.

"Hey, I do know you, you're the Suit Guy right?" asked Cory.

"Suit Guy?" said Evelin.

"Sure that's what all the girls call him in my old year."

Evelin lifted her eyebrow as she does and smiled across at Milton, "Did you hear that Suit Guy? You have a following."

"Well, they'll need to call me Milton, as I've decided to stop wearing them."

"What do you mean?" said Evelin.

"The suit ... it's not me, I don't want to be 'the suit guy' anymore. I realised while I sat in prison with my parents, I did a lot of thinking. I realised I was forced to be the grown up in my family dynamic and as I'm in high school, I can't drag the past around with me anymore. You as well Eve, it's doing us no good."

"You have been thinking," said Cory.

"Sure have," said Milton removing his tie and throwing it off the balcony.

"But you're right, you can't let the past drag around behind you, latching on to your future," added Cory.

Evelin raised her eyebrow again.

"You know what I mean Evelin, we're young, we make our own future."

"Carpe Diem," said Evelin in a monotone whisper.

"Carp what?" said Cory.

"It's 'Seize the day' in Latin."

"Yeah, that's right!" said Milton taking off his jacket, and also tossing it off the balcony. They watched as the wind took hold of it and wrapped it around the scarecrow.

"We get the point, you can keep the pants on," said Cory.

Evelin said nothing. Past, present, future, they were all the same to her. It didn't matter where she went, her anxieties wouldn't leave her alone.

"It's not that easy, can't you see, it's not going away," whispered Evelin.

"What do you mean? What isn't?" asked Milton.

"I can't escape this," said Evelin turning up her hands, "I can't just stop wearing a suit."

"Escape what Eve?" said Milton as he held onto her hands.

"Myself. I can't escape myself."

Montë and Palia found themselves alone on the quiet hallway side of the kitchen door. Forced to obey Garon's orders they ran from the showdown in the kitchen and there they anxiously waited. Sorrowfully they listened, it wasn't long before Chef Barbadoa and his apprentice had won the battle; and it was then the frightful black shadow appeared and ordered them to find Belleny.

"The witch!" whispered Palia. "She sounds furious! She want us alive?"

"Quick we must hide, they'll be coming this way! Find the others and Belleny!" said Montë. "Did you hear, Garon pushed her and Bateau through a doorway. I heard him slam it. He shouted for her to run. She can't as well run far in a cupboard can she?"

"But I didn't see any other doors?" questioned Palia, "he must have opened the back door. Maybe she's outside!"

"No, the Apprentice locked us in," said Monté.

"Either way I'm not going back in the kitchen till they leave."

"She can't be too far, we must find her first."

Together they raced from the kitchen and into a winding hallway. They took paths away from the loud echoing laughter that clawed through the adjoining corridors. There were plenty of places to hide, but the castle was overrun, conversations crept along the walls and the bustle of footsteps scraped at the stone floor.

This castle is infested! thought Palia. *Don't worry Belleny we'll find you.*

After they had checked several rooms, Palia and Monté discovered one chamber that looked like a storage area for the banquet.

"What a mess! Such monsters," said Palia.

"Hmm, something terrible has happened here," said Monté.

"Hello, Belleny are you in here?" whispered Palia.

There was no reply.

"I thought so!" Monté pointed to the small storeroom door in the wall and ran towards it. A slippery oily goo dripped out and onto the floor. In it he noticed a handful of black feathers and picked one out. "This is the door all right. I'm sure she was here; Garon's feathers are everywhere."

"Belleny! Bateau! Are you in there?" whispered Palia into the shoot.

They both waited in silence and sadly shook their heads.

Monté grabbed Palia and said, "Let's go back to the kitchen and see if they're hiding in a cupboard, you know how good she is at hiding."

"I'm not sure Monté, I don't want to say it but—"

"Then don't say it."

"Yes, you're right, we can't give up just yet."

Together they ran back towards the kitchen. Surprisingly the castle seemed deserted, silent and only the lanterns crackled as they flickered along the hallways.

"Was it this way?" asked Palia.

"I think so, they all look the same. No, I'm sure it was this way," said Monté taking the corridor to the right and walking up another set of stairs.

"This is ridiculous, where's the kitchen?!" snapped Palia.

"I think we took a wrong turn," said Monté.

"What made you think that?" said Palia.

"I would have remembered them and that!" said Monté, pointing up at several large statues ushering them down a corridor fit for a king. "Look's like we've found the way to the great hall," he said.

Palia shook her head and agreed, "Should we look? I hope she's not down there?"

Monté peered round the statue, his ears darted up and his heart hit hard against his chest, "Oh no Palia ... that was—"

"Belleny!" cried Palia, "we have to save her!"

"Where could the others be, Danté and Kale? We need their help, we can't do this alone," said Montë.

"Kale! How dare he lure the Princess into this horrid place? He better have a plan to save her, or was this his plan all along?" said Palia.

"Please Palia, you're stronger than this, you need to stay focused."

"I'm sorry but this is not the way it was supposed to turn out!"

"Shhh. I can sense Agarus! He's close by!"

"What where?" asked Palia looking down the corridor for him.

"It's faint, but he's in there too, I'm sure of it."

"Captured as well! We're doomed as doomed can be."

"No Palia, he's hiding, I can feel he's okay. Nervous but safe."

Montë started to wander towards the great hall.

"Where do you think you're going?" yelped Palia as she darted up behind him. "Wait Montë!"

"If you can Palia, swoop in and take Belleny out of this horrid place at any chance you get," said Montë. "I'm sure Agarus won't be far from our side, and Kale and Danté, even Sharpie no doubt is aiming his potions at the witch as we speak."

"Do you think?" paused Palia looking hesitant.

"It's the only way to think," said Montë.

"We've finally been set free from Lucretia's curse, to be trapped by her once again after all these years."

"At least we'll go as ourselves, as the White Knights, like Esdaile always wanted," said Montë.

"Yes you're right, Esdaile would be proud of us," said Palia.

Together they continued through the corridors until neither could go no further without entering the great hall. Several figures up ahead moved and disappeared as a body of creatures converged sealing the ballroom.

"We're getting close, too close, Montë! So many of them, hundreds!"

"Quiet now Palia."

"Sorry, I don't know if I'm anxious or excited, it's been so long since I've felt like this," she squeaked. "Oh no someone's coming!"

"Keep calm," said Montë, "like Danté said, we're as strange and muddy as they all are, we'll blend in. Just keep your feathers black, act like the rest of them and stay out of the witch's sight ... she's the only one that's seen us before."

"And them! The Chef's are up ahead, I'm sure of it!" squawked Palia.

Montë couldn't see as far as Palia and the corridor had little lighting, but he knew the two silhouetted Giants were going to be bad either way.

"Quick in here!" he said pulling her into a doorway.

With trembling knees, Palia waited by the door, listening as the enormous figures stomped down the hall and grumbled about fetching extra tables. One reached for the door and with a massive fist pulled it shut. "Doesn't anyone shut doors around here!" he grumbled as they continued on.

Palia's chest felt numb from her rapid heart beats.

"That was too close," whispered Montë.

"It wasn't them," said Palia. "I tell you Montë sometimes I'm my own worse—"

"Shh!" said Montë cutting her short. He shook his head as he raised his finger to his lips and turned her head around slowly. It felt as if they had walked into a surprise party and the lights had switched on. In a desolate room, adjoined to the ballroom, a hundred strangers stood wall to wall. Montë and Palia waited for a horrible surprise! But there was none. Compared to the hall on the other side this place was dead silent and deathly cold.

"What are they? Who are they?" asked Palia.

"I don't know. Come on, let's go," said Montë. "I don't like this place any better that out there," he whispered.

Palia felt like closing her eyes as he walked her forward. She stepped carefully hoping not to bump into any of them, dead or alive they were haunting.

Montë glimpsed up at one of the figures and its expression was frozen as if howling endlessly in pain. He turned to another whose hands clawed at the air as if waiting to be struck by lightning, and indeed he also looked as if he had. He waved his hand in front of its worried face; it did nothing.

"What is this place?" whispered Montë. "It's so cold in here."

"Statues?" questioned Palia. "Are they carved from charcoal? They're ghastly, but well done."

"A lot of soldiers, it's like a toy room for a giant," said Montë.

"Look there's also children and women?" said Palia.

Montë reached forward and touched a soldier's hand. His carbon black skin was smooth yet cold like steel. With a dry crack, the soldier's hand broke off at the wrist. Montë looked inside and gulped. Its hard black flesh continued all the way to the bone which remained white. Shocked, Montë let go with a gasp and dropped it on the floor.

"They've been turned into charcoal!"

"The Witch has done this! So many!" gasped Palia.

"They must be King Morne's people. Sharpie's lucky he ran away."

"Montë! There she is!" gasped Palia hovering in the air.

"Lucrecia!" panicked Montë.

"No, our Belleny! I'm sure it's her! Yes and Bateau!"

Palia pointed to the very end of the room; past the charcoal figures, up to the large frosted crystal doors, through the slight gap between them, past the silhouettes of horrifying creatures and up the stairs to a kneeling Belleny and Bateau by her side.

This time Palia took off towards them and pulled at Montë along with her. She weaved through the haunting statues at top speed and crept up against the wall beside the crystal door.

"Palia!" cried Montë as the room roared with laughter and then came to a hushed silence. "We must wait!"

Sitting nestled in the shadows, they listened to the witches strangled and maudlin voice, taunting as she explained to Belleny that she wasn't Lucretia as they once understood, and there were two witches. She being the most powerful and devious, her name was Varin Eel. Lucretia was her prisoner, drained of her powers and trapped alive in a crystal coffin.

"Hideous creatures how dare they laugh at our Belleny!" snapped Palia.

"They're not, they're laughing at Dillon and Garon. Oh no, they look—"

"Let me see. Oh no, Dillon looks, please no," cried Palia.

By their necks, they were brought into the great hall by Chef Barbadoa and his apprentice. With all eyes on the Varin Eel, Montë and Palia took their chances and moved closer, although it was a sorrowful sight. They watched as Varin Eel towered over Belleny and pushed her to the ground with one hand, and tore off her frightening mask with the other.

The creatures roared in unison and continued into a wild thunderous cheer.

As Varin Eel sentenced, Garon and Dillon, they were thrown into cages and wrenched up by ropes as thick as a pirates forearm, up to the ceiling rafters. She then proceeded the walk down into her shadow and disappear. Leaving the creatures to entertain themselves and wait for her return and the redeeming.

"Did you see that! She walked inside her shadow!" said Palia.

"At least she's gone. How will we ever get them down from there?" questioned Monté.

"We must wait here. Wait for the others, a signa—" said Palia. She held her hand to her mouth as Belleny screamed. Yanked by her hair and thrown into a cage. Bateau was thrown close behind and together hauled to the roof to hang beside Garon and Dillon's cages.

"At least they are out of harms way up there," said Monté.

"For how long ... poor Belleny, I can't believe there's another witch!" said Palia. "At least one of them is silenced."

"Yes, but, it doesn't seem right?"

"Of course it does. Lucretia deserves all that's come her way," said Palia.

"She could help us? We could set her free?" said Monté.

"What! snapped Palia. "Are you forgetting she's the witch that put a curse on us! Turned us into frail freaks. She's the reason Belleny is in a cage and—"

"I know Palia," said Monté before she could continue, "but we also got to meet Belleny and Bateau and to be with her for all those years. Lucretia is going to be mad. Who know how long she's been trapped in there?"

"Do you have another plan?" said Palia.

"We have our original plan, Scissor Salt, but I doubt it could destroy a sorceress like Varin Eel, but it's worth a try. I only have a few small bags left, nearly all of it was spoiled and spent on Raveene," said Monté.

"Poor Raveene, I hope he's all right. Taken away with that giant Gretn Maramon, what a failed mission," said Palia.

"Palia you're not helping."

"Sorry, but look what's out there, and what they did to them ... even if we did get them free, they're severely injured, Garon probably can't walk let alone fly."

"Lucky we split up. The others couldn't possibly had a worse time than us."

"True we really got the short straw," she said.

"Shh quiet, someone's coming," said Monté.

The door from which they entered opened up and a small herd of creatures poked their heads inside. Palia and Monté held their breaths behind a wall of charcoal figures.

"They've got to be in here," growled Sniffler, his pointy nose was as long as his head. He sniffed walking towards a statue and pointed to its broken hand. "Hands don't just fall off."

"Sometimes they do?" said Tarber, the winged feeble one, who looked like a goat fused with a cockroach, "my brother once went fishing and as he was winding—"

"Shut up you fool, split up and get away from me," growled Sniffler, "and don't break anything, we're not even supposed to be in here. We don't want to be strung up by our necks."

"You must be able to smell them Sniffler?" asked Oberok, his bony bug-like face peering around the blackened bodies.

"Not with your stinky carcass beside me! I said split up!" he snapped.

Montë tugged at Palia's black feathers, "Let's get out of here."

"Out? Out where?" whispered Palia.

"Up there," pointed Montë through the gap in the door.

"Are you crazy? Behind the witches coffin?! Then what?" squeaked Palia trying to keep her voice down.

Montë smiled and nudged his head towards the door, pushing it ever so slightly. The great hall came into full view. The sounds and sights were overwhelming.

A horror zoo, thought Palia as she peered inside. "Wait!" she said as a two-toed ogre stopped by, his axe swinging hands only inches from Montë's face.

It was then the voice of Agarus came into Montë's head, *Montë!*

"Agarus?" said Montë out loud.

Palia looked up, "He's in there!"

Palia! You're here at last. I can sense you both. They think I'm one of them. I'm sitting in the middle of this mess. You won't believed what's happened! You need to find a safe place. I'll help you.

Agarus pushed back his stool, climbed onto the table and stood up so all eyes were upon him. Even Belleny and Bateau got up and watched in bewilderment as he ran along the tables, kicking plates of porridge slop into faces while doing spinning kart wheels. Stunned the creatures watched on as he rose up to the roof and turned on the point of his tail, then dropped into a roll and ran back, proceeding to do flips like a gymnast.

As a finale he pounced into the air, his long serpent tail becoming a giant whip, he hooked around Garon's cage. In giant circles, he swung while hanging upside down by his tail.

The crowd went berserk cheering on his wild antics.

"Go Edgar!" cheered Four Eyes.

"Incredible! That fellow belongs in a circus!" said the Baron.

Garon instantly woke as he was thrown from side to side.

"Now!" cried Montë and together they ran out into the open and along the wall like mice and up the throne room stairs.

"Hey someone opened the door," ordered Tarber.

"It's them!" roared Oberok, pushing aside a statue and jumping forth. Like dominoes, the statues began to fall.

"Get them!!" shouted Sniffler as carbon soldiers came crashing down upon him.

Montë reached the crystal coffin and ducked behind its stand. Palia dove down beside him.

"We made it!" whispered Montë.

"I'm afraid not," cried Palia as Oberok and Sniffler proceeded towards them up the stairs.

"Push it!" shouted Palia leaning against the coffin.

"What, no! Lucretia is inside."

"Just push!" shouted Palia heaving with all her might.

Montë shook his head and pushed hard against it, "We should run! We can't possible move this!"

But as he spoke the coffin slid from its stand as if they were two slabs of ice.

Lucretia's tomb slid off like a toboggan and came rushing down the stairwell. Agarus swung upwards watching as the crystal coffin slid down with full force collecting the bodies of Oberok and Sniffler along its way. The monstrous crowd rose from their seats with a mass snarl. Everyone stared at Palia and Montë, then down to the coffin where its lid was cracked open and Lucretia's bluish-white claws grasped at its edges.

Belleny screamed, "Run Palia run! Get out of here Montë!" From high above she watched as the morbid creatures proceed forward like rats from a sewer, clawing across their tables and revealing their weapon of choice.

"Come on Agarus! These must be the intruders the witch warned us against, you want the reward don't ya!" said Four Eyes.

"Are you sure?" said Agarus as Four Eyes jumped across his table and joined the hunt.

Palia took to the air; her wings beating hard and fast to rise above Montë. With each flap, her black wings turned a brilliant bright white, and she continued to change until her entire body was complete.

A scruffy and scared Montë stood alone at the top of the stairs, nowhere to run, nowhere to hide.

"Look out!" pointed Belleny as a feverish minion leaped up the stairwell in front of the others, revealing loaded crossbows attached to each arm. Without hesitation, and with a sneering laugh, he pointed them up at Palia and fired them both simultaneously. Belleny caught her breath, flinched and turned away before they connected. Garon also looked away; he knew all too well the creature would have to be cross-eyed to miss at such close range.

Montë couldn't see what happened to Palia, all he could see were the creatures hideous faces and snarling hateful expressions as they stabbed their blades and claws hard against his body. They were like zombies crowding around him as if he was their last meal.

"I'm sorry Princess!" he cried out, "you must save her Palia!"

These were his last words.

And through the gaps between the monstrous faces he watched as the white feathered Palia fell from above.

Curled in a ball Montë's eyes closed and now remained shut.

The shouting voice of Agarus cried out in his mind. He held his chest where the blade's had hit; the claws had scraped and with a tear he waited to die. But the creatures didn't give up there and one after another they took turns hitting him. His heart sunk listening to them grovel and drool, speaking of endless helpings, for the one that brought her his head.

But the wait to die lingered, the terror arrived but the death never came. The beasts became furious, and each hit him harder and harder. One held him up by his neck while another drove its blade in deep. But the sword seemed to slide around Montë, again and again.

"Take of his armour! It's obviously enchanted!" one roared ripping his chest plate to the ground and stabbing his knife into Montë's heart. It too slid off his dirty black coat.

"Just cut off his head already!" said another.

Montë peered down; he was not bleeding, and he realised there was also no real pain. He seemed to be fine and every stab, slash, whip and cut from the creatures weapons appear to fall to the side, not penetrating the skin but sliding off as if he was made of bronze.

Palia had felt the same thing as the arrowheads hit her, but penetrate her no, they seemed to slide off and merely knocked her about.

"How did you miss from there you idiot! Get out of the way!" roared another, reaching back and throwing his knife at Palia.

"Ha ha! A direct hit," he roared. But his spotless blade falls at his feet as Palia continues to circle above them.

She can't believe it either, nor can Belleny, Bateau or Garon, who returned their gaze when they hear the creatures confusion.

"What's happening to them?" said Agarus swinging up to face Garon.

"Agarus! Where did you come from!" said an aching Garon, "Get us out of here!"

"Look!" said Belleny.

One by one the raucous creatures became silent and froze like the charcoal statues. Their eyes turned white, and they dropped whatever weapon they were holding. Even Montë fell to the ground.

"Belleny! Dillon!" cried Palia as she circled the cages. She stared in at poor Dillon, but he remained curled up in a black ball, unconscious.

"Palia!" waved Belleny, "You're alright!"

"Do you know what's going on Palia? How did you do that?" said Bateau.

"It's Lucretia," pointed Palia, "look!"

Lucretia's hands extended out of the coffin, her glowing white fingers weaved together, her thumb and forefingers pushed up and outwards.

"She's helping us?" said Belleny.

"A protective spell?" said Palia, "Look at Montë! He's shaken, but alright!" she waved down as Montë climbed the tower of minions to wave back. "I'm all right!" he shouted.

Belleny waved back and signalled him to look across at Lucretia. It was then he realised what had happened and why the horde were stuck.

"She's frozen them as well?" said Bateau.

"I can't believe it!" said Garon shaking his head, "how could she do that?"

But Lucretia's hand wavered and the creatures moved ever so slightly.

"I don't think she can hold them for much longer," said Garon.

"Please, help us down at once," said Belleny.

"Of course Princess," said Agarus as he leapt onto the cage's chains and swung down to the giant who pulled them up there. He too stood in a zombie-like daze. "Here we go," said Agarus pushing against the beast's arm to get a good grip on the lever. Its skin wet and greasy moved more than its arm did. *Please don't wake, please don't wake,* he prayed. The chains gnarled together and shook the cages. Bones, feathers and straw scattered below.

"Hold on!" called Agarus and eased Garon down the best he could. Agarus was strong, but he was no giant, and the heavy chain slipped through his hands. Garon fell with full force.

"Garon!" cried Belleny as she blinked, and he was gone. Shortly a loud crash and a grumbling Garon indicated he had reached the floor in one piece. Garon climbed out of the debris and shuffled backwards. He had landed on top of several creatures, but even they stay frozen in a trance.

"Are you alright? Sorry, but you weigh—"

"I'm a little bruised but I'm fine Agarus. Now please be careful with the next one!" said Garon.

Agarus nodded and lowered the Princess and Bateau. Garon watched nervously as the frozen creatures twitched and drooled as Belleny descended slowly to the floor.

"Weren't we supposed to give you a silent whistle before we attacked?" said a familiar voice.

Garon spun round and shook his head. There stood Danté next to Kale with Rel perched upon his shoulder. "We have got to get out of here!" crowed Garon.

"What's going on? Where is the witch! How come they're not moving?" said Danté, running to their aid.

"It got to be a spell! Quick this can not hold for long!" said Kale, running through the creatures.

"Kale! Danté!" said Belleny waving down at them.

"What about me?" said Rel.

"Oh yes, of course, Rel, it's so good to see you too."

"Looks like you found the witch first," said Danté.

"Hold tight Belleny," he said as the cage meets the stone floor with a heavy clang.

"Quick give me a hand here," said Garon and with all their might, Danté, Kale and Garon grabbed the cage door and lifted it off it's hinges. With a chuckle, they threw it on top of a crowd of the witch's minions. Although they fell, and one moaned, they still didn't wake.

Belleny runs into Garon's arms, "Thank you! Are you all right? I can't believe what they did to you, I thought you were dead."

"There, there Princess, it's time to go home," said Garon.

"Wait, where is she?" said Kale.

Garon poked his beak across to the crystal coffin and snapped, "Your witch is over there."

"Lucretia!" whispered Kale.

"Lucretia's helping us," said Belleny.

"What do you mean?" said Danté.

"She's been trapped by another, a sorceress call Varin Eel."

"You're joking, there's another one! Then where is she?!" said Danté.

"There had to be," said Kale and he took off towards Lucretia.

"Don't get too close!" said Garon, "we're leaving!"

Garon looked up at the huge figure nearby, "Danté, you think he looks scary, you should see Varin Eel."

"Yeah well, you don't want to see what's in the basement, this ugly bag of knuckles is its breakfast," Danté lowered his head.

"You were in a fight?" said Belleny.

"Where's Sharpie," said Garon cautiously.

Danté frowned and said, "He didn't make it."

"Curse her! Curse all of them!" roared Garon, "We have got to get out of here. Come back with a real army."

Palia remained latched onto Dillon's cage as Agarus lower him to the ground. She called his name to no response. When the cage hit the floor, his door swung wide open.

They needn't lock it, thought Garon, *poor guy they really did a number on him.*

"Dillon, Please wake up!" said Belleny running into the cage.

A low and sad moan crept from his lips and slowly his eyes open, "Belleny? Please tell me I'm in the Jungle Room."

"Oh Dillon, I'm so sorry we must get you up and out of here at once."

Dillon leant up against the cage wall and sighed, "This definitely isn't the Jungle Room."

"Can you walk?" asked Palia.

"Here Dillon I'll help you," said Montë.

"Belleny, hop on, I have to get her out of here. Kale lets go! Now!"

Kale stood before Lucretia her weaken body drained of life force.

"Kale, is that you my boy?" said Lucretia. Her eyes remained closed as she reached out towards him.

"Yes it's me, hold on I'll get you out of this."

"We have to get out now!" roared Garon as Belleny and Bateau secured themselves.

"Agarus, can you carry her?" asked Kale.

Agarus looked across Montë, who shrugged; then he turned to Palia, who slowly moved her beak from side to side. There was the witch that turned them into the embodiment of fear and sadness, stole them away from Gonzo and their circus life. A burning hatred remains inside him, growing with each and every day of the journey.

"Of course he will," said Belleny, "we must."

"Why Belleny? She should rot here with the rest of them," snapped Palia.

"No, she has done her time."

"But—"

"No, we must forgive her," added Belleny.

Agarus looked across at the White Knights and nodded, "As you wish."

Slowly he dipped his head and twisted in and out of the creatures to kneel at Kale's feet.

"Thank you Agarus," said Kale.

Agarus looked inside the coffin and gasped, "Lucretia!"

Her body was light and skeletal. Kale easily removed her from the coffin and onto Agarus.

"Were getting you out of here," said Kale pulling the harness tight and strapping in her legs.

"I'm sorry," she whispered and with that she collapsed, falling forward against Agarus with her arms either side.

Bateau's ears darted up as the silence of the room returned to the monstrous voices and sounds once again. The spell Lucretia held them in was broken and the creatures continued where they left off, stabbing into the air where Montë once stood and wondering where Palia had disappeared to? Or how they ended up with a cage door on their heads?

"Time to go!" said Montë, while he and Palia pick Dillon up to his feet. Belleny held Bateau tight as Garon moved around, jumping up onto a table, then with wings out wide up to the top of the throne room staircase, the others follow at once.

The beasts dawdle around, confused and in a daze, but it didn't take too long to remember what they were doing.

Like monkeys, they jump around screaming and circling the alter.

Kale removed his black blade and with both hands waving it from side to side, "Stand back," he shouted.

"Oh no, not those two," said Garon, as Chef Barbadoa and his horrid apprentice stomp in.

Barbadoa took of his hat, threw it on the ground and ordered, "Shut the doors!"

"He's going to eat you raw," said one of the creatures.

"This time you're dinner! Who wants a roast!" said Barbadoa.
It was then the room began to chant,
"Roast! Roast! Roast!"

Danté removed his bow and aimed an arrow across the front row. "Get back! You don't know what you're doing, save yourselves before it's too late!" he screamed. "You're forest creatures, not monsters! You can be saved!"

"Saved! You should be so lucky!" one heckled as the mass of grotesque surged forward.

"Listen to him, please we don't want to hurt you!" said Belleny waving her blade in the air.

"You just hold on up there!" grumbled Garon.

"Roast, roast!" yelled a half goat beast as it crept up the steps. Garon made a lunge for the creature and kicked downwards, clawing the goat man in the face and tossing him upwards and over, back into the crowd.

"Who's next?" snarled Garon and whispered to Kale and Danté, "We can't hold them back, do you have any trick's up your sleeve?"

"Tricks Garon? Do you mean forbidden magic tricks?" asked Danté.

"This is no time for—" grunted Garon.

"Go for the bird, if you miss you might hit the little ones on top," screeched a scaly figure pointing up at Garon.

This amused the front row of the witch's archers and one by one they aimed their bows up towards Garon, Belleny and Bateau.

"Fine Magic! We'll all be dead without it!" roared Garon.

Everyone turned to the ceiling as a large figure was launched into the hanging cages and came crashing down amongst its own. With a monstrous roar, the giant beast that pulled up the cages fell to its knees and was dragged across the crowd as the minions started to collapse from the back.

"Look out!" screamed Belleny.

Danté jumped backwards into the air, fired an arrow and landed behind the witch's throne. A minion's harpoon stabbed through the chair stopping only inches from his face.

"That was close," said Danté peering round the chair and down the stairwell. The warrior creature lay lifeless in the arms of others as black blood seeped from the arrow lodged in its forehead.

"Dillon smiled as the chef Barbadoa was next, crawling through the air and landing with a crunch. The witch's minions tumbled over each other, shouting in pain and confusion.

In a maudlin sounding chorus, the creatures cried "Run! It's the witch's beast!"

"Oh no, it's Drokura!"

"Drokura, Drokura is out!"

"Run for your lives!"

Aggravated and hungry, a very surly Drokura burst through granite, shale and river stone castle walls, destroying the wooden door into splinters. Drokura flicked his tentacles back and forth, curling up and swiping them across the room. Mobs of creatures jumped onto the dark blue tentacles and stabbed their knives and teeth into it, but this only made the ancient underworld beast furious, throwing them down on the tables like small ants.

"Garon, it's Drokura!" shouted Kale, "The creature in the boiler room!"

"What? Oh no! He's breaking out?!" said Danté.

"Drokura?" said Garon, "What is that thing?"

"The walls are starting to crack, he's going to pull this place down with him," said Kale.

"We'll be crushed!" cried Belleny.

"Quick follow them!" said Palia taking to the air. "I'll show you where to go, stay clear of that thing."

In a line, the travellers followed Palia down towards the stairwell.

Belleny held on tightly and squeezed her eyes shut as Garon jumped up and over the fallen corpses.

An opaque shadow shrouded the walls and window glass, as it crept into the centre of the room. Belleny pointed back towards the alter as the lantern light returned, "Varin Eel!" she screamed, watching as the eerie figure climbed out of her oily shadow as if walking up a steep flight of stairs!"

Varin stepped out of her pooling black shadow revealing her entire body. Higher and higher she rose, exposing her spidery legs as they hooked back at the knee and her clawed toenails that scraped hard against the stone floor. She hunched over and reached back inside her shadow, dragging out a large heavy cauldron and pushed it across the stone floor. Her poisonous potion splashed around as if it was alive. She scanned the room and the chaos erupting around her while the destructive sounds of Drokura below destroying the boiler room and eating his victims echoed out. Furiously the evil witch screeched with all her malice and rage, pointing at Belleny, "Look what you have done! I will not rest till I kill you all. Run all you want, there is no escape from me."

Drokura's tentacles were bloodied black and squelching, scaling across the room, reaching out from the debris to snatch at anything and anyone. Varin realised her pet had become a ravenous destroyer and offered it the entire cauldron. Despite its size, Drokura moved fast and curled a limb around the pot, but Varin held it firm, wiped the black blood from its wounds and said, "Wait! First you must help me stop those that did this to you." Varin bared her teeth as Drokura took the cauldron and pulled it down inside the stairwell, "That's a good boy. Now drink up, don't spill a drop!" she snarled.

And just as quickly as she had appeared, the sorceress walked back down into her shadow and disappeared into a pool of snake-like shadows.

Belleny couldn't believe that they were now outside, but she knew it was far from over, the ground and sky was littered with creatures and she knew they were so far from home.

"They're going to be furious, this is worse that I could imagine," she sighed.

"We still haven't killed a witch," grumbled Garon as he stared at Lucretia's limp body slumped over Agarus.

"There will be no killing, Belleny must escape now, take her Garon and go!" said Kale.

"What about you?" said Belleny. "I can't leave you behind."

"You don't have a choice," said Garon stretching his wings out wide.

"Look out! In the sky, it's Varin Eel on the creature she arrived on!" said Palia.

"I guess none of us are flying out of here then," said Bateau.

"Damn her!" growled Garon. "Wait, no, there's no one riding it, it's escaping.

"But there were others, some could still be chained at the stables," said Kale.

"We'll we're not going to find out waiting here."

Suddenly Kale froze, the sound of a glass shattering high pitched shriek filled the night sky

"Even the Kylen's are taking to the air on their winged steeds trying to escape, come this way!" said Kale, jumping up and over fallen debris and making his way along a wooden fence. But his face dropped as they arrived and watched as the witch's minions scrambled over the winged beasts like rats on a floating carcass.

"Damn it! We're too late!" said Danté.

"Over there!" called Garon, spotting another as it dragged a metal chain and half the stable with it, whipping its wings from side to side, in pain it screeched out as they approached.

"I can see why they left this one alone," said Rel yawning as he woke up.

"Drokura's come out to play," said Kale as he approached it cautiously.

"A Kylen?" asked Belleny.

Kale stood still and raised his arm, "Rel, let her know we are friends, we would like to fly her back to the kingdom, she will be safe there."

Rel leapt off Kale's wrist and fluttered towards the winged beast. It bit at him like a dog snapping flies as he continued to casually hover in front of its face. Eventually, it stopped and stared at him in wonderment. Rel began to whisper the faintest of words into it's pricked ears and the creature lowered its head to the ground, stopped flapping its wings and resisted from kicking the chain secured around its leg.

Rel returned to Kale, "If you could remove the chain it will be most grateful."

As he approached, blade in hand, it squawked and rose up, towering above him.

Belleny's eyes bounced from the winged beast and back to the castle. Shivering as the witch's creatures crawled about in every direction and Drokura continued to tear the castle apart.

"It will be all right, you will be safe," said Kale resting his hand against the winged creature. In a swift movement, he stabbed the lock with his blade and turned it forcefully. The shackle dropped to the ground revealing a raw bloody ankle. At once the beast drove its wings down around him and took to the sky.

"Wait!" whispered Kale, "Please take her."

He turned back to the others and shrugged, then stared across at Lucretia as she rose up from upon Agarus.

Rel climbed back on Kale's shoulder and they watched it join the other escapees in flight, fading off into the forest shadows.

Kale turned to the others, their eyes now on Drokura as more and more of the horrifying ancient was exposed. "I'm sorry, we'll have to walk."

"Ungrateful thing!" grumbled Garon kicking at the dirt.

"It was scared," said Kale.

"We all are," said Montë holding up Dillon the best he could, "I don't think Dillon can walk back."

Danté came to his assistance and said, "We can go back to Sharpie's hideout, we will be safe there."

Before they could answer Rel whistled and pointed up into the air.

"Hold that thought," said Danté as four of the witch's faithful winged creatures appeared for a last battle, one without a chain, the rest dragging them below from their legs.

"Look out!" roared Garon, "the witch's minions, that damn thing brought them back! The poison runs deep in its veins."

"I'm too weak to fight," said Dillon.

"Someone take Lucretia off my back, I have to protect Dillon," said Agarus.

With all eyes on the sky, they watched as the winged beasts circled and the creatures that rode them screeched wildly in the air. It was then that they began to swoop. But instead of picking them off one by one the winged beasts rose up vertically into the sky and spiralled around with their wings out, throwing the witch's minions off their backs and breaking their necks as they tumbled onto the jagged rocks below.

"I don't believe it!" said Belleny as it began to rain with screaming bodies.

"Look out everyone!" said Garon, dodging from side to side.

One by one the spiralling creatures flew back and landed nearby, they too wanted to be released from the sorcery and evilness that had enslaved them for all this time. Belleny and Bateau climbed on first and patiently the winged beasts waited while Kale fastened them in tightly.

"Here Belleny, it'll be cold up there, but don't worry you're going to be home before you know it," said Kale. He wrapped her in a cape that he had taken from the body of an unfortunate skydiving creature.

"But our ride looks sick, it's turned white," said Bateau nervously as its large black eyes turned to look back at him.

"No, this one's called Pepper, aren't you boy!" said Belleny.

It was then it screeched out and lashed its tongue back at them like a overjoyed dog.

"Alright you're set. So which way do we go?" said Danté.

"I know the way!" shouted Belleny, taking out her silver pendant and excitedly watching as the delicate white alphena crab spun around and stopped sharply, pointing the South Westerly direction home.

"Hold on you two!" roared Garon.

"Come on Orphans! Last one back is a rotten egg!" shouted Belleny as they too took control of their creature and Montë steered it into the air behind them.

"This is just like riding Yeena at the circus!" exclaimed Dillon.

Danté took the reins of his ride and like a little boy jumped up excitedly, "Let's go Kale! They're beating us!"

Kale held Lucretia tight in his arms and watch as the castle collapsed in flames. The giant Drokura seemed as big as the castle itself as it crawled out of the debris and tumbled forward into the muddy moat.

"Are you ready Rel?" said Kale, watching as he too stared into the castle's flames.

"This will not be the last time we will see Drokura or his master," said Rel.

"I know, but we got what we came for. Let's go home."

— PART FOUR —

Face to Face

CHAPTER 63 - KIKAAN RETURNS

Witnessing the rays of light streaming from Crystalon Castle up into the night sky was a breathtaking vision, with dazzling shards of luminous blue and white light surging upwards. Belleny was so excited, even though beyond exhausted, as she was finally back in her beloved royal kingdom of Mare-Marie, minutes from the castle and most importantly her father.

As they approached, they were spotted immediately by Castle Wardens and from out over the high castle walls a squad of Kylen riders took to the air and surged towards them.

"Garon, there are soldiers coming our way!" yelled Bateau.

"Yes, we better let them know it's us," said Garon, as he whistled a unique melody to alert the wardens they were a Royal party. Despite being some distance away, the guards returned a response and the largest winged kylen resonated its lights rhythmically. Upon approaching they swooped below the clouds to rise up beside Garon at the front of the pack.

"Commander Quick it's you, you're back! Oh no! Where's the Princess?" shouted the soldier Kostis.

"Ah Kostis, indeed we are. She's all right, just a little exhausted," said Garon revealing the Princess wrapped snugly within his wing fold.

Gustus appeared on the opposite side of Garon, his kylen flapped hard as it lifted his enormous body.

"And Gustus, I knew you wouldn't be far," said Garon.

"Commander! Oh, it is a good day. You look—" said Gustus with a hesitant pause.

"Terrible?" said Garon.

"Yes," said Gustus, "but triumphantly so."

"You missed out on quite an adventure men," said Garon.

"Someone had to mind the fort sir," said Gustus disappearing as his ride began to dip through the clouds.

"And how is our King?" asked Garon.

"King Vera ... he's been quite unpredictable with the Princesses absence," said Kostis, "and the others?" he said looking back at the flying beasts.

"Yes they're fine, we have an extra guest though, she'll need a room prepared."

"Yes sir!" said Kostis.

Both soldiers signalled off with a nod and with a tug of their reigns they dove and soared upwards as if the laws of gravity was irrelevant, disappearing into the clouds towards the great castle.

Kostis and Gustus arrived back at the castle gate and perched upon a large leafless tree. Dismounting with a leap, "I'll go ahead Gustus, the king will want his message immediately!"

Kostis took off at once and sprinted down the halls and corridors till he reached the king's quarters. He banged hard against the royal door. There was no answer, but Kostis could hear the muffling sounds of growls and the beating of tin-like drums. He pounded harder.

"Who goes there at this untimely hour?" shouted King Vera, as the sound of falling vases and a dressing table tumbled within the room.

"King Vera! Urgent news, Princess Belleny has returned!" he shouted at the door.

The door was wrenched open and a dishevelled King Vera stood in the doorway. Kostis stepped backwards as the king was dressed in large furry bear skin trousers, a horned helmet with his chest bare. He grabbed Kostis by the shoulders and pushed him against the wall.

"My Belleny! Returned! How dare you tell such vicious lies!" he roared, "I'll throw you into the Pit of Nothingness myself!"

"Your majesty I tell no lies, I have seen her with my own eyes, she rides with Garon the Quick and will be arriving as we speak."

In a wave of joy, King Vera was overcome with happiness and he hugged Kostis so hard his armour began to buckle against his bare chest. Noticing the sound of the armour denting the king let go and stood back.

"Is she healthy?" He waited for what felt like an eternity for Kostis to answer, but Kostis' attention was distracted by the dent in his chest plate.

"Soldier are you a mute?" shouted King Vera.

"The Princess is healthy and in good spirits Sir, but she is exhausted. It seems they did have an extra traveller with them, a lady and they requested a guest room be prepared, she didn't look too well. I thought she was dead."

"A guest is with them? See to it a room is prepared. I must go at once!" said the King.

"Splendid Sir, with respect may I suggest you change out of your ..."
Kostis pointed down at the king's bear skin legs.

"No time!" said the King grabbing his sleeping gown off the door and running out the door.

Inside the castle walls, Belleny and the travellers had arrived; utterly relieved and excited to be far from Varin Eel, her minions and her poisoned beast, Drokura. The Orphans were exhausted and looked forward to collapsing in the Jungle Room. Bateau held his head up over Garon's scruffy feathers and waved goodbye as Kale carried Lucretia in his arms, lead by Gustus to a room where she could recover.

"Don't worry Garon, I'll make sure father cools his temper down," said Belleny, "I'm sure if anyone is in big trouble it will be me."

"Garon! You sack of festering feathers, I'll have your head!" shouted King Vera coming at them in his sleeping gown, slippers and dragging a large broad sword in both hands ready to behead.

Belleny ran forward and King Vera paused looking up with teary eyes. He dropped his sword with a loud echoing clang as she lunged into his warm embrace.

"Are you okay? Tell me you're okay! What's this black stuff all over you? What were you thinking?! Don't you ever leave like that again!" said the king clustered with emotions.

"I'm all right father, I'm so sorry for disappearing the way I did," said Belleny, "I don't know, something came over me, a regretful impulse, from being inside for so long. Garon took care of me, everyone did."

King Vera looked up and stared over her shoulder at Garon with a frown. "You're lucky I don't have you roasted tonight," he said pointing a finger at him.

"I've heard that a lot lately,"muttered Garon.

"Come here and give me a hug you silly old bird!" said the king as he reached forward and grabbed Garon in a warm embrace, "You must tell me everything, you seem to be missing some feathers?"

"You're not going to like who we brought back with us," said Garon.

"Now don't be angry father," added Belleny.

"Why would I be angry?"

"Brace yourself, it's Lucretia," said Belleny.

"What? The witch is here? What is the meaning of this nonsense?"

"It is true," said Garon, "she saved us."

"I will explain everything," said Belleny, "but first I must get out of this outfit and wipe this blood off me."

"Blood!" cried the King.

"It's not mine, so that's all that matters," said Belleny, "I have so much to tell you, you won't believe the —"

It was then that the King frowned down and put his hands on his sides, "You'll have plenty of time to tell every single last detail, as you're grounded young lady, no more going outside until I'm long gone!"

"But you don't understand! I can never be stuck inside again," said Belleny.

"I'll be the judge of that, go and get in the royal baths, the sight of you covered in oily stuff is making me feel ill."

"What are you wearing?" said Bateau pointing with his tails at the king's furry pants. The king looked down at his open gown and closed it quickly.

"Just go and have your bath! I'm glad you all made it back in one piece."

"Not all of us," said Belleny.

"Oh?" replied the king.

"Raveene was attacked by ferocious bugs, but hopefully he was saved by an invisible giant, Gretn Maromon. Garon we must go back and find out," said Belleny.

"You must be joking! Inside now!" roared the King, "Garon can go, the whole kingdom can go, but you my dear are not going anywhere!"

CHAPTER 64 - REUNITED

"I have to get off this balcony; it's making me feel sick," said Evelin groaning a little at getting up.

Cory pulled her back down instantly, "No you're not."

"What?" scoffed Evelin and Milton simultaneously.

"You heard me, I want to tell you something."

"Um ... go on," said Evelin curiously.

"I was thinking about what Astina said, and she may be right you know."

"Who's Astina?" said Milton.

"I'll tell you later," said Evelin.

"She's a witch," began Cory, "more importantly, what she said."

"Not now Cory I know you don't like her," said Evelin.

"Just think about it, before you go and lock yourself inside for the rest of holidays."

"I have thought about it, it's all I think about," said Evelin.

"And ... " said Cory.

"And nothing, I'm happy staying inside."

"What do you mean you're not going out?" said Milton.

"I don't want to, I have everything here in the Plastic Palace, I have BC, my paper fish, loads of books, records—"

"But—" started Milton.

"Look, I'm going through my own private journey and things are a little out of control at the moment," said Evelin.

"But you seem fine to me," said Milton.

"I know, but inside I'm not and I can't control it, I'm seeing a therapist, I have been for ages and I have an inner demon, I've seen it."

"A therapist? What demon? What do you mean? No way ... are you possessed?" said Milton.

"Possibly," said Evelin.

"You are not! Not possessed by the Devil at least," said Cory.

"I was hypnotized and I saw it clear as day, I saw it deep inside me, a whirlpool of darkness. I stopped it, but then it came back and it tried to drown me."

"Hypnotized? Cool!" said Milton.

"You can drown in your dreams Evelin, it doesn't mean you're dead when you wake up," said Cory.

"I don't know, a part of me is. If I stay inside I don't feel anxious, the whirlpool goes away."

"Oh, but where is the whirlpool exactly?" asked Milton.

"Nonsense! You're a defeatist, you are the whirlpool so suck it up and get on with it," said Cory as if channelling Astina Francis.

"Cory what are you saying?" said Evelin.

"I won't hear of it, you are lying to yourself, and if I have to I'm going to drag you outside kicking and screaming, I will!"

"You're crazy," said Evelin.

"No doubt I am, but you my dear are not. Come on we're going to book you an appointment to see this shrink of yours."

"Why?" said Evelin.

"You're in No Man's Land, you need to go back under hypnosis and defeat this inner whirlpool. And get off these meds!"

"I'm booked to see Esta next Friday."

"Next Friday! That's out of the question. "Let's ring her now, we'll go tomorrow at the latest. What's her number I'll ring her?"

"But—" said Evelin.

"No buts, shouldn't, couldn't, can't, won't and maybes! I'm dedicating the rest of my life to helping you Evelin Boots!"

"Is this because you feel guilty?" asked Evelin.

"Don't be stupid of course not, but if I have to I'll give myself up," said Cory.

"Give yourself up?" said Milton.

"No don't!" said Evelin.

"I wasn't really going to, but it's good to see you're still on my side."

"You girls are so confusing, I think you're both a little—"

"Don't say it Milton," said Cory.

"Evelin, what have you two done?"

Evelin looked at Cory, then across to Milton, "We burnt down the school library," she said in her softest monotone voice.

"Eve!" coughed Cory with a smile, "Well I burnt it down, Evelin merely supplied me with the ignition fuel."

"Very funny. Eve doesn't even have a lighter," smiled Milton pushing her shoulder.

Evelin shook her head.

"Sorry Cory, I had to tell Milton, he's the only person I can trust and I just can't keep this secret from him, it's hurting me."

"Understood, but this goes no further, you hear me boy?" said Cory pointing her unlit cigarette at him.

"Are you guys for real? Does Robin know?"

Evelin shook her head again. Her eyes didn't lie.

"No wonder you feel like crap! Your conscience must be out of control Evelin, that happened ages ago, why on earth did you do it? And why wasn't I invited?"

"You know Milton, you're right, I feel a lot better already now you know," said Evelin.

"I bet you do, a ton of weight off your shoulders."

"I don't," grinned Cory, "now I have to kill both of you."

"Okay let's call Esta, I can't wait until the end of the week."

"The demon slayer," said Milton.

"I hope so," said Evelin.

"That's the spirit Eve," laughed Cory.

The trio dialled the therapist and Esta Green picked up the phone. Instantly she recognized Eve's voice, "Hello Evelin."

"Tell her you want to see her right away," said Cory pushing in.

"Who's that? Are you all right Eve?" asked Esta.

"Yes I'm all right, sorry that's my friend Cory, I would like to book an appointment."

"You're booked in for Friday Evelin, would you like to come in sooner?"

"Yes, I want to finish where we left off."

"With the hypnosis?"

"Yes, I'm ready, I want to defeat my whirlpool."

"Oh, that's wonderful Eve, would you like to come tomorrow?"

"Tomorrow, yes please."

Cory nodded her head, trying her best not to grab the phone.

"That's fine, I'm free after lunch so come round when you're ready."

"Thank you."

"Thank yourself," said Esta.

"Tell her we're coming too," whispered Cory.

"Can I bring two close friends?"

"Of course, if that live wire Cory can sit still, of a second, of course you can," chuckled Esta.

"Yes, she will, see you tomorrow Esta."

"Bye Eve."

Evelin put down the receiver and took a breath.

"Done, tomorrow, after lunch."

"Do you want us to watch?" said Cory.

"I don't mind, I might need your strength. You heard Esta though, you'll have to be chilled."

"Yeah, I know, don't worry I'm always prepared," said Cory.

It was then that Robin entered the kitchen, "What's going on in here then? Stirring up trouble I hope."

"You have no idea Mr. Boots," said Milton.

"Milton, Welcome home old man. How are your folks?"

"Locked up," replied Milton.

"Hmm, you'll always have a family here," said Robin.

"Thanks, Mr Boots. Hey, I better go, my aunt will be wanting to talk to me. How are we getting to the appointment tomorrow?"

"Oh, I didn't think about that," said Evelin.

"What appointment?" asked Robin.

"I was about to tell you, I just booked a session with Esta. I think it's best if I see her sooner rather than later," said Evelin.

"Are you all right?" said Robin.

"Not at all, but I'm going to defeat my inner demon."

"Well, that is good news, I can drive you in the truck. You could all hop in the back like little pigs?" said Robin.

"I think we should probably catch a taxi," said Evelin.

"Hey, I know Miss Davis has a new station wagon, she wouldn't mind taking us I'm sure," said Robin.

"Ooo Miss Davis," called Milton over his shoulder as he was walking out the front door.

"Are you still here?" shouted Robin.

"Sure why not? Ring her, it's a good idea," said Evelin.

"Is it?" said Robin.

"Of course it is," said Evelin, "we'll kill two birds with one stone."

It took a while for Belleny and the travellers to accept the very different outcome of their recent quest and accept that Lucretia was now on their side and a new inconceivable darkness was their nemesis. The most profound truth was to do with Kale's heritage. He was the son of Lucretia and the day she was expelled from the kingdom for sorcery against the crown, both little Kale and his mother fled and climbed Poskar's watery stairs, and ventured off on their own path never to return. At first, Lucretia was welcomed at the Temple of Thought and she remained there until moving to Castle Morne to continue her sorcery under a new king and queen.

Kale spent his childhood and adolescence at Castle Morne, tucked away in the tower, being schooled in spiritual and magic theory and practice. His mother would visit him on occasion, but when these visits became more sporadic and finally stopped, he felt unloved and presumed she had abandoned him.

When kale heard of the rumours of a suffocating and growing darkness, he couldn't believe it was true. An army of minions? Taking over the castle, giant creatures and the land poisoned and rotting? His earliest and most honest memories were of his mother's generosity and good nature and he couldn't believe that she would turn to the dark arts and abandon the light. How had she become so malicious and vengeful? Was she so embittered by the banishing from the Mare-Marie kingdom?

Now more than a decade later, Lucretia was back in Mare-Marie and laying peacefully in bed on crisp white sheets her mind and heart were cleared of doubt and anger. Kale stared at his weakened mother's hand and fondly stroked her pale and transparently thin hands. He felt her squeeze his hand in return and with a little movement she smiled, her eyes remaining closed.

Kale looked down at his own hands and pulled back when he saw he was still covered in Drokura's blood. He pulled back gently and wiped his mother's hand clean with a cloth and went to the next room to clean up. He was still wearing his leather headgear and slowly unlatched the mouthpiece letting it fall to the side like an aviator's pilot cap. He stood up and walked towards the small bathroom and inspected himself in the bathroom mirror. With a moistened towel, the steamy water removed the muck from his lips and chin, revealing underneath his preserved skin. Pushing back his headgear it exposed his face letting his cloud white hair become free. He dipped his head under the warm running water and washed away the grime and reflected on their arduous journey and their quiet achievements.

Patting his face dry with a clean white towel, he fondly noted his eyes were the same opalescent pea green colour as were his mothers and his hair the same silvery white flock but his formed a long point as it hung down his back.

"Kale—" called Lucretia pushing herself up, "if you would please come here, I have something important to tell you. I tried to stop her once ... I tried everything I could.

"Mother, you are not to blame for this. It's not your burden to carry alone. Varin Eel is far away," soothed Kale.

"She cursed the water ... it changed everything ... she has this Drokura creature that will devour everything," Lucretia shut her eyes and he felt her retract and slip back into silence.

A knock at the door startled Kale and Jodin the maid appeared in the doorway with King Vera and the Orphans standing behind her, all peering earnestly into the room.

"Come in," beckoned Kale.

"I've brought warm towels and Vallene tea," said Jodin.

"Thank you," replied Kale, "Vallene tea is my mother's favourite."

Kale reached for the teapot and poured a small ramekin cup's worth of warm brew, "here mother, please drink, it's Vallene tea, it will revive your strength."

She whispered faintly, "Thank you my boy."

King Vera walked in holding his crown to his chest as a mark of respect. The Orphans peered inside and saw Lucretia on the bed and to her side sat Kale, his face revealed to them, they could now see how much they resembled each other.

"Kale welcome back. You are a noble and brave soldier and I thank you for protecting my daughter —the King looked downwards at Lucretia and asked softly—is she all right?" He approached the bed looking at Lucretia's faint and gaunt body under the bed sheets.

She could sense him standing nearby, her old friend and recent enemy and slowly her eyelids rose revealing her green opaline eyes.

Before he could speak, she read his thoughts, "We all make mistakes King Vera, it's a pity sometimes others pay dearly for them," said Lucretia.

"I was wrong to banish you from Mare-Marie before talking to you first. I was threatened by your ways, I was scared and upset."

"You tore me from my life, my only son. I was cast out before I could explain myself, then the darkness tracked me down and saw me as a vessel to channel evil. Before I knew I was being fooled I could not resist the temptation of Varin Eel's dark arts," said Lucretia looking up at Kale with wet eyes, then back up to the king.

The King gasped as her skin seemed to grow finer and more transparent and sink into each enclave of her skull as she spoke.

"Please Vasilis I must repent of this guilt and grief before I pass," she raised her voice but softened it with a pat on his hand. "I put a curse on your daughter, the spell kept her locked inside the castle without the need of a physical boundary. She became fearful and pessimistic. First I used the Seed of Doubt but then double the spell as assumed she would inherit the strength of her mother to one day overpower it. With the encouragement of the White Knights she was always going to fear the worst of everything—I wanted to hurt you, for you also to live with the pain of never seeing your daughter grow up and be happy."

Lucretia placed her hand on her heart.

"The Seed of Doubt?" questioned the King.

"The White Knights delivered it with them, she planted it in her room."

"The tree Winta!" snarled the King, "that cursed weed is in her room!"

"You did a terrible thing Lucretia," sighed King Vera, "of which I may struggle to forgive you."

Lucretia sat up and he leant in close, "I cannot shake the grief I caused you. I want you to know I didn't try to escape when I was captured and entombed by the necromancer Varin Eel. I lay trapped inside her crystal coffin, it was my due sentence."

King Vera looked into her eyes and Lucretia let go of his arm and slipped her fingers into the teapot handle. Kale went to help, but she still had strength and power, picking it up like it weighed nothing. She poured the amber tea and placed the pot back, then with a sip, she sighed and continued, "The night that monster Varin Eel appeared from the darkness, it was the last night of my so-called freedom. I heard the screams of the King of Morne. I quickly went upstairs to his quarters. I was too late and watched the witch kill him thrusting a dagger into his heart and his queen, her claws around the Queen's throat as her legs quivered."

"Mother stop, you need to rest," said Kale.

Lucretia lay back down and closed her eyes, "Please, forgive me my Lordship."

The King was silent and muttered to himself as if pondering his deepest thoughts, "We must go, she needs rest," and they silently left leaving Kale and Lucretia in the room.

*

Garon was relaxing deep in the swirling hot water of the royal baths, his giant wings stretched out to cleanse the caked mud and oily black tar as he bathed. The steaming water rose around Belleny's head and Bateau watched from a dry stone nearby as he never really loved getting his fur wet. Belleny felt rejuvenated as the hot water removed the mud and crusted blood from her skin, she cleaned her toes and hands and washed her hair.

"That's enough for me, I'm turning all wrinkly like Varin Eel," said Belleny, but no one laughed. Grabbing a huge white bathrobe that looked like a polar bear hugging her, she stood on the edge of the steaming bath water.

"You know she's still out there," said Garon.

Belleny stopped and turned on her heels to face Garon, "She's coming here to the castle isn't she, with that giant Drokura?" Belleny need not wait for an answer, hung her head and walked out of the bath house.

Garon waited until she left and closed his eyes. He opened his eyes when he could hear the scuffling footsteps of King Vera approaching. From his quick waddle, he could tell he was most upset.

"Garon! Where is she now?!" said King Vera.

"You just missed her, she retreated to her room," said Garon calmly.

"Good. Hopefully, she stays there. Wait, first I have to get rid of that damned tree!"

"Tree?"

"I've just spoken to Lucretia, the Orphans weren't the only trick up her sleeve, also that horrid tree Winta in the Princess's room. I'm a fool to not see it."

"I'll have it chopped down immediately," said Garon.

"Thank you, let me do the first swing. Lucretia brings terrible news of this Varin Eel, I fear the kingdom is still in great danger!"

King Vera gulped and said, "she stabbed King Morne and his Queen and killed all of his men, without the aid of an army."

"I know," said Garon.

"And what of this witch's giant? Does it still walk? Danté speaks of it as a living nightmare?"

Garon was silent, he froze at the thought of Drokura.

CHAPTER 66 - REUNION

Belleny ran into her room shouting, "Winta! I made it back!" But once inside she paused and looked at the haunting tree as if she were suddenly afraid. *Creepy,* she thought as she only recognized how strange and unnatural it was to encourage a dark and haunted tree to flourish and take over her chamber. Belleny went straight inside her walk in robes and found Esdaile lying on the ground close to where she left him, hidden between two long rows of mannequins.

"Esdaile, I'm back with the White Knights. I now know what happened, I know everything."

Belleny hugged Esdaile and walked quickly to a mannequin which wore her clothes chosen for today. She paused and stared fondly at the delicate dress fabric it was draped in. After such an adventure, in the same dirty wild outfit, she just couldn't wear the pale yellow dress presented before her. *I can't fight a witch in a yellow dress.*

"Bateau! I'm glad you're here. Look at all this, a piece of clothing taken from over five different mannequins—I have changed! Who knows what I'll wear tomorrow ... if there is a tomorrow."

"Of course there will be a tomorrow," said Bateau collapsing on her bed. Hey, cheer up. Varin Eel may be dead for all we know? That beast of hers was on fire when we left. I can only imagine if it tried to cross that river it'd be halfway down the endless waterfall."

"That's not what Garon thinks, or Danté, he said they're probably on their way here. I overhead that Drokura was unstoppable."

Bateau said nothing and he watched Belleny change into her bold and practically new outfit, it reminded him of the circus troupe changing before a show and the memory of Gonzo saddened him.

"I'm just getting myself prepared," said Belleny watching him in the reflection of the mirror. She walked by him and up to her masks, choosing a feathered faced character from her collection.

"Exotic," said Bateau, "good to see you in a little colour."

"Thank you. I want to look empowering when we go and see Lucretia."

"But I just got up here and I'm getting comfy—"

"Oh Bateau, I carried you halfway across Mare-Marie, and I don't mind caring you downstairs."

"But shouldn't we wait here? The King's orders—and aren't you a little angry at her? With what she did to you and the Orphans?"

"No, I know it was wrong, but I forgive her."

"You forgive her?" asked Bateau sitting up and winding his tails around each other.

"Of course, I have a new life ahead of me, I can't be carrying grudges around, we all make bad decisions."

"Don't I know it," said Bateau stretching forward with a grin. Belleny scooped him up and together they left her room and descended the staircase. It wasn't long before she could see Jodin walking up towards her, "Jodin!"

Jodin looked up and paused, *it sounds like Belleny, but she, no she couldn't be—smiling? Is it another impostor?*

"B ... Belleny is that you?" asked Jodin, dropping the sheets she carried and ran towards her.

Bateau jumped from Belleny's arms before he was squashed between them, "Of course it's me, you won't believe where I've been and the things I've seen, oh how I missed you terribly!"

"Oh Belleny!" said Jodin, who hugged her so hard that Belleny felt as if she had been lifted from the ground. "You had us all thinking the worst, day after day, night after night, Oh Belleny I don't know what I would have done if—"

"I know, I know," said Belleny, "It was irresponsible and a big mistake to vanish the way I did. But boy what an adventure!"

"It's fine, I'm just glad you're back now. You are ever so brave. I'm so proud of you. I can't believe there are two witches! Lucretia's too beautiful to be a witch—oh and her son, he looks just like her," said Jodin.

"Does he now?" said Belleny raising an eyebrow in an animated manner.

"I've got to see this," said Bateau.

"We're on our way there now, is Lucretia resting?" asked Belleny.

"She was exhausted after she talked to King Vera," said Jodin.

"They made their peace for now. She's really upset about the old curse and the Orphans. Punished herself by staying in that other witch's crystal coffin, how awful."

"I must see her at once," said Belleny.

When they arrived at Lucretia's room, it was guarded by two footmen and a small creature that Belleny had never seen before.

"Princess Vera it is a miracle you have returned safely," said one of the guards.

"Thank you, the miracle that saved us is in there. I have to ask, who is this little one, is he yours?" she pointed at the strange creature facing the door.

"It's with the King, it appeared a few weeks ago.

"So my father is not in there with her?"

"No Princess, he has gone to talk with Garon the Quick. Only the witch and her son are inside."

Belleny opened her locket and watched the grey triangles shape change and point at the creature. Anxiously she waited as they broke apart and formed into a rose shape and then back into an arrow. *A friend!* she thought relieved. She knelt down to the creature that sat patiently as if they weren't there, "Hello, what's your name? My name is Belleny and this is Bateau, do you know Lucretia?"

The creature's eyes stared at the door intensely as if listening to the conversation in the other room, it removed its gaze only for a second to scan Belleny and Bateau and then back to the wooden door.

"Fine, I guess we better go in," said Belleny. She knocked gently on the door. There was no answer. Shrugging her shoulders she looked at Bateau.

"Are you sure this is the right room?" said Belleny to the soldiers.

One of them replied, "Yes Princess, of course!" Quickly he double checked and opened the door ever so slightly. Bateau peeked inside and pulled Belleny's head forward with his tails.

"Look! That must be Kale, asleep against the bed," said Bateau.

"Oh my, it is," she whispered.

The door creaked as they pushed their heads against it. Kale woke and with sharp battle-hardened instinct, he drew his blade before them. Seeing his friends, he returned his blade.

Belleny remained behind the door and asked, "Should we come back tomorrow?"

"No—it's fine, please come in Princess, you to Bateau."

"Thank you, there is a little someone out here as well. I think it wants to say hi," said Belleny.

"Oh, who?" said Kale.

"I don't really know?" she said, looking down at the rose petal covered creature.

Kale stood and approached the door and through the gap peered at the soldiers with a nod, he smiled at Belleny and Bateau and then down at the strange little creature.

"I see, hello Capette—you are a faithful little one," smiled Kale patting the small flower-like creature. Instantly it raced through the gap and caressed Lucretia's face.

"She is Lucretia's familiar, come in Princess, Bateau—no more guests please guards."

Belleny opened the door and followed him in slowly with Bateau tight in her arms. She didn't know where to look first. There lay Lucretia as if she was dead. Silently asleep and somewhat beautiful, just as Jodin mentioned, and there was her son Kale—unveiled for the first time. Belleny witnessing his entire face without his mask locked her eyes onto his and he in return stared into hers.

She quickly spoke, "You can stay here until you see fit to leave. My maid tells me my father came here earlier? And a truce was made," said Belleny.

"Yes. I'm not sure if the White Knights will ever truly forgive her, or yourself," said Kale.

"Of course I do, these events were beyond our control. Blame can only point to more pain. We must move on."

"Thank you, Princess. I'm afraid we've pinpointed the source of our anguish, our battle with Varin Eel is far from over."

"But she could be dead?" said Bateau.

"Yes," said Belleny, "you saw the castle fall down. It went up in flames!" she whispered, watching Lucretia's eyelids flicker, "nothing could have survived that, not even her giant."

It was then that Lucretia opened her eyes and spoke, "No! She hides in shadows my dear. Even the burning flames of fire cast a hollow darkness."

Lucretia shuddered and a teary smile came over her. She raised a thin, translucent hand toward Belleny.

"It doesn't matter," said Belleny taking her hand into hers, "You're safe here, you don't have to leave the kingdom."

"No Princess, with respect, you're wrong about that. No one is safe while the necromancer stalks us, especially here."

Drokura's limbs were lodged under the twisted pipes, shifting swathes of blue granite blocks and a ton of fallen rubble that crashed around him as Castle Morne collapsed. With his free tentacles, he scrapped the thick dust from his eyes and bore witness to a roaring fire above. It devoured the thick red curtains lining the castle walls. What he couldn't see was the castles ceiling, saturated with a lake of rolling flames as if a dragon had exploded on the roof. Huge beams of timber were being scorched as opaque smoke billowed in and around the chambers. He could feel the poisonous potion race through his veins, manifesting itself into every cell and mutating like a virus. But this sickness gave him strength like never before. The giant bones in his legs felt as if they were growing and the torn muscles repaired by each turbocharged cell in his body. It had been an age since he had been able to unfurl and stretch them out, forever enclosed in the confinements of the boiler room. He clawed his strange crab-like feet into the rubble and pushed up, he pushed so hard his back raised the collapsing boiler roof like hot lava rising the crust of the earth. The roof splintered, and all the furniture sitting above it came tumbling down. Heaving himself with clawed fists he punched through the roof, releasing a vacuum of swirling hot and cold air from above. With oxygenating gills, it filtered the poisoned air and emerged out of the smokey grey vapour vortex of the burning castle.

The lucky ones who escaped turned back and stood frozen in fear as Drokura rose its head and continued to stand so high that it seemed to be higher than the castle itself. Bellowing his lungs out, he lifted his deep blue crusty head high above the flames and reached his tentacle arms out for the winds to grab and claw at, howling at a momentary release. This ancient creature that had laid dormant opened its two-dozen black eyes, reflecting the fiery chaos surrounding it. The flames did little but warm the greasy crust covering its face and body, coated layers from so many years stuck underground. Its tongue was a hideous creature within itself. It poked and flicked like a five metre eel, hiding in the cave of the enormous and terrible mouth, and lashed across its face, scraping the thick black icing-like dirt encrusted around its eyes.

Drokura clawed over the rubble and pulled himself up and over the debris to freedom, out onto the hard muddy ground on the other side.

He felt the oily sacks on his back had heated up to the point of boiling. He clawed behind and scraped his claws across and they began to burst and pour down his back like hot tar. In pain and anger, he rose up on his hind legs, towering over the crumbling castle. He then felt the poison pumping through his entire body, mutating him with each and every pump of infected blood bubbling through his veins. The sickness within him grew with the mutations. Drokura shivered uncontrollably; he felt hot then cold and then he collapsed, falling to his knees. Like the rapid flow of the poisonous Cassan River, Drokura regurgitated across the mountain a wave of thick chunky black vomit.

The lucky creatures that escaped weren't so lucky.

"Drokura!" screamed Varin Eel from above.

Drokura looked up into the night sky and saw a huge creature flying above. With a violent roar, he reached out attacking it, flinging thick black poison into the air with every swing.

"Stop that at once!" she screamed down at him.

With every eye, Drokura could see her, perched high on her flying best, pointing at him with her bony claws. She flew in closer, and he stood still staring, his eyes glowing a sickly yellow with rage.

"Look what they've done to you, quick get in the moat at once before you burn to death!" shouted Varin.

Drokura was so fuelled up he didn't realise his condition. He was seeping black blood from wounds across his back, and his body was covered with flaming cinders; several curling limbs now hung lifeless by his side and dirty dry blood stuck to his dark blue skin.

Yanking his immense frame, he stumbled forward and dove into the deep murky water. He swam across the moat like a giant mutant dog, sloshing and sprouting jets of muddy water. He dipped his head deep under and cooled his stinging skin, moaning in relief as the pain diminished. There was silence in the mud, and he could only hear a faint crackle of the burning castle.

Drokura poked his head out of the muddy water, sniffing at the air and with his many eyes he peered up at Varin Eel.

"Drokura you can't hide in there forever. Half your body is still on the land. I will take you to the sea—a vast ocean, you will be free to swim." Varin watched him stare off as his eyes reflected the burning castle.

Yes, you will be an easy one to control. Clasping her claws tight, she began to chant as her minions watched eagerly from afar. She reached out to him and pulled back with force. As if he was on an invisible leash his head yanked up. Yes, always easy with the big dumb ones. She was in control of him now.

Drokura's back and curling tentacles rose out of the moat, and he released gallons of muddy water through the vents on the side of his neck.

"Come my pet. You can't fight on an empty stomach. I will make you stronger, unstoppable."

Drokura stood upon the muddy embankment wiping the muck from his body and revealing more of his enormity.

Several poisoned sacks hung by his sides while others had drained completely. The clear cysts behind his arms were full of yellow grease as dead pupa swirled about as he moved forward.

Varin smirked as he followed her command, "Follow me!" she roared.

Varin lead Drokura up and across the mountain to the other side; to the place she found so long ago, to the rock that pierced down like a giant shard into the Veelin River.

"The Stone of Thorns!"

She smiled as it came into view. "There Drokura! Drink the water will make you unstoppable."

Like the river, the surrounding trees had become monsters twisting together and forming a barricade, letting no one enter for miles but as Drokura tore forward he crushed them down like paper trees.

"Drink!" said Varin.

But Drokura refused and shook his head wildly.

"You will drink, or you will die!" she roared.

News of the White Knights spread throughout Gonzo's entire circus, but what sparked equivalent frenzy was the vision that Malom Gipanick foreshadowed.

Malom, on occasion, could astral travel and on this particular morning he awoke in a blanket of nervous sweat, "Monster!" he blurted out as his wife leapt backwards from the bed.

"Who are you calling a monster? I'm just trying to get my cookbook you've gone and rested your feet against!"

"No, not you dearest, I saw a monster, in my dreams."

"Oh Malom, you must stop the night snacks, no more toasted cheese sandwiches! You've gone and had one of your cheese dreams."

"You're the only cheese in my dreams woman, I must tell Gonzo at once," he said strapping on his overalls.

"This was more than just a nightmare; it was a premonition!"

"Right then, if you hurry the store will still be open. Can you pick up some milk while you're out."

"Bah woman, go milk yourself!"

Malom ran to Gonzo's cabin, and he was relieved when Eddie answered the door and Gonzo was awake.

"Malom, is everything all right?" asked Eddie.

"No, it's not Eddie. It's sensational news about the White Knights, but regrettably I bring bad news."

"You better come in then, looks like it's one of those days."

Malom stepped inside and instantly saw Garivin knocked out in the corner of Gonzo's cabin.

"Don't mind Garivin, he's just taking a little nap," said Eddie.

"What seems to be the problem Malom?" asked Gonzo.

"A giant like no other, flames in the darkness, a castle in ruins!"

"A premonition," said Gonzo.

"The Crystalon Castle?" questioned Eddie.

"No, it was Castle Morne! I could tell from the giants skull and its bones surrounding the mountain, that place is frightening even from above."

"Castle Morne!" said Gonzo his fist tightening, "but that's where the White Knights are known to be! What army did this?"

"No army Gonzo, an ancient. I followed the giant the best I could before the missus woke me up, hideous thing it was."

"The creature or your missus?" said Eddie.

"You won't be laughing when I put this in your face!" said Malom waving his fist in the air.

"There, there Malom settle down," said Eddie, who was clearly the strongest.

Malom took a seat and told them how he had followed the path of destruction sewn by Drokura. It had torn through the muddy currents of the Cassan River and dodged being swept off the endless waterfall by wading along the poor Bridge's to the other side. It conquered the Baroque Woods by smashing its way through the thorny branches as if they were sand. Drokura caught his breath at the Porcelain Ponds, and it was there that Malom witnessed the creature in clear sight. It washed the thorns away, and the black oils from its body; dark blue and black rings covered its sweaty skin. With tentacles twisting from its back, the giant stood in a daze with enormous clawed fists by its side. It stretched all its limbs out wide as if electrified.

"If what you've seen is real, and not a dream, we're all in trouble," said Gonzo.

"Yes I hope so. So much devastation left in its path, if it is real, the creature moves fast. I last saw it on the edge of the Valley, Tjaman's land, near the Temple of Thought," said Malom.

"Tjaman can hide in the valley, but if it continues South—" said Gonzo.

"The kingdom isn't equipped to take on a giant; it will destroy them."

"Yes Eddie, it will be bad news," said Gonzo. "You didn't happen to see the White Knights did you Malom? Together they could bring down any giant."

"Sorry Gonzo, I was transfixed on the creature, but I saw something else just before I woke.

"Go on," said Gonzo transfixed.

"I'm certain a witch fly's by its side. Possibly controls the beast."

Gonzo closed his eyes and took a slow deep breath, "Are you sure? A witch."

"What? On this giant's shoulder? Going for a joy ride?" said Eddie.

"Quiet Eddie."

"No, above the giant circled a winged beast with a dark figure at its helm, I flew in close; it was just as frightening as the creature below it."

There was silence and after a moment Gonzo stared up Eddie, then turned across to Garivin and back, "I have a feeling everything is connected. If your right Malom we must get to the castle before they do."

Jacqueline Davis pulled into the Boots' driveway and Robin, who had been hiding behind the curtains beside the front window, spotted her immediately and raced back into the kitchen.

"Eve, she's here!" he shouted into the intercom attached to the wall.

Evelin replied back down it from her room, "Well, she's come to see you, go and let her in."

"I can't believe Miss Davis has appeared back in our lives," said Cory as she was sitting at the end of the bed and gazing into the aquarium.

"Believe it," said Evelin.

"They're a good match I guess. I think every stupid boy in my year had a crush on her, then she moved to Yellow Tree High, they were devastated, it was a hormonal implosion."

"Gross," said Evelin. "She doesn't teach anymore."

"Right, what does she do now then?"

"She has a bakery in town."

"Oh, so I guess she's filled out then."

"No, not really, I think she has a high metabolism, or she doesn't eat her own cakes."

"Hmm, I could eat a cake right now," said Cory getting up.

"No doubt she brought some treats for Robin ... or a basket of eggs," said Evelin.

"Eggs? Yuck, no thanks."

"Come on, we better go downstairs, Robin will be rattling on."

"What about you, how do you feel?"

"Nervous, I feel jumpy."

"Don't you worry Eve, I'll be right by your side. You're a good kid Boots."

"Hey, you're only a year older than me."

The girls descended down to the kitchen to find Robin about to give Miss Davis a tour of the kitchen. He was demonstrating his craftsmanship and running his palm over the kitchen bench top.

"And this is the kitchen bench which I crafted from a deceased hull of an old 40ft Double ended Ketch ... ah, that's a boat."

"Not to mention the cupboard doors, chairs, and pantry," said Evelin.

"Oh, hello Evelin," said Miss Davis stepping forward and shaking her hand.

"Hi Miss Davis," said Evelin. "You remember Cory?"

"It's been a while, but I never forget a student, but I'm also in your father's book club at the library. He talks about you more than the books we're discussing, photos too."

"He shows photos? Argh that is so embarrassing ... thanks, Miss," said Cory raising her brow.

"We best be off," said Evelin. It's going to be a bit of a ride.

"OK Eve, just cruise you have plenty of time, and remember ... call me if you need to," said Robin.

Cory and Evelin left the kitchen and rode their bikes across the street where Milton was waiting. They rode through the leafy suburban streets and headed toward the beach and ultimately Esta Greens. It wasn't long before they crossed Hammer Park and the wind picked up pushing them from behind. Milton and Cory could smell the salt in the air and knew they were getting close, but Eve spotted gulls flying overhead and could hear the waves crashing. She rode up ahead with Cory racing beside her.

"Come on Milton, slow poke!" shouted Evelin.

Before they knew it, they were standing on the corner, at the very top of the Clair Street that wound it's way along the coast. Eve pointed to the last building on the cove. They looked at Esta's ramshackle house and pondered a thousand and one thoughts between them. Evelin thought it moved further away from the other houses with each visit. The gulls hovered high above the house in the blasting sea winds, and several perched themselves behind the smoking chimney, whose fire was as usual, ablaze in the middle of the day.

So rough, wild, nothing could survive out there, thought Evelin turning her gaze to the crashing waves and rolling white caps.

Today the ocean seemed to be unusually rough and the wind took hold of Evelin's hair. Cory smiled as her hair did the same and like a couple of young witches, they pointed and laughed at each other.

Together they rode on and when they arrived parked the bikes by the beach. As they locked them to a rickety wooden fence, Evelin said,

"Hey, thanks for coming guys. This means a lot to me, we're a few minutes early, but we could probably go straight up, plus it's freezing ... and I'm getting quite anxious."

Evelin turned towards Milton, his gaze set on the ocean, "You want to come with us or stay here? I don't mind, I'm happy knowing you're nearby."

"If it's okay, I think I should pass this time around Eve. I'll probably start laughing and mess it all up, and anyway someone's got to keep an eye on the bikes, just look at the state of this driftwood fence."

"That's fine. Find me a lovely shell won't you?" asked Evelin.

"As if ... maybe a crab," he grinned.

"Come on Cory, let's go up then. See you soon Milton."

Together, arm in arm, the two girls pushed their feet through Esta's sandy driveway and towards the house. A fiery-haired figure stood out on the porch.

Cory asked, "Is that her?"

"Sure is."

"Wow, you didn't tell me she was a witch."

"Now Cory, play nice."

Esta stood on the front porch with Mr. Barnaby in her hands. The girls ran up the staircase and noticed how the wind was blocked by the lattice walls, not even a leaf blew around.

"Hello Eve, beautiful day. I just love it when it's windy on the beach. You must be Cory, my name is Esta, and this is Mr. Barnaby."

"Hello," said Cory tying up her hair.

"Hi Esta, yes very windy, pushed us most of the way. The ocean looks angry," said Evelin.

"The waves are alright, they're just playing around with each other, they do that."

"Who're playing?" asked Cory.

"The wind and the sea. Come on in girls we have work to do," said Esta pointing at their shoes.

Once they got inside Evelin followed Esta into the room on the landing at the top of the staircase and she showed Cory the view from the balcony. They scanned across the cove and spotted Milton as he was the only human dot on the beach. Evelin watched the crashing shoreline then looked out to the jagged horizon. There was nothing but a dark green wash, a stormy sea that surged and sucked, continuously devouring itself over and over.

"Come inside girls, please close the doors, we don't want a gull blowing in here like last week," said Esta.

Cory smiled and pushed Evelin inside, closing the doors behind her. It was warm, the fire was stoked and several cats took front seat.

"Right then, Cory you can sit beside Eve and Eve, please—"

"Hop on the couch," said Evelin.

"Yes, dear."

Evelin sighed, she knew Esta's introduction only too well, but she accepted this and laid down.

Cory moved the hair from Evelin's eyes, "I'll be right here," she said.

"Now we're going to go back, in the water, to where we were last. You understand don't you Eve? This is the only way."

"Yes, can Cory hold my hand?"

"At times she can, but not always, don't forget you are the one who needs to take control. And you will." Esta then turned a stern eye to Cory. "Now Cory remember it's a privilege you are here, please understand you must follow any directions I give you as well. Do not interfere, no matter what Evelin may say or do."

Evelin's eyes rolled up towards her, "Cory?"

"Of course! Not as if this is an exorcism."

"Call it what you wish," said Esta. "Are you ready Evelin?"

"I guess ..."

"Good, I'm going to count to twenty and with each number I want you to open your eyes and then close with the next. We're going to go straight back to the coral, underwater, yes?"

"Yes," said Evelin.

"Good let's begin. One ... open your eyes ... two—close your eyes now ... three ... open ... four ... close them ... five ... six ... seven ... eight ... nine ..."

It was then that Cory watched on in awe as Eve closed her eyes with the soothing counting and ascent of the numbers and then her eyes began flickering under her eyelids. Esta moved forward and picked up Evelin's arm by the wrist and dropped it. It fell like a wet towel and to Cory's amazement Evelin was under.

Kostis and Gustus sat on watch high above the Crystalon Castle's main drawbridge. "It's just the way things are my friend," said Kostis, "living creatures are classified into species, which in turn belong to larger groups of families. New species are still being discovered and named, and the important thing is to determine if it's a completely new species or a variant. The law of the land allows if you find something before someone else has, then you can call it whatever you like."

"So if I found a Zempadom with the head of a Catlor Beetle, I could call it anything?" Gustus enquired innocently.

"Don't tell me you found one?"

"Not yet."

"Good it sounds like it would leave a nasty bite. But yes that's right. For example, the Yellow-Bellied Ilk neither has a yellow belly, nor is it really an ilk. And the Toothy Weasel, is not really a weasel, it's more of an overgrown Helmette Mouse with the top half of a bird's beak—and how many beaks have teeth—apart from a Dina-Schniza which technically isn't a bird but a Wimble?" quizzed Kostis.

"I guess you're right, you're very clever Kostis," said Gustus, "I thought creatures were called such things because there were no more names left."

"Language means there are many word combinations and many descriptions for things that need naming. Words can make an infinite number of names, but you still must be original with your combinations. The good news is Mare-Mare is becoming quite fertile, a change is in the air can you sense it? Just the other day an enormous list of undiscovered creatures were newly named and announced. It's as if they're falling from the sky. Just imagine finding something new and naming it for the rest of its life.

"Like the King Gustus Beetle?"

"Yes, I like the sound of that. But what if you discovered a unique porcelain mouse that had wings, what would you call it?"

"A flying porcelain mouse?" shrugged Gustus.

"See, completely unoriginal and a to be frank a little too obvious."

"Oh ... then ... the King Gustus Beetle!" said Gustus proudly.

"Yes much better. This is why some of us call things exactly what they're not. You see?" said Kostis.

"I see something, look at that trail of dust out there—Gustus pointed into the distance with is large stubby fingers—I think someone's coming or going. I didn't see anyone? Did you?"

"Open the gate you idiots! I must warn the King at once!" came a sharp voice from below.

"Sergeant Toroto! Ahh, I see, are you in a hurry or are you just zipping around at your usual pace?" shouted Kostis.

"Open the drawbridge you slow-witted fool! Sound the alarms, a beast is coming, a savage giant from unknown lands!" Sergeant Toroto jumped up and down shouting as his tiny Raeen bird joined him.

"He sounds serious, better let him in," said Kostis.

Gustus leant slightly on the drawbridge lever and instantly the door rose. Toroto and his bird squeezed though the first signs of a gap and together raced off. Only a trail of dust could be seen as they disappeared inside.

"Even you would look like a giant to that little guy," smiled Gustus.

"No my friend, I'm afraid something is coming."

King Vera pointed at the towering stairwell and ordered Belleny and Bateau, "Both of you must go to your quarters at once!"

"Father what's going on? It's Varin Eel isn't it?" asked Belleny.

"Stop asking questions, please go to your room!"

"I am, I was just—"

Toroto raced into the room before she could continue and said, "Greetings your Majesty, Commander Garon, oh my Princess Belleny it's my honour."

"Hello, little one. Oh, I remember you at the singing reeds. Your little bird is so cute! Who made your suit, it's adorable."

"You do? He is? It is? Well, my wife sews most—"

"Belleny! I will not ask again!" roared King Vera.

"Fine I'm going, but I want to be informed at once at the fist sign of danger!"

Garon waited for Belleny to reach her stairwell before he asked,

"At ease Sergeant, something positive to report I hope?"

Toroto shook his head, "I'm afraid not, The Watchers have confirmed that an ancient, a giant belonging to the sea is heading South towards the kingdom."

Drokura! thought Belleny, who paused waiting and listening in.

"Does it come alone?" asked Garon.

"No Sir, it does not. Someone travels with it, high in the clouds on a savage, winged beast."

"Varin Eel!" gasped Belleny.

"Belleny, to your room I said," roared her father.

Kale entered the room dressed in his dark leather armour and headgear, he held a large staff, one end a blade and the other a large metal claw.

"Kale!" said Belleny, "Drokura is on his way here and Varin Eel!"

"Yes, Princess. You must—"

"I know, I know, return to my room. Come on Bateau we have to prepare," she said, holding him in her arms.

"Belleny!" said Garon.

"Yes Garon."

"Stay up there, that's a double order."

Belleny's head dropped to the floor. "Yes Sir," she said firmly and left.

"Where is their current location?" asked Kale.

"My scouts first sighted the giant in the far north of the Baroque Woods, just south of Castle Morne."

"So Drokura survived the collapse of the castle," growled Garon.

"But then the creature went west even though the terrain was most difficult," said Toroto, "the scouts followed as it travelled to the Veelin River. It was drawn to a strange black rock, nearly as tall and unnerving as the giant himself. It looked as if it had fallen from the sky and stabbed straight into the Veelin River. We've never seen it before."

"Most unnerving. Go on," said Garon.

"The river surrounding it seemed to be severely poisoned, black and muddy. We believe it is from this rock, that the North is being poisoned and the river is spreading its poison our way."

"And the witch and her giant, why would they go there?" asked Kale.

"This is where it gets worse. Of all things the giant drank the black water surrounding the rock and reports say it doubled in size," said Toroto.

"This must be the source of the witch's potion!" said Kale.

"A bleeding stone," said the King, "it has to be removed at once!"

"Last reports the enemy was spotted on the edge of Kay Kasa. Their arrival into Mare-Marie kingdom is imminent. I dare say it will have no obstacles crossing the valley, nor across the baron Tonerae Mountains.

Once they reach the Highland Forest, it will level the trees, but perhaps the Slate Cliffs may prevent it from advancing any further, the vertical ascent is a deathly steep drop even for a giant.

"Hmm and if it passes the cliffs?" asked King Vera.

"Once it finds a path through the Woven Woods, the enemy could reach the Crystalon Castle by the early hours of the morning," added Toroto.

Kale shook his head and said, "The Slate Cliffs will only stall them once they get down and through the Woven Woods there will be nothing to stop them. We must gather all Kylen riders and bring it down before it steps foot on this side."

"Kale go get Danté," said Garon, standing up tall, "I'll assemble an army of Kylen riders. King Vera we'll need to barricade the perimeter walls and line the Queens Garden hedge with every last one of your men. We must prepare for the worst."

Poskar peered through the metal barred gates, his gaze followed the curve up along the watery stairway. Anxiously he felt the presence of a shadow thief and something more than monstrous up ahead.

There you are. His eyes widened as Drokura's monstrous silhouette appeared at the top of the Slate Cliffs. As it leant forward, he could see its chest pumping in and out, inhaling through it's gargling gills and dripping black blood from skin wounds back into the Veelin River below. Its enormous legs stood solid, as its heavy tentacles continuously moved and swirled around its body as if they were powered by their own brains. Poskar gasped as he saw a black shadow zip in and out of a cloud.

"You are forbidden to pass Varin Eel! Return to the black hole from which you crawled from, or your next move may be your last."

Harrowing laughter came from above, "Oh Poskar you seem to forget, I've taken over much more than just any old shadow, you can't stop me anymore, no one can."

Poskar raised his hand up to the witch, bending his long white fingers towards her, "You will fall."

"Fool! We could be powerful allies, free to devour any shadow we wished."

"You have gone too far Varin Eel, you know that is not how it works!"

"All you warlocks are the same," she croaked. "You have lived way too long on borrowed time. Forward Drokura! Crush this insolent pest!"

Drokura obeyed and with surprising speed, lashed his tentacles into the water and drove his body forward, down the river stairwell. Poskar remained behind the massive gates. Drokura surged forward and bashed his fists into the gates, and with his tentacles pulled at the metal bars with immeasurable force. The gate didn't budge and Drokura screamed out in anger, spitting chunks of foul blackness through the gate but Poskar didn't move.

"Why don't you go back and try jumping from the cliffs?" said Poskar.

"I don't think that will be necessary," said Varin Eel as she appeared from out of an oily shadow on his side of the gates. Standing tall on her spidery legs she snarled, "You and I are the same Poskar, stop fooling yourself."

"There is a difference between us. I will not be bought cheaply on whims and fancy.

Drokura continued to latch his arms around the gate, like a giant squid out of water, he grabbed at everything and nothing, feeling for an exit. His two dozen eyes were inky black and absorbed as much light as possible to glimpse his prey. His tentacles almost twice as long as his body seemed to flourish and grow longer in the water.

"Take your hideous beast and return from whence you came, you have no business entering the kingdom," said Poskar furiously.

Varin Eel crept forward and said, "Oh but I do shadow thief, I have an appointment with King Vera and his dear Princess."

It was then Poskar felt Drokura's tentacle wrap around his leg and tighten the grip. With an open hand, he summoned a great power from within and forced the white ball of light against Drokura's flesh, scorching the skin like toffee in the sun. The giant screeched and retracted furiously.

Varin whipped out with her long thin arms, scraping at the dry ground in front of him. In a flash, Poskar banged his staff against the ground and he leapt into the air. His face stricken with panic for a second then his expression was of relief as his shadow reappeared on landing. But Varin didn't give up and with each scrape he was forced to jump back and back until his back was up against the gates.

Drokura venomously latched outward, grabbing him and pinning his arms around Poskar's neck, strangling him tightly against the iron bars. Varin knelt down in front of Poskar and clawed the ground before him. His shadow bubbled and like half dry paint solidified into an oily pool. She held it high up in front of him.

Poskar screamed out in agony, watching helplessly as Drokura tightened his grip.

"Hush now, what's good for the goose," mocked Varin as her own shadow morphed into a seething and hungry swarm of rats, whipping and twisting around the shadow devouring it as it tried to escape. She pushed it deep into the ground and her shadow consumed the blackness.

"What a shame it is to lose your shadow, and you powers—prepare to die," said Varin lifting her hand towards him.

Drokura released Poskar and lifeless he collapsed to the floor, the tainted water gushing against his translucent grey face and his floppy corpse. Drokura pushed up against the iron gate and felt it buckle beneath his weight. With a joyous roar, he tore the metal from their hinges and forced himself inside, along with a Tsunami of oily crashing waves.

"Danté? What's happening to you?" gasped Kale.

"The pain! Poskar!" cried Danté collapsing to his knees. He had experienced such an exacting pain rip through his entire body only once before; the day Poskar took his own shadow.

Danté leant down on his hands and limb by limb he fell to the floor as if he were a marionette with his strings cut one by one. Kale called for help as Danté's eyes became black smoky pearls and lifeless.

"Don't worry I know who can help," said Kale picking him up with both arms.

"What's happened?" called Garon as he ran towards them.

"It's Danté, he collapsed," said Kale,

"Oh no, what's happened to his eyes! This is witchery!" said Garon

"I'm afraid you're right, we must get him to my mother at once."

Together they took Danté to Lucretia's room and placed Danté on the bed next to her.

Belleny came running into the room with Bateau in her arms, "Danté! What's wrong with him? He looks poisoned. Tell me he'll be okay!"

Kale held up his hand and silenced her, waiting patiently for Lucretia to open her eyes, "Mother can you hear me, Danté is unwell, his eyes lifeless—I fear a dark sorcery has been bestowed upon him."

Lucretia frowned at first and then opened her eyes. She nodded slowly and turned to the lifeless Danté, "It was only a matter of time I'm afraid. His other half is dead."

"What other half?" said Garon.

"His shadow," said Lucretia.

"But Poskar has his shadow," said Belleny.

"Not anymore ... Poskar took good care of it. Without a doubt, it's been ripped from beneath him and eaten by another shadow thief."

"Varin Eel," added Kale.

"She can't destroy it, but now it is hidden in the darkness of her own, unattached, lost amongst the others she has stolen. I'm afraid he will be dead by sunrise if it is not returned to its owner, no one can survive for long without one."

Belleny hung her head and held Danté's hand. She turned to Kale with watery eyes. Lucretia continued,

"Shadows are known to go astray, even swap with others during the night. If they attach to someone else you can survive, but if they are eaten by a necromancer like Varin Eel ... his body will dry up and blacken like charcoal," said Lucretia.

"Like those we saw in Castle Mourne! No! Not Danté!" cried Belleny.

Kale tightened his fist and said, "Damn that also means they've reached the Slate Cliffs ... poor old Poskar."

"We must prepare for an attack," said Garon.

*

Meanwhile, Drokura was lumbering along the Slate Cliff perimeter, looking up at the towering wall of rock above.

"Move Drokura! Move! We're so close!" screamed Varin as she circled the giant, but he was stuck between the Slate Cliffs and the enormous wall of the Woven Woods. Drokura pushed hard against the tree's, but the huge trunks wouldn't budge.

"Stop!" roared Varin, "Drokura get back up the cliff, see if you can crawl over this weed!"

At the same time the evil was clambering over woodland and rocks, Belleny returned to her chamber as she couldn't bear to see Danté lying lifeless and couldn't stand the thought of him withering into charcoal.

"Don't worry Belleny, I'm sure Kale will get his shadow back ... somehow," said Bateau gingerly touching her arm. "Shh, a moment, do you hear that? Listen, there's music in the distance ... I don't believe my ears!" said Bateau.

"What? What is it?"

"It's Gonzo, it's the song of the Horgons! The convoy of the Great Gonzo Circus!"

"Gonzo, this is Denkar, we've arrived at the border!"

Denkar seated high up on his driving seat, squinted one eye and looked through a long telescope, "There is still some distance to travel. I see many Kylen riders circling in the sky, I see soldiers lined up on the far side of the castle, no signs of danger, but it looks as though they're preparing for something big."

"We better get down there. Camp the Horgans down, we'll fox across at once. Over and out." Gonzo put down the receiver and looked up at his strong man Eddie, "Doesn't look good Eddie, looks like Malom Gipanick's premonition was very real. Get our strongest folk together, we're going to the castle at once."

Gonzo raced out of his cabin, pushing the carriage door as it clipped heavily against the hanging bell, it was the only sound to be heard as it echoed down the ravine. With a grin he lunged and grabbed onto a large harpoon needle as a choice of weapon and ascended a ladder that lead up to the flying fox, that was perched against his cabin wall. Stopping half way up on a wooden plank that stuck out like a diving board he walked to the very end and pointed down at them.

"All right people listen up, Mare-Marie and its kingdom are in grave danger, we have suspicions the very witch that stole our White Knights is to blame. She has with her an ancient creature, a giant, who has already destroyed one castle and is heading to the Crystalon Castle as we speak! We will do our best to help them, we ride from here. Gather your courage and be prepared for war. There's a annual bonus of your wages, for the person who finds where Bateau or any of the White Knights are kept and in addition I'll give my entire bottle collection to the giant slayer!"

With an explosive cheer from the crowd and a round of applause, Gonzo climbed the ladder all the way to the very top of the flying-fox. With his harpoon in hand, he locked it into a giant crossbow bolted to the stand and with all his force pulled back and cranked and cocked the weapon.

"Need a hand boss?" asked Eddie, who was not far behind him. Eddie hooked a large coil of rope through the harpoon's eyelet and locked it. He then aimed the spear into position.

"Wait!" said Gonzo opening up his jacket. He took from his shoulder a coil of brightly lit canisters and clipped them to the harpoon.

"Good thinking Gonzo."

"Go for it Eddie."

Eddie lit the fuse and they stood back with their fingers in ears.

"Fire!" roared Gonzo as he pulled the trigger, launching the needle into the air and towards the castle. One by one the canisters exploded in the night's sky releasing huge clouds of vibrant colour and sparkles.

"Wow! Look at that!" said Kostis running around to get a better view as the harpoon soared through the air with a trail of colour and light.

"It's magic!" said Gustus.

"Yes but it's coming right for us!" said Kostis taking cover.

"Gustus get out of the way!" he cried out, but Gustus was clearly more interested in the harpoon's sparkles and colours and with only seconds until full impact he reached out with his giant hands.

"What are you doing?" shouted Kostis squinting his eyes, "it's a harpoon, not a ball, you can't catch it!"

But it was too late and the flash of the weapon made Kostis shut his eyes tightly and he shook his head slowly, "Why? Why did you only have half a brain and not a full one, why?" Kostis banged his hand against the ground.

"Look I caught it!" said Gustus pulling at the rope attached.

"What? You caught it? You big fool! Quick pull it around this pillar and tie it on, it's the end of a flying-fox, their flying-fox to travel the length of the ravine," said Kostis pointing up at the giant Horgons.

"I know! It's The Great Gonzo Circus! I'm so excited Kostis!"

At once Gustus wound the rope, secured it and flicked it with his thick forefinger, it was taut and both Kostis and Gustus waved their arms in the air for the go ahead.

"Looks like we're good to go on that side boss," said Eddie peering through his telescope.

"This is going to be fun!" said Gonzo stretching from side to side, "I'll see you at the castle."

Like a fish to water Gonzo attached his personal flying-fox handle and jumped into the air, hundreds of metres off the ground and raced off down towards the castle.

"Now that's how you do it people!" shouted Eddie latching onto the flying-fox and with that sped off behind Gonzo.

"Look Kostis! Here they come!" Jumped Gustus clapping his big hands together.

"Well, move to the side, unless you're going to catch them as well."

*

It was high up in Belleny's tower, Bateau and the Princess watched as the blackened silhouetted shapes zipped through the night air towards the castle.

"They're coming! Gonzo's coming Bateau!" said Belleny. "Come now, we must go tell the Orphans!"

Belleny grabbed her jacket and mask and ran for the door. She couldn't believe it, such terrible things were happening on one side of the castle yet on the other a long-awaited reunion was about to finally unfold.

Belleny's anticipation was exacerbated by the loud call of the Horgons as they woke up the White Knights in the Jungle Room and like little children running around at Christmas they giggled and grabbed at each other giddy for the meeting of their old and dear friends.

It wasn't long before Gonzo and his circus folk gathered at the castle gates, joyously greeting and being towered over by Gustus running between his legs and in a stream of colour they followed Kostis inside the castle walls in a glorious procession of light and noise.

King Vera met with Gonzo with welcoming arms.

"The great GONZO!" roared the king.

"The pleasure is all mine!" said Gonzo, "I hear you have a giant problem."

"You could say that," said King Vera, "I also have two witches and a daughter that won't do what she's told."

"We are here to help," said Gonzo pointing up at his strongman Eddie.

"The necromancer Varin Eel and her giant Drokura are headed here, it will take a lot of good men to win this."

"Then we'll send out the women first!" laughed Gonzo. But his laughter turned into a light splutter.

"Are you all right Gonzo?" said Eddie.

"The White Knights!" said Gonzo, his hands shaking on his chest.

"Oh yes," chuckled the king, "they've been here all along!"

"What do you mean?" said Gonzo grabbing the king.

"Let me explain Gonzo!"

Eddie retrieved Gonzo as King Vera quickly explained what had happened to them. Gonzo watched as four white figures came down the stone path under a long archway and skipped forward on the polished stone floor. To Gonzo, it was an incredible dream and with a loud and glorious cry he stumbled forward with his arms open wide.

"My friends!"

Gonzo!" they shouted in unison.

The White Knights raced forward and launched upon him, nuzzling him over and over, "Gonzo! We're back!" they shouted.

"Look how beautiful you have grown. Where have you been all this time?" Gonzo looked at them and paused, "But where is Barera?"

"Poor Esdaile," sighed Palia.

"He's not with us anymore Gonzo," said Dillon.

"We've been under a terrible curse, we had no idea who we were," said Montë.

"My poor White Knights, such sad news," said Gonzo.

Belleny approached silently and stood next to her father. To see her smile again brought a tear to his eye.

Gonzo looked up at her, "And you must be Princess Belleny, the girl that broke the witch's curse ... I can't say in words how grateful I am."

Belleny stood a little closer and looked into all of Gonzo's big watery eyes, "I had the help of one very special person."

"Who might that be so I can praise them as well?"

"Your two-tailed friend," said Belleny and paused as Gonzo whispered, "Bateau?"

Gonzo's face started to wobble, the big round eyes on the side of his head filled like pools and his mouth wobbled as tried to speak.

"B ... Bateau, is here? My little boy!" he cried out dramatically, falling to his knees, "This is the happiest day of my life!" He rolled onto the ground as the Orphans still overjoyed stuck to him like glue. Bateau hid behind a structure in the archway, listening to Gonzo's joy he wanted to gloat quietly to himself at the love and commotion. Belleny turned to call Bateau from out of hiding. Before she could speak she watched as Gonzo, the fat little circus master, ran down the corridor swiftly sweeping up little Bateau and holding him up to the air.

"My little Bateau! Ha ha ha! It's you, it's really you! We're all back together again!"

The embrace was enough to make Eddie cry.

"So you didn't leave me?" said Bateau.

"What? Leave you! No! Never!" said Gonzo.

"Garivin said you wanted to get rid of me. I was on Kabela's roof sleeping when all of a sudden he started pushing me into a dirty sack. He told me I was nothing but a troublemaker and I talked too much and that you wanted me out of the circus. Next thing I know I woke up in an alleyway."

"It was all Kabela's fault, we'll have no more trouble from her," said Eddie.

"Eddie it's good to see you!" said Bateau.

"You too my little friend, it's been quiet without you around."

"Gonzo, I hate to disrupt this glorious reunion, but Varin Eel and her giant is on her way, I have to help my men defend the castle."

By now Varin Eel had forced Drokura back to the top of the watery, stone stairwell, his poisonous black blood pooled into the water below.

"Move!" said Varin pulling him with her claws in the air.

Drokura tipped forward, towards the cliff edge and he fell across the treetops. He cleared the gap easily and landed heavily upon the Woven Woods snapping through sixty trees in the middle of the canopy.

"To the castle!" she roared.

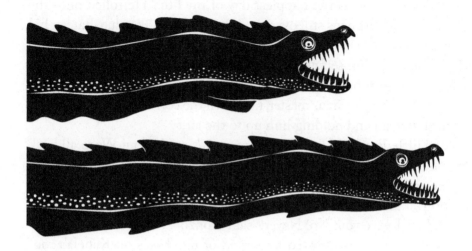

C ory looked on aghast as Evelin's body began to twitch and she muttered, "The sea, it's rough, the swell it's pulling me under!"

"Go into the water Evelin, it will be calmer underwater. That's right dear, remember it's you Eve, who is in control," said Esta calmly, "let the swell become a ride, go with the flow, as they say."

Evelin struggled still under and Cory felt it was like looking at her best friend through a glass bottom boat. She could see a physical Eve, but her mind and conscious was elsewhere.

"No Esta, I'm afraid, I don't want to go down," she said as the water sucked her with its full force and pulled her down towards the bottom. It spun her upside-down and pulled her sideways, nudging her towards a wall of green thick reeds. Darkness surrounded her as they swamped their wet clammy limbs over her body and the swell continued to pull her out into the endless blue. Evelin felt lifeless as the water became deeper, distant and the swell lost all of its strength.

"Are you all right Eve?" asked Esta.

"I am now, I'm drifting," she whispered.

"I see something in front of me ... bright colours ... it's coral."

Evelin drifted slowly towards a rocky ledge, its entire surface covered in a flourish of hues and movement. As she approached, the beautiful clusters of sea anemone stretched out with their coloured tentacles and held her fingers, twisting her around, and pulling her back against the coral wall.

"Hey, what are you doing? You're tickling me," she said as she laughed.

"Who's tickling you Evelin?" asked Esta.

"The sea flowers," she replied.

Cory watched on in disbelief, *Sea flowers? Where is she? I've never seen her giggle like a kid before.*

Evelin effortlessly pulled herself from the sea flowers, but they persistently tried to coil and pull her back. She noticed her hair drifting weightlessly around her, then she watched as it moved to the side and off her face. The water had begun to swirl and the sea flowers held on tighter.

Instantly Evelin panicked and turned in every direction, "The whirlpool, it's back! I want out!" she cried as the water surged before her.

Cory rose towards Evelin, but Esta held out her hand silently in front of her as a sign to sit back down.

"You destroyed the whirlpool before and you can do it again Eve, it has no power unless you give in to it, do not be afraid," said Esta.

"Oh no, they're here! Get away!" cried Evelin, as she yanked herself free and climbed to the top of the ledge.

There was nowhere for her to duck or hide as two horrifying shapes circled her.

"No! Please you're scaring me," she cried.

Cory reached out holding Evelin's hand.

Esta nodded that it was all right and said, "What's scaring you Evelin? Remember you are in control."

Eve's voice deepened to an octave lower than normal, "The giant Eels, they're here."

Giant eels? thought Cory as her hand was squeezed tight within Evelin's grip. She nervously looked across at Esta for reassurance.

The eels approached slowly from behind and passed by either side of Evelin. Their jaws opening and closing as if they were stretching without reaching satisfaction.

"Leave me alone!" mouthed and bubbled Eve under the water.

Cory turned to Esta with anxious eyes, "Wake her!" she said.

Esta held out her hand to silence Cory, as a gust of sea wind shook the patio doors.

"Why do you hate the eels Eve? Why are you afraid of them?" asked Esta.

"They scream at me because they know the truth."

"What do they know?"

"That I'm a bad person," said Evelin.

Oh no, she's going to tell her about the library!

Please Eve don't tell her!

Don't say anything!

Cory squeezed Evelin's hand, hoping she would feel her inner thoughts somehow.

"You're not a bad person Evelin, no matter what an eel may think," said Esta as the fire crackled behind them.

The eels began to circle around her, disappearing behind the peak of the ledge to reappear in front of the growing whirlpool.

"Are you here to kill me?" sobbed Evelin as the eels stared back at her in silence. "I'm too weak, I can't hide anymore, go on just take me, we both know I don't deserve to be here."

Cory looked up at Esta and shook her head nervously.

"Why don't you deserve to be here?" asked Esta.

"You know, don't you?" said Evelin staring back at the eels as if it was a competition.

"Can I talk to the eels Eve?" asked Esta.

"Yes you can try. They just scream at me without making a noise. Be quick, the whirlpool is growing!"

"Trust me, they can talk, you just hold on Eve and relax. Eels can you hear me?" asked Esta, her tone sent shivers down Cory's spine. She felt Evelin's grip loosen and slip, her hand flopped and hung beside her.

There was silence.

Evelin jolted once on the couch and a frown dawned across her face.

"Of course," said Evelin representing one of the eels, her voice cold and harsh.

A demon?

She is possessed! thought Cory.

Esta continued as if the giant eels were there in the room with them, "Eels can you hear me?"

"Of course," said Eve.

"Good. Why do you haunt Evelin? Do you wish to hurt her?" asked Esta.

"We can't hurt her, even if we wanted to," said the Eels, Evelin's voice cracked as she spoke.

"But do you want to?" asked Esta curiously.

"Of course—she wants us to."

Chapter 75 - Calam is Sentenced

Calam Zouraa observed very little of the world and cared less about current events. He associated himself with himself and he liked it that way. For those who were unlucky enough to meet him, these folk usually detained passengers, they all became saddened at the sight of his prison cart trailing away into the distance. It wasn't simply the fact that they were now stranded in the middle of the desert filled with Vicious Candar, but Calam held no judgment towards anyone and he listened to their stories. The good and the bad.

Tonight the fine Lightning Grass of the Lacetin Plains glistened as small sparks of electricity trickled along their thin-leafed bodies. Calam took his time in the rolling fields where it was an easy ride on the gentle grassy slopes. He deserved the rest and so did his newly replaced Kick-Horses. They had done well, nearly as quick as his last set of animals who had been sucked alive into the desert sand by the malicious Viscous Candar.

Calam noticed the wild Lacetin buffalo huddling low to the ground like large hairy rocks. Within the darkness of their broad-horned skulls, sharp wide eyes stared back at him, watching but not blinking.

What's got into them? he thought. With a quick scan of the area, he continued on. He drove his steeds to the top of the last long sloping hill and brought them to a halt. His kick-horses ducked low and munched down on the grass, knowing there would be no more. He could see clearly and scanned the area ahead, it was vacant, flat and as usual the still shallow pools of water remained.

Not a soul in sight, he thought, staring out into the wan and dreamy distance.

Sitting on the horizon sat a continuous spark on the edge of the night sky. He took out his telescope and he could see the shimmering white shell walls of the Crystalon Castle. Although the telescope's lens was cracked, he could still make out the bright, colourful flashes in the sky made from Gonzo's circus.

A festival? Damn! I miss out on everything! That's got to be where everyone is? Maybe it's a food festival? he thought.

Calam's heavy prison cart travelled noisily down the grassy hill. The sound of metal spiked wheels and his horses hooves began to change as the surface morphed from a soft grassy trail to a black sandy plain. Their pointy hooves stabbed into the sand, spraying fans of sand and fine droplets of water through the air with each pool of water they hit.

He had arrived at The Land of the Mirrored Lakes and tonight the pools of water reflected the moonlight hovering above him.

"Slow down girls, I think we all need a drink," said Calam.

With heads down, the kick-horses soaked up the water, viciously dragging their parched tongues through the shallow pools lapping the water eagerly.

Calam climbed down off his cart and shook his thick coat, like diamonds the white sand of Veehn fell onto the black silt ground. He was always glad to reach the pools, although salty the water gave the steeds vigour and increased their stamina. With their heads down the giant steeds towered over Calam. As he passed each one, he gave them a pat and checked their hooves.

"Settle down now, what's wrong girl?" said Calam calming one of the steeds as it began to snort and flare its nostrils. The others began flicking their tails and kicking their front legs.

Calam noticed the pools of water began to ripple. Not just by the kick-horses but across the whole desert.

"What could be doing that?" said Calam, "Stay calm girls, it's probably just a—oh no it can't be—an Ancient!"

From out of the darkness the moonlight shone across Drokura's oily, blood-covered body as he stomped through the exploding pools of water. His body squelched and dripped thick black poison with every step.

Calam's heart raced as he tried to get his horses together. He watched as the giant screamed out loud in a terrifying roar. Its arms came down hitting the ground with an enormous thud, as its tentacles whipped at the pools. It leant back up, and as if cleaning, slid its tentacled arms across its body. Oily black muck fell off in thick wads. As a child, it scraped it off its face and threw it into the air. Like black rain, it flew far and fell hard, covering Calam and his cart exploding like paintballs, splattering against the horse and wheels.

Calam tried not to scream out loud as the black tar seeped into his eyes and stung as if they were splashed with fuel. His kick -horses, stricken with fear, tried to tear themselves loose and kicked in every direction, thrusting the cart forward and sideways in heaving jolts. The sounds of their chains crashing against each other was enough for Drokura and he found them easily. With violent steps, he moved straight towards them. Calam swung his hammer at the bolted chains, hoping to set the frantic steeds free. The horses rose up on their hind legs, "Hold on, wait I'm trying to set you free!" said Calam but it was too dangerous. He cracked his whip at the oily ground beside them. "Just go! Take the damn cart and go!" he shouted.

The kick-horses legs quivered nervously and their hooves slid on the oily ground. Drokura lunged forward, squeezing one of the horses by its waist and pulled it up to its mouth. One after another the horses, still harnessed together by the chains, were lifted towards the creature's mouth.

"Drokura that's enough! Save your strength!" shouted Varin, "soon you can unleash your fury on an entire army."

Even Varin Eel couldn't believe what the oily water by the Stone of Thorns had done to Drokura. He had transformed beyond her wildest dreams. But to control him she knew would take more than words.

Like a cat in trouble for playing with a mouse, Drokura would also have some fun before he would let go. He wrapped his tentacles around the kick-horses and holding one, squeezed it like a tender pea.

"Drop them!" roared Varin with a throaty snarl. Obeying his master, Drokura dropped the horses and whimpered as he pulled back and inspected his now sore limb from where she touched him. Varin lowered her hand and said, "There will be plenty to crush at the castle Drokura, now get a move on!"

Calam lay hidden in the oily muck as the giant stood above him and unlatched its strangling grip. As the cart came smashing down he leapt aside as the horses crashed upside-down. The watery pools turned from moonlight silver, to red, then to black. Calam held back from screaming as he saw the bodies of his poor broken steeds, the ones that were still alive, kicked and cried, scraping their legs and rocking as they tried to stand up.

Drokura continued his playful rampage. He pushed the horses aside like simple play toys and shoved the prison cart out of his way. Calam held on tight as the cart spun and came to a halt as the horses acted like an anchor. With a thumping heart, he watched as the giant stomped off, with the witch close by on her monstrous flying creature.

"Oh no, he stopped!" said Calam peering from his cart."

Please be quiet girls! Please don't come back! he prayed.

Drokura stood quiet as if he was in a trance. The water had washed his eyes and the silvery white puddles surrounding him had caught his many eyes. The giant looked deep down into his reflection. But not as a creature of horror and disgust, he saw through his abnormalities, he recognised his old self and at once remembered a time before he became a vessel of evil. The vision he saw was of Trylis the water serpent, spirited and flowing with luminous liquid blue colours and iridescent light. The water turned into an opaque reflection and the vision was gone.

Calam helped his weakened horses to their feet and watched nervously, *What is it doing? What does it see?* he wondered.

"I said move Drokura! Forward at once!" shouted Varin as she lifted up her bony arm and clenched her fingers into a claw, strangling Drokura's feeble consciousness and controlling him once again.

Lucretia sat up and swung her legs over the side of the bed, her strength was quickly returning. She sat up in the empty room and stared across at Danté knowing he was trapped inside his own body. Soon he would dry up, his flesh and mortal self no longer part of this world morphing into a carbon statue, his soul an eternal prisoner.

"Danté, I know you can hear me," she said softly.

He did not move.

"I know you heard me speak of the consequences of having no shadow, especially when one has lost theirs to a shadow thief," she paused and leant over, slipped her long delicate fingers through his cold and pale his hands.

"I can't make you a shadow Danté, but I can release you before you're trapped in the eternal darkness," she said clenching his palm tight and pinching it in several places. "It has been said to be a pure state, energised as a spirit form."

With rapid gasps, Danté sat up in a possessed manner and cried, "Please Lucretia let me out! I feel like I've have been torn in half! I can't stand it any longer!"

"If I let you out, you can never return to this body—any body."

"Please Lucretia, I understand," he whimpered, "the darkness, it's limitless, suffocating—I don't belong here!"

Danté's chest heaved with every breath as his body began to shake.

"If you survive you will become more than a spirit, an enigma, but always remain Danté Vakares."

Danté gasped the words, "Thank you!" He turned his head towards her and opened his eyes which were completely opaque and black.

"Oh Danté! You poor thing it won't take long," said Lucretia.

"Do it ... please Lucretia," he begged through gritting teeth.

Lucretia placed her hand against Danté's forehead and spoke the pattern of select words, each verse getting louder and louder. Her long white hair rose around her face as if electrified and floating in water. Danté opened his mouth wide and Lucretia could see the swirling black darkness inside him. She continued to weave her spell until she fell back and tumbled over the side of the bed frame. Simultaneously Danté fell back into the bed, his eyes closed and his expression was calm and his tight fists relaxed.

Inside the Lost Realms of Light, Danté was walking in pure darkness, a place void of form. He was shifting from form into pure energy.

Back in the room Lucretia lay silently, and with a gentle smile she watched through teary eyes as a phantom, a strange luminous light emerged from Danté's corpse.

"Lucretia, you have freed me!" said Danté, his voice a symphony of sound and white light. His body levitated and floated in the centre of the room, as light emitted all over it. He moved forward and reached out, touching her gently on the hand. Lucretia's eyes widened as her colour returned and her blood raced through her body.

"What am I? He asked, his body swirling round as if underwater.

"You are free," said Lucretia.

His new form glistened as it floated above his old body. He stared down at it and smiled.

The phantom Danté looked at this reflection in the mirror, and like an apparition he wafted around the room. He moved his twisting hand across the table and like a ghost passed through the teapot and the cups as if they weren't there. No! He grumbled and he grasped at the teapot once again and this time he took it off the table.

"I seem to be here, yet not?" he said.

"You have left the restraints of form, you have no obstacles, your mind is your will," she said.

Then like a frightened squid his body changed colour, rippling in a wave of dark light, "I can hear her so clearly now. She's so afraid."

"Who?" asked Lucretia.

"I don't know … I must go, beyond the mountainous borders, far across the sea—a girl beckons me, she needs me and I feel this stronger than ever before. I must go to her, this is my destiny."

"You are free, follow your destiny Danté," said Lucretia, hair was changing as she spoke, from silvery white to a rich chocolate brown.

"Farewell Lucretia, thank you! I will be back."

Lucretia smiled as he disappeared through the window. She turned to his crumpled body on the bed, slowly it turned black like coal and then crumbled to dust beneath the sheets.

Without delay, Danté flew East towards the Sea of Sorrow, his destination the Untouched Tower. With the land of Mare-Marie far below him, he wafted through the clouds and on the horizon he could see the white spray from the ocean smashing hard against the Zale Mountain's shoreline. The foamy whitewash blasted into the air like a watery volcano and came crashing down on the other side. Sorrow filled him as he approached the mountain as he could see that the sea had risen and it was not long before it would either crush the mountain or overflow. *This can't be happening, is this really the end of Mare-Marie?*

Albeit the brevity of the short but super joyous reunion between Gonzo and the White Knights, he rejoined his circus folk to help barricade what protective items they could muster to shield the inner castle walls. They found rice bags covered in hessian, wooden barrels, ploughing barrows and slabs of stone. Belleny was cradling Bateau in her arms and standing high up on her balcony watching the townsmen scurry about below, they were speechless as an illuminated shape drifted off into the distance. Apart from Lucretia, it was unknown to all that Danté was now free from his death sentence and floating on his way through the night sky to the Unknown Tower.

"Did you see that Bateau?" she asked.

"How could I? I'm in your arms?"

"Father!" she fumed stomping to the door. She pushed and pulled at the handle. It didn't budge.

"I know you're out there! I demand you let me out at once!" she roared banging hard against the door.

The soldiers Gustus and Kostis were on guard out the front, ordered by King Vera, it was to be locked shut and kept closed until further notice.

"Sorry, Princess orders by King Vera, for your own safety you must stay in your room," said Kostis.

"I order you to let me out at once, I'll have you thrown into the Pit of Nothingness!"

"He said you would say that," said Kostis.

"But something came out of the castle walls! A strange creature, it flew right by my window!"

"He also said you would say something like that too," said Kostis nodding his head at Gustus.

"You better keep it locked, just in case it comes back," said Gustus.

"Hmph, idiots!" Belleny kicked the door and returned to her balcony.

"I guess locking it isn't a bad idea," said Bateau. "It might return."

"Fine!" said Belleny and she stomped back to the balcony. Through it she noticed far in the distance the Kylen riders circling and beaming their lights upon one spot.

What's going on out there? she thought.

"It's the giant, it has to be Bateau! Pass me my sightseer, please."

"Now Princess, it can't be him. It can't be, it took us days to get here, and we flew," he said approaching with her telescope in his tails.

"Hmm, thank you," she said and squinted through the tube.

"See anything?" he asked.

Belleny watched for some time, and it was when she began to breathe heavily that Bateau asked, "What's wrong Princess? What's out there?"

Silently she passed back the telescope and said, "It's him."

"It can't be," said Bateau and he scanned the distance and found the kylen's flashing lights. As they rocked back and forth, the shape of Drokura was revealed. "I don't believe it, he's huge, even bigger than before, they won't be able to stop him ... let alone Varin Eel."

"Where is she? I couldn't see her? She can't be far," cried Belleny squeezing her brooch tight.

The castle shook as if Drokura was jumping outside their window.

"What's happening?" screamed Belleny as she fell to the floor, she tried to stand but the castle continued to shake and it took several seconds before it subsided.

"The land, it moved!" said Bateau.

"How is that possible? Could the giant do that?" said Belleny.

"Listen to them! I hope the circus is all right," said Bateau.

The cries of the Horgans bellowed out over the land. From high up on the Oryan Mountains, they too shook and were lucky not to fall down the steep ridges.

Belleny and Bateau watched as Drokura pushed through the forest out into the open Rain Fields. Thunderous step by thunderous step he approached the large hedge barrier of the Queen's Gardens with tremendous force.

The soldiers' anxious voices rose and echoed up towards them, and the name Drokura was on their shaky lips.

Like black darts, Garon and Kale returned with the Kylen riders. The flying soldiers gave all their best, but even their harpoons did nothing to the enormous giant. Drokura's eyes were guarded behind sliding tentacles and protrusions covering his face, and the black oil that continued to pour from his skin made it hard to see even his face at times.

"Aim for the beast's eyes! It can't attack what it can't see!" yelled Garon swooping down from high above. The King's men roared and cheered as he flew by and twisted along the barricade. Kale followed by his side and leapt from his kylen to land upon the garden's giant hedge wall.

"Here it comes men! Defend the Queen's Gardens as you would defend the castle!" roared the King.

Kale tied a satchel of seeds to his arrows and he pulled back on his bow, "Wake up Rel, this is no time to be sleeping!"

"I would rather be asleep than awake to see this," said Rel.

"Light this up Rel, quick now!"

Rel coughed and flicked his tongue as a small flame spat from his thorny lips. They hit the dangling wicks that were joined to Kale's arrows.

With all Kale's strength, the silent archer fired three arrows, one headed east, one west and another dead straight. Screaming through the air the two on either side went wide and curved in homing in on Drokura as he swung his arms in defence. Each arrow hit hard, piercing deep, one hit his palm, one in a curling tentacle and the last in the chest. The giant wailed out loud, but they were merely splinters to the enormous beast.

"What happened?" said Rel.

"Wait for it," said Kale, then as Drokura took his first step forward the heated up seeds attached to the arrows exploded, filling the beast with light on all sides and across his chest. The soldiers cheered wildly, but the giant was not impressed. His furious roar filled the valley as he smashed his sticky limbs hard against the ground and drove forward with full force.

"Hold on men!" yelled Garon.

Drokura's enormous body slammed hard and heavy against the giant hedge wall, shaking men off the scaffolding to land back in the Queen's Gardens below.

Fear paralyzed the soldiers as the yellow oily eyes of Drokura stared down in anger.

"Fire! Fire at once!" roared the King.

The soldiers pulled back on their bow and arrows and froze as the oily blood seeped from the creature's enormous skull and dripped down and around them.

"He said fire!" shouted Garon and their nervous arrows left the barrier in a dense wall. Like a thousand needles, they covered Drokura from head to toe. Like shooting at hot larva, the arrows stuck into the dripping black oil and fell off the giant.

"Now Eddie!" said Gonzo pointing as the giant stumbled towards them.

"Not yet Gonzo," he replied as he aimed his flying-fox harpoon, anxiously waiting for a clear shot at one of the creature's eyes.

"Oh, here he comes!" cried a soldier running past.

Then Eddie found it. With a mere release of the trigger, his harpoon fired off towards Drokura, passing his wailing tentacles to pierce deep into his forehead.

"Damn! I missed!" said Eddie.

"Oh no, you didn't!" said Gonzo as Drokura roared backwards, twisting his tentacles around the harpoon. As he struggled to pull it out, the King's men reloaded and once again he ordered them to fire. But the arrows became a joke and even the harpoon was removed like pulling out a thorn.

"Look out Eddie!" said Garivin, whom Gonzo had dragged into the battle.

But it was too late, Drokura had reached around Eddie and squeezed him tight. Garivin ran along the hedge and leapt from the ledge, stabbing hard into Drokura's twisting arm. It dropped Eddie but in return threw Garivin far and hard into the garden below.

Enraged he then slid his destructive arms along the wall swiping off all those upon it. Screaming soldiers fell into the gardens below, some smashing through tree branches, others caught painfully in sculptures.

Drokura began to latch onto the ever-growing hedge and hooked his first step up, caring less of the stray arrows that seemed to do nothing more than stick into his poisonous tar exterior.

"Look out my lord he's coming over!" shouted a soldier climbing down the barricade.

"Hold your places!" roared the King, but even he knew there was little chance of stopping the giant.

"That's far enough!" said Dillon dressed in his battle armour and turning his white fur black.

"No let him take a few more steps," said Agarus. He too had become black once again and wore a suit of leather armour.

"Are you ready Montë?" said Palia as he flew upon her back.

"Just don't drop me in his mouth!" he replied.

"White Knights!" called Gonzo holding onto the hedge far below.

Kale watched as Drokura left the ground and clawed upwards. With blazing arrows, he fired one after another but the creature continued. He held back as Drokura pushed himself up onto the hedge and the White Knights launched into the air with Palia swooping in low as she dropped Montë right on to Drokura's head.

Like a game in the Jungle Room they flipped and jumped through Drokura's tentacles like vines. At each one slicing and cutting them with their claws.

Drokura wailed and swung all of his limbs at once. Flinging black oily muck across the Queen's Gardens as plants shrivelled up and rotted on contact.

The ground began to shake violently once again and Drokura lost his footing, falling off the giant hedge wall to land heavily and disgustingly on the ground.

The White Knights dangled from the hedge like Christmas ornaments.

"Drokura is down!" they cheered.

"Not for long," grumbled Garon, swooping low with the King upon his back. He landed next to Kale.

"It's happening—today is the day," said Kale as Garon helped him to his feet.

"Yes, the Zale Mountains, they've finally given up," said Garon.

The King held his hands to his face and cried, "The sea has won."

Chapter 78 - Home sweet Home

Belleny and Bateau were trapped in her quarters, they had watched everything from her balcony high above. Not only had she witnessed Drokura attack, but she also witnessed Varin Eel as she flew past on her winged creature.

"Drokura was just a deterrent, she's coming for me!" said Belleny in a panic.

"Open the door! Varin Eel is here, she's outside the castle!" screamed Belleny.

"Sorry, Princess but orders are orders," said Kostis.

"And when orders are orders they're—" said Gustus.

"You fools, we'll be dead if you don't escape! Do you hear me?" cried Belleny.

But they returned with silence. There was a dull thud against the door and the sound of buckling armour.

"What's going on out there?" said Belleny. "Bateau? She's ... she's out there isn't she?"

"Meeooow," said Bateau with a strange cat-like meow. He curled his tails around each other.

"Oh Bateau, now is not a good time to lose your voice. What do we do? We're trapped in here!"

Belleny jumped back as an oily black shadow slid under the door and sniffed up at her.

"Get away from me!" she screamed.

Belleny stomped at the shadow with her heel, picked up Bateau and ran towards the balcony.

Varin Eel's harrowing laughter echoed down the stairwell as she slammed open Belleny's door.

"Get away from me! I'll jump!"

"Oh Princess, you are no fun, we can't have that!" scowled Varin. Like Drokura, she too had drunk the pure black water by The Stone of Thorns. She had grown, towering on spidery legs as her leech-like shadow clawed and sniffed about like a pack of wolves. As if she was setting them free, her shadow raced along the floor and yanked Belleny forward by her leg.

Bateau hooked his claws into it as if the shadow was a living creature. It threw him aside and dragged her forward.

"No! Bateau! Help! Garon!" cried Belleny.

In a moment of clarity, she grabbed the whistle from around her neck and blew into it with all her might.

Chapter 79 - Abreaction

The fire inside Esta's room and the sea wind that bellowed out along the cove reflected Evelin's state as she laid under Esta's trance. Hypnotized, she found herself deep underwater in a strange place far from here and now.

Esta was in conversation with the giant eels that haunted Evelin, "And why would Evelin want you to hurt her?" she asked them.

"It's obvious," said Evelin in a harsh voice, "she can't do it herself."

Cory stared nervously at Evelin, *Poor Eve, this is crazy, is this all my fault?*

Esta spoke to the Eels as if they were in the room, "Of course she can't, she knows full well she isn't supposed to hurt herself, she's trapped, she feels guilty doesn't she?"

Cory gulped. *Esta was good, too good. She wasn't going to let up was she?*

Cory held Evelin's hand and thought hard, *Go on Eve, I'll forgive you if you tell her I did it ... that's alright with me.*

"Guilty, so guilty," said the Eels together. "We feed off it, she attracts us with her guilty scent."

"I see," said Esta, "and what does this whirlpool want with her?"

"You fool," said Evelin, "she created the whirlpool to take her away from it all."

"Just tell her the truth Eve, let yourself go!" said Cory.

"Shh Cory!" snapped Esta.

"Thank you Eels, I'm going to talk to Evelin now."

"Eve are you there?" continued Esta in a firm tone.

Evelin jolted as she did before and whispered, "Yeah."

Esta leant in close and said softly, "Do you understand now? You need to forgive yourself Eve and forget about the past. I don't know what you have done, or think you have done, but it's dragging you down here, you've created a whirlpool of darkness, it won't help you, do you understand?"

Esta and Cory watched as tears began to pool along Evelin's eyes and she began a deep sobbing that made Cory well up beside her.

Esta held out her hand to Cory, signalling that this was good for Evelin, "Good it's okay to cry Eve."

"Yes," she sniffed.

"You can say it out loud or silently, but you need to let it out, you can't hold on to this any longer, we forgive you, forgive yourself."

Evelin nodded and Cory squeezed her hand tight, this was it, the truth would be out.

"I—" started Evelin and she paused as the tears continued.

"Yes Evelin," said Esta, "you can keep it to yourself, just forgive yourself, let go of your guilt, such a pointless emotion."

Cory was teary and through a trembling lip, she looked across at Esta, "I—" she began, but Evelin spoke out over her.

"I ... I killed my mother," sobbed Evelin, her sorrow breaking Esta's heart and concealing Cory's confession.

"Oh Eve, you poor little angel," said Esta trying to control herself from embracing her and waking her from such a deep trance.

"It was an accident Evelin, you are not to blame and no one blames you."

"Accident or not, it's true," said Evelin.

The eels closed their mouths for the first time, they hung their heads and moved beside her as the whirlpool turned faster. She began to feel the whirlpool's current and watched as loose coral and reeds were sucked in.

Esta leant in close, "Evelin you need to understand that life and death is a mystery, you can't put a right or wrong to it, it just is, your mother wouldn't want you to carry such a burden. Nor would your father."

"Poor Robin ... I don't care anymore," said Evelin, it was then that the coral wound tight around her limbs and held her as she gave up. Evelin shook on the chair and sank deeper into submission.

Cory looked across at Esta, "What's happening to her?"

"Abreaction," whispered Esta removing Cory's hand from Evelin's.

The fire began to surge, bellowing from the wind outside.

"Evelin on the count of three I'm going to click my fingers and I want you to open your eyes and awaken feeling refreshed and relaxed. One, two and three." Esta clicked her fingers hard in front of Evelin's face.

There was no response.

She tried again, but nothing.

"Shake her! Wake her up!" said Cory.

"We can't, it's too dangerous to wake her in this state," said Esta.

"Eve, can you hear me?" said Cory.

There was silence and only the fire could be heard.

Then Evelin murmured in the Eel's voice, "No, she's gone."

"Don't do this to yourself Evelin, please come back, I love you," said Cory.

"You need to let her go," said Evelin.

"No! You need to let her go!" demanded Cory.

Evelin could hear, but she was drifting further away. The whirlpool spun before her, bleak and mesmerizing. But the corals held her back. She looked at the tentacles of the yellow Anemone on either side.

"Why won't you let me go?" she asked. They moved forward and caressed her face and pulled her back once again.

Am I wrong? I'm so sorry.

"Eels can you help me?" she asked.

The giant eels turned their heads towards her, "But why would we?"

"Because I can't do this alone."

"Will you forgive us?" they said.

"You are me, I created you."

"Well then?" asked one of the Eels.

"Yes I forgive you," said Evelin.

"Good," they whispered.

In a flash, the eels took off towards the whirlpool and together they disappeared into the swirling darkness. They wrapped around each other, twisting and turning, as she once saw in her aquarium, and a flash of electricity cracked violently within the whirlpool. Like a thundercloud underwater, the whirlpool twisted and turned trying to escape their shocks.

Evelin watched on as the swirling dark circle began to shrink and pull into itself. Like water sinking down inside a plug hole it spun wildly before it vanished before her eyes.

Evelin felt the coral let go, and as if she couldn't breathe, she quickly swam to the surface and upon breaking through, gasped for air.

Back in Esta's room Evelin instantly woke. With a teary smile, she sat up.

"Oh Evelin!" said Cory wrapping her arms around her.

"Don't worry, it's over," she said.

Chapter 80 - The Inner Child

Danté ventured deep into the rising Sea of Sorrow, his old body left behind, his new self, now embodied in a strange, wondrous and luminous body. Which could now fly and easily push against the ferocious winds that raced above the ocean. His mind was impervious, determined to reach the tower and its mysterious floating orb above it, but ultimately to find the one who called out to him, for so very long. His destiny feared none, pulling him forward.

With no escape from the ocean's monstrous voice, he was forced to listen to the violent swells that roared up at him. His surroundings were a fierce and watery hell.

I can't be too late, I can't be! Where is it? Don't tell me it's gone?

Danté hovered over the sea and scanned the never-ending waters. Continuously the waves clawed up at him, trying to pull him under. With a shaky glance, he looked back at the mountain, but it had disappeared behind a wall of ocean spray, a misty haze that took away all his bearings.

What was that? He rose several meters higher in the blink of an eye and scanned inside the crashing, cavernous waves.

There, there it is again! What is it? Below him, something swam and lit the water in a bright electric flash. It disappeared. Then fifty meters away, he saw it again.

Something swimming in the sea! Nothing could survive in there ... But it does! He told himself in disbelief.

The glazed skin of the swimming creature glistened as it moved through the water smashing through each and every wave that it came across.

"A serpent!" he yelped.

Danté took off at once, this creature had potential to do him more than harm. *No! Not now, he begged, not when I am so close! How long has it been following me? And why? This can't be the one that calls me.*

The bright electric flashes continued to follow him and the cloud in turn began to mimic its electric light show. Danté pushed on but found he was losing the battle, the tower could be anywhere and the serpent was clearly following him. Danté stopped, turned and watched the beast as it circled below.

This creature must be here for a reason? he thought, *Like the tower and its orb.* And there he waited as the serpent left the peak of a giant tidal wave and headed straight up. Like a dragon without wings, it twisted in the sky and dove into the thick clouds above. Danté watched as its spiky fins cut through the thick grey and its body flashed towards him.

Is this it? thought Danté, *I cannot defend myself with this new body.*

From above the serpent sank down before him like a giant snake, its dark blue and red speckled chest was beauty in every sense, but Danté only acknowledged fear in its presence. He had already seen and escaped death today and this beast was formidable. Slowly it circled him, with each and every turn its big scaly eyes never once left him.

"Who are you? What do you want with me?" shouted Danté over the fierce weather.

"My name is Ruegeris Bimatherous, I am the protector of the girl child," it spoke in heated waves as it roared through its demonic jaws.

"The girl child? What child?" said Danté.

"You don't know?" he questioned as his body swayed back and forth as if underwater.

"No, how could a child live out here? How do you?"

The serpent did not answer, it remained silent as it observed Danté.

"Are you going to kill me Ruegeris?"

"Perhaps," it said and circled him once again and after a long pause added, "Perhaps not."

"I just want to know what's out here! The temple, the floating orb, does it even exist or am I going mad? Someone calls me, they always have, but I could never reach them ... till now."

"You have seen the sphere?" said Ruegeris.

"Yes it floats above the Untouched Temple, somewhere out here in this wild ocean."

"She calls you?" questioned Ruegeris.

"Yes even in my sleep, but now the sea is so loud I'm afraid I'm too late."

"Soon," growled Ruegeris. "It tries to keep her safe, it is supposed to protect her, like me, but it creates more harm than good ... it's overprotecting," said the serpent, its mouth's full of jagged teeth and darkness. "Are you here to take her away, now that I must leave?"

"I don't know what you're talking about. I've never seen this girl child? I can't even find her out here."

"But you have heard her?"

"Yes I hear her, she's afraid, she cries."

"No, she weeps," said Ruegeris.

"She sounds so sad," said Danté.

"Very," groaned Ruegeris.

"Please, take me to her."

The giant serpent circled slowly once again and stared back into his eyes.

With a flash of light, Ruegeris said, "This way," and took off, his long body rolling past at great speed, his tail whipping behind him.

Danté gasped for the fear of the creature shook within him, *I'm so close, now I'm shown the way. A child? Out here? How could it be?* thought Danté.

He followed Ruegeris and watched as he flew and dipped into the clouds above, flashing his body so Danté could follow. Then he saw it. As if it was a mirage, a sparkle of light shone out in the distance. He knew he would have never found it without Ruegeris.

"There it is!" he cried out to the wild waves below, and with all his energy flew directly towards it.

"Thank you Ruegeris!" he shouted.

Ruegeris bowed his head, dove into the ferocious water and began to circle the temple.

The closer Danté got to the strange structure the more the weather turned savage and unpredictable, closing in on him with a dense cloud that rained down hard, pushing him lower and lower. He couldn't believe that any building could be built let alone survive within this ferocious sea, but there it was. It was just as beautiful as Danté imagined. Sparkling golden walls rose high to a giant chalice like structure, where floating at the very top of its goblet shape hovered an enormous stone sphere defying all gravity.

He looked down below as Ruegeris flashed like lightning. The sea suffocated the golden temple and now a whirlpool had wrapped itself around it. He climbed higher and higher as the water rose along its golden walls. He watched Ruegeris circle against the wild currents, slowing its surge.

Danté had made it in due time, he knew it wouldn't be long before it disappeared under the rising swell. Flying in close he observed the stone-like orb, it was exactly the same colour as Tjaman's and Palace's. He caught his reflection in the policed surface, unfamiliar, a phantom.

The orb began to crystallize in his presence, compelled to touch it Danté nervously extended his hand and reached out. In an instant, he was absorbed downwards and continued to fall into the bowl of the chalice structure, falling straight through the solid gold surface and within the cup.

Instantly the thunderous sounds of the clouds above, and the crashing surge of the ocean smashing against the temple walls disappeared. Danté hovered at the end of a large queen sized bed, its silver-white sheets tucked tightly into a beautiful golden bed frame that melted into the floor as if they were one. Out of each corner rose four ornate pillars, entwined with solid gold vines and delicate flowers, and across it was draped an intricate white lace roof.

Danté lowered himself to the ground and stood admiring such wonder. The floor was warm and comforting and he began to feel solid in his new body. Then he heard a voice and instantly turned to where it was coming from. At the end of the bed, dwarfed by four huge white pillows and an assortment of dolls, was a child, a small human girl. Red-eyed, she sat crouched against the puffy headrest, her sheets pulled up to her face.

"Hello, don't be afraid," he said.

Danté could tell she was shaking, although he sensed it was quite warm. Bundled in her sheet, her pale white arms were wrapped tight around her knees. She said nothing and stared at him.

"Please don't be afraid," he continued and carefully rose towards the bed and towards her.

"Where's Ruegeris?" she said, her voice laden with worry.

"Outside, I have been looking for you and he brought me here."

The girl turned and peeked through her long dark hair, only to flinch back as Danté approached closer. He paused, trying his best not to startle her, although he knew it was hard.

"And who are you?" asked Danté.

"I am the inner child, Eve," she said.

"Don't be afraid Eve, why are you all alone out here? How did you get here?"

"I feel I've always been here, it's been so long, with Ruegeris and the sea."

"You're crying? Please don't be scared. Are you hurt?"

"No, not anymore, these are tears of joy, it's finally over and now you have come for me, am I right?"

"What's over?" said Danté.

"The suffering, please—you have come for me, don't leave me," she said.

"Of course," said Danté, "I will stay or take you away. I never knew you were out here, but you have been calling me all my life."

"I'm glad," said Evelin sitting up on her knees, her smile so innocent. Like sunlight through stained-glass windows Danté began to glow, his emotions so intense, electric cells started to ripple in waves along his new body, and with arms outstretched they embraced.

"I will never leave you, I am eternal," he said.

"Yes, we are. Thank you Danté," she smiled.

"I will take you to the Crystalon Castle, you will be safe."

Evelin felt the electricity in Danté's body and within his words, she stared at him and from the corners of her eyes a tear trickled continuously down her cheeks.

"Don't cry, it's going to be all right," he said.

"No, I must!" she whispered and the temple began to shudder and the golden roof above tore like paper as the sea wind gushed inside.

Danté and Evelin looked up as the crystal orb pulled away from the temple and soared up into the clouds. Ruegeris also watched from below and sped off towards the open roof as the ocean roared out at him.

"Goodbye my friend!" roared Ruegeris down at the ocean as he entered the temple, curling himself around the open roof and blocking the fierce winds.

"Hold on!" he roared.

The orb continued high into the clouds and paused as it hung in the sky once again, then as if gravity had come back one hundred fold, the giant sphere dove into the ocean with the impact of a fallen star. The angry sea exploded outward, creating a tidal wave of gigantic proportions. Within minutes, it arrived at the Zale Mountains and hit with full force. With giant cracks and dismantling peaks, the mighty waves tore straight through. The Sea of Sorrow had been released and with its ravaging rapids it poured into the valleys of Mare-Marie leaving nothing untouched. The people, locked away in their homes, hiding from Drokura, watched as the bellowing water rose around them. The prophecy had been foretold, but never did they dream it would be so savage, and so quick.

The ferocious power of the gushing water did not cease. It continued to pour over the mountains with full force destroying it as it went. It tore across the desert and gushed along the Slate Cliffs, there was nowhere in Mare-Marie that it didn't devour. Even the high north felt its fury as it broke in from above and poured down the Mountains of Morne.

The Stone of Thorns was torn from the Veelin River and its poisons flushed away. It crumbled as the salt water corroded it into pieces. Creatures ran from the water, but it sank into even the deepest muddy hole. Coughing and spluttering they swam to the surface.

In the South, the tidal rapids hit hard against the castle. Drokura held up his arms and cried for help as the water arrived and crashed down upon him. It loosened his footing and picked him up with ease as he tumbled backwards as if he had been dumped by the whole ocean.

The castle walls took the full force of the sea, it held on strong, driving the currents along its walls and around to the Pit of Nothingness on the other side. The rushing water dove deep into the Pit, its vast echoing chasm engulfing the water that poured in. The strange bird-like creatures on the blackened trees took flight and circled the enormous drain hole.

The White Knights gasped for air as the water came gushing around the hedge wall like a broken dam. Dillon grabbed Agarus by the arm and together they climbed, but the water was too strong and whisked them away. Palia frantically flew above, looking for anything white and silky, then out of the corner of her eye, she spotted Monté grasping for air and disappearing below. She dove deep underwater and clawed around his shoulders ripping him free.

It seemed that as quick as the sea came, was as fast as it went. It took the giant Drokura and its oily poisons with it, down into the Pit of Nothingness. Garon, the King and Kale landed on the castle wall and scanned the flooded land.

Survivors clambered up the giant hedge and many in the town floated to the surface in their strange underwater houses. It was as if everything had been washed, everything was sparkling as the sun began to rise and the black, empty scar called the Pit of Nothingness was now nothing short of a glistening lake.

"Look down there, it's them, near the pit!" said Kale waving out to the White Knights, whose wet white coats stood out amongst the deep blue water.

But as they waved back they noticed inside the pit were giant bubbles appearing on the water's surface and a dark shadow rose from beneath. Their waves turned into frantic gestures.

"Get away! Drokura is back! In the pit!" they shouted.

But the White Knights were too far away to understand, and too exhausted to notice the silent dark limbs climbing up through the surface.

"Quick get on, we must do something!" said Garon to Kale.

"Get back to the castle Vera!" said Garon, who watched a white fear fall upon his face.

"Look Garon over there, another giant!" said the King.

"Don't worry it's Maramon! He's with us!" said Garon, as he spun around and rose into the air with giant flaps.

The King shook his head in disbelief as Garon and Kale sped off towards the giant creatures. He turned and ran off along the hedge wall back towards the castle.

The transparent giant Gretn Maramon, who once warned them of the witch and the darkness in the north, approached the Pit of Nothingness.

Together Garon and Kale watched helplessly as Drokura appeared from below.

Drokura's tentacles were the first to appear, he peered up at them with his many eyes. With a painful cry, he pushed himself up and fell back down into the water.

Garon and Kale watched from above as Maramon approached the

edge and with his long bony arms drove them into the water and grabbed Drokura tightly. He pulled Drokura's colossal body to the water's edge. The exhausted Drokura didn't put up a fight or squirm as water and air circulated through his system and his cleared ventricles and gills as Maramon wiped away the remaining black muck. Drokura's silvery blue-scaled body was revealed as it shone and glittered in the golden morning light.

Gretn Maramon spoke loud but softly, "Trylis, it's me, your friend Maramon, can you hear me?"

There was silence as he slowly looked up, falling away from his face the black oil easily disintegrated in the salty water, revealing the creature's silvery skinned face, his once yellow eyes were now full of the deepest, bright pooling whites.

"Trylis ... Gretn?" he said, in a wondrous watery voice. "What has happened to me? Am I free?"

"Yes my friend, rest now, you have been through more than enough."

"Please ... forgive me," said Trylis.

"Of course."

The evil known as Drokura was no more, free from Varin's poisonous curse and cleansed by the Sea of Sorrow, the beautiful old water creature Trylis had returned to himself.

Garon, Kale and the White Knights watched in amazement as Gretn helped Trylis climb to the banks of the pit. They sat and stared at their giant and incredible reflections as the waters continued to pour in and across Mare-Marie.

In a panic, Garon pointed skyward toward Belleny's tower and said, "Did you hear that Kale?"

"No. What is it?" he asked even though deep down inside he knew exactly who and it was.

"Shh wait ... there it is again! It's faint, but I'm sure it's my alert whistle! Up there. Oh no, it's got to be the Princess! Get on, it looks like Varin Eel has distracted us with her beast!"

"Wait here Rel! Go, Garon, Go!" said Kale and in one smooth movement he leaped into Garon's saddle. Garon rose his wings and brought them down with all his strength and fury.

"Keep clear of her shadow!" cried Rel, left behind in a cloud of feathers.

From the top of the giant hedge, Garon launched at full speed, darting towards the flooded land before swooping up in full flight.

"White Knight's to Belleny's tower at once!" roared Garon as he raced past like a black mist.

"Varin Eel has the Princess!" said Kale.

"Go! We're on our way!" said Dillon.

The White Knight's rallied at once.

*

Silently Varin Eel crept forward in the darkness of Belleny's quarters. Her long spidery legs sank deep into her slithering, oily black shadow. As she circled Belleny, she snarled with a poisonous satisfaction, "No point screaming child, not even your big dumb bird can save you now!"

"What do you want from me?" cried the Princess.

"Oh, I think you know and if you don't, you'll find out soon enough." Varin rose her hand and the dim lantern flames crackled up high.

"Ever so dark in here, even for me—so this is the cursed tree? Such strange oddities, are you sure you're not a child of the darkness?"

Bateau scampered to his feet as the two soldiers, Gustus and Kostis entered the room in a trance.

"I command you fools—shut the door and lock it," ordered Varin.

"Shut the door," repeated Kostis as he slammed the heavy door and Gustus sealed the entrance with his iron spear.

In a fearful panic, as Varin turned, Belleny seized her blade from her boot and slashed it across the cold shadow that coiled and tugged at her leg.

Varin twisted back at once. Her physical self did not appear to be in pain, but it was her shadow that wailed and flipped about like a hooked fish.

"Oh yes indeed, you are a wicked thing," gnarred Varin through barbed teeth. "Fools, bring her to me."

Gustus stomped forward, but he was too heavy and slow to grasp the agile Princess. But he was large and found it easy to corner her.

"Leave her alone! Snap out of it Gustus!" said Bateau as his voice returned. He leaped up on Gustus, and then again to reach his beetle-like face and blind his bulbous bug eyes with his tails.

Varin grinned at the sight of the struggle and then turned to the door. She listened to King Vera as he raced up the stairwell pleading and swearing, "Belleny! I'm coming! Don't you lay a finger on her witch!"

"Isn't that sweet? Here comes daddy dearest," said Varin, then spat a sticky black phlegm against the door handle. It seemed to secure it further.

With loud thunderous fists, he helplessly banged against the rooted door and ordered his men to break it down at once.

"Witch! Open this door!" he roared, but this made Varin laugh, an evil, sinister laugh that made Belleny's body quake with fear.

"Don't worry, I'll open it soon enough, once I'm finished with your daughter," mocked Varin.

"Get away from me you Kostis!" cried Belleny.

With nowhere to run the possessed soldiers grabbed both the Princess and Bateau. In anguish they kicked and screamed to no avail.

"That's it, bring her to me. I like to be hand fed," said Varin lurching in and out of her shadow.

Belleny watched in horror as Varin removed her hood and revealed her hideous face in the light of the fiery lanterns. Like her black-flesh arms and bony claws, her unapproachable visage consisted of a skinless skull coated with a thin layer of black, dripping, tar-like oil. Haunting polished eyes peered through, preying on a frightened and fearful Belleny. In the harrowing silence of a course breath, Varin snarled, parting her blue lips and revealing her long, glass, fang-like teeth. She licked the oil from her lips as Garon and Kale landed outside on the balcony.

"For a recluse, you are a popular one," said Varin.

"Kale! Garon!" cried Belleny from within the firm claws of Kostis.

"Not quick enough bird!" snarled the witch. She held up her hand and her shadow raced forward, slithering like eels. They began to control the vines outside and they ferociously whipped around Kale and Garon, strangling them with their leafy grips.

"Get off me!" roared Garon, trying to remove his blade, but the vines pulled his wings behind his back, tied his legs together and lifted them both off the ground.

The room was swamped with shadows as the sorceress began to chant and the lantern's flames grew wilder.

"Yes, take care of them for me. Now, where were we, yes appetizers!" Varin lunged forward with claws out and tore Bateau from Gustus.

"No! You can't!" cried Belleny.

"Leave him alone!" roared Garon.

"Quiet out there!" said Varin, she snarled and threw Bateau at Garon with full force. The vines momentarily parted and he flew straight out.

"Oh, I missed," said Varin.

Garon and Kale were forced to watch, unable to reach out to catch Bateau as he grasped for a hand. In the blink of an eye, he disappeared, falling at a great speed through the clouds and to the solid ground miles below.

"Bateau," wept Belleny.

"Bateau," mimicked the witch.

"You beast!" roared Belleny with a vengeance in her eyes.

"What's worse? You thought I was going to eat him? What a laugh, such a disgusting vermin," said Varin. "Enough games." She knelt down and clawed at the two soldier's shadows. Dragging her nail along them like a pool of water. Instantly the soldiers woke from their trance, shook their heads and scuttled away. Varin scraped her claws up in front of them snatching at their shadows as they stretched like melted black plastic. With a terrified gasp, they both fell to the floor, half stumbling, half crawling.

Outside, King Vera relentlessly pounded against the door.

Belleny continuously tried to break free, but Varin's shadow now latched even tighter around her leg, "Be still child! Silence her," said Varin, as her shadow whipped out and slapped Belleny hard across the face.

Gustus and Kostis shook in agonizing pain, their own shadows peeled up from beneath them, now a lifesize black scab ripped from their flesh.

"No! You can't have them!" said Belleny as she reached across the table and grabbed one of her solid glass ornaments. With both hands, she stabbed it deep into the shadow before her. Instantly it let her go and she continued forward.

Her heart felt for Bateau and the voice of Kikaan roared from deep inside, "Fear me, witch!"

Swiping back her blade and raising it before her.

"Fear me!!" growled Varin snarling down at her and exhibiting an expression of pure horror.

It was then Gustus, still in excruciating agony, stood up and strangled the necromancer by the throat with his giant hands. The room filled quickly with Varin's gagging howl as her shadows whipped about as if on fire.

"Kostis! Help!" cried Gustus as he began to sink into her shadow as if quicksand. Garon and Kale watched helplessly as Varin started to overpower Gustus and crawl herself out.

"Belleny! Get out of there! Now!" yelled Garon.

But she had other ideas, ideas that were fueled by pain and anger, she lurched forward and drove her blade into Varin's hood. The black metal blade remained lodged deep in her skull. Instantly Gustus and Kostis gasped for air as if they were underwater and regained consciousness. They were released from their crippling curse as their shadows fell to the ground like wet, black paint and rejoined them.

With trembling hands, Belleny let go of the blade and stood back.

Varin was motionless, but her shadow was animated and coiled around her like a pool of eels.

"Get away. Run!" roared Garon.

"Princess! This way," said Kostis helping her to her feet.

Gustus held out his arm and shielded Belleny towards the door, but in horror he watched Varin clasp her claws around his thick wrist and in one go pulled the blade from her head.

"Not so fast," she growled and with an immense energy she returned, slamming the soldiers against the wall, collecting a wall of glass sculptures in the motion. She wrenched her body back to Belleny, who was trying to remove the wedged spear from the door.

"You are a little witch aren't you?" said Varin, "Why would I waste my time eating their shadows when all I'm really here for, is yours?"

Varin Eel towered over Belleny. She hunched forward, pinning the Princess against the door, snatching and squeezing her face. Black gore dripped down from Varin's skull and covered a screaming Belleny. It pooled under the door. King Vera watched in horror as it surrounded his boots.

"I'll kill you Varin Eel!" he roared.

"So you've said, old man! I'd like to see you try from out there."

Varin stabbed her claws into the ground beside Belleny and pinched at her shadow.

"A stubborn one," said Varin as she tugged at it, now with a hand full of claws.

"You have no idea what this will do to me!" said Varin opening her gruesome mouth and baring her black tongue and piercing glass teeth.

"Belleny! Be strong," cried the King. At that moment, he fell to his knees. The tower began to shake as if the ocean had triggered a second tidal wave to wipe out the remains of the land.

But outside it was a giant figure who raced up the tower at great speed and coiled around the balcony.

"Raveene!" shouted Kale and Garon.

Raveene's appeared before them with Rel riding upon his enormous skull.

He grinned and with a wink he held his breath to remain weightless. With a giant claw, he tore into the vines while they fought back with vigor, but it wasn't long before they dropped Kale and Garon to the ground. Kale instantly removed an arrow, with pace and finesse, he fired. Then one after another, refusing to stop until they were all impaled deep inside Varin Eel. Varin spoke not a word as they lodged into her collarbone, through her ribs and into her sternum.

Belleny reached up and grabbed at her shadow as it hung from Varin's grip. As quick as light, her shadow returned to her.

"Run here, Belleny, run!" said Garon as he stumbled wildly through the vines. But the balcony doors then slammed shut in his face. As if returning from the dead, Varin Eel's piercing black eyes opened. Belleny suddenly felt her whole body yank backward then forward, headfirst into her giant mirror, smashing it into a thousand pieces. Motionless she lay unconscious on the floor.

The lantern flames danced wildly around the room shouting, "Get up Belleny! Get up!" but as she opened her eyes it wasn't the lanterns speaking, it was Varin Eel.

"You're all pathetic!" laughed Varin, stepping up on Gustus, who was now unconscious on the chamber floor.

Belleny awoke and touched her face. *Blood!* She felt her warm blood trickling down her face. Covered in a mixture of the witches blacken oils. Through stinging eyes, she summoned all her strength and sprinted inside her change room.

"Such childish games," said Varin watching her every move. She moved to the doorway overlooking the enormous change room, and the rows and rows of mannequins, her eyes scanning furiously.

"What is this witchery? No! Enough of these games!"

Varin and her poisoned shadow entered the room. One after another, she tossed the mannequins aside.

"What have we here?" she questioned, finding Esdaile, the White Creature, lying silently before her. She approached the White Knight and held up its heavy skull by its wispy white mane.

"Yes you want games, let's have some fun," she scowled, "go sniff her out for me beast!"

Varin mouthed a haunting spell and it was with her claws she tore at her own shadow and in her hand an oily black creature snapped about wildly. She threw it on the ground and like a pool of black blood it surrounded Esdaile then fastened to his body.

Esdaile lay lifeless and his dead fish eyes morphed into shiny, pitch black beads. He moved and made a low growl that resonated throughout the entire change room. Slowly he rose to his feet, his fur draped from his skeleton and along the white shell floor. He took off at once, sniffing the air, tracking Belleny's scent.

Esdaile? But he's dead. That witch has cursed him alive! thought Belleny as she violently trembled beneath a mannequin's flowing gown. She could hear his thick black claws tapping against the solid floor. He was getting close. Knowing it was only a matter of time before he sniffed her out, she made a dash for it. Esdaile followed her sent just as fast, his large frame pushing the mannequins over four at a time.

Stop! Please! Esdaile it's me Belleny!

He appeared before her and looked into her eyes. With the power of telepathy, he read her thoughts, but he was confused and frowned down at her.

Belleny held out her arms, "I forgive you Esdaile."

These words seemed to have an overpowering effect and Esdaile looked down at her and shook his head. She touched his face and graced him with a smile.

"Princess," he growled softly under heavy breath. "What has become of me? I don't feel well."

"That's because you ... you're dead," she said nervously.

"Dead?"

"You jumped, from my balcony."

Esdaile paused and stared into her eyes. He reflected on the past. He remembered.

"You brought me back, up here."

"Yes," she whispered, "I could sense you weren't completely gone."

"But why am I in this state now?" he asked softly.

"A necromancer summoned you from the dead. She wants to kill us all. Look at your shadow, it's not yours. You're under her spell."

The shadow moved like a bag of rats and sniffed up at her leg.

"No, no more!" said Esdaile and clawed down hard upon it.

Varin Eel crowed out from the entrance, "Have you found that little rat? Careful not to kill her—not yet."

Esdaile turned towards the entrance and snarled, "I have her!"

"Good, bring her to me! You can be rough."

Esdaile leaned forward and bit hard into his new and poisonous shadow, it whipped about and then recoiled beneath him.

"Take care Princess, I am so proud of the young lady I see before me."

"Esdaile wait! Please, don't leave me here!"

But it was too late he was gone.

Racing towards Varin, he moved with such velocity that his long mane streaked behind him and shifted from white to pitch black. The White Knight was too quick for Varin and with claws outstretched he brought her down, tearing her oily flesh from her bones and hooking his teeth around her neck. He dragged her back into the room and ripped her from her own shadow, and into the hollow trunk of the tree Winta.

Belleny's heart was racing, she heard Varin's harrowing screams and ran to the doorway to watch as Esdaile hold his ground, growling with his sight focussed inside the hollow of the tree.

"You fool, you're dead!" snarled Varin stepping out of Winta, but Esdaile launched forward and clawed her back inside.

The tree Winta shook as if alive as they struggled inside her.

A loud hiss was heard from deep within and with a loud crack Esdaile came flying backward into the room, smashing hard against the wall and snapping branches along with him. Varin held out her arm, her shadow had returned within her claws.

"Esdaile!" cried Belleny running to his side and in anger she picked up a fallen lantern and threw it at Winta. As if covered in fuel the tree lit up in flames and fire raced along its wiry black branches.

Forgive me Winta! thought Belleny. She stood back as the fiery branches twisted and curled into itself, burning and into gnarled charcoal splinters.

At first Belleny thought the light was moving Varin's wicked shadow, but then realised it was trying to escape the flames. Reaching for another lantern she threw it hard against the tree. Varin screamed, leaping from within the hollow and on landing tumbled forward, Esdaile had snapped her long spidery legs.

Varin scavenged about and held her small sliver of a shadow, cradling it like a baby. The shadow dregs twisted and turned.

"What have you done? What you have done?!" she screamed up at Belleny.

In a flash, the balcony doors flew open, torn off their hinges on both sides.

"You trying to give an old bird a heart attack?" squawked Garon as he darted inside, swooped up Belleny and launched himself towards the chamber door. With an all mighty kick, Garon dislodged the spear and swung the door wide open. King Vera and The White Knights tumbled forward followed by a barrage of soldiers. Instantly King Vera took Belleny and scooped her up in his mammoth bear arms.

"You're bleeding!" he cried.

"I'm alright father! Be careful she's not dead!" cried Belleny.

"She will be," said Garon.

"Oh Belleny!" said King Vera, he squeezed her tight only releasing his hold to pull out his mighty sword and roar, "Where is this vile creature! Bateau take the princess out of here at once!"

"Bateau! You survived!" cried Belleny as he jumped into her arms.

"He was lucky, I heard him howling on the way down," said Palia.

"Thank you Palia."

"Kale was right Belleny, you are the chosen one! You killed her!" said Dillon pointing at the withering witch.

"No, I'm not, she's not dead—not yet. It was Esdaile who brought her down," said Belleny.

"Esdaile?" gasped the White Knights.

Belleny looked up and pointed toward the White Creature on the floor. "I'm sorry, but I've kept him all along. Varin's curse brought him back to life to capture me, but he attacked her ... and now he's—"

The White Knights ran to his side.

"Barera!" cried Montë holding him tight, "Thank you, my friend."

"He always was the hero," sniffed Palia.

"Barera! Esdaile! Can you hear me?" said Dillon.

"Is that you Aelios," whispered Esdaile and slowly his eyes opened and closed.

"Careful Kale she's wounded, but still very much dangerous!" roared Garon as he drew his blade and approached Varin, curled up beneath the tree. Varin twisted, clawing herself away as they circled the remnants of the burnt Winta. The tree's charcoal exterior continued to crackle and cinder.

"Get away from me!" snarled Varin. Her eyes turned dark with anger.

Garon dug his talons into her blistered chest as she twitched furiously, kicking her broken legs across the floor.

"Drokura will crush you all!" said Varin wailing and scratching up her skinless arms and fingers.

"Drokura is dead, the sea has seen to that," said Garon, clawing down upon her rising arms.

Varin spat up at them, "No! You will pay with your lives, I am fear, I will always exist! I'm a Shadow Witch!"

"Silence!" said King Vera, "destroy this abomination at once!"

"With pleasure," said Garon, as he pushed down hard against her throat.

The witch squirmed and coughed, laughing up at him.

"Kill her already!" said the King fuelled with anger.

"I'm trying, but the Necromancer won't die!" growled Garon.

With a gasping cackle Varin Eel smirked up at them, "I'll curse every last one of—"

"Enough of your curses!" said Belleny, she raced forward—and to their astonishment—drove her black blade deep into Varin's breastplate, piercing her stone heart.

Instantly Belleny was yanked into the air by Garon. She looked down and covered her mouth as Varin's black flesh withered and converged into an oily pool. It collected at the foot of the tree, her skin pulled taught across her skeletal remains.

The witch was dead.

Chapter 82 - Girl of the Wind

"It is done," said Danté, floating across the balcony like an apparition. "It was your destiny Belleny, you are the one."

His strange serpent body was illuminated and glowing in the Mare-Marie twilight. He was drawing tender nudges from Raveene's giant snout and next to him was the young girl who smiled and tickled Raveene's chin as the serpent Ruegeris Bimatherous flew over to join the throng.

"It's good to see you too Raveene, I'm glad to see you got rid of those bed bugs!" smiled Danté.

"Who are you!" gasped Kale as he rose his blade before him.

"I'm pretty sure that will go straight through me Kale."

"Wait ... is that you—Danté?" asked Kale, recognizing the voice but not the illuminated creature before him.

"What witchery is this!" roared the King as he held Belleny behind him.

"Serpent what have you done with Danté!" snapped Garon.

"Oh no, it's eaten him!" said Bateau, "he's still alive—inside!"

"Oh, Bateau please, don't be afraid. Yes, it is I Danté Vakares, in the flesh ... well the flesh is gone but I remain my friends."

"Danté I don't believe it!" said Kale, "but how could this be?"

"More magic," said King Vera.

"It was indeed. Lucretia, she released me from my decaying mortal self and unlocked me so I could manifest into my pure form."

"Are you alright?" asked Kale.

"I feel more alive than ever before and without your mother's help I would never have reached the Untouched Tower," said Danté.

"You actually made it?" said Garon in disbelief.

"Not on my own," Danté pointed out to Ruegeris, who circled the temple, "this magnificent serpent was my guide."

"Welcome home Danté, it's so good to see you!" said Belleny skipping over to see her old friend.

"Good to see you to Belleny."

"Well, not really see you, if you know what I mean," said Bateau.

Garon frowned at Varin's oily remains and grumbled, "So is she coming back?"

"Fear needs more than to be just silenced," said Kale.

Garon huffed and clawed the witch's cloak, then threw her bones into the burning hollow of Winta.

"Who are you little girl?" asked Belleny.

"She is the treasure that has been calling me from her ocean tower. My friends this is Eve and out there is Ruegeris Bimatherous, he is her protector from the sea."

"I don't believe it! Out there! You must be very special," said Belleny.

"She is the lost key to Mare-Marie," said Danté, "she is free from her temple and the sea but will need somewhere safe to stay."

"If I recall, we have a tower built just like mine, you can live here with me if you like?" said Belleny.

"Thank you, Princess. I would like that very much, I have been so very lonely," smiled Evelin.

"You must take a look outside Belleny, your kingdom is cleansed, it is truly a magnificent sight across the sea," said Danté pointing to the East.

Garon walked across the room and removed a heavy latch covering another neglected balcony. As if by magic the doors swung open to reveal a sunrise just appearing over the horizon in the valley and where the sea had drained into the shimmering Pooling Pit. Beyond the demolished Zale Mountains, the sky and sea mirrored one another and it was difficult to make out where the heaven's started and the water finished. It was as if a crystal path had been etched into the horizon, a gateway into to a new dimension.

"Oh, my ... it's beautiful, look father!" said a teary Belleny.

"The ocean is calm, it is welcoming us once again," said Danté.

"We could go for a swim!" said Dillon to the others. "We could sail the sea!" added Monte.

"The sea, calm ..." whispered Belleny and turned back with a youthful smile, "yes, I can't wait to sail it!"

"No! You're not going anywhere!" whimpered King Vera pushing his side of the balcony door shut.

Belleny stared out through the half-open door, at the sea and then across at her furious father.

Silence fell upon the awkward situation and to the White Knights' ecstatic surprise, Esdaile stood up and approached King Vera, his white mane soft and pure tumbled down and trailed behind him.

"Esdaile!" said Belleny. She ran forward, holding him tightly as he continued over to the King.

"Don't worry Princess, I can control it," said Esdaile calmly as his shadow flickered then returned and moved softly with each step.

He stood next to King Vera and laid his heavy white paw upon his shoulder. With his other he pulled the balcony door back open. Esdaile and the King stared silently into the distance. One by one, the White Knights approached as did Garon, Kale, and Rel; they all stood in silence.

King Vera shook his head and turned back at a sullen Belleny with Bateau in her arms.

"King Vera," said Garon, "all little birds must learn to fly."

In silence, they contemplated the past, the future and most importantly the present. The King with a light sniffle began to nod his head and with a teary smile he turned to Belleny, "You are a formidable and very brave girl. Your mother would be proud as I am. Your destiny is your own. You have my blessing behind every step of the way. You do what you will. I'll be there just behind you, we all will be."

From a distance came a shadow, slithering across the surface of the clouds like a minnow darting across the smooth pebbles of a stream. And then a voice carried along with it, faint at first, but familiar, "Boots? Evelin Boots?"

Evelin knew it could be no other than the Weatherman and sure enough as he landed before her in an explosion of cloud, it was.

"It is you Boots!" he grinned as his moustache curled with excitement.

"Weatherman how nice it is to see you again."

"Oh really? It is? Oh yes, yes indeed of course it is," he replied, removing his top hat, adjusting his silvery white fringe, and carefully placing the hat back on top. Evelin smiled as he then proceeded to dust the floor before her and pull together a comfy stool made of the finest white cloud. "There you go! Or stay ... or sit for that matter."

"Thank you. I will sit."

"Good. So, Boots, you're back?" questioned the Weatherman as he quickly squeezed together a makeshift throne of cloud and sat down as if a King.

"Yes, it looks like I am," replied Evelin with a cheeky grin.

"It's been a while, or ... has it?"

"It has been a long while."

"Are you well?" he asked. "You look well ... well your hair's the same, I give you that. Thunder at the back, lightning at the front."

"Yes, you're right. I am, much better. Good days and bad, of course."

The Weatherman inspected his gloves and said, "Life's a full course."

"It certainly is," she said with a smile.

Evelin looked up to the ocean rolling behind the clouds above them.

"The Eels, how are they?" she asked.

"Still long and slippery. Behaving more or less, but between you and me, they're irreplaceable," said the Weatherman.

"I can imagine," smiled Evelin.

"I know you can, would you like to bring up a storm or two with me, put them to work? Now where are they? Nowhere to be seen, of course."

"It's OK, I'm afraid I can't stay for very long. I'm starting to wake I think."

The Weatherman paused and lowered himself concerning, "Oh that's a shame, so you're still afraid?"

"No—I'm not anymore, I don't let it get the better of me," she replied.

"Good for you, I knew my advice would eventually sink in."

"Yes, thank you," laughed Evelin as she shook her head.

"Goodbye, Weatherman, until we meet again."

"Goodbye, Boots. It was a pleasure."

"It was indeed, oh and Weatherman,"

"Yes?"

"If you see the Eels, do let them know ... they've got a friend."

THE END

THE
OTHER SIDE
OF EVE

I sincerely hope you enjoyed, The Other Side of Eve.

I would be grateful if you take a moment and leave a review on;
Amazon.com & Goodreads.com
It will help spread the word and excite new readers to enjoy.

Please find a special gift waiting for you online.
http://theothersideofeve.com/readers-gift/
Password: Bateau

Visit the official website for news, illustrations and latest writings.
I am currently writing the prequel to, The Other Side. To be kept up to
date please follow me the author, Paul Ikin on Twitter @paulikin

Thank you!

Paul Ikin

www.theothersideofeve.com

CPSIA information can be obtained at www.ICGtesting.com
Printed in the USA
BVOW08s1449300715

410891BV00002B/98/P